PRAY
FOR THE DYING

Quintin
Jardine

PRAY
FOR THE DYING

headline

First published in 2013 by
HEADLINE PUBLISHING GROUP

3

Cataloguing in Publication Data is available from the British Library

978 0 7553 5698 0 (Hardback)
978 0 7553 5699 7 (Trade paperback)

Typeset in Electra by Avon DataSet Ltd, Bidford-on-Avon, Warwickshire

Printed in the UK by CPI Group (UK) Ltd, Croydon, CR0 4YY

Headline's policy is to use papers that are natural, renewable and
recyclable products and made from wood grown in sustainable forests.
The logging and manufacturing processes are expected to conform to the
environmental regulations of the country of origin.

HEADLINE PUBLISHING GROUP
An Hachette Livre UK Company
338 Euston Road
London NW1 3BH

www.headline.co.uk
www.hachette.co.uk

For Eileen, for ever, or as close to that as we can manage.

PreScript

From the *Saltire* newspaper, Sunday edition:

Strathclyde Chief Constable believed dead in Glasgow Concert Hall Shooting

By June Crampsey

Mystery still surrounds a shooting last night in Glasgow's Royal Concert Hall in which a woman was killed in a VIP seat at a charity concert, inches away from Scotland's First Minister, Clive Graham MSP. The identity of the victim has still to be confirmed officially, but it is believed that she was Antonia Field, the recently appointed Chief Constable of the Strathclyde Force, the second largest in the UK after London's Met.

The killing was carried out by two men, who were themselves shot dead as they tried to escape, after murdering a police officer and critically wounding another.

A security cordon was thrown round the hall immediately after the incident, but reporters could see what appeared to be three bodies outside in Killermont Street, one of them in police uniform. A fourth man, said to be a police officer, was taken away by ambulance, and a spokesman for Glasgow Royal Infirmary confirmed later that he was undergoing emergency surgery for gunshot wounds.

Edinburgh Chief Constable Bob Skinner, husband of Scottish Labour leader Aileen de Marco who was a guest of the First Minister at the fund-raiser, took command at the scene. Briefing media in Glasgow City Chambers, he refused to name the victim, but did say that it was not his wife, nor was it the woman who had accompanied her to the concert, believed to be Edinburgh businesswoman Paula Viareggio, the partner of another senior police officer in the capital, Detective Chief Superintendent Mario McGuire.

Most of the eyewitnesses refused to speak to journalists as they were ushered away from the concert hall. Many seemed to be in shock. However, world-famous Scottish actor Joey Morocco, Master of Ceremonies for the evening, told the *Saltire* as he left, 'There was complete confusion in there.

'The conductor, Sir Leslie Fender, had just raised his baton and the house lights had dimmed when I heard three sounds that I know now were shots, one after the other. Then everything went completely dark, pitch black, and someone started screaming.

'Before that, though,' Mr Morocco continued, 'I was standing in the wings and I was facing the audience. In the second or two before the lights went out, as the shots were fired, I saw movement in the front row. There were three women on the First Minister's left.

'Aileen, she's a friend, by the way, she was sat furthest away from him, then her companion, Paula, and then the lady who'd arrived with Mr Graham. I don't know her name, but somebody said she's the chief constable. I saw her jerk in her seat then start to fall forward. That's when the lights went out.

'The emergency lighting came on automatically, after a few seconds. It wasn't much good, but I could make out that the seat next to the First Minister was empty and that there was a shape on the floor.

'There was panic after that. I heard Mr Graham shouting for help, then I could just make out a policeman rushing forward. I think it was Mr Allan, the assistant chief constable. I tried to use the mike but it was useless with the power being out, so I jumped up on to the conductor's podium and yelled to everyone to stay in their seats and stay calm until the lighting was restored. But the people in the rows nearest the front, some of them realised what had happened and they started to panic.

'Mr Graham was brilliant. He stood up, called out to everyone to stay where they were, for their own safety. It was an incredibly brave thing to do,' Mr Morocco added. 'He might have been the target himself and the gunman might still have been there, but he put himself right in the line of fire, then he took off his jacket and put it over the woman on the floor. That's when I knew for sure that she was dead.

'Thing is,' he explained, 'she was wearing a red dress. Normally at a big public event Aileen wears red, her party colours, but last night, for some reason, she didn't. So I'm wondering if she was the intended target and whether the gunman just made a mistake.'

Addressing journalists in a hastily convened briefing in the Glasgow City Council Chambers, after being asked by the First Minister to take charge of the situation, Mr Skinner refused to comment on Mr Morocco's speculation.

'It's way too early to be making any assumptions,' he said firmly. 'We believe we know who the shooters were, but we're a long way from understanding their motives.'

Asked whether Al Qaeda might be involved, he replied, 'I'm not ruling that out, but the gunmen were not Muslim and the nationality of a third person involved in the plot makes that highly unlikely. However, I can tell you that this was a well-planned operation carried out by people with special skills.

'We've been able to establish already that the hall was blacked out by an explosion that took out the electricity substation serving the building. It was remotely detonated as soon as the shots had been fired. We're also sure that the two men gained entrance to the building dressed as police officers, and ditched their disguises before trying to escape.'

He refused to go into detail on how they had been killed, or by whom.

When I spoke to him later, by telephone, he explained that neither of the victims could be identified before their next of kin had been told. He added that the First Minister was under close protection at his home, and that his wife was also being guarded at a secret location.

One

'I put Paula in harm's way, Mario,' Bob Skinner murmured, as he gazed at his colleague, their faces pale in the glare of the freestanding spotlights that had been set up to illuminate the scene. 'I am desperately sorry.'

Never before had Detective Chief Superintendent McGuire seen his boss looking apprehensive, and yet he was, there could be no mistaking it.

'How exactly did you do that, sir?' he replied, stiffly. 'Your wife invited my wife to chum her to a charity concert. Given that Aileen is a former and possibly future First Minister of our country, most people would regard that as something of an honour.'

'Someone tried to kill her,' Skinner hissed. 'There was intelligence that a hit was being planned. You know that; I knew it. I was asleep at the fucking wheel, or I'd have considered that as a possibility.'

'Then it was Paula that saved her life, Bob,' McGuire pointed out, more gently. 'If she hadn't told Aileen that she was wearing a red outfit, on account of her being so pregnant it was the only thing that would fit, then Aileen would have worn her usual colour.'

The chief constable frowned. 'But Paula isn't wearing red.'

'No, she found something else. Thank your lucky stars again that she didn't think to tell Aileen about it. Stop beating yourself up, man.

Nobody's going to blame you for anything, least of all me. Paula's all right, she's off the scene, and that's an end of it.'

Skinner nodded towards the splayed body, a few yards away from where they stood, in front of the auditorium stage of Glasgow's splendid concert arena. 'She would blame me, if she could.' He put a hand to an ear. 'If I listen hard enough I reckon I'll hear her. Five minutes, that's all it would have taken. If we'd got to our informant five minutes earlier . . .'

'You'd probably have been caught in traffic,' his colleague countered, 'and got here no quicker. Okay, if the Strathclyde communications centre hadn't been on weekend mode, you might have got the word to ACC Allan and prevented the hit . . . but they were and you didn't.'

'Speaking of old Max,' Skinner murmured, 'how is he? I didn't have time to talk to him when he met us at the entrance. "She's dead," he said. That was all. I assumed it was Aileen. I didn't wait to hear any more. I just charged inside and left him there.'

'He's wasted; complete collapse. When I got there he was sitting on the steps in the foyer with his face in his hands. He had blood on them; it was all over his face, in his hair. He was a mess.' He paused. 'The guy you were with, the fellow who took Paula and Aileen away. I only caught a glimpse of him. Who is he?'

'His name's Clyde Houseman. Security Service; Glasgow regional office.'

'He's sound?'

'Oh yes.' Skinner's eyes flashed. 'Do you think for a minute I'd entrust our wives' safety to him if I wasn't sure of that? I told him to take them to the high security police station in Govan and to keep them there till he heard from me. And before you ask, there's a doctor on the way there to check Paula out, given that she's over eight months gone.'

'But she was fine, as far as you could see?' McGuire asked, anxiously.

'Yes, like I said. Obviously, she got a fright at the time . . . not even Paula's going to have the woman in the seat next to her shot through the head without batting an eyelid . . . but when I got to her she was calm and in control. Far more concerned about Toni Field than about herself.'

'Did she see . . .'

'Not much. Even when the emergency lighting came on, it wasn't far short of pitch dark, and Clive Graham got between her and the body, and made his protection officers rush her and Aileen out of there, into the anteroom where I found them. Aileen screamed bloody murder, of course.'

'Was she in shock?'

'Hell no. It wasn't from fright. She just didn't want to leave. I'm a cynic where politicians are concerned, and my wife's no different from any of them, maybe worse than most. She wanted to be seen here alongside Clive Graham, who appears to have been a complete fucking hero. He'll get the headlines and Aileen was livid that she'll be seen as a weak wee woman, hiding behind her husband. I wasn't fucking wearing that, mate. I told Houseman to get them out of there, regardless of what she wanted, and I sent Graham's people back to do their job.' He grunted. 'You know that actor guy, Joey Morocco? Didn't he turn up on the bloody scene while all this was going on, demanding to know that Aileen was all right!'

'Morocco? The movie star? What's his interest in Aileen?'

'The very question I put to him, but she said they were old friends. News to me, but they were all over each other. I might as well not have been here. He offered to take the girls to his place, but I told him that unless it was bomb-proof like the Govan nick, that wouldn't be a starter. Then I told him to clear out, with the rest of the civilians.'

'How long are you going to keep them there?'

The chief constable's eyebrows rose. 'Christ, Mario, I haven't thought that far ahead. I've been here for twenty-five minutes, that's all, trying to keep this crime scene secure till the forensic team arrive. Anyway, this isn't our patch. That's an operational decision for . . .'

'Indeed.'

Both police officers turned towards the newcomer. McGuire, irked by the interruption, frowned, but Skinner knew the voice well enough. 'Clive,' he murmured in greeting, as the First Minister stepped into the silver light, with his two personal protection officers no more than a yard behind him. He was tartan-clad, waistcoat and trousers, but no jacket. The chief constable guessed that garment was draped over the body of Toni Field.

The woman had been his arch-enemy. She had been a surprise choice as head of the Strathclyde force, a job for which he had declined to apply, in spite of the entreaties of his wife and of the retiring chief. Most Scots assumed, therefore, that she had been appointed by default, but Skinner recognised the quality of her CV, and even more important its breadth, with success in the Met and England's Serious Crimes Agency added to relevant experience as chief constable of the West Midlands.

She and Skinner had been on a collision course from their first meeting, when it had become clear that Field was in support of the unified Scottish police force advocated by Clive Graham's government, and that she expected to be appointed to lead it, regardless of his own ambitions.

As it happened, those no more included heading Graham's proposed force than they had inclined him towards Strathclyde. Skinner was firmly against the idea, on principle. He had shunned the

Glasgow job because he felt that a force that covered half of Scotland's land mass and most of its population was itself too large.

He had always believed that policing had to be as locally responsible as possible, and when he had discovered a few days earlier that his wife, the First Minister's chief political rival as leader of the Scottish Labour Party, intended to back unification and help rush it through the Holyrood parliament, their marriage had exploded. Aileen had moved back to her flat, ostensibly for a few days, but they knew, both of them, that it was for good.

'How are you?' he asked the First Minister. He had no personal issues with him. His position and that of his party had been clear from the start; his wife's, he was convinced, was based on political expediency, pure and simple.

'In need of another very stiff drink,' Graham replied. 'Yes, I've already had one, but I suspect I'm going to get the shakes pretty soon. What happened . . . it hasn't quite sunk in yet. Please brief me, on everything. I can't get any sense out of the locals, and my protection boys don't know any more than I do.'

Both Skinner and McGuire realised that he was making a determined effort not to look at the thing on the floor.

'Are the ladies safe?' he continued.

'Yes,' Skinner replied.

'The pregnant one? She's . . .'

'My wife,' McGuire whispered.

The First Minister stared at him.

'This is DCS McGuire,' Skinner explained. 'My head of CID. I had promised my kids some attention today, so Aileen invited Paula to use the other ticket.' Not a lie, not the whole truth. 'And yes, thank you. She's okay. Obviously Mario here will be keeping her in cotton wool from now on, but she'll be fine, I'm sure.'

'That's good to hear. Now, do you believe there's a continuing threat?'

'No, I don't, but we shouldn't take any chances.'

'What happened? None of us really knows, Bob. Who was it? Did they get away?'

'It was a professional hit team. Originally there were three, but one of them, the planner, died a few days ago, unexpectedly, of natural causes. The body was dumped in Edinburgh. The other two didn't think for a minute we'd identify him, but we did, and as soon as we knew who he was, we knew as well that something was up. We guessed the venue, but we got the target wrong. We thought they were after the pianist, the guy who was supposed to be playing at this thing.'

'Theo Fabrizzi?'

'Yes. For all his name, he's Lebanese, and he's a hate figure for the Israelis. We didn't find out any of this until the last minute. When we did, we got him out of here. You were probably told he'd been taken ill, but that was bollocks. The guy's a fanatic, a martyr with a piano; he wouldn't back off, so we arrested him and took him away, spitting feathers, but safe.'

'My God,' the First Minister exclaimed. 'Why wasn't I told this at the time?'

'We were too busy sorting the situation out,' Skinner shot back, irritably. 'Or so we thought. And there was another reason,' he added. 'I shouldn't have to tell you that your devolved powers do not include counter-terrorism. That's reserved for Westminster.

'As soon as we identified Cohen, the planner, MI5 got involved, with the Home Secretary pulling the strings. There had been intelligence that a hit was planned in the UK, but no details. With Cohen and his team in Scotland, assumptions were made, and we all bought into the piano player as the target. Then the Home Secretary got brave . . . God save us all from courageous politicians in fucking bunkers in Whitehall, Clive . . . and decided that she wanted her people to catch the rest of the team. She declared that it was a Five operation, and that the police shouldn't be alerted, in case of crossed wires.'

'So how did you get involved?'

'I was in play by that time, having asked them for help in identifying Cohen.'

Graham's face was creased into a frown that made him unrecognisable as the beaming man on the election posters. 'But if . . .' he growled.

Skinner nodded. 'There was someone else involved, the man who supplied the weapons. My MI5 colleague and I got to him,' he paused and checked his watch, 'less than ninety minutes ago. We interrogated him and he told us that from a remark by one of the shooters, when they collected the guns last night, the target was definitely female.

'Obviously that changed everything. At that point . . .' he paused, '. . . well, frankly, it was fuck the Home Secretary's orders. We headed straight through here. I tried to stop the event, but in all this mighty police force, Clive, I could not find anyone willing to take responsibility, until it was too late. You know what happened then.'

'What about the terrorists? Did they escape in all the confusion? Nobody can tell me, or will.'

'They're dead. They were making their escape when we arrived. They'd just shot the two cops manning the door.' He sighed, shuddered for a second, and shook his head. 'Fortunately my Five sidekick was armed or we'd have been in trouble. We didn't negotiate. Captain Houseman killed one. I took down the other one as he tried to run off. But don't be calling these guys terrorists, Clive. They weren't. No, they were . . .'

He broke off as his personal mobile phone . . . he carried two . . . sounded in his pocket. He took it out and peered at the screen, ready to reject the call if it was Aileen spoiling for a renewed fight, but it was someone else. 'Excuse me,' he told the First Minister. 'I have to take this.'

Graham nodded. 'Of course.'

He slid the arrow to accept, and put the phone to his ear, moving a few paces away from the group, skirting Toni Field's body as he did so.

'Hi, Sarah,' he murmured.

'Bob!' she exclaimed. Skinner's ex-wife was cool and not given to panic, but the anxiety in her voice was undeniable.

'Where are you? Are you okay? What's happened? I've just had a call from Mark. He told me he heard a news flash on radio about a shooting in Glasgow, at an event with the First Minister and Aileen. That's the event that she and Paula were going to this evening, isn't it? He says someone's dead and that your name was mentioned. Honey, what is it? Is it Aileen?'

'Shit,' he hissed. 'So soon. They're not saying that, are they, that it's Aileen?'

'I'm not sure what they said but Mark was left wondering if it might be. He's scared, Bob, and most of all he's scared for you.'

'In that case, love, please call him back and calm him down. Yes, I am at the scene, yes, there is a casualty here, and others outside, but none of them are Aileen or anyone else he knows. And it's certainly not Paula. They're both safe.'

'But how about you?' Her voice was strident.

'You can hear me, can't you? I'm okay too. I might not be in the morning, when it all sinks in, but I am fine now, and in control of myself.' As if to demonstrate, he paused then lowered his voice as he continued. 'Are you alone?' he asked. 'Are you at home?'

'Yes, of course, to both.'

'Good. In that case, I need you to do a couple of things. Call Trish,' their children had a full-time carer; their sons had reached an age at which they refused to allow her to be called a nanny, 'and have her take the kids to your place. As soon as you've done that, get hold of my grown-up daughter. I'm guessing she hasn't heard about this yet, or she'd have called me, but Alex being Alex, she's bound to find out soon. She may be at home; if not, try her mobile . . . do you have the number?'

'Yes.'

'Fine, if you can't raise her on either of those, try Andy's place. Tell her what I've told you. I don't have time to do it myself; the fan's pretty much clogged up with shit here.'

'Where will you be?'

'That remains to be seen, but I'll keep you in touch.'

'When will you be out of there?'

'Same answer.'

'When you are,' she told him, 'come here first. It's important that the kids see you as soon as they can.'

'Yes, sure.'

'What about Aileen?'

'What do you mean?' Bob asked.

'Will she be coming back with you?'

'No,' he replied, with a sound that might have been a chuckle or a grunt, 'not even in protective custody. I told you last night, she and I are done.'

He glanced to his right. The First Minister and McGuire had been joined by a youngish man, in a dark suit. Strained though it was, his face was familiar to Skinner, but he found himself unable to put a name to it. Graham caught his eye, and he realised that they were waiting for him to finish his call. 'Now, I must go,' he said.

'Take care,' Sarah murmured.

'Don't I always?'

'No.'

A brief smile flickered on his lips, but it was gone before he returned his phone to his pocket. He rejoined the group, and as he did so he remembered who the newcomer was. They had met at a reception hosted by his wife, during her time as Clive Graham's predecessor in office.

'Bob,' the First Minister began, 'this is . . .'

'I know: Councillor Dominic Hanlon, chair of Strathclyde Police Authority.' He extended his hand and they shook. 'I'm sorry for your loss.'

Hanlon whistled, softly. 'I could say something very inappropriate right now. It's an open secret that you and Toni didn't get on.'

'You've just said it, Mr Hanlon,' Skinner snapped. 'You're right; it's as far from appropriate as you can get. Are you implying I'm glad to see her dead?'

'No, no!' The man held his hands up, in a defensive gesture, but the chief constable seemed to ignore him.

'Colleagues don't always agree,' he went on, 'any more than politicians. Like you two for example; anywhere else you'd be at each other's ideological throats.' He felt his anger grow, make him take the councillor by the elbow. 'Come here,' he growled. He pulled him towards the body on the floor, knelt beside it and removed the covering jacket, carefully.

'This is what we're dealing with here, chum. Look, remember it.' The back of the head was caked red, and mangled where three bullets had torn into it. The right eye and a section of forehead above it were missing and there was brain tissue on the carpet.

Hanlon recoiled, with a howl that reminded the chief constable of a small animal in pain, as he replaced the makeshift cover.

14

'Poor Toni Field and I might have had different policing agendas,' he said, 'but we each of us devoted our careers to hunting down the sort of people who would do that sort of thing to another human being. You remember that next time you chair your fucking committee.'

'I'm sorry,' the younger man murmured.

'You want to know how I feel?' Skinner, not ready to let up, challenged. 'I feel angry, so walk carefully around me, chum.'

'Yes, of course,' Hanlon said, patting him on the sleeve as if to mollify him. 'Surely, the chances are it wasn't Toni they were after. Everybody outside is saying it's Aileen that's been shot . . . our Aileen, we call her in Glasgow. There's folk in tears out there.'

'I thought it was her myself until the First Minister told me otherwise. Only the people in the front row could possibly know what's really happened and I doubt if any of them do. They all think it's Aileen because that's the natural assumption. I think these people made a mistake, and shot the wrong woman.'

'For God's sake, man!' Graham barked, beside him. 'This is Aileen's husband, don't you realise that?'

'Yes, of course! Sorry.' The councillor seemed to collapse into his own confusion.

Skinner held up a hand. 'Stop!' he boomed. 'Enough. We'll get to that, and to Dominic's theory. First things first.' He turned to McGuire. 'Mario, did you come through here alone?'

'No, boss,' the massive DCS answered. 'Lowell Payne, DCI Payne, our Strathclyde secondee, he's with me. He's outside in the foyer; it was sheer chaos when we arrived, with no sign of anybody in command, so I told him to take control out there, calm people down as best he could, and move them out the other exit, so they wouldn't go past bodies outside.'

The chief nodded. 'Well done, mate. My priority was in here when

I arrived. With Max Allan not making any sense, all I could do was get hold of a uniformed inspector and tell him to contain the audience within the hall, until we could be sure that there was no further threat outside. Where is everyone?'

'Payne said he would gather them in the foyer and in the smaller theatre. There's enough back-up lighting for that to be managed safely.'

'Okay, that sounds fine. Now, you shouldn't really be here at all, but you charged through here like a red-taunted bull as soon as you heard your wife might be in danger. Whatever, your priority will always be her. Get yourself off to the Govan police station, pick her up from there and take her home.'

'What about Aileen?' McGuire asked.

'She stays there, till someone in authority says otherwise. Find Clyde Houseman and tell him from me that he takes no instructions from anyone below chief officer rank. On your way, now.'

He turned back to the politicians. 'Now. You two were working up to say something before Dominic here put his foot in it. What was it?'

'We've got a crisis, Bob,' Graham replied. 'Strathclyde is in trouble, and that's putting it mildly. The chief constable is dead, the deputy chief took early retirement a fortnight ago, Max Allan, the senior ACC, has just been taken away in an ambulance with severe chest pains, and the two other ACCs are far too new and inexperienced in post to move into the top job, even on a temporary basis . . . and even without the force facing one of the highest-profile murder investigations it's ever known, as this will become.'

Hanlon nodded, vigorously. 'As you've just pointed out to me, Mr Skinner, graphically, this is a major crime, and even if Toni's killers . . . and the killers of one, maybe two police officers . . . are lying dead in the street outside, the matter isn't closed.'

'Maybe three, maybe four,' Skinner murmured.

The Police Authority chairman blinked. 'Eh?'

'How did they get the uniforms? We don't know that. Did they bring them, or did they take them from two other cops we haven't found yet?'

'My God,' Hanlon gasped. 'I hadn't thought about that.'

'Bob,' the First Minister intervened. 'This investigation needs a leader. This whole force needs a leader and it needs him now. We don't have time for niceties here. I want to appoint you acting chief constable of Strathclyde, pending confirmation by an emergency meeting of Dominic's authority. That will take place tomorrow morning.'

'Me?' Skinner gasped. 'Strathclyde? The force whose very existence I've opposed for years? Is there nobody else? What about Andy Martin? He's head of the Serious Crime and Drug Enforcement Agency. He could do the job.'

Graham shook his head. 'He could, I agree, but everybody knows he's your protégé, not to mention him being your daughter's partner. He'd be seen as second choice, and I can't have that. I need the best man available, and that is you. Please, help me. Your deputy in Edinburgh is more than capable; she can stand in there. Please take the job; in the public interest, Bob, even if it does go against your own beliefs.'

Skinner stared at him. 'You've really boxed me in, man, haven't you?'

'It's not something I'd have chosen to do.'

'No, I believe you. That's the way it is, nonetheless.' He sighed. 'Fuck it!' he shouted, into the darkness of the empty hall.

'Can I take that as a yes?' the First Minister whispered.

Two

'And you've agreed?'

'What else could I do, Andy? The Police Authority meets tomorrow to confirm it formally, and it'll be announced on Monday. But it's for three months, that's all. I've made that clear.'

There was a silence on Andy Martin's end of the line, until he broke it with a soft chuckle. 'Would that be as clear as you've made it to anyone who would listen that you would never take the job under any circumstances?'

'Yes, okay, I have said that,' Skinner conceded. 'But,' he protested, 'who could have predicted these particular circumstances?'

'Nobody,' his best friend conceded. 'That's why the "any" part of it was a mistake. Now let me make a prediction. However hard it was for you to get into the job, it will be harder for you to get out.'

'Nonsense! I said three months and I meant it. They'll be glad to see me go, Andy. The politicians will hate me here; remember, most of them are followers of my soon to be ex-wife.'

'Your what?' Martin exclaimed. 'Come on, Bob. Alex told me you'd had a row over police unification, but I'd no idea it was that serious. You'll get over it, surely.'

'No, we won't. Too much was said, too much truth told. This isn't like when Sarah and I broke up, or you and Karen. We haven't drifted

away from each other like then, we've torn the thing apart. Besides . . .'
He stopped in mid-sentence. 'No, that's for another time. I have things
to do here. First and foremost, I've got a very messy crime scene to
manage. Second, I've got to face the press.'

'Where are you going to do that?'

'I've told the press office to use the City Chambers. Hanlon, the
Police Authority chair, is going to fix it. I could have done it on the
front steps of the concert hall, but I want to move the media, or as
many as I can, away from there, so the people who were in the
auditorium can leave as easily as we can manage. They're having to go
that way, into Buchanan Street, since there are still three bodies lying
in Killermont Street.'

'I know Hanlon; he'll want to sit alongside you.'

'You're right. He's asked if he could, and not only him. Clive
Graham tried it before him. I've told them both that they're not on.
This is the assassination of a high-profile public figure we're dealing
with and I'm damned if I'm having anything that sniffs of political
posturing alongside it.'

'Hah!' Martin exclaimed. 'That's already happened. I've just
seen that Joey Morocco guy vox-popped on telly, outside in
Buchanan Street. The way he tells the story, the First Minister's
something of a hero, standing up in the line of fire when the emergency
lights came back on. Graham's going to have to give himself a gallantry
medal.'

'Stupidity medal more like.' Skinner paused. 'Did Morocco say
who the victim is?'

'No, but he did say it isn't Aileen, or Paula. They are both unhurt,
yes?'

'Yes, fine, I've spoken to them both, before I had them rushed out
of here. Aileen wanted to stay and wave the red flag, of course.'

'Ouch! Bob, can I do anything? Personally, or through the agency?'

'Yes, you can. I'd like you to take Alex to Sarah's, and stay there with her. I don't believe for a second there's any sort of threat to them, but I'm feeling a bit prickly, and I want all my family under one roof and looked after till I can get to them.'

'I understand. I'll do that. Now, Alex wants to speak.'

Skinner could picture his elder daughter snatching the phone from her partner's hand. 'Dad!' Her voice had the same breathless tone as Sarah's, a little earlier.

'Be cool, kid,' he told her. 'The panic's over; there's no hostage situation or anything like that. Andy will tell you as much as he can. I have things to do and then I have to go to the Royal Infirmary. We have a cop there fighting for his life and I have to see how he's doing. Go now. I'll see you when I can.'

He ended the call and walked back towards the pool of light in front of the stage. The First Minister had been escorted away by his protection officers, and Councillor Hanlon had gone to the Glasgow council headquarters, to have them made ready for the media briefing to come. But Skinner was not standing guard alone.

'I've just spoken to your niece,' he said to Detective Chief Inspector Lowell Payne. 'I didn't tell her you were involved, though, in case she phoned Jean. There's enough anxiety in my family without spreading it to yours.'

There was a personal link between the two men, one that had nothing to do with the job. Ten years after the death of Skinner's first wife, Myra, Alex's mother, Payne had married her sister.

'Thanks, Bob. I appreciate that.'

'Don't mention it. Listen, Lowell, this job I've taken on, temporary or not, I have to be on top of it from the start. That means I need to get up to speed very quickly on the basics of the force, areas where my knowledge may be lacking: its structure, its strengths and its weaknesses, as perceived within the force.

'I'm going to need somebody close to me, to advise me and instruct me where necessary, a sound, experienced guy. You've got twenty-five years plus in the job, all of it in Strathclyde. Will you be my aide, for as long as I need one? Officially, mind; you'll come off CID for the duration and operate as my liaison across the force. You up for it?'

The DCI seemed to hesitate. 'Are you not worried there might be talk, about you and me being sort of related?'

'No, and anyway, we're not. My daughter being your niece does not make you part of my family, or me part of yours.'

'In that case the answer's yes.'

'Good. Now, what's happening outside?'

'Everybody's calm, and they're leaving. They're all potential witnesses, I know, but there's no need to ask them all for contact details, since they're all on a central database. They all booked through the internet, so they all had to leave their details.'

'Good man. Not that we'll need to go back to any of them. None of them can answer any of the questions we need to ask.'

'Those being?'

'Who sent the hit team, and why?'

Payne frowned. 'Why? Does there have to be a why these days, when terrorism is involved, and politicians are the target?'

'Doesn't matter. It's our job to look for it.'

'And mine to help you.'

Skinner turned. He had recognised the voice, from many similar scenes over many years. The man who faced him was clad in a crime-scene tunic, complete with a paper hat that failed to contain the red hair that escaped from it. Looking at him the chief wondered if he would have recognised him in ordinary clothes, or, God forbid, in uniform.

'Arthur,' he exclaimed. 'You're looking as out of water as I feel. What the hell are you doing in Glasgow?'

'You should know, boss,' Detective Inspector Dorward replied. 'You approved the set-up. Ever since forensic services were pulled together into a central unit, we've gone anywhere we're needed and more than that, we've had a national duty rota at weekends. I drew this straw. And bloody busy I've been. I'd not long left a very messy scene in Leith when I got the call to come through here.' He paused. 'But I could ask you the same question. Why are you here?'

'I was following a line of inquiry. It led me here.'

Dorward raised an eyebrow. 'Oh aye,' he drawled. 'I know what that means. So far I've counted four bodies on the ground. Any of them down to you?'

'Just the one.'

Dorward nodded towards the figure under the jacket. 'Not her, though?'

'Definitely not. Now don't push your luck any further, Arthur.'

'Fair enough, Chief; in return, you get your big feet off my crime scene.' He looked at Payne. 'And you.' He paused. 'Here, weren't you at Leith?'

The Strathclyde DCI nodded.

'Then what the fuck's going on here? What's the connection?'

'Never mind that,' Skinner told him. 'This is what matters. For openers, we need you to recover the bullets that killed our victim here, for comparison with the ones that were recovered from the two bodies in Leith.'

'Are you saying they'll be the same?'

Skinner nodded.

'And if they're not?'

'Then we're all going to find out how deep shit can get. Go to work, Arthur.'

'Errr . . .' a deep contralto voice exclaimed from the relative darkness beyond the floodlights, 'can we just hold on a minute here?'

Its owner stepped into the bright light. She was tall, around six feet, and wore, over an open-necked white shirt, a dark suit that did nothing to disguise the width of her shoulders. Her hair was dark, swept back from a high forehead, her eyes were a deep shade of blue, but her nose was her dominant feature. A warrant card was clipped to the right lapel of her jacket.

She eyed Skinner, up and down, no flicker of recognition on her face. 'So who the hell are you, to be giving orders at my crime scene?' she asked, slowly.

The chief constable took his own ID from a pocket and displayed it. She looked at it, then shrugged.

'That doesn't answer my question,' the woman retorted. 'That says Edinburgh. Okay, the earth might have moved for me last night, but not that much. As far as I know, this is still Strathclyde.'

Payne took half a pace forward. 'Cool it, Lottie. This is Chief Constable Bob Skinner, and you know who I am.'

She frowned at him. 'Sure, I know who you are. You're a DCI and you're in strategy. I'm serious crimes, which this as sure as hell is, from what I was told and what I saw outside. That puts me in command of this crime scene.' She nodded sideways, in Skinner's general direction. 'As for our friend here . . .'

'Sir,' Payne sighed, 'I must apologise to you, on behalf of the Strathclyde force. My colleague here, DI Charlotte Mann, she's got a reputation for being blunt, and sometimes she takes it to the point of rudeness. Lottie, get off your high horse. We know what's happened here . . .'

'I don't,' she snapped back. 'I know there's a dead cop outside in Killermont Street, and two other gunshot victims, but I don't know how they got there. I don't know who's under that jacket . . .'

'You'd better take a look, then,' Skinner told her.

'You speak when you're spoken to . . . sir. And don't be trying to tell me my job.' She stepped across to the body.

'Be careful over there,' the blue-suited Dorward warned, but she ignored him as she lifted the jacket from the prone form.

'Bloody hell!' she exclaimed as she observed the shattered head. She peered a little closer, then looked over her shoulder, at Payne. 'Lowell,' she murmured 'is this . . . ?'

He nodded.

'And the two men outside?'

He nodded again. 'The shooters.'

'So you see, Inspector,' Skinner said. 'We do know what's happened here.'

The DI glared at him. 'You might, chum, but the procurator fiscal doesn't, and it's my job to investigate these incidents and report to her. So you can shove your Edinburgh warrant card as far as it'll go. It means nothing to me. As far as I'm concerned, you're just another witness, and for all I know you might even be a suspect. My team should all be here within the next few minutes. Do not go anywhere; they will be wanting to interview you.'

'Aw, Jesus!' Payne laughed, out loud. 'I've had enough of this.' He glanced at Skinner. 'May I, sir?'

'You'd better,' the chief conceded. He moved aside, letting the DCI step up to his CID colleague and whisper, urgently and fiercely in her ear, then catching her eye as she looked towards him, nodding gently, in answer to her surprise.

She walked towards him. 'They didn't waste any time filling the chair,' she said.

'They . . . they being the First Minister and the Police Authority chair . . . felt that they didn't have a choice. I was asked and I accepted: end of story. It'll be formalised on Monday, but as of now you take orders from me and anyone else I tell you to.' He paused. 'Now, Inspector, tell me. How are your traffic management skills?'

Lottie Mann held his gaze, unflinching. 'The traffic will do what I fucking tell it, sir,' she replied, 'if it knows what's good for it. But wouldn't that be a bit of a waste?'

Skinner's eyes softened, then he smiled. 'Yes, it would,' he agreed, 'and one I don't plan to have happen. I know about you, Lottie. ACC Allan told us all about you, at a chief officers' dinner a while back.'

For the first time, her expression grew a little less fierce. 'What did he say?' she asked.

'He said you were barking mad, a complete loose cannon, and that you were under orders never to speak to the press or let yourself be filmed for TV. He told us a story about you, ten years ago, when you had just made DC, demanding to box in an interdivisional smoker that some of your male CID colleagues had organised, and knocking out your male opponent inside a minute. But he also said you were the best detective on the force and that he put up with you in spite of it all. I like Max, and I rate him, so I'll take all of that as a recommendation.'

Mann nodded. 'Thank you, sir. Actually it was inside thirty seconds. Can I take your statement now . . . yours and the guy I was told you arrived with?'

The chief grinned again. 'Mine, sure, in good time. My colleague, no. His name won't appear in your report and he won't be a witness at any inquiry.'

'Spook?'

'Spook. That reminds me.' He turned to Payne. 'Lowell, there is bound to be at least one CCTV camera covering the Killermont Street entrance. I want you to locate it, them if there are others, and confiscate all the footage from this afternoon. When we have it, it goes nowhere without my say-so.'

'Yes, sir.'

As the DCI left, Skinner led Mann away from the floodlight beam and signalled to Dorward that he and his people could begin their work. He stopped at an auditorium doorway, beneath a green exit sign and an emergency lamp.

'Lottie, this is the scenario,' he said. 'On the face of it, a contract hit has taken place here. I can tell you there have been rumours in the intelligence community of a terrorist attempt on a British political figure. So, it's being suggested there's a possibility Chief Constable Field was mistaken for the real target: my wife, Aileen de Marco, the Scottish Labour leader. Aileen usually wears red to public functions. This evening she didn't, but Toni Field did.'

'That suggestion's bollocks,' she blurted out. 'Sir.'

His eyebrows rose. 'Why?'

'A couple of reasons. First, and with respect . . .'

The chief grinned. 'I didn't think you had any of that.'

'I do where it's deserved. I know about you too. And I know about your wife. She's my constituency MSP, and she's a big name in Glasgow, even in Scotland. But not beyond. So, killing her, it's hardly going to strike a major blow for Islam, is it?'

'Go on.'

'Okay. You say this is a contract hit. So, let's assume that the two guys outside weren't amateurs, however dead they might be now.'

'Far from it. They were South African mercenaries, both of them.'

'Right. That being the case, they're going to have seen photographs of their target. Your wife is about five eight and blonde. Toni Field was five feet five with her shoes on and she had brown hair. But even more important, Aileen de Marco is white, and Chief Constable Field was dark-skinned. These people knew exactly who they were here to kill, and they didn't make a mistake. That's my professional opinion. Sir.'

Skinner gazed at the floor, then up, engaging her once again. 'And mine too, Detective Inspector,' he murmured. 'But let's keep it to ourselves for now. The media can run with whatever theories they like. We won't confirm or knock down any of them. Tell me,' he added, 'what did you think of Toni Field?'

'Honestly?'

'I don't believe you could tell it any other way.'

'On the face of it, she was a role model for all female police officers. In reality, she was a careerist, an opportunist and another few words ending in "ist", none of them very complimentary.

'I liked DCC Theakston, but she had him out the door as fast as she could. I more than like ACC Allan, he's the man I've always looked up to in the force, and she had her knife out for him as well. She might have been a good police officer herself, but she didn't know one when she saw one. I have a feeling that you might.'

'I believe I'm looking at one.' He pushed the door open. 'Come on. You're with me.'

'Where? I'm supposed to be in command here.'

'Mmm. True,' he conceded. 'Okay, get your team together, and give them dispositions. You need to search the building for anything the shooters left behind. The weapon they used was a Heckler and

Koch, standard police issue, so the assumption is, they must have worn uniforms to get in.

'Tell your people to find those, and then find out whether they're authentic. If so, we need to establish whose they were, because we're looking for those owners. Beyond that the work here's for Dorward and his people. Once you've got your people moving, I have to do a press conference, and I want you with me.'

'Me?'

'Absolutely. I think Max was wrong to hide you away. You're a gem, Lottie; the Glasgow press deserve you. Just mind the language, okay?'

Three

'Can I get you coffee?' the Lord Provost of Glasgow asked.

Bob Skinner smiled. 'That's very kind of you,' he replied, 'but given that it's nine o'clock on a Saturday evening, if we accepted you'd either have to make it yourself or nip out to Starbucks. No, the use of your office for this short meeting is generosity enough. Now, if you'll . . .'

Dominic Hanlon took the hint. 'Come on, Willie,' he murmured. 'This is operational; it's not for us.'

'Oh. Oh, aye.' The two councillors withdrew.

The Lord Provost was still wearing his heavy gold chain of office. Skinner wondered if he slept in it.

'Right,' he said, as the door closed. 'We'll keep this brief, but I wanted a round-up before we all left.' He looked to his right, at Lottie Mann, and to his left, at Lowell Payne, who had joined them as the press briefing had closed.

The conference had been a frenzied affair. It had been chaired by the Strathclyde force's PR manager, but most of the questions had been directed at Skinner, once his presence had been explained.

'Can you confirm the identity of the victims, sir?' the BBC national news correspondent had asked. She was new in the country, and new to him, sent up from London to make her name, he suspected.

'Sorry, no,' he had replied, 'for the usual next-of-kin reasons, not operational. However,' he had added, halting the renewed clamour, 'I can tell you that the First Minister is unharmed, as is the Scottish Labour leader, Aileen de Marco, who was also present.'

'Joey Morocco says the victim inside the hall was female, and that she was sitting next to the First Minister.'

'Joey Morocco was there. I wasn't. I'm not going to argue with him.'

'Why isn't the First Minister here?'

'Because he was advised not to be.'

'By you, sir?'

'By his own protection staff.'

'Does that mean there's a continuing threat?'

'It means they're being suitably cautious.'

'There are two men lying in Killermont Street, apparently dead. It's been suggested that they were the killers. Can you comment?'

'Yes they were, and they are both as dead as they appear to be.' Skinner had winced inwardly at the brutality of that reply, but nobody had picked up on it. 'As is the police officer they murdered as they left the hall,' he had continued. 'His colleague is in surgery as we speak.'

'Are you looking for anybody else?'

'You're asking the wrong person. I'm here by accident, remember. That's a question for Detective Inspector Mann of Strathclyde. She's the officer in charge of the investigation.'

Lottie Mann had handled herself well. She had given nothing away, but she had made it clear that the multiple killings at the concert hall would be investigated from origins to aftermath, like any other homicide.

The one awkward question had been put by a *Sun* reporter, with whom Mann had history, after arresting him for infiltrating a crime scene.

'Aren't you rather junior to be running an investigation as important as this one?'

She had nailed him with a cold stare. 'That's for others to decide. I was senior officer on duty tonight and took command at the scene, as I would have in any circumstances.'

'By the way, you did fine in there, Lottie,' Skinner told her, in the Lord Provost's small room. 'You did fine at the scene as well; took command, took no shit from anybody, and that's how it's supposed to be.'

'To tell you the truth, sir,' she confessed, as subdued as he had seen her in their brief acquaintance, 'I was in a bit of a panic when I heard that ACC Allan had been taken away. I hope he's all right.'

'He is,' Payne reassured her, 'reasonably so. I called the Royal on my way down here. They gave him an ECG in the ambulance, and there's no sign of a heart attack. They're going to keep him in, though; apparently his blood pressure's through the roof and he's in shock.'

'How about the wounded man?' the chief asked. 'What's his name, by the way?'

'PC Auger. Still in surgery, but the word is that he'll survive. He was shot in the chest, but the bullet missed his heart and major arteries. It did nick a lung, though, and lodge in his spine.'

'And his colleague?'

'Sergeant Sproule. His body's been taken to the mortuary.'

'Who's seeing next of kin?'

'Chief Superintendent Mayfield,' Payne told him. 'She's divisional commander.'

'Okay. And Toni's next of kin? Was she married? I don't know,' Skinner confessed. 'She and I never got round to discussing our private lives.'

'I don't know either, sir. Sorry.'

'No reason why you should, but raise the head of Human Resources, wherever he is, and find out. Whoever her nearest and dearest is needs to be told, and fast.'

'Yes, they do,' Lottie Mann said, 'because the whole bloody world will soon know she was there if it doesn't already. Chief Constable Field was a big Twitter fan. She posted every professional thing she did on it. No way she won't have tweeted that she was chumming the First Minister to a charity gig.' She scowled. 'I'd ban that fucking thing if I could.'

Skinner whistled. 'Thank God you didn't say that to the press.' He smiled. 'Max Allan would never let either of us forget it. Lowell,' he continued, 'do you know where the other ACCs are?'

'Yes,' he replied. 'I thought you'd need to know that. Bridie Gorman's on holiday, in Argyll, I'm told, but ACC Thomas turned up at the concert hall just after you'd left. He was for taking command, but I told him that he'd better speak to Councillor Hanlon down at the City Chambers. He did, and when he'd done that, he went off in what I can best describe as the huff.'

'Oh shit,' the chief constable sighed. 'That I did not need. I know Michael Thomas through the chiefs' association. He was very much in the Toni Field camp on unification of the forces. In fact, at our last meeting, when things got a bit heated, I told him to shut the fuck up unless he had something original to say.' He smiled. 'Don't worry, though, Lowell. I'll make sure he doesn't hold it against you when I'm gone in three months.' He paused. 'Till then, don't worry about him. You might still be only a DCI in rank, but working directly for me as acting chief, you'll be taking orders from nobody else. Now, have you located the CCTV footage?'

'Yes, sir. There was only one camera, and I'm getting the footage. CCTV monitoring in the city is run by a joint body that's responsible for community safety. Councillor Hanlon and ACC Gorman are on the board, and in a situation like this one, we get what we want. In fact, they were expecting a call from us. Their manager said the monitor person crapped himself when he saw what happened.'

'I'm not surprised.'

'What do you want me to do with it?'

'I want you to keep it close to you. I want to see it on Monday, and obviously Lottie has to have access as senior investigating officer, but, Inspector, you and you alone are to view the footage.'

She frowned. 'What am I going to see there?' she asked.

'I don't know for sure, but if I'm right, I'll be in shot . . . Christ,' he chuckled, 'what have I just said? . . . and so will someone else, with me. If that's so, he is absolutely off limits.' He paused. 'Lottie, I hope you didn't have a big date tonight . . .'

'Only with my husband and son,' she said. 'We were going for a Chinese.'

'Well, I'm sorry about that, but I need you to go back up to the concert hall, resume command, and make sure that everything in this operation is done exactly by the book. By now they'll have found shell casings, probably in one of the lighting booths overlooking the stage, and those two discarded police uniforms. Let's just pray they don't have bullet holes in them.' He gave her a card. 'That's my mobile number. Keep me in touch.'

She smiled. Until then Skinner had not been certain that she knew how. 'Yes, boss. But . . . I'm only a lowly DI. There's a whole raft of ambitious guys above me on the CID food chain, including my two line managers. What do I do when one of them turns up and says he's taking over?'

'One, you ask him why it's taken him so long to get there. Two, you tell him he'd better have a bloody good answer to that question for the acting chief constable, first thing on Monday morning. Thing is, Lottie, Max Allan was the ACC responsible for criminal investigation. He won't be around for a while, and in his absence CID will go straight to me. To be frank, even if he was, that's how it would be. It's the way I work. Questions?'

Payne and Mann shook their heads.

'Good. You know where to get me if you have to. Get on with what you have to do. I'm off to stick my head in the lioness's mouth.'

Four

'Y ou really are a fucking fascist at heart, Bob, aren't you?' she hissed.

'If that's how you want to see me,' he retorted, 'then honestly, I don't give a damn. I got you out of there because there was a belief that you, not Toni Field, was the target of those people. And you know what? If they had shot Paula instead, who was sat between the two of you, Toni would have done exactly the same as I did. She'd have got you out of there, and fast.'

'I should have stayed in the building,' she insisted.

'Why? You're not First Minister any more, Clive Graham is. You were a fucking liability in there, Aileen, somebody else to worry about. I couldn't have that. Plus,' he hesitated for a second, 'you happen to be my wife. I didn't bend any rules to protect you, but believe me, if I'd had to, I would have.'

'That's irrelevant,' Aileen de Marco shouted. 'I should have stayed there. It was my duty; I'm the constituency MSP. I should have been there but instead I'm hiding in this bloody fortress like some kid who's afraid of the dark.'

'No, you were hidden, if you want to put it that way, because there was a chance you might still have been at risk.'

'Does that chance still exist?'

'I don't believe so,' he replied, 'although I can't be certain.'

'But I'm free to leave here?'

'To be honest, you always were. Don't tell me that hadn't occurred to you. But you stayed here. Aileen, you're allowed to be scared! A woman has just been shot dead, a few feet away from you. You may not have noticed this, but her blood is spattered on your dress. The assistant chief constable is in hospital suffering from shock. I am strung out my fucking self! So what's your problem?'

'I was detained, man, against my will. Can't you see that? I'm a politician, and as such I can't be seen to be showing weakness in the face of these terrorists.'

He threw up his hands. 'Okay, Joan of Arc, go. There isn't a locked door between you and the street, and I will arrange for a car to take you wherever you want to go, even if it's back to our place in Gullane.'

'Hah!' she spat. 'The only time I'll be back there is to collect my clothes. I've got somewhere to go tonight, don't you worry, and I will not have a police guard outside the door either.'

Skinner stood. 'You bloody will. You may leave here, but you will have protection, wherever you are. That's Clive Graham speaking, not me. He's ordered it, and I've had arrangements made. For the next couple of days at least, you will have personal security officers looking after you. That is not for debate, but don't worry, discretion is included in their training.'

It had been a casual remark, meaning nothing, but she flushed as he said it and he realised that he had touched a nerve.

'I don't want to know, Aileen,' he murmured.

'As if I care,' she snorted. 'Isn't life bloody ironic? You and I go to war because I'm for police unification and you're against it, yet here you are in command of a force that covers half of Scotland.'

'Temporary command,' he pointed out.

'So you say, but I know you better than that. You may not have volunteered for this job, but now you're in it, you won't want to let it go. Up to now you've chosen your own pond, and been its biggest fish. Now one's been chosen for you, by fate, but your nature will still be the same. Once you get your feet under that desk in Pitt Street, Fettes will never be quite big enough for you again. That's how it will be because that's how you're, like it or not!'

Five

'You might have told me you were goin' to be on the telly, Mum,' Jake Mann mumbled, as he disposed of the last of his cereal. 'I'd have told all my pals to watch.'

'I didn't have much notice of it, Jakey,' Lottie replied. 'Anyway, I wouldn't have wanted you to do that, given the subject.'

'You should have combed your hair.'

She raised an eyebrow and glared at the nine-year-old. 'Maybe, but my hairdresser wasn't available at the time. I could have done with a bit of lippie as well, but the make-up room was in use.'

'You were good, though,' Jake said, reaching for his orange juice.

'Good?' she boomed.

'Brilliant,' he offered. 'Pure dead brilliant.'

'You're getting there, kid.'

'Who was that big man alongside you?'

'That was Mr Skinner. He's from Edinburgh, but he's going to be our chief constable for a while.'

'Is that right?' a voice from the doorway asked.

Lottie turned, and frowned. 'Hey,' she exclaimed, 'the Kraken's awake.'

'The Kraken of dawn,' Scott Mann moaned, as he shambled barefoot into the kitchen, in T-shirt and shorts.

'Dawn? It's half past eight, for Christ's sake.'

'Aye, and you didnae get in till midnight.'

'Sorry, but you saw what happened. Didn't you?'

'Not really. The telly didn't show much. They just said the chief constable was deid, that was all, even though you and the guy Skinner wouldnae say so.' He looked at her as he lifted the kettle to check that it was full, then switched it on. 'Izzat right?'

She frowned. 'It's right.'

'How?'

She nodded towards their son. '*Pas devant l'enfant.*'

'Eh?'

'It means "Not in front of the child", Dad,' Jake volunteered. 'Mum's always saying it so I looked it up on the internet.'

'That's your mother all over, Jakey. She got an O grade in French at the high school, and she thinks she's Vanessa Paradis.'

'Hah, and you'd just love it if I was, sunshine. I'm closer to being her than you are tae Johnny Depp, that's for sure.' She paused. 'He's nearer my height and all.' Her husband was stocky in build but he stood no more than five feet eight. 'Yes, that's a deal, you can have Vanessa and I'll have Johnny.'

'Naw!' Jake protested.

Lottie laughed. 'Chance would be a fine thing, wee man. On you go if you're finished; see what's on CBeebies.'

Their son needed no second invitation to watch television. He grabbed a slice of buttered toast and sprinted from the room.

'So?' Scott asked, as the door closed. 'What did happen?'

'Three bullets in the head from a professional. The thing was very well planned. They blew the power as soon as they'd fired. They shot two cops on the way out . . . Sandy Sproule and Billy Auger . . .'

'Aw, Jesus,' her husband exclaimed. 'I ken Sandy. Is he . . .'

'Yes, I'm afraid so. He died instantly. Billy Auger will live, but they're not sure he'll walk again. Spinal damage.'

'Bastards.'

'Ye can say that again. They'd have got away too, had not Skinner and another bloke arrived just seconds after they'd shot them. I've seen the video. The other guy did for one of them straight away. His buddy ran for it, but Skinner picked up Sandy's carbine and put two rounds through him. Never batted a fucking eyelid either, either on the tape or later, inside the hall. The only thing he was sorry about was that if he'd just wounded the guy he might have given us a clue tae who sent him. But he said that from that range all he could do was aim for the central body mass, as per the training manual. That is one fucking hard man. I couldn't have done that, I'll tell you.'

Scott squeezed her hand. 'You know what, love? I'm glad about that.' The kettle boiled. 'Want another?' he asked.

She handed him her mug. 'Quick one. I've got to be out again. I've had crime scene people workin' all night up at the hall and in Killermont Street. I've set up a temporary murder room, I have to get up there to pull everything together. Killermont Street's still closed to traffic and there's another event due in the hall tonight. Some golden oldie rocker; it's a sell-out and they're desperate not to cancel, so time is, as they say, of the essence.'

Her husband stared at her. 'Can they do that? Just open the place the night as if nothin's happened?'

'As long as they put a patch in the carpet,' she said. 'They won't get the blood and the brain tissue out with bloody Vanish, that's for sure. And they'll have to get joiners in to fix the boards in front of the stage. They had to dig a couple of flattened bullets out of there. They'll maybe keep the lights low all the time, that'll help.'

His eyes widened. 'Imagine. Somebody's goin' to be occupying a seat tonight, and last night a woman was . . . Wow.'

'Ah know,' she agreed. 'It's a bit ghoulish. Listen, Scott, if I could, I would close the hall tonight as a mark of respect. Any polis would. But the hall manager says that people will be coming from all over Scotland to hear this guy. Some'll have left already.'

'Not any polis,' he said.

She looked at him, surprised. 'Come again?'

'Ah still have pals in the job,' he replied, 'even though I've been out for five years. From what they tell me, Antonia Field won't be missed by too many people. A lot of people, me included in my time, liked Angus Theakston, the deputy chief, and I know you did too. It's an open secret that she more or less sacked him. A guy Ah know worked in his office. He says they had a screamin' match one day that folk in Pitt Street could have heard, and that Mr Theakston put his papers in next morning, and was never seen in the office again. She treated old Max Allan like shit too, my pal said. The only one she had any time for was Michael Thomas.'

'He's a fucking weasel,' Lottie muttered. She sipped her tea. 'You never told me any of this before.'

'Ah was told on the QT. You're a senior officer; Ah didn't want to get my pal intae bother.'

'Eh?' she exclaimed. 'Do you actually think that I would come down on a guy because of something you told me?'

'Come on, hen,' he protested, 'you're a stickler and you know it. We used tae work thegither, Ah've seen you in action, remember; been on the receiving end too.'

'Aye,' she retorted, 'and had your own back too. Let's not go there, Scott. Just don't keep anything else from me. Okay?'

'Okay.'

'Good, now I've got to go.'

'When'll you be back?'

'Soon as I can.'

'You've forgotten, haven't you?'

'Forgotten what?'

'We promised Jakey we'd take him to Largs.'

'Bugger!' she swore. 'I'm sorry, Scott.'

'Don't say sorry tae me. Save it for the wee man.'

'Aw, don't be like that. You know what it's like. Look, when I say as soon as I can, I mean it. But I will have to put a report on Skinner's desk first thing tomorrow, ready to go to the fiscal. And I will have to work out where the hell we go from here, given that our new acting chief's gone and killed the only possible bloody witness.'

His expression softened. 'Ah know, love, Ah know.'

She picked up her purse from the work surface and extracted three ten-pound notes. 'Here,' she said. 'Take him wherever he wants to go with that.'

He raised an eyebrow. 'You're takin' a chance, aren't you?'

She frowned. 'I'd better not be.' She headed for the door. 'Have fun, the pair of you. See you.'

Six

The bedroom door creaked as she opened it, jerking him from a dream that he was happy to leave. 'Are the kids awake yet?' Bob mumbled, into the pillow.

'Are you joking?' Sarah laughed. 'It's five past nine.'

Their reconciliation, which had come after a burst of truth-talking only a day and a half before, had taken them both by surprise, but the next morning neither of them had felt any guilt, only pleasure, and possibly even relief.

Their separation and divorce had not been acrimonious. No, it had been down to a lack of communication and each one of them had concluded, independently, that if they had sat down in the right place at the right time and had talked their problems through in the right spirit, it might not have happened at all.

'You what?' Bob rolled over and sat up in a single movement. He was about to swing a leg out of bed, but she sat on the edge, blocking him off.

'Easy does it,' she said. 'They don't know you're here.'

'They'll see my car.'

'No they won't. You parked it a little way along the road, remember.'

'Alex and Andy?'

'They left after you crashed. That was quite an entrance; five minutes to midnight. Your first words, "Gimme a drink," then you polished off six beers inside half an hour.' She paused, then murmured, 'I can always tell, Bob, the more you drink, the worse it's been.'

'I know,' he admitted. 'And the bugger is, the older I get, the less the bevvy helps.'

'So I gather. You did some shouting through the night. It's just as well this house is stone, with thick walls. How do you feel now?'

'My love, I do not know.' He reached out and tugged at the cord of her dressing gown. She slipped out of it, and eased herself alongside him.

She held his wrist, with two fingers pressed below the base of his thumb. 'Your heart rate is a little fast.'

'Probably the dream. It was a bastard.'

'Are you ready to tell me what happened?'

He slipped his right arm around her shoulders. 'I told you last night. Toni Field is dead, and somehow I let Clive Graham talk me into taking her place for three months. Three months only, mind, even though Aileen and Andy both say once I'm there they'll never get me out.'

'Hey,' Sarah murmured. 'Maybe the witch knows you better than I thought.'

'You think so too?' He shook his head, and a slight grin turned up the corners of his mouth. 'And here was me thinking you and I were making a new start.'

'Then let me put it another way. Sometimes you don't know where your duty lies until it's brought home to you. You've been frustrated since you became chief in Edinburgh; I can see that. You were never really keen on the job, without really knowing why. When you were talked into taking it, you found out. It was more or less what you'd been doing before, but it made you more remote from your people and more authoritarian.

'But Strathclyde's different. You've always known why you didn't want that job; you grew up there in a different time and you feel that force is too big, and as such too impersonal. Now that you've been forced into the hot seat by circumstances in which, in all conscience, you couldn't decline, you might find the challenge you've been needing is to change that. You get what I'm saying?'

'Yes.' He paused. 'But I'm a crime-fighter.'

'I know,' she agreed, 'but even Strathclyde CID's remote, isn't it? If you can bring that closer to the people in every one of the hundreds of communities within the force's area, then won't they feel safer as a result, and won't that be an achievement?'

'Okay,' he nodded, 'I can see your argument. Maybe you're right . . . and maybe if this new unified force does happen it'll be even more important to have someone in charge who thinks like I do. But probably you're wrong. The chances are I'll be back in Edinburgh by November. The chances are also that the unification will happen and I'll walk away from it.' He hesitated, and his forehead twisted into a frown. 'That's the way I feel right now.'

'So tell me why,' she whispered. 'Although I think I can guess, having seen this before.'

'I killed someone,' he whispered, 'one of the South Africans. His name was Gerry Botha. He probably didn't murder Toni Field, not personally, but he was part of the team that did: not just her, but three other people in the last forty-eight hours, and God knows how many more in other places, before that. I've shot people before in the line of duty . . .' He sighed. 'Christ, darlin', most cops never handle a firearm, but I'm always in the firing line. At the time it's a decision you have to make in a split second. I've never been wrong, or doubted myself afterwards, but there comes a time when you have to think that however evil the life you've just snuffed out, someone brought it into being.

'Gerry Botha and his sidekick Francois Smit, they probably have mothers and fathers still alive, and maybe wives and maybe kids who see completely different men at home and who're not going to have them to take them to rugby and cricket or the movies or to the beach any more, like I did yesterday with ours before all this shit happened, and when I start to play with all that in my head I start to think, "Oh God, perhaps that man wasn't all that different from me, just another guy doing the best he can for those he loves." And that's when it gets very difficult.' He leaned back against the headboard, and she could see that his eyes were moist.

She kissed his chest. 'Yeah, I know, love. That's why you, of all people, understand why I prefer to be a pathologist, rather than to work with people with a pulse. But,' she said, 'if I was a psychologist, I'd be telling you to take that thought and apply it to Botha's victims and to imagine how their nearest and dearest are feeling today, then to ask yourself how they'd feel about you if you'd funked your duty? Toni Field, for example; did she have a family?'

'No, she's never been married,' he told her. 'According to the Human Resources director, her next of kin was her mother, name of Sofia Deschamps. He was able to get the mother's details from her file; he accessed it from home. I'm not too happy about that, but it's an issue for later.

'Mother lives in Muswell Hill; a couple of community support officers broke the news to her last night. Apparently there was no mention of a father on her file. The mother was a single parent, Mauritian. Antonia must have Anglicised the name at some point, or maybe the mother did, for she graduated as Field.'

'I guess now they can confirm that she's the victim.'

'Yeah. The press office is going to issue a statement at twelve thirty, after the Police Authority's emergency meeting. That will ratify my . . .

temporary . . . appointment, and I'll be paraded at another media briefing at one.'

'What about your own Police Authority?'

'Good question. The chairperson's a Nationalist, one of the First Minister's cronies. He was going to talk to her last night, but I'll have to give her a call as well, to ask for her blessing, and to get her to nod through Maggie as my stand-in and Mario's move up to ACC Crime.' He took a breath.

'And I'll have to talk to Maggie myself; I can go and see her, since she doesn't live far away. Then I'll need to call in on Mario . . . not to tell him about his promotion, he knows about that . . . but to see how Paula is the day after. And I suppose I'll have to go to Fettes and change into my fucking uniform . . .'

Sarah rolled out of bed and grabbed her dressing gown from the floor. 'Then what the hell are you still doing lying there? Get yourself showered . . . but don't you dare put my Venus leg shaver anywhere near your chin . . . then dress and come downstairs to surprise our children. I'll make you breakfast and then you can get on the road.'

'Yes, boss.' He grinned.

'You'll see,' she added, 'it'll be good for you, this new challenge.'

'If I'm up to it.'

'That's bullshit. You do not do self-doubt, my love.'

Bob frowned. 'No, you're right, not when it comes to work. In everything else though,' he sighed, 'I'm a complete fuck-up. Three marriages; soon to be two divorces. Are you sure you want to get close to me again?'

She put her hands on his shoulders, and drew him to her. 'Even in our darkest moments,' she whispered, 'even across an ocean, I was never not close to you. You see us? We're each other's weakness and strength all rolled into one. This time, strength comes out on top.'

He nodded, stood, took hold of her robe, and kissed her. 'Sounds good to me.'

He headed towards the bathroom, then stopped. 'Will you keep the kids here tonight?'

'Yes. Will you come back here?'

'Mmm. What do you think? Do you want me to, I mean? What will the kids be thinking? This has all happened pretty quick; Aileen being gone, you and me . . .'

'What do I think?' she replied. 'To be brutally honest, I think that Mark won't bat an eyelid, that James Andrew will be pleased . . . he didn't like her and, believe me, I never said a word against her to him . . . and that Seonaid will barely notice she's gone.'

He nodded. 'Okay then. I'll see you later.'

He was stepping into the en-suite when she called after him. 'Hey, Bob?'

He looked over his shoulder. 'Yeah?'

'If you did walk away from the job,' she asked, 'do you have the faintest idea what you'd do?'

'Sure. I could collect non-executive directorships, get paid for sitting on my arse and play a lot of golf, but that wouldn't be my scene. No, if I do that I'll become a consulting detective; I'll become bloody Sherlock.'

Seven

*H*e *looks tired and tense,* Paula Viareggio thought. *But he also looks more alive than I've seen him in a couple of years.*

'I am perfectly fine, Bob,' she assured him. 'Honestly. The police doctor checked me out last night and he said exactly that. He checked both of us out in fact. The baby's good too. For a while afterwards I did wonder if he'd stick his head out to find out what all the fuss was about, but it seems he's keeping to his timetable.'

'You're some woman, Paula,' Skinner chuckled. They were sitting around a table on the deck of the prospective parents' duplex. The sun was high enough to catch the highlights in his steel-grey hair.

'No, I'm just like all the rest. I had my few moments of sheer terror, and I know I'm never going to lose the memory, of the noise more than anything else, the sound of the bullets hitting the poor woman.'

'Hey, enough,' her husband said quietly.

'No, Mario, it's all right; I yelled my head off at the time, because I was afraid . . . I was scared for two, as well. But once something's happened, it's happened. You can't go back, you can't change it, but the danger's over and talking about what happened won't bring it back. So no worries, big fella; I won't be waking up screaming in the night.'

'I'm glad you feel that way,' the chief constable said, 'because there

49

is a formal murder investigation going on in Glasgow and it would be useful if you could give my DI a statement, for the record.'

'I won't have to go through there, will I? I couldn't be arsed with that.'

'No, of course not. You don't need to leave home. Knock it out on your computer, print it, sign it with Mario as witness, then scan it and send it to DI Charlotte Mann.' He dug a card from his pocket and handed it to her. 'Her email address is on that.'

'Will do. Is Aileen having to do the same?' She paused. 'That is the one thing that gets to me, Bob: the idea that she was the real target.'

'Then don't dwell on it,' he told her. 'Because I don't believe she was, and neither does Lottie Mann.' He looked at his colleague. 'How about you, Mario?'

The swarthy detective shook his head. 'Probably not.'

'But what does Aileen think?' Paula asked.

'I've never been good at working that out,' Skinner replied, 'but whatever she believes, she won't mind having people think she was. There's more votes in it.'

She stared at him, shocked. 'Bob, that's not worthy of you. The poor woman was terrified last night.'

'Maybe, but she was spitting tin tacks when I spoke to her last at the thought of Clive Graham taking credit from it.'

'Get away with you, you're doing her an injustice.'

'I wish I was, but I'm not.' His expression changed, became quizzical. 'Did she tell you anything last night about the two of us?'

Paula hesitated. 'No, she didn't say anything specific; but looking back, there was something about her, something different.'

'We're bust,' he said. 'Sorry to be blunt, but it's over. The press will catch on eventually. When they do, we'll call it "irreconcilable differences". That'll be true, as well.'

'The police unification issue? Mario told me you were at loggerheads about it.'

He nodded. 'That's part of it, but not all. She was planning to turn me into a backroom politician. Aileen has ambitions beyond Scotland that I knew nothing about. She had this daft idea that I would help her fulfil them.' He snorted. 'As if.'

He stood, straightened his back, and smoothed his uniform jacket. 'Now I must go. Wouldn't do if I was late for my unveiling.' He turned to Mario once again. 'Okay, ACC McGuire. I have no idea when I'll see you again, but I'm glad the promotion's come through. It probably won't make any operational difference to you, as you'll still be head of CID under the new structure, but you'll be doing the job from the command corridor, where you've belonged for a while now.'

A smile lit up McGuire's face. 'Thanks, boss.'

'You're out of date. Maggie's the boss, for the next three months. She'll need support though; be sure to give her all you can. And have your people do something for me too.'

'Of course.'

'Freddy Welsh. The armourer, the man that young Houseman and I arrested yesterday. The man who supplied the weapons for the concert hall hit and God knows how many others. Clyde and I didn't have time to ask him all the questions we needed to, but they're still relevant. Technically, it's part of Lottie Mann's investigation, but he's in your hands, so your people should handle the interrogation.

'I want to know who placed the order for the weapons. Was it Cohen, the man who put the operation together, or was it someone else? Somebody sent that team after Toni Field . . . yes, Paula, fact is we're certain she was the target . . . and we must find out who it was and why they did it.'

'I'll handle it myself,' the new ACC said. 'But it's a pound to a pinch of pig shit, Bob; his lawyer will have advised him by now to keep his mouth shut.'

'Then keep his lawyer out of it. Welsh is going away for years for illegal possession of firearms, and conspiracy to supply. We don't need to charge him over his involvement in Field's assassination, so you can interview him as a potential witness, not a suspect.'

'Okay, but I'll bet you he still won't talk. His customers aren't the sort you inform on.'

Skinner smiled. 'If that's how it is, you give him a message from me. If he holds out on us, I won't hesitate to hand him over to MI5, and Clyde Houseman. My young friend made quite an impression on Freddy at their first meeting. I don't think Mr Welsh will be too keen on another session. Now, I really am off.'

McGuire saw him to the door. 'Well,' he said as he rejoined his wife in the sunshine. 'Is this our morning for surprises? The big man enticed to Strathclyde, not to mention him and Aileen being down the road.'

'Indeed,' Paula laughed. 'And maybe get yourself ready for another. When she saw that Joey Morocco last night, before the concert, and it was all going off . . . mmm, that was interesting.'

Mario looked at her, intrigued, reading her meaning. 'She looked like she wanted to eat him, did she?'

'Oh, I think she has, in the past. In fact I know so, 'cos she told me. And I'm pretty certain she fancies another helping.'

Eight

'God, but you're hot stuff when you're angry, Aileen de Marco,' Joey Morocco gasped.

She smiled, looking down on him as she straddled him. 'Then look forward to mediocrity, my boy, because I won't stay mad for ever . . . unless you can come up with ways of winding me up.'

'What if I told you I'm a Tory?'

'Hah! That might have worked once, but now I'd just feel sorry for you, 'cos you're an endangered species in Scotland.' She raised an eyebrow, reached behind and underneath her and took his scrotum in her right hand, massaging him, gently. 'You're not, are you?' she asked.

'Absolutely not! Absolutely not!'

'Just as well,' she laughed, releasing him.

'You don't need to stop that, though.'

'Yes, I do. I'm knackered.' She pushed herself to her feet, bounced on the mattress as if it was a trampoline, and jumped sideways off the bed. 'Besides, have you seen what time it is?'

'No; a gentleman removes his Tory Rolex, remember.'

'And this lady keeps on her nice socialist Citizen. For your information it's gone half past twelve.'

'Missed breakfast, then,' he observed, with a cheerful grin. 'Have we still got fairies at the bottom of the garden?'

'My unwanted guardians, you mean?' She crossed to the window and looked outside, taking hold of a curtain and drawing it across her body. 'Yup. They're parked across your driveway too; that's a clear sign to anyone that there's something going on here. I thought the protection people were supposed to be subtle. Here,' she added, 'do you ever have paparazzi hanging around?'

'Yes,' he exclaimed, sitting upright, suddenly alarmed, 'so get your face away from the window.'

She stayed where she was, looking back over her shoulder, and letting go of the curtain. 'Why? Would I be bad for your image? Would your fans not approve of you with an older woman?'

'I'm not worried about my image, Aileen,' he protested. 'I'm concerned about yours. You're married to a bloody chief constable, remember, and you're a top politician. You can't afford scandal.'

She left the window and winked at him. 'Not to "a chief constable", Joey; to "The Chief Constable". Bob's taking over the Strathclyde job; it's an emergency appointment. There was nobody else there anyway.'

Her reassurance was wasted on him. 'Jesus Christ,' he said, 'so these guys outside, they report to him?'

She shrugged. 'I suppose they do. But can you see them being brave enough to go to him and say, "By the way, sir, your wife's shagging Joey Morocco"? Somehow I don't. But even if they did, frankly I would not give the tiniest monkey's. I wouldn't lose my party job over this, for I'm divorcing Chief Constable Skinner just as fast as I can, or he's divorcing me, if he gets in first.' She read his concern. 'Don't worry, Joey. You won't be caught in the middle. The split between Bob and me, it's not about sex, it's about ambitions that could not be further apart. You and me? We're just a bit of fun, right?'

He hesitated, then nodded.

'That's how it was when you were starting out on that soap on BBC Scotland, fun. Now you're in big-budget movies, moved upmarket, and I'm free and soon to be single again, but it's still just fun, convenient uncomplicated nookie, no more than that. You're a sexy guy and I'm a crackin' ride, as my coarser male constituents would say, so let's just enjoy it without either of us worrying about the other. Deal?'

His second nod was more convincing. 'Deal.'

'Good, now what do you do for Sunday lunch these days?'

'Usually I go out for it. Today, maybe not; I'll see what's in the fridge.'

'Do that, and I'll get showered and dressed. No rush, though. I'd like to lie low here for the rest of the day, if I can.'

'Of course. We might even manage breakfast tomorrow?'

'Sounds like a plan. Thanks. You're a sweetheart. It really is good to have somewhere to hide out just now. Actually, I'm a chancer,' she admitted. 'I brought enough clothes with me for two nights.' She shuddered. 'God, was I glad to get out of that dress, with the bloodstains. I felt like Jackie Kennedy.'

He winced at the comparison as she went into his bathroom. She had left her phone there the night before, after brushing her teeth. She switched it on, then checked her voicemail.

There were over a dozen calls. One was from her constituency secretary, one from Alf Old, the Scottish Labour Party's chief executive, another from her deputy leader . . . *Probably cursing that the bastard missed me,* she thought . . . several from other parliamentary colleagues, not all of her party, and three from journalists who were trusted with her number. She had expected nothing from her husband.

As soon as she was showered and dressed she called the secretary, an officious older woman with a tendency to fuss. 'Aileen, where are you?' she demanded, as soon as she answered. 'I've tried your flat, I've tried your house in Gullane. I got no reply from either.'

'Never you mind where I am,' she retorted sharply. 'It would have been nice of you to ask how I was, but I'm okay and I'm safe. Anybody calls inquiring about me, you can tell them that. I may call into the office tomorrow, or I may not. I'll let you know.'

No reply from Gullane? she mused as she ended the call, but had no time to dwell on the information as her phone rang immediately. She checked the screen and saw that it was the party CEO, trying again. 'Alf,' she said as she answered.

'Aileen,' he exclaimed, 'thank God I've got through. How are you?'

'I'm fine, thanks. I'm safe, and I'm with a friend. I'm sorry I didn't call you last night, but things were crazy. The security people got me off the scene, by force, more or less. Even now I have protection officers parked outside, like it or not. The First Minister insisted.'

'Good for him. Now . . .'

'I know what you're going to say. Silence breeds rumours.'

'Exactly. I've had several calls asking where you are, and whether you might have been wounded.'

'Then issue a statement. Have they confirmed yet that it's Toni Field who's dead?'

'Yes. Strathclyde police announced it a wee while ago.'

'In that case we should offer condolences . . . I'll leave it to you to choose the adjectives, but praise her all the way to heaven's gate . . . then add that I'm unharmed, and that I've simply been taking some private time to come to terms with what's happened. I suppose you'd better say something nice about Clive Graham as well, but not too nice, mind you, nothing that he can quote in his next election manifesto.'

'Mmm,' Old remarked. 'I can tell you're okay.'

'I'll be fine as long as I keep myself busy,' she told him. 'I'm sorry if I seem a bit brutal, but even without what happened last night there's a lot going on in my life.'

'Do you want to take some more time out? Everyone would understand.'

'They might,' she agreed, 'but in different ways. There are plenty within the party who'd think I was showing weakness. I don't have to tell you, Alf, as soon as a woman politician does that the jackals fall on her. I've handled stress before; I'm good at it.' She paused. 'I'll be back in business tomorrow; I have to be. The First Minister will come out of this looking like fucking Braveheart, so we have to keep pace. We need to come out with something positive. You know that Clive and I were planning a joint announcement on unifying the Scottish police forces?'

'Yes, you told me.'

'Well, I want to jump the gun. Have our people develop the proposition that what happened in the concert hall illustrates the need for it, that it was a result of intelligence delayed by artificial barriers within our police service that need to be broken down. Then set up a press conference for midday tomorrow. We don't have to say what it's about. They'll be all over me anyway about last night. But I want to be ready to roll with that policy announcement.'

'Will do,' Old said, 'but Aileen, what about your personal security? I know the police don't believe there's any continuing threat to you, because I spoke to the DI in charge this morning, but they can't rule it out completely.'

'I told you,' she snapped, 'I've got bodyguards. But so what? If people want to believe there is someone out to get me, let them. Remember Thatcher at Brighton? The same day that bomb went off she was on her feet, on global telly, making her conference speech and saying "Bring it on". That's the precedent, Alf. I either follow it or I run away and hide. Now get to work, and I'll see you tomorrow.'

As Old went off to follow orders, Aileen thought about returning some of the other calls but decided against it. Instead she trotted downstairs. 'Joey?' she called as she went.

'I'm in the kitchen. Telly's on: you should see this.'

She had had no time to learn the layout of the house when she had arrived late the night before, but she traced his voice to its location. The room looked out on to a large rear garden surrounded by a high wall, topped with spikes. 'No place for the photographers to hide here,' she remarked.

'No. I had the fencing added on when I bought the place. It does the job.'

'So what's on the box that I should see?'

He turned from the work surface where he was putting a salad together and nodded towards a wall-mounted set. It was on, and a BT commercial was running. 'Sky News,' he replied. 'They've been trailing a Glasgow press conference and somebody's name was mentioned. In fact . . .'

As he spoke, the programme banner ran, then the programme went straight to what appeared to be a live location: a table, and two men, one of them in uniform.

'Is that who I think it is?' Joey asked. 'I spoke to him last night; didn't have a clue who he was. No wonder he got frosty when I asked about you.'

She smiled, but without humour or affection. 'That's him. I told you earlier what this is about. Observe and be amazed, for it's one of the biggest U-turns you will ever see in your life. Here, I'll do the lunch.'

As she took over the salad preparation, Joey Morocco watched the bulletin as Dominic Hanlon introduced himself to a roomful of journalists and camera operators. There was a nervous tremor in the councillor's voice, a sure tell that the event was well beyond his comfort zone. He began by paying a fulsome tribute to the dead Antonia Field, and then explained the difficult circumstances in which the Strathclyde force had found itself.

'However,' he concluded, 'I am pleased to announce that with the approval of his Police Authority in Edinburgh, Chief Constable Robert Morgan Skinner has agreed to take temporary command of the force for a period of three months, to allow the orderly appointment of a successor to the late Chief Constable Field. Mr Skinner, would you like to say a few words?' He looked at his companion, happy to hand over.

'In the circumstances,' Skinner replied, 'it's probably best that we go straight to questions.'

A forest of hands went up, and a clamour of voices arose, but he nodded to a familiar face in the front row, John Fox, the BBC Scotland Home Affairs editor.

'Bob,' the reporter began, 'you weren't a candidate for this job last time it was vacant. Are you prepared to say why not?'

The chief constable shrugged. 'I didn't want it.'

'Why do you want it now?'

'I don't, John. Believe me, I would much rather still be arguing with Toni Field in ACPOS over the principles of policing, as she and I did, long and loud. But Toni's been taken from us, at a time when Strathclyde could least afford to lose its leader, given the absence of a deputy.

'When I was asked to take over . . . temporarily; I will keep hammering that word home . . . by Councillor Hanlon's authority, on the basis that its members believe me to be qualified, as a police officer I felt that I couldn't refuse. It wouldn't have been right.'

Fox was about to put a supplementary, but another journalist cut in. 'Couldn't ACC Allan have taken over?'

'Given his seniority, if he was well, yes, but he isn't. He's on sick leave.'

'What about ACC Thomas, or ACC Gorman?'

'Fine officers as they are, neither of them meets the criteria for permanent appointment,' he replied, 'and so the authority took the view that wouldn't have been appropriate.'

'Did you consult your wife before accepting the appointment, Mr Skinner?' The questioning voice was female, its accent cultured and very definitely English. Aileen was in the act of chopping Chinese leaves; she stopped and if she had looked down instead of round at the screen she would have seen that she came within a centimetre of slicing a finger open.

She saw Bob's gaze turn slowly towards the source, who was seated at the side of the room. 'And why should I do that, Miss . . .'

'Ms Marguerite Hatton, *Daily News* political correspondent. She is the Scottish Labour leader, as I understand it. Surely you discuss important matters with her.'

'You're either very smart or very stupid or just plain ignorant, lady,' Aileen murmured. 'You've just lit a fuse.'

A very short one, as was proved a second later. 'What the hell has her position got to do with this?' her estranged husband barked. 'I'm a senior police officer, as senior as you can get in this country. Are you asking, seriously, whether I seek political approval before I take a career decision, or even an operational decision?'

'Oh, really!' the journalist scoffed. 'That's a dinosaur answer. I meant did you consult her as your wife, not as a politician.'

On the screen Skinner stared at her, then laughed. 'You are indeed from the deep south, Ms Hatton, so I'll forgive your lack of local knowledge. I suggest that you ask some of your Scottish colleagues, those who really know Aileen de Marco. They'll tell you that there isn't a waking moment when she isn't a politician. And I can tell you she even talks politics in her sleep!'

'Jesus!' Aileen shouted. 'Joey, switch that fucking thing off!'

'Relax,' he said, 'it's not true.'

The woman from the *Daily News* was undeterred. 'In that case,' she persisted, 'how will she feel about you taking the job?'

'Why should I have any special knowledge of that?' He looked around the room. 'No more questions about my wife, people.'

On camera, John Fox raised a hand. 'Just one more, please, Bob? How is she after her ordeal last night?'

'Last time I saw her she was fine: fine and very angry.'

'Where was that, Mr Skinner?' Marguerite Hatton shouted.

'You've had your five minutes,' he growled. 'Any more acceptable questions?'

The woman beside Fox, Stephanie Marshall of STV, raised a hand. 'You weren't a candidate for the Strathclyde post last time, Chief Constable, but will you put your name forward when it's re-advertised?'

Watching, Aileen saw him lean forward as if to answer, then hesitate.

'If you'd asked me that last night,' he began, 'just after Dominic asked me to take on this role, I would have told you no, definitely not. But something was said to me this morning that's made me change my attitude just a wee bit.

'So the honest answer is, I don't know. Let me see how the next couple of weeks go, and then I'll decide. Now, ladies and gentlemen, I must go. We have a major investigation under way as you all realise, and I must call on the officer who's running it.'

Aileen reached out and grasped the work surface, squeezing it hard.

'What are you doing?' Joey chuckled.

'I'm checking for earth tremors. You might not know it but what he just said is the equivalent of a very large mountain starting to move. I can't believe it. I told him last night he'd never leave Pitt Street once he got in there, but I didn't think for one second that he'd actually listen to me. It's a first.'

He reached out and patted her on the shoulder. 'No, dearie, it's you that wasn't listening to him. His words,' he pointed out, 'were "this morning", not "last night". So whoever made him think again, it wasn't you.'

'You're right,' she whispered. 'Which makes me wonder where the hell he was this morning.'

'While I'm wondering about something else,' Joey said. 'Why did that *News* cow ask where he'd seen you last night?'

Nine

'I'm sorry about that *News* woman, sir,' Malcolm Nopper said. 'I've never seen her before. I can't keep her out of future press conferences, but I'll do my best to control her.'

Skinner looked at the chief press officer he had inherited from Toni Field, and laughed. The media had been escorted out of the conference room in the force headquarters building and the two men were alone. Nopper eyed his new boss nervously, unsure how to read his reaction.

'How the hell are you going to do that?' the chief constable asked. 'Sellotape over her gob? So you didn't know her? I didn't know her either, and it would have been the same if she'd turned up in Edinburgh, on my own patch. She's a seagull; we all get them.'

'A seagull, sir?'

'Sure, you know, they fly in, make a noise, shit on you, then fly away again. As for controlling her, you don't have to. If she turns up at one of my media briefings in future . . . not that I plan to have many . . . I'll simply ignore her. You can do the same at any you chair.'

'I tend not to do that, Chief,' Nopper said. 'When an investigation's in process, I let the senior investigating officer take the lead.'

'Not any more. Lottie Mann will have to go before the media later on. From something that Max Allan told me a while back, I guess she hasn't had any formal media training. Am I right?'

'None that I can recall,' the civilian agreed.

'I know she'll be fine, but I'm not sure she does, so she must have a minder. I'll be there but if I go on the platform it'll undermine her. As you said, she's the SIO. So you'll be there, you'll introduce her and you'll pick the questioners. Ms Hatton will not be one of them. Your regulars won't mind that. In my experience they don't like seagulls either.'

'As you wish, Chief.'

'Mmm. Where will you hold it? Do you have a favourite venue?'

'No. Normally it would be where it's most convenient for the officer in charge.'

'In that case we do it here in Pitt Street, in this room. I spoke to DI Mann on the way through here. She'll be finished at the concert hall by two. She and I agreed that given the nature of this investigation it's best that it be centrally based, rather than in a police office that's open to the general public. Nobody else will be using this room this afternoon, will they?'

'Not as far as I know, but suppose somebody was, you want it, you get it.'

'Okay, set it up for four. That'll give Lottie time to brief me, and it will give me time to get used to my new surroundings.'

As he spoke, a figure appeared in the double doorway.

'Lowell,' Skinner called. 'You found us. DCI Payne is going to be my executive officer during my stay here,' he explained to the press officer. 'When you want to get to me, you do it through him. That'll be the case for everyone below command rank, but be assured, I will be accessible; his job won't be to keep people out, but to help them in.'

He moved towards the exit. 'Your first task, Lowell. Show me to my office. I knew where it was in Jock Govan's time, but I have no clue now.'

As one of her first signs of her new-broom approach, Antonia Field had rejected the office suite used by her predecessors and had commandeered half a floor in the newer part of the headquarters complex. 'Have you decided where you're going to live, sir?' Payne asked as he led the way up a flight of stairs towards the third floor.

Skinner stopped. 'Lowell,' he said, 'I don't expect to be "sirred" all the time by senior officers, least of all by you. You want to call me something official, call me "Chief". When there's nobody else around and you ask me something you'd ask me over the dinner table, call me Bob, like always.'

'Fair enough. Although,' he added, 'it was really a professional question, since I'll have to know where to raise you in an emergency.'

'True. The answer is that as much as possible I plan to live in my own house. I will have a driver and I plan to use him.'

'That's in Gullane?'

'Sure. Where . . .' He halted in mid-sentence. 'Ah, you thought I might stay in Aileen's flat.'

'Well, yes.'

'That won't be happening. It will become apparent soon, if only because we're both public figures, that she and I are no longer together.'

Payne was silent for a few seconds, as they resumed their climb. 'I see,' he murmured. 'I'm sorry to hear that. So that's why you weren't with her at the concert.'

'That was part of the reason. Anyway, it's not public knowledge yet, although I came close to making it so in my press briefing, when that bloody *News* person wound me up. It is something I'll have to deal with, and soon, but not right now. Once we've both calmed down, we may issue a joint statement, but we're both too hot to discuss that just now.

'So,' he continued, 'Gullane is where you'll reach me most of the time. When I have to stay here I'll use a hotel; Hanlon's already said he'll pick up the tab for that . . . without me even asking, would you believe.'

They reached the top of the stairway; Payne turned left, and headed along a corridor that was blocked by a glass doorway, with a keypad. He opened it with four digits and led the way into a complex with more than a dozen rooms around a small central open space, with four chairs surrounding a low table, on which magazines were piled.

'This is it, Chief, your new command suite. Your office is facing us.'

Skinner stared ahead. 'It's got glass walls,' he exclaimed.

'Relax,' his aide said, noting his indignation. 'There are internal blinds between the panels. I'm told that Chief Constable Field kept them open all the time.'

'That will change; they'll be closed permanently. I never did like people watching me think.'

'There's a bathroom and a changing room as well. They have solid walls,' he added.

'Just as well, or I'd be going back to Jock Govan's old suite. Do I have a secretary?'

'Of course, but she isn't here today. I called her and told her what was happening, about you, and your appointment. I didn't want her finding out from the telly. She offered to come in, but I told her not to.'

'What's her name?'

'Marina Deschamps.'

'Mmm,' Skinner murmured, then he blinked. 'Deschamps, you said? Wasn't that Toni's birth name?'

Payne nodded. 'Yes. It's her sister; the chief brought her with her. She insisted on it, apparently, before she accepted the job.'

'Eh? The bloody Human Resources director didn't think to tell me that last night.' He frowned. 'What about the mother? Are we flying her up here?'

'The Met took care of that. They got her on to the first Glasgow flight this morning.'

'I wish to hell they'd left her down there.' He sighed. 'I know I have to pay her a courtesy call, but I'll leave that until tomorrow. Meantime, the sister should be regarded as on compassionate leave. Does she have a contract of employment?'

'I don't know for sure, Chief, but I'd imagine so.'

'She's a civilian, yes?'

'Yes.'

'Okay. Tell the Human Resources director that her contract will be honoured. If she wants to stay here in another capacity, she can. If she wants to leave, then she may do so at once, but she'll be paid as if she'd worked a full notice period, whatever that is. Then tell him to find me a replacement, pronto, someone with full security clearance, mainly to manage my mail and yours.'

They had been walking as they talked, and reached Skinner's new office as he finished issuing his orders. The door was locked, but Payne took a ring with three keys from his trouser pocket and handed it over. 'I had the lock changed,' he said. 'Easier than searching through Ms Field's things and getting Marina's back from her.'

'Good thinking.' He detached a key from the ring, used it to unlock the door, then handed it to the DCI. 'Yours,' he said then stepped inside. As he did so he felt a sudden and unexpected shiver run through him. 'Weird,' he murmured. 'I have never imagined doing this, not once.'

He looked around. The room was larger than the one he had left in Edinburgh, but furnished in much the same way. His desk was on the left, facing a round meeting table, with six chairs that slid underneath it. Beyond, there was another door; he could see through the unscreened glass wall that it led into another office.

He pointed towards it. 'Secretary's room?'

'Yes,' his aide replied.

'Where are you going to go?'

'I hadn't given that any thought.'

'Where's the deputy's office?'

'That's the one beyond the secretary's.'

'Then use that. It's vacant.'

'Okay, Chief, thanks.' Payne walked behind the desk and opened a door behind it. 'Your personal rooms are through here,' he said. 'There's a safe in the changing room, but apparently nobody knows the combination, unless Marina does. I'll ask her. If she doesn't I'll . . .' He smiled. 'Actually I'm not sure what I'll do.'

'Too bad Johnny Ramensky's dead,' Skinner chuckled.

'Yeah: the last of the legendary safecrackers. As for the rest,' the DCI continued, 'all of Ms Field's things have been removed, from the changing room and the bathroom, and everything from the desk as well, that wasn't office-related. Her business diary is still there, so you can see what she had in her schedule. There are also some files. I had a look at them, a very quick look, and then closed them up again. They seem to contain her observations on her senior colleagues.'

'Then take them away and shred them,' Skinner instructed him. 'I don't want to know about her prejudices and her grudges.' He grinned. 'I prefer to develop my own. What's the general view of Michael Thomas?' he asked. 'You can be frank, don't worry.'

'Unfavourable,' Payne replied, without a pause for thought. 'I knew him as a constable, way back, after I'd made sergeant. He was "Three bags full" then, before he started to climb. Much later I was stationed in his division for a while when he was a chief super. He virtually ignored me. He has a reputation for efficiency, but also for being a cold fish. He was a big supporter of Toni Field, at least he kissed her arse regularly enough.'

'I know that from ACPOS. He was her regular seconder in the debate on unification. What about Bridie Gorman?'

'Now she is well liked. She spends a lot of time out of the office, in the outlying areas of the force. I think that suited her, and suited Chief Constable Field as well, for they were complete opposites, as cops and as people.' Payne scratched his chin. 'Obviously I don't know what perceptions were outside Strathclyde, but the view in here was that Field planned to get rid of every chief officer apart from ACC Thomas. She'd already axed the deputy, and it was common knowledge that Mr Allan was next.'

Skinner nodded. 'Yes, I could tell that at ACPOS too. She didn't even try to be civil to him. Any word on him, by the way?'

'Yes, I checked. He's still in hospital, suffering from what they're now describing as shock. They're going to keep him in for a couple of days. I don't know how he'll feel about coming back.'

'Then see if you can find out for me. Go and visit him, this evening if you can. Max is only a few months off the usual retirement age. If he's up to talking about it, tell him that if he'd like to come back, I'll be happy to see him, but if he doesn't, I'll sign him off for enough sick leave to take him up to his due date.'

'Yes, Chief; I was planning to go and see him anyway. He's always been good to me.'

'Fine. Now who's here, in the building now?'

'ACC Thomas is. He said he'd be in his office, and that he'd like to see you as soon as possible. And ACC Gorman's in as well. She came down from Argyll overnight.'

'Does she want to see me too?'

'No, she said to tell you she was about if you needed her, that's all.'

Skinner smiled. 'Okay then, let's talk to her; I can spare a few minutes before I have to see Lottie. Ask her to drop in, then give Mr Thomas my apologies, tell him that I'll fit him in tomorrow morning, and that he's free to salvage what's left of his Sunday.'

As Payne left, he walked over to the desk, tried the swivel chair for height, and found, as he had expected, that it was set far too low. He stayed in it for only a few seconds, then pushed himself out. There was something not right about it, something that made his spine tingle. He knew what it was without any deep analysis. Less than forty-eight hours before, Toni Field had been sitting in it, and at that very moment she was lying in a refrigerated drawer in one of the city's morgues, unless she was being autopsied by Sarah's opposite number in the west.

He knew that he would never feel comfortable in her old seat, and so he wheeled it over to the secretary's office, and left it in there with a note saying, 'Replace, please,' scribbled on a sheet torn from a pad.

He had just stepped back into his own room when he heard a knock on the door. 'Come in,' he called.

'I can't,' a female voice shouted back. 'This door self-locks. It can only be opened with a key or from the inside.'

He stepped across and admitted his visitor. ACC Bridget Gorman was in civvies, light tan trousers and a check shirt. 'Afternoon, Chief,' she said. Her manner was tentative, not that of the Bridie Gorman he knew.

'Hey, Bridie, last week at ACPOS it was Bob,' he told her. 'It still is, okay? Come in and have a seat.' He showed her across to the table and pulled out two of the chairs.

She glanced across to the desk, taking in the missing swivel but saying nothing. 'Wouldn't be right,' he replied to her unspoken question. 'I feel bad enough being here.'

Gorman frowned, and her forehead all but disappeared behind a mop of black but grey-streaked hair. 'I know,' she murmured. 'It's just awful. And it could have been Aileen.'

'No,' he said. 'I don't believe it could, and neither does DI Mann.' He explained why.

She nodded. 'Yes, I can see that. Somebody like them, they'd know exactly who they were shooting, I suppose. But why? Why Toni Field?'

'They didn't need to know that.'

'But they'd know who wanted it done.'

'Not all the way up the chain, not necessarily.'

'Do you think it was related to something here?'

'Come on, Bridie,' Skinner murmured, 'you know the rule: speculation hinders investigation.'

'Aye, I suppose I do. Did you say that Lottie Mann's involved?'

'She was on duty; she took the shout.'

'Granted, but . . . Lottie can be like a runaway train. Max Allan was always careful how she was deployed.'

'I know that,' he conceded. 'But last night was chaos. The hall was full of headless chickens, but she turned up and took charge, even put me in my place. I liked that. It means she's my kind of cop. What's her back story? She said she has a family, but that's all I know about her.'

'That's right,' she confirmed, 'she has. Her husband used to be a cop too. His name's Scott, as I recall. I've got no idea what the wee boy's called.'

'Used to be, you say?'

'Yes. He left the force a few years back. No, that's a euphemism; he was encouraged to resign. He had a drink problem and eventually it couldn't be tolerated any more. The job probably didn't help, for he seems to have got himself together after he left it. The last I heard he was working in security in a big cash and carry warehouse out near Easterhouse.' She smiled. 'There's a story about Lottie and an interdivisional boxing night . . .'

'I've heard it. Max Allan told me.'

'Aye but did he tell you the name of the cop she flattened? It was Scott; that was how they met.'

Skinner laughed, softly. 'There's a love story for you. Somebody should make the movie.'

'Fine, but who would you get to play Lottie?'

'That would be a problem, I concede. Gerard Butler in drag, maybe.' A name suggested itself. 'Joey Morocco?'

'Mr Glasgow? Our movie flavour of the month? He looks good, granted, but I wonder sometimes if there's any real substance to him. I'm pretty sure I'd back Lottie against him over ten rounds.'

'Maybe I'll make that match,' the chief murmured. 'It would fill Ibrox Stadium. Bridie,' he said, his tone changing, 'I know you're as surprised to see me here as I am to be here.'

She contradicted him. 'No, I'm not. What happened, happened. I think they've done the right thing. This force always needs a strong hand; Max is too old, I don't have the experience in the rank, and neither does Michael, whatever he might think.' She frowned, concern in her eyes. 'How is Max, by the way?'

'He's okay, but it remains to be seen whether he'll be back. But whether he is or not . . . I have to get some hierarchy in place here. That means I need to appoint a temporary deputy chief. Even if Max was here, I'd want that to be you. Are you up for it?'

She was silent for a few seconds. 'How can I say no?' she asked when she was ready. 'But what are you going to tell Thomas?'

'I don't plan to explain myself, if that's what you mean, Bridie. The Police Authority gave me the power to designate my deputy, and you are it.'

She smiled, and said, 'This might sound daft, Bob, but . . . what will I have to do as deputy?'

He returned her awkward grin and replied, 'To be honest, I don't know yet, not in any detail, because I don't know yet what the demands of the job will be on me. Mind you, they have just cast doubt on my plans to go to my house in Spain in a couple of weeks' time, something I'll have to break to my children. Holidays might prove to be out of the question.'

'Aw, what a shame,' she exclaimed, like a kindly aunt. 'The poor wee souls.'

'It might not be a complete disaster. I'll ask their mother if she can clear some time to take them instead.' He sighed. 'As for your question, all I can say is that you'll deputise for me whenever it's necessary.'

'I'd better go and practise looking important then,' the ACC chuckled. 'Was there anything else for now?'

'No. My usual practice is to have a morning session with my senior colleagues. I'll probably carry that on here; Lowell Payne will advise everybody. He's going to be my aide while I'm settling in here, maybe for longer.'

'Good,' she declared. 'I like Lowell. He tends to fly below the radar; that may be why he hasn't risen higher.'

'I don't think he's bothered about that. I know him well, from outside the force, and I'm glad to have him alongside me.' He stood. She thought he was indicating the end of the meeting and was in the act of rising, but he waved to her to stay seated.

'I'm just about to call Lottie up here, to give me an update on her investigation. You stay here and sit in; belt and braces. Christ, after what happened to Toni, none of us can be sure we're going to see tomorrow.'

Ten

'I could get to like this,' Aileen said. 'Bob's garden in Gullane is nice too, but it overlooks the beach. He refuses to plant trees to give it a bit of privacy; says he likes the view.' She picked up her glass from the wrought-iron table. 'Well he's bloody welcome to it!'

Don't get to like it too much, Joey Morocco thought. He had been on the astonished side of surprised when Aileen had called him the night before, almost raving about being imprisoned by her husband and seeking sanctuary for a day or two, but they had enjoyed regular liaisons a few years before, and the occasional fling since.

Their history together had been enough to overcome his caution about taking another man's wife under his roof, even when the man was as formidable as Bob Skinner was said to be.

Nonetheless, when she had defined their renewed relationship, *'just fun, convenient uncomplicated nookie, no more than that'*, he had been relieved. He was bound for Los Angeles in a few days, for the film project that was going to make him, he knew, and the last thing he wanted was a heavy-duty woman in Scotland with her claws in him.

'Are you sure that's really what you want?' he asked. 'To end your marriage?'

'Bloody certain,' she replied. 'I don't actually know what drew me to him in the first place.' She grinned. 'No, that's not true, I do. I

75

wanted to find out if he matched up to the waves he was giving out. Very few do, in my limited experience.'

'Did he?'

'At first, yes. Then I made the mistake of marrying him. It all got mediocre after that, but I suppose that's life. I'll learn from it, though; once is enough.'

He smiled.

'And you're relieved to hear that, I know,' she said. 'Don't worry, Joey. My career is all planned out, and it doesn't take me within six thousand miles of where you're going.' She looked around the suntrap garden once more. 'But this is nice. I like it here; it suits me. I'm guessing that when you go to the US, you won't be back here very often, so if you need a tenant, let me know.'

'I will,' he promised. 'The way my commitments are, I won't be back for at least a year, so that might work. You'd be a house-sitter, though, not a tenant.'

'No,' she declared. 'It would have to be formal. I couldn't be seen as your bidey-in, even though you were never here.'

He shrugged. 'Whatever,' he murmured, hoping secretly that it would all be forgotten by the next morning. 'Want another drink?' he asked.

Aileen pressed her glass to her chest. 'No, I'm fine,' she said. 'I'm not a big afternoon drinker . . . or evening, come to that. You've seen me in action before. You know I can't handle it.'

'True,' he conceded. 'If you're sure . . . I think I'll get another beer, if you don't mind.'

'Not a bit.'

He wandered back into the kitchen, and took another Rolling Rock from the fridge. He had just uncapped it when the phone rang. He frowned, irked by the interruption, wondering which of the few people with access to his unlisted number had a need to call it on a bloody Sunday, when they all knew it was the day he liked to keep to himself.

'Yes,' he barked, not choosing to hide his impatience.

'Is that Joey Morocco?' a female voice asked.

'Depends who this is.'

'My name's Marguerite Hatton. I'm on the political staff of the *Daily News*.'

'And I'm a bloody actor, so why are you calling me?' *Hatton, Hatton*; the name was fresh in his mind. Of course, the woman from the press conference, she who had tried to give Aileen's husband a hard time, and had her arse well kicked.

'I'm trying to locate Aileen de Marco,' she replied. 'I'd like to talk to her about her ordeal last night and how relieved she feels that the killer got the wrong woman.'

'So?' he challenged. 'Why are you calling me?'

'You're quoted as saying, last night as you left the concert hall, that you're a friend of hers,' she explained. 'I'm calling around everyone; the Labour Party, Glasgow councillors, anyone who might know her, actually, but she seems to have disappeared. Do you have any idea where she might be?'

'Why should I? And if I did, do you really think that I'd betray her by setting you on her? If you want to find her, ask her husband, why don't you?'

'I rather think not,' Hatton drawled. 'Can you tell me about your relationship with Ms de Marco, Mr Morocco?'

'No,' he snorted. 'Why the hell should I do that?'

'But you did say you're a friend of hers.'

'Yes. So what? Aileen has many friends. She's Glasgow's leading lady. Ask a real journalist and they'll tell you that.'

'Oh, but I'm a real journalist, Mr Morocco,' she told him. 'Be in no doubt about that. How long have you known Ms de Marco?'

'For a few years.'

'How close are you?'

'We are friends, okay? Is there any part of that you don't understand?'

'What's the nature of your friendship?'

'Private. Now please piss off.'

'I don't think so.'

He felt himself boil over. 'Listen, hen,' he shouted, lapsing into Glaswegian in his anger, 'you want to talk to me, you go through my agent or my publicist. By the way, both of those are owed favours by your editor, so don't you be making me have them called in.'

'He owes me a few as well, Joey,' she countered. 'I keep bringing him exclusives, you see. When did you last see Ms de Marco?'

'Fuck off!' he snapped and slammed the phone back into its cradle.

'You've been a while,' Aileen said, as he rejoined her.

'I had a nuisance call,' he replied.

'There's a number you can call that stops you getting those.'

'It doesn't always work. But hopefully that one's gone away to bother somebody else.'

Eleven

'How's the force reacting to Mr Skinner's appointment?' Harry Wright of the *Herald* called out, from the second row of the questioning journalists gathered in the Pitt Street conference room.

'Come on, Harry,' Malcolm Nopper began to protest, but Lottie Mann cut across him.

'How would I know?' she replied, her deep booming voice at a level just below a shout. 'I'm just one member of this force, and for the last,' she made a show of checking her watch, 'twenty hours, minus a few for sleep, I've been leading a murder investigation. I think I can say for everybody that we're all still shocked by what happened to our former chief constable. As for the new chief, he's keeping in close touch with my investigation, but he's confirmed me as the lead officer.'

'Ladies and gentlemen,' Nopper exclaimed, 'people, I know these are unique circumstances, but I remind you that we're here to discuss an ongoing inquiry into a suspicious death.'

A few explosions of laughter, some suppressed, some not, came from the gathering at his blatant use of police-speak. Skinner winced, and reflected on his insistence that the chief press officer should take the chair at the briefing. He had slipped into the room at the first call for order, and was standing at the back, half-hidden behind a Sky News camera operator.

'Okay,' Nopper sighed, shifting in his seat before the Strathclyde
Police logo backdrop as he tried to rescue the situation. 'At least that
got your attention. My point was that this is a murder we're here to talk
about and that it should be treated just like any other, regardless of
who the victim is. Now can we stick to the point?' He looked towards
the *Herald* reporter. 'Harry,' he invited, 'do you want to ask a proper
question?'

The man shrugged. 'I thought that was, but never mind. Detective
Inspector, you were able to confirm for us that the police victims are
Chief Constable Field and Sergeant Sproule. Now can you tell us
anything about the other two men? Do you know who they are . . .
were, sorry?'

Lottie straightened in her chair, and took a deep breath, in an effort
to slow down her racing heart. 'We believe so,' she replied, speaking
steadily. A murmur rippled through the media, and she paused to let
it subside. 'They've been identified as Gerard Botha and Francois
Smit. They were both South African citizens, and they've been
described to us as military contractors.'

'Mercenaries?' a female *Daily Record* hack shouted.

The reporter was so suddenly excited that Lottie suspected she had
spent her career waiting to write a crime story that didn't involve
domestic violence, homophobia or dawn raids on drug dealers. 'If you
want to use that term,' she said, 'I won't be arguing with you.'

'Who gave you that description?' John Fox asked, from his
customary front and centre seat.

'Intelligence sources,' the DI told him.

'MI6?'

Lottie looked him in the eye, then gave him the smallest of winks.
'Be content with what I've given you.' She came within a couple of
breaths of adding, 'There's a good boy,' but stopped herself just in

time, realising that Pacific Quay's top crime reporter was someone she did not need as an enemy.

Fox grinned. 'I had to ask, Lottie. These men were the killers, yes?'

She nodded. 'Yes.'

'To what degree of certainty?'

'Absolute.'

'Do you know as certainly how they came to die?'

'Yes,' the DI said. 'But with the greatest respect, I'm going to tell the procurator fiscal before I tell you. Fair enough?'

The BBC reporter shrugged his shoulders slightly as if in agreement, but some others tried to press the point. She held her position until eventually Harry Wright changed the angle of approach.

'DI Mann, the concert hall had security cover and the event was policed, yet these two men seem to have smuggled a weapon in there regardless. Is your investigation focusing on your own security and on the lapses that allowed this to happen?'

'We know how they did that too, but again I'm not able to share it with you.'

'Same reason, I suppose,' Wright moaned. 'The fiscal gets to know before the public.'

She shook her head, firmly. 'No. It's information that we have to keep in-house for now. There are aspects of it that we need to follow up.'

'Continuing lines of inquiry?'

'Sure, if you want to say that, I'm content.'

'DI Mann, why isn't Mr Skinner sitting alongside you?' Marguerite Hatton cried out from the side of the room.

'Relevant questions only,' Nopper exclaimed. 'Anyone else?'

'I'll decide what's relevant,' the woman protested. 'I'll disrupt this press conference until you answer. Why isn't the new chief constable present?'

'He is!'

Every head in the room, apart from the two seated at the table, turned at Skinner's bellow.

'Satisfied?' he boomed. 'DI Mann is leading this investigation and she enjoys my full confidence.'

'How is your wife today, Mr Skinner?' Hatton shouted back.

Slowly, the chief constable walked towards her. A press office aide stood at the side of the room, holding one of the microphones that were available so that every reporter's questions could be heard. He held out his hand for it and took it, then stopped.

He knew that the TV cameras were running and that still photographs were being shot, but made no attempt to have them stop.

'Lady,' he said, into the mike, 'I don't know who you think you are, or what special privileges you expect from me, but you're not getting any. You're here at our invitation to discuss a specific matter, and now you're threatening disruption, as everyone here has heard. I'm not having that. One more word from you and I'll have you ejected.'

'This is a public meeting,' she protested.

'Don't be daft,' he snapped back at her. 'It's a police press conference. I mean it. One more word and you are on the pavement.' He held her gaze, his eyes icy cold, boring into hers, unblinking, until she subsided and turned away from him.

'Okay,' he murmured. 'As long as we're clear.' He looked at the platform. 'Carry on, Malcolm.'

'Thank you, sir,' the chief press officer said.

The *Daily Record* reporter raised her hand. Nopper nodded to her. 'Can we take it that Chief Constable Field's relatives have been told?'

'Of course,' he replied. 'We released her identity, didn't we? Her mother arrived in Glasgow this morning.'

Shit, Skinner thought, *they're going to love you for that when the media turn up on their doorstep.*

'Did they identify the body?'

Malcolm Nopper put a hand to his mouth, to hide a laugh.

'They knew who she was, Penny,' John Fox pointed out.

Twelve

'So you're the armourer,' ACC Mario McGuire said to the man who faced him across the table in the Livingston police office. There was nobody else in the interview room.

Freddy Welsh was a big man, one with 'Don't cross me' in his eyes, but someone had. There was a deep blue bruise in the middle of his forehead and his right hand was bandaged. For all that, he still looked formidable. 'I don't recognise that name,' he murmured.

'Maybe not, but it seems that other people do. People like Beram Cohen.'

'Never heard of him.'

McGuire leaned back and sighed. 'Look, Mr Welsh, can we stop playing this game? You've never been in police custody before, so I appreciate you're only doing what you've seen on the telly, but really it's not like that. There's no recording going on here.

'You've already been charged with illegal possession of a large quantity of weapons. We have the gun that was used in last night's murder in Glasgow, and we are in the process of proving beyond any doubt that it came from the crate that was found yesterday afternoon in your store. You can take it that we will do that, and as soon as we do, the Crown Office will have a decision to make.'

'And what would that be?' Welsh asked.

'Are you really that naive, man?' McGuire laughed. 'Do I have to spell it out? The kill team that executed Toni Field are all dead.'

The prisoner's eyelids flickered rapidly. He licked his lips.

'You didn't know that?' his interrogator exclaimed.

Welsh shook his head. 'I've been locked up since last night, and I wasn't offered my choice of newspaper with breakfast this morning. How would I know anything? I don't even know who this bloke Tony Field is, or how Glasgow comes into it.'

'Antonia Field,' McGuire corrected. 'The Chief Constable of Strathclyde. She was the victim. Your customer, Mr Smit, put three rounds through her head. You told my colleague Mr Skinner it was a woman he and Botha were after, and you were right.'

The other man frowned, as he took in the information. McGuire had assumed that he knew at least some of it, but it was clear to him that he had been wrong. 'And they're dead?' he said.

The ACC nodded in confirmation. 'Yeah. Cohen, the planner, the team leader, he died of natural causes, a brain haemorrhage, but you knew that much. As for the other two, Mr Skinner and the other man you met,' as he spoke he saw the shadow of a bad memory cross Welsh's face, 'arrived on the scene too late to save Chief Constable Field, but they did come face to face with Smit and Botha as they tried to escape, over the bodies of two other police officers they'd just taken down. They were offered resistance and they shot them both dead.'

The armourer started to tremble. McGuire liked that. 'Yes,' he went on, 'dead. It's one thing being the supplier, Freddy, isn't it? You've been doing that for donkey's years, supplying the weapons to all sorts, but never being anywhere near them when the trigger was pulled. Not like that here, though. You're too close this time, and it's scary. Isn't it?'

He reached into his pocket and pulled out two photographs and laid them in the table. One showed the body of Antonia Field, the other that of Smit.

'Go on, take a good look,' he urged. 'That leaky grey stuff, that's brain matter. Awful, isn't it?'

Welsh pushed them back towards him.

'You don't like reality, do you?' he said. 'It's not good to be that close.' He leaned forward again. 'Well, you are, and far closer than you realise. That woman, her whose photo I've just shown you, when that was done to her, my wife,' his voice became quieter, and something came into it that had not been there before, 'my heavily pregnant wife, was in the very next seat. When I got her home last night she was in a crime scene tunic that Strathclyde Police gave her, because the clothes she'd been wearing before had Toni Field's blood and brains splattered all over them, and she couldn't get out of them fast enough.'

He stopped, then reached a massive hand across the desk, seized Welsh's chin and forced him to meet his gaze.

'So far I know of four people who I hold responsible for that, Freddy. You are the only one left alive, and that puts you right in it, because now only you can tell me who commissioned this outrage. And you will tell me.' He laughed, as he released Welsh from his grasp.

'You know, Bob Skinner suggested that if you didn't cooperate, I should get the MI5 guy here to persuade you. But I don't actually need him. He's just a spook with a gun, whereas I am a husband who's going to wake up in cold sweats, for longer than I can see ahead, at the thought of what might have happened to my Paula and our baby if that sight you supplied with your Heckler and fucking Koch carbine had been just a wee bit out of alignment.

'I've been playing it cool up to now, because Paula's amazingly calm about it and I want to keep her that way, but that's been a front. Inside I've been raging from the moment it happened. Now I can finally let it out. You're a big guy, but you're not tough. There's a hell of a difference. I'm probably going to beat the crap out of you anyway, but what you have to tell me may determine when I stop.'

He sprang from his seat and started round the table.

Thirteen

'So what have your people got?' Skinner's jacket . . . while he disliked any uniform, his hatred for the new tunic style favoured by some of his brother chiefs was absolute . . . was slung over the back of the new swivel chair that had been in place by the time he had returned from the press briefing. He had refused all requests for one-on-one interviews, insisting instead that these be done with Lottie Mann, as lead investigator.

His visitor was as smartly dressed as he had been the day before, but the blazer had given way to a close-fitting leather jerkin. *No room for a firearm there*, the chief thought. Just as well or security would have gone crazy. The garment was a light tan in colour almost matching Clyde Houseman's skin tone, but not quite, for his face sported a touch of pink. 'Have you caught the sun?' he asked.

The younger man smiled. 'Did you think I'd just get browner?' he responded. 'I'm only one quarter Trinidadian, on my father's side. The rest of me gets as sunburned as you. And the answer's yes. I went for a run this morning, a long one; not on a treadmill either but around the streets.'

'Where did you go?'

'Along Sauchiehall Street, then down Hope Street to the Riverside; over the Squinty Bridge, along the other side for a bit then I crossed back further up, past Pacific Quay. Up to Gilmorehill from there, round the university, and then home.'

'Is that your normal Sunday routine?'

'Hell no. Normally I go out for breakfast somewhere. There are a few places nearby.'

'Where is home?'

'Woodlands Drive.'

Skinner's eyebrows rose slightly. 'Woodlands Drive, indeed. I had a girlfriend who had a flat share there, in my university days. Louise.' His eyes drifted towards the unfamiliar ceiling, and then back to his visitor. 'Are you married, Clyde?'

Houseman shook his head. 'Half my life in the Marines and special forces, seeing action for most of it, then on to MI5. No,' he chuckled. 'I couldn't find the time to fit that in. Not that I had any incentive, given the happy home I grew up in.'

The two men's first encounter had been in a squalid housing estate in Edinburgh, when Skinner had just made detective superintendent. Houseman had been a street gang leader, son of a convicted murderer and a thief, until the scare the cop had thrown into him had made him rethink his entire life and join the military.

'Hey,' the chief constable said, 'mine wasn't that great either. It didn't put me off marriage, though, not that I've been very fucking good at it. I've had three goes so far. My first wife died young, car crash, second marriage ended in divorce, and now the third's going the same way.'

'You and the politician lady?'

'Yeah. She had this notion that I should help her fulfil her ambitions, which are substantial. That would have involved me following behind, in the Duke of Edinburgh position. Not my scene, I'm afraid, so we're calling it a day.'

'Won't that be tough on your kids?'

'No. The three young ones are very close to their mother, and as for my adult daughter, she'll wave Aileen a cheerful goodbye. Having made a similar mistake herself she reckons I was daft to split up with Sarah in the first place, and I'm coming to agree with her. They say that Alex and I are absolutely alike, but that's hardly surprising, since I pretty much brought her up on my own.'

He sighed. 'I know why you went for the run, incidentally. To clear your head after what happened last night. We all have our own way of dealing with the shitty end of the job, the things we see, and sometimes the things we have to do; I've been known to go running myself, but usually I get pissed first, to give me something to run off, so it'll hurt that wee bit more. Sometimes I wish I was a Catholic like my friend Andy, so I could go to church and get absolution. But no, not me; I have to do it the hard way.'

Without warning he swung his chair around and sat upright, his forearms on his desk. 'But enough of that. I asked you what your people have got, if anything, on the origin of this hit. We've discounted the notion that Aileen was the target, so, who wanted Toni Field dead?'

Houseman looked back at him, his expression serious. 'I'm not sure I have the authority, sir,' he replied.

Skinner shook his head. 'No, Clyde, I'm not having that. I know there's recent history between your team and Strathclyde and that your deputy director told you to keep your distance from our Counter-terrorism and Intelligence Section. But that was then and this is now.

'Amanda Dennis may have told you she thought it was leaky, but I know damn well that she didn't like or trust Toni Field, and didn't want any involvement with her. I've known Amanda for years, and I worked with her on an internal investigation I did in Thames House a few years ago. I can lift that phone right now and have your order rescinded, but save me the bother, eh?'

The spook gazed at him for a few seconds, then shrugged. 'I'm sure you're right,' he said, 'and I don't fancy breaking into Amanda's Sunday, so okay. The truth is we've got nothing yet. But that's no disgrace, since we've concentrated our efforts since last night on the source of the intelligence that London had, that there was going to be a political hit somewhere in Britain.

'Twenty-four hours ago, that was my colleagues' firm conviction. Today, they're saying they were conned. The threat was bogus; somebody in Pakistan was trying to buy entry into Britain for his family. In short, back to square one.' He smiled. 'Now, since we're sharing, how about you?'

'Fair enough,' Skinner conceded. 'We've been working on the basics. We have one potential witness to interview. You met him yesterday evening: Freddy Welsh. He may have dealt only with Beram Cohen, but it's possible that the order for the weapons was placed by somebody else.'

'Do you want me to talk to him again?'

'I don't think that'll be necessary. Mario McGuire's going to see him.'

'McGuire? Your colleague? The man whose wife was sitting next to Toni Field?'

He nodded. 'The same. Freddy isn't going to enjoy that; not at all.'

'Did you tell him to go hard?'

'No, but I couldn't stop him even if I tried. You and I might have scared Freddy last night, but that was a gentle chat compared to what the big fella's capable of.'

'He won't go too far, will he?'

'He won't have to. I expect to hear from him fairly soon. In the meantime, there is one thing that I will "share" with you, to use your term. Remember, our assumption yesterday was that Smit and Botha were going to get into the hall disguised as police officers?'

'Only too well,' Houseman said, with a bitter frown. 'If the police communications centre hadn't been on Saturday mode, we might have got the message through in time to stop them.'

'That's something I will be addressing now I'm in this chair,' Skinner promised, 'but don't dwell on it. My fear was that those uniforms would have been taken from two cops and that we'd find them afterwards, probably dead.'

'Yes. You're not going to tell me you have, are you?'

'No; the opposite in fact. We've found the uniforms, along with the discarded police-type carbine that Welsh supplied, in the projection room where they took the shot from, but I don't have any officers missing, and the tunics were undamaged . . . no bullet holes, stab wounds or anything else.

'They were also brand new, and were a one hundred per cent match for the kit my people wear. Trousers, short-sleeved undershirt, stab vest with pockets, and caps with the usual Sillitoe Tartan around them. Same for the equipment belt and the gear on it, Hiatt speedcuffs, twenty-one-inch autolock baton, and a CS spray.

'Okay, all British police forces wear similar clothing these days, but all these things were identical,' he stressed the word, 'to ours. The Strathclyde insignia is sewn on the armoured vest, and the manufacturer was the same . . . that's telling, for the force changed its stab vest supplier not so long ago. In addition to that, we found two bogus cards on lanyards. Well, they were bogus in that the names were made up, they'd been created from blanks that my people believe were genuine.'

'Could Welsh have supplied the stuff?'

'You saw his store yesterday. There was nothing there other than firearms, boxed.'

'In other words,' the MI5 operative murmured, 'what you're saying is that . . .'

'We're doing a thorough stock check now, but it looks as if the clothing and body equipment came from our own warehouse. I've also asked for checks to be done in every other force that uses Hawk body armour. In other words, Clyde, the hit team had inside help. Somebody in this force supplied them.'

'Then you've got a problem, sir.'

Skinner leaned back in his chair, making a mental note to adjust it to deal with his weight. 'Actually, Clyde,' he murmured, 'I've got two.'

Houseman frowned. 'Oh? What's the other?'

'It's why I asked you to come here,' the chief replied. 'It takes us back to sharing. I need to know what you took from Smit's body yesterday, when I was busy shooting Gerry Botha, and where it led you. I've seen the CCTV, remember. You were very slick, and very quick, but it's there.' He took a deep breath, then let it out in a sigh. 'Fifteen years ago, son,' he said, 'I gave you a serious warning; don't make me have to repeat it, far less follow through on it.'

Fourteen

'You don't need to see the tape, Danny,' Lottie Mann said, in a tone that would have blocked off all future discussion with anyone but Detective Sergeant Provan; he had known her for too long.

He persisted. 'Are you going to show it to the fiscal?'

'She's got it already. The chief had it sent over to her office after he'd shown it to me.'

'So what's on it?' The stocky little detective puffed himself up, his nicotine-stained white moustache bristling, a familiar sign of irritation that she had seen a few hundred times before, mostly when she had been a detective constable on the way up the ladder, before she had passed him by. 'This is a police inquiry and I'm second in seniority on the team. I'm entitled to bloody know.'

'News for you, Dan. You're third in the pecking order. The new chief constable might have told the press that I'm SIO on this one, but make no mistake, he is. This man Skinner is miles different from Toni Field in most ways, but in one they're very much alike. She was on the way to creating a force in her own image, flashy, high-tech.'

'Don't I know it,' Provan grumbled. 'Fuckin' hand-held devices in all the patrol cars. She'd have had us all wearing GPS ankle bracelets before she was done, so she could tell where every one of us was all the time.'

Lottie smiled; she had a soft spot for her sergeant that she never showed to anyone else. While it was a little short of the truth to say that he was her only mentor . . . Max Allan had been that also, if anyone ever was . . . he had always been her strongest supporter, even though he had known from their earliest days as colleagues that he had plateaued, while she was on the rise.

'I wouldn't go quite that far,' she said, 'but aye, that's along the lines I meant. Skinner, if he sticks around, he'll change us too, but it'll be far different from the Field model. And I'll tell you something else, when it comes to CID, it will always go back to him. So, Danny my man, don't you be under any illusions about who's really heading this investigation, 'cos I'm not.'

'Okay,' he replied. 'That's ma card marked. So if Ah want to know what's on that video Ah go an' ask Skinner. That's what ye're saying, is it?'

'Jesus!' the DI exploded. 'You're as persistent as my wee Jakey. I never said I wouldn't tell you. The recording shows four people being shot. Three of them are dead, and Barry Auger could be left in a wheelchair.' She described it in detail, as she had done to her husband a few hours earlier. 'Don't feel left out because you haven't seen it, Danny. I wish I hadn't. Poor Barry and Sandy, they never had a chance.'

'So much for body armour,' the sergeant muttered.

'It's no' going to stop a bullet at close range,' Mann replied. 'Anyway, Sandy was shot in the head, twice. He was a goner before he hit the ground. The guy Smit was getting ready to finish Barry when Skinner and the other bloke arrived.'

'Aye, the other bloke. What about him?'

'Not one of ours. Youngish bloke, maybe mixed race, looked military.'

'You're kidding,' the DS exclaimed. 'When I was coming in, there was a bloke just like that at reception, and I heard him ask for the chief constable's office. Light brown skin, dark hair, creases in his trousers, shiny shoes; a fuckin' soldier for sure. Who is he? What is he?'

'Skinner hasn't said outright, but you can bet he's MI5. I know they've got a regional presence in Glasgow but I've never heard of them being involved with us before.'

'So how come they were this time?'

'The chief had an investigation going in Edinburgh, and this man got pulled in.'

'Linked to this one?' Provan asked.

'Aye. They've got a man in custody, the arms supplier.' She held up a hand. 'Before you get excited, he knows nothing that's going to help us. I just had a call from an ACC in Edinburgh. He told me he just finished interrogating him and he's satisfied he's not holding anything back.'

'So the only possible line of investigation we've got are the uniforms they wore.'

'Right enough; and the fact that they were ours, not fakes,' she confirmed. 'But that's not going to be general knowledge either, Danny. If Smit and Botha did indeed have an inside contact, we know one thing, he'll be on his guard. We have to be careful.'

'Agreed, but can Ah ask, how certain are we they're frae inside?'

'Every single item that we found was what an officer would wear or carry, yet they came from a range of suppliers. If they got them anywhere else they'd have had to know who every one of those is, and some of that stuff isn't public knowledge, not even under Freedom of Information rules. But it's the CS spray that's the clincher; that stuff's military, and each canister has a serial number. We know that the two we found came from our store, because the numbers are in sequence and they were missing from the stock.'

'Right. How do we handle it?'

'Quietly,' Mann declared. 'All police equipment's held in a secure store in Paisley. Operationally, ACC Thomas has oversight of all supplies. He checked on the numbers for me personally . . . he let me know it was a big favour, mind . . . and he's agreed that we can interview the civilian manager, as long as we're discreet. We're off to Paisley, first up tomorrow morning.'

'Just the two of us?'

'Absolutely,' the DI replied. 'Discreet is the word.'

Provan nodded. 'Fair enough. Now, there's one other thing that Ah've been wondering, a question I haven't heard anyone raise since last night.'

'What's that?'

'How did these two fellas get there, and how were they plannin' tae get away? This was a well-planned operation, so I doubt they were going down tae the Central Station to catch the London train.'

Lottie Mann's eyes widened. 'You know, Dan, life's really not fair. You should be the DI, not me. Smit and Botha had nothing on them, nothing at all. No ID of any sort, no wallets, no car keys, nothing.'

'In that case, Lottie,' the DS chuckled, 'maybe Ah should be chief constable, for if the new guy really is runnin' this investigation like you say, then he's missed it as well.'

Fifteen

Clyde Houseman's face grew even more pink, but with embarrassment.

'Come on,' Skinner snapped. 'Out with it.'

'I'm sorry, sir,' the man replied, 'but it's like this. I'm a Security Service officer, and what we were involved in yesterday . . . well, I felt at the time it was one of our operations, and not police, and when I was sent to see you yesterday, by my boss, it was on the basis of bringing you inside, not deferring to you.'

'And you kept thinking that way even though three of our people had been shot?' the chief constable countered.

'Even though. I'd just taken someone down myself, and in those circumstances it was my duty to protect the interests of my service: standard practice. So I did what I did. I meant to report to my deputy director straight away, but I was caught up in the situation and couldn't. I tried to call her this morning, but so far I haven't been able to raise her, and I don't want to go anywhere else. She's my immediate boss.'

'Even Amanda Dennis has to turn her phone off some time,' Skinner said. 'Clyde,' he continued, 'I understand what you're saying, but I'm not buying it. Like it or not, this was a very public crime and the investigation has to be seen to be thorough. I can't have you withholding evidence. So come on, man, and remember this: I've already protected the interests of your service. Only one police officer has seen that tape of you and me taking care of the South Africans, and that's how it's going to stay. She's assuming that I've given it to the procurator fiscal, the prosecutor's office, because I let her believe that, but in fact it's still in my desk. The deputy fiscal in charge of the investigation knows about it, because I've told him; he understands the sensitivity and he's prepared to forget that it ever existed.'

'Where is it now?'

'Locked in my desk, for now, till somebody comes up with the combination of the bloody safe that Toni Field left behind.'

'Thank you for that,' Houseman murmured. 'But do you trust your people? Leaks can happen, and the last thing that either of us wants is for that video to wind up on YouTube.'

'At the moment, I trust them more than I trust you,' Skinner pointed out, 'and I will until you cough up what you took from Smit's body. Look, I don't want to, but I will bypass Amanda and go to your director if I have to, even though he is a buffoon.'

'Sir Hubert would probably back me up.'

'No he wouldn't,' the chief chuckled. 'Do you have any idea of what would happen if I even hinted to the media that MI5 was getting in the way of my investigation? You're forgetting who's been killed here. Toni Field was a big name in the Met, plus the Mayor of London was said to be her biggest fan. All of their weight would come down on Thames House if I dropped the word. Plus,' he added, 'I've got the tape. You're worried about YouTube, son? If I chose I could edit it, destroy the footage of me shooting Botha, and leak the rest myself. If I chose,' he repeated. 'Not that I would, but I won't have to, because you're going to . . .' he smiled, '. . . share with me again. Aren't you?'

Houseman sighed, then reached inside his leather jerkin. For an instant Skinner tensed, but what he produced was nothing more menacing than an envelope.

'I had a hunch our meeting might go this way,' he said, 'so I brought the things along.'

He handed it across to the chief, who took it, ripped it open and shook its contents out on to the desk: a car key, with a Drivall rental tag bearing a vehicle registration number, and a parking ticket.

Skinner picked up the rectangle of card and peered at it with the intense concentration of a man who had reached the age of fifty and yet was still in denial of his need for reading spectacles.

'Have you done anything with this yet?'

His visitor shook his head. 'I decided to wait for instructions.'

'On whether to hand it over to me or not?'

'Yes, more or less.'

'Now you've done it, story's over as far as I'm concerned. If Amanda gives you a hard time, although I don't believe she will, you can tell her I coerced you into it. So,' he held up the ticket, between two fingers, 'you know where this is for?'

'It doesn't say on it.'

'Maybe not, but given the exit they chose, the likeliest is the multi-storey on the other side of Killermont Street, beside the bus station. One way to find out.' Skinner pushed himself to his feet. 'Gimme a minute.'

He picked up his uniform jacket from the back of his chair, and stepped into the private room behind it. When he emerged, three minutes later, he had changed into the same slacks and cotton jacket that Houseman had seen the day before.

'We're going ourselves?' the younger man asked.

'Of course. I seize every chance that comes up to get out of my office; there may not be too many more, now I'm here.'

He led the way out of his room, but instead of heading straight for the exit, he turned left, stopping at the second door. He opened it and called to the occupant. 'Lowell, I have an outside visit; I could use your help.'

Payne had been working on the chief constable's forward engagement diary. He closed it and crossed swiftly to the door. 'Where are we going?' he asked, then reacted with surprise as he saw Houseman for the first time.

Skinner did the introductions on his way to the lift. 'Clyde's come in with some new information,' he added. 'He's found the vehicle Smit and Botha were using yesterday. Well, that's to say, we know where it might be.'

'Should we call Lottie?' the DCI asked.

'Yes, we should, but we won't until we've got something to tell her.'

They rode the lift down to the sub-level that accessed the police headquarters park, then took Payne's car, which he had left in the space allocated to the deputy chief. The journey along Sauchiehall Street and Renfrew Street to the Buchanan Street bus station took only two minutes, five less than it might have on a weekday. Skinner smiled as they passed the McLellan Galleries, his mind going back thirty years to a visit to an art exhibition, in a foursome with Louise Bankier and a couple of their fellow students, when he had spotted, on the other side of the big room, Myra, his fiancée, with a spotty guy he had never seen before. They were heading for the exit, hand in hand, with eyes only for each other. He never had found out who the bloke was, but it had never occurred to him to ask. He had been too wrapped up in his own guilt over Louise; indeed the close encounter had been the beginning of the end of that relationship.

He was still dwelling on the past as they approached their destination. In case his daydream had been noticed, he took out the Drivall car key and made a show of peering at the number written on the fob, until he gave up and handed it to Houseman, and his younger eyes.

'We're looking for a Peugeot,' he announced, after the briefest study, 'registration LX12 PMP. Doesn't say what colour it is.'

Payne ignored the official entry point and drove to the office instead. The way was blocked by a barrier. A staff member, in a Day-Glo jacket, came out to meet them. The DCI showed his warrant card, and the parking ticket that Skinner had handed to him. 'That one of yours?' he asked.

The attendant studied it. 'Aye,' he confirmed. 'It's dated yesterday afternoon. Left overnight, eh, and no' picked up yet. Stolen car? There's nae TV in here so we get them.'

'Not necessarily, but we need to find it. Is the park busy?'

'Jam packed, but go on in.' He pushed a button at the side of the barrier, and it rose.

'Okay. Two ways of doing this,' the chief declared. 'We either drive through very slowly, and hope we get lucky, or we do the sensible thing and split it. Lowell, drop me on level two, Clyde on four and you go to the top and park. We work our way down till we find it. You've both got my work mobile number, and I've got yours; either of you find the car, you call me and I'll alert the other.'

Payne did as he was instructed. As each of them reached his starting point, he realised that the multi-storey was spilt into sub-levels, making it bigger than it had looked from the outside. They searched their separate areas as quickly as they could but nonetheless almost fifteen minutes had passed before Skinner's mobile rang. By that time he was at ground level.

His screen told him that it was Houseman who had made the discovery. 'I'm on level five,' the spook said. 'At the side, overlooking the street.'

'Good spot. Be with you in a minute; I'll tell Lowell.'

'There's no need. The way this place is built he can see me from where he is.'

Skinner took the stairs, two at a time. As he stepped out on to level five he saw Payne, on his left, coming towards him down a ramp.

The Peugeot was a big saloon model, in a dark blue colour. Skinner took the key from his pocket and worked out by trial and error which button unlocked it. Houseman was in the act of reaching for the driver's door handle when Payne called out to him.

'No, not without gloves.' He smiled. 'Sorry,' he said. 'It's a CID reflex.'

'Understood,' the MI5 man conceded. He took a handkerchief from his pocket and used it to open the door.

Skinner stepped up behind him and looked inside, then slotted the key in to light up the dashboard. 'Satnav,' he said.

'So?' Houseman murmured.

'With a bit of luck they'll have used it. With even more, they won't have deleted previous entries. When did they collect the uniforms and equipment? Where? That may give us a clue.'

'Mmm.'

'And if they did pick up the gear from an inside source, he may have left us a print, or a DNA trace.'

'That's if he's on the database,' Payne pointed out. 'If he is inside, how likely is that?'

'Come on, Lowell,' Skinner chided. 'Think positive.' He glanced into the back of the car, saw it was empty, then withdrew the key and closed the driver's door, leaning on it with an elbow. Moving round to the back of the vehicle, which had been left perilously close to the wall of the building, he pushed a third button on the remote. There was a muffled sound and the boot lid sprang open.

'Jesus Christ!' the DCI yelled, jumping backwards in alarm and astonishment.

His companions stood their ground, gazing into the luggage compartment.

'Surprisingly capacious, these things,' the chief constable murmured, 'aren't they, Clyde? You'd get at least two sets of golf clubs in there, no problem. Maybe two trolleys as well.'

'Beyond a doubt.'

Two medium-sized blue suitcases lay on their sides, at the front of the boot, but there had still been more than enough room for the rest of the load to be jammed in behind them: the body of a man, knees drawn up and his arms wrapped around them. The eyes were open, staring, and there was a cluster of three holes in the centre of his chest.

'So, chum,' Skinner wondered. 'Who the hell were you, and why did you wind up here?'

Sixteen

'That's Bazza Brown,' DS Dan Provan announced.

Lottie Mann frowned. 'Are you sure?'

'Trust me. Real name Basil, but nobody ever called him that, unless they wanted a sore face. The first time Ah lifted him he was sixteen, sellin' what he claimed were LSD tabs on squares from a school jotter. They wis just melted sugar, but nobody ever complained; he wis a hard kid even then, and he had a gang.'

'When was that?' Skinner asked. He had never met the wizened little detective before but he found himself taking an instant liking to him, and to his irreverence.

'Goin' on twenty-five years ago, sir. He moved on frae there, though. The next time I picked him up he'd just turned twenty-one and he was sellin' hash. He got three years for that, in the University of Barlinnie, and that, you might say, completed his formal education. He's never done a day's time since, even though he's reckoned . . . sorry, he was reckoned . . . to be one of the big three in drugs in Glasgow.'

'So how come he wound up in a car boot sale?'

'Ah can't tell you that, sir. But Ah know you're going to want us to find out.'

The chief grinned. 'That is indeed the name of the game, Sergeant.'

He and Payne had called in Mann and her squad at once. They

had left the car untouched. Indeed the only change in the scenery since they had made their discovery lay in the absence of Clyde Houseman. Skinner had decided that it would be best if he made himself scarce.

He had expected Lottie Mann to be blunt when she arrived, and had been ready for her challenge.

'Can I ask what the fuck you're doing here, sir? I've got people out showing pictures of Smit and Botha to every car park attendant in Glasgow, and what do I find? You and DCI Payne, with their bloody car key!'

'Inspector!' Lowell Payne had intervened, but his new chief had calmed his protest with a wave of his hand.

'It's okay. DI Mann is well entitled to sound off. I was given some information, Lottie, and I decided to evaluate it myself, and to bring you in if I reckoned it was worth it. Get used to me: it's the way I am.'

'Oh, I know that already, sir,' she retorted. 'Just like I know there's no point me asking who your source was.'

'That's right, but now the result is all yours.'

She had given one of her hard-earned smiles, then gone into action.

The photographer and video cameraman were finishing their work as Provan announced the identity of the victim and he and Skinner had their exchange. They had been hampered slightly by a silver Toyota parked in the bay on the right, but the two to the left were clear.

As they packed their equipment, the elevator door opened, beside the stairway exit, and a woman stepped out, pushing a child in a collapsible pram with John Lewis bags hung on the back. She frowned as she moved towards them. 'What's going . . .' she began.

Payne moved quickly across to intercept her, holding up his warrant card. 'Police, ma'am. Is that your Toyota?'

'Yes, but what . . . It's not damaged, is it? I can move it, can't I?'

'It's fine, but please don't come any closer. If you give me your car key I'll bring it out for you.'

'It's not a bomb, is it?' The young mother was terrified; Payne smiled to reassure her.

'No, no, not at all. If it was I wouldn't be within a mile of it myself. It's just a suspicious vehicle, that's all. We're checking out the contents. You just give me your keys and don't you worry.'

He reversed the Toyota out of its bay and drove it a little way down the exit ramp, then helped her load her bags and her child, who had slept through the exchange.

'Did she see anything?' Mann asked the DCI as he returned.

'No, or you'd have heard the screams. But we need to get a screen round this, now we've got the room.'

'It's on the way, with the forensic people. We'd better not touch anything till they get here. That peppery wee bastard Dorward's on weekend duty and he'll never let me forget it if I compromise "his" crime scene.'

'It's well compromised already, Lottie,' Skinner pointed out. 'Anyone got a pair of gloves?' he asked. 'I want a look at these suitcases. I'll handle Arthur's flak. I've been doing it for long enough.'

Provan handed him a pair of latex gloves. He slipped them on and lifted one of the blue cases from the boot, laid it on the ground and tried the catches, hoping they were unlocked and smiling when they clicked open.

'Clothing,' he announced as he studied the contents, and sifted through them. 'It looks like two changes: trousers, shirt, underwear, just the one jacket, though, and one pair of shoes. Everything's brand new, Marks and Spencer labels still on them. Summer wear. Mmm,' he mused. 'What's the weather like in South Africa in July?'

There was a zipped pocket set in the lid of the case, which also sported a Marks and Spencer label on its lining. He unfastened it, felt inside and found a padded envelope. It was unsealed; the contents slid into his hand.

'Wallet,' he said. 'Looks like at least three hundred quid. One Visa debit card in the name of Bryan Lightbody. A passport, New Zealand, in the same name, but with Gerry Botha's photo inside. Flight tickets and itinerary, Singapore Air, Heathrow to Auckland through Singapore, business class, departure tomorrow evening.'

He lifted the second case from the car and checked its contents. 'An Australian passport,' he announced when he was finished. 'It and the bank card are in the name of Richie Mallett, and the flight ticket's Quantas to Sydney, again Heathrow tomorrow night. So that was the game plan. Drive to London, fly away home and leave us scratching our arses as we try to find them on flights out of Scotland.'

'Well planned,' Lottie Mann observed.

'Yes, but that's not what these guys did. The man Cohen was the planner. He made all the arrangements, bought the air tickets, hired the car.'

'The car,' she repeated, then turned to Provan. 'Get . . .'

'Ah'm on it already,' he retorted, waving the car key with his left hand while holding his mobile to his ear. 'Yes,' he said, 'that's right, Strathclyde CID. I'm standing over one o' your cars just now, and Ah need to know whose name is on the rental contract.' He paused, listening.

'Because there's something wrong wi' it, that's why.' He waited again.

'Maybe there wasn't when it left you, Jimmy, but there is now. There's a fuckin' body in the boot. Or dae all your vehicles come with that accessory? No, Ah won't hold on. The registration's LX12 PMP;

you get me the information Ah want and get back to me through the force main switchboard. They'll transfer your call to my mobile. Pronto, please, this is very important.'

As Provan finished, Skinner tapped him on the shoulder. 'Have you ever done a course,' he asked, 'on communication with the public?'

The sergeant pursed his lips, wrinkling his two-tone moustache in the process, and looked up at him. 'No, sir, I can't say that Ah have.'

'Then I will make it my business, Detective Sergeant,' the chief told him, without the suggestion of a smile, 'to see that you never do.'

'Thanks, gaffer,' the little DS replied, 'but even if you did send me on one, at my age I wake up sometimes wi' this terrible hacking cough. Knocks me right off for the day, it does.'

Skinner laughed out loud. 'I could get to like it here,' he exclaimed. Then he turned serious. 'Now prove to me that you're a detective, not some fucking hobbit who's tolerated because he's been around for ever. There's a begged question in this scenario. I'm not wondering about the guy in the boot. You knew who he was, and I know what he was. No, it's something else, unrelated. What is it?'

As Dan Provan looked up at his new boss, two thoughts entered his mind. The first of them was financial. He had over thirty years in the job, and his pension was secure as long as he didn't punch the chief constable in the mouth, and since that struck him as being a seriously stupid overreaction, it wasn't going to happen. So the 'daft laddie' option was open to him, without risk.

But the second was professional, and pride was involved. He had survived as long as he had because he was, in fact, a damn good detective, and as such he was expert in analysing every scenario and in identifying all the possible lines of inquiry that it offered.

A third consideration followed. Skinner hadn't asked him the question to embarrass him, but because he expected him to know the answer.

He frowned and bent his mind to recalling as much as he could of what had been said in the previous half hour. He played the mental tape, piece by piece, then ran through it again.

'It's the flights,' he said, when he was sure. 'The two dead guys had plane tickets out of Heathrow. Yes?'

'Yes.'

'Right. Now if everything had gone to plan, the two hit men, Smit and Botha, or Lightbody and Mallett, or Randall and fuckin' Hopkirk deceased, whoever they were, if it had all gone to plan, they'd have driven straight out of this car park, almost before the alarm had been raised, headed straight down to London, dumping our friend Bazza in some lay-by along the way, and got on a fuckin' plane. Right, boss?'

Skinner nodded. 'You're on a roll, Sergeant, carry on.'

'Thank you, gaffer. In that case, even as we're stood here, they could have been sipping fuckin' cocktails in business class. Except . . . their flights were booked for Monday, for tomorrow. So what were they supposed to be doin' in those spare twenty-four hours?'

The chief constable smiled. 'Absolutely. Top question. You got an answer for that one?'

Provan shrugged, 'No idea, sir.' He nodded towards the boot of the Peugeot. 'But if we find out what they were doing with poor old Bazza Brown there, maybe that'll give us a clue.'

Seventeen

'He's a marginally insubordinate little joker, but I do like him,' Bob chuckled. 'He and that DI, Lottie, they're some team.'

Sarah smiled across the table, on which the last of their dinner plates lay, empty save for the skeletons of two lemon sole. She raised her coffee cup. 'Could it be that Glasgow isn't the cultural wasteland you thought it was?'

'Hey, come on,' he protested. 'I never said that, or even thought it. I'm from Motherwell, remember; I'm not quite a Weegie myself, but close. I have a Glasgow degree; I spent a good chunk of my teens in that fair city. West of Scotland culture is in my blood. Why do you think I like country music and bad stand-up comedians?'

'So part of you is glad to be back there,' she suggested.

'Sure, the nostalgic part.'

'Then why did you ever leave?' she asked in her light American drawl. 'Myra was from Motherwell as well and yet the two of you upped sticks and moved through to Gullane in your early twenties.'

'You know why; I've told you often enough. I liked Edinburgh, and I liked the seaside. I wanted to work in one and live by the other. I've never regretted that decision either, not once.'

'But what made you choose it over Glasgow? I can see you, man, and your pleasure now at being back there. There must have been an underlying reason.'

He leaned back in his chair and gazed at her. 'Very well,' he conceded. 'There was. I didn't like being asked what school I went to.'

'Uh?' she grunted. 'Come again? What's that got to do with anything?'

His laugh was gentle, amused. 'You've lived in Scotland for how long? Twelve years on and off, and you don't know that one? It's code, and what it actually means is, "Are you Protestant or are you Catholic?" Where I grew up that was a key question, just as much as in Belfast, and for all Aileen and her kind might try to deny it, I'm sure it still is in some places and to some people. The answer could determine many things, not least your employment prospects.

'Why the school question? Because through there, education was organised along religious lines; there were Roman Catholic schools and non-denominational, the latter being in name only. They were where the Protestants went. So, your school defined you, and it could mean that some doors were just slammed in your face.'

'Wow,' Sarah murmured. 'I know about Rangers and Celtic football clubs, of course, but I didn't think it went that deep.'

'It did, and for some it still does. Both those clubs condemn sectarianism but they still struggle to eradicate it among their supporters. I decided very early on that I didn't want any kids of mine growing up in that environment, and Myra agreed. That's what was behind our move.'

'But now you're back you like it?'

'Hey, love, it's been one day. My reservations about the size of the Strathclyde force are as strong as ever. What I'm saying is that I like the people I've met so far. Mann and Provan, they're good cops and pure Glaswegian, both of them.'

'What school did they go to?'

'As for Lottie, I have no idea.' He winked. 'But the Celtic supporter's lapel badge that wee Provan was wearing still offers something of a clue. He may miss their next game,' he added, 'if they don't get these killings wrapped up soon.'

'Yeah,' Sarah said. 'The body in the boot must have been a bit of a shaker.'

'It was for Lowell, that's for sure. He jumped out of his skin. Me too, to be honest, but I've gotten good at hiding it.'

'Why was he there, the dead guy?'

'I guess they didn't want to leave him wherever he was killed. The provisional time of death was Friday evening some time; with the hit being planned for Saturday, they may not have wanted to muddy the waters by having him found.'

'Meaning the police might have made a connection to them?'

He nodded. 'It would have been a long shot, but that would have been the thinking.'

'Mmm.' She frowned. 'But I didn't mean why was he in the boot; I mean why were they involved with him at all?'

'We all asked ourselves that one. It seems that the late Mr Brown was a reasonably heavy-duty Glasgow criminal, but I doubt very much that Mr Smit and Mr Botha met him to do a drug deal on the side.'

'Are you still sure those are their real names?'

'Oh yes, we know that. We can trace them all the way back to the South African armed forces. Lightbody and Mallett were aliases. It remains to be seen whether they actually lived under those names, one in New Zealand, one in Australia. We'll need to wait for the passport offices and the police in those countries to open before we can follow them up.' He checked his watch; quarter to nine. 'New Zealand should be wide awake now, Australia in an hour or two. Anyway, whatever their fucking names, what were they doing with a Weegie hood?'

'Yes, any theories?'

'Only one, the obvious. Mr Brown must have been involved in the supply of the police uniforms and equipment, and they must have decided not to leave him behind as a witness.'

'So why did they leave the arms dealer alive?' Sarah wondered.

'Because he's part of that world, I'd guess, and was in as deep as they were. A small-timer they'd have seen as a weakness.'

Sarah refilled her cup from a cafetière. Bob, who had given up coffee at her suggestion, almost at her insistence, topped up his glass with mineral water.

'But the tough questions are, why was he in the chain at all, and who introduced him? There we do not have a Scooby, as wee Provan would probably say.'

'Good.' She smiled. 'Enough for tonight, Chief Constable. No more shop, just Bob and Sarah for a while. I've been thinking about what happened a couple of nights ago, you and me having a nice quiet dinner and ending up in bed together.' She took his hand, studying it as she spoke. 'I have to ask you this, Bob, because it's been gnawing away at me, knowing from personal experience how unpredictable you are when it comes to women. Are you and the witch definitely a thing of the past? Is there any chance of a reconciliation?'

He sipped some water. 'Given our history,' he began, 'I suppose I deserved that "unpredictability" crack. But you can take this to the bank: Aileen and I are through. Sit her across from you and she would give you the same answer. She'd probably add also that we're not going to walk away as friends either. Each of us married a person without knowing them at all. Before too long we found we didn't even like each other all that much.'

'Do you think you know me now?' she asked.

'None of us can live inside someone else's head, but if I don't know what makes you tick by now . . .' He leaned forward and looked deep into her eyes. 'I always did like you; now I know more. I never stopped loving you either.'

'But let's not put it to the test by getting married again. Agreed?'

Bob nodded. 'Agreed. But is that because you don't trust me? If it is, I understand.'

'Amazing as it may sound, I do trust you. No, it's because right now, the way we are . . . I don't think I've ever felt happier, and I don't want to risk that.'

'Fair enough. Now, with the kids upstairs in bed, can we do something old-fashioned, like watching television?'

She laughed. 'How very couple-ish! Yeah, let's.'

She was flicking through the channel choice when Bob's work mobile sounded. 'Bugger,' he murmured. 'I must give this Edinburgh phone back to Maggie and get a new one from Strathclyde. Chances are this is for her.' He looked at the caller identification. 'No, it's not. Lowell,' he said as he accepted the call, 'what's up? News from down under?'

As Sarah watched him, she saw his eyes widen, a frown wrinkle his forehead for a second then disappear. 'You're fucking kidding,' he exclaimed. 'So that's what the bloody woman was leading up to. Don't apologise, man, I know you had to tell me, but worry not; it won't ruin my night. I just wish I could be a fly on a certain wall, that's all.'

He ended the call as Sarah laid down the TV remote.

'Well?' she demanded. 'What bloody woman? Aileen?'

'As it happened, no,' he told her, 'another bloody woman, but not unconnected. What you asked me earlier on, whether there was a cat's chance of the two of us staying together.' He laughed. 'If you doubted me at all, then, by Christ, you're going to be a happy woman tomorrow morning.'

Eighteen

'Are we all set for tomorrow, Alf?'

'Yes, but I've brought it forward to eleven thirty. The phone's never stopped ringing all day, and the place is going to be packed out. If you want to do follow-up interviews and get them on the midday news we'll need to start a bit earlier than noon.'

'Agreed,' Aileen said. 'And the announcement: do they have that ready?'

'Yes,' the party CEO replied. 'I've just sent you a draft by email. If you clear it, I can tell the policy staff to go home for the night.'

'I'll do that right now.'

'Thanks. I must go now, Aileen. For some reason the switchboard's just lit up like a Christmas tree.'

She cradled the phone and turned to Joey Morocco, who was removing silver boxes from a brown paper bag. She smiled. 'You must do this a lot,' she remarked. 'I heard you at the front door; you were on first-name terms with the delivery boy. "Thank you, Wen-Chong." I take it that means we're having Chinese.'

'I see that being married to a detective's rubbed off on you,' he said. 'Sure, first-name terms with him, with Jeev from the Asian up in Gibson Street, with Kemal from the kebab shop and with Jocky.'

'Jocky? Who the hell's he?'

'Pizza. That's the Italians for you; much more interbred with the indigenous population.'

She looked over his shoulder. 'What have we got?'

'Chicken, brack bean sauce,' he replied, mimicking a Chinese accent, 'plawn sweet and sowah, clispy duck and pancakes, and lice; flied of course.'

'Sounds great. I just need five minutes on my laptop and I'll be ready.'

She wakened her computer from the sleep state in which she had left it earlier in the evening, and searched her email inbox. It was full of messages from friends, anxious, she guessed, for news of her safety, but Old's was near the top and she found it with ease.

She opened the attachment, which was headed, 'Draft Statement: Unified Police Force', scanned it quickly, made a few changes to bring it into her delivery style, then sent it back with a covering note that read, 'Final version clear for use.'

She had just clicked the 'send' button when a tone advised her that another message had hit the inbox, once again from Alf Old. Almost simultaneously, her mobile rang, and the screen showed that he was calling. She made a choice; the phone won.

'Aileen.' Even although he had only said her name, the chief executive, famed for his calmness, sounded rattled. 'I've just sent you an email.'

'I know, it just arrived. I haven't opened it yet.'

'Then you'd better do so.'

Not only rattled, she realised; he was angry also.

She opened the message. There was no text, only an attachment, headed 'P1', in PDF form. She clicked on it and an image appeared, as quickly as her ageing laptop would allow.

It was a newspaper front page, with the masthead of the *Daily*

News, and beneath it a headline. 'Road to Morocco: married Labour leader goes to ground.' Most of it was taken up by a photograph, taken from a distance with a long lens, but the face was all too clearly hers, looking out of Joey Morocco's bedroom window, with a curtain held across her, but not far enough to cover her right breast, which the newspaper had chosen to cover with a black rectangle.

'Fuck!' she screamed.

'Exactly!' Old barked. 'What the hell were you thinking about, Aileen?'

'It's not what you think,' she protested.

'Then what the hell else is it? Anyway it doesn't matter what I think, it's what the readers of the *Daily News* think, them and the readers of every other paper that the photographer sells it on to, once they've had their exclusive. They've already given it to BBC, Sky and ITN, for use after ten, to sell even more papers tomorrow morning.'

'Is it on the streets yet? Can we stop them?'

'It will be any minute now, and no we can't. We could go to the Court of Session and ask for an interdict preventing further publication. We might get it, we might not, probably not. Anyway, the damage is done.'

Her anger had risen up to match his. 'But how did they get it?' she asked. 'How did they know I was here?'

'They didn't. I spoke to the editor of the Scottish version; he's a mate and he was good enough to call me, and to send the page across. He said it was taken by a freelance photographer, a paparazzo, who stakes out Joey Morocco's place periodically, just in case.

'She saw a car parked across his driveway, with two guys in it who had Special Branch written all over them . . . her words . . . so she found a vantage point out of their sight and hung around, just in case. She got lucky; saw a face at the window and a bit more, snapped off as many shots as she could, then legged it.

'It was only when she downloaded the photos on to her laptop in her car that she realised how lucky she was. She got straight on to the *News*. That's her best payer, apparently.'

'Bastards!' she hissed, then chuckled, taking herself by surprise. 'It's the wee black sticker I really hate. It's suggesting that my tits are too misshapen for a family newspaper: that they might put folk off their breakfast.'

'Then cheer up,' Old growled. 'There's another one inside, on page three, appropriately enough, with you looking over your shoulder, as if to make it crystal clear that there is somebody else in the room with you. There's a lot more of you on show there, and they haven't covered that up.'

'Who wrote the story?'

'Marguerite Hatton. She's on their political staff. They flew her up from London overnight.'

'That's the bitch that gave Bob trouble earlier on at his press conference. She'll rub his nose in it now.'

'Or he will rub yours.'

'I couldn't care less about him. Why do you think I'm at Joey's?' As she spoke, she became aware of a figure in the doorway, holding a plate in each hand. 'I've got some apologising to do to him.'

'Well, do it on the way to the emergency exit. You have to get out of there, for a fucking army's going to land on his doorstep as soon as the telly news breaks. Get your bodyguards to pull right up to his door, jump in their car and have them get you the hell out of there.'

'To where, though?' Joey had moved in behind her and was studying the image on the laptop. 'It'll be just as bad at my place.'

'To Gullane?' Old suggested. 'Give yourself time to come up with a cover story? Maybe even do a happy families shot tomorrow.'

'Not a fucking chance. I tell you, we're history. Anyway, I'm going to be in Glasgow tomorrow.'

'Eh?' he exclaimed. 'You're not going ahead with the press conference, are you?'

She gasped. 'Of course, man. We'll never have a bigger crowd. I will not back down from this. It's not going to kill me, any more than that guy did last night, so it can only make me stronger.'

'Then go to my place. Nobody will think to look there. I'll call Justine and tell her you're coming.'

Nineteen

'She's done what?' Sarah looked at him, astonished. 'Let herself be photographed in a lover's bedroom the morning after she's come within an inch of her life?'

'That's what they're going to say,' Bob acknowledged.

'She will argue, of course, that Morocco's an old family friend and that his girlfriend was there too.'

'I don't think so,' he replied. 'She won't lie her way out of it; too big a downside if she's caught, as many a politician's found out to their cost. She'll front it up; I know her.'

'And blacken your name in the process?'

He shook his head. 'She'll have a tough time doing that. She doesn't realise it but I have more friends in the media than she has. Speaking of whom, I expect that some of them will be calling me in the next hour or so, on my mobile and at Gullane. I think it would be best if I go home, so that I'm there to answer them.'

'Aww!' she moaned. 'I was looking forward to you staying.'

'Me too, but if I do, there's an outside chance that someone might doorstep me here in the morning. I don't want you and the kids caught up in this, in any way.'

She stood with him as he rose to leave, picking up his jacket from the back of the sofa. 'How do you feel about this?' she asked.

'Her being all over the tabloids.'

'I've had some of that myself in my career,' he answered, 'and I didn't like it. Am I embarrassed by it? Not a bit. People may talk about me behind my back, but none will to my face, so fuck 'em. Am I angry? No, because I don't have a right to be. It could have been me looking out of your bedroom window and all over the papers in the morning.'

'Are you sorry for her?' she murmured.

'Only if he's a lousy fuck, and not worth it. She will win out of this. I don't know how, but she will.'

She walked him to the door and hugged him there, looking up into his eyes. 'So what do we do?'

'Tomorrow we go to work, each of us, and Trish takes care of the kids as usual. I'm going to be as busy as the Devil's apprentice all this week, so we'll see each other when we can. With a bit of luck we'll be able to keep the weekend free.'

She kissed him. 'That's a plan,' she said. 'Now be on with your way and answer those phone calls.'

The first came, on his work mobile . . . he had switched his personal phone off as he left Sarah's . . . as he was turning on to the Edinburgh bypass. He had been expecting it.

'Bob.' The voice that filled the car through its speaker system was no longer aggressive, as it had been the last time he had heard it, but there was nothing fearful or tentative about it. 'I have something to tell you.'

'No, you don't,' he replied, speaking louder than usual, to allow for road noise.

'You've heard, then.'

'Of course I have. The editor of the *News* called my people. I don't know him but he said that he'd given you advance warning and was offering me the same courtesy. Of course, he also asked me for a comment.'

'And did you give him one?'

Skinner laughed. 'Shouldn't I be asking you that question, in a different context? Not that I need to; from what I've been told the answer's pretty fucking obvious. Oops, sorry, unfortunate choice of word. Bet you're glad now I persuaded you to spend that time in the gym.'

'Bob!' she snapped. 'Did you give the man a quote?'

'Don't be daft,' he retorted. 'Of course I didn't. Nor will I to anyone else, and I'm bloody sure quite a few people will be asking over the next couple of hours. What about you?'

'Nothing so far; they don't know where I am now. But I'm seeing the press tomorrow morning.'

'How about Joey? What's he going to be saying?'

'That I'm an old friend and that he offered me a place where I could recover from my ordeal in private.'

'Is he going to refer to me?'

'What would he say about you?'

'Not about me: to me. Some people might expect him to say "Sorry". That's the big media word these days, isn't it? People under the spotlight all have to utter the "S" word, whether they are or not.'

'Do you expect that?'

'Hell no. I'm sorry for him, if anything. He didn't bargain for all this crap.'

'Well,' she said, beginning to sound exasperated, as if she thought he was playing with her, as he was to a degree, 'what are you going to say?'

'Tonight, nothing. Not a fucking word, about you or against you, or anything else. What time's your press briefing tomorrow?'

'Eleven thirty.'

'In that case,' he declared, 'at ten o'clock, we're going to issue a joint statement through Mitchell Laidlaw, my lawyer at Curle Anthony Jarvis. It will say something along these lines: on Thursday . . . or whenever, you pick the day . . . you and I agreed to separate permanently because of profound and irreconcilable differences that have developed between us. You draft it, let me see it and we'll take it from there. You okay with that?'

'Mmm.' The car was silent, for long enough to make him wonder if the connection had been lost.

'Aileen?' he exclaimed into the darkness.

'I'm still here,' she replied. 'Thinking, that's all. I'm not sure I want it going out through your daughter's law firm.'

'Listen,' he retorted. 'You don't have a regular bloody lawyer that I know of. I can hardly use the Strathclyde Police press office for this, and I'll be damned if I'll have the end of my marriage announced by the Labour Party. Alex will have no sight of the statement, I promise.'

She drew in a deep breath, loudly enough for him to hear it clearly. 'Okay,' she agreed. 'What else do you want to put in it?'

'The minimum.'

'Should I say that we intend to divorce?'

'I include that among the minimum. Don't you? If you want you can say that we'll do it when we've completed the legal period of separation. Unless you want to marry Joey straight away, that is.'

'Don't be funny.'

'Sorry. How's the guy taking it anyway?'

'He's been lovely,' she said.

'I'm assuming that you and he had been over the course in the past. Yes?'

'For God's sake!' Aileen protested. 'Do you think he was a quick pick-up?'

'Not at all; hence the assumption. What else is he likely to say?'

'Nothing beyond what I told you. And he's going to leave for America tomorrow, a few days earlier than planned.'

'He probably thinks that's very wise on his part. I mean, hanging around in a city after being caught banging the chief constable's wife, all sorts of misfortunes might come your way. But tell him not to worry, if he is worrying, that is.'

'I will. And I'll tell him as well that he's probably done you a favour.'

'What do you mean by that?' he asked.

'Isn't it obvious? When you show up somewhere with another lady on your arm, everybody's going to say, "Aw, is that no' nice, after what the poor man went through." I could even hazard a guess as to who she might be.'

'Don't bother yourself, Aileen. You just get on with your brilliant career. I wish you every success.'

'And you get on with yours, my dear. And you remember what I said. Now you're wedged in the Stratchlyde chief's chair, you'll find it impossible to leave. And when the new single force is created, and your case against it has been knocked back, as you know will happen, you'll want that job too, because you won't be able to help yourself. The one and only thing that you and I have in common, my dear, is this: we are both driven by ambition.'

'You could not be more wrong. I have only one motivation.'

'Oh aye,' she said, mockery in her voice. 'And what's that?'

'Love.' He continued, cutting off her gasp of derision. 'Send me your draft. I'll be home in fifteen minutes.' He ended the call.

He thought about his final exchange with Aileen for the rest of the journey to Gullane. Never before had he encapsulated his driving forces in one word, but he realised that it was entirely appropriate. He loved his children, all of them with equal intensity, and he loved Sarah. And he loved his job as well, because it was his vocation, and it enabled him to be the best he could be for all of them.

He had never loved Aileen. He realised that. He had been attracted to a personality as powerful as his own, but had discovered that they could not co-exist in the same union. Eventually each had sought to dominate the other and the marriage had broken apart. This was not to say that Aileen was incapable of love herself. She had her tender side, but she would always be a leader, never a follower, and her soulmate, if he existed, would have to know that and be compliant.

The draft joint announcement was waiting for him as an email attachment when he reached home and turned on the computer in his small office. He read through it, found it factual and unemotional, and forwarded it, unamended, in a message to Mitchell Laidlaw asking him to issue it to the media at 10 a.m. next morning through his firm's PR company. He copied the mail to Aileen, then sent Laidlaw a text message from his personal mobile advising him that it was on its way.

He had expected no reply until the morning, but within a minute, his phone rang.

'Bob,' Mitch Laidlaw exclaimed. 'What a shocker. This is completely out of the blue. This will shake a few people.'

'Clearly you haven't seen the telly news tonight. From what I'm told it has already.'

'No, I missed that. We were watching a film. Why, has it leaked?'

'Not in the way you mean, but . . . go online and look at the *Daily News* website, you may find that explains a lot.'

'Intriguing, but I will. There's no chance of any . . .'

'No, chum; not a prayer. We both know what we want to say and we're not backing off from it. When your PR people put it out, they can add that I'm making no further comment. What Aileen chooses to do is up to her.'

'What about the legal side of it?' the solicitor asked.

'We haven't discussed that. Look after my kids' interests if it becomes necessary; that's all the instruction I'll give you at this stage.'

'I will do. The fact is, you're pretty much divorce-proofed after the last time.'

'Ouch!' Skinner winced. 'You make me sound like a recidivist.'

'Two's above average in our community, Bob.'

He laughed. 'I know, but I'm coming round to the view that the first one doesn't count.'

'Oh yes? What does that mean?'

'Nothing; just idle banter. Now, go on with you.' As he spoke his landline rang out, on his desk. He peered at the caller display. 'Incoming from my daughter,' he said. 'I suspect she has seen the TV news.'

He killed the mobile call and picked up the other. 'Yes, Alex.'

'Pops,' his elder daughter exclaimed in his ear, 'what the hell is this about Aileen and tomorrow's press? I've just had a call from Andy. He's been watching . . .'

'I know. Kid, go easy on her; it wasn't her fault.'

'Wasn't her . . .'

'Alexis,' he said, using her Sunday name for added emphasis. 'Stop and think back, not very far back, to a time when someone was out to make trouble for me, and you left your bedroom curtains open. You with me?'

'Yes, Pops,' she murmured. 'I suppose I live in a glass house.'

'We all do,' he replied. 'Fortunately, you've minimised the chances of a repeat by moving to a penthouse.'

'I know. I suppose I'm only angry because of the effect her behaviour might have on you.'

'Well, don't be. While she was with Morocco, whose bed do you think I was sleeping in? Where did I go on Saturday, when I got free of the concert hall and Glasgow? Where did you and Andy see me?'

'At . . .' she paused. 'You and Sarah? You're back together?'

'Let's just say we've got a hell of a lot in common, with three kids and a lot of personal mileage.'

'Plus the fact that she loves you,' his daughter pointed out, 'and that's the main reason why she came back from America and took the job at the university.'

'Plus the fact that I love her,' he conceded. 'But the key word, darling, is "discreet". Aileen will find out eventually, and the last thing I want is for her to get vindictive. So neither I, nor any member of my family or circle of friends, is going to say a single hard word about her. She had every right to be with Morocco, with or without the horror at the concert hall, but as it happens the guy was there for her when she chose to go to him. So be cool, promise me.'

'I promise. What are you going to do?'

'We, that's Aileen and me, have done it already through Mitch, but you're not to be involved. Don't talk to anyone, not even people within the firm. Understood?'

'Yes.'

He heard a sound, indicating that there was a call waiting. 'On you go now,' he said. 'I'm in for a busy hour or so.'

'Pops,' she sighed. 'Don't be so Goddamned conscientious; do what anyone else would to and unplug the phone from the socket.'

'Is that your legal advice?' he chuckled.

'No, it's pure Alex, and I'm not advising, I'm ordering. Just bloody do it.'

'Yes, boss,' he replied, then, not for the first time in his life, did as she had told him.

Twenty

'I think I preferred it when you were just another DI, and Max Allan kept you in the background.' Scott Mann stared at the kitchen wall clock; it showed five minutes to midnight. 'What the hell time's this tae be comin' in?'

His wife stared at him. 'Don't you bloody start,' she warned. 'The number of times I've asked you that question. That and "Where the hell have you been?" although it was always all too obvious.'

'Ye'll never let me forget, will ye?'

'Bloody right I won't; not when you start digging me up about my work. I've had the day from hell and I don't need you narking at me. I didn't ask to catch the shout to the concert hall last night, but I did and that's the end of it. Okay?' She barked out the last word.

He winced and glanced towards the ceiling. 'Shh,' he whispered. 'Ye'll wake the wee man. He's no' long asleep. He tried to stay awake for you. Ah made him put his light out at half nine, but he did his best tae hang on.'

She smiled, with a gentleness that none of her colleagues would have recognised. 'Wee darlin',' she murmured. An instant later she glared at her husband. 'As well for you though that it's the holidays, and tomorrow's not a school day.'

'Well it's no',' he shot back, 'and that's an end of it.'

'Aye fine,' Lottie sighed, deciding that further hostilities were pointless. 'Where did you go, the pair of you?' she asked.

'We got the bus out tae Strathclyde Park. There's a big funfair there; he had a great time. Ah got him a ticket . . . a wristband thing, it was . . . for all the rides.'

'What about you? Did you go on any?'

'Shite, no! Me?'

'Come on, Scottie,' she chuckled. 'You're just a big kid at heart. What was it? Too dear for both of you?'

'No, Ah just didnae fancy it.'

'Did I not give you enough money?'

He shook his head. 'No, no,' he insisted. 'I had enough if Ah'd wanted.' He paused. 'Have you eaten?' he asked.

'Yes,' she lied. 'I had a sandwich earlier. I just want a cup of something then I'm off.'

In truth, she would have considered committing murder for a brandy and dry ginger, but she refused to keep alcohol in the house, unless they were entertaining, when she bought wine for their guests. She had seen her husband drunk too often to do anything to undermine his constant, daily, effort to stay sober.

'Ah'll make you a cup o' tea,' Scott said. 'Go and take the weight off your plates.'

She did as he told her, slipping off her shoes and her jacket, then slumping into her armchair. She was almost asleep when he came into the living room a few minutes later, carrying what she saw was a new mug, with the theme park logo, and a plate, loaded with cheese sandwiches and a round, individual, pork pie.

'Eaten?' he laughed. 'My arse! Where are you going tae get a sandwich anywhere near Pitt Street on a Sunday night? Wee Danny Provan's no' going to run out and get you something, that's for bloody sure.'

She squeezed his arm as he laid her supper on a side table. 'You're a good lad, Scott,' she murmured.

'Ah do my best,' he replied. 'Honest, Ah really do.'

'I know.'

'So,' he continued, 'how's it goin'? Have you solved the case yet? No' that there's much to solve.'

She laughed. 'Oh, but there bloody is. For a start, we've established who the two dead guys were.'

'Ah thought you knew.'

'We knew who they had been, through our "intelligence sources",' she held up both hands and made a 'quotation mark' gesture with her fingers, 'so called. But now we know about them. That's why I'm so late in. One of them went under the name of Bryan Lightbody. He lived in Hamilton, New Zealand, with a wife and a wee boy Jakey's age, and he owned four taxis there.

'The other one was known as Richie Mallett, single, well-off, low-handicap golfer. He lived in Sydney, in an apartment near somewhere called Circular Quay, and he had a bar there. Both of them seem to have been very respectable guys, apart from when they were moonlighting and killing people.'

Scott whistled. 'They'll no' kill any more, though.'

'No, but they did leave us a wee present.' She broke off to demolish half of the pork pie. 'Do you remember when you were in the job,' she continued, when she was ready, 'hearing of a guy called Bazza Brown?'

He frowned. 'Remind me,' he murmured.

'Gangster. Fairly small time in your day, but come up in the world since then.'

'Mmm,' he said. 'Aye, but vaguely.'

'Well, they'd heard of him,' Lottie declared. 'We traced their car this afternoon, and we found Bazza shut in the boot.'

'Eh?' her husband exclaimed. 'So he must have been in it all night. Was he still alive?'

'No.'

'Did he suffocate?'

'I don't think so. I doubt if he'd time before they shot him in the chest.'

His eyes widened. 'Fuck me!' he gasped.

She chuckled. 'Those may very well have been his last words.' She ate the other half of the pie and washed it down with a mouthful of tea.

'No' much use to you dead, though, is he?' Scott remarked, recovering his composure. 'He'll no' be much of a witness.'

'He's not going to tell us a hell of a lot,' she conceded. 'But nevertheless, even dead, he's a lead of sorts. We think we know why he was involved with them. I don't believe for a minute that he was behind the whole thing, too small a player for that, but if we can find who he was in touch with before he died, that may lead us to whoever ordered Toni Field killed.'

'My God,' he whispered. He looked at her, frowning. 'You're sure she was the target, and no' the de Marco woman?'

Lottie nodded. 'Oh yes,' she replied. 'There's no doubt about that now, sunshine. The crime scene team found her photo, tucked away in Botha's false passport.'

Twenty-One

'Sod this!' Skinner muttered. When he had plugged his landline into the wall ten minutes before six o'clock, it had told him that nineteen messages had been left for him. In theory his number was private and unlisted; he knew that some of the Scottish news outlets had acquired it by means he had chosen not to investigate, but he had no idea how many. The call counter gave him a clue. Making a mental note to have it changed, he held his finger on the 'erase' button until the box was empty. If any friends or family had called him, he guessed they would have rung his personal mobile as back-up.

He switched that on; there were no message waiting, but he had only just stepped out of the shower when it rang. He answered without checking the caller. No journalists had the number . . . no active journalists, but there was a retired one who did.

'Bob,' a deep familiar voice rumbled, the accent basically Scottish but overlaid with something else.

'Xavi,' Skinner exclaimed. 'How are you doing, big fella? And those lovely girls of yours?'

Xavier Aislado, and his ancient half-brother, Joe, were the owners of the *Saltire* newspaper. Their father had escaped from Civil War Spain to Scotland, and eventually they had chosen to return, although in different circumstances and at different times.

Xavi, after a promising football career cut short by injury, had been the *Saltire*'s top journalist, and had been responsible for its acquisition by the media chain that Joe, thirty years his senior, had built in Catalunya.

Their family structure was complicated. Xavi's mother had left him behind as a child, and had gone on to have twin daughters, by a police colleague of Skinner. One of the two had taken over from Xavi as the *Saltire*'s managing editor, although she had been completely unaware of their relationship until then.

'We're all fine,' he said. 'Sheila and Paloma are blooming and Joe's hanging in there. He wasn't too well during the winter, but he's got his love to keep him warm too. But more to the point, what is happening in your life? June called me at some God-awful hour about a story that everybody's chasing, about your wife. She and I want you to know that we owe you plenty, so if it's all balls, you have open access to the *Saltire* to help knock it down. If it's true . . . we'll ignore it if that's what you want.'

'I appreciate that, Xavi,' Bob assured his friend. 'As it happens it is true, but we're proposing to deal with it like two grown-ups. Tell June to be ready for a joint statement this morning; that should put a lid on it.'

'How about this man Morocco? Look, I've been there; I know how you're liable to be feeling about him.'

'Liable to be,' he agreed, 'but I'm not. Morocco's a relative innocent in this carry-on, so don't go looking to give him an editorial hard time. Let him stay a Scottish celebrity hero. Between you and me, the guy's done me a favour.'

'If that's what you want, I'll pass it on to June.' He chuckled, a deep sound that made Skinner think of one of his vices, a secret that he shared with Seonaid, his younger daughter: a spoonful of Nutella, scooped straight from the jar. 'I don't tell her anything, you understand. On the *Saltire*, she's the boss.'

'I'm sure.' Bob frowned. 'Has she brought you up to date with what happened on Saturday, in the Glasgow concert hall?'

'Yes, she has. From what she told me, it rather complicates the Aileen situation. She had a narrow escape and went running to Morocco, not you.'

'She didn't. Have a narrow escape, that is. She wasn't the target.'

'You can say that for certain? I thought there was still some doubt about who they were after. A couple of our Spanish titles are running the proposition that the First Minister himself was the target, and they missed.'

'Then you should kick someone's arse. Clive Graham might not mind the publicity, but the truth is that the one thing we did know for sure was that the target was female, and we said so at the time. Now we know definitely that it was Toni Field. My team in Glasgow haven't announced it yet, but they will this morning. Press conference at ten o'clock, the same time as my lawyer will issue our statement, Aileen's and mine, about our decision, last week, to pull the plug on our marriage.'

'Now there's a coincidence. Sorry,' the Spanish Scot murmured, 'that was my cynicism showing through.'

'Hey, Xavi,' Skinner laughed, 'I've learned many things from you. One of them is how to minimise a story, as well as how to maximise it. Tell June . . . sorry, suggest to her, that she forget about us and concentrate on Glasgow this morning. There were developments yesterday, significant developments, and they're going to blow political marriages off the front page.'

'Any hints?'

'Just one. I don't want anyone approached before the press

135

conference, but your crime reporter might be well employed doing all the research he can on a man named Basil "Bazza" Brown.'

'Thanks for that. Will you be at the media briefing?'

'No, I have someone else to see before then. I'll need to go, in fact; my driver's due to pick me up in under fifteen minutes.'

'Fine.' Aislado paused, then added, 'You and Strathclyde, Bob. I know how you've always felt about it, so how the hell did that happen?'

'A chapter of accidents, mate. Aileen says that now I'm there it'll be my Hotel California. You know, I can check in any time I like but I can never leave. I'm not so sure about that, though. I have many things to sort out in my head over the next few weeks.'

'Well, if you'd like somewhere to sort them out undisturbed, you're welcome to visit us. I know you have your own place in L'Escala, but we have a guest house here now, and it's yours for as long as you need it, if you don't want anyone to know where you are.'

'Cheers, appreciated. I may take you up on that.'

'Okay. Bob, one last thing. If we do go looking for this man Brown after ten o'clock, where are we likely to find him?'

'In the fucking mortuary, mate.'

Twenty-Two

'I'm too old for this shit, Lottie,' Dan Provan moaned.

'Agreed,' DI Mann retorted. 'But you're here and you're all I've fucking got as a second in charge, so get on with it, eh? Oh and by the way, you're not too old to collect the overtime.'

'There is that,' the sallow sergeant conceded. He smiled. 'Keeps us both out the house as well. How's your Scottie gettin' on?'

'He's fine. Moans a bit but he's doing great in the battle against the bevvy; that makes me happy. He took the wee guy to the big shows in Strathclyde Park yesterday. A year ago, even, I'd never have trusted him to do that.'

'Theme park,' Provan corrected her. 'The shows are what you and me went to when we were kids.'

'Maybe you did. My dad never took me anywhere. All his spare money went on that bloody football team. "Follow, Follow",' she sang, off-key. 'I remember my mum making me hide from him many a Saturday night . . . well, maybe not that many, for they didn't lose all that often, but when they did and he got in with a couple of bottles of Melroso in him, nobody was safe.'

'No' even you?' He looked her up and down, trying to tease her. In all the time they had worked together she had never before mentioned her childhood.

'Not when I was eight or nine. If my mum gave me and my big brother money for the multiplex on a Saturday night, we knew there was going to be trouble.'

Provan frowned. 'Did he . . .'

'Batter my mum? Oh yes. Don't get me wrong, he was a quiet man all the rest of the time.' She shook her head. 'Listen to me, defending him.'

'What happened to him?'

'Stomach cancer happened to him, when I was twelve. Then I grew up, joined the police, got married, and found myself in the same situation as my mother had. She warned me, ye know, but I never listened.'

'Scott was like him? Is that what you're saying?'

She nodded.

'Just as well you could handle him,' the sergeant said, 'like you proved at that daft boxing night.'

'Not all the time. There were re-matches, Danny, without the gloves and the head guard. I didn't always win. That was around the time when he was fuckin' up his police career through the drink. When that finally happened I gave him an ultimatum. I gave him two of them, to be honest. The first was that if he ever raised a hand to me again, I would leave him. The second was that if he ever raised a hand to Jakey, I'd kill him. He believed both of them; he's been off it, more or less, ever since. He still goes AWOL every now and then, but he comes back sober, and that's the main thing.'

'Then good for him. He's gettin' on fine at work too, is he? In that cash and carry place o' his?'

'Yes. He's a supervisor now. The head of security's due to retire in a couple of years, and Scottie's in with a chance of getting the job.'

'Mibbes he could find somethin' for me if he does,' Provan muttered. 'Like Ah said . . .'

She sighed. 'I know, I know, I know. You're too old for this shit: but you're here, and we're both standing in it, so just you keep on shovellin', Danny. I've got another press briefing at ten o'clock. By then I'd like an answer from that car rental company.'

The sergeant nodded; a small shower of dandruff settled on the shoulders of his crumpled, shiny jacket. 'Aye,' he said. 'They should have been back tae us by now. Time tae rattle their cage.' He checked the number on the key-ring fob, then snatched his phone from its cradle and punched it in.

'Drivall Car Hire,' a young female voice chirped. It made him feel older than ever.

'DS Provan, Strathclyde CID,' he announced. 'Ah spoke to somebody in your office last night. The lad said his name was Ajmal; Ah wanted some information about one of your cars that we found in Glasgow. He was going to get back to me, but I'm still waitin'. I need tae speak to him, now.'

'I'm sorry, caller,' the irrepressible youth replied, sounding anything but regretful. 'Ajmal's off duty today.'

'Then go and get him,' Provan barked, 'or dig up your manager! This is a major inquiry Ah'm on.'

The girl sniffed. 'There's no need for that tone of voice, sir. If you hold on I'll see if Mr Terry's available; he's our manager.'

'You do that, hen.' He sat and waited, but not for too long.

'Sergeant err . . .' a querulous male voice began. 'I'm sorry, Chantelle didn't catch your name.'

'Provan,' the Glaswegian growled. 'Detective Sergeant Provan.'

'Thank you, sorry about that; I'm John Terry, the general manager. This will be about our vehicle LX12 PMP, is that right?'

'Indeed.'

'We have been acting on this, I assure you,' Terry declared. 'My

139

colleague Ajmal left me a note when he went off duty. The vehicle hirer has died and you're trying to find out who he was through us, is that the case?'

'I suppose it might be possible, sir,' Provan said, 'that a guy hired a vehicle, shot himself three times in the chest, shut himself in the boot and disposed o' the gun, but we don't really believe that.'

The manager gulped. 'Pardon? I didn't quite catch all of that.'

'Okay, mate. Let me spell it out for ye', in words of one syllabub.'

'My God,' Terry exclaimed, before he was finished. 'Mr Provan, I think we've had a little language difficulty here. Ajmal's English is not the best, and your accent is, let's say, quite regional.'

No, let's fuckin' no' say! With difficulty, the detective managed to keep his thought to himself, as the manager continued. 'Ajmal left me a note with the registration number of the vehicle and the information that a man had been found dead in the vehicle and that the Glasgow police wanted the name of the hirer. What you've just told me is news to me and shocking news at that.'

'Well, now that we understand each other,' Provan said, weighing each word to avoid further 'language difficulties', 'maybe yis can get me the information Ah need.'

'Oh, I have that already, Sergeant. The office where the vehicle was hired . . . it's in Finsbury Park . . . was closed last night. I spoke to the person in charge five minutes ago. The vehicle was rented a week ago yesterday, for return by five p.m. yesterday evening. The hirer's name was Byron Millbank, address number eight St Baldred's Road, London. I happen to know where that is; it's very close to what was Highbury Stadium, the old Arsenal football ground, before they moved to the Emirates.'

'Did he have a UK driving licence?'

'I don't know, but I assume . . .'

'We don't deal in assumptions, Mr Terry. Will they have a record in your other office?'

'Oh yes. And a photocopy. Not everyone does that but we always do; take a photocopy of the plastic licence and the paper counterpart.'

'In that case,' Provan told him, 'I need you tae get back on to your other office and get those photocopies faxed up to me. Haud on.' He found a number that he had scrawled on a pad on his desk for another inquiry, a week before, and read it out to Terry.

'I'm afraid we don't have fax machines in our regional offices any more,' he said. 'Old technology these days.'

'Well, find one, please. Go to the Arsenal if ye have tae; they're bound tae have one.'

'Oh, we won't have to do that. We can scan the copies and send them.'

'Eh?'

'Scan them, Mr Provan. Turn them into JPEGs.'

'Eh?'

'Photographic images. Then we can send them to you as email attachments.' Terry giggled. 'Or don't you have email in Scotland?'

Nancy! Provan, an old-school homophobe, kept another thought to himself. 'Oh aye, sir, we have. It runs on gas, right enough, but we get by.' He read his force e-address, then spelled it out, letter by letter. 'Soon as ye can, please; Ah need it within the next half hour.'

'You'll have it in ten minutes.' Terry paused. 'Can I send somebody along from our Glasgow Airport depot to collect our car?'

'Eventually,' the DS told him. 'Ah'm afraid your car's a crime scene, sir. Ah'm no' sure how long we'll need to hold it for. When we're done with it, we'll bring it back to you. We'll even clean aff the bloodstains fur ye.'

He hung up and turned to Mann. 'A name for ye, Lottie. The car was hired by somebody called Byron Millbank.'

'What do we know about him?' she asked.

'Eff all at the moment, but we should have a wee picture soon, off his driving licence. Meantime, his name's enough tae go searchin' for his birth certificate.'

'Maybe,' the DI cautioned. 'That's assuming it's his real name. Let me see the image as soon as you get it, and blow it up as large as you can. I want to let the big boss see it.'

Twenty-Three

'When it arrives, have them forward it to my email,' Skinner told Lowell Payne, raising his voice slightly as his car overtook three lorries that were travelling in convoy along the busy motorway that links Scotland's capital with its largest city. 'I'd like to see it as soon as I get to the office, although I'm not sure when that will be. I'm not looking forward to my next visit, although it's one I have to make.'

'I'll do that, Chief. I was planning to attend the press briefing. Should I do that?'

'Mmm.' He considered the question for a few seconds, as he held his phone to his ear. His Strathclyde driver was new to him; Bluetooth was not an option. 'Maybe not. The media will be aware by now of your role as my exec, and I've been dodging the buggers since last night. But tell DI Mann she should make it clear that we now know for sure that Field was the target. She doesn't need to say how, but she should rule out any other possibility one hundred per cent. Do we video these events ourselves?'

'I don't know,' Payne admitted. 'I've never been involved in one as formal as this.'

'Then find out. If they don't, make sure it happens. I've always done it in Edinburgh. I like my own record of events.'

'Understood. I'll tell Malcolm Nopper.'

'Thanks. Something else I'd like you to do. The force area is massive, as we all know; I don't plan or expect to set foot in every police station on a three-month appointment, but nonetheless I imagine I'm going to be travelling quite a bit. I want to be in complete touch at all times, so I'd like you to fix me up with a tablet computer.'

'An iPad?'

'That or equivalent, as long as it gets me internet access everywhere I go and has a big enough screen for me to read. With one of those I'll be able to read emails at once, wherever I am.'

'You'll have one before the day's out.'

'Thanks.' As he spoke, his driver signalled then eased to the left, leaving the motorway. Skinner knew where they were, well enough; Lanarkshire had been his territory until he was into his twenties, even if it had changed since his departure.

'Why the hell do they call this Motherwell Food Park?' he mused aloud.

'No idea, sir,' his driver replied, believing that an answer had been required. 'Why would they not?'

'Because it's in bloody Bellshill, Constable; it's miles away from Motherwell.'

'Is that right, sir?'

'Trust me on it; I was born in Motherwell, and my grandparents, my father's folks, they lived in Bellshill. Where are you from, Constable Cole? What's your first name, by the way?'

'David, sir; Davie. I'm from Partick; that's in Glasgow, sir.'

Skinner laughed. 'I know that well enough. I did some sinning there or thereabouts in my youth. Used to hang out in a pub called the Rubaiyat, in Byres Road.'

'That's not quite Partick, sir, but I know where you are. It's still there.'

'But not as it was; it was gutted, or "refurbished" to use the polite term for architectural vandalism, back in the eighties. It had a lounge bar . . . where you could take your girlfriend; never to the public bar, mind, men only there . . . called "The Bowl of Night". Very few of the punters had a clue where the name came from, but it was famous nonetheless. There was never any trouble there, either.'

Careful, Bob, he told himself. *Steer well clear of memory lane, or you could get to like this bloody place all over again.*

'Were you Chief Constable Field's driver, Davie?' he asked.

In the rear-view mirror, he saw the young man's eyes tense. 'Yes, sir. I wasn't on duty on Saturday, though. She told me she was being collected by the First Minister's car. I think she was quite chuffed about that.'

'So you've been to her home before?'

'Oh yes, sir, often. We're not far from it now.'

They were moving down a steep incline that led to a complex motorway interchange. To his left, he saw a series of fantastic twisted shapes, the highest of them a wheel. 'What the hell's that?' he asked.

'Theme park, sir,' his driver informed him. 'They call it M and D's.'

'My younger son would love it,' he chuckled. 'He's the family action man. The older one would turn his nose right up; he's our computer whizz kid.'

'That whole area's called Strathclyde Park, sir,' Constable Davie went on.

'Oh, I know that,' Skinner murmured. 'It used to be wilderness. In fact, the Motherwell burgh rubbish tip was there, right next to a football ground that used to be covered in broken glass and all sorts of crap. It was all taken away when the park was created and they diverted the River Clyde to make the loch. I was a kid when they did it, but I remember it happening.'

Nostalgia, nostalgia, nostalgia. Stop it, Skinner! And yet, he reminded himself, none of those he thought of as his second family, Mark, James Andrew and Seonaid, had ever set foot in the town that had raised him.

He shook the thoughts from his head as Davie drove through the interchange and off by an exit marked 'Bothwell'. Almost immediately he took a left, then made a few more turns, the last taking them into a leafy avenue called Maule Road. 'This is it, sir,' he said, drawing to a halt outside a big red sandstone villa, built, Skinner estimated, in the early twentieth century.

'Pretty substantial,' he remarked. 'When did Chief Constable Field move in here?' he asked his driver. 'Given that she was only in post for five months.'

'Three months ago, sir. For the first few weeks she and her sister lived in an executive flat on the Glasgow Riverside.'

'Right.' He stepped out of the car, then leaned over, beside the driver's window; it slid open. 'I can't say for sure how long I'll be,' he murmured. 'If I'm any longer than half an hour, I want you to toot the horn. I'll pretend it's a signal that I've had an urgent message.' He smiled. 'I'll never ask you to lie for me, Davie, but it's always good to have an escape plan.'

'I understand, sir.' Constable Cole frowned, as if wanting to say more, but hesitant.

The chief read the signal. 'Out with it,' he said.

'Thank you, sir. It's presumptuous of me, but I wonder if you'd express my sympathies to Marina and her mother.'

'Of course I will. You've met them both?'

'Yes, sir. I saw Marina pretty much every day, with her working so close to the chief, and I met Miss Deschamps when she stayed with them a couple of months ago. I think she came up to see the new house,' he added.

146

'What are they like?' Skinner asked. 'Mark my card, Davie.'

'They're both very nice ladies. Marina's younger than the chief by a few years and not all that like her physically, or in personality, come to that. Miss Deschamps . . . she's very particular about that, by the way, sir. Marina's a Ms but her mother is definitely Miss . . . Miss Deschamps is quiet, doesn't say much, but she was always very polite to me. She tried to tip me when we got here.' He grinned at the memory. 'The chief did her nut, but she just smiled and shook my hand instead.'

'Thanks.' The chief constable stood straight, walked through the villa's open gateway and up to the vestibule. He rang the bell and waited.

He was about to press the button again when the front door opened. A tall, slim woman stood there; her hair was honey-coloured, and her skin tone almost matched it. The overall effect, Skinner mused, had the potential to cause traffic accidents.

She looked up at him, but not by much. 'Yes?' she said.

'Bob Skinner,' he told her. 'I believe you're expecting me. My aide called yesterday, yes?'

Her hand flew to her mouth. 'Of course,' she exclaimed. 'I'm so sorry. It's just . . .' She broke off, looking at his suit.

'I'm sorry,' he murmured. 'I should have thought this through. It's my habit to leave my uniform in the office and travel in civvies. Please don't feel slighted.'

'I don't, honestly,' the woman assured him. 'I always thought my sister overdid the uniform bit.' She extended her hand. 'I'm Marina Deschamps,' she said, as they shook. 'Come in, my mother is through in the garden room.'

She led the way and he followed, through a hallway, then along a corridor. He guessed at her age as they walked. A few years younger than her sister, Davie had said. Toni had been thirty-eight, so Skinner placed Marina early thirties, somewhere in age between her sister and his own daughter.

The corridor led them into a small sitting room that might have been a study at some time in the life of the old house, before what most people would have called a conservatory was added. As far as the chief could see it was unoccupied.

'Mother,' Marina called out, 'our visitor is here.'

Sofia Deschamps had been seated in a high-backed wicker armchair, one of a pair, looking out into a garden that was entirely paved and filled with potted plants of various sizes, from flowers to small trees. She rose and stepped into view. She was almost as tall as her younger daughter; indeed they were very much alike, twins with a thirty-year age difference.

'Mr Skinner,' she said, as she approached him. 'Thank you for calling on us.' Her accent had strong French overtones, and she held her hand out in front of her, as if she expected him to kiss it, in the Gallic manner. Instead, he took it in his.

'I wish I didn't have to,' he replied. 'I wish that Saturday had never happened, that Toni was still in Pitt Street and I was still in Fettes, in my office in Edinburgh. My condolences to you both.'

'Thank you.'

It occurred to him, for the first time, that both women were wearing black; inwardly he cursed himself for his pale blue tie. Sofia's face was drawn, and her eyes were a little red, but there was an impressive dignity about her, about both of them, for that matter. 'It's still fairly early,' she murmured, 'but please, allow me to fetch us some coffee.'

'No, no, ma'am,' he protested, 'that isn't necessary.'

'I insist.' She stood her ground; refusal would have been impolite.

'In that case, thank you very much, but if I may I'll have water, sparkling if you have it, rather than coffee. My . . .' He paused; he had been about to describe Sarah as 'My wife'. '. . . medical adviser says I drink far too much of the stuff, and she's made me promise to give it up.'

'A pity,' Miss Deschamps murmured, with a hint of a smile. 'We should allow ourselves the occasional vice.'

'My medical adviser is my vice.' He said it without a pause for thought. 'That's to say,' he added, searching for an escape route, 'she's my former wife, and I've learned that it's too much trouble to disobey her.'

'In that case I will not press you further. Excuse me, I will not be long.'

His eyes followed her as she headed for the door. She might have left sixty behind her, but she had lost no style or elegance; even at that early hour she was dressed in an ankle-length skirt and high heels.

Marina was less formal, in black trousers and a satin blouse. 'Please,' she said, 'sit down.'

Skinner listened for French in her accent; there was some but less than in her mother.

'Maman is being discreet,' she continued. 'She knows I want to ask you about my employment situation, and she doesn't want it to appear as if we're ganging up on you.'

'That's very decent of her,' the chief said, as he sat, facing her, on a couch that matched the armchairs, 'but there's no rush to consider that. I know that you acted as Toni's personal assistant. My assumption has been that you wouldn't want to continue in that role with her successor, but that's a decision you can take in your own time.

'I've already given instructions that you can have all the time you feel you need. My temporary appointment is for three months; if you want to take all that time to decide what you want to do, or at least until a permanent successor to your sister is selected, that'll be fine by me.'

Marina shook her head. 'There's no need, sir,' she replied. 'I have a job, and I'd like to carry on doing it.'

Skinner stared at her, unable to keep his surprise from showing. 'You want to work for me?' he exclaimed.

She nodded.

'Look,' he said. 'I have to be frank about this. You know your sister and I were not exactly the best of friends.'

Marina smiled, then nodded. 'Oh yes. She was very clear about that. But that was more political than anything else. You had different views on certain things, but that didn't affect what she thought of you as a police officer. We both know she was a big supporter of a unified Scottish force.'

'Sure, she made that clear enough in ACPOS, and I made my opposition equally plain. We had some robust discussions, to say the least.'

'Oh she told me. But what you probably do not know is, her big fear was that she would talk you round to her view. She rated you very highly as a police officer; in fact she said you were the best she'd ever met. She wanted the top job, no mistake about that, but she didn't think she'd have a chance if you went for it.'

'Indeed?' Skinner murmured.

'Indeed.'

'So where does that take us, Ms Deschamps?'

'I have no personal issues with you, sir,' she replied. 'Fate has put you in what was my sister's office. I'm a top-class secretary with personnel management qualifications, and I like to work with the best. Therefore . . .' She held his eyes with hers.

'Let me think about it,' he said. 'I like to have a serving officer as my assistant, and I've already appointed someone to that position, pro tem. To be frank, I'll need to get to know the job before I can judge whether there will be enough work left for you. But first things first; you and your mother have a funeral to organise, albeit with all the help that the force can give you. Once that's over, we can talk. Fair enough?'

'Fair enough,' she agreed.

Out of nowhere, Skinner remembered a problem. 'There is one thing, though. Do you have the combination of the safe in the chief's office?'

Marina sighed. 'I did,' she replied. 'It was seven three eight two seven six. But Antonia always changed it at the end of the week. It was usually the last thing she did on a Friday; sometimes she'd tell me the new number there and then, but if she didn't have a chance it would wait until Monday. Last Friday she didn't tell me. You can try the old number, just in case she forgot to make the change, but if it doesn't work, I fear I can't help you.'

She looked up as her mother returned carrying a tray, loaded with two tiny espresso cups, and a bottle of Perrier with a glass.

'No ice,' Sofia Deschamps declared as she placed them on a small table at the side of the couch. 'I refuse to dilute the mineral with melted tap water, as so many do.'

'I couldn't agree more,' Skinner told her. 'When my late wife and I were very young, we went on a camping holiday to the South of France. Everybody told us not to drink the water there, so we didn't. But we had ice in everything, so everything tasted of chlorine.'

'If that was the only side effect,' she countered, 'you were lucky.'

He winced. 'It wasn't; I was being delicate, that's all.'

'Your late wife,' she repeated. 'And earlier you mentioned your former wife.'

'Three,' he said, anticipating the question. 'Three and still counting.'

'Maman!' Marina exclaimed, her tone sharp.

'Ah yes.' Her mother held up a hand. 'I am sorry. That was indiscreet; we have seen this morning's papers.'

'No apology necessary,' he assured her. 'All it means is that our separation is public knowledge. It wasn't the way I'd have chosen for it to be revealed, but these things happen. Have you ever been married, Miss Deschamps? Or am I making a false assumption? Have you reverted to your birth surname?'

'No, you are correct. I have always chosen to avoid marriage. Antonia's father, Anil, was a member of the Mauritian government of the day . . . you see, we have politicians in common. Marriage with him was never possible, since he had a wealthy wife, to whom he owed his position.

'Marina's father was an Australian, with business interests in Port St Louis. He spent part of the year there, the winter, usually, and the rest in Australia, or travelling in connection with his business. He was something of an entrepreneur.' She pronounced the word with care, balancing each syllable.

'We had a very nice apartment there, and a very pleasant life. Not that I was a kept woman,' she was quick to add. 'I had a very good job, in the Mauritian civil service, and I maintained my own household. He did not contribute, because I would not allow it, even though we were together for seventeen years. I had a good income. We are a wealthy country, you know; close to Africa and yet a little distant from it too.'

'I know,' Skinner replied. 'Mauritius is one of the many places on my "To do" list.'

'You will like it.'

'Why did you leave?' he asked her.

'To be with my daughters. Marina's father was very good to both my girls; he more or less adopted Antonia, and when she came to university age, he got her a place in Birmingham, where she did a degree in criminology.'

'She first joined the police in Birmingham as well,' Marina added. 'She had a specialised degree and that got her fast-tracked. Well, you'll have seen her career record, I'm sure. She never looked back.'

'How about you?' he put to her. 'Were you ever tempted to join the force?'

'That never really arose, not in the same way. My father died when I was sixteen. I was very upset, and any thought of university went out of my mind . . . not that I had Antonia's IQ anyway. I stayed in Mauritius and went to college; I did a secretarial course and a personnel management qualification. I came to Britain eight years ago, when Antonia was senior enough to point me at a job with the Met support staff.'

She smiled. 'That's not as bad as it sounds; I had a very stringent interview, and I must have been vetted, for I was attached to SO15, the Counter-Terrorism Command, for a little while. But when Antonia became a chief constable . . . back to Birmingham again . . . things changed. She insisted that I go with her, to run what she always called her Private Office. The rest you must know.'

Skinner nodded. 'I've been told. Ladies,' he continued, 'you'll be aware that since Saturday evening, a full-scale murder investigation has been under way. I'm keeping in close touch with it, and I know that DI Mann, the senior investigating officer, will want to visit you fairly soon to interview you for the record. Meantime, is there anything you would like to ask me?'

'Of course,' Sofia exclaimed, 'but why would he need to interview us?'

'Detective Inspector Mann is a lady, Maman,' her daughter murmured.

'Then she, if you must. Why would she? What do we know? In any event, can this not be an interview? You're her boss now, after all, as my dear Antonia was.'

'Yes but she is in day-to-day charge.' He paused. 'If it makes you happy, I can go over some of the ground she'll want to and report what you say to her. If she's comfortable with that, fine. If not, she can come and visit you again. Okay?'

'Yes,' Marina Deschamps replied, at once. 'But Maman is right. Why do you need witness statements from us?'

'Because we're now certain, beyond any doubt, that Chief Constable Field was the target. These men weren't after my wife, or the First Minister. They were pros, hit men; they knew exactly who they were there to kill, and they did.'

'*Oui*,' Miss Deschamps whispered. 'We saw my daughter's body yesterday. They covered half her face with a sheet, but I made them take it off. We know what was done to her. So yes, I understand you now. What do you need to know?'

'Her private life,' Skinner said. 'I can tell you that we'll be going back through her entire career, looking at what she's done, people she's put away, enemies she may have made along the way who have the power and the contacts to put together an operation like this.'

'Such an impersonal word: "operation". You make it sound like a military thing.'

'It was,' he told her. 'Smit and Botha were former soldiers, and Beram Cohen, the planner, had an intelligence background. They didn't work cheap, and they weren't the sort of men you can contract in a pub. The very fact that the principal, as we'll call the person who ordered your daughter's death, was able to contact Cohen, tells me that he is wealthy and well-connected.

'I know about some of the successes that Toni had as a police officer and I'm aware that she may have upset some very nasty people in her time. Trust me, we will look at these, using outside agencies wherever we need to.'

'Outside agencies?'

'He means the British Security Service, Maman,' Marina volunteered.

'Not only them. The FBI, the American DEA; we'll go anywhere we need to. But alongside that I need to know about any personal relationships your sister may have had. Unlikely as it may seem, did she ever have a romance that ended badly?' He hesitated. 'Did she have any personal weaknesses?'

'Of course not!' Sofia exclaimed.

'I'm sure she didn't,' Skinner said, deflecting her sudden anger, although privately he counted naked ambition and ruthlessness towards colleagues as ranking fairly high on the weakness scale. 'But the questions must be asked if we are to do our best for you in finding the person who had that done to her, what you saw yesterday. Marina, you understand that, don't you?'

'Yes, I do. I knew my sister well enough. Personal weaknesses? Was she a gambler, closet drinker? No, she was tight with her money and she didn't touch a drop. She didn't mortgage beyond her means either; she was shrewd with the property she bought. For example, she picked up this pile at the bottom of the market, after making a big profit from her house in Edgbaston.'

She stopped and looked at her mother. 'Personal relationships?' she repeated. 'Maman, cover your ears if you like, but this is the truth. I don't think Toni ever had a romance in her life, certainly not in the years that I've lived with her in Britain.

'Relationships, yes; she's had six of them. Make no mistake, she was robustly heterosexual. But none of them were about love; all of them were about her career. I'm not saying that she bedded her way to the top, but every lover that she had was a man of power or influence, one way or another.'

'Might any of them have been the sort of man to take it badly when she pulled the plug on him?' the chief asked.

'No, I would not put any of them in that category. Everyone she brought home . . . and she told me she never played away . . . was as cynical as she was.'

'Were they cops?'

'A couple were. There was a DAC . . . deputy assistant commissioner . . . in the Met, about five years ago, and an assistant chief from Birmingham before him. I'm sure that neither of those two were in a position to advance her career directly, but they knew people who were.

'More recently, from what she told me, the men she's been involved with have been . . . how do I put it? . . . opinion formers, movers and shakers outside the police force. There was a broadcast journalist, a civil service mandarin in the Justice Ministry, and another man she said was a very successful criminal lawyer.'

'You're telling me what they were but not who,' Skinner pointed out. 'Can you put names to any of them?'

Marina smiled. 'No, because Antonia never did, and since we didn't live together until she became the chief in Birmingham, I never saw any of them. "No names, no blames", was what she always said, whenever I asked her. It used to annoy me, until I realised that given her background and mine . . .' She broke off and looked at her mother. 'I'm sorry, Maman,' she said, 'but this is the truth. She never had a proper father as such, far less than I did. We were secret daughters in a way, both of us, but her most of all.

'Given that history, that upbringing, it was perfectly natural that Antonia should have woven a cloak of secrecy around her own personal life. And me? I am exactly the same. Most observers, looking at me, would say that my life is a mystery.'

Sofia nodded. Her eyes were sad. 'I wish I could deny that,' she sighed, 'but it is true. That is my legacy to both of my daughters.'

Twenty-Four

'Bingo,' Skinner exclaimed, as he gazed at the photograph on his monitor. He turned to his exec. 'It may say Byron Millbank on his driving licence, and that may not be a top-quality image, but I rarely forget a face . . . and never, when I've seen it dead. That is Beram Cohen, one-time Israeli paratrooper, then a Mossad operative until he was caught using a dodgy German passport while killing a Hamas official, most recently for hire as a facilitator of covert operations.

'As you know, Lowell, he's the guy who recruited Smit and Botha, procured their weapons through Freddy Welsh in Edinburgh, then went and died, inconveniently for them, of a brain haemorrhage a few days before the hit.'

'Could we have stopped it if he hadn't?' Payne asked.

'There would have been even less chance. The evidence we had would still have led us to Welsh, but no sooner; we probably wouldn't have got to the hall as quickly as we did.

'Even if we had been lucky and got the two South Africans, my guess is that Cohen would have been in the car and would have taken off. He'd have been on the motorway inside two minutes. He would have got clear, dumped the guy Brown's body, so it would never have been linked to our investigation, and we'd have had no clue at all, nowhere to go.'

He scratched his chin. 'Cohen dying might have been convenient for us, but as it turned out it wasn't a life-saver. Speaking of Bazza Brown's body,' he continued, 'lying a-mouldering in the boot of a Peugeot, and all that, I'd like an update on that side of the investigation.' He checked his watch. 'Mann's press briefing should be over by now; ask her to come up, please.'

The DCI nodded and was about to leave when Skinner called after him. 'By the way, Lowell, are we any nearer being able to open that bloody safe, or do we seriously have to explore the Barlinnie option? Toni's sister gave me a number, but as she warned me, it had been changed. She did it weekly, apparently; there's security,' he grumbled, 'then there's fucking paranoia.'

Payne laughed. 'It's in hand, gaffer, but the Bar-L route may be quicker than waiting for the supplier to send a technician.' He paused. 'By the way, how did your visit go? How are the mother and sister?'

'As bereft as you would imagine,' the chief replied, 'but they're both very calm. I was impressed by Marina,' he added. 'She's not a bit like her half-sister. Toni, it seems, was the love child of a Mauritian politico; she must have inherited the gene. Marina, on the other hand, struck me as one of nature's civil servants, as her mother was.'

'And her father? Is he still around?'

'No, not for some years; he never was, not full-time. Sofia seems to have valued a degree of independence.' Skinner pointed to the anteroom at the far end of his office, the place that Marina Field had filled. 'Have you lined up any secretary candidates yet?'

'Yes. Human Resources say they'll give me a short list by midday.'

'Then hold back on that for a while. We can call up a vetted typist when we need one. Marina says she wants to carry on in her job, working for me. I've stalled her on it, until I decide whether I want that.'

'How long will you take to make up your mind?'

Skinner grinned. 'Ideally, three months, by which time I'll be out of here.'

Twenty-Five

'It is for these reasons,' Aileen de Marco concluded, reading from autocue screens in the conference room of the ugly Glasgow office block that housed her party's headquarters, 'that I am committing Scottish Labour to the unification of the country's eight police forces into a single entity. The old system, with its lack of integration and properly shared intelligence and with its outdated artificial boundaries, bears heavy responsibility for the death of Antonia Field.

'Not only do I endorse the proposal for unity, I urge the First Minister to enact it without further delay to enable the appointment of a police commissioner as soon as possible to oversee the merger and the smooth introduction of the new structure.'

'Any questions, ladies and gentlemen?' Alf Old invited, from his seat at the table on the right of the platform, then pointing as he chose from the hands that shot up, and from the babble of competing voices. 'John Fox.'

'Is this not a panic reaction, Ms de Marco,' the BBC reporter asked, 'after your narrow escape on Saturday?'

'Absolutely not.'

'What would you say to those people, and there may be many of them, who think that it is?'

'I'd tell them that they're wrong. Scottish Labour took a corporate decision some time ago to support unification; we're quite clear that it's the way forward. On the other hand, the party in power seems less committed. Yes, I know the First Minister says that it's the way forward, but there are people on his back benches who aren't quite as keen.

'We've been reading a lot this morning about the First Minister's personal courage . . . and I have to say that I admire him for the way he displayed it on Saturday, when even the senior Strathclyde police officer on the scene collapsed under the strain.

'What I'm saying today is that it's time for him to bring that courage into the parliament chamber and join with us in getting important legislation on to the Scottish statute book.'

She paused, for only a second, but Marguerite Hatton seized on her silence.

'Do you have anyone in mind for the position of police commissioner, Ms de Marco?' she asked.

Aileen glared down at her from behind her lectern. 'There will be a selection process,' she replied, 'but I won't have anything to do with it.'

'Would you endorse your husband's candidacy?'

'I repeat,' she snapped, 'I will not have anything to do with the selection process. I'm not First Minister, and even if I was, the appointment will be made by a body independent of government. The legislation will merge the existing police authorities into one and that will select the commissioner.'

'Then my question still stands,' the journalist countered. 'Will you endorse your husband's candidacy?'

'I'm sorry, Ms Hatton,' she maintained, 'I'm not going there. I'm the leader of the Scottish Labour Party, and I'm sure that I'll have political colleagues on the new authority, but it won't be my place to influence them in favour of any candidate.'

'Or against one,' she challenged, 'if you believed he was entirely wrong for the job?'

Aileen paused. 'If I believed that strongly enough about someone,' she replied, 'I'd say so in parliament.'

'So do you believe your husband would be the right man for the post, even though he's an authoritarian bully?'

'Now hold on a minute!' Alf Old barked, from the platform. 'This press conference isn't about individuals. It's about important Labour Party policy. However, I have to tell you that I've met the gentleman in question and I don't recognise your description. Now that's enough out of you, madam. Another questioner, please?'

Hatton ignored him. 'But isn't that why you and he have just announced your separation, Aileen?' she shouted. 'Isn't that why you ran into the arms of another man after your terrifying ordeal on Saturday, because Bob wasn't there for you?'

Aileen de Marco had known more than a few intense situations in her life, and she was proud of her ability to stay calm and controlled, whatever the pressure. And so, it was agreed later, her outburst was entirely atypical, which made it all the more shocking.

'Bob's never been there for me,' she yelled. 'Why the hell do you think I'm divorcing him, you stupid bloody woman?'

Twenty-Six

'John, go easy on her, will you?'

'Bob, I'm BBC. We don't run big lurid headlines on our reports and we don't editorialise on politicians. We just run what we've got on the record, and in this case that's Aileen screaming at the Hatton bitch then storming out of the room. We can't ignore that, because it's there. STV have got it, and that means it'll be on ITN national at lunchtime. Sky have got it and they won't hold back. Plus I saw a couple of freelance cameras there, so it could even go international.'

'Bugger,' Skinner sighed. 'And you're the nice guys, aren't you?'

'Exactly,' John Fox said. 'You know what Hatton will do with it, and the rest of the tabloids. Thing is, Bob, it's not just Aileen that's been caught up in it.'

'Don't I know it. I was never there for her, she said.'

'Do you want to react to that?'

'To the media in general, no, because anything I say will be used in evidence against either Aileen or me. To you, because I trust you or we wouldn't be speaking right now, I'll say I'm sorry she feels that way, and I'll add that lack of communication is one of the factors behind our separation.' He paused, then added, 'Hell, you can use this as well, on the record. I find it contemptible that she was goaded into her outburst after what she went through on Saturday night.'

'I will use it too. How about Hatton calling you an authoritarian bully?'

Skinner laughed. 'Jesus, John, I'm the acting chief constable of the UK's second biggest police force. If that doesn't make me an authority figure, I don't know what would. As for me being a bully, I appreciate Alf Old putting her straight, and I hope that others will as well.'

'I wouldn't worry about that,' Fox told him. 'It's a wee bit close to defamation, so most sensible editors . . . including Hatton's . . . won't repeat it. I was only covering my back by asking you about it. Besides, no tabloid editor in his right mind's going to want to fall out with you.' He laughed. 'Not that that implies you're a bully, mind.' He was silent for a second or two. 'Can I ask you something else? he murmured.

'Sure.'

'I told you what she said about Max Allan. Do you want to counter it?'

'I'd like to, but I can't, because it's true. Max was first into the hall when the emergency lighting came on. He could see very little, and at first he thought it was Paula Viareggio who'd been shot, not Toni. Max has known Paula since she was a kid; he and his wife live closer to Edinburgh than Glasgow and so they do nearly all their shopping there. They've been customers of the Viareggio delicatessen chain for twenty years, since the days when Paula worked behind the counter.

'He thought that was her on the floor, and he just buckled. The poor guy's career's probably at an end, and an ignominious one at that, thanks to Aileen. The next time I speak to her she and I are going to have very serious words about it. You can be sure of that.'

'I agree,' the journalist murmured. 'True or not, it was well out of order. But Bob, off the record this time, why did she put herself up there to be shot at? Sorry, that was an unfortunate choice of words in the circumstances.'

'Maybe but I know what you mean. My informed guess would be that her reasons were purely political.'

'Did you know about Labour supporting unification?'

'Of course I did. This is very much between us, chum, but it was the last straw as far as our marriage was concerned.'

'I guessed as much. There's a piece on the *Saltire* website that nobody's noticed yet. It was blown out of the printed edition by the Field shooting, but it's got your stamp all over it. Everybody knows that paper's your house journal, with June Crampsey being a retired cop's daughter.'

'Mmm,' Skinner murmured, 'do they indeed? I'll need to watch that, but I won't lie to you about my input to that article; you're right. I was a bit steamed up at the time. But if you're going to have a girn about me playing favourites, don't, because I'm doing it just now. Nobody else is getting past the switchboard here and I'm taking no other media calls anywhere else.'

'I appreciate that,' Fox chuckled. 'In the spirit of our special relationship, is there anything else you'd like not to tell me? About the Field investigation, for example.'

'Not a fucking word, mate; you're not that special. However, you might like to call another chum of yours, the First Minister. I reckon Aileen will have put his nose mightily out of joint.'

'Thanks for that, and the rest. Cheers.'

The chief was unfamiliar with the telephone console on his desk, but he had noticed a red light flashing during the last couple of minutes of his conversation with Fox. As he hung up he discovered what it was for as the bell sounded, almost instantly. He picked up the receiver, expecting to hear the switchboard operator, or Lowell Payne, but it was neither.

'Yes,' he began.

'Bob,' a male voice snapped back at him, 'can't you keep that bloody wife of yours under control?'

'Hello, Clive,' he replied. 'Funny you should call. Your name just came up in conversation.'

'I'm not surprised. Your ears must have been burning too. Do you know what Aileen's done?'

'Yes.'

'When did you know?'

'I first became aware of it about ten minutes ago. Clive,' Skinner asked, 'what the fuck are you on about? Haven't you read any newspapers today?'

'No I haven't. I'm not in the office. I've spent the last thirty-six hours incommunicado, comforting my distraught wife. She's under sedation, Bob. I'm still trying, but failing, to make her believe that I wasn't the target . . . although the truth is, I'm not a hundred per cent sure of that myself.

'But more than that, it's not just the thought of me with my brains on the floor that's got to her, it's the notion that if she had come with me, and not Toni, she'd have copped it. So you'll see, Bob, reading the press hasn't been at the top of my agenda. My political office has only just emailed me the unification press release Labour have put out.'

'And that's all they've sent you?'

'That's all.'

'Then you should shake up all your press people, in the party and in government. Somebody should have told you that two hours ago my dear wife and I announced that we've split. They should also have told you to check out today's *Daily News*. You're going to have fun with that come next First Minister's Questions at Holyrood, I promise you.'

He heard the First Minster draw a deep breath, then let it out slowly. 'Then I apologise, Bob,' he said, quietly. 'The government people are supposed to brief me constantly on what's happening in the media, partly to ensure that I don't make any embarrassing phone calls like this one. I told them, firmly, to leave me alone, but when the troops are afraid to override your orders when necessary, that makes you a bad general.'

'Or an authoritarian bully,' Skinner murmured.

'What?'

'Nothing. You can tell Mrs Graham to calm down. We have absolute proof that Toni was the target. They were set up and waiting for her.'

'Are you certain?'

Skinner snorted. 'I appreciate that you're a politician, but even you must know what "absolute" means.'

'But how did they know she'd be there?' the First Minister asked, sounding more than a little puzzled.

'When did you invite her to accompany you?'

'Two weeks ago.'

'Yeah, well, one day later Toni posted the engagement on bloody Twitter, and on the Strathclyde force website. She set herself up.'

'But who'd want to kill her? I know she was abrasive, but . . .'

'I've got a team of talented people trying to find that out,' the chief replied, 'and I imagine that right now they're waiting in my assistant's office.'

'Then I won't delay you further. Again, I'm sorry I went off at half cock.'

'No worries. For what it's worth, I reckon I know why Aileen broke ranks on unification. You might not realise it, if you've been cloistered since Saturday, but you've become something of a media hero, thanks to Joey Morocco's eyewitness account. He's seen a few things up close in the last couple of days, has our Joey. With the election coming up, Aileen couldn't let that go uncountered. It's the way she thinks.'

'I suppose it is, and I might even understand it. It won't do her any good though. I've seen our private polls: Labour will be crushed, and her career will be over.'

Bob laughed. 'Don't you believe it, Clive. She has a plan for every contingency. She's like Gloria Gaynor: she will survive. Get on with you now. Go and give your wife the good news.'

Twenty-Seven

'Will I survive this, Alf?' Aileen asked, leaning forward across the table, with a goblet of red wine warming in her cupped hands.

'I'll treat that as rhetorical,' the chief officer replied. 'You've just locked up the female vote within the party; as for the men, they were eating out of your hand anyway.'

'But tomorrow's coverage will be all about me dropping the bomb on that twat Hatton, and not about the policy initiative I announced.'

'Aileen, you and I both know that is bollocks; the announcement doesn't matter. We don't make policy any more, the SNP do.'

'But they need us to get unification through fast,' she countered.

'No, they don't. You and Clive Graham agreed to rush it through before the election so that it doesn't become an issue that the Tories could score with, but the Lib Dems are for it as well, and even in a minority situation their votes would see the bill through. That's if he tables it at all. The poll's in a few weeks, and you've just removed police structure as an issue anyway by announcing that we're for it.'

'You're saying that if I've pissed him off with my challenge he might walk away from our agreement.'

'Indeed I am.' He glanced around the basement restaurant to which they had retreated, checking that they were still alone and that no journalists had followed them there. 'But so what? It's irrelevant alongside the campaign that's ahead of us. With everything that's happened, are you sure you're ready for it?'

She looked him in the eye. 'How long have you known me, Alf?'

He scratched his chin. 'Twenty years?' he ventured.

'Exactly, since our young socialist days. And in all that time have you ever known me not to be up for a battle?'

'No,' he admitted. 'But you've never been in circumstances like these before. You've had a horrendous forty-eight hours.'

'Horrendous in what way? My marriage has broken up. That happens to more than ten thousand of my fellow Scots every year, and probably as many again who end cohabiting relationships. And although the statement Bob made me agree to was bland and consensual, the idiot woman Hatton just succeeded in portraying me as the partner who's been wronged. Don't you imagine that was in my mind when I staged my walk-out?'

'Are you saying that wasn't spontaneous?'

She hesitated. 'No, I'm not, but even before I reached the door I could see the positives in it. Can't you?'

'I suppose so,' he admitted.

'Exactly. So, my other personal disaster: what of that? My body was all over today's *Daily News*, and by now it'll have gone viral on the internet. But I've read the story, there and in all the other papers. Not one has said that Joey was actually in the room, because no way can they prove it, so their lawyers wouldn't let them. Neither of us will ever admit that he was, so what am I, Alf? A victim of the paparazzi, that's what, and that's how the party has to spin it. Understood?'

'Understood,' he agreed, 'but you didn't have to spell it out. Our communications people have been doing that since the story broke, both here and in London. You probably don't know this, but the shadow Culture Secretary in Westminster is going to demand that the government legislates to make invasion of privacy a go-to-jail offence. They won't do that, of course, because it can't afford to piss off the *News*, but they'll make sympathetic noises.'

'I'll bet they will. The last thing they want is Clive Graham with an absolute majority.' She smiled. 'Do you still think I'm not up for a fight?'

Old grinned back at her. 'No, and I never did. So, why did you ask me if you'd survive?'

'I only meant within the party, man. What's the feeling in our shadow cabinet and on the back benches? Are they scared by what's happened? Is my sleekit deputy Mr Felix Brahms likely to seize the day and challenge me for the leadership?'

'As far as I can tell, there won't be a revolt. You certainly needn't worry about Felix. I spoke to him last night. Yes, he was making opportunistic noises, but I put a stop to that.'

She frowned. 'How?'

'You don't want to know.'

'Yes, I bloody do. Out with it.'

He looked around again; a waiter was approaching with an order pad, but he waved him away. 'A friend of mine in Special Branch up in Aberdeen, the Brahms fiefdom, dropped me a word about him. They were worried about him being a security risk as shadow Justice Secretary.

'He's been having it off with a woman, a well-known local slapper called Mandy Madigan, whose brother Stuart is currently remanded in custody charged with the murder of a business rival, that business being prostitution and money-lending.'

'What a creepy bastard!' Aileen exclaimed. 'I like his wife, too. What are we going to do about it?'

'Nothing,' he replied, firmly. 'You've put a hint of sex into the campaign; that's just about okay, given the way that you and Bob have dealt with it. We do not need any more sleaze, though. When Brahms called me about your situation, I had a sharp word with him, told him what I knew. He swears he didn't know about her family background, and he's going to put an end to it. The Grampian cops will keep the affair to themselves, but he'd better be a choirboy from now on.'

'My God,' she chuckled. 'You're making me feel like the singing nun by comparison. Well, maybe not quite, shagging a movie star and all, but still.' She paused. 'Poor Joey; he called me this morning, on his way to the airport. He's quite upset, worried that he might have done for my career. I must call him once he gets to Los Angeles, and tell him he's probably put my approval rating up a few points.'

'Any chance of him supporting you in the campaign?'

'Hell no, he's a Tory. I know, before you say it, I seem to be making a habit of sleeping with the enemy. At least I'm not going to marry this one!'

'Is Bob going to make trouble down the line?'

'For me, no. I've got a funny feeling that I've done him a favour by cutting him loose. Not politically, either. He's got nothing to gain from it.' She frowned, suddenly. 'That said, I must ring him and apologise for what I said at the press conference. He'll have heard by now, for sure, from one of his inner media circle, Foxie, or June Crampsey. I don't want to fall out with him any more than I have done.'

'Why should that bother you?' the chief executive asked. 'You don't think you can win him over on unification, do you? He made his views pretty clear in the *Saltire* at the weekend.'

'Did he? That passed me by, not that I care. It'll go through regardless. And once it's there, who knows what he'll do. I'm quite convinced that if Toni Field was still alive he'd go for it. He's a cop first, second and third; it's all he knows, and most of what he cares about, apart from his kids.

'He's also a pragmatist. If that's right, that he said his piece in the press, all he was doing was getting at me. He knows he won't win. Deep down he also knows that if Field had been there to go for the police commissioner job, he'd have done whatever was needed to stop her, and that would have meant putting himself forward.'

'Christ, you're making it sound as if he was behind the shooting.'

Aileen smiled, but her eyes stayed serious. 'He's shown himself capable of pulling the trigger, on Saturday and more than once before that in his career. But no, I wouldn't go that far.'

'Now she's dead, what will he do?'

'My guess is that he will go for it, and I've told him as much. He spent years telling himself he didn't want to be chief in Edinburgh. Since he was talked into it, he's been saying the same about Strathclyde, but I sensed a change in him when his refusal to put his name forward last time left the field clear for Toni Field, and he saw what a political operator she was. He said something to me once about power only being dangerous if it was in the wrong hands. He could have been talking about her.'

'And his are the right hands, are they?'

'He'd never say so. He'd leave it to the politicians he dislikes so much, and the media he uses so skilfully, to do that. But he believes it all right. He hides it well, but Robert Morgan Skinner has a massive ego, tied to an absolute belief in his own rectitude. And when it comes to power, he's the equivalent of an alcoholic; one taste and he's hooked. Mind you, he'd tell you the same thing about me, and he'd be right too.'

She sipped her wine. 'I want to stay on good terms with him,' she continued, 'because I will need to be. Whatever the polls say, and however badly our colleagues in London have fucked things up for all of us, I intend to be First Minister after the election and, as such, we will have to co-exist.'

Old nodded. 'I can see that.'

'But,' she added, 'there's something else. I want to stay as close to his investigation as I can, because I want to know who killed Toni Field just as much as everyone else does. Who'd want her dead?' she asked. 'She hadn't been in Scotland long enough to have upset the criminal fraternity that badly. Yes, she may have hacked off someone dangerous in her earlier career. But can you recall another case of a senior British cop being assassinated by organised crime? I can't. However, like I said earlier, the late Toni was an intensely political animal. Who knows who she's crossed in that area. Make no mistake, politics can get you killed, and if there is any whiff of that, I want to know about it.'

Twenty-Eight

'I'm fine, Bob, honestly. I lost it for a second or two in there, but that's enough when the red lights are on the cameras. I'm simply calling to apologise for what I said about you. It was unforgivable; if you want, I'll put out a statement through my press office retracting it and saying that I was provoked.'

'Let it be, Aileen. I'm not worried about it. What you said is bloody true, anyway, so I won't ask you to lie for me.'

'Thanks,' she said. 'I appreciate that. You couldn't do something about that Hatton woman, could you?'

'No need. She's done it to herself. I've just taken yet another call from her editor, made no doubt on the advice of his lawyer. This time he was grovelling over what she called me. He's ordered her back to London this afternoon, even offered to sack her if I insisted on it. I said I didn't want that, but that he should tell her, so she can see that I have a magnanimous side after all.'

'But if she ever comes back to Glasgow, she'd better not have any drugs in her handbag?'

He laughed. 'You said that, I didn't. Now, I must go; I've got people outside waiting to brief me on the Toni Field investigation, and I cannot get off the fucking phone.'

'Then I won't keep you. How's it going, by the way? I gather from

Alf . . . I'm with him just now; we're hiding out in the Postman's Knock, the bistro down the road . . . that they've determined that she was the target.'

'That's right. My turn to apologise; you should have heard that from us, not him. I'll know more when I've seen the team, but we have several lines of inquiry. Not least, we want to know what the hell a dead Glasgow gangster was doing in the boot of the shooters' getaway car.'

'My God!' she exclaimed.

'Indeed, and you should be pleased to hear it. Lottie Mann was going to break that news at her press briefing. It should deflect some of the coverage of yours. By the way, you'd better call Clive Graham. He practically blew the wax out of my ears a few minutes ago, in the ludicrously mistaken belief that I've got any influence over you.'

'Oh, sorry again,' Aileen said. 'I was planning to do that anyway. Bob, will you keep me up to date on the inquiry?'

'Eh?' he exclaimed. 'Why should I do that?'

'Well,' she murmured, 'I do have a personal interest in knowing why I've had to throw away a very expensive evening dress.'

'There is that,' he admitted. 'Yes, I suppose we could. I'll be briefing the First Minister, so I could persuade myself that I should do the same for the leader of the Opposition, given that the election's coming up.'

'Thanks, you're a love.'

'No, I'm not. I'm chief constable and you're a constituency MSP on my patch. When are you seeing Joey again?' he asked.

'Maybe next time we're in the same city, maybe not, maybe never.' His question took her by surprise; she returned the challenge. 'When are you seeing Sarah?'

His reply took one second longer than it should have. 'Next time I pick up the kids.'

'Sure,' she sniggered, 'sure. Bob, I didn't get where I am by being stupid.' She let her words sink in, realising that her shot in the dark had found a target. 'But don't worry about it, I don't care. Whatever works for you, that's fine by me. As for her, just you be certain that getting even with me isn't her main aim.'

'It isn't,' he said, 'but let's not discuss it further. Now please, let me speak to my team. I promise I'll keep you informed, as far as I can.'

'Thanks, I appreciate that.' He thought the conversation was at an end, but, 'Bob, one more thing. I don't want to have to go back to Gullane again, ever. I'd like you to pack up everything I have there, clothes, jewellery, books, music, personal papers, everything that's mine, and have it couriered through to my flat. Would you do that for me?' She laughed, without humour. 'What am I talking about? Would you do it for us? I imagine you don't want me there again either.'

'Of course I'll do that. I'll deliver them myself.'

'Thanks for the offer, but no, let's keep it impersonal.'

'If that's what you want, fine; I'll do it as soon as I can.'

He hung up, then dialled Lowell Payne's extension number, ignoring the 'call waiting' light that continued to flash on his console. 'I'm clear,' he told his exec as he answered. 'Ask Mann and Provan to join me. Have the sandwiches I ordered arrived yet?'

'Yes, they're on a trolley outside your door; and tea in a Thermos.'

'Good. Listen, I want you to get on to the switchboard and tell them that from now on nobody gets through to me without being filtered through you; not the First Minister, not the Prime Minister, not even the monarch. Most of them won't get through; whenever you can, please refer them to Bridie Gorman or, where it's his area, to

Thomson. Also I've changed my mind about having an office mobile through here; I don't want one. You've got my personal phone number. If anything's urgent and I'm not in the office, you can use that.'

'Yes, Chief.'

Skinner headed for the side door to retrieve the sandwich trolley; Lottie Mann and Dan Provan were entering through his anteroom as he returned. 'Welcome,' he greeted them. 'Sit at the table.'

He pulled the trolley alongside them, then poured three mugs of tea. 'Help yourself to sandwiches,' he said. 'Sincere apologies for keeping you waiting so long, when you have other more important things to do. Bloody phone! Bloody journalists! Bloody politicians! The least I can do is feed you.'

Provan grunted something that might have been thanks followed by a grudging 'Sir'. The chief looked at him, pondering the notion that if he judged a book by its cover, the scruffy little DS would be heading for the remainder store.

'How long have you been in the force, Sergeant?' he asked.

'Thirty-two long years, sir.'

'It's a bind, is it?'

'Absolutely, sir. Ah have to drag ma sorry arse out o' bed every morning.'

'So why are you doing it, for what . . . fourteen or fifteen grand a year, less tax and national insurance? That's all you're getting for it in real terms. With your service, you must be in the old pension scheme, the better one, and you'll have maxed out. It'll never get any bigger than it is now as a percentage of final salary. You could retire tomorrow on two-thirds of your current pay level. Tell me,' he continued, 'where do you live?'

'Cambuslang, sir.'

'How do you get to work?'

179

Provan reached out and took a handful of sandwiches. 'Train usually, but sometimes Ah bring the car.'

'But no free parking in your station, eh?'

'No, sir.'

'No. So retire and that travel cost is no more. Are you married?'

'Technically, but no' so's you'd notice. She's long gone.'

'Kids?'

'Jamie and Lulu. He's twenty-six, she's twenty-four. He's a fireman, she's a teacher.'

'That means they're off your hands financially. So why do you do it, why do you drag your shabby arse out of bed every morning for those extra few quid?' He laughed. 'Jesus, Sergeant, if you stayed at home and gave up smoking you'd probably be better off financially. You're more or less a charity worker, man. You're streetwise, so you'll have worked this out for yourself. So tell me, straight up, why do you do it?'

'Because I'm fuckin' stupid . . . sir. Will that do as an answer?'

'It will if you want to go back into uniform, as a station sergeant. Somewhere nice. How about Shotts?'

'Okay,' Provan snapped. 'I do it because it's what I am. Ma wife left me eight years ago because of it, before Ah'd filled up the pension pot, when Lulu was still a student and needin' helped through uni. Sure, Ah could chuck it. Like you say, I'd have more than enough to live on. Except I'd give myself six months and ma head would be in the oven, even though it's electric, no' gas. The picture you're paintin's ma worst nightmare, Chief.'

He paused and for the briefest instant Skinner thought he saw a smile. 'Besides,' he added, 'the big yin here would be lost without me. Ah'm actually pretty fuckin' good at what Ah do. But why should Ah go and advertise the fact?'

'The suit's a disguise, is it?'

'No,' Lottie Mann intervened. 'Dan wears clothes, any clothes, worse than any human being I have ever met. Even when he was in uniform they used to call him Fungus the Bogeyman.' She dug him in the ribs with a large elbow. 'Isn't that right?'

The DS gave in to a full-on grin. 'It got me intae CID though.' Then it faded as he looked the chief constable in the eye. 'What you see is what you get, Mr Skinner. No' everybody's like you or even Lottie here, cut out to play the Lone Ranger . . . although too many think they are. Ah don't. Every masked man on a white horse needs a faithful Indian companion, and that's me, fuckin' Tonto.'

The chief picked up a sandwich, looked at it, decided that the egg looked a little past its best, and put it back on the plate.

'Nice analogy, Dan,' he murmured, 'but it doesn't quite work for me. I speak a wee bit of Spanish, just restaurant Spanish, you under-stand, but enough to know that "Tonto" means "Stupid", and that, Detective Sergeant, you are not. I'm not a uniform guy myself, as the entire police community must know by now, so the wrapping doesn't bother me too much as long as it doesn't frighten kids and old ladies, but what's inside does.

'I took a shine to you yesterday, but to be sure you weren't just the office comedian, I pulled your personnel file and the first thing I did when I got here today was to read it. As far as I can see the only reason you're still a DS is because that's what you want to be. You've never applied for promotion to inspector, correct?'

'Correct, and you're right, sir. Ah'm happy where I am. It's no' that I'm scared of responsibility, I just believe Ah've found my level,' he paused, 'Kemo Sabe.'

Skinner chuckled. 'In which case, Dan, I'll value you for as long as I'm here. So, how much of the trail have you two sniffed out?'

'Thanks to you, Chief,' Mann replied, as soon as she had finished the last sandwich, the one that he had rejected, 'we now know that the man who rented the Peugeot was the planner of the operation, Beram Cohen, the guy you've got in the mortuary through in Edinburgh.

'We've established through HMRC that under the name Byron Millbank he's lived and worked in London for the last six years, for a mail order company called Rondar. It operates one of those tele-shopping channels on satellite telly. Three years ago he married a woman called Golda Radnor, the boss's daughter, we're guessing, going by the fact that her name's the company's reversed, and eighteen months later they had a wee boy, named Leon Jesse. According to the General Register Office, Byron was born in Eastbourne thirty-two years ago, father unknown, mother named Caroline Anne Millbank, died on the last day of the last century.'

'Pity,' Provan muttered. 'She missed the fireworks.'

'I doubt if she was ever alive to see them,' Skinner countered.

'Do you think those records are faked, sir?' Mann asked.

He nodded. 'And clumsily, by somebody with a knowledge of poetic history. I studied it as an option in my degree. Look at the names: Byron Millbank, out of Caroline Anne. Lord Byron the poet, and two of his most famous women, Lady Caroline Lamb and her cousin Annabella, the one he wound up marrying.'

'Where does Millbank come from?'

'That was Annabella's family name, only it was spelled differently, as I recall.' He laughed. 'I don't know where all that came from. I must be turning into Andy Martin; he's got a photographic memory for everything. However,' he continued, 'there's a second context, and one that's more likely to be connected. It used to be a secret, but now one of the most famous buildings in London is Thames House, on

Millbank: it's the MI5 headquarters. Whoever set up Cohen's identity practically signed their name.'

'Aye, sir, but,' Provan interposed, 'how do you know that Cohen's no' the alias?'

'I know because I'd never heard of him until Five told me who he was, and told me about his career in the Israeli military and then its secret service. I guess,' he continued, 'that Mr Millbank had a driving licence.'

Mann nodded.

'And a passport?'

'Yes, sir.'

'Neither of them more than six years old?'

The DI opened the folder she had brought with her, searched through her notes, then looked up. 'That's right. Both issued a couple of months before he shows up on the payroll of Rondar, and on the same day.'

'To make absolutely sure,' Skinner instructed, 'I want you to go to the DSS and see if his records go any further back with them. My dollar says they don't. Before then Cohen was in Mossad, until he was caught up in an illegal operation and got thrown out.'

'But what does it mean, sir?' Dan Provan asked.

'Probably nothing at all, as far as our investigation's concerned. My reading is that British intelligence did the Israelis a favour by looking after one of theirs. They gave him a legitimate front and if he continued to take on black ops under his old identity, that was all right with them. They told me about one where he had used Smit and Botha; that was American-sponsored, in Somalia. I suppose he was what the spooks call an asset, but now it looks as if he wasn't fussy who he worked for.'

The sergeant blew out his cheeks. 'This is a' new stuff for us, gaffer. How do we go about investigatin' MI5, for Christ's sake?'

'You don't,' the chief told him. 'Yes, Byron Millbank, he'll need to be followed up, but I'll take care of that. I want you two and your team to focus on Bazza Brown. Am I right in believing that the media haven't made any connection between his murder and the Field assassination?'

'So far they haven't. As far as they know, Ronnie Edgar from Townhead's the SIO on that case, and they've only just found out it's Bazza that's dead. They've been told we're still tryin' to identify the victim.'

'Good. From what I've heard of Brown's history, now that we have released his name, the first thing the press will do will speculate that it's gang wars. That'll be fine by me. Let them chase that hare as long as they can. Meantime, you need to look at his family and his associates. Do you know them?'

'I know the main one; that would be Cecil, his brother,' Lottie Mann replied. 'Younger by two years, but they were as inseparable as twins.'

'Cecil?' Skinner repeated. 'Basil and Cecil? Not exactly Weegie names.'

Provan's eyes twinkled. 'Remember that old Johnny Cash song, about a boy called Sue? Their old man, Hammy, he had the same idea. He gave them soppy names, and the pair of them grew up as the hardest kids in Govan. The muscle was equally divided, but Bazza got a' the brains. Ah've lifted Cec in my time. He's no' likely tae help us.'

'Lift him again; tell him it's on suspicion of conspiracy to murder Toni Field. If the brothers were that close, we have to go on the assumption that whatever the connection was to Smit and Botha, Cecil was part of it. See how he reacts under questioning. Whether he was involved or not, he'll be thinking revenge. If you tell him there's nobody left for him to kill, he might just cooperate.'

'He might, sir. Just don't build your hopes up, that's all Ah'm sayin'.'

'Understood. Now, what else do you have to tell me?'

'The satnav in the rental car, sir,' the DI said. 'We've looked at it and it was used. Since they've had it, they've been to several locations. One was in Edinburgh, and another in Livingston.'

'The first would be when they first met up with Freddy Welsh, their armourer, when Cohen upped and died on them. The second was when they collected the weapons from Welsh's store. We know that already. Anything we don't know?'

She nodded. 'We've found out where they were living. Their journeys were to and from a hotel out on the south side; it's called the Forest Grove. It's a quiet place, family run, with about a dozen bedrooms. They were booked in for a week, Sunday to Saturday, full board, signed in as Millbank, Lightbody and Mallett. Millbank said they were there for a jewellery convention, and that the other two worked for the South African branch of his firm. The owner knew him; he'd stayed there before, a couple of times.'

'Do we have dates?'

'Yes, boss. And yes, we've checked for unsolved crimes to match them. There were none, neither in Glasgow, nor anywhere else in Scotland. But there was a watch fair in the SECC each time, so it looks like he was there on legitimate business.'

'Fair enough; good on you, for being thorough. Who paid the bill?' he asked.

'The man the hotel people knew as Lightbody. He settled up on Saturday lunchtime, then they left. The owner, his name's MacDonald, remarked to him that he hadn't seen Mr Millbank for a couple of days, and that his bed hadn't needed making. Lightbody said that he'd been called away to a meeting in Newcastle and that he'd flown back to

London from there. Mr MacDonald thought that was odd, for his daughter had serviced the room the first morning he was gone and his stuff was still in it. Thing about the bill, though, sir, it was settled in cash, old-fashioned folding money.'

'New Bank of England fifties?'

Mann's looked at him, surprised. 'How did you know that?'

'Our investigation in Edinburgh last week, after we found Cohen's body, led us to a kosher restaurant in Glasgow. The three guys ate there, and that's how they paid. Does MacDonald still have the notes?'

'I'm afraid not, sir. They went straight into his bank's night safe. I've got somebody contacting his branch though; they're probably still there.'

'Good. The notes from the restaurant are in Edinburgh. If we can match them up with these and they are straight from the printer, we might be able to trace them to the issuing bank and branch.'

'Wouldn't that have been Millbank's?' the DI pointed out.

Provan shook his head, causing another micro snowstorm. 'Ah don't see that. If he's had two identities, he's going tae have kept them completely separate.'

'For sure,' Skinner agreed. 'It may be that he had a separate Beram Cohen account, or a safe deposit box, but there's also a chance the cash came from the person who bought the operation. If we can trace its movement in the banking system, you never know.'

'If we can recover them,' Mann said. 'I'll chase it up.'

'Do that, pronto. Anything else from the satnav?'

'Yes, one other journey, but I'm not getting excited about it. On Friday, they went from the hotel to the Easthaven Retail Park, not far from the M8 motorway.'

'Indeed?' the chief said. 'Why are you writing that off?'

'Because it seems they went there to shop and to eat, that's all. We found receipts in the car for two shirts, and a pack of underwear from a clothes shop, and for two pizzas, ice cream and coffee from Frankie and Benny. The next journey programmed was the second last, the one to Livingston; the last being from their hotel to the car park next to the concert hall, where we found the car.'

'Yes, you're probably right; sounds like a refuelling stop, no more.' He frowned. 'Forensics. What have they given us?'

'They say that Bazza was shot in the car. They dug a bullet out of the upholstery, and found blood spatters. Other than that, they've given us nothing we didn't have before.'

'Post-mortem report? What about that? Has Brown been formally identified? I don't want as much as a scratch in him until that's done. If we ever do put anyone in the dock for this, he can't be allowed to walk out on a technicality.'

'That's done,' she said. 'His wife did it first thing this mornin'. Pathology's not holding us up but still I'm not pleased about it. Either Dan or I will have to be there as a witness. That's going to use up the rest of the day for whoever it is, with there being two of them.'

'Two?'

'Yes, there's Bazza, and there's the one on Chief Constable Field.'

'Of course.'

'Yes, I'd hoped that could be done yesterday, but it turns out it wasn't.'

'Bugger that,' the chief grumbled. 'What was the problem?'

'The chief pathologist was away on what he said was "family business", then this morning the so-and-so went and called in sick. I don't fancy his deputy, not since his evidence cost me a nailed-on conviction in the High Court last year. I said I wasn't having him do them, so they've called somebody through from the Edinburgh University pathology department.'

'Professor Hutchinson?'

She shook her head. 'No, sir. I asked for him but he wasn't available either. Instead they've sent us his number two. A woman, they said. I hope she's up to the job.'

Skinner's eyebrows rose. 'Oh, she is, Inspector, she is. I can vouch for her. As for you being there,' he continued, 'your priority has to be keeping the investigation up to speed.'

'Fair enough, sir. I never mind not going to post-mortems. Do you want me to send a couple of detective cons along instead?'

'No, Lottie, you leave that to me to sort out. The autopsies may be only formalities, but given that my predecessor's going to be on the table, our representative has to be appropriate in rank. Luckily, I know the very man for the job.'

Twenty-Nine

Every so often, in the office where he spent most of his time, Detective Chief Superintendent Neil McIlhenney would find himself daydreaming. When he awakened it was always with a start as he looked out of his window. He was still well away from being used to life in the Metropolitan Police Service, and he wondered if he ever would.

When a move south, on promotion, had been offered to him he had taken no time at all to accept. There had been more involved than his own future. Louise, his wife, had taken time out of her acting career to have a family, but he had known there would come a time when she would want to go back to work, and London was where she was known and where the opportunities arose.

As she had put it, she was beyond the 'age of romance', in that lead roles in major movies were no longer being offered, but it had always been her intention to go back to the stage when she passed forty, as she had a few years earlier. They had been in London for only a few weeks, yet she was in rehearsal for a major role in a West End play and the arts sections of the broadsheets were trumpeting her return.

The sound of his mobile put an end to his contemplation; he looked at the screen and smiled when he saw who was calling.

'Good morning, Chief Constable,' he said. 'I'm guessing this isn't a social call.'

'Why shouldn't it be?' his former boss challenged. 'We have lunch breaks in Strathclyde too. I take it you've heard what's happened.'

'How could I not, even if I hadn't had my best mate call me on Saturday night, as soon as he got Paula back to Edinburgh? He was crying, Bob; Mario. Can you believe that? He started to tell me what had happened and then he broke down, sobbing like a baby. Was Paula really that close to the victim?'

'Their heads couldn't have been any more than three feet apart when Toni Field's was blown open,' Skinner told him.

He shivered. 'God, it doesn't bear thinking about. How is she?'

'Most people, put in her situation, would be under sedation right now. Clive Graham's wife still is, and she wasn't even there. Maybe at another time Paula would be too, but at the moment she's completely focused on the baby, so, once she was sure he was okay in there, she was fine. I was with them yesterday morning and saw no sign of a delayed reaction. She's still on course to deliver in a couple of weeks.'

'Yes,' McIlhenney said. 'That's something else I won't be around for, but I'll get up to meet wee Eamon as soon as I can. You know Mario's calling him after his father, don't you?' He paused. 'It's not plain sailing for me, you know, being down here. To move or not to move, it was my choice; Lou didn't put any pressure on me. If I'd said no, we'd have got by, but I want what's best for all of us, Lauren, Spence and wee Louis, and this is it. That said, I miss you lot and not being around for Mario when he really needed me, that was tough.'

'I can imagine. But I admire you nonetheless, for making the move. I have to admit, you're so Edinburgh that I didn't think you'd have the balls.'

'Thanks, pal.' The DCS chuckled. 'By the way, does Joey Morocco still have his? He had a small part in one of Lou's movies a few years back. She says he had a reputation for nose candy and shagging anything female and alive, the latter probably being optional.'

'Fu—' Skinner snorted. 'You are one of the few guys in the world who could say that and get away with it. Yes he has, maybe more by luck than judgement. Aileen and I are history, but what you saw in the papers probably happened because of that, rather than the other way round. I've got no beef with Morocco, but there's a freelance photographer here in Glasgow who should leave town sharpish.'

'That sounds as if you're planning to be there for longer than the three months Mario told me about. I called him back yesterday,' he explained, 'just to make sure he was all right.'

'Ach, Neil, I'm not planning anything. This whole thing . . . it's so bizarre, so bloody terrible, and with the Aileen situation too, I haven't had time to gather my thoughts. I just don't know any more. What I do know is that I'm at the head of the highest profile investigation of my career, and I'm going to consider nothing else until it's done. Speaking of which . . . you were right. This isn't a social call.'

'Some things never change. Go on, Chief, let me hear it.'

'Okay, but you're not due anywhere soon, are you? It's best that I fill you in from the start, and it'll take a while.'

'No, I'm clear for an hour. I was just about to go for lunch, but I can do without that.'

'Thanks. Knowing how you like your chuck, I appreciate that.'

He ran through the events of the previous few days, from the discovery of a body in a shallow grave in Edinburgh, through the chain of events that led to the assassination of Chief Constable Antonia Field, then gave McIlhenney the story of the investigation as it stood.

The chief superintendent stayed silent throughout, but when Skinner was finished, he asked, 'Am I right in thinking that you've run all these checks on your planner, this man Cohen, alias Byron Millbank, without any reference to my outfit?'

'You're spot on, chum. I chose not to involve the Met until I absolutely had to, and that time is now. Make no mistake, this is a Strathclyde operation, but I am going to need to interview people in London, and I will need assistance. I propose to phone your commissioner and ask for it, but what I do not want is for the job to be handed to anyone who might have been personally acquainted with Toni Field. I know she had an affair with a DAC, but I don't have a name.'

'Couldn't you ask the Security Service for help? I know you're well in with them.'

'I could but I don't want to. Their paws are all over Beram Cohen's false identity.'

'Forgive me for asking the obvious, but couldn't Beram Cohen be the false name? They told you about him, after all.'

'No, because there's no trace of Millbank any further back than half a dozen years.'

'Right, box ticked. So, boss . . . listen to me; old habits and all that . . . cut to the chase. Why are you calling me? As if I can't guess.'

'I'll spell it out anyway,' Skinner told him. 'When I call my esteemed colleague, I want to ask him to lend me someone I know and who knows the way I work. But I don't want you press-ganged. Do you want to take this on, and can you?'

'Of course I want to,' McIlhenney replied. 'Can I, though? I'm heading up a covert policing team down here. I have officers operating under cover, deep and dangerous in some cases. I don't run them all directly, but I have to be available for them, and their handlers, at all times.'

'Not a problem. All I'm talking about here is partnering one of my guys in knocking on a few doors. Millbank was a family man, so there's a wife to be told. He had a legitimate job, so that will have to be looked at. I need to know whether there was any overlap between his life and that of Beram Cohen, and if there was, to see where it takes us.'

'Who will you give me? You can't know anyone through there yet, apart from the assistant chiefs.'

'Wrong, I do. I'm going to send my exec down. He's a DCI and his name is Lowell Payne.'

'That's familiar. Isn't he . . .'

'Alex's uncle, but our family link is irrelevant. He's been involved in this operation almost from the start. He's the obvious choice.'

'In which case,' McIlhenney exclaimed, 'I'll look forward to meeting him.'

Thirty

Anger writhed within Assistant Chief Constable Michael Thomas like a snake trapped in a jar. He had seen enough of Bob Skinner, and the way he dominated ACPOS meetings, to know that he did not like the man.

He was ruthless, he was inflexible, he was politically connected and in Thomas's mind he had an agenda: Skinner was out to mould the Scottish police service in his own image, planting his clones and protégés in key roles until they came to dominate it.

He had done it with the stolid Willie Haggerty in Dumfries and Galloway, with quick-witted Andy Martin in the Serious Crimes and Drug Enforcement Agency, and most recently in Tayside, with Brian Mackie, 'The Automaton', as some of his colleagues had nicknamed him.

When Antonia Field had been appointed chief constable of Strathclyde and he had taken her measure, he had been immensely pleased. Finally there was someone on the scene with the rank, the gravitas and the balls to tackle his enemy head on. The truth, that he was afraid to do so himself, had never crossed his mind.

She had identified him from the beginning as her one true supporter among the command ranks in Pitt Street, and he had demonstrated that at every opportunity. She had been in post for less than a month when she took him to dinner, and laid out her vision of the future.

'Unification is coming, Michael,' she began. 'My sources among the movers and shakers tell me that the Scottish government is going to create a single police force, as soon as it deems the moment to be right. I will make no bones about it; I want to be its first chief.

'As head of Strathclyde I should be the obvious choice, but we both know there's a big obstacle in my way. I need allies if I'm going to overcome him, and in particular I need you. You're the only forward-thinking policeman in the place. Theakston, Allan, Gorman, they're all old-school thinkers; they're not going to be around long. Back me and you'll be my deputy inside a year, and again when the new service comes into play. Are you up for that?'

'Of course, Toni, of course.'

After dinner she had taken him to bed, to seal their alliance, she said, although there were times later, after he felt the rough edge of her tongue, as everyone did, when he wondered whether it had been to give her an even greater hold over him, insurance against his ambition growing as great as hers. It had been a one-off and when it was over she had more or less patted him on the bum and sent him home to his wife. There had been no hint of intimacy from then on; he wondered whether there was a new guy in the background, but that was one secret she did not share with him.

For all that, she had been as good as her word and he had been almost there: DCC Theakston gone to enforced early retirement, and Max Allan with his sixty-fifth birthday and compulsory departure only four months in the future. Within a few weeks he would have been deputy. And beyond that?

She had been right about the new force. It had come up in ACPOS, and while Skinner had won the first battle, by a hair's breadth, the next round would be theirs, and the First Minister would be able to claim chief officer support as he moved the legislation. The enemy would be marginalised and unable to go forward as a candidate for commissioner, having fought so hard and publicly against the creation of the job.

Toni had promised him that she had no ambition to grow old, or even middle-aged, in Scotland. She was bound for London, back to the Met when its commissioner fell out with the Mayor, as all of them seemed to do. 'I have levers, Michael, and I will use them, when the time comes. When I go, the floor will be yours.'

Three shots, inside two seconds, that was all it had taken to put the skids under his entire career. He had been doing a spot of evening fishing with his son near Hazelbank when the call had come through. 'An incident reported at the concert hall, sir,' the divisional commander had told him. 'A shooting, with one reported casualty.'

He had known that Toni would be at the hall that night . . . for the previous fortnight she had been full of her 'date' with the First Minister . . . and so he had almost stayed on the river, but a moment's reflection had convinced him that the smart thing would be to tear himself away and rush to the scene. He had arrived to discover that Toni was the reported casualty, and that Max Allan was another, having suffered some sort of collapse, suspected heart attack, they were saying. Her body was still there, with crime scene technicians working all around it in their paper suits and bootees. He had tried to take charge of the shambles, and that was when DCI Lowell bloody Payne had told him about Skinner being there.

He hadn't believed the man, until Dom Hanlon had told him Skinner had taken command, and that he would have to live with it, even though the guy had no semblance of authority. Outrageous, bloody outrageous. Then next day, to cap it all, they'd gone and appointed him acting chief.

That was when the grief had set in, for his own foiled prospects as much as for his fallen leader. He knew where he stood with Skinner, a fact confirmed when he had chosen Bridie Gorman, whom Toni had sidelined almost completely, as acting deputy. He had been considering resignation, quite seriously, when he had been called to the chief constable's office, urgently. Twenty-four bloody hours and suddenly it was urgent.

There he had been, Toni Field's arch-enemy behind Toni Field's desk. God, it had been hard to take.

He hadn't expected subtlety and there had been none. 'Michael,' Skinner had begun, 'you don't like me, and I don't like you much either. But that's irrelevant; if everyone in an organisation this size were bosom buddies it would get sloppy very quickly. Far better that some of us are watching out for each other, and that there are some rivalries in play.

'I had two CID guys in Edinburgh who could have been twins, they were so close; indeed, twins they were called, by their mates. Eventually they rose until they were at the head of operations. It didn't work out; things started to slip through the net, because each one overlooked the other's weaknesses and mistakes. At least that's not going to happen with you and me, in the time I'm here.'

'In that case,' Thomas had ventured, 'wouldn't that make me an excellent deputy?'

The response, a frown. 'Nice try, but no. In my ideal world, people like you and me would be elected to our post by the people we seek to command, not appointed by those who command us, or by boards of councillors. I've been here a day and I've worked out already that if we did that, you wouldn't get too many votes.

'I don't doubt your ability as an officer, not for a second, but what I've seen in ACPOS and heard since I've been here make some believe that you're not a leader. Forgive me for being frank; it's the way I'm built.

'However,' Skinner had continued, 'even though I chose ACC Gorman as my deputy when necessary, you are still my assistant and that I respect. So let's work together, not against each other, for as long as I'm here. I'd like to meet with you and Bridie tomorrow morning, so that you can both brief me on your areas of responsibility. Meantime . . . there's something quite important that I'd be grateful if you could handle. It's not going to be pleasant, but it needs a senior officer.'

And that was how Michael Thomas had come to be standing, seething with anger, in an autopsy theatre, gowned and masked, looking, not for the first time, at the naked body of Antonia Field. The pathologist had followed him into the room. She was a woman also, a complete contrast to Toni, and not only in the fact that she was alive. She was tall, fair-skinned, and the strands of hair that escaped her sterile headgear were blonde.

'You're the duty cop with the short straw in his hand, I take it,' she said. 'I'm Dr Grace.' She turned and nodded towards a young man. From what Thomas could see of his face, his skin tone looked similar to that of Toni. 'And this is Roshan, who'll be assisting me.'

He realised, to his surprise, that she was North American, possibly Canadian, possibly US; he had never been able to distinguish the respective accents.

'ACC Thomas,' he replied. 'Given the circumstances, I felt it was appropriate that I come myself.'

'And I don't imagine Bob tried to talk you out of it,' she murmured, through her mask.

He looked at her, puzzled. 'I'm sorry?'

'Chief Skinner. He's my ex, my former husband. The older he gets, the more squeamish he gets.'

'I see.' The bastard had set him up!

'That said, he's been to more than his fair share. How about you?'

'I've spent most of my career in uniform,' he told her, avoiding a straight answer.

'Ah, so you'll have seen mostly suicides and road fatalities. They have a pretty high squeamishness quotient.'

'Mmm.'

She looked at the man. His eyes told her what the rest of his face was saying. 'You've never been to an autopsy in your life, have you?'

'No,' the ACC confessed.

'So here you are, looking at somebody you knew and worked with, who's now dead and you're going to have to watch me cut her open and take her insides out, all in the line of duty?'

Thomas felt his stomach heave, but he mastered it. 'That sums it up pretty well,' he conceded. 'I suppose your ex would say "Welcome to the real world", or something like that.'

'That sounds like a Bob quote, I admit. Since he didn't, I assume you didn't tell him you've never done this duty before.'

'Of course I didn't.'

'Ah,' she exclaimed, 'the macho thing. The traditional pissing contest, in yet another form. As a result I've got somebody in my workplace who's liable to faint on me or, worse, choke himself to death by barfing inside a face mask. You should have told him, and he'd have sent someone else, because he knows that's the last thing I need. And by the way, he isn't an ogre, either.'

'Well, I'm here now, Doctor,' he replied stiffly, 'so we might as well take the chance. I'll make sure I don't land on anything important when I fall over.'

'Not necessary.' She peeled off her mask. 'You're a legal necessity but in practice don't have to watch every incision or every organ being removed. This is not going to be a complicated job. Cause of death is massive brain trauma caused by gunshot wounds; we know that before I touch her. But the law needs a full report and that's what it will get.

'You can go sit in the corner and read a book, or listen to your iPod. If I find something I believe you need to look at up close, I will tell you and you can look at it. But that's not going to happen. And from what I've seen of our next customer, that's going to be the case with him as well. He was shot from so close up that some of his chest hairs are melted. So go on, get out of my space.'

He looked at her, gratefully. 'Thank you,' he said. He started to move away, then paused. 'Doctor Grace,' he ventured, 'this is a silly thing to ask, I know, but Toni and I, well, we were friends as well as colleagues. Be gentle with her, yes?'

'As if she were an angel,' Sarah replied, feeling pity for the man, then adding, in case he thought she was being sarcastic, 'Who knows, by now she may be one.'

Thirty-One

'Ye cannae do this,' the prisoner protested, 'ma lawyer's no' here. I'm saying nothin' till he gets here. And this charge! What the fuck yis on about? Conspiracy tae fuckin' murder? That's pure shite. Ah never murdered onybody.'

'Technically that's true, Cec,' Dan Provan admitted. 'The jury was stupid enough tae convict you of culpable homicide, and the judge was even dafter when he gave you five years. But the boy ye killed was just as fuckin' deid, so let's no' split hairs about it.'

'We can do it,' Lottie Mann assured him. 'We can do pretty much what we like.'

'Oh aye?' Cecil Brown stuck out his jaw, with menace, then took a closer look at the expression on her face and realised that aggression was not his best option.

'Oh aye.' She pointed at the recorder on the desk. 'That thing is not switched on. When your brief gets here it will be and we'll get formal, but until then, tell me what business you and your brother had with the South Africans.'

He stared back at her. When they had arrested him, the DI's impression had been that he was genuinely surprised. As she studied his big, dumb eyes, that feeling moved towards certainty. 'What fuckin' South Africans?' he asked.

Provan leaned forward. 'Son,' he murmured, 'off the record, who's your biggest rival in Glasgow?'

'Ah don't know what you're talkin' about.'

He laughed. 'Of course you do. Don't fanny about, Cec. I'm askin' you who you've got in mind, what mind ye have, that is, for toppin' your brother. Paddy Reilly? Specky Green? Which of those have you crossed lately? Which of those are we liable tae find in the Clyde any day now?'

When the sergeant floated the second name he saw Brown's eyes narrow; very slightly but it was enough. 'It's Specky, right? Let me guess; you and Bazza ripped him off on some sort of a deal, or moved gear intae one of his pubs. So you're thinkin' it was him that bumped off the boy. Well, if ye are, ye're wrong.'

'Aye, sure.' The tone was a mix of scepticism and contempt. 'Ah might be thick, but no' so thick Ah'd believe youse bastards.'

'He's not kidding, Cecil,' Lottie Mann assured him. 'This is how it was. We found your brother's body yesterday afternoon crammed into the boot of a car in the multi-storey park next to the Buchanan Street bus station. It had been there for a day, and it was starting to hum.

'It was a hire vehicle from London, and it was meant to be the getaway car for the two men, those South Africans I mentioned, who shot and killed our chief constable in the Royal Concert Hall on Saturday evening. Unfortunately for them, they didn't get away, and they're no longer,' her eyes narrowed and she smiled, 'in a position to assist us with our inquiries.' She paused, letting the slow-moving cogs of his mind process what she had said.

'Now we don't actually believe,' she went on, 'that you and your brother were the masterminds behind a plot to kill Ms Field, but the fact that we found him where we did, and also that our forensic team will prove that he was killed by the same gun that was used to shoot two police officers outside the hall, that puts you right in the middle of it.'

Cecil Brown's mouth was hanging open.

'Yes,' she continued. 'I can see you get my point. So we need you to tell us what your role was, and how Bazza came to meet up with those guys. You help us, before your brief gets here to shut you up, and your life will be a hell of a lot better. For openers, you will have a life.

'We are going to put somebody in the dock for this, make no mistake, and at the moment you're all we've got. I'm not talking about five soft years for manslaughter here, Cecil. If you're convicted of having a part in Chief Constable Field's murder you'll be drawing your old age pension before you get out.'

'Personally, laddie,' Dan Provan yawned, 'Ah'd love tae see that happen. You sit there and say nothing and we'll build a case against ye, no bother.'

'Ah don't know anything!' the prisoner shouted. 'Honest tae Christ, Ah don't. Bazza said nothin' tae me about any South Africans.'

'What did he tell you?'

'Nothin'.'

'Come on,' the DS laughed, 'when did your big brother keep secrets from you? The pair of you wis like Siamese twins. You lived next door tae each other, drove the same gangster motors . . . what are they, big black Chrysler saloons . . . ye both married girls ye'd been at the school with, ye shared a box at Ibrox. Come on, Cec. You cannae expect us to believe that Bazza was involved in the shooting of the chief bloody constable and he kept you in the dark about it.'

'Man,' the surviving Brown brother protested, 'ye're off yir heid. Bazza would never have got involved in anything as crazy as killin' the chief constable, or any fuckin' constable. The amount of shite that would have brought down on our heids! It's the last thing he'd have wanted. He had nothin' to do with it.'

'But he had, Cecil,' Lottie Mann boomed. 'Like it or not, he was with Smit and Botha, the two men who shot Ms Field. He was involved with them, and he could have identified them, so they killed him when they had done whatever business they had with him.'

'If you say so,' the prisoner muttered, his lip jutting out like that of a rebellious child. 'But he never telt me about it, okay?'

She sighed. 'Yes, right. Let's say I accept that, for the moment. Did Bazza keep a diary?'

'Eh?'

'Did he keep any sort of written record of his life; his meetings, deals, and so on?'

'In a book, like?'

'Book, computer, tablet.'

'Ah don't know. Maybe on his phone.'

'We don't have that,' Mann said. 'Would he have had it on him?'

'Oh aye, a' the time.'

'Did he have a contract or did he use a throwaway?'

'He had a top-up. He took it everywhere, even tae the bog.'

'Then Smit and Botha must have dumped it after they killed him.' She leaned closer to him. 'Cec, we want whoever was behind them. So do you, for your brother's sake. Help us.'

He met her gaze. 'How can Ah, if Ah don't know anything?'

'Where's Bazza's car?'

Brown turned, at Provan's question. 'Parked outside his hoose,' he replied.

The DS looked at the DI, eyebrows raised, as if inviting a response. It came. 'Did Smit and Botha pick him up from home?' she asked.

'Naw. Ah'd have seen them,' Cec volunteered, with certainty.

'We've got CCTV. It covers both houses. Ah checked it this mornin', as soon as Senga told me he was deid. Ah was looking for Specky, or his boys. There was nothin', other than us, the paper boy and the postie.'

'So that makes us wonder. How did he get to wherever he met them?'

'Ah suppose Ah must have took him.'

'Where? When?'

'Friday evenin'. Ye know that big park with a' the shops, beside the motorway? Bazza asked me if Ah'd take him there for seven o'clock. He said he was meetin' a burd. He always had bits on the side,' he added, in explanation. 'Our cars are a wee bit obvious, so if he is . . . when he wis . . . playin' away he liked tae use taxis. Ah took him there and Ah dropped him off, in the car park, must hae been about seven, mibbes a wee bit after.'

'And that was the last time you saw him?'

'Aye.'

'But you didn't see the woman?'

'Naw.' His eyes were fixed on the table. 'There couldnae have been one, could there? Ah must have delivered him tae the guys that killed him.'

'Then it's too bad for him he didn't tell you what was going on. You could have hung around and watched his back.'

'Fuckin' right,' Cec muttered.

'Is there anything else?' Mann asked him. 'Anything that could help us?'

'I wish there wis. If Ah could, Ah would, honest.'

'You know what,' she said, 'I think I believe you. Cec, you're free to go, but I warn you, we've got search warrants for Bazza's house, and for yours, and for the office of that so-called minicab company that you run. We're enforcing them right now, going through the records, and looking for anything that'll tie your brother to those guys. If we find something, and you're involved after all, you'll be back in here before you've even had time to take a piss.

'In the meantime, my advice is to watch your back. If the man we're after gets it into his head that Bazza might have confided in you, he might decide that it's too big a risk to leave you running around loose.'

Brown's eyes seemed to light up with a strange intensity, that of a man with two bells showing on a one-armed bandit and the third reel still spinning. 'Ah hope he does, Miss. Ah'd like tae talk tae him.'

Thirty-Two

'So there you have it. Sir Bryan Storey, the Met commissioner himself, has approved your trip. Funny,' Skinner mused, 'I met that man for the first time at a policing conference a few weeks ago. D'you know what he said, "Ah, you're Edinburgh, are you?" as if he was a Premier League manager and I was mid-table Division Three. Just now when I spoke to him, he was almost deferential. It seems that this office does have clout nationally, more than I'd realised.'

'I don't have to report to him when I get there, do I?' Lowell Payne asked.

'No, not even a courtesy call. I doubt if he's spoken to a DCI since he got the final piece of silver braid on his cap. You just catch the first London flight you can tomorrow, go to New Scotland Yard and ask for Chief Superintendent McIlhenney. He'll be waiting for you.'

'What's he like, this man?'

The chief smiled. 'Try to imagine a quieter, more thoughtful version of Mario McGuire; but when he has to, Neil can be almost as formidable. The division he works in, covert policing, has some tough people in it. He'd never be any good in the field himself because he's too conspicuous, but he will always have the respect of the people who are.'

'How do we play it with Millbank's family?'

'You should take the lead in the questions. You're the investigator, in practice; Neil's just your escort. He knows that and he's
okay with it. I'd suggest you begin by being circumspect. Remember,
we've only just identified Cohen under the name Byron Millbank.
Now we have done, Storey's going to send two female family support
officers to break the news to his widow, but you'll be going in soon
after.'

'How much will they have told her?'

'Only the basic truth, that he died suddenly, of a brain haemorrhage,
and that he had no identification on him at the time, hence the delay
in getting to her. It's your job to fill in the rest, and find out as best you
can whether she has a clue that her old man had another identity. The
book's open on that. My bet is that she doesn't, but you reach your
own conclusions, gently.'

'Once we get past gentle, what then?'

'You don't,' Skinner told him, with emphasis. 'You ask to see her
husband's computer, to check his calendar, recent contacts, all that
stuff. Kid-glove stuff, Lowell. It's only if she doesn't play ball that you
have to make the request formal, and take it all away.

'It should be the same with his workplace, this teleshopping outfit.
It's pretty obvious that it's a family business, given the similarity with
the wife's maiden name, so unless you find a box of Uzis in his desk,
you maintain the front that it's a formal sudden-death inquiry, required
by Scottish law, and that all we're doing is confirming his appointments,
movements, etc.'

'Understood.' Payne stood up. 'When do you want me back?' he
asked.

'When you're done; that's all I can say. I have no idea how this
thing will go, but I do know this. An outside agency has an interest in
it, and I want to head it off. So, any leads that are thrown up have to

be followed up, fast. If you need to stay tomorrow night, or even beyond that, so be it.'

'Okay, I'll take enough clothes and stuff for a couple of days.' He smiled. 'There's just one thing, though, Bob. It's our wedding anniversary on Thursday, and I've got a table booked at Rogano. If it comes to it and I have to cancel, I'd appreciate it if you call Jean and tell her, and say that it was your fault.'

Skinner whistled. 'There ought to be no absolutes in the field of human courage,' he said, 'but it would take an absolute fucking hero to do that. If necessary, her niece and I will take her to Rogano ourselves, and I'll pick up the tab.'

'That's a deal. Hopefully it won't come to that. Here,' he added, 'what will you do for an assistant while I'm away? You're still on a learning curve here.'

'Yes, and I'm going to rely on my ACCs to instruct me. Mr Thomas and I had a getting to know you session earlier on. I asked him to attend the post-mortem on Toni Field and to sit in on Bazza Brown's while he was there.'

'Oh shit,' Payne murmured.

The chief frowned. 'What?'

'Maybe I should have told you, but I never thought to, because it was no more than office gossip. Not long after Field arrived, when she lived on the Riverside, a couple of PCs in a Panda car saw Michael Thomas leaving her apartment block at three in the morning. The story was all round the force inside a day. ACC Allan heard about it and put the word out that anybody who even thought of posting it on Twitter or Facebook would wind up nailed to a cross.'

'Indeed?' Skinner murmured, with a thin smile. 'Typical Max; he's too nice a guy for his own good. Yes, it sounds like I really have put Thomas on the spot. Was this a continuing relationship?'

'I'm pretty sure it wasn't.'

'How sure?'

'Not a hundred per cent, I admit. Why?'

'Oh nothing. Between you and me, Marina Deschamps gave me a rundown on her sister's sex life. It hadn't occurred to me till now, but the numbers didn't quite add up.' He nodded, as if he had reached a conclusion, then spelled it out. 'That's made my mind up,' he said. 'I'm going to tell Marina she can come back to work. If any more Toni skeletons pop out during this investigation, it'll be useful to have her around.'

'Do you want me to . . .'

'No, I'll call her myself, after I've told the fiscal that I want the body released tomorrow morning.'

'The fiscal here doesn't like to be told, Chief,' Payne warned.

'Then I'll make it seem as if it was his idea all along.'

'He's a she.'

'Aren't they all these days? When my dad was in practice just after the war, there wasn't a single female solicitor in the burgh. Now the majority of law graduates are women, like our Alex. It's magic; it hasn't half shaken up the establishment. What's her name?'

'Reba Paisley. Mrs.'

'Get her on the phone for me, please. Then you'd better get off home, once you've booked your flight.'

'Will do. By the way,' he volunteered, 'that bloody safe; you were right. It was installed at Chief Constable Field's request and we do not have the technical capability in-house to open it. I've asked our plant and machinery people to source the supplier and get someone to deal with it.'

As Payne headed back to his own office to make the call to the procurator fiscal, the regional chief prosecutor, Skinner moved from the table to his desk. As he eased himself into his seat . . . not a patch on my Edinburgh chair, he grumbled, mentally . . . his mobile buzzed and vibrated in his pocket, signalling an incoming text. He dug it out and read it.

'In Glasgow. Can I blag a lift? We came in Roshan's car. Be about 6. Sarahx.'

He keyed in a reply, awkwardly because of the thickness of his index finger; he had never mastered using his thumbs on the mini-keyboard.

'I know, & what ur doing. Sure. Take a taxi to Pitt St when ur done. L Bob.'

He had no sooner sent the message than the phone rang. 'Chief Constable,' he said as he picked up.

'Procurator fiscal,' an assertive female voice replied. 'What can I do for you, Mr Skinner?'

'Nothing, Mrs Paisley. I don't ask for favours. Let's get that clear from the start.'

'So this is a social call?'

'Yes, partly.'

'Even "partly" makes a change. In the time she was here I never once heard from your late predecessor.'

'You won't be wanting to hang on to her then,' Skinner chuckled.

'To tell you the truth,' the fiscal replied, 'I hadn't given that any thought.'

'What's your normal procedure with homicide victims?'

'I don't have one. I make my judgement on a case by case basis, but it's my judgement, I stress. It's not a call that I delegate to a deputy. In this case . . . is the PM done?'

'As we speak.'

'Who are the immediate family?'

'Mother and sister.'

'Are there any prospects of further arrests?'

'Further?' Skinner repeated. 'We never actually got round to arresting Smit and Botha.'

He heard a sound that might have been a chuckle. 'You know what I mean. Because if there are, defence counsel might want access to the body.'

'I know that, but it isn't an automatic right. I can't say for sure we will ever trace the people in this chain of conspiracy, let alone guessing when. We're interviewing the brother of the man found dead in the getaway car, but I don't believe he will be able to help us.'

'Why not?'

'Because he's still alive. If Cec knew anything, he'd probably be in the cooler next to his brother.'

'How about if I authorise release for burial only?'

'Toni Field was born in Mauritius. What if her mother wants to take her home there?'

'It would be a lot easier in an urn than a coffin. Is that what you're saying?'

'I'm not saying anything, only asking questions.'

'But good ones,' Paisley said. 'Tell you what. If the post-mortem report satisfies me that there are no unresolved questions about the death, the family can have her, and do whatever they like with her.'

'That's fair enough,' Skinner agreed. 'I'll tell them. The only unresolved questions about the death aren't related to the autopsy. There are only two: who wanted her dead and why.'

'Do your people have any ideas about either of those issues?'

'I don't encourage my people to deal in ideas, only evidence. As I speak they're looking for any that's to be found. When they have more to report, they will, to both of us. Good to talk to you; you must come here for lunch some time.'

'That will also be a first,' the fiscal remarked. 'I'll look forward to it.'

As he hung up, Skinner scribbled, 'Lunch Pitt St with fiscal: arrange,' then called the switchboard and asked to be connected with Marina Deschamps. It was her mother who came on the line. 'I regret that Marina is unavailable,' she said. 'Will I do?'

'Of course, Miss Deschamps. I want to talk to you about Antonia's funeral.'

'Good, for we were going to call you about that. We contacted an undertaker, but he said that he had no access to her body.'

'Not yet,' he agreed. 'There are issues in any homicide, but once the fiscal has some paperwork in place, everything should be all right. What I want to talk to you about is the form of the funeral. Antonia was a chief constable, and she died in office. If you want a private family funeral, so be it, but it's only right that her force should pay its tribute. I'm happy to organise everything for you, if that's what you would like. Did she have a religion?'

'She was raised in the Roman Catholic Church,' she fell silent for a few seconds, 'although she was not a regular visitor, I must admit.'

'Nonetheless. Cardinal Gainer, in Edinburgh, is a friend of mine. I'm sure he would officiate, or approach his opposite number in Glasgow.'

'That is very generous of you, Mr Skinner. I would like to talk to Marina about it when she returns.'

He heard a sound, in the background, as if someone was calling out. 'Is that her now?' he asked.

'No, it's just street noise. We will call you, Mr Skinner. Thank you very much.'

Thirty-Three

'Anything on Bazza's computer, Banjo?' Lottie Mann called out to a detective constable who was seated at a table on the other side of the inquiry office, working on the confiscated PC. He rose and crossed towards her.

'No email account that I can find, and that's disappointing. He was very big on porn sites, though,' he advised her. 'Nothing illegal, nothing that Operation Amethyst would have hit on; all grown-ups, all doing fairly monotonous and repetitive stuff. Strange; from what I saw of Mrs Brown when we raided the house, he shouldn't have needed any diversions like that. There are some pictures of her on the computer that bear that out, and a couple of videos.'

'*Chacun à son goût.*'

The DC nicknamed Banjo . . . his surname was Paterson, but none of his colleagues made the connection to the man who wrote the words of 'Waltzing Matilda' . . . stared at her. 'Eh?' he exclaimed.

'It's the only French I know,' she said. 'It means there's no telling what you'll find under a guy's bed when you take a look. Or something like that.'

'I'll take your word for it, boss. I only speak Spanish and a wee bit of Mandarin Chinese.'

'Smart bastard,' she snarled. 'What else?'

'Video games; the thing was wired up to a big high-def screen. And casinos, he was quite a gambler, was our Bazza. He played roulette and blackjack mostly, but poker as well, from time to time. He also had an account with an online bookie, and bet heavily on the horses and on boxing.'

'Was he any good at it?'

'He seems to have been. He paid through a credit card; I've looked at the records and most months there was more going in than coming out. He had a system for roulette and he only ever backed favourites.'

'That's not a complete surprise; Bazza's old man had a bookie's licence and a couple of betting shops. As I recall, Bazza ran them for a while after he died, then sold them on to a chain. So yes, he'd a gambling background. He backed the wrong horse, though, when he took up with the South Africans. How about Cec?' she asked. 'Did he have a PC?'

'Cec couldnae spell PC,' Dan Provan muttered.

'Possibly not,' the detective constable agreed. 'He's got a PlayStation and that was it. He likes war games; anything where people get blown to bits. He also likes porn, but DVDs in his case. We could nick him for a few of those if you want.'

'Can't be arsed,' Mann said. 'What about their office?'

'Definitely non-ecological. They don't give a shit about how many trees they kill. All their records are on paper. However, they did fail to hide a list of addresses. They didn't connect to anything so we're having a look. Our search warrant was broad enough to let us go straight in.' Paterson smiled. 'Now for the good bit. Uniform have visited just one so far, a four-bedroom villa in a modern estate near Clydebank; it's a cannabis farm, and you can bet the others are too.'

She laughed. 'Poor old Cec; it's not his week. He's probably home by now; have him rearrested and brought in, then hand him and that address list over to Operation League. He's their business now.' She turned to Provan. 'Bilbo,' she began.

He glared at her. 'The chief wis bad enough,' he growled. 'No' you as well.'

'What do we have on Bazza as a force? Is there an intelligence report on him?'

'Now there's a hell of a question to be askin' a garden fuckin' ornament like me.'

'Okay, Dan,' she laughed, 'I'm sorry.'

'No more funnies?'

'No more funnies.'

'Good, because that really was a hell of a question. Ah've got a mate, a good mate, in what we're no' supposed to call Special Branch any more, in Counter-Terrorism Intelligence Section. He's jist told me that the chief . . . the old chief, no' the new one . . . asked for updated files on all organised crime figures as soon as she came in. When SCT went to work on Bazza, they asked the National Criminal Intelligence Service for input, and a big red sign came up, warnin' them off.'

'What does that mean?'

'It means he wis a fuckin' grass, Lottie; he was protected. And if it wasnae for us, and it wasn't, it must have been for MI5. They've got a serious crime section.'

'Jesus!'

'You'll get brownie points wi' the new chief when ye tell him that, eh?'

'Maybe. But have you thought through the implications?'

'Sure,' Provan admitted, 'but Ah'm no' paid enough to spell them out. Ye'd better go and see the gaffer.'

'I will do. While I'm up there, you concentrate on the only other line of inquiry we have with Bazza. Have we got the CCTV tapes from the Easthaven Retail Park yet?'

'Aye, and I've cleared up something; nothin' major, just a point for the record. We know that Smit and Botha were at Easthaven and that Bazza went there too, to meet them. We know from the gaffer that the South Africans were in Livingston on Friday, collecting their weapons. Ah've checked with the team in Edinburgh, spoke to a DC called Haddock, bright-soundin' kid . . .'

'Nothing fishy about him?' Mann murmured.

'Whit . . . ach, be serious, Lottie. He said that there was no mention of a third man bein' with them. So, Bazza must have been in the boot o' the motor by then.'

'Fair enough, fills in the timeline. Take a look at that video and see if it shows them meeting, then we'll join all the dots. What does the recording cover?'

'Two cameras, all day Friday, midnight to midnight. But there's a clock on it so Ah'll speed run it back to just before seven and go from there.'

'Fine, you do that. I'll go and see the boss.'

Thirty-Four

'You do realise, Lottie,' a frowning Skinner said, 'that I should be water-boarding the wee man until he tells me who his contact in CTIS is. That section is supposed to be completely confidential. Information like that shouldn't be passed on outside the reporting chain.'

'That's why I didn't bring him up here with me,' the DI replied. 'But you'd be wasting your time, boss. He'd drown before he told you. Dan's old school.'

'Don't I know it. That's why the tap's not running. I won't press the point, for now, but I won't forget it either. Make sure he knows that, so that his mate, whoever he is, will get to hear about it.'

'Understood, boss. I'll drop a word in his ear.'

'Don't be too friendly about it. I know he was your mentor, but you're his line manager, not the other way around. Now, since he has given us this information . . . you know what it suggests?'

'I think so,' she said, 'if it was the Security Service that flagged Bazza Brown as off limits . . . and who else would it be?'

'Drugs enforcement,' the chief suggested, 'but that's unlikely. I can and will check it, though. If that was the cause of the red notice, it would have come from Scotland. The head of the SCDEA and I are close. He'll tell me if it was his mob that were running Brown. Indeed,

I've got a feeling that if it was them, he'd have been in touch with me by now to let me know.

'So, let's say that Bazza was on the books of MI5's serious crime section. If our speculation that they fixed Beram Cohen up with a new identity is well founded, then he would have as well, and that's our link.'

'What do you want me to do about it, boss?'

'Absolutely nothing,' Skinner replied, almost before she had finished her question. 'As far as you're concerned, you never had the information you just brought me and neither did Dan. He shouldn't have been given it in the first place, and if he made any written note of his conversation, it must be destroyed.'

'Yes, sir.' She rose from the chair that faced the chief constable's desk. It was low set, so that whoever sat behind the desk was always looking down on his visitors, an intimidating tactic that Skinner disliked, and vowed that he would change. 'Since I was never here,' she said, 'I'd better make myself scarce.'

He laughed. 'You do that, Lottie. Concentrate on the video you told me about. If you can show Bazza Brown meeting Smit and Botha, you can wrap up the inquiry into his murder, and pass that on to Reba Paisley's office. Why he met them, if we're right about that, she doesn't need to know. How they came to know him, that's completely off limits.'

'Fine, I'll report back on the first part as soon as we've nailed it down.'

He watched her as she left then reached across his desk for the phone, only to be interrupted by his mobile signalling another incoming text. 'Done here. Scrubbing up, then on my way. Sarahx.'

No reply needed; he smiled as he put it back in his pocket, then picked up the other instrument, selected 'direct dial' and made the call he had been intending.

'Mario? How are you settling into my old office? Do you like the view? You can see every bugger who comes in and goes out. Useful at times.'

'Sure,' the newly appointed ACC conceded, 'but they can see me.'

'Not if you angle the blinds right.'

'I'll try that. Have you got any other advice for me?'

'Yeah, keep your eye on David Mackenzie; he's after your job.'

'I worked that one out for myself, Bob, quite some time ago. Anything else? Anything serious?'

'No, but a question. How's Paula?'

'Blooming. No sign of delayed shock, post-traumatic stress or any of that crap, I'm relieved to say. Maybe because she's got too much on her mind. She saw her consultant again this morning, at his request. When he checked her over yesterday, he thought he might have got her dates wrong. Now he's sure, he's given her to the end of the week to get the job done herself, or he's going to induce labour.'

'They did that with Myra, when she had Alex. As I recall, it started with castor oil. Tell her that; the threat alone might be a trigger.'

'I will. Now let me ask you one. How's Aileen? First off, I'm sorry about you two, and about all the other shit. She's had a very tough forty-eight hours, man.'

Skinner felt his forehead tighten. 'Are you saying I made it worse?' he asked.

'No, absolutely not,' McGuire insisted. 'I wasn't implying that. I understand how things are between you. It was a straight question.'

'In that case, she's fine. She and I spoke not that long ago and everything's okay. We've put our situation on the record, so the press will have to be very careful with what they say about her. I know she had that bother at her press conference this morning, but given the trouble the Hatton woman's been making, it'll work for her rather than agin her.'

'Good. Now would you like to come to the point?'

'What makes you think there is one?' Skinner asked.

'How long have we known each other? About fifteen years? I'm not saying you never call me just to pass the time of day, but I don't recall you ever doing it from the office, not once.'

'Christ, is that true? You know, McIlhenney said much the same earlier. What does that say about me?' He sighed. 'The sad thing is, you're right. I've got a situation here, I need it resolved, but I can't be bothered going through channels. It would take too long. Instead, I'm looking for a simpler solution. Do you remember a wee guy called Johan Ramsey?'

'Wee Jo? Of course. A master of his craft, if ever there was one.'

'It didn't stop him getting lifted a few times though. Do you know where he is now?'

'As a matter of fact I do. He's here in Edinburgh, on parole after his last sentence. We were advised when he was released.'

'Good,' Skinner declared. 'That's what I wanted to hear.'

'How come?' McGuire laughed. 'What do you want with him?'

'I want to employ him.'

'You what?'

'I mean it. I've got a job for him. There's a safe in my office here. Toni Field had it installed, and only she knew the combination. I don't have the time to wait for some bloody company in the south of England to free up one of their specialists, so I want to hire one of my own. I'd like you to pick him up, and invite him to join me here tomorrow morning, to see what he can do. Tell him there's a hundred in it for him, regardless, cash, and that his probation officer will never know. Can you do that for me, ACC McGuire? Make it work and I'll buy you lunch after your first ACPOS meeting.'

'Hell, Bob, you don't need to bribe me to get me to do that. That's a first, and it's going in my memoirs.'

'That's fine,' Skinner grunted, 'but you'd better make it clear to wee Jo that if it winds up in his, then next time he gets sent down, I will make certain, personally, that parole is off the table.'

Thirty-Five

'In my office, please, Dan,' Lottie Mann said as she returned to the investigation suite.

'Absolutely,' Provan muttered, but too quietly for her to hear, and he rose from his seat and followed her into a small room at the end of the open area.

'See that friend of yours in CTIS?' she began, without preamble. 'Whoever he is, you'd better warn him that where he works careless talk costs lives, and in this case it's his that's on the line. On Toni Field's watch there would probably have been a leak inquiry over what he told you. There won't be this time, but probably only because Skinner likes you too much to use a nutcracker to get the name out of you.

'We are not to follow up what you were told. Instead we're to wrap up Bazza's murder, pass the file to the fiscal and mark it case closed, then get on with the main investigation, which is still, unlike Field, very much alive. That's the way it is, Dan. You are from Barcelona. You know nussing.'

'Ye've got the accent wrong,' the DS said. 'Ah'm old enough to have seen *Fawlty Towers* when it wis new. Unfortunately, Lottie, Ah don't know nothin'. In fact, Ah know too fuckin' much.'

'Oh, I know that,' she laughed. 'Too much for your own good.'

'No, love,' he sighed, 'for yours.'

She stared at him. 'What are you on about, Detective Sergeant? Can we just keep up the pretence that I'm your senior officer?'

'No, we can't.'

Her eyes narrowed. A spasm of something strange ran through her, and she realised that it was fear. 'Dan,' she murmured, 'what is this?'

'This, Lottie, is me doin' something Ah shouldn't. By rights Ah shouldn't be talking to you alone. There should be a senior officer in this room right now, probably the chief constable himself. There isn't, because Ah care about you, lassie, and I want you to know about this from me, first. This might have to be another of those conversations that never happened, like mine with Alec in CTIS, but this is a hell of a lot more serious.'

He reached across her desk and switched on her computer; it was an old-fashioned tower type, probably on its last legs, and took an inordinate length of time to boot up.

'Dan,' she said once more, as they waited, but he hushed her, with a finger to his lips.

'They store the CCTV recordings on DVDs,' he told her, as he loaded a disk on to the computer's player tray, and slid it into position, then settled into the DI's chair so that he could control playback.

'I started at the end, like Ah said,' he began. She looked at the screen and saw a still image of an empty car park, and with numerals in the bottom right corner. 'These things can hold eight hours at a time,' he explained. 'They have a bank of recorders tae cover the whole park. When one disk gets full, another starts, so it's constant. Ah thought I'd have to go a' the way back tae seven, but . . .'

He clicked a rewind icon, three times; the image began to move, as did the time read-out, fast, backwards. Provan's finger hovered above the mouse until the clock showed seven twenty-eight, when he clicked again, freezing the recording once more.

'Ah nearly missed this first time. Watch.' He clicked on the 'Play' arrow and the images started to move.

Mann peered at the screen. The park was almost as empty as it had been before; only a few cars remained. Then she saw a silver saloon roll into view, moving jerkily, for the camera was set to shoot only a few frames per second. It came to a stop and as it did so, a figure walked towards it, his speed enhanced. He was carrying a large parcel. She could just make out a face in the front passenger seat, and a hand, beckoning.

'Bazza,' Provan murmured. 'Now see what happens.'

The man she took to be Brown opened the rear door, slid into the back seat, and closed it behind him. Everything was still for a few seconds. Then she saw what seemed to be three flashes, inside the Peugeot, as if someone was sending a Morse message with a torch. Immediately afterwards, the car zoomed off, at high speed.

'That was the execution of Bazza Brown,' the DS said.

'No doubt about it,' his DI agreed. 'So?'

'So, what was wrong with that picture?'

'Enlighten me,' she growled. 'Stop playin' games, Dan.'

'This is no game, kid. The parcel.' He emphasised the word. 'Where did Brown get the fuckin' parcel? Cec never mentioned that. As far as he was concerned he was takin' his brother to meet a bit on the side. And what was in it? Did he take her chocolates? If he did, it's the biggest box of Black Magic Ah've ever seen.'

'True,' she murmured. That cold feeling revisited the pit of her stomach. Her old crony was taking her somewhere, and she had a bad feeling about their destination.

'Then there was the time,' the DS continued. 'Bazza wanted to be there for seven, yet the South Africans never turned up for another half hour. So Ah ran the recording back to the time Cec told us, like this.' He rewound once more, stopping at six fifty-eight, with a large black car in shot, near to where the Peugeot had pulled up.

Provan let the recording go forward, and Mann saw Bazza Brown step out of his brother's Chrysler, and into the last half hour of his life. He went nowhere, but stood his ground, pacing up and down, waiting, as Cec drove away.

And then a door opened; it was set in the side of a large warehouse building at the top of the frame. A figure stepped out. He was carrying a large parcel, and he walked towards Brown. There was no handshake between the two, barely a glance exchanged, it seemed, as the bundle was handed over. The second man seemed about to turn on his heel, when Provan froze the screen.

'I need you to confirm, ma'am,' he said, 'that the man with Brown is who I think he is.'

Standing behind him, Lottie leaned over and grasped his shoulder, and the corner of the desk, for support.

'Oh no,' she moaned. 'Oh my God, no. You know it is, Danny. You know it's my Scott.'

The sergeant let out a sigh that seemed bigger than he was. 'Ah've never wished in ma life before,' he murmured, 'that Ah wasnae a cop. But I do now, so that somebody else could be doin' this.'

He stood, and gave her back her own chair. Then he went to the door, opened it and beckoned to Banjo Paterson, who crossed the office and joined them.

'Detective Inspector,' Provan announced, his accent vanishing in the formality of his voice, 'in view of what we've just seen, and what you've confirmed, in spite of my subordinate rank I have got no choice but to ask you to remain here with DC Paterson while I take this matter to senior officers.'

Thirty-Six

'So this is where it all happens,' Sarah Grace said, with a smile in her tone as she looked round the room that had become his. 'This is the nerve centre of Scottish policing.'

'A week ago,' Bob told her, 'I would have denied that suggestion, with all the vehemence at my disposal. Today, I'm forced to agree with you.'

'I prefer the command suite in Edinburgh,' she confessed. 'It has a more, I dunno, a more lived-in feel about it. This is all very antiseptic, very impersonal.'

'Honey child,' he laughed, 'don't you think that might be because I haven't had time to stamp my personality on it?'

'Maybe. I'm sure you will . . . as long as that doesn't involve importing that coffee machine you inherited from your old mentor Alf Stein.'

'It won't, I promise you. You told me I should give myself a caffeine holiday and that's what I'm doing. I haven't had a coffee this week. Are you pleased with me?'

She grinned. 'Yes and no. If you really are sticking to it, that might mean I have to give up too. When you're around, at least. Speaking of which,' she added, 'do you want to stop off tonight? The Gullane house will be empty, since the kids are with me.'

'I think I would like that very much, although I do have something to do there, before the place can be truly empty.'

'Can I help?'

'Mmm,' he mused. 'No, I don't think so. I don't reckon either of us would feel right if you did.'

'Ah,' Sarah whispered. 'I think I can guess what you mean. Clearing out all the evidence, yes?'

'Yes, at the other party's request.'

'Then you're right. That is something you should do on your own . . . unless it involves a bonfire, in which case I'll be happy to help.'

'Hey, hey!'

'I'm joking,' she said. 'The strangest thing happened to me this morning. I saw the newspapers and all of a sudden I found that I don't bear that woman any ill-will, not any more, however she might feel about me.'

'To be honest with you, Sarah,' Bob confessed, 'I don't believe she feels any way about you, and I doubt that she ever did. She thought I was somebody I'm not. Now she's found out the truth, she's happy to make me, and everything to do with me, part of her past.'

'Does that include not trying to take you for plenty in the divorce?'

'That hasn't been mentioned,' he grinned, 'and I'm not going to raise the subject.'

He loaded a handful of documents and files into his attaché case, an aluminium Zero Halliburton that Sarah had given him as a birthday present a few years before, clicked it shut and picked it up. 'Come on,' he said. 'Constable Davie, my driver, will be waiting for us in the car park.'

He turned, and was in the act of heading for the door that led directly into the corridor when he saw a small, crumpled, moustachioed figure in his anteroom, his hand raised as if he was about to knock on the door.

'What the hell?' he murmured. 'Hold on a minute, love,' he told his ex-wife. 'There's something up here. Detective sergeants don't turn up uninvited in the chief's office without a bloody good reason.'

He signalled to Dan Provan to enter, but the little man stood his ground. 'What the fu—' Skinner muttered. 'Sit down for a minute, Sarah,' he said. 'Maybe the wee bugger's scared of strange women.'

He walked towards the glass doorway, then stepped through it into the outer office. 'Yes, Dan?' he murmured. 'Where's your DI and what can I do for you?'

'She's detained, sir, downstairs in the office.'

Skinner had a low annoyance threshold. 'What the fuck's detaining her? Has it paralysed her phone hand?'

'No, sir, you don't understand. Ah've detained her. Out of bloody nowhere she's become involved in the investigation. The rule book requires that Ah do that and report the matter to senior officers, plural. In this case, Ah don't think that means a couple of DIs.'

The chief's face darkened; looking up at him, Provan, experienced though he was, felt a chill run through him.

'Where is she?' Skinner murmured.

'She's in her private office, boss. DC Paterson's with her; Ah've ordered him not to allow her to make any phone calls or send any texts.'

'You've done that to Lottie?' Skinner said, and as he did he realised how upset the sergeant was. 'Right, let's hear about it, but not here.'

He opened the door behind him and called out to Sarah, 'Urgent, I'm afraid. Hang on please, love; I'll be as quick as I can.' Then he led the way into the corridor and along to ACC Gorman's office, relieved to see through the unshaded glass wall that she was behind her desk. He rapped on the door, and walked straight in.

'Bridie, sorry to interrupt, but something's arisen that DS Provan feels he has to bring to the top of the reporting chain. He's been around long enough to know the rule book off by heart, so we'd better hear him out.'

'Of course.' Skinner's deputy rose. 'Hi, Dan,' she said. 'You look as though the cat's just ett your budgie.'

The little sergeant sighed. 'Ma'am, if it would make this go away Ah'd feed it the bloody thing maself.'

'So what do you have to tell us?' she asked.

'To show you,' he corrected her. 'Is your computer on?'

'Give me a minute,' she said, then pressed a button behind a console that sat on a side table.

The command suite computers were of more recent vintage than those in the floors below, and so it was ready in less than the time she had requested.

Provan inserted the DVD he had brought with him into a slot at the side of the screen. 'This is CCTV footage,' he explained to the two chief officers, 'from the Easthaven Retail Park. It was taken on Friday evening. Our investigation established that the two men who killed Chief Constable Field went there at that time, and later Bazza Brown's brother, Cec, told us that he took Bazza there as well. Now, please watch.'

He played the recording in the same way that he had shown it to his DI twenty minutes earlier, stopping as the Peugeot roared away from the park.

'That's your homicide wrapped up,' Skinner remarked. 'But where did the parcel come from?'

'Watch again,' Provan replied, rewinding the recording by half an hour, showing Brown's drop-off by his brother, the unexpected encounter, and the handing over of the package. Once again, he froze the action to show the newcomer's face.

'I see,' the chief constable murmured. 'Are you going to tell me who that is, now?'

It was Bridie Gorman who answered. 'I can tell you that,' she hissed. He looked at her and saw that her eyes, normally warm and kind, were cold and seemed as hard as blue marble. 'That is Scottie Mann, one-time police officer until the bevvy got the better of him, and still the husband of Detective Inspector Charlotte Mann. What's the stupid fucking bastard gone and done? Dan, what was in the parcel? Do you know?'

'I would bet my maxed-out pension, ma'am,' the veteran detective declared, 'that it was two police uniforms and two equipment belts.'

Thirty-Seven

'I'm sorry that took so long,' Bob told Sarah as he stepped back into his office, 'but it had to be done straight away, and by nobody other than my deputy and me.'

'What's happened?' she asked. 'Can you tell me?'

'In theory no, I can't, but bugger that. If I don't I'll be brooding over it for the rest of the night. Bridie Gorman and I have just found ourselves in the horrible position of having to interview, under caution, the senior investigating officer in the Toni Field murder. Her husband turned up not just as a witness, but as a suspect in the conspiracy. That's what wee Provan came to tell me, and it must have been bloody tough on him, because the two of them are bloody near father and daughter.'

'Oh my. How did it go?'

'We put the question directly to her and she swore that she had no knowledge of her husband's involvement, and that if she had she would have declared it.'

'Do you believe her?'

He nodded. 'Yes, we do. The poor woman's in a hell of a state. She alternates between being tearful and wanting to rip her old man's heart out . . . and she's big enough to do that too.'

'What happens now?'

'Scott, the husband . . . the ex-cop husband,' he growled, his face twisting suddenly in anger, 'will be arrested. In fact it's under way now. Provan's taking a DC and some uniforms to their house to pick him up. Their son will see that happen, I'm afraid, but there's no way round that. DC Paterson and the uniforms will take him away and Dan . . . he's the boy's godfather . . . will stay with him till Lottie gets back.' He chuckled, savagely. 'She wanted to make the arrest herself! I almost wish that was possible. It'd serve the guy right. No chance, though; she's out.'

'You mean she's suspended?' Sarah looked as angry as he did.

'No, of course not.' He smiled to lighten the moment. 'Calm down. No need to get the sisterhood wound up. She's on an unanticipated holiday, that's all. She can't continue on the inquiry, because she's been hopelessly compromised.'

'Who'll take over from her?'

'Dan will,' Skinner replied, 'reporting to me, just as she's been doing. I could parachute in another DI, indeed maybe I should, given his closeness to the family, but Scott was a cop himself and it would be difficult to find someone who had never crossed his path.

'Anyway, Provan's forgotten more about detective work than most of the potential candidates will ever learn, and he's still got enough left in his tank to see him through. He won't interview Scott, though. Bridie and I will do that, tomorrow morning. Not too early, though, I want him to stew in isolation for a while. Now,' he declared, 'let's you and I get out of here. Change of plan; we'll take the train, then a taxi to yours. I can't have PC Davie drive me through to Edinburgh at this time of night.'

They took the lift down to the headquarters car park, where PC Cole was waiting. The chief constable introduced the extra passenger, 'Doctor Grace, the pathologist, from Edinburgh University,' then apologised for the delay, a gesture that seemed to take his driver by surprise. His reaction rose to astonishment when Skinner told him that the destination was Queen Street Station.

'Are you sure, sir?' he exclaimed.

'Certain. You can pick me up from there tomorrow as well. I'll let you know what train I'm on.'

The train was on the platform five minutes from departure as they settled into its only first-class compartment. Sarah grinned. 'I'm on expenses, or I would be if you hadn't bought my ticket. What's your excuse?'

'I'm not quite sure,' he confessed, 'since everything happened very quickly at the weekend, but I think I am too. But the truth is that I prefer first, on the rare occasions that I take the train, simply because there's less chance of me meeting an old customer, so to speak.'

'And that would worry you?' she asked, eyebrow raised. 'Are you feeling your age?'

'No to both of those, and not that it's likely to happen, but I'd rather avoid those situations. I'm not just talking about people I've locked up; there's councillors, journalists, defence lawyers. I don't like to be cornered by any of them, because I don't care to be in any situation where I have to watch every word I say.'

'I can see that,' she conceded.

No other passengers had joined them by the time the train left the station.

'This preference of yours for privacy,' Sarah ventured, as it entered the tunnel that ran north out of Queen Street, 'would it have anything to do with you not wanting to be seen with me?'

'What?' He laughed. 'Don't be daft.' He reached out and took her hand. 'There is no woman in the world I would rather be seen with.'

'Apart from Alex.'

234

'Alexis is my daughter, and so is Seonaid, our daughter, yours and mine. We made her and I am very proud of that, even though I was fucking awful at showing it for a while. You are different, you are you, and I love you.'

'This hasn't happened too soon, has it?' she wondered. 'A week ago, if you'd asked me, I'd never have imagined you and me, here like this, now.'

'Me neither,' Bob admitted, 'but I am mightily pleased that we are. It should never have been any other way. I was stupid, and not for the first time in my life. Feeling my age, you asked. Well, maybe I am, in a way. It's led me to a point where I'm honest with myself about my weaknesses, and the things I've done wrong in the past, and strong enough to be able to promise you that I will never let you down again.'

'You realise that if you do,' she whispered, as the train passed out into the open with leafy embankments on either side, 'I will do your autopsy myself, before they take me away?'

He gave her a big wide-open smile, a rarity from him. 'Yes, but I don't need that incentive.'

When the door slid open, they were both taken by surprise. 'Tickets please.'

The guard's intervention ended the moment. They were passing through the first station on the route before Sarah broke the silence. 'When did you eat last?' she asked.

'Good question; probably sometime between one and half past; sandwiches with Mann and Provan, my office. They were crap. The bread was turning up at the edges by the time we got round to them.'

'That sort of a day, uh?'

He nodded. 'That sort. How about yours?'

She scrunched up her face for a second or two. 'Usual blood and guts, but pretty run-of-the-mill, as my job goes.'

'No surprises? No complications?'

'None, in either case. The two cadavers I'll be looking at tomorrow . . . remind me of their names again? Not that it matters.'

'Smit and Botha, also known as Mallett and Lightbody.'

'Well, one thing I can tell you about them right now is that they were very good at their job, and humane too. Neither of their victims had any time to think about it. Mr Brown died on Friday evening. He may have seen the man who was killing him, but he died instantly. He still had a surprised expression on his face.'

'I know,' Bob reminded her. 'I saw him in his second-to-last resting place. And,' he added, 'I've just seen a recording of him being shot.'

'Why didn't they kill the detective inspector's husband?'

'Because he never saw them, otherwise, you're right, poor Lottie would be a widow.'

'Then too bad for Mr Brown that he did, otherwise his life expectancy would have been pretty good. He was a fit guy.'

'And how about Toni?'

'Same with her, as you might expect, given her job. She was killed even more humanely than Brown, if I can use the term. She would not have had the faintest idea of what had happened to her. Well,' she corrected herself, 'maybe a few milliseconds, but no more than that. She'd have been brain-dead even before the force of the impact threw her out of her seat. If that's some small comfort to her family, you might like to tell them.'

'I have done already. I saw her mother and sister this morning.'

'How were they?'

'Very dignified, both of them. I've let the fiscal talk herself into releasing the body as soon as she gets your report.'

'Then I'll complete it and send it to her before I move on to Smit

236

and Botha.' She paused. 'But how about her husband? How about the child?' she asked. 'Or is it too young to understand?'

He stared at her, a slight, bewildered smile on his face. 'Husband?' he repeated. 'Child? What child?'

'Hers of course, Antonia Field's. I assumed she was married or in a familial relationship.'

'No, never,' Bob said. 'She was never married, and she lived with her sister. What makes you think she had a child?'

'Hell,' she exclaimed, 'I might not be a professor of forensic pathology yet, but I do know a caesarean scar when I see one.'

He sat up straight in his high-backed seat. 'Well, honey, that is news to me, and neither her mother nor her sister . . . who wants to come back to work for me . . . gave me the slightest hint of its existence.'

'Then tread carefully if you decide to tackle them about it. Yes, she has a scar, and there were other physical signs of child-bearing. However, there is no way I could guarantee that her baby was delivered alive.'

'I accept that, but the odds are heavily in favour of that. If a kid goes full-term or almost there . . .'

'That's true, but Bob, where are you going with this? Suppose she did have a baby and kept quiet about it in case it harmed her career; that's not a crime.'

'In certain circumstances it might be. An application for the post of chief constable requires full disclosure.'

'But honey, she's dead. Does it really matter?'

'Probably not at all.' He grinned. 'But it's a mystery and you know how I feel about them. How old was this scar? Can you tell?'

'I can take a guess. I'd say not less than one year old, and not more than three.'

'Okay. One year ago she was chief constable of the West Midlands;

if she had it then it would have been a bit noticeable. But hold on.'

He raised himself from his seat and took his attaché case down from the luggage rack. He spun the combination wheels and opened it.

'I've got Toni's HR file in here. Let's take a look and see what that tells us.' He removed the thick green folder, then closed the case again, putting it on his knee to use as an impromptu table.

'Let's go back three years. Then she was a Met commander, on secondment to the Serious and Organised Crime Agency; she built her legend there knocking over foreign drugs cartels. If she'd taken time out to have a kid, that would have been noticed and recorded. It isn't, so we can rule it out. So where does that take us?'

As he read, a smile split his face. 'It takes us to her becoming the chief constable of West Midlands, just over two years ago.'

'She couldn't have been there long,' Sarah remarked.

'She wasn't. She barely had time to crease her uniform before the Strathclyde job came up. But, it says here that before she was appointed to Birmingham she took a six-month sabbatical, which ended a week before she was interviewed. That fits like a glove,' he exclaimed.

'It does,' Sarah agreed. 'But what do you do about it?'

'I could simply ask her family, but you're right; there could be sensitivities there. It's even possible they don't know about it. Marina gave me a pretty full rundown of her sister's sex life and didn't mention her being pregnant. She may have assumed that I knew from her record, but on the other hand, is there any reason why she should? If the child was safely delivered, it could have been put up for adoption. Toni was the sort of woman who wouldn't have fancied any impediment to her career ambitions.

'So no,' he decided, 'I won't take it to Sofia or Marina. Instead I'll do some digging of my own. I have a timeframe, her full name,

Antonia Maureen Field, and her date of birth; they'll be enough for the General Register Office to get me a hit. But I'm not counting on it.'

'No?'

'No. I have a feeling that there's another possibility, one that might even be more likely.'

'You love this, don't you?' Sarah chuckled. 'The thrill of the chase, and all.'

'It's what I do, honey,' he replied. 'It's the part of the job that I've always loved. These days, I don't have too many chances to be hands on, so I take every one that's going.'

'Including interviewing the guy tomorrow morning? Surely you don't really have to do that. An ACC alone's pretty heavy duty, isn't she?'

'Oh, I have to do it, make no mistake. Not only was he a police officer until a few years ago, his wife still is. I've come to rate her in the last couple of days, and to like her a lot too. This bastard's gone and compromised her career and even put her in a situation where she had to be formally detained for a short while.

'Tomorrow morning, he's going to have me across the table, and if he thinks that his obligatory lawyer will prevent me from coming down on him like an avalanche, he's kidding himself.'

'It's a new thing in Scotland, isn't it, the prisoner's right to a lawyer?'

Bob nodded. 'Indeed, but to be frank, I don't know how we got away with the old system for so long. It doesn't bother me anyway; I'm at my best when I don't say a word.'

Sarah grinned, as a gleam came into her eye. 'You can say that again, buddy,' she murmured.

Thirty-Eight

'Where is ma daddy, Uncle Dan?' Jake Mann asked, not for the first time. His godfather realised that there was no ducking the question.

'I told ye before, Jakey, it's all hush-hush, but maybe this'll explain it. Ye know your daddy used to be a policeman.'

The child nodded, with vigour. 'M-hm.'

'Well, it's like this. They've asked him to go back and help them again. Yer mum and I, we've been asked no' tae talk about it, not even tae you.'

'Wow! Secret squirrels?'

'That's right, secret squirrels; undercover.' He ruffled Jake's hair. 'Now away ye go to your bed, like yer mum asked ye to a while back.'

'Okay.' He hugged his honorary uncle and ran into the hall, heading for the stairs, as if he was fuelled by excitement.

'You're a lovely wee man, Danny Provan,' Lottie said, from the kitchen doorway. 'I'd never have thought of that.' She was carrying two plates, each loaded with fish and chips still in the wrapper. She handed him one and settled into her armchair. 'It won't hold up for long, though,' she sighed. 'Eventually, this is going to hit the press.'

'Eventually,' he conceded, 'but these are special circumstances. The husband of the SIO bein' lifted? Okay, it's bound to leak within a day or two, but Ah'd expect the fiscal tae go to the High Court and get an interdict against publishing Scott's name, at least until the trial begins, maybe even till he's convicted.'

'There's no doubt he will be, is there?'

'Ah'd love tae say he's got a chance, but Ah can't. We found the wrapping from the parcel in the car. You know as well as I do that the forensic people will find fibres on it and match them to a police uniform.'

'It's as well for him he is done,' she barked. 'I could bloody kill him, for what he's done to Jakey; it'll be hellish for him at school. Ye know what kids are like. I tell you this, even if by some miracle he does get out of this, he and I are done. He's never coming back here. Never!'

'Come on, Lottie, Scott wouldnae harm his laddie for a' the tea in China.'

'And what about me? Do you think he hasn't harmed me?'

'No, Ah don't,' the sergeant admitted. 'I concede that. Ah want you to know, hen,' he added, 'that this has been the worst day of my police career. What I had to do this afternoon . . .' His voice trailed away, as if he had run out of words.

'But you had to do it, Dan,' she countered. 'As you say, you had to do it. If you hadn't, I'd have thought the worse of you, and so would you and all, for the rest of your life. You've always been a hero to me, since I was the rawest DC in the team, but never more so than this afternoon.'

Thirty-Nine

'You'll be DCS McIlhenney, then,' Lowell Payne said as he approached the hulking, dark-suited stranger who stood at the entrance to the platform at Victoria Station where the Gatwick Express arrived.

'How do you work that out?' the other countered.

'The boss's description was enough. That and the fact that you've got his warrant card hung around your neck.'

'Ah. I deduce that you are a detective. DCI Payne?'

They shook hands. 'That's me. It's a pleasure to meet the other half of the Glimmer Twins.'

'You know my Latino compatriot?' he asked, surprised. 'Bob never mentioned that.'

'Yes, I do. I was involved in the investigation in Edinburgh that led up to the shit that happened at the weekend. That's how I met Mario. He and I got to the Glasgow concert hall not long after the shooting. Now I find myself right in the middle of the follow-up.'

'You were there?' McIlhenney's eyes flashed. 'How's Paula? McGuire says she's all right, but I couldn't be quite sure that he wasn't spinning the truth to keep me off the first plane.'

'Trust me, he wasn't,' Payne assured him. 'She's a tough lady. Everything happened so fast that I don't think she had time to be scared. She was fine when we got there, shaken, but well in control of

242

herself. From what the boss said when he called me last night she still is. Mind you, you can think about booking a flight this weekend, from what I hear. The baby's expected by the end of the week.'

'Is that right? That's terrific.' He laughed. 'Mario has no idea how much his life is going to change. He reckoned nothing could ever slow him down, but this will. Who knows? I might even get to overtake him.'

He read the question written on Payne's face. 'He's always been first to every promotion,' he explained. 'Then when I get one, he lands another. It's the same again this time. I come all the way to London to make chief super, he stays in bloody Edinburgh, and gets the ACC post.' He beamed. 'There's a longer ladder here, though; he'll be struggling from now on. He's got one more rung left in him, max, while I could have two in the Met.'

'Good for you guys,' Payne said. 'I'm not on a ladder any more. I won't see fifty again, I've reached my level, and I'm happy with it.'

'Don't write yourself off,' McIlhenney murmured, 'not if you're working for Bob Skinner.' He frowned, rubbing his hands together. 'Now,' he continued, 'enough career planning. You and I have got a grieving widow to interview.'

'Does she know she's a widow yet?'

The chief superintendent checked his watch, as they walked towards the station exit. 'She should by now. We ran some checks on her and found that she's not in employment, so we guess that she's a full-time mum. The family support people were going to call on her at nine thirty, and I've had no message to say that she wasn't in. It's going on ten now, so hopefully by the time we get there, she'll have had time to absorb what's happened.'

'Or not, as the case may be,' the visitor countered. 'It's the worst possible news they'll have given her. She might not be capable of talking to anyone.'

'In that case, we get a doctor, we sedate her and while she's in the land of nod we search the place, quietly but carefully.'

'Can we do that?' Payne wondered. 'Legally, I mean?'

McIlhenney opened his jacket, displaying an envelope in an inside pocket. 'I've got warrants,' he said. 'Everything the Met does these days has to be watertight. We are all book operators now. I hate to think how Bob Skinner would get on down here. He'd do his own thing, because that's all he knows, and wind up on page one . . . just like his bloody wife! That was a shocker; it blew me right out of my seat when I saw those pictures. Some of my brother officers think it's funny, fools that they are, to see the big man embarrassed like that. How's it going down in Pitt Street?'

'Very quietly. The new chief's reputation travels before him. One of our ACCs might be found chortling in a stall in the gents, but he's got his own secret to protect, so he's poker-faced in public.'

'Sensible man.' McIlhenney slowed his pace as they approached a waiting police car. 'I can't get over Aileen getting herself compromised like that. She always struck me as super-cautious, given her political position. What doesn't surprise me, though, is that the marriage was up shit creek even without the Morocco complication.'

'No?'

'No. Those are two of the most powerful people, personality-wise, that I've ever met. I never thought it would last. Just as I never thought he and Sarah would actually split, even though she can be volatile and though Bob doesn't have quite the same control over his dick that he has over everything else. McGuire tells me that Sarah's back in Edinburgh. Is that right?'

'So I believe. I have met her, you know. For example, a few years back, at my niece's twenty-first . . . well, she's my wife's niece, really. Sarah and Bob weren't long married at the time. She was well pregnant at the time.' McIlhenney was staring at him, puzzled. 'Alex,' he explained. 'Alexis, Bob's daughter. I'm married to her mother's sister, although Myra had died well before I came on the scene.'

The chief superintendent beamed, then laughed. 'Jeez,' he exclaimed, 'the man's like a fucking octopus; his tentacles are everywhere. He's had a family insider in Strathclyde CID all this time and he's never let on.'

'Oh, come on,' Payne protested, 'you're making it sound like I was his snitch. I rarely saw him, other than a few times when he came with Alex to visit our wee lass, or family events, like weddings and such, and before now our paths only ever crossed the once professionally, way back when I was a uniform sergeant and he'd just made detective super.'

'Maybe so, but I'll bet when you did see him, you spent a hell of a lot more time talking about policing than about Auntie Effie's bunions.'

'Mmm,' the DCI murmured. 'We don't have an Auntie Effie, but yes, I suppose you're right. It was mostly shop talk. Mind you, I'm not a golfer, and I don't follow football, so there wasn't much else on the agenda.'

'Wouldn't have made any difference,' McIlhenney assured him. 'Come on, let's get on our way.' They slid into the back of the waiting police car. 'You know where we're going?' he asked the constable at the wheel.

'Yes, sir,' the driver replied. 'There was a message for you while you were away,' he added. 'The family support gels say it's okay for you to go in. The lady's been advised, and she's okay to speak to you.'

'I hope she's still okay after we've finished,' the chief superintendent grunted.

The car pulled out of the station concourse and into the traffic. 'Tourist route, sir?' the constable asked.

'Not this trip. We can show DCI Payne the sights later.'

The visiting detective had no more than a tourist's knowledge of London, and so he sat bewildered as they cut past New Scotland Yard and along a series of thoroughfares that might have been in any developed city in the world, had it not been for the omnipresence of the Union flag and the Olympic rings, and for the Queen's image beaming from shop windows displayed on a range of souvenir products from clothing to crockery. The sun told him that they were heading roughly north, and occasionally a sign would advise him that Madame Tussaud's lay a mile from where they were at that moment, or that they were passing an underground station called Angel, or that the Mayor of London wished him an enjoyable stay in his city.

They had been on the road for twenty minutes when McIlhenney pointed out of the window to his left, indicating a modern steel edifice, its clean lines sharp against the sky. 'The Emirates Stadium,' he announced. 'Home of Arsenal Football Club.'

'Are you a fan?'

'No,' he chuckled. 'Spence, my older laddie, won't allow it. He plays rugby, pretty well, they say, and I usually follow him on winter Saturdays. Not that we've had too many of them down here, not yet. Next season, though; he's been accepted by London Scottish. Dads on the touchlines can be bad news at junior rugby, but they like me, being a cop.'

And a brick shithouse into the bargain, Payne thought. 'The stadium. Is that where we're heading?'

'Not quite. We're going to the Gunners' old home, Highbury. In fact,' he paused as they made a turn, 'there it is.'

Ahead the DCI saw a tall building with 'Arsenal Stadium' emblazoned in red along its high wall, with a wheeled gun underneath.

'Who plays there now?' he asked. As he spoke he glanced forward and caught in the rear-view the constable driver giving him a look that might have been scornful, or simply one of pity.

'Nobody, sir,' he volunteered. 'It's been turned into flats and stuff. They weren't allowed to knock down the front of the main stand . . . more's the pity. Should have bulldozed the lot, if you ask me.'

'I take it you're not a follower.'

'God forbid! No, I'm Totten'am, till I die.'

'You don't want to get into that, Lowell,' McIlhenney advised. 'Serious London tribalism.'

'When you've been on uniform duty at an Old Firm match,' the visitor countered, 'nothing else can seem all that serious.'

'Before I came down here, I might have agreed with that.'

The driver indicated a right turn, then waited for oncoming traffic to pass. Reading the street sign, St Baldred's Road, McIlhenney tapped him on the shoulder. 'Don't turn in there. Pull over here and we'll walk the rest; this vehicle would tell the whole neighbourhood that something's up.'

'Sir.' The PC changed his signal, then parked twenty yards further on. The two detectives climbed out, and crossed the street.

St Baldred's Road told a story of comfortable middle-class prosperity. The Millbank family home was four doors along, on the left, a brick terraced villa, smart and well-maintained like all of its neighbours.

A blue Fiesta was parked outside, out of place between a Mercedes E-class, and a Lexus four-wheel drive with a child seat in the back. Payne glanced inside the little Ford and saw two female uniform caps on the front seats. *Discretion seems to be the watchword in the Met these days*, he thought.

The door opened before they reached it; one of the pair, a forty-something, salt-and-pepper-haired sergeant, stood waiting for them. 'How is she?' McIlhenney asked, quietly, as they stepped inside.

'Shocked, but self-controlled,' the woman replied. 'She's got a kid, little Leon. In my experience that usually helps to keep them together.'

'The child's here? Not in a nursery?'

'He's here, outside in his playground. Molly, PC Bates, my colleague, is looking after him. I'm Rita,' she added 'Sergeant Caan.'

'Has she called anyone? Friends, family?'

'No, not yet. She said something about having to phone her mother, to let her know. I said we could do that for her. She felt she had to do that herself, but she hasn't got round to it yet.'

'Do you know,' Payne began, 'if we're right in our assumption that the husband worked for her family business?'

Rita Caan nodded. 'Yes, spot on. The mother runs it; Golda's father's dead.'

'Thanks, that's helpful; one less question for us. Have you picked up anything else?'

She frowned at him. 'Other than the fact that she's four and a half months pregnant, no.'

'Doctor on the way?' McIlhenney asked.

She sighed. 'Of course he is. It's standard in a situation like this. She didn't want to bother him, but we persuaded her that he'd want to be bothered. He's coming after his morning surgery.'

'Good. Sorry, Sergeant. I wasn't doubting you; I just had to know for sure. Let's see her, then, before the doc gets here.'

'Okay. She's in the living room. This way.' She led them to a solid wood door, as old as the house, tapped on it gently, then opened it. 'Golda,' she called out. 'My colleagues have arrived. Chief Superintendent McIlhenney and Mr Payne, from Scotland. Mr McIlhenney is too, as you'll realise very quickly, but he's one of ours.'

The widow was in the act of rising as they stepped into the room, which extended for the full length of the house, with double doors opening into the garden. As Payne looked along he saw a ball bounce into view, and heard a toddler's shout, as Caan's colleague retrieved it.

'Don't get up, Mrs Millbank, please,' McIlhenney insisted. 'I'm the local,' he added, 'he's the visitor. First and foremost, we are both very sorry for your loss.'

'Thank you,' Golda Millbank, née Radnor, said. Her voice was quiet, but strong, with no hint of a quaver. 'Please, can you tell me what happened to Byron? All that Rita could say is that it was a brain thing.'

'That's correct,' Payne confirmed. 'An autopsy was performed; it showed that your husband suffered a massive, spontaneous subarachnoid cerebral haemorrhage. Death would have been almost instantaneous, the pathologist said.'

'When did this happen?'

'Last week.'

'Last week?' she repeated. 'Then why has it taken so long for you to tell me?'

'When your husband's body was found,' the DCI explained, 'he had no identification on him. It took the police in Edinburgh some time to find out who he was.'

'What does Edinburgh have to do with it?'

'That's where he was found.'

'But he was supposed to be in Manchester, then in Glasgow, at a jewellery fair, and then in Inverness, visiting one of our suppliers. I don't understand why he would be in Edinburgh.'

'When was he due home, Mrs Millbank?' McIlhenney asked.

'Not until today; I expected him back this evening.'

'When was the last time you spoke to him?'

'On the day he left for Scotland. Byron doesn't like mobile phones; he won't have one. When he's away on business, I don't expect to hear from him, unless he sends me an email. He tends to do everything through his computer. He has a laptop, a MacBook Air. It goes everywhere with him; he says that all his life is on it.'

'When did you meet him?' The DCS kept his tone casual.

'When he came to work for my parents' business; I called in there one day, a few months after he started. Neither my father nor mother were there but he was. He introduced himself and,' she smiled, 'that was that.' She shook her head. 'He was such a fit, strong man. I can't believe this has happened.' She stared at McIlhenney, and then at Payne. 'Are you telling me the truth?' she asked. Her voice was laden with suspicion. 'Has somebody killed my husband?'

It was Payne who replied. 'No, absolutely not. I assure you, his death was completely natural. I can get you a copy of the post-mortem report, if it'll help you. I can even arrange for you to speak to the pathologist, Dr Grace. She's one of the best in the business, I promise you. If there had been any sign of violence, or anything other than natural causes, she'd have found it.'

'Then why are you here?' she demanded. 'You two, you're detectives, you're not wearing uniforms like Rita and Molly. And you, Mr Payne, you've come all the way from Scotland. Would you do that if there was not something more to this?'

'When he died, Mrs Millbank, he was unattended, not seen by a doctor,' the DCI explained. 'That makes it a police matter; nothing sinister, a formality really, but we have to complete a report.'

'Very good, but such things must happen every day. For a senior officer to come down to London . . . please, Mr Payne, don't take me for a fool.'

He glanced at the DCS, who nodded. 'Very well, there is more to it,' he admitted. 'Can I ask you, Mrs Millbank, how much do you know of your husband's background, of his life before you two met?'

'I know that he was born in Eastbourne, that he never knew his father and that his mother is dead. He spent some time in Israel, was a lieutenant in the army, but left because of his opposition to the Iraq war, worked in mail order and finally for an investment bank, before he joined Rondar . . . that's our family business.'

'How about friends, family? Did you ever meet any of them?'

'He has no family, and as for friends, when he left the army, he left them behind too. We have friends, as a couple, but that's it.'

'Has he ever mentioned a man called Brian Lightbody, from New Zealand, or Richie Mallett, an Australian? Or have you ever heard of either of them indirectly?'

She shook her head. 'No. Those names mean nothing to me. Why do you ask?'

'Because we know that your husband ate with them in a kosher restaurant in Glasgow, on the day he died, and that they were all registered in the same hotel, and that the other two told staff they were there for the jewellery fair.'

'So?' she retorted. 'That's your explanation surely. I don't know everybody in the business, and if they were jewellery buyers also, they do tend to be in the same place at the same time.'

'Sure, but . . . Mrs Millbank, Lightbody and Mallett weren't jewellery buyers, and those weren't their real names. I'm not free to tell you at this stage who they were, but we do know, and we do know their real business.'

'Are you saying they killed Byron?'

'No,' Payne insisted, 'I am not, but they were with him when he died. There is physical evidence that one or both of them tried to revive him after he collapsed. When they failed, they removed all the identification from his body, including his clothing, and concealed him. Then, after a day or so, they called the police and told them where he could be found.'

Golda Millbank opened her mouth but found that she could not speak. She looked towards Rita Caan, as if for help. 'Is this . . .' she whispered.

'I don't know any of it,' the sergeant told her. 'It's not what I do. Molly and me, we're only family support, honest.'

'It's true, Mrs Millbank,' McIlhenney said. 'We're here to find out everything you knew about your husband and about what he did.'

'I know all about him,' she insisted. 'He was a good husband and a faithful family man. Or are you trying to tell me that he had a piece on the side?'

'Not for a second, but suppose he did, that wouldn't be our business. Let me chuck another name at you. Beram Cohen; Israeli national. Mean anything?'

Both he and Payne gazed at her, concentrating on her expression, looking for any twitch, any hint of recognition, but neither saw any, only utter bewilderment.

'No,' she declared. 'I've never heard of him.' She rose from her chair. 'I have to phone my mother. She needs to know what's happening here.'

'Where will she be at this moment?' the DCS asked.

'She'll be at work.'

'In that case, I'm sorry, but we'd rather you didn't contact her.' He paused. 'Look, Mrs Millbank, I'm as satisfied as I can be that you know no more about your husband than you're telling us. But let me ask you, how successful is the family business? I could find out through Companies House, but if you know, it would save time.'

She took a deep breath, frowning. 'I can tell you that. I'm a director, so I know. Frankly, it's been on its last legs since my father died three years ago. We're being out-marketed by other companies and we don't have the expertise in the company to reverse the trend. Mummy's trying to sell it, but there are no takers.'

'Byron wasn't a director?'

'No, Mummy wouldn't allow that. She didn't want a situation where she could be outvoted. There's just the two of us on the board; I'm unpaid of course.'

'How about Byron? Was he on a good salary?'

'Thirty-five thousand. He had to take a pay cut at the beginning of last year, down from fifty.'

'In that case, living in his house must be a stretch,' McIlhenney suggested. 'This isn't the cheapest part of London, from what I'm told. How long have you lived here?'

'We bought it when Leon was on the way, and moved in just after he was born. But it's okay, we get by easily, because we don't have a mortgage.'

'Lucky you. Did your father leave you money?'

'No. It was Byron. He made a pile in bonuses working with the bank, and never spent it. He wasn't the type to buy a flashy sports car or anything like that. No, one way or another we've always been comfortably off.' Her eyes narrowed. 'Are you saying . . .'

'I'm not saying anything,' the DCS replied. 'I'm asking. We're trying to build up a complete picture of Byron. To do that we need to search, where he lived, where he worked, everywhere we can. Was he a member of a sports club, for example?'

'He played squash, but otherwise he wasn't the clubbable sort. He ran, on the streets, he cycled and he did things like chins and press-ups . . . he could do hundreds of those things . . . but always on his own.'

'So all his private life was here in this house?'

'Yes.'

'Did he have a computer here?' Payne asked.

'We have one, yes, but it's mine and he never used it. I've told you, he had his laptop, his MacBook, and he took that with him when he left.'

'Can we look in your machine nonetheless? Just in case he was able to access it without you knowing about it.'

She let out a sigh, of sheer exasperation. 'Yes, if you must, but honestly, Byron wouldn't do that, any more than I would look in his. That's assuming I could get into it. He used to laugh about it and say that breaking his password was as likely as winning the Lottery.'

'If that's so,' McIlhenney said, 'I wouldn't like to try to access it, just in case it spoiled my luck for the jackpot.'

'No worries of that happening,' Payne pointed out.

'You mean you didn't find it,' the widow asked, 'among his effects?'

'I told you, we didn't find anything, Mrs Millbank. Not even his clothes.'

She shuddered and for a second her eyes moistened, her first sign of weakness. 'How awful,' she whispered. 'Robbing a dead man. How could they have done that? Of course I'll help you in any way I can. What do you need to see?'

'That computer for a start,' the DCS replied. 'If you could take us through it, looking for any files you don't recognise, and at its history, its usage pattern. Then if we could look though his belongings, and examine any area where he might have worked at home.'

'There wasn't one. He never did. But you can look. If it'll help, you can look; anything that'll help you find those so-called friends of his.'

'Oh, we know where they are,' Payne said.

'Then what are you looking for?'

'I'm afraid it's one of those situations where we won't know until we find it. And if we do,' he added, 'we might not be able to tell you, for your own protection.'

Her forehead wrinkled. 'That sounds a little scary. You can't tell me anything?'

'No more than we have already.'

'Nothing? What about that name you mentioned, the Israeli man, Beram Cohen. Where does he fit? Who is he?'

The DCI looked at his escort colleague, raising his eyebrows, asking a silent question. McIlhenney hesitated, then nodded.

'I'm sorry, Mrs Millbank,' Payne replied, 'but he was your husband.'

Forty

'Thanks, Bridie,' Skinner said, as the ACC rose from her chair at his meeting table, their morning briefing session having come to an end. 'I'll give you a shout when I'm ready to start interviewing Scott Mann. He can stew for a bit longer.'

'His lawyer's not going to like that,' she pointed out.

'Then tough shit on him. The Supreme Court says he has a right to be there, but we still set the timetable, up to a point, and we haven't reached that yet. He can wait with his client.'

Gorman liked what she heard; her smile confirmed it.

'Do something for me,' he continued. 'Ask Dan Provan to come up here, straight away. With Lottie being stood down, he's carrying the ball, and I need to speak to him.'

The third person in the room was on his feet also, but the chief waved him back down. 'Stay for a bit, Michael, please. I'd like a word.'

ACC Thomas frowned, but did as he was asked.

'I want to apologise to you,' Skinner began as soon as the door had closed behind Gorman.

'For what, Chief?' *For which of the many ways I've been offended?* he thought.

'For asking you to attend Toni Field's post-mortem. It's been suggested to me since then that your relationship might have been more than professional. If I'd been aware of that at the time, no way would I have asked you to go.'

'Even if the suggestion was untrue?'

'Even then, because I wouldn't have been quizzing you about it. If you and she had a fling away from the office, so what? When I was on my way up the ladder, and widowed, I had a long-standing relationship with a female colleague. Nobody ever questioned it and if anyone had they'd have been told very quickly to fuck off.'

'Then I accept your apology, and I appreciate it, sir . . . although it wasn't really necessary, since it was my duty as a senior officer to attend the autopsy.'

Skinner grinned. 'Which means, by implication, that if it was yours, then it was mine even more, and I shirked it.'

'I didn't say that.'

'No, but if you had I couldn't have argued, 'cos you'd have been right. The truth is, I've seen more hacked-about bodies than you or I have had years in the force, combined, and I tend not to volunteer to see any more. I should have stood up for that one, though.'

Thomas shook his head. 'No, you shouldn't,' he said.

'How do you work that out?' the chief asked.

'Because the examination was performed by your ex-wife, who still speaks of you with a smile and a twinkle in her eye; in my book that disqualifies you as a witness. Suppose that she'd made a mistake, and her findings had been challenged by the defence in a future trial and you'd wound up in the witness box. You'd have been hopelessly compromised.'

Skinner stared at him. 'Do you know, Michael,' he murmured, 'you are absolutely right. It's years since I attended one of Sarah's autopsies, but I have done, when we were married. I shouldn't have, unarguably. I should have known that, so why didn't it dawn on me?'

'I'd guess because the possibility of her slipping up didn't enter your head,' Thomas suggested. 'She does seem very efficient.'

'She's all that. She gave up pathology for a while, when we went our separate ways, but I'm glad she's back. I confess that the very thought of what she does turns my stomach from time to time, but I can say the same about my own career.'

'Is it public knowledge?'

The chief blinked. 'What?'

'Toni and me. Does everybody know?'

'From what I gather, most of the force does.'

'Jesus!' The ACC stared at the ceiling. 'It's never got back to me, then. I've never heard a whisper, not once. And once is the number of times it happened so how the . . .'

'You were unlucky. You were seen by the wrong people, the kind whose discretion gene was removed at birth. Max Allan did what damage limitation he could, but for what it's worth, when Lowell Payne gets back from a wee job I've given him, I'm going to ask him to root out the people who started the story. Then I'm going to draw them a very clear picture of their futures in the force. What's the shittiest part of our vast patch, Michael? Where does no PC want to be posted?'

'I'll give it some thought,' Thomas growled.

Skinner nodded and pushed his chair back. 'You do that,' he declared. 'Let's you and I start again, with a clean sheet,' he added, extending his hand.

As the two men shook, Skinner's phone rang. 'Need to take this,' he said. 'It might be Payne.'

It was.

'We've just left Mrs Millbank, Chief,' his exec told him. 'We got nothing from it. Neither of us believe that she had a clue about her husband's previous, or any idea about his sideline. It helped their lifestyle, though; the family business is pretty well fucked, but they live debt-free and drive a nice Lexus.'

'But no clue to where he kept his Cohen money?'

'Yes and no. The wife, widow now, told us that he had a computer, an Apple MacBook Air laptop that he was never parted from. His life was in it, was how she put it. Am I right in thinking that hasn't shown up anywhere?'

'You are,' Skinner agreed. 'Nothing of his has turned up. He was buried naked, wrapped in a sheet. Leave that with me, Lowell. I'll check it out and get people moving if I have to. Where are you off to now?'

'To check out his workplace, in the Elephant and Castle, wherever that is. It'll be a shock for his mother-in-law, or maybe not, depending on how she felt about him. From what I gather, Byron, or Beram, wasn't much bloody good as a buyer. That's what the father did, and the business has been suffering since his death.'

'Let me know how you get on. Then we can decide whether there's anything else to be done in London.'

'Will do, boss.'

The chief constable flicked a button on his console to end the call, another for an outside line, then dialled a number that was ingrained in his memory, yet which he had never called before.

A female voice answered. 'Yes?'

'Bet you got a shock when that rang,' he said. 'Theory being that it's for your private calls, and not routed through the comms centre.'

'Are you kidding?' Maggie Steele replied. 'This is the fourth call I've had on it. One was from Chief Constable Haggerty in Dumfries, another was from Archbishop Gainer, and the third was from old John Hunter, the freelance journalist, who's got onset dementia and asked me for a prawn biryani with naan bread. He got me mixed up with the

Asian takeaway. Are there any of your friends who don't have this number, Bob?'

'One or two. How are you getting on?'

'Okay, but I still feel a wee bit overawed. It feels strange, sitting in this chair, and you on the other side of the country. Only for three months though, yes?'

'That's the duration of my appointment,' he agreed, 'or my loan if you'd rather put it that way.'

'Can I have a straight answer to that question? You will be back, won't you?'

'That's my intention.'

'Bob! Don't prevaricate. Have you been seduced by the bright lights and the glitter balls of Glasgow already?'

'No, but . . .'

'I knew it!' she declared.

'No, really. I still have three months in my head, for reasons that are more than just professional.'

'The kids, I imagine.'

'And Sarah,' he added, 'but keep that very much to yourself. I know that you and she didn't always see eye to eye, but much of that was my fault. It's best for us as a family that she's here, and that we get along.'

'But? I can still hear it, hanging there.'

'But, there are good people through here, Mags, and they need leadership. There is no successor here, from within, and frankly, nobody else in Scotland either, except possibly for Andy, and he wouldn't want it.

'The force has already been disrupted and demoralised by Toni Field, God rest her, by her blind ambition and her half-arsed ideas. I'll hear about the likely runners when the job is advertised. If I don't fancy any of them, I won't rule out applying for the post myself.

'As I say that, I'm thinking that it sounds incredibly conceited, but I am a good cop and I do believe that I'm capable of doing the job, in spite of the misgivings I've always held about the size of this effing force.'

'That's not conceited,' she retorted, 'it's the plain truth. And beyond that,' she asked, 'will you go for the police commissioner post, if unification happens?'

'I haven't thought that far, but if I can overcome my doubts about policing half of Scotland, I suspect I'll be able to do the same about the rest.'

Maggie laughed. 'Now there's a sea change, after what you were saying in the press last weekend. If it's what you want, Bob, or what you feel you have to do, good luck, although I'll worry about who we might get here as your permanent successor.'

'I'm listening to her,' he said.

'Nice of you to say so, but I don't have the seniority. The councillors on the Police Authority won't have it.'

'The councillors will have it, because I'll bloody tell them. Their political parties all owe me favours and I will call them in, make no mistake.'

'But maybe I don't want it,' she suggested.

'Bollocks,' he laughed. 'You do, because your late husband would have insisted on it.'

He heard her sigh. 'You've got me there. Stevie would. Hell, though, my in-tray's stacked high here, and yours must be even bigger.'

'True, but I didn't just call you to shoot the breeze. I need your help in our top-priority investigation, Toni Field's assassination. You weren't really involved when it began, but are you up to speed now?'

'Yes,' she confirmed, 'fully.'

'In that case, you'll know it all began when we found the body of a man in Edinburgh, having been directed by the people who left him there, his ex-soldier buddies. They're now dead, having been killed on the scene after the Field hit. We've found their car, and what was in it, including the body of a well-known Glasgow hoodlum. Although we haven't linked his death to them, but there was nothing there that referred back to Cohen. Everything that he had is missing. That includes a MacBook Air laptop . . . you know, the super-light kind . . . and that's what we would most like to find.

'It may no longer exist. Freddy Welsh told me he burned his clothes but he didn't mention the computer. Maybe that went into the fire as well, but maybe not. Either way, Freddy needs to be asked; use Special Branch. Have George Regan go to see him. He's been well softened up, so he'll talk with no persuasion.

'If he can't help us, I would like you to institute a search, city-wide, but looking initially at the area near Welsh's yard, where Cohen died, and around Mortonhall, where he was found. Will you do that for me?'

'Of course. What's on the computer?'

'I don't know; his wife in London said his whole life was on it, but maybe that means nothing more than his iTunes collection and photographs of her and their kid. On the other hand, there may be the key that unlocks all the fucking boxes.

'We know already all there is to know about Byron Millbank; that's the alias he was given by somebody's friends at MI5. If what the widow told Lowell Payne and Neil McIlhenney is literally true, the MacBook, if it still exists and we can find it, may tell us everything we need to know about Beram Cohen, including the name of the person who paid him to kill the chief constable of Strathclyde, and why.'

'We'll get on it right away,' Steele promised.

'Thanks,' Skinner said. 'It's a long shot, I know, but if you don't buy a ticket, you won't win the raffle.'

Forty-One

'Where have you been, Sarge?' Banjo Paterson asked, as Provan came into the room. 'The DI was on the phone looking for you.'

'Did ye tell her I'll call her back?'

'No. I thought you might not want to. It's awkward with her being suspended.'

'She's not fuckin' suspended!' Provan yelled, flaring up in sudden fury. 'She's on family leave. If I hear that word used once more Ah'll have your nuts in a vice, son.'

The DC backed off, holding up his hands as if to keep the little man at bay. 'Sorry, sorry, sorry.'

'Aye, well . . . just mind your tongue from now on.'

'Understood. So,' he continued, 'where have you been? You went out that door like a greyhound. I've never seen you move so fast.'

'Doesnae do tae keep the chief constable waiting,' the DS said, a smirk of bashful pride turning up one corner of his mouth.

Paterson whistled. 'A summons from on high, eh? What did he want?'

'He wants us to do a wee job for him. Ah need you to get intae your computer and find me a phone number for the equivalent of the General Register Office in the Republic of Mauritius . . . wherever the fuck that is.'

263

'It's in the Indian Ocean. Give me a minute.'

Provan looked on as he bent over his keyboard, typed a few words, clicked once, twice, a third time, then scribbled on a notepad. 'There you are,' he announced, as he ripped off the top sheet and handed it over. 'That's the number of the head office of the Civil Status Division, in the Emmanuel Anquetil Building, Port Louis, Mauritius.' He glanced at the wall clock. 'I make that fifteen seconds short of the minute.'

'Since you're that fuckin' clever, can you access birth records through that thing?'

'I doubt it, but I'll have a look.' He turned back to the screen and to his search engine, but soon shook his head. 'No, sorry; not that I can see. You'll have to call them.'

'Will Ah be able to speak the language?'

'Possibly not; it's English.'

'Cheeky bastard,' the DS growled, but with a grin. He dialled the number Paterson had given him. The voice that answered was female, with a musical quality.

He introduced himself, speaking slowly, as if to a child. 'I am trying to find the record of a birth that may have taken place in your country two years ago.'

'Hold on please, sir. I will direct you to the correct department.'

He waited for two minutes and more, becoming more and more annoyed by the sound of a woman crooning in a tongue he did not understand, but which he recognised as having Bollywood overtones. Finally, she stopped in mid-chorus and was replaced by a man.

'Yes, sir,' he began. 'I understand you are a police officer and are seeking information. Is this an official inquiry?' His voice was clipped and his accent offered a hint that he might have understood the lyrics of the compulsory music.

'Of course it is,' Provan replied, his limited patience close to being exhausted, 'as official as ye can get. It's a murder investigation.'

'In that case, sir, how can I be of help?'

'Ah'm lookin' for a birth record. Ah don't know for certain that it'll be there, but ma boss has asked me to check it out. All we have is the name of the mother, Antonia Field.'

'What is the date?'

'We don't know that either, just that it was two years ago, in the period between January and June. The lady took six months off work tae have the child, so our guess is that it was probably born round about May or early June.'

'Field, you said?'

'Aye, but when she lived in Mauritius she was known as Day Champs.'

'Pardon?'

'Day Champs.'

'Are you trying to say Deschamps, officer?' He spelled it out, letter by letter.

'Aye, that's it.'

'Very good. I will search for you. If you tell me your number, I will call you back. That way I will know that you really are a police-man.'

'Fair enough.' Provan gave the official the switchboard number, and his own extension, then hung up.

With time to kill, he wandered into Lottie Mann's empty office, sat at her desk, picked up the phone and dialled her number.

She answered on the first ring. 'Dan?'

'Aye. How're ye doin', kid?'

'Terrible. Wee Jakey isn't buying the story about his dad any more. I've had to tell him the truth, and it's breaking his wee heart.'

'Maybe he'll be home soon,' the sergeant suggested, knowing as he spoke how unlikely that was.

'Get real, Dan,' she sighed. 'There's more. On Sunday I gave Scott thirty quid to take the wee man out for the day. They went to that theme park out near Hamilton. It occurred to me, that's a hell of a lot more than thirty quid's worth, so I had a rummage in his half of the wardrobe. I found an envelope in a jacket pocket, with four hundred and twenty quid in it. The envelope had a crest on the back: Brown Brothers Private Hire.'

Provan felt his stomach flip. 'Lottie,' he murmured. 'What are ye telling me this for? Ah'll have tae report it now.'

'No you won't. I've done that already, I called ACC Gorman and told her.' She paused. 'Here, did you think I was going to cover it up? For fuck's sake, Danny!' she protested. 'Don't you know me better than that?'

'Aye, right,' he sighed. 'Ah shouldae known better. Sorry, lass.'

'Have they interviewed him yet?' she asked. 'The big bosses?'

'They'll just be startin' about now. Ah'm no long back frae seein' the chief. He was just gettin' ready to go down there, him and Bridie.'

'Then God help my idiot husband. There's no prizes for guessing who'll play "bad cop" out of that pair, and I would not like that bugger sitting across the table from me. Why were you seein' him anyway?' she asked. 'Are you telling me there's been a development?'

'No, just something he asked me to handle for him.' As he spoke he heard a phone ring outside, then saw Paterson pick up his own line. The DC spoke a few words, then beckoned to him. 'I think that's ma contact now,' he said. 'Ah'll need tae go. Ah'll call ye if I hear anything from the interview.'

Forty-Two

The chief constable paused outside the door of the interview room. 'Who's his solicitor?' he asked his deputy.

'Her name's Viola Murphy,' Bridie Gorman told him. 'She's a hotshot in Glasgow, a solicitor advocate . . . that means . . .'

'I know what it means. She takes the case the whole way through, from first interview to appearing in the High Court. I know about her too. She was one of my daughter's tutors when she did her law degree. Alex couldn't stand her.'

'Will she know you?'

'Not personally. She might from the media, though.'

'Of course, she's bound to. How do you want to play this?'

'Very simply. We're going to walk in there and inside five minutes Mr Mann is going to be singing like a linty. He'll tell us everything we want to know. And you know what? It might even be true.'

Gorman was sceptical. 'Mmm. I know Scott. He used to be a cop, remember, a DC. He's interviewed people in his time, so he'll know what's going on in here. He'll know that he has a perfect right not to say a single word, and you can bet that's how Viola bloody Murphy will have advised him to play it.'

'We'll see. You keep her in her box and let me have a go at him. Remember, the right to silence goes both ways.' He opened the door and stepped into the interview room.

Scott Mann was seated at a rectangular table. His solicitor was by his side, but she shot to her feet. 'I don't appreciate being kept waiting like this,' she protested.

Skinner ignored her. He and Gorman took their places and she reached across and switched on the twin-headed recorder, then glanced up and over her shoulder to check that the video camera was showing a red light.

'I mean it,' Viola Murphy insisted. 'I am a busy woman, and you've kept me sitting here for an hour and a half. I promise you, as soon as this interview is over I'll be complaining to your chief constable.'

Now there's a real kick in the ego, Skinner thought. *She doesn't know who I am after all.*

'For the purposes of the tape,' the deputy began, 'I am ACC Bridget Gorman, accompanied by acting Chief Constable Bob Skinner, here to interview Mr Scott Mann, whose legal representative is also present.'

Murphy glared at Skinner, but could not hide her surprise at his presence. He could read her mind. *If the top man is doing this interview himself, my client is in much deeper shit than I thought.*

'Well? Get on with it,' she snapped.

'Ms Murphy,' Gorman said, 'you're here to advise Mr Mann of his legal rights and to ensure that these aren't infringed. But you don't speak for him, and you don't direct us.'

As they spoke, Skinner fixed his gaze on Scott Mann, drawing his eyes to him and locking them to his as if by a beam. He held him captive, not blinking, not saying a word, keeping his head rock steady. The silent exchange went on for almost a minute, until the prisoner could stand the invisible pressure no longer and broke free, staring down at the desk.

'Look at me,' the chief murmured, just loud enough for the recorders to pick up. 'I want to see what we're dealing with here. I want to see what sort of person you are. So far I've seen nothing; a nonentity in the literal sense of the word. They say you were a cop once. They say you're a loving husband and father. I don't see any of those people; they're all hiding from me. Look at me, Scott.'

'Mr Skinner!' Viola Murphy yelled, her voice shrill. 'I won't bloody have this! I protest!'

His head moved, very slightly, and his eyes engaged hers. She stared back, and shivered, in spite of herself.

'No you don't,' he told her, in a matter-of-fact voice. 'You sit there, you stay silent and you do not interfere with my interview. If you raise your voice to me again and use any more abusive language, I will suspend these proceedings and charge you with breach of the peace, and possibly also with obstruction. Then we will wait for another lawyer to arrive to represent both Mr Mann and you.'

'You're joking,' she gasped.

'I have a long and distinguished record of never joking, Ms Murphy. I advise you not to test me.' He turned back to Mann who was looking at him once more, astonished. 'Okay,' he said. 'I have your attention again.'

He fell silent once more, then reached inside his jacket, and produced what appeared to be three rectangles of white card. He turned the top one over, to reveal a photograph, of Detective Inspector Charlotte Mann, then laid it in front of her husband.

'For the tape,' he said, 'I am showing the prisoner a photo of his wife, a senior CID officer.'

He turned the second image over and placed it beside the first.

'For the tape,' he said, 'I am showing the prisoner a photo of his son, Jake Mann.'

He turned the third over and put it beside the other, watching Mann recoil in horror as he did so.

'For the tape,' he said, 'I am showing the prisoner a close-up photo of the body of Chief Constable Antonia Field, taken after she was shot three times in the head in the Royal Concert Hall, Glasgow, on Saturday evening.'

He paused, as the shock on the prisoner's face turned into something else: fear.

'What I'm asking you now, Mr Mann,' he continued, 'is this. How could you betray your wife and compromise her career, how could you condemn your wee boy to the whispers and finger-pointing of his school pals, by being part of the conspiracy that led to Toni Field lying there on the floor with her brains beside her?' His gaze hardened again; in an instant his eyes became as cold as dry ice. He reached inside his jacket again and produced a fourth image. It was grainy but clear enough.

'For the tape,' he said, 'I am showing the prisoner a photograph of himself in the act of handing a parcel to a second man, identified as Mr Basil Brown, also known as Bazza.'

He glanced at the solicitor. 'To anticipate what should be Ms Murphy's next question, we know that Mr Mann was not receiving the package because that image was taken from a CCTV recording that shows the exchange. However, Ms Murphy, your client did receive something from Mr Brown and that is also shown on the video.'

His hand went to his jacket once more, but this time to the right side pocket. He produced a clear evidence bag and slammed it on to the table. 'For the tape,' he announced, 'I am showing Mr Mann an envelope which his wife discovered today in their home and sent to us. It bears the crest of Mr Brown's taxi firm and contains four hundred and twenty pounds.

'It hasn't yet been tested for fingerprints and DNA but when it is we're confident it will link the two men. We can't ask Mr Brown about this as he was found dead in Glasgow on Sunday. However, Mr Mann, we don't need him, or even that evidence. We've recovered the paper from the package you handed over and we've got your DNA and prints, and his, from that. We can also prove that the package contained two police uniforms, worn as disguises by the men who assassinated Chief Constable Field.'

He stopped, and locked eyes with Mann yet again. His subject, the former detective, and veteran of many interviews, was white as a sheet and trembling.

'All that means,' Skinner continued, 'that we can prove you were an integral part of the plot to murder my predecessor, and it is our duty to charge you with that crime.

'You'll be lonely in the dock, Scott; it'll just be you and Freddy Welsh, the man who supplied the guns. Everybody else in the chain is dead, bar one, the man who gave the order for the hit, recruited the planner and funded the operation.' He paused. 'I think we've reached the point,' he went on, 'where you bury your face in your hands and burst into tears.'

And Mann did exactly that.

Skinner waited, allowing the storm to break, to run its course and then to abate. When the prisoner had regained a semblance of self-control, he asked him, 'What's your story, Scott? For I'm sure you have one.'

'My client,' Viola Murphy interposed, 'isn't obliged to say anything.'

The chief sighed, then smiled. 'I know that as well as you do,' he replied. 'And you know as well as I do that given the evidence we have against him, if your client takes that option and sticks to it, then the best he can hope for is a cell with a sea view.

'Silence will be no defence, Ms Murphy. The best you will be able to offer will be a plea in mitigation, and by that time it will be too late, because once he's convicted, the sentence will be mandatory. I'm offering the pair of you the chance to make that plea to me now, and through me to the fiscal, before he's charged with anything.'

'He said he was only borrowin' them,' Scott Mann blurted out. 'He said he would give me them back.'

'Okay,' the chief responded. 'Now for the big question. Did he tell you why he was borrowing them?'

'He said it was for a fancy dress dance, for charity. He told me that he and Cec wanted tae go as polis, and that they wanted it to be authentic.'

Skinner leaned forward. 'And you seriously believed that?' he exclaimed.

'I chose to. The fact is, sir, Ah didn't want to know what they were really for, because I didn't have any choice.'

'What do you mean by that? You had a very simple choice. You could have told your wife that Bazza Brown had asked you to acquire two police uniforms for him, and let her handle his request. Jesus, man, even if your half-arsed story is true, by not telling Lottie and co-operating with Brown, you condemned a woman to death.'

'I ken that now,' Mann wailed. 'But like I said, I didnae have any choice. Bazza's had a hold on me from way back, since I was a cop. It's no' just the drink that's a problem for me. Ah'm an addictive personality. Anything I do, I do it to the limit and beyond.'

'Drugs?'

'Not that: gambling. Horses, mostly, but there was the cards too. Bazza's old man was ma bookie, and then he died and the brothers took over. Bazza gave me a tab, extended credit, he called it, but what he was really doin' was lettin' me pile up debt. One night he introduced me to a poker school. Ah did all right early on, but I think that was rigged, to suck me in. Then I lost it all back, but Ah was beyond stoppin' by then. Bazza kept on stakin' me, letting my tab get bigger and bigger. It got completely out of control, until before I knew it I was about seventy-five grand down, on top of twelve and a half that I'd owed him before.'

He paused, and his eyes found Skinner, reversing their earlier roles. 'That was when I was truly fucked. He pressed me for the money, even though he knew I didnae have it. He got heavy. He threatened me, he threatened Lottie and he even threatened wee Jakey, even though he was only a baby then.

'I threatened him back, or Ah tried to, told him he was messing wi' a cop and that I could have him done. He laughed at me; then he put a blade to my throat and told me that it would be the easiest thing in the world for me to be found up a close in an abandoned tenement with a needle hangin' out my arm and an overdose of heroin in ma bloodstream. And Bazza did not kid about those things. So I agreed tae pay him off in kind.'

'How?' the chief murmured.

'I became his grass, within the force. I told him everything we knew about him. Every time he was under surveillance he knew about it. If one of his boys was ever done for anything, Ah'd fix the evidence, or I'd give Bazza a list of the witnesses against him and he'd sort them.'

'You mean he killed them?'

'No, he never needed to go that far. That would have been stupid, and he wasn't.'

'So you were his safety net within the force?'

'Aye. And I got uniforms for him, once before.'

'You did? When?'

'About six months before I was kicked out. He gave me the same story: a fancy dress party. That time he did give me them back, after they'd been used in a robbery at an MoD arms depot. All the guys that were in on it were caught eventually, apart from Bazza.' He frowned. 'That was a funny one, a Special Branch job rather than our CID.'

And I know why, Skinner thought. *Bazza was off limits on the NCIS database because he'd grassed on his accomplices in the robbery . . . or possibly set the whole thing up for MI5.*

'How did you get the uniforms, then and this time?' he asked.

'I've got a friend who works in the warehouse. I asked for a favour.'

'I don't imagine it was done out of the goodness of your friend's heart.'

Mann shot him a tiny smile. 'It was, as it happened.'

'Eh?' The chief constable was taken aback. 'So why did you have that cash from Bazza Brown?'

'Ah told him that Ah had to pay the supplier.'

'What's your friend's name?'

'Aw, sir. Do ye really need it?'

Skinner stared at him, then he laughed. 'Are you kidding me? Of course we do. The guy's as guilty as you are, almost. Name, now.'

'Chris McGlashan,' the prisoner sighed. 'Sergeant Chris McGlashan. And it's no a guy; it's Chris, as in Christine. Please, sir,' he begged. 'Can ye no' leave her out of it? Can you not say I broke intae the warehouse and stole them?'

'Why the bloody hell should I do that?'

'She'll deny it.'

'I'm sure she will, but we'll lift her DNA as well, from the package and the equipment.'

'Aw Jesus, no! Lottie . . .'

The obvious dawned. 'Aw Jesus, indeed!' Skinner exclaimed. 'You stupid, selfish, irresponsible son-of-a . . .' he snapped. 'This Chris, she's your bit on the side, isn't she? You're an addictive personality right enough, Scott. The booze, the horses, the women . . . Is she the only one you've been two-timing Lottie with, or have there been others?'

Mann seemed to slump into himself. 'One or two,' he sobbed.

'Mr Skinner,' Viola Murphy ventured, 'is this relevant to your investigation?'

'Probably not, but it does demonstrate what a weak, untrustworthy apology for a husband and father your client is . . . let alone what a disgrace he was as a serving police officer.'

He turned back to his subject. 'How did Bazza react when you were chucked out of the force, Scott? I don't imagine you could have worked off all that ninety-odd grand, just in doing him favours.'

'He was okay about it, more or less. He told me he'd still come to me for info, and that he'd expect me to get it through Lottie, but he never really did, no' until this business. To tell you the truth, I half expected tae wind up in the Clyde, but nothin' happened.'

'No, you idiot,' Skinner's laugh was scornful, 'because the debt was never real! The poker school, where you supposedly lost all that dough. Did it never occur to you that it wasn't just the first few hands that were rigged in your favour, but that the whole bloody thing was rigged against you, to set you up? Who were the other guys in the school? Did you know them?'

'A couple of them; they were Bazza's drivers in the taxi business.'

'Then they must have been on bloody good tips, to be able to sit in on such a high-roller card game. You got taken, chum, to the cleaners and back again, just like everyone else who was involved with your friend Mr Brown. Did you really never work any of this out?'

'No. Now you say it, I can see how he done it, but honest, sir, he had me scared shitless most of the time and on a string. He was even the reason I got chucked off the force.'

'What? Are you saying he fed you the booze?'

'It had nothin' tae do wi' the booze. The station commander caught me liftin' evidence against Cec, one time he got arrested for carvin' up a dope dealer that had crossed the pair of them. I photocopied the witness list. He walked in on me while Ah was doing it, and saw right away what it was about. He gave me a straight choice: either Ah resigned on health grounds and blamed alcoholism, or I'd go down for pervertin' the course of justice.'

'Why did he do that?'

'For Lottie's sake, he said.'

'And who was this station commander, this saviour of yours?'

'Michael Thomas,' Mann replied. 'ACC Thomas, he is now. He was a superintendent back then.'

'Indeed?' Skinner murmured. 'And what happened to Cec? I don't recall any serious assault convictions on his record.'

'The charges were dropped anyway. The two key witnesses withdrew their evidence. They must have got to them some other way.'

'Not through you?'

'No. I never knew who they were. Ah never got that far. They must have had another source in the force.'

Forty-Three

'Do you ever feel like you're in a movie, or a TV series?' Lowell Payne asked.

Neil McIlhenney laughed. 'All the bloody time. My wife's an actress, remember. As a matter of fact, she's just been offered the lead in a new TV series, about a single mother who's a detective, but it would have meant spending months at a time out in Spain, so she turned it down. Why d'you ask? Are you a frustrated thesp?'

'Hell, no. No, it's being down here, in this place, where all the names come straight off the telly. Highbury earlier on; now it's the Elephant and bloody Castle, for God's sake. Makes me feel like Phil Mitchell.'

'Nah, you've got too much hair, mate.'

'Where does the name come from anyway?'

'I'm told by my cockney colleagues that it goes back to one of the worshipful companies that had an elephant with a castle on its back on its coat of arms. Somehow that became the name of a coaching inn on this site, about two hundred and fifty years ago.'

'So it's got fuck all to do with real elephants, or castles.'

'Absolutely fuck all.'

The two detectives were standing on the busy thoroughfare they had been discussing, having been dropped off by their driver in the bus lane that ran past the Metropolitan Tabernacle Baptist Church, a great grey pillared building.

'Where's the office?' the visitor asked.

'On the other side of the road, on top of that shopping complex; that's what I'm told.'

Payne looked at the dual carriageway, and at the density of the fast-moving traffic. 'Crossing that's going to be fun,' he complained.

'No. It's going to be dead easy,' his companion replied, heading towards a circular junction. At the end of the road was a subway, running under the highway and surfacing through the Elephant and Castle tube station. 'The office should be just around the corner here,' he said, as they stepped out into the sunlight once more.

They walked up a ramp that led into a shopping centre, and found the block without difficulty, and the board in the foyer that listed the tenants, floor by floor.

'There we are,' McIlhenney declared. 'Rondar Mail Order Limited, level three, north. Just two floors up.'

They took the elevator, at Payne's insistence. 'I'd an early start, and I am knackered. Buggered if I'm walking when there's an option.'

As they stepped out, they saw, to their left, the Rondar logo, emblazoned across double doors of obscured glass. There was no bell, no entrance videophone, so the two officers walked straight through them, into an open space furnished with half a dozen desks and a few tables. At the far end, there were two partitioned areas, affording privacy. They counted five members of staff, all female, all white, all dark-haired, all in their twenties.

'Fuck me,' Payne whispered, 'it's like a room full of Amy Winehouses. I'm sure you don't have to be Jewish to work here, for that would be illegal, wouldn't it, but I'm even surer it helps.'

The woman seated at the desk nearest to the entrance looked up at them. They judged that she was probably the oldest of the five. 'Yes?' she said.

'Mrs Radnor, please,' the DCS replied, showing her his warrant card. 'Police. I'm Chief Superintendent McIlhenney, from the Met, and this is Chief Inspector Payne, from Strathclyde.'

'Aunt Jocelyn's busy, I'm afraid. She's making a new product video, and can't be disturbed.'

McIlhenney smiled. 'I think you'll find that she can. But we'd all prefer it if you did it, rather than us.'

For a moment or two, the niece looked as if she might put up an argument, but there was something in the big cop's kind eyes that told her she would lose. And so, instead, she sighed and stood. 'If you'll follow me.' They did. 'Can you tell me what this is about?' she asked as they reached the private room on the right.

'Family matter,' Payne told her.

'But I'm . . .' she began, swallowing the rest of her protest when he shook his head. 'Wait here, please.' She rapped on the door and stepped inside.

They waited. For a minute, then a second, and then a third. McIlhenney's fist was clenched ready to knock, when it reopened and Jocelyn Radnor, glamorous, late fifties and unmistakably Golda's mother, stepped out. She did not look best pleased, even under the heavy theatrical make-up that she wore.

'Gentlemen,' she exclaimed, 'I haven't a clue what this is about, but it had better be worth it. I've been trying to get that bloody promo right for an hour now, and I had finally cracked it when Bathsheba came in and ruined it.'

'We're sorry about that,' McIlhenney said, lying, 'but it is important, and better dealt with in your office.'

'If you say so,' she sighed. 'Come on.' She led them into the other room; they found themselves looking down the Elephant and Castle, back towards the tabernacle. The furniture had seen better days, but it was quality. She offered them each a well-worn leather chair and sat in her own. 'What's it all about, then? "A family matter," my niece said.'

'We want to talk to you about your son-in-law,' Payne replied.

She tilted her head and looked at him. 'You're one too?' She chuckled. 'Scotland Yard is finally living up to its name. What about my son-in-law?' she asked, serious in the next instant. 'Why are you asking about Byron?'

'We'll get to that. Can you tell us, how did he come to work for you?'

'We needed a buyer, simple as that. Jesse, my late husband, always handled that side of the business, from the time when he founded it. That was the way it worked; he bought, I sold. Eventually, there came a time when he decided to plan for what he called "our retirement". What he really meant was his own death, for he was twenty years older than me and had heart trouble, more serious than I knew. So he recruited Byron.'

'How?'

She frowned at the DCI. 'I don't know; he recruited him, that's all. I can't remember.'

'Think back, please. Did he place an ad in the newspapers, or specialist magazines? Did he use headhunters?'

Her eyebrows rose, cracking the make-up on her forehead along the lines of the wrinkles that lay underneath. 'That was it. I asked where he found him and he said he had used specialists.'

'Do you know anything about his career before he joined you?'

'Jesse said he had worked for other mail order firms, in his time, and for a bank, but he never specified any of them.'

'Doesn't he have a personnel file, Mrs Radnor?' McIlhenney asked.

'Please, officer,' she sighed, with a show of exasperation. 'This is a family business. We don't need such things. I know he was born somewhere on the south coast, although I can't remember where, I know that he never had a father and that his mother is dead, I know that he's nowhere near as good a buyer as my husband was, I know that he's a very good husband to my daughter, and I know that he spent some time in Israel, a lot of time.'

'How do you know that last bit?'

'The accent would have told me, if he hadn't. He didn't get all of that in Sussex. I asked him about it, not long after he joined us; he said that after his mother died he went to work in a kibbutz.'

'Do they have mail order in kibbutzes?' Payne murmured.

'Of course not, but after that he stayed in Tel Aviv for another few years, or so he said.'

'You didn't believe him?'

'Let's say he was never very specific.' She paused. 'Look, to be absolutely frank, my guess has always been that when Jesse took him on he was doing a favour for a friend from the old days.'

'The old days where?' the DCI asked.

'My late husband was a soldier in his earlier life, a major in the Israeli army. He fought in the Six Day War, back in sixty-seven. He didn't come to Britain until nineteen seventy-two.'

'But he kept his links with Israel? Is that what you're saying?'

'Yes, through work with Jewish charities. He had a couple of friends at the embassy as well.'

'So, Mrs Radnor,' McIlhenney murmured, 'if we told you that the man you've known all these years as Byron Millbank was known before that as Beram Cohen, am I right in thinking you wouldn't be all that surprised?'

'Not a little bit.' She gazed at the DCS. 'So what's he done, that you're here asking about him?'

'He's died, I'm afraid.'

Jocelyn's hands flew to her mouth, but she regained her composure after a few seconds. 'Oh my. That I did not expect. Golda, my daughter, does she know?'

'Yes, we've just left her. You'll probably want to go to her when we're finished here.'

'Of course. When did this happen? Where? And how?'

'Last week, in Edinburgh, of natural causes.' He carried on, explaining how it had happened and what his companions had done with his body.

She listened to his story without a single interruption. 'What was he doing with these men?' she asked, when he was finished.

'Planning a murder,' he replied. 'You've probably heard of the shooting of a senior police officer in Glasgow on Saturday evening. Your son-in-law organised the whole thing. The two guys who buried him were his comrades, soldiers like he was in Israel, working these days for money, not for flags.'

'Yes,' she acknowledged, 'I read of it. His buddies, they're dead too, yes?'

'Killed at the scene.'

'So Byron was a soldier. That's what you're saying?' McIlhenney nodded. 'Israeli army, I guess.'

'That and more. Latterly he was Mossad, the Israeli secret service.'

'So was my husband,' she told them, 'in the old days, and for a while after he came to Britain. It all fits. So why did they send him over here?'

'From what I'm told, he'd become an embarrassment, so he was relocated. He kept in touch with his old community though. The concert hall killing wasn't the only job he did, not by a long way. I guess it all helped pay for your daughter's lifestyle.'

'I have wondered about that,' she admitted. 'And Golda, does she know any of this?'

'Only that her husband had another identity.'

'Am I allowed to tell her the rest?'

'If you want to, but do you? Isn't being widowed enough for her to be going on with?'

'True,' she agreed. 'So why did you tell me?'

'Because you don't strike me as the sort of person who'd fall for a phoney cover story when we say we need to take Byron's computer and all the other records he kept in this office.'

'I'll take that as a compliment,' Jocelyn said.

'So, can we have it?'

'I imagine that's a rhetorical question, and that you have a warrant.'

'Call it a courteous request, but yes, we do.'

'Warrant or not,' she retorted, 'I'd be happy to cooperate, and let you take everything you need. Unfortunately, someone's beaten you to it.'

'Eh?' Payne exclaimed. 'What do you mean? Nobody else knows about this branch of the investigation.'

'That's irrelevant. This is London, Chief Inspector, and there's a depression. Two nights ago we had a burglary. The thieves took a few pieces of not very valuable jewellery, and they took Byron's computer. Of course, I reported it to your people, as we have to for the insurance claim, but frankly, they didn't seem too interested. That's how it is these days.'

Forty-Four

'What do you think, Bridie?' Skinner asked. They were in her office; she held a mug of coffee in a meaty hand, he held a can of diet Irn Bru.

'I think,' she began, 'that I accept his story about the fancy dress. Okay, he knew he was being spun a line, and that he chose not to ask questions, but I don't believe that Scott Mann would knowingly be a part of any conspiracy to murder, or that if we charged him with that, we'd get a conviction.

'However, we can tie him to those uniforms beyond reasonable doubt, so he's not walking away. I would propose that we charge him with theft, and his girlfriend, assuming we do get her DNA from the packaging. We'll get guilty pleas for sure, I could read it in Viola Murphy's dark Satanic eyes.'

The chief gave a small nod. 'I agree with that. What about McGlashan? Do we let her resign quietly or do the full disciplinary thing?'

'Formal,' Gorman replied, without hesitation. 'If I could I'd put her in the public stocks in George Square.'

Skinner laughed. 'I once suggested to my soon to be ex-wife that her party should propose that as a way of dealing with Glasgow's Ned hooligan problem. She took me seriously, started arguing that the rival gangs would turn out in force to throw rocks at them. So I started arguing back to wind her up. She got angrier and angrier, wound up calling me a fucking fascist. Looking back, it was maybe the beginning of the end. We won't go that far with this lady, but yes, I agree, she has to be made an example of.' The humour left his expression. 'The consequences might be worse than an hour being pelted with rotten fruit. Imagine how Lottie's going to react when she finds out.'

His deputy sighed. 'Need she?'

'She's bound to. Her husband's going to court and so's his girlfriend. We'll make sure there's no mention of a relationship during the hearing, but she'll figure it out, for sure. It might be best for the pair of them if the sheriff puts them out of her reach for a few months.'

'Do you think he will?'

'I'm bloody sure of it. They've got to go down.'

'And what about the elephant?' she asked.

'Which one would that be?' he murmured.

'The great big one in this bloody room: Michael Thomas.'

'I've been trying to pretend it isn't there,' the chief admitted.

'But it is,' Gorman insisted. 'Scott Mann claims that Thomas caught him photocopying a witness list for the Brown brothers, and hushed it up. For Lottie's sake, indeed. Do you buy that?'

'No. Not for a second. If what Mann says is true, then he had an obligation to call in another officer to corroborate what had happened and then to charge him.'

'So why didn't he?'

'I'll let you speculate on that, Bridie,' Skinner said. 'I'm too new here.'

'If you insist. The witnesses against Cec Brown were nobbled anyway, and as Scott said, that suggests Bazza had another source. According to his story, Michael Thomas saw the list, and we know that he kept quiet about Mann nicking it. That has to raise the possibility that he was that source. If he'd done what he should have, the investigation would have gone all the way to Brown, the witnesses would have been protected and both brothers would have been finished.'

'I can't argue against that. So what do you suggest we do about it? Get the brush out again and sweep it under the carpet? After all, Brown's dead and it will only be Scott's word against his.'

'We couldn't do that, not even if we wanted to, and I don't believe that either of us do. Viola Murphy heard the accusation, and she has the copy of the recording that we were bound by law to give her. She's riding the bloody elephant in the bloody room!'

'Colourful but true. What's your recommendation?'

'We take a further statement from Mann, not as an accused person, but as a witness, and we give it to the fiscal. What do you say? New or not, you are where the buck stops.'

'Yes and no,' the chief said. 'Action has to be taken, but not by us. I suggest that you call in Andy Martin, and the Serious Crimes Agency. I don't want to do it myself, or to be involved, because Andy's in a relationship with my daughter. That might not have mattered in the past, but we have to be spotless here. His people have to take the statement, and have to decide what happens after that. Almost certainly that will not involve the local fiscal. For all we know she could be a member of the Michael Thomas fan club. See to it.'

'Will do, Bob. After the statement's taken, what will we do with Scott?'

'We charge him, and his girlfriend as soon as we have a DNA match. Murphy will probably apply for bail. Likely she'll get it, since we have no strong grounds for opposing it, so we might as well let them go, until their first court appearance.'

'What about Lottie?' Gorman asked. 'Are you going to tell her about this . . . new development?'

'Hell no! Dan Provan can do that. I'm nowhere near brave enough.'

Forty-Five

Detective Sergeant Dan Provan sat at his absent boss's desk staring at the notes he had made. He was unsure of the significance of what he had discovered. Instinctively he doubted that it had any relevance to the investigation on which he was engaged. But one thing he did know: it was well outside his comfort zone as a police officer.

He had spent most of his thirty-something year career catching petty thieves and putting them out of business, sorting out those who thought that violence was an acceptable means of self-expression, or in one short but horrible chapter, pursuing and prosecuting those he would always refer to only as 'beasts', sicko bastards who preyed upon children, their own on one or two occasions, leaving them with physical and emotional scars they would carry through life.

Always, those issues had been clear, and he had known exactly what he was doing and why. But this stuff, Glasgow hoodlums coming up with big red 'hands off' notices on the national intelligence database, and the latest, Mauritian mysteries, it was all unfocused, and way outside the rules of the game that he was used to playing. Yet it excited him, gave him the kind of thrill he had experienced as a young man, before it had been washed away by a river of sadness and cynicism.

When the door opened he did not look up. Instead he growled,

'Banjo, will you fuck off! Did Ah no' say Ah want to be alone in here?'

'Indeed?' a strong baritone voice replied. 'Anyone less like Greta Garbo I cannot imagine.'

Provan gulped and shot to his feet. 'Sorry, sir,' he said to the chief constable. 'Ah thought it was DC Paterson. Around here we're no' used to the brass comin' tae see us. Always it's the other way around, and usually for the wrong reasons. As a matter of fact,' he continued, 'I was just about tae ask for an appointment wi' you.'

Skinner laughed. 'You make me sound like the fucking dentist. Sit down, man, and relax. Before we get to your business, I've got another task for you. Not a very pleasant one, but I reckon you'd rather do it that anyone else.'

'Sounds ominous, gaffer.' He took a guess. 'Scott Mann?'

'Got it in one. ACC Gorman and I have not long finished interviewing him. He's going to be charged.'

'Conspiracy to murder?' the DS murmured.

'No, he'll only be charged with theft. We're satisfied that he had no specific knowledge of why Bazza Brown wanted the uniforms. He's heading for Barlinnie though, or Low Moss.'

'Still,' Provan countered, 'all things considered, that's a result for him. It'll no' be nice for Lottie and the wee fella, but a hell of a lot better than if he got life.'

'True, but it's not as simple as that. There will be a co-accused, Sergeant Christine McGlashan, who works in the store warehouse.'

Provan stiffened in his chair. 'Christine McGlashan?' he repeated. 'She used to be a DC, until she got promoted back intae uniform. She worked alongside Scott in CID and it was an open secret that he was porkin' her. But that was before he met Lottie. Are you gin' tae tell me he still is?'

The chief constable nodded. 'I'm afraid so. You'll see that's why

289

you're the best man to explain the situation to Lottie. That said, if you think it's Mission Impossible, you don't have to accept it. This tape will self-destruct in five seconds and I'll handle it myself.'

'No, sir, Ah'll do it. You're right; it's best she hears that sort of news from someone who knows the both o' them.'

'Thanks, Dan. None of this is going to go unnoticed or unrewarded, you realise that?'

'Appreciated, boss, but that "Thanks", that was enough. There's no way you could reward me, other than promotion to DI, and I wouldn't accept that. I am where Ah want to be. If you can make sure that for as long as Ah'm here Ah'll be alongside the Big Yin, tae look after her, that'll be fine.'

'For as long as I'm here myself, I'll make sure that happens. That's a promise, Dan.'

'In which case, Ah hope you stick around.' He frowned. 'What's happenin' tae McGlashan?'

'She'll have been arrested by now, and on her way here. You and Paterson can interview her, but make sure you listen to the recording of Mann's interview first. Once you've done that, you can charge them both, then release them on police bail, pending a Sheriff Court appearance.' He took a breath, then went on. 'Now, what were you coming to tell me?'

'The thing you asked me tae do, sir,' Provan responded. 'Ah've got a result, sort of. There's a hospital in Port Louis . . . that's the capital of Mauritius,' he offered, with a degree of pride. 'It's called the Doctor Jeetoo. Its maternity department has a record of a patient called Antonia Day Champs. She had a baby there, a wee girl, on May the twenty-third, two years ago. It was born by caesarean section, and she was discharged a week after. The address they had for her was in a place called Peach Street. I checked the local property register; it said it's owned by a woman called Sofia Day Champs.'

'Toni's mother,' Skinner volunteered. 'She got knocked up and went home to Mum.'

The sergeant sniggered. 'Makes a change from goin' tae yer auntie's for a few months, like lassies used tae do in the days before legal abortions. Ah wonder why she didnae have one herself, given that she was such a career woman. Her clock must have been tickin' Ah suppose.'

'Who knows?'

'I spoke to the ward sister. She said she remembered her. She said that a woman came to visit her when she was in, but no husband. There was one man came to visit her, though; much older, about seventy. The sister heard Sofia call him "Grandpa". She said his face was familiar, like somebody she'd seen in the papers, but that whoever he was he was pretty high-powered, because the consultant was on his best behaviour when he was there, and Antonia had a room tae herself.'

'Then I guess that could have been her father. Marina told me he was a bigwig in government, and Sofia was his mistress. So what about the birth registration, Dan?' the chief asked. 'That's what I'm really interested in.'

'Then you're no' goin' tae like this. Mauritius is more modern than ye'd think. All the latest records are stored on computer. The doctor who attends the birth gives the parents a form tae say that it's happened, but that's the only written record, apart from the official birth certificate that the parents are given when they register it. And you have tae do that; it's the law. The government guy Ah spoke to checked the whole period that she was out there after the twenty-third of May, and there is no record of a birth bein' registered. He's in no doubt about that.'

'Bugger!'

The DS held up a hand: it occurred to Skinner that one day he would make an excellent lollipop man. 'However,' he declared, 'he did say that he'd found an anomaly. On the thirtieth of May, a week later, there were forty-six births notified, but when he looked at the computer, he noticed that number seven two six four is followed by seven two six six. There's a number missing; he had his computer folk look at it. They said it had been hacked. How about that then, boss? D'ye think Grandpa was powerful enough to have the record removed?'

'I doubt it, Dan,' Skinner replied. 'But I know someone who is.'

Forty-Six

'So much for the tour of the capital,' Lowell Payne grumbled.

'We drove past the Tower of London, didn't we?' Neil McIlhenney pointed out. 'And if you went up on the roof here and found the right spot, you'd be able to see the top of Big Ben. Not only that, you've seen the home of the mighty Arsenal Football Club. All for free too, in the most expensive city I know.' He grinned. 'Tell you what. You check in with the King in the North and I'll take you for a pint and a sandwich. It's getting on past lunchtime and I'm a bit peckish myself.'

'I've been trying but he's not in his office, and his mobile's switched off.'

'Maybe he's still doing that interview you told me about.'

'If he is and the bloke hasn't been charged yet, he'll be entitled to get up and walk out.'

'He's probably still hiding under the table. Big Bob doesn't like bent cops, even ex ones. Try him again, go on.'

The DCI took out his phone and pressed the contact entry for Skinner's direct line. He let it ring six times, and was about to hang up when it was answered.

'Lowell?'

'Yes, Chief.'

'How's it going down there? Got anything useful?'

'Some, but don't get excited. We've worked out how an Israeli ex-paratrooper and disgraced spook hit man came to get a job as a jewellery buyer with a London mail order company. His late father-in-law was Mossad, once upon a time.'

'Surprise me,' Skinner drawled, with heavy sarcasm. 'How did you find that out?'

'We decided to be forthcoming with his mother-in-law. She was equally frank in return; she told us.'

He chuckled. 'Giving the guy a job, that's one thing; marrying your daughter off to him might be taking it a bit too far.'

'You'd think so, but the impression we're getting is of a popular, charming bloke. The wife's devastated. It was just starting to hit home when we left.'

'How about the mother-in-law? How did she take it?'

'Calmly. She was upset, of course, but it didn't come as a bombshell to find out that poor Byron had a second line of business. Before we left, she told us she hoped he was better at that than he was at the jewellery buying.'

'Did you get anything else from your visit, apart from a compendium of Jewish mother-in-law jokes? Did you take his computer?'

'No, and that's the real news I have for you. Somebody beat us to it; Rondar Mail Order had a break-in last Friday night. A few small items were taken, but the main haul was Byron Millbank's computer. I'm sorry about that, boss, but this trip's been pretty much a waste of time.'

'Like hell it has,' the chief retorted. 'There are three possibilities here, Lowell. One, the break-in was exactly that, a routine office burglary. Two, it was an inside job, staged to hide something incrim-inating from the sharp eyes of the VAT inspectors. Three, someone who knew about Byron's background, and the fact that he was no

294

longer in the land of the living, decided to make sure that nothing embarrassing had been left behind him. I know which of those my money's on. You've had a result, of sorts, Lowell. What was only a suspicion until now, it's confirmed in my book. The cleaners have been in, and not just in London.'

'But what have they been covering up?'

'Work it out for yourself. It's too hot for any phone line, especially a mobile that can be easily monitored. The thing that's getting to me is that they've been too damn good at it. If I'm right, I know what the big secret is, but I can't even come close to proving it, and the bugger is that I don't believe I ever will. Our investigation into Toni Field's murder is dead in the water, as dead as she is.'

'Are you sure?' Payne asked.

'I don't believe in miracles, brother.'

'What do you want me to do, then?'

'You might as well come home. Get yourself on to an evening flight. I'll see you tomorrow.'

As the DCI ended the call, he realised that McIlhenney was gazing at him. 'How did he take it?' he asked.

'He reckons that's it. We're stuffed. He's going to close the inquiry. He sounded pretty pissed off. I know he hates to lose.'

The chief superintendent shook his heard. 'No,' he said. 'You don't know. He refuses to lose. You wait and see. He's not finished yet.'

'He says he doesn't believe in miracles.'

'Then he's lying. When he's around they happen all the time.'

Forty-Seven

'Bastards!' Skinner exclaimed. The room was empty but there was real vehemence in his voice. 'It's like someone's farted in a busy pub. You're pretty sure who it was but you've got no chance of proving it and the more time passes, the more the evidence dissipates.'

Frustrated, he reached for his in-tray and began to examine the pile of correspondence, submissions and reports that his support team had deemed worthy of his attention. He had planned that it would go to Lowell for further filtering but his absence had landed it all on his desk.

'Commonwealth Games, policing priorities,' he read, from the top sheet on the pile. 'One, counter-terrorism,' he murmured. 'Two, counter-terrorism, three counter-terrorism, four, stop the Neds from mugging the punters.' He laid the paper to one side for consideration later, probably at Sarah's, and picked up the next item, a letter.

It was addressed to Chief Constable Antonia Field, from the Australian Federal Police Association, inviting her to address its annual conference, to be held in Sydney, the following December.

He scribbled a note, 'Call the sender, tell them about Toni's death. If he asks me to do it, decline with regret on the ground that I have no idea where I'll be in December,' clipped it to the letter and dropped it into his out-tray.

He worked on for ten minutes, finding it more and more difficult to maintain his concentration. He felt his eyes grow heavy and
realised for the first time that he had missed lunch. A week before he
would have poured himself a mug of high-octane coffee, but Sarah
had made him promise to give up, and he had promised himself
that he would never cheat on her again, in any way. Instead, he
took a king-size Mars Bar from his desk drawer and consumed it in
four bites.

As he waited for the energy boost to hit his system, he picked up his
direct telephone, found a number and dialled it.

He hoped that it would be Marina who answered rather than Sofia;
and so it was.

'Bob Skinner,' he announced.

'Good afternoon. This is a pleasant surprise . . . do you have
something to tell us about Antonia's death?'

'No, sorry. In fact I have something to ask you. When were you
going to get round to telling me about Toni's child?'

He counted the silence; one second, two seconds, three . . .

'Ah, so you know about that.'

'Of course. You must have realised that the post-mortem was bound
to reveal it.'

'Yes, I suppose I did. Maman and I hoped you wouldn't regard it as
relevant. It isn't really, is it?'

'Probably not,' he agreed, 'but when we set out to create a picture
of someone's life, it has to be complete. We can't leave things out,
arbitrarily, for personal, or even for diplomatic, reasons.'

'No, I accept that now. We should have volunteered it.'

'What happened to the child?'

'She's here, with us. When you visited us the other day, she was
upstairs, playing in the nursery that Antonia made for her there. She

was born in Mauritius, two years ago. Her name is Lucille; she's such a pretty little thing. Normally she lives in London, with Maman, in a house that Antonia's father bought for them. He is widowed now, and when he heard of the child he was overwhelmed. He had never recognised my sister as his daughter, not formally, not until then.'

'Does he know she's dead?'

'Oh yes. Maman called him, straight away. She said he was very upset. So he should have been. I don't care for the man, even though I've never met him.'

'Who's Lucille's father?' Skinner asked.

'I don't know,' Marina confessed. 'Antonia never told me, and she never told Maman. But she registered the birth herself, in Mauritius. You should be able to find out there.'

'That's right,' he agreed, 'we should.' *We should*, he thought, *but some bugger doesn't want us to.*

'When you do, will you let me know, please. Maman and I have been looking for Lucille's birth certificate among Antonia's papers, but we can't find it.'

'Sure, will do. But until then we're guessing. Those men friends you told me about, her lovers: she never gave you any clue to their names?'

'No, not really. She gave one or two of them nicknames. The DAC in the Met, for example, she called him "Bullshit", for whatever unimaginable reason. The mandarin she called "Chairman Mao", and the QC was always "Howling Mad". Other than that, she never let anything slip.'

'You mentioned five men in her life,' the chief said, 'but when we met you said she'd had six relationships in the time you lived with her. Was the sixth Michael Thomas?'

She laughed. 'Him?' she exclaimed. 'You know about that?'

'The whole bloody force seems to know about that. He was seen leaving the flat she was renting, far too late for it to have been a work visit.'

'Then that was careless of her, and not typical. It was very definitely a one-night stand. It was also the only time that she ever had a man when she and I were under the same roof. Actually, I found it quite embarrassing,' she confessed. 'The walls were thin.' He heard what might have been a giggle. 'It's very off-putting to hear your sister faking it. Next morning I complained. She laughed and said not to worry, that it had been what she described as "tactical sex" and wouldn't happen again.

'No,' she continued, 'her most recent relationship was still going on, and had been for at least three months. I'm more than a little surprised that I haven't heard from the poor man; he must be distraught, for they were close. For the first time I sensed that there was no motive behind the relationship, nothing "tactical" about it.'

'I don't suppose she told you his name, either.'

'Ah, but this time she did,' Marina exclaimed. 'That's why I believe it was serious. She told me he is called Don Sturgeon, and that he works as an IT consultant. She never brought him home and she never introduced us, but I saw him once when he came to pick her up. He is very attractive: clean-cut, well-dressed, almost military looking.'

Skinner felt his right eyebrow twitch. 'Indeed?' he murmured. 'Anything else that you can recall about him?'

'Yes,' she replied at once. 'His skin tone; it's almost the same as mine. It made me wonder if he was Mauritian too, and that's what she saw in him.'

'In this life,' the chief observed, 'anything is possible. Marina,' he exclaimed as a picture formed in his mind, 'are you doing anything, right now?'

'No. Maman is with Lucille, so I'm free.'

'Then I'd like you to come into the office, quick as you can.'

Forty-Eight

Lowell Payne had seen the interior of Westminster Abbey several times, but only on television, when it had been bedecked for royal weddings or draped in black for funerals, and packed with celebrants or mourners. As he stepped inside the great church for the first time, he found himself humming 'Candle in the Wind' without quite recalling why.

It was the sheer age of the place that took hold of him, the realisation when he read the guide that its origins were as old as England itself, and that the building in which he stood went back eight centuries.

He knew as little of architecture as he did of history, but he appreciated at once that the abbey was not simply a place of worship, but also of celebration, a great theatre created for the crowning of kings and, occasionally, of queens.

In common with most first-time visitors, he paused at the tomb of the Unknown Soldier, wondering for a moment whether the occupant's nearest and dearest had been told secretly of the honour that had been done him. 'Somebody must have known,' he whispered as he looked down, drawing an uncomprehending smile and a nod from a Japanese lady tourist by his side.

He moved on and found a memorial stone, commemorating sixteen poets of the First World War, recognising not a single name.

Charles Dickens he knew, though, and the Brontë sisters, and Rabbie Burns, and Clement Attlee. Stanley Baldwin was lost on him, but somewhere the name Geoffrey Chaucer rang a bell.

His mobile did not ring, but it vibrated in his pocket. He took it out, feeling as if he was committing a form of sacrilege, until he realised that half of the tourists in the place were using smart-phones as cameras.

He read the screen and took the call. 'Chief,' he said, keeping his voice as low as he could, and moving away from the throng of which he had become a part.

'Where the hell are you?' Skinner asked. 'You at the station already?'

'No, I've got time to kill, so I'm doing the tourist thing. Does the name Stanley Baldwin mean anything to you?'

'Of course. He was a Tory prime minister between the wars, and even less use than most of them. He took a hard line on Mrs Simpson and made the King abdicate, but he didn't mind Hitler nearly as much. Bloody hell, Lowell, what did you do at school? You'll be asking me who Attlee was next.'

'No, I know about him. What can I do for you?'

'Cancel your return flight. I'd like you to stay down there overnight. Can you do that?'

'Sure. Has there been a development?'

'Maybe. I'm not sure. But if something plays out . . .' His voice drifted off with his thoughts for a few seconds. 'I'll know in a couple of hours, but meantime you just hang on down there. I'll be back in touch.'

The conversation ended with as little ceremony as it had begun, leaving Payne staring at his phone. 'If you say so, Bob,' he murmured. 'I wonder if I can put a West End show on expenses.'

Forty-Nine

Skinner smiled as he gazed at the ceiling. *Stanley Baldwin*, he thought. He guessed where Payne had been when he had reached him. The abbey was one of his favourite stopping-off places when he was in London.

London. For all that the prospect of an independently governed Scotland was looming, the great monolith in the south remained the centre of power. He had decided that he would vote 'Yes!' with his heart in the referendum, but he had no illusions over the difficulty his country faced in extricating itself from the British state, if that was what the majority chose.

Scotland might become a nation, fully self-governing, a member of both the European Union and the UN, but it would still share a head of state and an island with its English neighbours and their common problems of security would remain. He knew better than most what that would mean. MI5 would continue to operate north of what would have become a national border.

Even if a future first minister had access to its work and to those of its secrets that affected his interests, he would have a very small voice in decisions that affected its remit and its funding, and no control at all over its activities. Strings would continue to be pulled in secret, by secret people, like his friend Amanda Dennis and her immediate boss,

Sir Hubert Lowery, the director of the service.

It would be up to the new Scotland to come to terms with the need to have its own counter-espionage service, to protect itself against potential threats from wherever they came, even if that was Westminster. He had discussed this with Clive Graham, at a meeting so private that he had kept it from Aileen. Whatever their differences on the unification of the police forces, the two men were agreed that if the time came, their country would need its own secret service. There was also an understanding over the man who would head it.

His smile was long gone when the phone sounded; he flicked the switch that put it on speaker. 'Yes?'

'Sir,' a woman replied, 'it's PC May in reception. I'm very sorry to bother you, and I wouldn't normally, but there's a man here, an odd-looking wee chap, and he's asking to see you. He won't give me his name but he says to tell you that he's been sent by Mr McGuire in Edinburgh. What should I do?'

'He's okay,' Skinner told her. 'He's a tradesman I need to solve a practical problem. Take him to the lift, then come up with him to this floor, straight away. I'll meet you there and take charge of him.'

He hung up and walked from his office. He was waiting by the elevator door when it opened less than two minutes later. A small wiry man with a pinched face and a jailhouse complexion stepped out.

The chief looked towards his escort. 'Thanks, Constable. I'll call you to come and collect him when we're done. By the way,' he added. 'I'm expecting another visitor quite soon. Let me know directly he arrives.'

She was nodding as the lift door closed, leaving Skinner alone with his visitor. 'Well, Johan,' he exclaimed. 'It's good to see you, under different circumstances from the usual.'

Johan Ramsey was dressed in baggy jeans and brown jerkin, over a

304

Rangers football top that his host judged, from its design, to be at least three seasons old. He was one of those people whose only expression was furtive. 'Is this legit?' he asked.

Skinner laughed. 'Johan, I'm the chief fucking constable; of course it's legit. A wee bit unorthodox, that's all. Come on.'

He led the way to his office, and into his private room, where he pulled aside the door that concealed the safe. 'That's the problem,' he said. 'My predecessor took the combination to her grave, and I can't open it. Six digits, I'm told.'

Ramsey took a pair of spectacles with one leg from a pocket in his jerkin, and perched them on the narrow bridge of his nose. He appraised the task for a few seconds, then nodded, and declared, 'A piece of piss,' with a degree of pride. 'If you'll just step into the other room, sir, Ah'll have it open in a couple of minutes.'

The chief's jaw dropped, then he laughed. 'Jo, if you think I'm leaving you alone in here, you're daft.'

The little man pouted. 'Professional secrets, Mr Skinner,' he protested.

'My arse! Jo, you're a professional fucking thief! I don't know what's in the bloody thing. Tell you what, I'll stand behind you, so I can't see your hands.' He took five twenty-pound notes from his wallet and waved them before the safe-cracker's eyes. 'And there's these,' he added.

'What about ma train fare?'

Skinner snorted, but produced another twenty. 'There you are: and a couple of pints when you get home. Now get on with it.'

'Aye, okay.'

He turned and hunched over the safe. The chief saw him reach inside his jacket again then insert a device that could have been a hearing aid in his ear. Everything else was hidden to him; all he could see were small movements of Ramsey's shoulders.

'A couple of minutes' he had said, and it took no longer, until there was a click, and the safe swung open.

'Piece of piss, Ah told ye. Three four eight five's the combination. Four digits, no' six.'

Skinner smiled as he handed over the notes. 'Do you know what "recidivist" means, Johan?' he asked.

'No, sir,' Ramsey replied as he pocketed them.

'No, I didn't think so. Do me one favour, even though it'll be a big one for you. Try not to get nicked again on my patch, whether it's here or in Edinburgh. This can't get you any favours, and I really don't want to have to lock you up again. Come on, let's get you back home. Remember, you were never here.'

His desk phone rang again as they stepped back into his office. He picked it up.

'PC May again, sir. Your next visitor's arrived.'

'Good timing,' he said. 'Bring him up, and you can take this one back.'

Fifty

'When will they be in court?' Viola Murphy asked, as soon as Dan Provan had finished reading the formal charges, and the two accused had been taken away to complete the bail formalities.

'Ah can't say,' he replied, 'but we'll let you know. Will you be defending them both?'

'Probably, unless either one of them changes their mind and decides to plead not guilty; in that event, there could be a conflict. Does Skinner mean it? Will he press for custodial sentences?'

'From what Ah hear you got on the wrong side of him. Did you think he's the kind that bluffs?'

'No,' the lawyer conceded.

'It's no' just him. ACC Gorman's of the same mind.'

'And you?'

'Listen, Viola, we all are. It's tough for me, personally, you must know that, but we cannae let this go by wi' a slap on the wrist, especially for McGlashan. If she goes down, he has tae and all. That would be the case suppose he wasn't an ex-cop and married to somebody who still is. The fact that he is just underlines it. The fiscal will demand jail. The best you can hope for is a soft-hearted sheriff that gives them less than six months.'

'I'll ask for a suspended sentence.'

'Ye better no'. He might hang them.' He winced. 'Bad joke, Ah know, but you know the bench. Sometimes, the more that lawyers chance their arm, the harder they go. Would ye like some advice?'

'I'll listen to it,' she said. 'Whether I'll act on it . . .'

'Okay. If I was in the dock, I'd want the youngest, freshest kid in your firm tae do the plea in mitigation. Ah'd even be hopin' that they made an arse of it, and the judge took pity on them. Because that's the only way those two will get anything like sympathy from any sheriff in this city.'

'Mmm,' she murmured. 'You may well be right. I suppose you should be; you've been around long enough to have seen it all. I'll have a word with my partners, and see what they think. Thanks, Sergeant.'

The door had barely closed behind her when it opened again. Provan looked up, to see Scott Mann framed there.

'Dan,' he began. 'Sarge.'

The older man bristled. 'Don't you fuckin' call me Sarge.' He jerked a thumb in the direction of DC Paterson who stood beside him, gathering notes and papers and putting them in order. 'That's reserved for colleagues, like Banjo here; for police officers, and that you're no'. And don't "Dan" me either. Mr Provan, it can be, but frankly Ah'd prefer nothing at all. Ah'd rather no' see you again.'

'Will ye put a word in for me?' Mann begged.

'What? Wi' the high heid yins? You must be joking.'

'No, I meant wi' Lottie.'

The DS started round the table towards him, only to be restrained by Paterson's strong hand, grabbing him by the elbow. He stopped, gathering himself.

'There is even less chance of that,' he said when he was ready. 'From now on, I will do all I can to protect Lottie from you. Now you fuck off out of here, boy, get off wi' your tart. And be glad you're leavin' in one piece. In the old days ye wouldn't have.'

Fifty-One

'Who was that little guy?' Clyde Houseman asked, as he settled into the chair that Skinner offered him. 'He wasn't the sort you expect to see on the command floor of the second largest police force in Britain.'

'Just a technician,' the chief replied. 'I had a wee problem, but he sorted it out for me.'

'Computer?'

He shrugged. 'You know IT consultants, they live in a different world from the rest of us. Some of them turn up and they're dressed like you, others, they're like him. I know which ones I trust more. I'm not a big fan of dressing to impress.'

The younger man winced and his eyes seemed to flicker for a moment. 'I do . . .'

Skinner laughed. 'Don't take it personally. I wasn't getting at you. You're ex-military, an ex-officer; you've had years of training in taking a pride in your appearance. Plus, you're not a computer consultant; you're a spook. Whatever, you look a hell of a lot better than you did as a gang-banger in Edinburgh half a lifetime ago.'

'Thank God for that.'

'Me, now? I've never changed. I joined the police force because I felt a vocational calling, and I followed it even though I knew that my old man had always hoped I would take over the family law firm eventually. I think he died hoping that. I never let myself be swayed, though. I applied to join the Edinburgh force, they saw my shiny new degree and they accepted me. And you know what? The first time I put on the uniform, I realised that I hated it. The thing was ugly and uncomfortable and when I looked in the mirror I didn't recognise the bloke inside it.

'It didn't kill my pride in the job, but it did make me want to get into CID as fast as I could. Look at me now; I'm a chief constable, but my uniform is hanging in my wardrobe next door. I'm only wearing a suit because I feel a wee bit obliged to do that, at least until I get settled in here.

'The real me might dress a wee bit sharper than the guy you passed at the lift, but it would still be pretty casual. So what you see here, to an extent it's a phoney. Old George Michael got it right; sometimes clothes do not make the man.

'But yours, though, they do. They mark you out, they define you. The military defined you. It made you; you became it. Before that you were no more than eighty kilos of clay waiting to be given proper form.

'I could see that when I came across you in that shithole of a scheme in Edinburgh. That's why I gave you my card that day: I thought you might see the light and get in touch. You didn't, but you still went in the right direction. If you had . . . you'd still be the man you are, but you'd just look a bit different, that's all.'

Houseman laughed. 'Scruffy at weekends, you mean? How do you know I'm not?'

'I know, because I've met plenty of soldiers in my time and quite a few were officers who rose through the ranks, like you. I'll bet you don't have a pair of jeans in your wardrobe. Am I right?'

'You are, as a matter of fact. Is that a bad thing?'

'In a soldier, no. In a lawyer, no. In an actuary, for sure no. When I hang out in Spain I see these fat blokes on the beach in gaudy shirts and ridiculous shorts, with gold Rolexes on their wrists and all of them looking miserable because their wives have dragged them there and they're starting to panic because they don't know who anyone else is and, worse, nobody knows what they are. My golf club's full of people who've never worn denim in their fucking lives, and that's okay, because if they did they'd be pretending to be something they're not.'

'Exactly. So what are you saying?'

'I'm trying to tell you,' Skinner said, 'that conformity is fine for normal people. But you, Clyde, you're not a normal person, you're a spook. You're a good-looking bloke, of mixed race, so you have an inbuilt tendency to be memorable. The way you dress, the way you present yourself, makes you unforgettable, and in your line of work, my friend, that is the very last thing you want to be. If they didn't teach you that when you joined up at Millbank, then they failed you.'

Houseman's eyebrows formed a single line. 'Point taken, sir. Any suggestions?'

'Nothing radical; the obvious mostly. Vary your dress, and when you go casual, don't wear stuff with big logos or pop stars on the front. Shop in Marks and Spencer rather than Austin Reed. Let your hair grow a bit shaggy. Don't shave every day. Wear sunglasses when it's appropriate, the kind that people will remember rather than the person behind them. Choose what you drive carefully.'

He smiled. 'That day you and I met, back in the last century, I was driving my BMW. That was an accident; normally I'd have been in my battered old Land Rover. If I had, you and your gang wouldn't have given it a second glance, and I wouldn't have had to warn you off.'

'Then whatever caused that accident, I'm grateful for it. You gave me the impetus to get out of there. Otherwise I might not have. I might have stayed a stereotype and wound up in jail.'

'Nah, I think you'd have made it. You were a smart kid. You'd have worked it out for yourself, eventually.'

'Maybe.' He pulled himself a little more upright. 'However, I'm sure you didn't call me here to give me fashion advice.'

'No,' Skinner agreed, 'that's true. I felt I should give you an update on the investigation, since you were in at the death, so to speak.'

'Thanks, sir. I appreciate that. How's it going?'

'It's not,' the chief sighed. 'It's stalled. All our lines of inquiry have dried up. There is no link between Beram Cohen and the person or organisation who sponsored the hit. We know how it was done, and even if it points in a certain direction, the witnesses are all dead. That's probably my fault,' he added. 'You had no choice but to take down Smit, but if I was a better shot I'd have been able to stop Botha without killing him.'

'There will be no further inquiries about our part in that?' Houseman asked.

'None. Everything is closed.'

Skinner rose to his feet, and his visitor followed suit. He moved towards the door, then stopped. 'I'm aware,' he said, 'that in Toni Field's time MI5 policy was to keep our counter-terrorism unit at a distance. It's okay, I'm not asking you to comment. Toni may not even have been aware of it, but I know it was the case. I just want you to know that while I'm here, I won't tolerate that. You can keep secrets from anyone else, but if they affect my operational area, not from me. Understood?'

Houseman nodded. 'Understood, sir.'

They walked together to the lift. The chief constable watched the doors close then went back the way he had come, but walked past his own room, stopping instead at the one he had commandeered for Lowell Payne. He knocked on the door then opened it halfway and looked in.

'Come on along,' he said.

Marina Deschamps put down her magazine, stood and followed him. 'This is all very surprising,' she murmured, with a smile. 'Even a little mysterious. By the way, did you solve the mystery of the safe?'

He nodded. 'This very afternoon. I've still to check its contents, but if there's anything personal in there I'll let you have it. As for the rest, you're right, but now I can show you what this visit's all about.'

He sat behind his desk and touched the space bar on his computer keyboard to waken it from sleep.

'This room has a couple of little bonuses,' he began. 'Having worked next door, you're probably aware that there's a security system. There's a wee camera in the corner of the ceiling and when the system is set, anyone who comes in here is automatically filmed, without ever knowing it.'

'Yes,' she agreed. 'Some evenings I would be last out of here, and so I had to be shown how to set it.'

'Yes, I imagine so. But did Toni tell you that it's more than an alarm?'

'No, she never did. It is? In what way?'

'It can also be used to record meetings. Clearly, if that happens, all the participants should be made aware of it, but if they weren't they'd never know.' He used his mouse to open a program then select a file. He beckoned to her. 'Come here and take a look at this.'

As she walked round behind him he clicked an icon, to start a video. There was no sound, but the image that she could see was clear and in colour. The chief constable with his back to the camera and facing him a sharply dressed, immaculately groomed man, whose skin tone was almost identical to her own.

'Ever seen him before?' Skinner asked, hearing an intake of breath from over his shoulder.

'Yes,' she whispered. 'That's Don Sturgeon. What's he doing here?'

Fifty-Two

'What d'you think of the beer?' Neil McIlhenney asked.

'It's okay,' Lowell Payne conceded. 'What's it called?'

'Chiswick Bitter. I don't drink much, not any more, but when I do it's the one I go for.'

'That's because it doesn't take the top of your head off,' one of their companions remarked, 'unlike that ESB stuff. Bloody ferocious that is. I've seen tourists staggering out of here after a couple of pints of that stuff. Not like you Jocks, though. You'd drink aviation fuel and never feel it.'

'I used to,' the DCS chuckled. 'Me and my mate. In those days we used to say that English beer was half the strength of a Scotsman's piss, but since I came down here I've developed an occasional taste for it. Travelling to work on the tube has its compensations.'

The other Londoner glanced at him. 'Where do you live?'

McIlhenney raised an eyebrow. 'Was that a professional inquiry? I've heard about you guys; you're never off duty.'

'No, not at all.'

'Richmond, actually.'

The man had his glass to his lips, he spluttered. 'You what? On a copper's pay? Maybe it should have been a professional question.'

'My wife's owned the place for years. When we lived in Edinburgh it was rented out. We used her flat in St John's Wood if we ever came down.'

'You're shitting us.'

'Oh no he's not,' Payne laughed. 'Ask him who his wife is.'

As he spoke, the phone in the pocket of his shirt vibrated against his chest. He knew who the caller would be without looking at it. He excused himself as he took it out, and stepped out into the street.

'Where are you now?' Skinner asked.

'I'm in a pub called the Red Lion, in Whitehall, with Neil McIlhenney and two guys he says are part of the Prime Minister's protection team. This might be a good night to have a go at him.'

'Given what happened on Saturday,' the chief pointed out, 'that's not very funny. Have you got a hotel?'

'Yes, the Met fixed me up with one near Victoria Station.'

'Good. I want you to meet me tomorrow morning. Victoria will do fine. I'll be coming up from Gatwick, same flight as you caught today.'

'I'll see you there. Where are we going?'

'I have a meeting, and given where it is and what's on the agenda, I'm not going in there unaccompanied.'

'Sounds heavy. Where?'

'Security Service, Millbank. I'm just off the phone with my friend Amanda Dennis, the deputy director. She's expecting us.'

Payne gasped. 'Jesus Christ, boss. Why are we going there? What's happened?'

'Nothing that I can slam on the table, point at and say "He did it", but enough for me to fly some kites and see how they react. I can see a chain of events and facts that lead to a certain hypothesis, but I can't see anything that resembles a motive. Still, what we've got is enough for some cage-rattling. I'm good at that.'

'I think I know that.'

'Then you can sit back and learn.'

'At my age I don't want to.'

'You're a year older than me, Lowell,' Skinner chuckled, 'that's all. One thing I want you to do in preparation for the meeting. When you call Jean, as I'm sure you will, tell her where you're going. I'll be doing the same with Sarah. I know, I said that Amanda's a friend, and she is, but in that place, friendship only goes so far.'

Fifty-Three

'Are you going to work in Glasgow for good, Dad?' Skinner's elder son asked, ranging over three octaves in that single sentence.

Mark McGrath, the boy Skinner and Sarah had adopted as an orphan, was at the outset of adolescence, and the breaking of his voice was not passing over easily or quickly. James Andrew, his younger brother, laughed at his lack of control, until he was silenced by a frown from his mother.

'I dunno, mate,' Bob confessed. 'Last week I'd never have imagined being there. On Sunday, when I agreed to take over, the answer would still have been no. But with every day that passes, I'm just a little less certain. But remember, even if I did apply for the job, so would other people. There's no saying I'd be chosen.'

Both of his sons looked at him as if he had told them Motherwell would win the Champions League.

'No kidding,' he insisted. 'There are many very good cops out there, and most of them are younger than me. I won't see fifty again, lads.'

'You'll get it, Dad.' James Andrew spoke with certainty, his father's certainty, Sarah realised, as she heard him. 'Will we have to move to Glasgow?'

'Never!' The reply was instant, and vehement.

'Come on, guys,' Sarah interrupted. 'It's past nine, time you headed upstairs. And don't disturb your sister if she's asleep.'

'She won't be,' Mark squeaked. 'She'll be practising her reading.'

'That's a bit of an exaggeration surely,' Bob chuckled. 'She might be looking at the pictures.'

'No, Dad. She's learning words as well; I've been teaching her. There's a computer program and I've been using it.'

Skinner watched them as they left, and was still gazing at the door long after it was closed. Sarah settled down beside him on the sofa, tugging his arm to claim his attention. 'Hey,' she murmured, 'come back from wherever you are. Whassup, anyway?'

'Ach, I was just thinking what a crap dad I've been. I should be teaching my daughter to read, not subcontracting the job to Mark. Last week I was all motivated, pumped up to do that and more. We had a great morning on the beach on Saturday, the kids and I, then I had a phone call, the shit hit the fan and I had to go rushing off, didn't I, and get it splattered all over me. Now I'm thinking seriously about taking on the biggest job in Scotland, when I've already got a job that's far more important than that.'

She turned his face to her, and kissed him. 'Bob,' she said, 'I love you, and it's good to see you taking your kids so seriously. But you always have done. You've been great with the boys all along, and you've never neglected Seonaid. It's taken you a while to realise that she isn't a baby any more, that's all. Me living in America didn't help, since that meant you missed a big chunk of her infancy, but I'm back now, and we can help her grow together.' She put a hand on his chest. 'That does not mean I expect you to become a house husband, because you couldn't. There's too much happening, too much at stake just now, and if you don't get involved in it, you'll regret it for the rest of your life.

'You can't walk away anyway, it's not in your nature. This thing tomorrow, this high-stakes meeting at MI5 that you're so worked up about, even if you're not saying so, you don't have to go there, do you? But you want to, you feel you have to. Isn't that right?'

'I set it up,' he admitted. 'Yes, it is a bit of a fishing trip, and there are other ways I could have played it. For example, I could just write a report, a straight factual account of the things that we know, and suggest certain possibilities. Then I could give that report to the Lord Advocate, who's my ultimate boss as a criminal investigator in Scotland, with a copy to the First Minister.'

'Why don't you?'

'Because they'd burn it. If I told them what I know to be fact and what I see as a possibility, they'd be scared stiff. If they acted on it, it could provoke a major conflict between them and the Westminster government. All in all, it's best that I keep it from them, and that I go and have a full and frank discussion with Amanda.'

'Bob,' Sarah ventured, 'are you suggesting that MI5 had something to do with Toni Field's murder?'

'No, I'm not, because the evidence doesn't take me there. Even if I thought they were capable of doing that, I can't see why they would. But I do know that they created the conditions for it to happen, and that they've been doing what they can to cover up. There's a piece of that I still don't understand, but I never will because they've been too good at it.'

'Okay,' she said. 'Here's what I think you should do. See this thing through to its conclusion, and let it go, however unsatisfactory the conclusion may be. Then apply for the Strathclyde job. You'll get it; even the boys know that. And once you're there, be everything you can be. Build your support staff so that you can delegate and not have to change every light bulb. Work the hours a normal man

321

does, and be the father that a normal man is expected to be.'

He grinned. 'And the husband?'

'Nah,' she laughed in return. 'You were always lousy at that; we're fine as we are.'

'Yeah,' he agreed. 'I'll go with that.'

'Would you like a drink? I put some Corona in the fridge for you. I take it it's still your favourite beer.'

'Absolutely, but I'll give it a miss tonight. Early start tomorrow. Hey,' he added, 'you realise that from now on I'll be able to tell whether you've got another bloke just by checking the fridge?'

'Yes, but how will you know I don't have another fridge somewhere, one with a combination lock just in case you do find it?'

Her joke triggered a memory. 'Bugger,' he exclaimed. 'I finally got into my own safe this afternoon, in the office. I haven't had a chance to check the papers that were in it. They're in my briefcase; mind if I go through them now?'

'No,' she replied, jumping to her feet, 'you do that, and I'll check that Madam Seonaid isn't halfway through *War and Peace* by torchlight under the duvet.'

As she left the room, he reached for his attaché case and opened it. He had brought the remnants of his in-tray with him, to be worked on during his flight to London, but the contents of Toni Field's safe were in a separate folder. He took it out and set the rest aside.

His dead predecessor's papers were contained in a series of large envelopes. He picked up the first; the word 'Receipts' was scrawled on the outside. He shook out the contents and saw a pile of payment slips, two from restaurants, three from petrol stations, five for train tickets, two for books on criminology bought from Amazon, another from a hotel in Guildford, *double room, breakfast for two*, he noted, recalling a policing conference in the Surrey town two months earlier that he had declined to attend. *Maybe she took Marina,* he thought.

Or possibly not. Might Toni have been capable of taking the so-called Don Sturgeon along for the ride, and slipping him on to her expenses?

He stuffed the slips back into the envelope and picked up the next. His eyebrows rose when he saw his own name written on the front. He was about to open it when he found a second envelope attached, stuck to it by the gum on its unsealed flap. He prised them apart and read another name, 'P. Friedman'. He looked inside, but it was empty, and so he laid it aside and slid out the contents of his own.

He found himself looking at two photographs of himself. From the background he saw that they had been taken surreptitiously at ACPOS, probably by Toni, with a mobile phone while his attention had been elsewhere. They were clipped on to a series of handwritten notes.

As he read them he saw that they were summaries of every meeting they had ever attended together, and one that had been just the two of them, when he had paid a courtesy call on her in Pitt Street in the week she had taken up office. That note was the most interesting.

Robert M. Skinner (Wonder what M stands for?)

The top dog in Scotland he thinks, come to let me know no doubt that he could have had my job for the asking . . . if he only knew. Tough on him; this is the season of the bitch. Sensitive about his politician wife. Eyes went all cold when I asked about her. Wonder if he knows what I do, about her screwing the actor guy every time he's in Glasgow. Or if he'd like me to show him the evidence. If he knew about the other one! But that definitely stays my secret, till the time is right.

Skinner's eyes widened as he read.

The man has testosterone coming out of his pores, which makes it all the more ironic that his wife plays away, as did the one before, from what I hear. As a cop, old school. He will not be an ally over unification. Question is, will he be an opponent for the job? Think he will, whatever he says; he's a pragmatist, used to power, and not being questioned. Also, will he stand for Scotland's top police officer being a woman, and a black one at that? Sexist? Racist? His sort usually are, if old Bullshit is anything to go by. Must work out a way to take him out of the game. Main weakness is his wife; use what I know and work on getting more on her. Other weakness his daughter, but she's protected by the dangerous Mr Martin so too much trouble. Summary: an enemy, but can be handled.

'No wonder this fucking woman got herself killed,' he murmured to himself. 'I might have been tempted to do it myself.'

He replaced the notes and the photographs, then turned to the next envelope. It was inscribed 'Bullshit'. It contained nothing but photographs, of Toni Field and a man. In one they were both in police uniform, but in the others they were highly informal. It was all too apparent that at least one of the participants had been completely unaware that they were being taken, most of all in one in which he was clad only in his socks.

Skinner stared. He gaped. And then he laughed. 'Bullshit,' he said. 'B. S. for short. B. S. for Brian Storey, Sir Brian bloody Storey, deputy assistant commissioner then, going by his uniform, but now Commissioner of the Metropolitan Police. And weren't he and Lady Storey guests in the royal box at Ascot a few weeks ago?'

His smile vanished. Was Brian Storey a man to be blackmailed and take it quietly? Maybe, maybe not.

He moved on to the next envelope. It was labelled 'Brum', another collection of candid camera shots of the star of the show with a West Midlands ACC, in line with Marina's account. Skinner knew the guy by sight but could not remember his name, a sign that the days when he might have been of use to Toni lay in the past.

The same was true of the men featured in the next two. The broadcast journalist had been a name a couple of years before but had passed into obscurity when he had signed up with Sky News. As for Chairman Mao, the only thing for which he was remarkable was the size of his penis, since Toni had been able, easily, to swallow it whole.

The fifth envelope in the sequence was 'Howling Mad'. There was something vaguely recognisable about the man, but if he was a QC as Marina had said, he would normally be seen publicly in wig and gown, as good a disguise as the chief constable had ever encountered. In addition, he was the only one of the five who was not seen completely naked, or in full face, only profile. However, there were a series of images possibly taken from a video, in which the pair were seen under a duvet, in what looked to be, even in the stills, vigorous congress.

'Howling Mad,' Skinner repeated. 'Who the hell are you, and why is that name vaguely familiar?'

His question went unanswered as he refilled the envelope and turned to the last. It was anonymous; there was no description of its contents on the outside. He upended it and more photographs fell out. They showed Toni Field as he had never seen her, out of uniform, without make-up, without her hair carefully arranged. In each image she was holding or watching over a child, at various ages, from infancy to early toddler.

He felt a pang of sadness. Little Lucille, who'd never see her mother again. One photograph was larger than the rest. It showed Toni, sitting up in a hospital bed, holding her child and flanked by Sofia and a man, Mauritian. He had given his daughter his high forehead and straight, slightly delicate nose. *And how much of his character?* Skinner wondered.

He was replacing the photographs and making a mental note to hand them over to Marina, after burning four of the others . . . the 'Bullshit' file was one to keep . . . when he realised that something had not fallen out when they did. He reached inside with two fingers and drew out a document.

He whistled as he saw it, knowing at once what it was even if its style was unfamiliar to him. A birth certificate, serial number ending seven two six five, recording the safe arrival of Mauritian citizen Lucille Sofia Deschamps, mother's name, Antonia Maureen Deschamps, nationality Mauritian, father's name Murdoch Lawton, nationality British.

In the days when Trivial Pursuit was the only game in town, Bob Skinner had been the man to avoid, or the man to have on your team. There was never a fact, a name or a link so inconsequential that he would not retain it.

'Murdoch,' he exclaimed. *'The A Team,* original TV series not the iffy movie, crazy team member, "Howling Mad" Murdock, spelled the American way but near enough and that's how Toni would have pronounced it anyway, played by Dwight Schultz. Hence the nickname, but who the hell is he?'

Sarah's iPad was lying on the coffee table. He picked it up, clicked on the Wikipedia app, and keyed in the name of the father of little Lucille Deschamps.

When Sarah came back into the room he was staring at the tablet's small screen, his face frozen, his expression so wild that it scared her.

'Bob,' she called out, 'are you all right?'

He shook himself back to life. 'Never better, love,' he replied, and his eyes were exultant. 'Can you print from this thing?' he asked.

'Of course. Why?'

'Because the whole game is changed, my love, the whole devious game.'

Fifty-Four

'Are ye sure you're all right, kid?' Since his visit earlier in the evening he had called her three times and on each occasion he had put the same question. Lottie understood; she knew that he was hurting almost as much as she was, but was incapable of saying so.

'I promise you, Dan, I'm okay. That's to say I'm not a danger to myself, or to wee Jakey. Nobody's going to break in here tomorrow and find me hanging from the banisters. Ask me how I feel instead and I'll tell you that I'm hurt, embarrassed, disappointed and blazing mad, but I'll get over all that . . . apart, maybe, from the blazing mad bit. I've made a decision since you called me earlier. Jakey's going to his granny's tomorrow and I'm coming back to work.'

'But Lottie,' Provan began.

She cut him off. 'Don't say it, 'cos I know that I can have nothing to do with the Field investigation, but there's other crime in Glasgow; there always is.'

'The chief constable said ye should stay at home until everything's sorted.'

'As far as I'm concerned it is sorted. Scott's been charged, right?'

'Right.'

'He's no longer in custody, right?'

'Right.'

'And I'm not suspected of being involved in what he did, right?'

'Right.'

'Thank you,' she said. 'In that case, there is no reason for me to be stuck in the house twiddling my thumbs. The longer I do that the more it will look like I'm mixed up in my husband's stupidity. So, Detective Sergeant, I will see you tomorrow. If the chief doesn't like it, the only way he'll get me out of there is by formally suspending me, and as you've just agreed, he doesn't have any grounds to do that. I won't come into the investigation room in Pitt Street. I'll go to our own office in Anderston instead.'

'Then ye'll see me there. The chief's told me to shut down the Pitt Street room. He says the investigation's went as far as it can, and there's no point in our bein' there any longer.'

'Why?' she asked, surprised. 'Have we run out of leads?'

'Worse than that. Everywhere we've gone, some bugger's been there before us. See ye the morra.'

As Lottie hung the wall phone back on its cradle in the hallway, her eye was caught by a movement. She looked at the front door and saw a figure; it was unrecognisable, its shape distorted by the obscure glass, but she knew who it was. She felt a strange fluttering in her stomach, and realised that she was a little afraid. She thought of calling Dan back. She thought of going back into the living room and listening to loud music through her headphones.

But she did neither of those things. Instead her anger overcame her nervousness, and she marched to the door and threw it open.

Her husband stood on the step, with a key in his hand, wavering towards the Yale lock that was no longer within reach. She snatched it from him.

'Gimme,' he protested.

'No danger. You'll not be needing it any longer.' She grabbed him by one of the lapels of his sports jacket and pulled him indoors.

'Aw thanks, love,' he sighed, misunderstanding her.

'Thanks for nothing,' she replied. 'You won't be staying. You're as drunk as a monkey and I'm not putting on a show for the neighbours, that's all.'

'Ach Lottie, gie's a break. I'm goin' tae the fucking jail, is that not enough for you?'

'That's the last thing I want, you pathetic twat,' she hissed. 'What do you think that's going to do for your son at the school? Every kid in the place will be pointing fingers at him and calling him names. The only thing that'll save him from being bullied is that all of them know me. As for your slapper, though, that McGlashan, they can stick her in Cornton Vale for as long as they like.'

'Leave Christine out of this,' Scott snarled, lurching towards her.

'I'd leave her out of the human race,' she retorted, her voice filled with scorn. 'And you take one more step towards me,' she added, 'and it won't be a police car that'll come for you, it'll be an ambulance. It was you that brought her into it. I hope you're happy that you've ruined her life as well as your own. If I didn't feel the contempt for her that any woman would feel, and that any good police officer would feel five times over, I could actually find it in my heart to be sorry for the poor cow. Do you have the faintest idea how cruel you've been in even asking her to do what she did, far less in talking her into it?

'I know you and she were at it before we met, and I suspect that you always have been, behind my big stupid plodding back. That can only mean that the daft bitch actually feels something for you. And that you've let her down just as badly as you've betrayed and shamed Jakey and me.'

She took him by the arm, as if she was arresting him and began to push him towards the door. 'Now go,' she ordered, 'and don't you ever come back here.'

'Lottie,' he pleaded, 'gie's a break.'

'Certainly. Which arm would you prefer?'

'Ah've got nowhere else tae go!'

'No? Why don't you just go to her place?'

'Aye, that'll be right. Her husband's lookin' for me as it is.'

'Her what? Well, I'll tell you what, you go down to the riverside and find yourself a nice bench to sleep on, so that if he comes here, I can tell him where to find you.' She opened the front door and thrust him outside. 'As soon as I get inside,' she warned him, 'I'm going to phone the station. If you're seen within a mile of this house for the rest of the night, you'll be lifted. But I won't tell them to arrest you. Oh no, I'll have them drive you to Christine McGlashan's house, drop you there and ring the doorbell. You think I wouldn't do that, you snivelling bastard?' she challenged.

He shook his head.

'Aye, damn right I would. You know, Scott, what I feel right now, looking at you? I feel ashamed that I let you father my son. Well, I tell you this. There is no way that I will let you pass your weakness on to him. It might hurt him for a bit, but you're never going to see him again.'

With that, Charlotte Mann slammed the door on her husband, walked quietly into her living room, slumped into an armchair, and wept as she had never wept before.

Fifty-Five

'It's bloody warm in this city,' Lowell Payne remarked, as they stood on the pavement outside Thames House.

'It can be in the summer,' Skinner conceded. 'I have this theory that all big cities generate their own heat. Mind you, it can be cold here too. I remember, oh, must be twenty years ago now, standing here on Millbank one evening in February, with a wind whistling up the Thames that felt as if it had come all the way from Siberia. That's still the coldest I've ever been in my life.'

'Are we going to get a chilly reception in here, d' you think?'

'No, I don't, but things may cool down quite a bit once we get going.'

'Who are we meeting?'

'I'm not absolutely certain. As things stand, our appointment is with Amanda Dennis, the deputy director of the service. Whether she has anyone with her, that may depend on whether she guesses why we're here.'

'What's my role?'

'You're a witness,' Skinner told him. 'Did you do what I suggested?'

'Tell Jean, you mean?' Payne frowned. 'No, I didn't, I'm sorry. You've known her for longer than I have, so I shouldn't have to tell you that if I just happened to mention casually that you and I were off to a top-level meeting with MI5 but I couldn't tell her what it was about, she'd have gone into full worry mode, and not slept a wink. Did you tell Sarah?'

'Of course. Sarah gave up worrying about me years ago.'

'Did you tell her what the meeting's about?'

'No, and she didn't ask. She's used to me moving in mysterious ways. She calls me God, sometimes.'

The DCI grinned and shook his head. 'What is it with you two?'

'What do you think?'

'Honestly?'

'Always. I'd expect nothing else.'

'I think that Aileen getting caught out with Joey Morocco came in very handy for both of you.'

'What does Jean think?' Bob asked.

'There's nothing for her to think about,' Lowell told him, 'as far as you and Sarah are concerned, not yet, but she'll be fine. They didn't know it at the time, but I heard her and Alex compare notes one day. Neither of them were too keen on Aileen.'

'I know that now.'

'I've got nothing against her, mind, but on the two occasions that I've met Sarah, I thought that she was a sensational woman and that the two of you together just filled the whole room.'

'Maybe we did at that, Lowell. We lost our way for a while, that was all. I hope we've found it again.'

'What's made the difference?'

'I've stopped living in the past. Recently, somebody very close to me told me that for the last twenty and a bit years, since Myra was killed in that bloody car, I've been in denial, that I've never accepted it, never moved on. I've come to accept that's true. It drove Sarah and me apart, and with Aileen . . . I made myself see Myra in her, when in fact they couldn't be more different. Myra was wild, self-indulgent and she lived her life on the spur of the moment. She was also promiscuous, as Jean may have told you, more than I ever was, even when I was single.

'Aileen, on the other hand, is one of the most calculating people I have ever known. I don't mean that unkindly, not any more, but everything she does is to a plan, and everyone around her must conform to it, even me.

'She supports police unification for two reasons. One, she does believe in it, but two, she thought that it would make me leave the force and help her achieve her real ambitions, which don't lie in Scotland, but down here, in Westminster.

'I'm sure she'll get there, but not with my help. As for me, as was said to me, my soul's been broken, but Sarah's helping me fix it, and I feel more at peace with myself than I have in years.' He checked his watch. 'And I'll be even more so when we've done our business here. Are you all set?'

'Yes, I'm ready.'

'Good. Come on then, I like to be bang on time when I visit this place.'

They entered the headquarters of the Security Service through a modest door to the right of the building's great archway, and stepped up to a reception desk that might have belonged to any civil service department. Skinner announced them to one of the uniformed staff. When he told the man that he had an appointment with Mrs Dennis, there was a subtle change in his attitude. He checked a screen that the police officers could not see, then nodded.

'Yes, gentlemen,' he announced. 'I'll let the DD know you're here and she'll send someone down to collect you.' He made a quick phone call, then filled in two slips, which he inserted in plastic cases and handed them over, one to each. 'These must be surrendered on leaving. Now, if you'll follow me, I'll check you in through our electronic security. It's just like an airport, really.'

'I know,' Skinner said. 'But I have a pacemaker so you'll have to pat me down.'

'That won't be necessary, Rashid,' a woman called out.

The chief constable looked over towards a line of lift doors and saw Amanda Dennis approach. 'Oh, but it will,' he insisted. 'I'm not having your lot plant a gun on me when we get upstairs then say I carried it in.'

She laughed. 'Damn it! There goes Plan A.'

The deputy director of MI5 was not what Lowell Payne had been expecting. In his mind he had pictured Dame Judi Dench, or someone like her. Instead he saw someone who was around fifty, with dark, well-cut hair and sparkling eyes that had none of the chilly aloofness that were a feature of her film and television equivalents.

'Hi, Mandy,' Skinner greeted her when the security search was over and he and Payne had retrieved their bags from x-ray. 'Good to see you; this is DCI Payne, Lowell, my sidekick, but you'll know that by now.' He kissed her on the cheek. 'You're looking better than ever. Still finding time for the toy boy?'

She winked. 'Shows, does it?'

'Does he still think you work in a flower shop?'

'No, it closed down. Now he thinks I'm a proof-reader in a law firm.' She grinned. 'Actually he knows exactly what I do. He's a bright enough chap to read the parliamentary reports where my name crops up occasionally. You know how it is, Bob. It's the junior ranks who have to be anonymous. Thanks to John bloody Major, the rest of us can't.'

'I know,' he sympathised, as they stepped into a lift. 'The Don

Sturgeons of this world have to be protected, but you and Hubert can walk around with targets on your backs.'

'Who on earth is Don Sturgeon?' she remarked, but did not wait for an answer. 'As for Hubert, why do you want to see me? He's the director, not me.'

'He's also a prat, a Home Office toady dropped in here because the Prime Minister of the day decided the place needed some new blood, after that wee scandal you and I uncovered a couple of years back. He may have been the transfusion, but you're still the heartbeat.'

The elevator stopped and they stepped out, then along a corridor. Mrs Dennis unlocked her office door and followed them into the room. It was oak-panelled and grandly furnished, in contrast to the utilitarian style of the reception area.

'Welcome,' she said. 'We'll use the conference table, but before we start, Bob, I assume you'd like coffee.'

He held up a hand. 'No thanks, Amanda, I've signed the coffee pledge, and Lowell here had a Starbucks on the way up from Victoria. By the way,' he added, 'he was propositioned by a whore, sorry, that's non-PC, by a sex worker in his hotel last night. Very English, could even have been public school. Three hundred quid. Isn't that right, Lowell?'

'Yes indeed, Chief. She said it was her way of paying off her mortgage.'

'Unluckily for her, he's a Jock, and a tight-fisted bastard like all of us. She wasn't one of yours, was she?'

'She could have been,' the deputy director replied. 'About a third of the women in this place fit that description. But if she was, she wasn't on duty. We tend to use Russian girls, or Polish. That's what our targets expect, and let's face it, chaps,' she winked, 'have you ever met a posh English girl who really knew how to fuck?'

Skinner laughed out loud. 'As a matter if fact I have, but you probably know about her. Likely she's on my file.'

'Come on, Bob,' she chided him. 'We don't keep files on senior police officers.'

'Of course you bloody do, Amanda. You keep files on everyone, apart from the odd militant Islamist who slips through the net and blows up a London bus. For example, you kept a file on Beram Cohen. I know that, because you sent my young friend Clyde Houseman through to see me last Saturday, to tell me who he was. What I didn't understand at the time was why MI5 should know about Cohen. He wasn't Islamic, he was Jewish. He wasn't an internal security threat to us. No, he was an Israeli secret service operative who got compromised and had to vanish.'

'Yes,' she agreed, 'and we helped, as you know by now. We did a favour via our friends in MI6, for their friends in Mossad, and took him on board.'

'You turned him into Byron Millbank?'

She frowned and the change seemed to add a couple of years to her age in the time it took. 'What a bloody stupid name! I was livid when I heard about it, but when it was done I wasn't involved. I was running our serious crime division then.'

'I imagine it flagged up with you as soon as my people ran a DVLA check on him.'

'Yes, that's how it happened.'

'And as soon as it did, you broke into the Rondar offices and removed his computer.'

'We did, as a precaution, although it turned out to be unnecessary. He seems to have kept his two identities absolutely separate.'

'But you knew he still functioned as Beram?'

'I did, and a very few others. Six advised us of a couple of operations he had undertaken for them and for the Americans. There was the one in Somalia, for example; that's how we knew of the connection between him, Smit and Botha. As soon as you came looking for him, trying to identify his body, I knew that something was up.'

'And you knew who the target was, but you didn't tell me,' Skinner said. 'Because MI5 wanted her dead.'

She stared back at him. 'Of course not,' she protested. 'Why the hell are you saying that?'

Lowell Payne had been following the exchange, fascinated; he had sat in on, or led, hundreds of interviews during his career, and he realised what Skinner was doing. As Dennis spoke, he detected a very subtle shift in her posture, as if she had slipped, very slightly, on to the defensive.

'Because I believe it's true,' the chief replied. 'Twenty-four hours ago, I was simply curious about the chain of events, mostly because of Basil "Bazza" Brown. As you said earlier, Mandy, you used to run the serious crimes operation in this place. Inevitably that would involve you in suborning criminals up and down the country and turning them into informants, either through blackmail or bribery.

'When we found Bazza's body in the boot of Smit and Botha's supposed getaway car . . . rented by Byron Millbank . . . and we checked him out through NCIS, they'd never heard of him. Now, Bazza might not quite have been one half of the Kray Twins, but he was a person of significant interest to Strathclyde CID and the Scottish Serious Crimes and Drugs Agency. So it just wasn't feasible that he wouldn't be on the national criminal database, unless he had been taken off it, and the only organisation I can think of with the clout to do that, is yours. Come on, he was an MI5 asset, wasn't he? Give me that much.'

She sighed, then smiled. 'I should have known,' she murmured. 'Yes, he was. I turned him myself.'

'Thought so. By the way, was Michael Thomas involved in any way, my ACC?'

'Yes, I had to involve him at one point, on pain of disgrace if he breathed a word. Why?'

'It answers a question, that's all. And gets him off a nasty hook.' He paused, straightening in his seat. 'Okay,' he went on, 'so you must see where I'm coming from. I've uncovered an operation in Scotland, planned by a man who is known to MI5. Then right in the middle, I find a key equipment supplier, eliminated to keep him quiet, and I discover that he was also known to you. At the very least that was going to start me wondering. You've got to concede that, chum.'

'Yes, okay, I do. But answer me this. If we were behind it, why did I send Clyde Houseman through to see you, to tell you who Cohen was? Surely I'd have kept quiet about it all.'

'No,' Skinner murmured. 'You wouldn't have taken that chance. If you had you'd have been betting that I wouldn't have found out about the operation on my own, without your help, and you know me too well for that. So you sent Clyde with his order, and with his personal connection to me to cloud my judgement.

'I bought into him, but now I've come to believe that his job was to make sure that the hit went ahead; not to help me, but to get in my way, and to keep me from getting to the concert hall on time, by any means necessary.'

'And I gave him orders to shoot you if he had to? Come on, old love,' she protested.

'No,' he conceded, 'just to fuck me about, to make sure we were chasing the wrong hare. It worked too. We didn't find out that the target was female until it was too late. Even then, when we did, I still assumed that it was political, as Clyde had said, and that meant that it had to be Aileen, my wife.'

'Bob,' Dennis murmured. 'This is all very flight of fancy. What on earth has brought it about?'

'Two things. First, you told me that official MI5 policy has been to steer clear of cooperation with the Strathclyde Counter-Terrorism Intelligence Section because you didn't trust Toni Field. But in fact I find out that you've had her under very close supervision, through Clyde Houseman, or Don Sturgeon, the identity he used to . . . how to say it . . . penetrate her.'

Amanda smiled and raised an eyebrow.

'Second,' Skinner continued, 'I've solved a mystery.'

'It seems to me that you've created one, but go on.'

'Toni Field's secret child, Lucille.'

'Her what?' Dennis exclaimed.

'Come on, Mandy, Clyde must have told you she had a kid. The scar was a clear giveaway, as we found at her autopsy. As soon as I heard about it, I found myself wondering why. Why did she have to hide the fact, take a sabbatical and fuck off to Mauritius to have the baby under her old name?

'A child wouldn't have been a roadblock in her career, not these days, and not even as a single parent, for Toni's mother's hale and hearty and still young enough to help raise her, as she is doing.

'So I started wondering who Daddy was, and I started to consider five people that Marina, her sister, told me about, five men in her life before they came to Scotland. The only problem was, Marina didn't know them by name, only nickname.'

'How inconvenient.' Her tone was teasing, but Payne, the shrewd observer, detected tension beneath it.

'Yeah. But somebody must have known one of them, somebody with the resources to hack into the Mauritian general registry and remove all records of the birth. If it hadn't been for the hospital patient log, we'd never have been able to prove it happened at all. Nice one, my dear. Tell me, did you have to send someone to Mauritius or were you able to do it without leaving this building?' He looked at her, inquiring, but she was silent.

'Yup,' he chuckled. 'This week, it's been a whole series of dead ends, until I found out about Mr Sturgeon and until a specialist thief of my acquaintance finally managed to get into Toni's safe, in what's now my office.' He picked up his attaché case and opened it. 'When I did, I found these.' He removed two envelopes and placed them on the table.

Amanda Dennis frowned and pulled her chair in a little. She reached out for the envelopes, but Skinner drew them back. 'All in good time,' he said. 'There were three others, but their subjects were of no relevance to this, so I've destroyed them. These two, though, they tell a story.'

He removed the contents of the envelope marked 'Bullshit' and passed them across.

As the deputy director studied them, her eyebrows rose and her eyes widened. 'Bloody hell!' she murmured.

'I wondered if you knew about him,' Skinner remarked. 'Now, I gather that you didn't. I expect you'll find that when Toni was appointed to both West Midlands and Strathclyde, Sir Brian Storey gave her glowing testimonials, both times. I don't like the man, so if you use these to bring him down, it won't bother me.'

He picked up 'Howling Mad' and reached inside. 'These, on the other hand, are a whole different matter.' He withdrew several photographs. 'I didn't know who this bloke was at first,' he said, as he handed them across, 'the one she's fucking, but I do now. Once he was Murdoch Lawton, QC, a real star of the English Bar. In fact he was such a big name that the Prime Minister gave him a title, Lord

Forgrave, and brought him into the Cabinet as Justice Secretary.

'There he sits at the table alongside his wife, Emily Repton, MP, the Home Secretary, the woman who controls this organisation, and to whom you and Hubert Lowery answer.'

She stared at the images. Even to Payne, that most skilled reader of expressions, she was inscrutable.

'Those are bad enough,' the chief constable told her, 'even without this.' He took Lucille Deschamps' birth certificate from the envelope and laid it down. 'You knew about it of course, since MI5 removed the original registration. Lawton knocked her up, fathered her child.' He sighed, with real regret.

'So now you see, my friend, how I'm drawn to the possibility that Toni Field was murdered by this organisation, to prevent her from advancing herself even further than she had already by blackmailing the woman at its head, and her husband.

'Amanda, I don't actually believe that you'd be party to that, which is why I've brought this to you and not to Lowery, who'd probably have the Queen shot if he was ordered to.'

Amanda Dennis leaned back, linked her fingers behind her head and looked up at the ceiling. 'Oh dear, Bob,' she sighed. 'If only you hadn't.'

As she spoke, a door at the far end of the room swung open and two people came into the room, one large, the other small, almost petite. Skinner had met the man before, at a secret security conference the previous autumn, not long after his appointment as Director of MI5, but not the woman. Nonetheless, he knew who she was, from television and the press.

Dennis stood; Payne followed her lead instinctively, but Skinner stayed in his seat. 'Home Secretary,' he exclaimed, 'Hubert. Been eavesdropping, have we?'

'No!' the director snapped. 'We've been monitoring a conversation that borders on seditious. To accuse us of organising a murder . . .'

'Go back and listen to the recording that you've undoubtedly made,' the chief constable said. 'You'll find no such accusation. I'm investigating a crime, and my line of inquiry has led me here. You people may think you're off limits, but not to me.'

As Sir Hubert Lowery's massive frame leaned over him, the chief re-called a day when, as a very new uniformed constable, he had policed a Calcutta Cup rugby international at Murrayfield Stadium, in which the man had played in the second row of the scrum, for England.

'Skinner,' the former lock hissed, 'you're notorious as a close-to-the-wind sailor, but this time you've hit the rocks.'

He pushed himself to his feet. 'Get your bad analogies and your bad breath out of my face, you fat bastard,' he murmured, 'or you will need some serious dental work.'

Lowery leaned away, but only a little. Skinner put a hand on his chest and pushed, hard enough to send him staggering back a pace or two. 'You were never any use on your own,' he said. 'You always needed the rest of the pack to back you up.'

'Bob!' Dennis exclaimed.

He grinned. 'No worries, Amanda. He doesn't have the balls.'

'Probably not,' the Home Secretary said, 'but I do. Let me see these.' She snatched up the photographs. 'The idiot!' she snapped as she examined them. 'Bad enough to get involved with that scheming little bitch, but to let himself be photographed on the job, it's beyond belief, it really is. Are these the only copies?'

'I'd say so,' Skinner replied, sitting once again. 'Toni was too smart to leave unnecessary prints lying around. Plus, she thought she was untouchable.' He took a memory card from the breast pocket of his jacket and tossed it on to the table. 'I found that among the envelopes. The originals are on it.'

Emily Repton picked it up, and the birth certificate. She walked across to the deputy director's desk and fed the photographs into the shredder that stood beside it. The memory card followed it. She was about to insert the birth certificate when Payne called out, 'Hey, don't do that! The child's going to need it.'

The Home Secretary gave him a long look. 'What child?' she murmured. The shredder hummed once again. 'Why did you give those up so easily?' she asked the chief constable.

'Because I'm a realist. I've been in this building before. I know what it's about, and I know that there are certain things that are best kept below decks, as Barnacle Hubert the Sailor here might say. But they're kept in my head too, and in DCI Payne's.'

'Sometimes it can be a lot harder to get out of here than to get in,' Repton pointed out.

'Not in this case,' Skinner told her. 'We're being collected in about half an hour from the front of Thames House by Chief Superintendent McIlhenney, of the Met. If we're any more than five minutes late, he will leave, and will come back, with friends.'

She smiled. 'See, Sir Hubert. I said you were underestimating this man. What's your price, our friend from the north?'

He pointed at Lowery. 'He goes. Amanda becomes Director General, as she should have been all along. Then you go.'

'What about my husband? Do you want his head too?'

'Nah. I imagine you'll cut his balls off as soon as you get him home for landing you in all this. I wouldn't wish any more on the guy.'

'I see.' She frowned and pursed her lips, calling up an image from the past as she stood in her pale blue suit, with every blonde hair in place. 'The first of those is doable, because you're right: Sir Hubert isn't up to the job, and Mrs Dennis is. The second, no, not a chance.'

'No? You don't think I'd bring you down?'

'I don't think you can. Okay, my husband had an affair with someone he met in the course of his work at the Bar and, unknown to him, fathered her child. I'll survive that . . . and it's all you have on me.'

Her mirthless smile was that of an approaching shark, and all of a sudden Skinner felt that the ground beneath his feet was a little less solid.

'Explain, Amanda,' she said.

'We didn't do it, Bob.' His friend looked at him with sympathy in her eyes, and he found himself hating it. 'When you asked to see me, I was afraid this was how it would develop. The thing is, we knew about the child, and we knew of Toni Field's ambitions, which were, granted, without limits, but we felt they were pretty much contained.

'We knew what the sabbatical had been about, even before she went on it. After we deleted the Mauritian birth record, we felt she had nothing to use against us, or against the Home Secretary, so we simply parked her in Scotland, with Brian Storey's assistance. I can see now why he was so keen to help.' She grinned, but only for a second.

'We made her your problem, Bob, not ours. No, we didn't know about the photos, but if we had, I'd have been relying on you or someone like you to find them, as you did. As for the birth certificate, well, we thought that had been dealt with.

'Oh sure, she still had her career planned in her head, Scotland, and then the Met as Storey's successor, but in reality, she'd never have got another job in England. Toni Field was a boil, that was all, and we thought we had lanced her, so there was no need to bump her off.'

'So why did you plant Clyde with her?' he asked. 'To check whether she had any more damaging secrets?'

'Bob, we never did! There was no liaison, there was no Don Sturgeon. Clyde never met the woman, I promise you.'

Skinner gaped at her as he experienced something for the first time in his life: the feeling of being a complete fool, dupe, idiot.

'This is bluff,' he exclaimed. 'Repton's laid down the party line for you.' But as he did, he thought of his own ruse with Houseman, and knew that she was right.

'I'm afraid not.' She rose, walked across to her desk, and produced a paper, from a drawer. 'This is a printout of the data we removed from the Mauritian files. It shows, along with everything else, the name and nationality of the person who registered the birth, and it even carries her signature.'

She handed it to him.

'Marina Deschamps,' he read, his voice sounding dry and strange.

'Exactly. She's how we came to know about the child, and who her father was. The same Marina who told you she didn't know any of her sister's lovers by name. Marina, who invented Toni's relationship with Clyde Houseman. Marina, who it is now clear to me had her half-sister killed.' She smiled at him once more, but with sadness in her eyes. 'My dear, I'm sorry, but you've been played. The scenario you have in your head, about the Home Secretary having Toni assassinated, to keep her husband's dark secret and to spare the government from possible collapse in the ensuing scandal, it's plausible, I'll admit, but it seems that Marina put it there. But don't feel too bad about it,' she added. 'She was an expert. She used to be one of us.'

'She what?' he spluttered.

'She worked here for five years, in MI5, with a pretty high security clearance. When she applied, she was with the Met, and Brian Storey recommended her for the job.'

'Doesn't that tell you something?' he challenged her. 'Given that Toni had Storey by the balls?'

'With hindsight it does. But he may have done it to get himself a little protection from her. Marina left here when Toni took the job in Birmingham. That was our idea originally; we wanted to keep a continuing eye on her and she agreed to do it. She sold it to her sister, so well that she thought it was her own wheeze. Marina's been keeping an eye on her all along.'

'Did Toni ever know she was a spook?' Payne asked, as his boss sat silent, contemplating what he had been told.

'No, never.' Dennis gave a soft chuckle. 'Believe it or not, she also thought Marina worked in a flower shop, of sorts, after she left the Met. I can and will check, but I'm certain that while she was here she would have been in a position to know about Beram Cohen, and his second identity, and that she'd have known about poor old Bazza too.'

She looked at Skinner. 'You do believe me, Bob, don't you? If you don't, there's an easy way to test me. Call her, at home. Send a car to pick her up, under some pretext or other. She won't be there, I promise you.'

He glared back at her. 'Then tell me why,' he demanded. 'Tell me why she did it.'

'If I knew,' Amanda replied, 'I would tell you, without hesitation. But I don't. I don't have a clue. All I can suggest is that you find her and ask her. However, if you do, and knowing you I imagine that you might, you must hand her over to us. None of the stuff that we've talked about here could ever come out in open court.'

'Don't you worry about that,' he growled. 'It won't.' He started to rise, Payne following.

'Hold on just a moment,' the Home Secretary said. 'We're not done yet, not quite. There is still the matter of your continuing silence on this business. I'm not letting you leave without that being secured.'

'How are you going to do that? I've got nothing to gain, personally, by going public, but if you knew anything about Scots law and procedures, you'd realise that having begun the investigation I'm bound to report its findings to the procurator fiscal.'

'Then it will have to be edited, otherwise . . .'

He looked at her, and realised that she was a rarity, a politician who should not, rather than could not, be underestimated. He had read a description of Emily Repton as 'a prime minister in waiting, but not for much longer'. Feeling the force of the certainty that radiated from her, he understood that assessment.

'Otherwise?' he repeated.

'Show him, Sir Hubert,' she murmured.

'No,' Skinner countered, 'I don't listen to him. You tell me.'

'Very well.' She reached out a hand; Lowery took a plastic folder from his pocket and passed it to her.

She selected a photograph and held it up. 'You seem to have recovered well from the public break-up of your marriage, Chief Constable. This was taken early this morning, as you left the home of your former wife.'

'So what?' he laughed. 'Our children are with her just now, and I wanted to see them.'

'But you have joint custody; you'll see them at the weekend.'

He snatched the image from her, crumpled it, and threw it on the floor. 'Go on, then,' he challenged her. 'Leak it and see what follows. I'll tell the Scottish media that it's a Tory plot to discredit me. See those two words "Tory plot"? In Scotland they're a flame to the touch paper. They'll be on you like piranha. You've got to do better than that.'

'I can. Your ex-wife is an American citizen. Now that you and she are no longer married, she's here because she's been given right to remain. That can be revoked.'

'We'd see you in court if you tried that.'

'It would have to be an American court; we'd have her removed inside twenty-four hours.'

'And twenty-four hours after that I'm on a plane to New York and we remarry. Come on, Home Secretary, up your game. You still need to do better.' And yet, as he spoke, he sensed that she could, and that her first two shots had been mere range-finders.

'If you insist,' she replied, and her voice told him that he had been right. 'It might come as a surprise to you to learn that your present wife's liaison with Mr Joey Morocco has been going on for years. It began before you met and it continued during your marriage.'

She took a series of photographs from the folder and handed them to him. He glanced through them; they showed Aileen and the actor at various locations: in a garden with Loch Lomond stretched out below them, on the balcony of her Glasgow flat, leaving a hotel in a street he did not recognise. None of them were explicit, but they displayed intimacy clearly enough.

He handed them back, and shrugged. 'Sorry, no surprise,' he said. 'Nor is it my business any more either. By the way, after the *Daily News* photos you might be able to sell those to *Hello!* or *OK!* but nobody else is going to buy them.'

'Probably not,' Repton conceded, 'but every newspaper in the country would run this, front page. The trouble with our modern celebrity culture is that it's so damn predictable. Where there are actors, there are the inevitable parties, with the same inevitable temptations. Most politicians have the sense to steer clear of them, but not, it seems, Ms de Marco.'

She took the last two items from the folder and gave them to him. The photographs had been taken in a ladies' toilet. There were three washbasins set into a flat surface, with a mirrored wall above.

The first picture showed two women, expensively clad, watching while a third, her face part-hidden by her hair, bent over a line of white powder, with a tube held to her nose. In the second, all three women were standing, their laughter, and their faces, reflected in the mirror.

He stared at it, then at Emily Repton with pure hatred in his eyes.

'The original is in a place of safety,' Sir Hubert Lowery barked. 'Not here, though, just in case Mrs Dennis feels obliged to do a favour for an old friend. I don't have to tell you . . .'

Skinner moved with remarkable speed for a man in his early fifties. He moved half a pace forward and hit the Director General with a thunderous, hooking, left-handed punch that caught him on the right temple. The man's legs turned to spaghetti and he was unconscious before he hit the floor.

'I've wanted to do that,' he murmured, 'ever since I saw him blindside our outside half at Murrayfield.'

'I did warn him,' Amanda Dennis remarked. 'I told him you'd want to hit somebody, and since he'd be the only man in the room . . .'

'He'll be all right,' the chief growled. 'His skull's too thick and his brain's too small for there to be any lasting damage.'

He turned to Emily Repton. Her eyes told him she had enjoyed the show. 'Spell it out,' he told her.

She nodded. 'Hard man, soft centre,' she said. 'Your marriage may be over, but I don't believe you would wish to cause Ms de Marco the damage, the distress and the disgrace that would follow publication of those images. The fact that it was a one-off doesn't matter. Her career would be gone, way beyond the U-bend, and so would her employable life. As indeed it will, if one single line in one single newspaper, or blog, should ever link my husband to Antonia Field and her child.

'You can write your report to the procurer physical or whatever he's called. It will say that your investigation has reached the conclusion that the balance of probability is that Chief Constable Field's killing was ordered and funded by Mexican or Colombian drug cartels that she compromised during her time with the Serious and Organised Crime Agency. There will be not the slightest hint of impropriety by the Security Service.'

She frowned. 'I'm not going to ask if you agree. There is no alternative on the table; you will do what you're told. Go back to Scotland, Mr Skinner, and be the big provincial copper in your little provincial pond. This is London; the power will always lie here. If you can't live with that truth, you could always resign.'

Skinner stared down at her, unblinking, until the coldness in his eyes made her shiver and look away.

'You really don't know me, Home Secretary,' he told her. 'My report's already dictated and that is more or less what it says. Even if my suspicions had been one hundred per cent right, there would have been no mileage for me in pulling this building down.'

He nodded towards Lowery, who was beginning to stir on the floor. 'Getting rid of him will do nicely thanks, and I've shown you why that has to happen.'

'Agreed,' Repton said.

'But you are right,' he continued, 'that I won't see Aileen broken by you. Hell, woman, I know you and Lowery set her up. Any idiot, even me, could see that. She can't hold her booze at the best of times, and I can tell from the photo she was rat-arsed when that all went off. I'm sure that if I could identify the two other women, I'd find that at least one was on Five's payroll.

'But that's by the by; I'll go along with your deal. Your husband's safe. If you're prepared to tolerate his adultery, that's your business. I've never met the man, so he really means nothing to me. Plus, I have no practical need to remove him, since he isn't in my sphere of influence.'

'That's pragmatic of you,' she mocked, her tone heavy with sarcasm.

'But you are,' he snapped, as he picked up his case. 'And you disgust me. You're the embodiment of everything I loathe about politics and politicians. Frankly, I don't want to be any part of any world in which someone like you operates, and there are only two things I can do about that. So I'll go back to my provincial, sub-national pond, and I will work out which one it's going to be.'

Fifty-Six

'No thanks, Amanda, I'll pass on that one personally. Maybe I'll send Lowell Payne instead. I was impressed by the way he handled himself the other day, and it's persuaded me that he's the man to take over what was a vacancy as head of CTIS.

'He's in post already. It wouldn't be right of me to come, when I might not be a police officer for much longer. You take care now, and watch your back as long as that woman's standing behind you.'

He ended the call and slipped his mobile into the big canvas bag that lay by his side.

'What was that about?' Sarah asked. They were sitting on a travelling rug on the beach at Gullane, watching their two sons trying to persuade Seonaid that the seawater was as warm as they said.

'Amanda Dennis,' he said. 'She's having a two-day review of the Field fiasco in London, on Monday and Tuesday. It's a natural response: what went wrong and how to prevent any recurrence. She said she's ordered Houseman and his entire Glasgow team down there, and asked if I wanted to attend.'

'Were you serious in what you said to her?'

'About Lowell? Sure. He never wavered in there and he turned out to be very good at reading people. He's a natural for the job, and it gives me grounds to give him an acting promotion, without anyone calling it nepotism. Mind you,' he chuckled, 'Jean wouldn't be too pleased if I send him off to London again so soon, so I don't think I'll pass on the invite.'

She shook her head. 'I didn't mean were you sure about Lowell. I was talking about the last part. Do you really mean that?'

'I think I do,' he said. 'I am edging myself towards walking away from the Strathclyde job and leaving the police service altogether, as soon as I can. All the way back from London I argued the toss with myself, and I still am arguing. It's doing my head in. I never wanted to destroy the Security Service itself, only to sort any people that might have crossed the line. I'm a realist, I understand how the world has to work at times. But given what I knew, or thought I knew, I had some questions that needed answers.

'As it was, I got it wrong, although not all of it: the Home Secretary did misuse her position by having Lowery delete the Mauritian birth record. Now I'm being blackmailed by Emily Repton herself, to save her husband's reputation and both their careers. You should have heard her, and seen her. That woman is fucking evil.'

'She threatened me? Really?'

'Yes, but we both knew that was crap; that was just her way of telling me how far she could reach into my life. I've taken legal advice since. Your passport may be American, but your children are British. There isn't a judge in Scotland who'd allow your deportation.'

'But her threat against Aileen? Is that for real?'

Bob nodded. 'Oh yes. She went with Morocco to a party in Glasgow, after the premiere of a movie he was in. They'd been watching the pair of them for long enough to be fairly sure she would go, especially since I was at a security conference that MI5 had set up.

'While Joey was away schmoozing the press, Hubert Lowery's two women got her shit-faced, possibly with a little chemical assistance, then set up the cocaine scene in the toilets. I know all this because Amanda made Lowery tell her as he was clearing his desk.'

'How did she make him cough that up?'

He gave a bitter laugh. 'She threatened to tell me where he lives. That was enough.'

'Can Amanda do anything about it, now she's in the top job?'

'Not with Emily Reptile as Home Secretary.'

'If you had been right, and Toni Field had been killed on Repton's orders, what would you have done?'

'As much as I could, although that might not have been a lot, since so many of the players are dead and so much of it is deniable.'

'Are you really satisfied that isn't what happened?'

He nodded. 'Yes, I'm sure. I got taken. As Mandy suggested, I did send a car to pick up Marina, as soon as I got out of there. She'd gone, right enough. Sofia thought she was just shopping . . . or so she said . . . but she hasn't been seen since. Amanda was right. The woman made me look like an idiot. Hell, I am an idiot! She fed me little hints to steer me in the direction she wanted, towards them and away from her.

'That last scene, her identifying Clyde Houseman as Toni's mystery lover, that was the final piece of the con. I bought it, like an absolute sucker, and went charging off down to London, to commit professional suicide.'

'It wasn't suicide,' Sarah insisted. 'You don't need to do anything so drastic as quit.' She paused. 'Don't go off on me for asking this, but could this depression from which speaking as a doctor, you are clearly suffering, be related to the fact that you feel humiliated, embarrassed, and maybe even a little unmanned by what this Marina woman did to you?'

'Why should I take the hump?' he asked. 'It's a fair question. But the answer's no. At the time, sure, I had a red face. Now, I see it the same as a golf game. Marina was good, and so was I. But where I shot a birdie, she had an eagle. When that happens out there on Gullane Number One, you don't give up the game. You say to the other guy, "Good shot," and then you stuff him at the next hole. If I leave the force, it'll be because I can't go after Repton from within it. But whatever happens, I'm going to find Marina Deschamps.'

She looked at him, a little afraid of the answer to the question she was about to pose. 'When you find her, what will you do?'

'I could eliminate her,' he told her. 'As long as I don't do it in the middle of Piccadilly Circus at rush hour, I really don't believe anyone would want to know. Too many guilty secrets.' He stopped, then laughed at the alarm on her face. 'I could,' he repeated, 'but don't worry, I won't. There is an alternative.'

He jumped up from the rug. 'Come on, let's go and paddle with the kids. The water can't be that cold.'

'Okay.' She took his hand and let him pull her to her feet, then laughed, as his phone sounded. 'I thought you were going to leave that at home,' she said.

'Force of habit. I'll ignore it.'

'Hell no,' she retorted, fishing it out of their beach bag. 'You'll fret if you do that.' She handed it to him. 'It's Mario.'

'Ah, that's different.' He took it from her and accepted the call. 'What is it?' he asked. 'Has Paula had the baby?'

'She has indeed,' the new father replied. 'Wee Eamon put in an appearance about half an hour ago. Like shelling peas, the midwife said, although not within Paula's hearing.'

'Big fella, that is absolutely great, I am so pleased for you both.'

'In that case, you're going to be even more pleased. About two hours ago a bloke walked into the St Leonards office with a bag that he found when he was sorting old clothes from one of those public recycling points. It was mixed up among them all, and there was a laptop inside it, wrapped in a shirt with a Selfridges label on it. The battery was flat, but the desk staff found a charger and plugged it in. When they switched it on, it said "Byron's MacBook". I reckon we've found your man Cohen's missing computer.'

Looking at Bob, Sarah saw his face light up, saw all his gloom and pessimism evaporate, and she knew that whatever he had been told, it had been a tipping point in his life.

'Mario,' she heard him exclaim, 'that's brilliant. It means the show's back on the road. I'd like it in Glasgow in my office, by Monday morning.' She thought he was about to end the call, but he went on, as if an afterthought had come to him just in time.

'One other thing,' he added. 'I want to see wee Ramsey again, but not in my office. Find him and tell him I'll be shopping in Fort Kinnaird at noon tomorrow and that I'll fancy a hot dog from the stall by the crossing. There'll be one in it for him as well if he turns up.'

Fifty-Seven

'Welcome back, Detective Inspector,' Skinner said, with feeling. He jerked his thumb in Provan's direction. 'This little bugger's been intolerable since you've been away.'

'Tell me about it,' Lottie chuckled. 'He's never been off the bloody phone. He'll be wanting to adopt me next.'

'Everything's all right at home, is it?' Her eyes went somewhere else for a second. 'Sorry,' he exclaimed. 'It's none of my business and if you don't want to talk about it, that's fine by me.'

'Not at all, Chief, not at all,' she replied. 'I had a tough couple of days, but I'm okay now. Scott's living with his brother out in Airdrie . . . at least that was the address they gave when he made his court appearance this morning. He turned up at the house again on Saturday, but he was sober, and it was only to collect his clothes.'

'Did you know that Sergeant . . .'

Her nod stopped him in mid-sentence. 'Yes, I was told. Her husband got himself arrested for thumping her. I'd have put in a word for him if he'd battered Scott, but he must have decided that hitting her was less risky. Maybe she's with him now. I don't know and I don't want to. Jakey's come to terms with the fact that his dad won't be back, and that's all I'm worried about.'

'Of course,' Skinner agreed. 'He's the most important person involved. Right,' he exclaimed, 'if we're all ready, let me explain to you what this is about.' He smiled. 'They thought it was all over . . .' he chuckled. 'But no, thanks to a large slice of luck, the game may still be on . . .' He rose, stepped over to his desk, and returned holding a laptop, which he laid on the table. '. . . and those who don't believe in miracles may like to have a rethink. That, lady and gentleman, is Byron Millbank's missing MacBook, the place where his wife told Detective Superintendent Payne that he kept his whole life. Normally,' he continued, 'there would have been a team of experts huddled over it for a week, trying to work out the password. In this case Byron gave us an unwitting clue, when he said to Mrs Millbank that the chances of getting into it were the same as winning the Lottery.

'So we had her rummage about among his personal things, and guess what she found? Yup, a payslip for a lottery season ticket.' He opened the computer to reveal a slip of paper, with six twin-digit numbers noted on it. 'There you are,' he said, and slid the slim computer across to Mann.

'Has anyone looked at it?' she asked.

'No, it's all yours. I want you and that bright young lad Paterson to get into it, and see if you can find anything that doesn't relate to the dull and fairly uneventful life of Mr Byron Millbank but to the rather more colourful world of Beram Cohen.'

'What about me, Chief?' Provan asked, with a hint of a rumble. 'Am Ah too old for that shite?'

Skinner threw him a sharp look. 'Almost certainly,' he said. 'But as it happens I've got something else in mind for you. I want you to get back on to your friends in Mauritius, and find the birth registration of Marina Deschamps. She's thirty-two years old, so the probability is that it will be a paper record. Birth date, April the ninth, so you'll know exactly where to look.'

'Marina Day Champs? The last chief's sister?'

'Not quite,' Skinner corrected him. 'The last chief's missing half-sister. There are things I don't know about that lady, and I want to.'

'Can Ah no' just ask her mother?'

'No chance. You do not go near her mother. Leave that to CTIS, Superintendent Payne's new team. She says she doesn't know where her daughter's gone, but we're tapping her phone, just in case. Like mother like daughters? You never know.'

Fifty-Eight

'The chief seems in better form today,' Dan Provan remarked, as they stepped back into the suite in Pitt Street that he had left the week before. 'When Ah saw him on Thursday, when Ah wis closing this place up, he wis like a panda that discovered he'd slept in and missed his big date wi' Mrs Panda.'

'Why's he interested in Marina Deschamps all of a sudden?' Lottie Mann pondered.

'How come you can say that and Ah cannae? Day Champs.'

'Possibly because I have a wider outlook on life than you, and expose myself to other cultures,' she suggested. 'You've got no interest in anything that doesn't involve crime, real or imaginary.'

'Maybe no,' but Ah'm shit hot at that. Ah've thought about puttin' ma name up for *Mastermind.*'

Beside him Banjo Paterson spluttered.

'You can laugh, son, but tell me, how many murders was Peter Manuel convicted of?'

'Eight.'

'No, seven. One charge wis dropped for lack of evidence. What was Baby Face Nelson's real name?'

'Who was Baby Face Nelson?

'Eedjit. Lester Gillis. What was Taggart's first sergeant called?'

'Mike?'

'Naw, he wis the second. It was Peter, Peter Livingstone.'

'Enough!' Lottie Mann laughed. 'If they ever have a "Brain of Cambuslang" contest you might be in with a shout, but until then stop showboating for the lad. All these things happened before he was born.'

'So did Christmas,' Provan retorted, 'but he knows all about that.'

He shuffled off to the desk he had adopted, and dug out the old-fashioned notebook that was still his chosen style of database. He opened it at the most recent entries and found the number of the Mauritian government. He keyed it in and waited.

'Mr Bachoo, please, Registry Department,' he asked. 'Tell him it's DS Provan again, Strathclyde Police in Glasgow, Scotland.'

Paterson grinned across at him. 'You didn't have any problem with that name,' he said.

'It sounds like a sneeze. Yes, Mr Bachoo,' he carried on, without a pause, 'it's me again. Ah've got another request for ye, another registration Ah'm trying to trace. This one goes back thirty-two years, but Ah've got a birth date this time: April the ninth. The name of the wean . . . Ah mean the child, is Marina Day Champs. Could ye do that for me?'

'Without difficulty,' the official replied. 'That period has not been computerised yet, and the records are kept on this floor. This time, could you hold on, please. Last week I was reprimanded for making a foreign call without permission.'

'Aye sure. Sorry about that; your bean counters must be worse than ours.'

'I beg your pardon?'

'Nothin', nothin'. Ah'll hold on.'

He leaned back in his chair, the phone pressed loosely to his ear, expecting more Bollywood music but hearing instead only the background chatter of an open-plan office. He glanced across at Paterson's desk but saw that it was empty, and guessed that the DC and DI were pressing on with their task.

He passed the time by listing, mentally and chronologically, the fictional officers who had been Jim Taggart's colleagues and successors, and the names of the actors who had played them. He was wondering, not for the first time, about the real relationship between Mike and Jackie, when he heard the phone in Mauritius being picked up.

'I have it,' Mr Bachoo announced, sounding pleased with himself. 'The child Marina Shelby Deschamps, Mauritian citizen, was born in Port Louis on the day you mentioned and registered on the following day. The mother was Sofia Deschamps, Mauritian citizen, and the father, who registered the birth, is named as Hillary, with two ls, Shelby, Australian citizen. I could fax this document to you; my superior has given me permission.'

'If ye would, Ah'd appreciate that.' He scrambled through the papers on the desk, and found the Pitt Street fax number, which he read out, digit by digit. 'Thanks, Mr Bachoo. Ah'm pretty sure that'll be all.'

'It was a pleasure, Detective Sergeant. As I believe you say, no worries.'

Provan smiled as he hung up, then added the name he had been given to his notebook. 'Hillary Shelby,' he murmured. 'Hillary Shelby.' And then he frowned, as another potential *Mastermind* answer popped out of his mental treasure chest.

'Hillary Shelby,' he repeated as he booted up his computer. 'Now that name definitely rings a bell.'

Fifty-Nine

'So what have we got here?' Banjo Paterson asked himself, with his DI looking over his shoulder. 'Standard MacBook screen layout. Let's see where he keeps his email. Mmm, he's got Google Chrome loaded up as well as Safari. Probably means he used that as his search engine. Let's see.'

He clicked on a multicoloured icon at the foot of the screen. 'Yes,' he murmured with satisfaction as a window opened. 'Big surprise, I don't think; the Rondar mail order site is his home page. Let's see what else he's bookmarked. Okay, he's got a Google account for his email.'

He clicked on a red envelope, with a two-word description alongside. 'Byron mail.'

'Auto sign-in,' he murmured. 'Lucky us, otherwise we'd have had to go back to the IT technicians to crack his password. His email address is Byron at Rondar dot co dot UK. Here we go.'

He inspected the second window. 'That's his inbox. He's got three unopened messages . . . What the hell?' He opened one headed 'National Lottery'. 'Oh dear.' It was half sigh, half laugh. 'The poor bastard's lottery ticket came up last Wednesday; he matched four balls and won ninety-nine quid.'

He hovered the cursor over an arrow and the next message opened.

It was from someone called Mike, confirming a squash court booking on the following Thursday for a semi-final tie in the club knock-out competition.

'Lucky boy, Mike,' Mann muttered. A wicked grin crossed her face. 'Let me in,' she told Paterson, leaned across him and keyed in a reply. *'Can't make it, have to scratch; good luck in the final.'* She hit the send button.

'Should you have done that, boss?' the DC asked, as she backed off.

'Maybe not, but the guy deserved to know. Go on.'

He moved on to the last unopened message. The sender was identified as 'Jocelyn' also using the Rondar mail system. 'The mother-in-law, as I understand it,' the DI told him.

'Mother-in-law from hell, in that case,' Paterson replied. 'Look at this.'

Mann peered at the screen, and read:

I have just received the latest quarterly management accounts. These show an operating loss of just under seventy-seven thousand pounds and make this the seventh successive quarter in which this company has lost money. Our auditors estimate that at this rate we will be insolvent by the end of the next financial year.

I have analysed the situation and have reached the inescapable conclusion that we have been on the slide since your father-in-law passed away. He and I always knew that the key to this business is not only what we sell but, as importantly, what we buy. We have to offer our customers attractive products at attractive prices while maintaining our profit margins. When Jesse was our buyer, we were able to do so very successfully. He was sure that when you took over from him, this would be maintained, but it is now clear to me that this confidence was misplaced.

I cannot allow this situation to continue, simply to sit on my hands and watch my company go out of existence. Son-in-law or not, I am going to have to relieve you of your duties and to declare you redundant. You and I both know that you are not suited to this line of work and never have been. So does Golda but she is too loyal to admit it. I intend to handle the buying function myself, with the assistance of my niece Bathsheba. When we are back in profit, Golda can expect to receive dividend income, but until then you are on your own.

'Lovely,' the DI said. 'Byron Millbank doesn't seem to have had a hell of a lot of luck.'

'Neither did Beram Cohen,' Paterson pointed out, 'culminating in them both being in a cool box in the mortuary.'

'Aye, but we're not so lucky ourselves. This doesn't tell us anything about Cohen, and that's what we're after. How about old emails? Could there be anything there?'

'I'm checking that, but I don't see anything. There's nothing filed or archived, not that I can see. I've checked the bin and even that's empty. He must have done that manually, the sign of a careful man.'

'What about the rest of it, other than his correspondence?'

'Gimme a few minutes. Please, gaffer.' He looked up at her. 'I don't really work best with somebody looking over my shoulder.' He smiled. 'A mug of tea wouldn't go amiss, though.'

'You cheeky bastard,' she exclaimed. 'I'm the DI, you're the DC; you're the bloody tea boy around here. However, in this situation . . . how many sugars do you take?'

'Me? None, thanks. Just milk.'

She left him in her room and crossed the main office. She glanced across at Provan, but he had his back to her and a phone to his ear.

She shook the kettle to check that it was full, then switched it on. And watched. And waited.

As she did, her mind wandered to her shattered family. Scott had been remanded on bail to a future court hearing, and to its inevitable conclusion. He had shown some contrition when he had come for his clothes, but she had smelled stale alcohol on his breath, and that had been enough to maintain her resolve. There would be no way back for him, no way, Jose.

And for her? There would be nothing other than her career, and bringing up her son. *I will not be making that mistake again*, she told herself. *There are no happy endings; sooner or later fate will always kick you in the teeth . . . and very much sooner if your husband is an alcoholic gambler who was shagging another woman within the first year of your marriage.*

The forgotten kettle broke into her thoughts by boiling. She made the tea, three mugs, one for Provan, stewed, as he liked it, distributed them and sat at her desk, waiting patiently for Banjo to finish his exploration of the dead man's double life.

Eventually he did, and turned towards her. 'Byron Millbank,' he announced, 'liked Celine Dion, Dusty Springfield, Black Sabbath, Alan Jackson, and Counting Crows, at least that's what his iTunes library indicates. He loved his wife and child, respected his late father-in-law but had no time for his mother-in-law. That's obvious from a study of his iPhoto albums. There's only one photograph of her on it, it's as unflattering as you can get and it's captioned "Parah", which I've just discovered is Hebrew for "Cow".

'He was a fan of Arsenal Football Club, not unnaturally, given where he lived. He had an American Express Platinum card, personal, not through the company. He had an Amazon Kindle account and his library included the complete works of Dickens and Shakespeare, the biography of Ronald Reagan and a dozen crime novels by Mark Billingham, Michael Jecks and Val McDermid.

'He had an Xbox and liked war games, big time. His most visited websites were Wikipedia, Sky News, the BBC and ITV players, the CIA World Factbook, and a charity called Problem Solvers.'

'Wow!' Mann exclaimed, with irony. 'How much more typical could this man have been? You're just described Mr Average Thirty-something.'

The DC nodded. 'Agreed. There is nothing out of the ordinary about him at all . . . apart from one thing. The charity: it doesn't exist. And that's where he does get interesting.'

Sixty

'It's not a charity at all, sir,' Paterson ventured. 'If you ask me, it's more of a doorway.'

'Explain,' Skinner said.

'It's the website, sir. It's called www dot problemsolvers dot org. Dot org domains used to be just for charities, but these days that's not necessarily so. To be sure I checked with the Charities Commission; they've never heard of it.

'On top of that,' the DC continued, 'it's weird in another way. It's password protected. I only got in because Millbank was careless in one respect: he saved his passwords on his computer, thinking, I suppose, that nobody else would ever use it.'

'When you did get in there, what did you find?' the chief constable asked.

'Nothing much; it's very simple. I'm sure he set it up himself. There's just the two pages. The home page has only six words: "Personnel problems? Discreet and permanent solutions." Then there's a message board. But there's no history on the site at all. He's wiped it all. However, there is one message still up on the board. It's possible that he left it there because the reply will go automatically to the sender, without Millbank ever needing to know who he was.'

'Not Millbank, Cohen,' Skinner countered. 'This is definitely

Beram Cohen. You've found him. What did the message say?'

'Confirm payment made as agreed, to sort code eighty-one forty twenty-two, account number zero six nine five two one five one.'

'Have you followed it up?'

'Not yet, sir.'

'Then do so, tomorrow morning. Wherever the bank is it'll have knocked off for the day by now. When you find it, trace the source of the payment and find out if any withdrawals have been made from it lately. Lottie, Banjo, that's good work.' He turned to Provan. 'Now, Sergeant, you're clearly bursting your braces to tell me something. It's your turn, so out with it.'

Sixty-One

'Is this not a real bore for you, Davie?' Skinner asked his driver, as they passed the clubhouse that welcomed golfing visitors to Gullane, and picked up speed. 'Same round trip every day, sometimes twice a day.'

'Absolutely not, Chief,' Constable Cole replied. 'I love driving, especially nice big motors like this one. I've done all the advanced courses there are, too. When I get moved out of this job, as I will, 'cos nothing's for ever, I'm going to try to get a spot as an instructor.'

'Good for you. But don't you ever miss the company? Most cops work in pairs. Most cops meet people through their work . . . even if some of those are rank bad yins.' He laughed at his own words. 'Listen to me,' he exclaimed. 'Second week in post and I'm lapsing into Weegie-speak already. I'm spending too much time with that wee bugger Provan, that's what it is. Maybe being a lone wolf isn't such a bad thing.'

'Maybe not,' Cole agreed.

'No, but seriously, does this never get to you? Don't you ever get the urge to see some action?'

The constable tilted his head back slightly, to help his voice carry into the back seat. 'The last action I saw, Chief, was over two years ago. We got a call to a cesspit of a housing scheme they'd used as accommodation for asylum seekers. Some of the neighbourhood Neds had given one of their kids a going-over and the dads went after them, mob-handed. It went into a full-blooded riot. My crew was sent in there with shields, batons and helmets, to re-establish order, we were told.' He chuckled. 'There hadn't been any proper order in that place for about five years, so they were asking quite a lot of us.

'Anyway, we waded in, and got the two sides separated. Just as well, because the local hooligans had turned out in force. They were winning the battle and there would have been fatalities if we hadn't stopped it. What we done, in effect, was protect the immigrants, but they never seen it that way. We had tearaways coming at us with swords and machetes, and behind us the foreigners were chucking bottles, rocks, all sorts of shit at us.'

Skinner glanced at the rear-view mirror as he paused, and saw him frown.

'Those riot helmets, sir,' he continued, 'they're pretty good, but if somebody drops a television set on you from the balcony of a third-floor flat, there's only so much protection they can give. It probably saved my life, but I still had a skull fracture, three displaced vertebrae in my neck and a broken shoulder. I was off work for nearly a year. When I came back they sent me on an advanced driving course. I did well at it. When Chief Constable Field arrived she wanted a full-time driver, and I got picked.'

'I see,' Skinner said. 'In that case, as long as I'm here, you'll be in the driving seat. Besides,' he continued, 'this is good for me too. Having you lets me get through shedloads of paperwork that I couldn't do if I drove myself, or if I took the train, for that would be too public. And the more of that I do while I'm travelling, the more time I have to put myself about, to see people, and, as important, to let them see me.

So,' he said, pulling his case across the seat towards him, 'time to shift some of it.'

He worked steadily for fifteen minutes until the car was half a mile from the slip road that joined the Edinburgh bypass.

'Davie,' he called, 'I want to make a detour, if you would. Go straight on, then take the next exit and head left, until you come to the second roundabout. You'll see a hot food and coffee stall. I'd like you to wait in the shopping centre car park, while I pick up a couple of bacon rolls. It's a lot less fuss to buy my breakfast than to make it myself.'

'I'm lucky, sir. I get mine made for me.'

'I'm lucky too. Looking out for yourself can be a price worth paying.' He grinned as he saw the driver's expression in the mirror. 'Don't mind me,' he said. 'I'm not always that cynical. The fact is, when we are together as a family, I enjoy making it for everybody.'

His directions were clear and accurate. PC Cole spotted the stall as he passed the first exit from the second roundabout, did a complete circuit and parked in the road facing the way he had come.

'Want anything?' the chief asked him.

'No thanks, sir, I'm fine.'

He relaxed in his seat as his passenger stepped out. He watched him in the nearside wing mirror as he sprinted towards the pedestrian crossing to catch the green light. Davie had never seen a senior cop who would go to work in a light tan cotton jacket; even the CID people usually wore suits, or expensive leather jackets in the case of some of the young, newly blooded DCs.

The stallholder must have known Skinner, he reckoned, for the boss smiled at him as he gave him his order. Or maybe he was only in a chatty mood, for he seemed to strike up a conversation with the scruffy wee man who was the only other punter there.

Whatever they were talking about, it must have been serious, for the other guy never cracked a smile, not even when the chief, his back half turned towards the car, slipped him something.

Christ, Cole thought, *the wee sod's on the scrounge. Not a bad guy, my boss. He likes getting the breakfast for everybody, even for a wee panhandler like that.*

Sixty-Two

It took almost no time at all to track down the bank account of Problem Solvers, once Banjo Paterson had opened the resource site that would take him there. He keyed in the sort code and number and clicked 'Validate', then leaned back with a smile on his face that broke all previous office records for smugness.

'There you are,' he announced. 'The account's held in the Bank of Lincoln, in an office in Grantham. There's no street address, only a PO box number, but there's a phone number.' He scribbled it in a pad and passed it to his DI.

'Thanks,' she said.

'Son,' Provan grunted, 'you better get a safe deposit box for a' these gold stars ye've been gettin', otherwise you might find yersel' bein' mugged on the way home.'

Mann took the note into her small office and dialled the number. 'Bank of Lincoln,' a cheery female voice answered. 'How can I be of service?'

'You can phone me back.'

'Pardon?'

'This is Detective Inspector Charlotte Mann, Strathclyde CID, Glasgow. I need to speak to your manager, urgently. If you call me back through my main switchboard number which I'll give you now,' she read it out, 'he'll know I am who I say I am. When you ring back, ask for extension one forty-eight.'

'Yes, madam. I won't be a minute.'

She was over-optimistic, by just under ten minutes, but did have the grace to apologise. 'I'm sorry to have kept you waiting, madam, but Mr Harrison, the branch manager, has only just become available. I'll put you through to him now.'

Mann had time to growl a curt 'Thank you' before the line clicked and a man spoke.

'Inspector, is it?'

'Detective Inspector.'

'I see. My name is Nigel Harrison, how can I help you?' There was a wariness in his voice. She had heard its like often enough in her career to know that assistance was not at the top of his agenda.

'I want to talk to you about an account that's held at your branch.' She recited the number. 'We believe that it's in the name of an entity calling itself Problem Solvers.'

'Let me check that,' the manager murmured. She waited, anticipating another long interlude, but he came back on the line after less than a minute. 'Yes, I have it on screen now. Problem Solvers; it's a charity.'

'So it says,' Mann retorted. 'I'd like to know about money moving in and out recently, within the last few weeks.'

'Ahh. I was afraid this conversation might take such a turn. I don't think I can help you there. I took the precaution of consulting my general manager before I returned your call, and was reminded that it's our head office policy to afford our clients confidentiality.'

'It's my policy,' she retorted, 'to get tough with people when I believe they're obstructing my investigation.'

She was sure she heard him sniff before he replied. 'If your questions are well founded,' he said, 'I'm sure the court will furnish you with the appropriate warrant.'

'I'm in no doubt about that,' she agreed, 'but I was hoping you'd be more cooperative. You're not, and that's too bad, because my questions are now going to move up a notch. You say this client of yours is a charity, yes?'

'Yes. We have a special account category for charities.'

'So it will be registered with the Charities Commission, yes?'

'Of course.'

'Sorry, Mr Harrison; it isn't.'

'But Mr Cohen assured me . . .'

'This would be Mr Beram Cohen, yes? The late Mr Beram Cohen?'

'The late . . .' the banker spluttered. 'Oh my! What happened?'

'He died. People do. So you see, he's got no confidentiality left to protect.'

'But Problem Solvers has.'

'A bogus charity? Tell me, sir, do the words "proceeds of crime" and possibly also "money laundering", which I'll throw into the mix just for fun, have any meaning for you?'

'What are you saying?'

'I'm saying that unless you cooperate with me, my next conversation will be with my colleagues in Lincolnshire Police. No more than an hour after that, they'll descend on you with that warrant you're insisting on, and they won't do it quietly. In fact, I'll ask them to make as much noise as they can. How will that go down with head office and your general manager?'

'Well . . .'

She had been bluffing, but his hesitancy told her that she was winning. 'I don't want to bully you, Mr Harrison, but this is urgent, and you'll be doing us a great service if you talk to me.'

She heard an intake of breath as he weighed up his options and made his decision. 'All right,' he sighed. 'Recent traffic through the account, you said?'

'Yes. Go back three months for starters.'

'Can do. I have it on screen, in fact. Two months ago, the charity received a donation of three hundred thousand pounds. One month later, two money transfers of fifty thousand pounds each were made, one to a bank in New Zealand, the other to Australia. Both of these were private accounts; that means I can't see the owner's name. That was followed by a third, for thirty thousand pounds, to a company in Andorra called Holyhead.

'The most recent transaction took place just under three weeks ago. Ahh,' he exclaimed, 'I remember that one. Mr Cohen called into the branch and made a withdrawal of fifteen thousand pounds in cash. It was potentially embarrassing, as my chief teller had let us get rather low on cash, and there had been a bit of a run that morning. We were forced to pay Mr Cohen his money in new fifties. Some customers would have been unhappy about that, but he said it was no problem.'

'I don't suppose you have a record of the serial numbers, do you?' she asked.

Harrison surprised her. 'As a matter of fact I do. Those notes were brand new; we were the first recipients. I can send that information to you.'

'Thanks. It would let us tick some boxes.'

'Anything else?'

'Oh yes,' Mann replied, 'the most important of all. Who made the payment of three hundred thousand?'

'That came from a bank in Jersey, from an account in the name of an investment company registered in Jersey. It's called Pam Limited.'

Mann felt her eyebrows rise halfway up her forehead, but she said nothing.

'Is that all?' Harrison asked her.

'Yes. Thank you . . . eventually.'

'Come on, Inspector. You must understand my caution.'

'I suppose.'

'What about the Problem Solvers account? Mr Cohen was the only contact we have with the organisation, whatever it is.'

'I'd suggest that you freeze it,' the DI told him. 'I have no idea what its legal status is, although Cohen's widow might fancy laying claim to it. Whatever, it's not my problem. I'll be reporting this; I'm sure someone will be in touch.'

'Your investigation,' Harrison ventured. 'You didn't say what it's about, but am I right in guessing that it's into Mr Cohen's death rather than this Problem Solver business?'

'No, you're not; it's into someone else's murder. You see, Mr Harrison, Mr Cohen's business was making people dead. Those were the sort of problems that he solved.'

Sixty-Three

'P am Limited,' Skinner repeated.

'Yes,' Mann confirmed. 'I checked with the company registration office in Jersey. According to the articles, it stands for Personal Asset Management. Its most recent accounts show that it's worth over two hundred and fifty million.'

'Who owns it?'

'According to the public record, its only shareholder is a man called Peter Friedman.'

'And who the hell's he?' the chief asked, frowning, then muttering, 'Although there's something familiar about that name.'

'Banjo ran a search on people called Friedman,' she told him. 'He came up with two singers, a journalist and an economist, although he's dead. The only references he got to anyone called Peter Friedman were a few press stories. He showed them to me; they all related to donations to good causes, charities and the like.'

'What, like Problem Solvers?' Skinner retorted.

'No, sir. Real ones, like Chest Heart and Stroke, Cancer UK, Children First, and Shelter. Only one of them gave any detail on him beyond his name and that was the *Saltire*, in a report on a charity fund-raiser dinner in the Royal Scottish Museum, in Edinburgh, six months ago. It described him as "a reclusive philanthropist"; nothing beyond that. If a wealthy man has that low a profile on the internet, then he really is reclusive.'

'Sounds like it. Friedman, Friedman, Friedman,' he repeated. 'Where the fu—' He slammed the palm of his hand on the table. 'Got it!' he shouted. 'It was . . .' He stopped in mid-sentence as he remembered who were in which loop, and who were not.

'I'll take the mystery man from here, thanks,' he told the DI. 'I've got another task for you, Lottie, for you and you alone. Thanks to Dan, we have Sofia Deschamps' address in Mauritius, but we don't know exactly where she lives in London, beyond that it's in Muswell Hill. She moved there very soon after Toni came back from her so-called sabbatical, to look after the child. Marina told me that Lucille's grandfather, Toni's dad, bought it for her. I took her word for that, like I swallowed everything else she fed me. She lied to me about other stuff, so maybe she lied about that too.

'I want you to dig deep, get the address and look into the purchase transaction. When it was bought, and if it was indeed an outright purchase, no mortgage, then I want to know exactly where the cash came from. And while you're at it, just for the hell of it, look into Toni's house in Bothwell, asking the same questions. Remember, don't involve the guys in this and report to me alone, as soon as you get a result. Use my mobile if you have to.' He gave her a card, with the number.

'I understand, sir,' Mann said. 'What do you expect to find?'

He smiled. 'Who knows? Maybe it's something to do with living at the seaside but I like flying kites.'

'Maybe you can show me how,' she replied. 'I'm going to have to find new ways to amuse my Jakey, with his dad out the picture.'

As soon as she had gone, he picked up the phone and made a direct call.

'*Sal-tire*,' a male telephonist announced, the confident public voice of a confident newspaper.

'June Crampsey, please. Tell her it's Bob. She'll know which one.'

'There may be other men called Bob in my life,' the editor said as she came on line.

'But you still knew which one this is.'

'It's my phone; it goes all moist when you call. Why didn't you use my direct line, or my mobile?'

'Because my head's full of stuff and I couldn't remember either number.'

'I thought you had slaves to get those for you.'

'That's Edinburgh. In Glasgow they're all lashed to the oars and rowing like shit to keep the great ship off the rocks.'

'Do I detect a continuing ambivalence towards Strathclyde?' she teased.

'It's a lousy job, kid, but somebody's got to do it. For now that's me. June, I need your help.'

'Shoot. You still have a credit balance in the favour ledger.'

'Six months or so back, you ran a story about some charity dinner in the RSM. It mentioned a man named Peter Friedman, a recluse, your story called him.'

'I remember that one.'

'How much do you know about him?'

'No more than was in the paper. He's a very rich bloke who keeps himself to himself. We ran that dinner to honour people who gave decent sized bucks to good causes last year. The guests were all nominated by the charities and we sent the formal invitations. His address was a PO box in Tobermory.'

'Tobermory?' he repeated.

'That's what I said. He lives on the Isle of Mull. That qualifies as reclusive, doesn't it?'

'Hey, I'm from Motherwell. Everything north and west of Perth's reclusive in my book. Your story: was there a photo with it?'

'Yes,' she replied. 'That's why I remember it so well. I had a photographer in the hall, snapping groups; real dull stuff, but I felt we had to do it since it was our gig. Your man Friedman was in one of them and he made a fuss about it. First he tried to bribe the photographer, then he threatened him. When neither of those worked he sought me out and asked me, more politely, not to use it. I said I'd see what I could do, then I made bloody sure that it went in.'

'Did you hear from him afterwards?'

'No. Fact is, I doubt if he even saw it. The next day was the Saturday edition; most people just read that for the sport and the weekend section.'

'Do you still have the photo in your library?'

'Of course, everything's in the bloody library. I'll have somebody dig it out, crop him out of the group and email it to you. What's your Strathclyde address?'

'Thanks, but use my private address. I don't want it on this network.'

'Okay, but what's this about, Bob? Why are you interested in him?'

'His name came up in connection with another charity donation,' Skinner replied, content that he was telling the truth. 'I like to know about people with deep pockets; maybe our dependants' support group can put the bite on him in the future. Thanks, June, you're a pal. You and that other Bob must come to dinner some night.'

'I'll take you up on that, only his name's Adrian. Now I'm wondering who the hostess will be. Cheers.'

He hung up, leaned back in his chair, his fingers steepled in front of his face, gathering his thoughts and seeing images flow past his mind's eye. He sat there until a trumpet sound on his phone told him that he had a personal email, and a glance confirmed that it was from June. He opened it, then viewed the attachment. As he did, possibilities became certainties.

The chief constable rose from his desk, left his office and his command floor, taking the stair down one level and walking round to a suite that overlooked Holland Street, and the group of buildings that once had housed one of Scotland's oldest and most famous schools.

He keyed a number into a pad, then pushed open a door bearing a plaque that read 'Counter-Terrorism Intelligence Section'. As he entered the long open room, a female officer looked up at him, first with a frown, then in surprise. She started to rise, but he waved her back down, and headed to the far end of the room.

A red light above Lowell Payne's door said that he was in a meeting. Skinner knocked on it nonetheless, then waited, until it was opened by a glaring man with a moustache.

'Aye?' he snapped.

'Intelligence section?' he murmured, as Payne appeared behind the officer.

'Chief.'

'Sorry to interrupt, Detective Superintendent, but you know me. Everything I do has "urgent" stamped on it.'

'Indeed. That'll be all for now, DS Mavor,' he said, almost pushing the other officer out of the room.

'Sorry about that,' he murmured once he and Skinner were alone. 'He was somebody's mistake, from the days when a guy might get dumped into Special Branch and forgotten about, because he was too rough-edged for the mainstream, or because he'd done somebody higher up a big favour in the witness box, and an SB job was his reward.'

'Where do you want him sent?'

'Anywhere that being rough-edged will be an advantage.'

'I'll ask Bridie. She'll have an idea. Now, I have a question, best put to somebody who was here six months ago and who'd know pretty much everything that went on then.'

'That would be DI Bulloch,' Payne replied at once. 'Sandra. You probably passed her on your way along here.'

'I did. At least she knows who I am, which is a good start.'

'I'll get her in.'

'Fine, but before you do, let me set the scene. When I got into Toni Field's safe finally, and found those envelopes, there was another. It was marked "P. Friedman" and it was empty. It was stuck on to the back of another, and I reckon that was a mistake on Marina's part.'

'Marina's?'

'Oh yes. Marina knew that stuff would be there for me to find, in time, once I'd got past her stalling me by giving me the wrong code for the safe. But she didn't intend me to find the Friedman envelope. She destroyed what was in it, but failed to notice that she'd left it in there. Now, let's talk to the DI.'

Sandra Bulloch was a cool one, neither too pretty nor too plain to be memorable, but with legs that few men would fail to notice, and that she probably covered up, Skinner guessed, when she went operational.

'Peter Friedman,' she repeated. 'Yes, sir, I remember him. It was Chief Constable Field's second week here; she called Superintendent Johnson and me up to her office, and told us that there was a man she wanted put under full surveillance. His name, she said, was Peter Friedman and he lived on Mull.

'I handled the job myself, with DS Mavor.' A small flicker of distaste crossed her face, then vanished. 'We found that he owned a big estate house up behind Tobermory, set in about forty acres of land. We photographed him from as close as we could get, we hacked his emails and we tapped his phones.

'He lived alone, but he had a driver, a personal assistant type, who also flew the helicopter that appeared to be his means of getting off the island. He left the estate once a day, that was all, to go down to Tobermory, in his white Range Rover Evoque, to collect his mail from the post office, and to have a coffee and a scone in the old church building next door that somebody's made into a shop and a café.

'He had no visitors and he never took or made a phone call that wasn't about his investments. Nor did he file any emails; they were all deleted after study. I assume that if he wanted to keep something he'd print it.

'The only thing we intercepted that was of any interest,' Bulloch said, 'was an email from a consultant oncologist, with a report attached. It didn't make good reading. It confirmed that Friedman had a squamous cell lung carcinoma, in other words lung cancer, that it was inoperable, and that no form of therapy was going to do him any good. It gave him somewhere between nine months and two years to live.'

'Ouch,' Skinner whispered. 'Did you report all of this back to Toni, to Chief Constable Field?'

'Of course, sir. We gave her a file with everything in it. She kept it and she ordered us to destroy any copies.'

'Which you did?'

Bulloch stared at him, as if outraged. 'Absolutely,' she insisted.

'Did she ever tell you why she wanted this man targeted?'

'No, and we didn't ask. Sometimes the chief constable knows things that we don't need to. For example, why you're here now, asking questions about the same man.'

He laughed. 'Nice one, Sandra. You're right; I'm not going to tell you either.'

His mobile sounded as she was leaving the room. The caller was Lottie Mann, with not one result, but two. He listened carefully to her, said, 'Thanks. I'll be in touch,' then ended the call.

'Lowell,' he asked, 'has our tap on Sofia Deschamps produced anything?'

'Nothing, Chief. Only a call from Mauritius, a bloke we think was Chief Constable Field's dad, going by his distress if nothing else. Nothing from Marina, though. In fact, when she was talking to the man, she said, "Now I've lost both my daughters, and I won't get either one back." I suppose that doesn't rule out her knowing where the other one is, but from the tone of her voice on the recording, I don't believe she does.'

'That's all right, I do. Pretty soon, I expect that everything will become clear. I'm tired of this business, Lowell,' Skinner sighed, 'tired of the entire Deschamps family and their devious lives. Tomorrow, the two of us will go on a trip. I'd like to meet this guy Friedman. Can you put me up at your place tonight? Otherwise it'll be an even earlier start for Davie.'

Sixty-Four

'Sailing is not something I do very often,' Bob remarked. 'In fact, the last time I was on a boat on this side of the country was when Ali Higgins took Alex and me for a weekend on her rich brother's schooner. It was a cathartic experience in an emotional sense.'

He was leaning on the rail of the Oban car ferry as it made a slow turn towards the jetty at Craignure, landing point for visitors to the island of Mull. Their driver, PC Davie Cole, was in the car, asleep.

'Funnily enough,' Lowell Payne said, 'I remember that; on your way there, the three of you were at Jean's dad's funeral. It was the first time you and I met.'

'You're right, it was. I think about that trip often, whenever I'm feeling low. I loved it. By the end of the voyage, I was talking seriously about jacking it all in and buying a boat of my own, doing the odd charter, that sort of stuff. Then the fucking phone rang, didn't it, and it all went up in smoke.'

'What if you had?' Lowell asked. 'Maybe you and Alison would be off in the Caribbean or the Med right now. Jean had hopes for the pair of you.'

'I know she had, but they were misplaced. We didn't last, remember; Ali was more career driven than me.' He sighed, and his eyes went somewhere else. 'But if we had bought our tall ship and made it work, she would still be alive. If I'd taken her away from the fucking police force,' he muttered, with sudden savagery, 'she wouldn't have been turned into crispy bits by a fucking car bomb.'

'You both made the same choice,' Lowell pointed out. 'And it could as easily have been you that got killed. A couple of times, from what I hear.'

'Yes I know that, but still. This fucking job, man, what it does to people, on the inside. Ali and I, we spent a couple of years banging each other's brains out, yet by the time she died, it was all gone and she was calling me "sir" with the rest of them.'

He was silent for a while, until he had worked off his anger and his guilt, and his mood changed. 'By the way,' he said quietly, 'I enjoyed last night. You and Jean, you're such a normal down-to-earth couple.' He gave a soft, sad laugh. 'As a matter of fact, you're just about the only normal down-to-earth couple that I know. And that lass of yours, young Myra, she's blooming. What is she now, thirteen? She reminds me a lot of Alex when she was that age. Prepare to be wound round her little finger, my friend.'

'There is a difference, though. You had to bring Alexis up on your own. Yes, I might be a soft touch, I'll admit, but Jean's there as a buffer; she takes no nonsense . . . not that Myra gets up to much, mind. She's a good kid. That is, she has been up to now. I suppose it all changes the further into their teens they get.'

'It does, and the trick is to accept that. There comes a time in every young person's growing up when they're entitled to a private life, in every respect. When it's a daughter, that can be difficult for dads, because we all inevitably remember the hormonal volcanoes we were at that age. I was no exception, and I'll always be grateful to Jean for being a really good aunt to Alex during that couple of years.'

'From what she said, and indeed from what I saw for myself, you were a great dad.'

'Ach, we all are to our girls, or should be. I'm beginning to learn that boys take much more managing.'

'Do you think that's what went wrong with Toni and Marina? The absence of a father's influence?'

He pursed his lips. 'In Toni's case, nah; I reckon she was just a bad bitch. As for Marina, maybe it was the opposite. The jury's still out on that.'

'What do you mean?' Payne paused. 'You realise I'm completely in the dark about this trip. You've hardly told me anything. Now it turns out we're going to see some recluse in Tobermory, and I still don't know why.'

'You will.' He pushed himself off the rail. 'Come on, let's go and see if Davie's awake yet. We'll be ready to offload soon.'

Twenty minutes later they were seated in the back of the chief constable's car, as PC Cole eased it carefully down the ramp then on to the roadway.

'I thought the terminal was in Tobermory itself,' Payne observed as he read a road sign outside the Caledonian MacBrayne building. 'Twenty-one miles away: I never realised Mull was so big.'

'I'd forgotten myself,' Skinner confessed, 'until I looked it up on Google Earth. I didn't think it would have street view for a place this size, but it does. Now I know exactly where we're going.'

'The post office?'

'No, the café place next door that DI Bulloch mentioned. The Gallery, it's called. We'll have a cup of something there and wait for Mr Friedman to arrive. It's a nice morning, and they've got tables outside.'

'What if he's already been for his mail?'

'There's no chance of that. This is the first ferry of the day, and the Royal Mail van was six behind us in the queue to get off. We'll be there before it.'

The Gallery was exactly as DI Bulloch had described it. A classic old Scottish church building, with a paved area in front with half a dozen tables, four of them unoccupied. It offered a clear view across Tobermory Bay and, more important, of anyone arriving at the post office, next door.

Cole dropped them off outside, then, on Skinner's instruction, reversed into a parking bay, thirty yards further along on the seaward side of the road, half hidden by a tree and a telephone box.

They took the table nearest the street, and the chief produced a ten-pound note. 'I'm not pulling rank,' he said, 'but since I actually know who we're waiting for, it's better you get the teas in. I'll have a scone too, if they look okay. They should be; you'd expect home baking in a place like this.'

As he took the banknote, Payne sensed the excitement of anticipation underlying Skinner's good humour. There was no queue in the café. He bought two mugs of tea and two scones, which looked better than okay, and was carrying them outside on a tray when he saw the Royal Mail van drive past, slowing to park.

There was no conversation as they sat, sipping and eating. The chief was relaxed in his chair, but his colleague noticed that it was drawn clear of the table, so that if necessary he had a clear route to the street.

And then, after ten minutes, a large white vehicle came into view, approaching from their left. It was halfway in shape between a coupé and an estate car. 'How many white Range Rover Evoques would you expect in Mull?' the chief murmured.

The car swung into an empty bay on the other side of the road. Its day lights dimmed as the driver switched off, then stepped out: not a man, Payne saw, but a woman, tall, in shorts and a light cotton top, with a blue and yellow motif.

Her hair was jet black, cut short and spiky. Although a third of her face was hidden behind wrap-round sunglasses, Oakley, he guessed, by the shape of them, the lovely honey-coloured tone of her skin was still apparent, and striking.

She was halfway across the road, heading for the post office, when Skinner put his right thumb and index finger in his mouth and gave a loud, shrill whistle. The woman, and everyone else in earshot, looked in his direction. But she alone froze in mid-stride.

She made a small move, as if to abort her errand and go back to the Range Rover, but the chief shook his head, then beckoned her towards them. She seemed to sag a little, then she obeyed, as if she was on an invisible lead and he was winding it in.

He stood as she drew near, reaching out with his right foot, gathering in a spare chair and pulling it to the table. 'Have a seat,' he said. He inclined his head towards Payne, never taking his eyes from hers. 'Lowell, you didn't get up to the command floor in the last chief's time, so you probably don't know her sister, Marina Deschamps, or Day Champs, as wee Dan Provan would say. Mind you,' he added, 'even if you did, you'd have had bother recognising her with the radical new hair and the designer shades. I probably wouldn't have been sure myself if she hadn't been driving her dad's car.'

'Her what?' Payne exclaimed.

'Her dad,' he repeated. 'Peter Friedman's her father. There's been a consistent feature in this investigation. Most of the players in it have had two names, making them hard to pin down. Byron Millbank was Beram Cohen, and vice versa when he had to be, Antonia Deschamps became Toni Field, in the cause of advancing her career like everything else she ever did, and even Basil Brown, gangster and MI5 grass, had to be called Bazza.'

'So what about Peter Friedman?' Marina asked, as she sat. 'What was he?'

'He used to be Harry Shelby.'

She removed the sunglasses, as if she was peeling them off her face, and stared at him, with eyes that were colder than he had ever imagined they could be. 'How did you find out?'

'MI5 erased the records of wee Lucille's birth,' he replied, 'but they had no reason to wipe out yours. It wouldn't have been that easy anyway, you being born before the computer era. When you steered me towards your conspiracy scenario, and I was stupid enough to embarrass myself, even endanger myself, by falling for it, you may have thought that I wouldn't survive professionally, maybe even personally. You certainly didn't envisage me coming after you, nor Five either, not after I'd handed them all Toni's blackmail leverage. For that's what your sister was, wasn't she? Inside Supercop, there was a nasty little blackmailer . . . as you well knew, for you were put alongside her to spy on her, and you found the evidence.'

'I . . .' she began, protesting, but he raised a hand, to stop her.

'I know you were, because Amanda Dennis told me so, and I know you did, because you left it for me, after you'd doctored it a wee bit. So come on, just nod your head, and admit it.'

She did.

'God knows what Toni got out of the civil servant,' Skinner continued, 'or the TV guy, or the other cop, but she got advancement from Storey, and I know now that she got a house out of the Home Secretary and her husband, the one your mother lives in in London. Her father didn't buy it, they did; they paid her off, and if that was known, the scandal would be compounded. That house was bought and paid for by Repton Industries, Emily Repton's family business. You knew that, Marina, and you didn't care a toss about it.

'But when she pulled the same stroke on your father, that was different. Lottie Mann traced both transactions right to the source of the money. She found out that the house in Bothwell was paid for by Pam Limited, Peter Friedman's investment company. Thanks to one single, unfortunate newspaper photo, Toni found out who Friedman really was. She contacted him and she sold him her silence, for five hundred and seventy-five thousand pounds, the cost of a nice big villa.' Skinner frowned. 'Or her silence for a while: and that was something you couldn't tolerate, the idea that she could unmask him any time she chose, so . . . you had your sister killed!'

'Half-sister,' she murmured. 'So prove it.'

He shrugged. 'I can't, not to court standards. Anyway, not only did your fiction add up, that Repton had her removed, it still does, for you could claim that everything you did was on their orders.'

'Do you really know it wasn't?' she challenged.

'Oh yes, I do. And I can prove that.'

'How?'

'It was your old man that paid Cohen to do the job, not them.'

'My God,' she said, 'you have been busy. You know that much?'

He nodded. 'Yes, I do.'

'In that case, tell me, Mr Skinner . . . I can see you're desperate to, you're so pleased with yourself . . . how did you find out who my father was?'

'I'm not pleased with myself,' he contradicted her. 'But I'm dead chuffed for Dan Provan, the guy I mentioned earlier. He's a walking anachronism of a detective sergeant, who's been hiding in Strathclyde CID for years. You probably never saw him when you were there, just as your path and Lowell's never crossed, but even if you had you wouldn't have noticed him. That's one of his strengths. The other is that he never forgets a criminal, if the crime is big enough to get his attention.'

He picked up his ever-present attaché case and spun the combination wheels to open it.

'I was never just going to forget about you, Marina,' he told her as he flicked the catches. 'I don't like being made to feel like an idiot. I take it personally. The first thing I did when I got back to Glasgow was send Provan to dig out your birth records from Mauritius. I wanted to build a complete picture of you and obviously I couldn't rely on the things you had told me, or the hints you had dropped, since you're as consummate a deceiver as your sister was.'

A flicker of a smile suggested she took that as a compliment.

'Provan discovered that your father was listed as Hillary Shelby,' he continued, taking a document from the Zero Halliburton and handing it to her. 'See? Hillary not Harry, and there's an Australian passport number. However, that surname niggled him, and the itch wouldn't go away. And that's where his special skills came into play. "Shelby," he told himself. "I know that name from somewhere." Dan isn't of the IT generation,' Skinner said, 'but he went to the computer and ran a Google search.' He grinned. 'He called it "that Bugle thing" when he told me about it. He did try the full name first off, but got zilch, so then he entered simply Shelby, on its own. He came up with a car designer, an actor, and three different towns in America, then at the foot of the page, he got Harry Shelby, and it all came back to him, and that pub quiz mind of his.

'Harry Shelby was an Australian financier, a real tycoon . . . or typhoon, as Dan called him. He built a business empire of considerable size in Australia, South Africa and in Hong Kong from the early seventies on. He started in minerals, then moved into currency trading, and pretty soon he had become a national business icon, stand-out even in an era in Australian history when there were quite a few of those around.

'In nineteen ninety-six, he was awarded a knighthood, in the Birthday Honours list. He was scheduled to be invested in Canberra, by the High Commissioner. Everything was set up, but the day before, Harry Shelby vanished, off the face of the earth. He was never seen again, and he never left a penny behind him, or rather a cent.'

'I remember that,' Payne exclaimed. 'It was big news for a week or so, internationally.'

'I confess that it passed me by,' the chief said. 'But nineteen ninety-six was a busy year for me; my mind was full of other stuff, on my own doorstep. Anyway,' he carried on, 'you can imagine that after Shelby disappeared, his whole life was dug up. It didn't take the investigators long to find out that in fact he ran out of business steam in the mid-eighties, after a series of bad currency deals that he managed to cover up. Everything he'd done after that had been a huge Ponzi scheme, paying investors with their own money, as he drew more and more in with the promise of attractive profits that were evidently being delivered. If Harry Shelby hadn't had such a big reputation, chances are he'd have been caught, but because he was such a hero he got away with it.'

He stopped to sip his tea, only to find that it had gone cold.

'Why did he run?' he asked, then answered. 'It may have been because he knew that all Ponzi fraudsters are caught eventually, unless they shut up shop before it's too late.' He paused. 'However, Provan happened upon another theory, one that the Australian authorities . . . Dan checked this with the Australian Embassy . . . believe to this day, possibly because it suits them so to do. They think, indeed they're pretty well sure, that a couple of his biggest investors were Americans,

Mafia figures, using his investment scheme to launder money. The scenario is, they caught on to the swindle, so they dealt with it the old-fashioned way. They made Shelby and his money disappear at the same time. On the day that he did, Australian air traffic control traced an unregistered flight out of Canberra heading for Tasmania. The investigators had a tip that Shelby was on it, until they dropped him out halfway there over the ocean.' He gazed at Marina. 'But we know that's not true, don't we?'

She stared back at him, silent. He took a photograph from the case, held it up for Payne to see, then passed it to her.

'That's Harry Shelby, aged about forty.'

He produced a second. 'That's Peter Friedman, photographed, to his annoyance, at a charity dinner last winter. He's over thirty years older, but I've had the images run through a recognition program, and it confirms they're one and the same man.'

He went back into the attaché and took out a third image. 'And that's you,' he said, 'from your HR file in Pitt Street. You can't hide from it, Marina. You are your father's double.'

She picked up his mug, and drank his cold tea in a single gulp. 'And proud of it,' she whispered.

'It was the newspaper photograph that did it, wasn't it?'

'Yes,' she agreed. 'Antonia was in her first month in Glasgow when it appeared. She read every newspaper, every day, to familiarise herself with the place, and she saw that. She used CTIS to trace him, then one day, just as you have, she turned up here, alone. When he got over the shock, he assumed that she had come to arrest him, but no. I mean, why would she have done that? There would have been nothing in it for her.

'Your assumption was correct; she did to him what she had done to Lawton and his wife. She showed him the brochure for the house and told him that she wanted it. She told him to forget about trying to vanish again, as she would know about it the moment his helicopter took off, or he boarded the ferry. But in truth she knew that there was no point in him running. He was dying, and even then the house was being turned into a hospice, a place for him to be as peaceful as he could be in his last days. So he bought the Bothwell place for her.' Her eyes flashed. 'He told me she should have chosen a bigger one.'

'Why did he go to the damn dinner? That doesn't sound like typical behaviour.'

'He was in Edinburgh, seeing an oncologist for tests,' she explained. 'It was that day, and he had a feeling the news wasn't going to be the best, so he went, in the hope it might cheer him up. As it turned out it did the opposite.'

'Does your mother know any of this?' Skinner asked.

'None,' Marina insisted. 'Maman is not a stupid woman. She had a good job in the civil service, but she was looked after by men for much of her life, first Anil, and then Papa. She's naive in some ways, so when Antonia told her that she had done well in property in Britain, she believed her.'

'How did Sofia meet your father?'

'He was part of an Australian business delegation to the island, in nineteen eighty, after her thing with Anil was over. Maman was in charge of official government hospitality. That's when it began.

'I was born two years later, and for all my childhood he spent as much time as he could with us. He was as good to Antonia as he was to me. That's what made her behaviour all the more despicable. You were right. She was just a nasty little blackmailer.'

'When did you get back in touch with him?'

'I was never out of touch. Gifts would arrive, and letters, never traceable, only ever signed "Papa". The theory is wrong, incidentally, about the Mafia. They were his partners in the Ponzi business, not his victims. They all made lots of money and when the time came to close it down, they helped him get away, and they planted the idea that they had killed him. In fact he lived in the West Indies for six years, as Peter Friedman. He moved to Mull ten years ago, around the same time as I came to Britain. It was then he told me his new name.'

'Whose idea was it for you to join MI5?' Skinner asked.

'A shrewd question, because I think you know the answer. Papa suggested it. The idea was that if the Australians started looking for him again, in Millbank I would be well placed to hear about it. By that time I was in a security department within the Met, so when I applied, it seemed a natural step, and I was accepted. Brian Storey was my boss then, and he endorsed me. Antonia never knew, though, not ever. The service, as it does, gave me a front as an importer for a chain of florists.'

'That sounds like an Amanda Dennis touch.'

'It was. She's a good teacher.'

'You were a good student, Marina. You could have been Amanda yourself, if you'd stayed the course, instead of letting them move you out to spy on your sister.'

'But if I had stayed, I wouldn't have been able to deal with her when the need arose.'

'By telling your father how to get rid of her? No, I don't suppose you would.'

'Papa never knew,' she said.

Both police officers stared at her.

'It's true, I swear,' she exclaimed. 'If I had told him he would have forbidden it, absolutely. All he ever did was make a donation of three hundred thousand pounds to a charity I told him about. He was a sucker for charities, especially those involved with cancer research; I told him it helped patients with difficult personal circumstances. I approached Cohen, using a contact email address I'd picked up in the service. I gave him the commission and he named his price. No conscience, that man, only a cash register. I also gave him Brown as a resource on the ground in Glasgow. I'm sorry they had to kill him, but not too sorry, as he was a traitor to his own kind. No, the decision was mine, and the orders were mine. Knowing what Antonia was, and what she might have become, I don't regret them. I'm sorry for Maman, and for Anil, and for Lucille, of course, but they will bring her up as if she was their own. Maman is still young and fit enough to see it through.'

'But what about Papa?' Skinner murmured. 'He isn't, is he?'

'Yes, Papa,' she sighed. 'I suppose you have come to take him away, as Antonia did not.'

'We haven't come to ask for a raffle prize for the policeman's ball, that's for sure. As for taking him away, we'll see about that. But I would like to meet him.'

'Then come with me, Chief Constable, and you shall.' She stood; Skinner and Payne followed suit. 'In your car? You have a car, I take it.'

'Yes, but Superintendent Payne can take that. I'll come with you, just in case the minder panics at the sight of strange vehicles. By the way, no nonsense up there, Marina. There are firearms in my car; that's a practice your sister introduced.'

'He isn't that sort of minder, I promise. Rudolf is a driver and a pilot, that's all.' As she spoke, they heard the heavy engine sound of an aircraft. She looked up and pointed, towards a helicopter above them, gaining height. 'In fact, that's him.'

'Hey!' Skinner exclaimed. 'Are you . . .'

'No. Papa is not with him. He's still at the house. Come and meet him.'

The chief frowned, still cautious, weighing her up, not anxious to be taken twice. 'Okay,' he said at last. 'Don't you want to collect your mail?'

'It can wait. Come on.' She led him across the road to the waiting Range Rover.

With the police car following close behind, they drove out of Tobermory, taking a narrower road from the one they had used earlier, passing a campsite on the edge of the small town, then climbing for two or possibly three miles, although its twists and turns made it difficult to judge distance travelled.

She slowed as they approached a gate on the right, with an unequivocal sign beside it: 'Private'. It was shut, but Marina pressed a button on a remote control and the barrier slid aside.

The surface of the estate road was gravel, but better than the one they had left. Their tyres crunched beneath them, early warning, Skinner thought, for anyone waiting.

The house itself was a grey mansion, large but not ostentatious. It reminded him of some of his neighbours on Gullane Hill, although the stone was different. She drew up at the front door, then waited until the second car stopped alongside and Payne climbed out to join them.

He was holding a pistol, in the manner of a man for whom it was a new experience. Skinner frowned and shook his head; he handed it back to Davie Cole.

'This way,' she said, leading them inside, walking briskly through a chandelier-lit hallway, and, ignoring a wide mahogany stairway, into a room on the far side of the house.

It was large, decorated with old-fashioned flock wallpaper. A bay window faced south over a sunlit garden, laid out in shrubs and fruit trees, with stone statuary among them. Soft music was playing, a female singer with a gentle voice; the chief guessed at Stacey Kent.

There was a smell about the room, a smell of disinfectant, a hospital smell, one that seemed fitting given the metal-framed bed that was positioned facing the window. Skinner saw an oxygen cylinder on the far side as they approached, and beside it, in a stand, a vital signs monitor.

All the lines on it were flat.

The man on the bed was old, but his face was unlined. He looked peaceful, with his eyes closed.

'Papa died just over two hours ago,' Marina murmured. 'Rudolf has gone to Oban to fetch an undertaker, and to take Sister Evans to the station. She's been with us for the last month. She did a great job; he was pain-free all the way to the end. The doctor from Oban was with him at the end. He was kind enough to stay overnight. He caught the first ferry back this morning.'

'I suppose I should say I'm sorry for your loss,' Skinner told her. 'And I am, honestly, even if he was a billion-dollar fraudster, and you're a sororicide . . . if that's a word. You are a first, Marina. I've come across plenty of conmen in my career . . . although not on your dad's scale, I admit . . . but I've never met someone who's killed her own sister.'

'What are you going to do with me?' she asked. Payne, standing on the other side of the bed, saw a hint of trepidation in her eyes, for the first time since their encounter in the café.

'What do you think?' the chief retorted. 'I'm duty bound to arrest you and charge you with murder. You've admitted it, and even if you recant that, I know enough now to put a case together.' And then he sighed. 'That's my duty, but the judge would be bound to knock out so much of my evidence on national security grounds that you would walk. Your problem would then be that you wouldn't walk very far, before you were hit by a runaway lorry, or killed in a random mugging, or died of a peanut allergy that nobody knew you had, or just plain disappeared.'

Her trepidation turned to undisguised fear as she acknowledged the truth in what he said.

'Who are you now?'

His question took her by surprise. 'My new identity, you mean?'

'Yes.'

'I have a Jamaican passport, in the name of Marina Friedman. My father obtained it for me, in case we both needed to move on in a hurry.'

'What was your next move? Your plan for life after Papa?'

'His will is with his lawyer in Jersey. It names me as his sole heir. He told me to go there, with the death certificate and my passport, to claim my inheritance.'

'That won't be happening now,' Skinner said.

'No, I realise that. So, what will you do with me? Will you save the expense of your abortive prosecution by handing me straight over to Amanda Dennis?'

He took a breath and blew out his cheeks. 'Like she would thank me for that,' he exclaimed. 'It would be better all round if I just shot you myself and buried you somewhere on this big island.'

She backed away, staring at him in sudden naked terror.

'Hey!' he exclaimed. 'Calm down. Better all round, but I'm not one of them, Marina. Besides,' he added, with a half smile and a nod in Payne's direction, 'there are witnesses, and your man Rudolf will be back from Oban soon. So,' he told her, 'here's what you do. You take whatever you can pack quickly, and as much as you can in the way of cash and valuables, you get in that car and you drive it straight on to the ferry. When you get to Oban, keep on driving, in any direction you can and in any direction as long as it is out of the jurisdiction of any Scottish police force.'

'But not Jersey, I take it.'

'No; there'll be nothing there by the time you get there. Whatever fortune your father's left isn't for you, it's for the people he swindled, even if some of them will be dead themselves by now.' He gazed at her. 'This is what's happened,' he said. 'Lowell and I arrived to arrest him, following my discovery of some papers in Toni's safe. Sadly, we were too late. You were never here. When Rudolf gets back and asks, "Where's Marina?" I will say, "Marina who?" That's the outcome. We get Papa, you get lost. We will be fucking heroes, Lowell and me, in Australia most of all. As for you, you will be alive.'

She looked at him, still doubting, until he nodded, to reassure her.

'You're a resourceful lady. You'll get by for a couple of years, and after that you can probably go back to Mauritius and become yourself again, because nobody will be looking for you. But don't ever show up here again, for I will know about it. You're getting away with murder, because that's what suits everybody best. But don't you ever forget it.'

PostScript

'Why did you decide to quit as leader? Were there knives out for you because of the Joey incident?'

Aileen snorted across the lunch table in a restaurant next to Edinburgh Castle. They had gone there after finalising their divorce, in the Court of Session, further down the Royal Mile.

'They wouldn't have been nearly sharp enough. No, to be frank I resigned because we are going to get absolutely slaughtered at the next Holyrood election and I don't want that on my CV. That twerp Felix Brahms will inherit it, now that I've endorsed him.'

'Foresighted as ever,' Bob chuckled.

'Of course, and there's this. I won't be a candidate in Scotland next time. One of our guys in a safe seat on Tyneside is about to retire early on health grounds. I've called in some favours; it's mine.'

'The divorce won't be a problem for you, will it?'

'I don't see it. We've settled on unreasonable behaviour as the grounds, not adultery. As for the *Daily News* pictures, they're old, cold news by now. Besides, it's a safe seat, like I said. The Lib Dems don't count there and as for the Tories, they're really too nice to use those sort of tactics.'

'Will Joey put in an appearance for you?'

'As if I'd ask him. Look, Joey and me, it's a thing from way back. I suppose I can confess now, there were other times while we were married, not just that one. Sorry if it dents your male ego, but there were.'

'I know,' he admitted. 'Toni Field had a file on you. It's long since gone into the shredder. Mind you, she did hint that there was somebody else, apart from Joey.'

Aileen's eyes widened. 'She did what? Any name mentioned?'

'No, and I'm sure I don't want to know.'

'Oh but you do. Who knows? It might come in useful to you one day. The US government ran a big hospitality shindig a couple of years back in the Turnberry Hotel. All the party leaders were there, and the champagne was fairly flowing. As usual, I had a wee bit too much, and God knows how it happened, but I woke up next morning with Clive Graham. So there you are. My deep dark secret, and Clive's, except . . . somewhere there may be CCTV footage of the two of us going into his room, and probably of me leaving. Find it and it could buy you a lot of influence.'

He sighed. 'My predecessor did that sort of thing, and it got her fucking killed.'

'What? She tried to blackmail Colombian drug lords?'

'Not quite. That was the official version. The true story's a lot different, but I'm not sharing, as the spooks say.'

She shrugged. 'Be like that. Here,' she went on, 'the way you said "My predecessor" there, it sounded as if you've made a decision.'

'I have. I've decided that I can't go back to Edinburgh. Mario and Maggie are getting on fine without me. They don't need me any more; if I went back I'd be a spare wheel. So my application for Strathclyde, permanently, is in the hat with the rest.'

'And you will get it, especially after all those headlines you got when you found that Australian fraudster.'

Bob laughed. 'You ain't kidding. The day I moved into Pitt Street, I inherited an invitation to address an Australian Police Federation conference. Since then I've had twenty-two more, from other organisations down under. Yes, I know I'll probably be confirmed in post. If not, I'll do something else. I might even retire and buy a boat.'

'And sail away, with Sarah and the kids?'

'They're all too young, and she's not ready.'

'It's cool, though? You and her?'

'Honestly? It is, for the first time really. We've discovered that being nice to each other, all the time, is all it takes.'

'Maybe I'll try that, next time.'

'Some chance of that,' he scoffed. 'You're a politician. By the way,' he added, 'the Turnberry tape did exist, kept carelessly by Toni in a plain envelope that I found deep in the desk that is currently mine. It does not exist any longer.'

'Thank you,' she whispered. 'To be honest, I was really worried about that, and not for Mrs Graham's sake.'

'It's nothing to be concerned about any more,' he replied, 'but this is.' He took an envelope from a slim document case that he had brought with him.

She took it from him and her face paled, as she studied its contents: two photographs of her, with two other women, in a ladies' toilet.

'What are . . . Bob, I think I know when those were taken, but . . .'

'You have to give up the booze, Aileen,' he said. 'You must. I didn't realise you had a problem, maybe because whenever we had a drink at home, you went straight to sleep, or else you got amorous and I put it down to my fatal attraction. But that's twice you've courted potential disaster, not counting the Morocco fiasco.'

'How did you get these?'

He smiled. 'The strangest thing happened a few weeks back.

Amanda Dennis called all her Scottish team down to London for a
two-day performance review. While they were gone, somebody broke
into their office, and opened the safe. I don't think they even know it
happened, not yet. All that was taken were those photos, and the
master tape. It's in there too. Somehow they found their way into my
possession.'

She gazed at him. 'You know, I could fall in love with you.'

'Nah, you didn't before, so how could you now?'

She laughed. 'Okay. Then how about a farewell shag? We could
get a room.'

He shook his head. 'I'm sworn to be faithful. You should try it too.
Besides, someone would be bound to photograph us. For example . . .'

He took another, larger envelope from the document case. 'These
are my parting gifts to you, Aileen, and my greatest. Where you're
going to be after your by-election, these will represent your ticket
straight to the front bench, and a fast track to the shadow Cabinet. In
this package you will see Toni Field doing what she did best. You'll
also recognise the bloke she's doing it to, and I think you will find that
you know his wife too. The stupid bloody woman actually believed I
wouldn't make copies! That same lady had you set up by those two
scrubbers, who are, incidentally, no longer Security Service staff, and
tried to use your moment of weakness to club me into submission and
silence.'

He lifted his glass and drank a toast, to her, to them, to their past,
and to their separate futures.

'Use them wisely, choose your moment, and when you do, make
certain sure that the damage to Emily Repton is terminal. "Provincial
copper" indeed. Doesn't she bloody know that we're a nation?'

THE FOREST YEARS

Other books by Louise Dickinson Rich

THE
FOREST
YEARS

Containing in One Volume

WE TOOK TO THE WOODS
MY NECK OF THE WOODS

by Louise Dickinson Rich

J. B. LIPPINCOTT COMPANY

PHILADELPHIA AND NEW YORK

THE FOREST YEARS

WE TOOK TO THE WOODS

TO MY BOYS
Ralph
Gerrish
Rufus
Kyak
Tom
This book is dedicated

CONTENTS

I

"Why Don't You Write a Book?"

DURING MOST OF MY ADOLESCENCE—SPECIFICALLY, BETWEEN the time when I gave up wanting to be a brakeman on a freight train and the time when I definitely decided to become an English teacher—I said, when asked what I was going to do with my life, that I was going to live alone in a cabin in the Maine woods and write. It seemed to me that this was a romantic notion, and I was insufferably smug over my own originality. Of course, I found out later that everybody is at one time or another going to do something of the sort. It's part of being young. The only difference in my case is that, grown to womanhood, I seem to be living in a cabin in the Maine woods, and I seem to be writing.

There is nothing that I so greatly admire as purposefulness. I have an enormous respect for people who know exactly what they are doing and where they are going. Such people are compact and integrated. They have clear edges. They give an impression of invulnerability and balance, and I wish that I were one of them.

I wish that I could say that, from the moment I first

thought about this kind of a life to the moment almost two decades later when I finally began living it, I had been working single-mindedly toward it. But it wouldn't be true. Actually I'd forgotten all about it long before. I did a lot of things—graduated from college, taught school, worked in an institution for the feeble-minded, went to Europe—but none of it was in preparation for an end. At the time it seemed end enough in itself.

I was shocked, therefore, to receive not long ago and within the same week, letters from two old friends saying virtually the same thing, although the writers are strangers to each other. What they said, in effect, was this: "Isn't it wonderful that you're at last doing what you always said you wanted to do! It proves that anything is possible, if one wants it enough to work for it."

My two friends, I thank you for your high opinion of my character, and I hate to have to disabuse you of it. It is wonderful—far more wonderful than you know—that I am doing what I once, without really believing it, said I was going to do. But if it proves anything, it is only that some people are fools for luck. Let me admit that not only is my living in the woods and writing an accident on both counts, but that until I received your letters I had been so busy coping with the situation that I hadn't even realized that I was living my old dream. It's a very queer feeling to wake up and find that the dream has sneaked up on you and become the reality.

There are differences, of course. My idea was a little log cabin in a sort of spacious park. There is nothing park-like about this northwestern-most corner of Maine. Here, between two ranges of mountains, the Boundary Mountains and the Blue Mountains, lies a high, wild valley, the basin that holds the Rangeley Lakes. The country is criss-crossed with ridges, dotted with swamps and logans, and covered with dense forest. There are very few people living here, and no roads down into what we call The Outside. There are a few narrow trails, but travel through the woods is so difficult, with the swamps and blowdowns and underbrush, that the lakes have remained what they were to the Indians, the main thoroughfare.

I like to think of the lakes coming down from the north of us like a gigantic staircase to the sea. Kennebago to Rangeley to Cupsuptic, down they drop, level to level, through short, snarling rivers; Mooselukmeguntic to the Richardsons to Pond-in-the-River, and through Rapid River to Umbagog, whence they empty into the Androscoggin and begin the long south-easterly curve back to the ocean. I like to say their names, and I wish I could make you see them—long, lovely, lonely stretches of water, shut in by dark hills. The trees come down to the shore, the black growth of fir and pine and spruce streaked with the lighter green of maple and birch. There is nothing at all on the hills but forest, and nobody lives there but deer and bear and wildcats. The people keep close to the lakes, building their dwellings in narrow clearings they have made by pushing the trees a little way back from the water.

Our own clearing is on the Rapid River, just below Pond-in-the-River Dam; and because Rapid River is not navigable, being the swiftest river east of the Rockies—it drops a hundred and eighty-five feet in three miles, with no falls, which is some kind of a record—we amazingly live on a road. It doesn't go anywhere. It's really a carry between two lakes, so it is sensibly called the Carry Road.

It starts at Middle Dam, on the Lower Richardson, and roughly follows the course of the river five miles to Sunday Cove, on Umbagog.

Middle Dam is quite a community. There is the dam itself, a part of the system for water control on the Androscoggin, with the dam-keeper and his family, Renny and Alice Miller and their three children, in year-round residence. Then in summer the hotel is open. We only call it a hotel; it's really a fishing camp. In winter it is closed, but there is a caretaker, Larry Parsons, who stays in with his wife, Al, and a hired man or two. So the permanent population of Middle Dam hovers at around nine, and that is comparative congestion. We get our mail and supplies through Middle, and it is the point of departure for The Outside, so its importance is all out of proportion to its population.

Sunday Cove, the other end of the carry, is something else again. The rutted, grass-grown road dips down a last steep hill and ends in the lake. There is an abandoned lumber camp rotting down on the shore, and a pair of loons living in the Cove, and that's all there is to it.

And halfway along, between road and river, is Forest Lodge, the sole address on the Carry Road, and our home.

When I said we lived in a cabin in the woods, I was speaking loosely. Forest Lodge is in the woods all right; there is nothing north or south of us but trees for so many miles that sometimes it scares me to think about it. But actually it consists of one cabin, one shack, one large house in the worst cracker-box style, and an assortment of lean-to's, woodsheds, work-shops, and what are euphemistically known as out-houses. These latter are necessary because we have no plumbing, and therefore no bathroom.

We get our water from the river and from a spring up back in the woods. We do our bathing in wash-tubs in front of the kitchen stove, and for other uses of the bathroom, we resort to the out-houses. This is no great hardship in summer, but in winter, with the snow knee deep, the wind howling like a maniac up the river, and the thermometer crawling down to ten below zero, it is a supreme test of fortitude to leave the warmth of the fire and go plunging out into the cold, no matter how great the necessity. We like to think, however, that it builds character.

The cabin, hereafter to be referred to as the Winter House, was the original Forest Lodge, built for a fishing camp. It is a low building with a porch and an ell, set on a knoll with a view up the river to the Pond-in-the-River. From the outside, it's not a bad little house, but everything that could possibly be wrong with it inside is wrong. The ceilings are too high and the windows are too small, although Ralph, my husband, ripped out the old ones and doubled the window space the first year we were here. The living-room, where we spend much of the time in winter, is on the north side, toward the woods, while the bedrooms, which we use only at night, are on the sunny, open side toward the river. The reason for this irritates me. In the country, the living quarters are always on the road side of a house, so that the inhabitants can keep tabs on the passers-by. In winter there are normally about three passers-by in seven months, here, but still the old rule holds. Apparently it's preferable to sit forever in sunless gloom than to lose one opportunity to speculate about someone's identity, starting point, destination, family connections, and probably discreditable purpose. We can't do anything about the arrangement, because the chimney is in the living-room, and that's where we have to have the stove.

That chimney is another wrong thing. It rises out of a fire-place—which is too shallow to draw properly—and instead of being in the wall, it is set out into the room about four feet. This splits the room into two parts, making the attractive and comfortable arrangement of furniture impossible. In winter the fire-place itself is of no use whatsoever, as anyone who has lived in the country in winter knows. A fire-place is pretty, and on chilly fall evenings, will keep you warm enough; but what you need in winter is a stove. So we have a stove. We boarded up our pretty fire-place, punched a hole in the side of the chimney, and set up an air-circulating wood heater. It isn't very attractive, and it takes up a lot of room, and set cheek by jowl with the fire-place, it looks silly. But it keeps us warm.

The only advantage of that half-witted chimney arrangement that has appeared to date is that the otherwise waste space behind it can be used as a woodbox. Ralph, known in these parts as "an ingenious cuss," cut a hole in the house, fitted it with a beveled door like an ice-chest door, and now we can put the wood in from outdoors. This doesn't sound like much of a triumph, but it is, nevertheless. Nothing will cool a house off quicker than opening and closing the front door forty times, while arm-loads of wood are brought in; and nothing will enrage and discourage the housewife more surely than the pecks of dirt and snow inevitably tracked onto her clean-swept floor. This little wood-box door, therefore, contributes largely to the peace and comfort of the Rich menage.

Why don't we just burn the Winter House down and forget about it? Because it's the only house that can be heated in really cold weather. Ralph has insulated it properly and finished the inside with really beautiful hand-rubbed pine paneling, and in spite of all I have said against it, it's not half bad, actually. It hasn't any kitchen, either, which is a point in its favor, odd as that may sound. We use the kitchen ell of the Big House all the year round, so the cooking odors that always collect in small country houses in the winter, no matter how often they are aired, never get into the Winter House.

About the last of May, or as soon as it is warm enough, we move down into the Big House, and the Winter House becomes the guest house for the summer. The Big House was built at a later date for a summer camp, and that is all it is good for in its present state. It is big and airy and the walls are too thin for warmth and it sprawls all over the place. I like it because it is on a high bluff over the river, with a view and sun-light and space to spread out in; because it has a huge stone fire-place that will take four-foot logs and really heat the living-room in the wettest, coldest September rain storm; because there is a wide porch over the river; because if I decide to eat some crackers and cheese before going to bed, I don't have to climb into a mackinaw and gum-boots as I do in winter, and cross a clearing in the cold to get them. And most of all I like it because I like to go upstairs to bed, instead of into the next room. For these reasons, we always put off moving out of it in the fall until the last possible moment, and we are rebuilding it so we can live in it all the year. Since Ralph is doing the work himself, for economic reasons, this is a slow process. At the moment the whole structure is balanced precariously on poles over the cellar he has dug beneath it. It looks both dangerous and sloppy, but he says it's perfectly safe, and when you're in a house, its external appearance needn't bother you. In fact, I should think a good way to buy a house would be by the looks of the house across the street, which is the one you see most of.

The house across the street here is the Guide's House, or what would be the servants' quarters, if we had servants. It's called the Guide's House because most people living in a place like this would be summer people, and they would employ a registered guide, who would live in the house across the road. It's a nice little shack, with a living-room and two bedrooms, and Gerrish lives there.

Gerrish works for us, but he is in no sense a servant. He has a guide's license, but that isn't important, because so have Ralph and I. It's a handy thing to own, around here. What Gerrish is, I suppose, is the hired help. We pay him to do certain things, which is the hired part. But since he is practically a member of the family, he does a great many other things for which we don't, and couldn't, pay him. That's the help part. We couldn't ever pay him, for example, for being so good and patient with our four-year-old Rufus, who, not to mince words, is often a pest, un-motherly an observation as that may be. Gerrish has to take his pay for that out of Rufus' adoration of him. We couldn't pay him, either, for being so dependable, and for always giving us a dollar and a quarter's worth of work for every dollar of his wages. We are very lucky to have found him. This is not a place that many people would care to work in. It is remote, not only from movies and stores, but from other people. There is nowhere to go except hunting and fishing, and nothing to see except woods and water. But luckily Gerrish likes it, and I think that he considers the Guide's House, his own undisputed realm, as home. Perhaps that is pay of a kind.

The one building here that looks as though it belonged in the deep woods is Ralph's shop, an old log cabin from long before our day. I can't say much about it, as it comes under the heading of sacred ground. It is full of tools and pieces of board that look like any other boards, but which have something special about them, so that they must never be touched, or even looked at. Hanging from the rafters are old car parts, lengths of rope, chains and boat seats, all of which are going to be used some day for some important project. In the middle is a pile of invaluable junk, and around the edges are kegs of nails and bolts. In my bridal innocence I used, when I needed a nail, to go and take one out of a keg. But it always turned out that I had taken (a) the wrong kind of nail for the job on hand, and (b) a nail that was being conserved for a specific purpose and was practically irreplaceable. So now when I need a nail I find Ralph and ask him to get me one.

He's usually easy to find. I have only to listen for the sound of a motor running. He is completely infatuated with gasoline motors, and collects them from the most improbable places. Once he brought home an old motor that someone had hauled into South Arm for a mooring anchor and then abandoned. It had been under water all summer and frozen into the ice all winter, but he dragged it the seven miles home on a hand sled, brooded over it, took it to pieces and put it together again, and now it runs the saw that saws our firewood.

We have only five miles of road to run a car on, but we are a four-car family. They aren't new models—the newest is a 1930 Model A and the oldest a 1924 Marmon—but they run, and they pay for themselves. All summer long Ralph hauls canoes and duffle across the carry for camping parties, and in the spring and fall the lumber company finds it convenient to hire him to tote their wangans up from Sunday Cove.

This lumber company is our privacy insurance, our guarantee that we won't wake up some morning and find new neighbors building a pink stucco bungalow down the river from us. With the exception of our two acres and a strip owned by a water power company, they own every foot of land for miles around. And they won't sell an inch to anybody. I won't go into reasons and company policy. All that matters is that, come hell or high water, they will not sell.

So here we sit in what amounts to a forest preserve of some hundreds of square miles; and in that "we" the reality differs again from the dream. I was going to live alone, remember. I don't, and that's quite all right with me.

Besides Ralph, Rufus, and Gerrish, there is Sally, Ralph's sixteen-year-old daughter by a previous marriage, and further proof that I am a fool for luck. A step-daughter could be a thorn in the flesh, which Sally certainly isn't. And there are Kyak and Tom, the dog and the cat.

We ourselves wouldn't have named Tom that, but we got him from a lumber camp that was moving out and didn't know what to do with him, so we had to take him as equipped. We compromise by saying that his full name is Thomas Bailey Aldrich, which isn't very suitable. He is the sort of cat that should be called Tom, regardless of banality. He is big and tough and mean, and he'd as soon as not fight the whole family at once. His idea of an average day is to get up at noon, trounce the dog for looking at him, go out and chase a deer away from the clearing, and set out the two miles for Middle Dam, there to visit with his girl, the Millers' cat, after half murdering her other three suitors. Then he comes home, looking so smug you could shoot him on sight, and sleeps until noon the next day.

Kyak, though we love him dearly, we have to admit is strictly an Art Dog. His grandmother was with Admiral Byrd at the South Pole, and his great-grandfather helped carry the serum to Nome. If they could see him, they'd turn in their graves. He is a very good example of the Siberian husky, with a white wolf mask, a rangy big body, and a curling plume of a tail; but he is completely nonfunctional. Try to put a harness on him, and he will lie down with all four feet in the air. Try to teach him to retrieve game, and he will look sorrowful and broken. The only thing he is good for, besides looking beautiful, is a watch dog, and he doesn't even do that well. He barks horribly at nothing, or at members of the family, and then amiably lets strange woodsmen walk right into the house. Then after they are in, and for all he knows, we are lying in a welter of blood, sometimes he remembers his responsibilities and stands outside barking hysterically. There's no use trying to do anything with him, except love him.

Around the blank space on the map where we live are some towns and some things that look like towns, but aren't. South Arm is one of these. We simply call it the Arm, and it's important, because it's at the beginning of the road to The Outside. Once you get off the boat from Middle Dam at the Arm, you have begun to leave the woods behind. There is still a long drive to Andover, the first village, but you can't help knowing that if you follow the road far enough you will land, not at a lonely cove tenanted only by loons, but in Boston or New York, or Butte, Montana. It makes a difference. The Arm itself is not imposing, consisting of a huddle of ramshackle wharfs and a string of tired sheds where people in here keep their Outside cars. But its implications are enormous.

Andover really is a town, with a school, two or three little stores, and a post office, whence comes our mail. Upton is a town, too, and our civic center, where we send Sally to school and where we go to vote. Most of the land around here is wild land, or unorganized territory—just squares on the map labeled C Township, or North C Surplus, or Section 37—but the back line of Upton runs north of us, so technically at least we live in organized territory. Upton has one hundred and eighty-two inhabitants and the loveliest view in Maine.

The only other town that concerns us is Magalloway, which is too small to be on the road map or to have a post office. But it does have the Brown Farm, where our telephone line ends. Let me say at once that the Brown Farm isn't a farm, and our telephone line isn't a telephone line, in the modern sense of the word. It is a fifteen-mile-long piece of wire, frail and uninsulated, strung haphazardly through the woods from tree to tree, and the private property of the lumber company, for communication with their various operations. We are hitched onto it only because once they cut down some of our trees by mistake, and extended this courtesy as reparation and apology. If it hasn't snowed lately, or the wind hasn't blown any trees down across the line, or if the wire hasn't sagged wearily into one of the many brooks it crosses, we can, by cranking three times on the battery-powered telephone which hangs on the kitchen wall, talk to the Millers. Or we can ring four times and talk to Cliff, an old hermit who lives down on Umbagog. Or we can ring twice and get the disembodied voice that is all I know of Joe, at the Brown Farm.

Although not a farm, the Brown Farm is a number of other things, including a hospital and de-lousing station for lumberjacks, a bunkhouse and mess-hall, a rest-cure for work-worn horses, and a store house for the tremendous amounts of food and equipment necessary in the lumber camps. There used to be a clerk in that store house who had a splendid graft. At that time the lumber company was using a brand of canned goods that gave premiums for the labels off the cans:—a pickle dish for ten labels, a baby carriage for five hundred, and, I suppose, a Rolls Royce for a million. The clerk isn't there any more, though. His label-removing activities—they buy canned goods by the car lot—left him no time for his duties; and besides, the cooks in the camps got bored with having to open twenty anonymous cans before they happened on the sliced beets they were looking for. He was about to retire, anyhow. He'd sold the things he didn't fancy himself, and had money in the bank.

Once, seven years ago, I saw the Brown Farm, but I didn't know then what it was going to mean in my life, so I didn't pay much attention. I don't remember what it looks like. I was the school-teacher-on-vacation, and my sister and I and some friends came up through this country on a canoe trip. We went through the Parmachenee section, and then we debated whether we should come back through the Rangeleys and along Rapid River or not. The guide insisted that this was the way to come—that although it involved a lot of work, the country was wild and beautiful and unspoiled enough to be worth a few paddle blisters, pack sores, and lame muscles. So we finally gave in, not too enthusiastically, being travel-frayed already.

And that off-hand decision, in which I didn't even have a major part, was the accident by which I now live in a cabin in the woods. As we walked along the Carry Road, we saw a man splitting wood in the yard of the only house we had seen in days, and we stopped to talk to him. He had just arrived there that morning, and he was about to build his first fire and cook his first meal. He invited us to stay and eat with him, because he felt like celebrating. He'd bought the place for a summer camp during the boom years, but he hadn't been able to come East from Chicago, where he lived, since 1929. Now, however, he'd sold some patent rights and not only was he going to spend the summer there, but if things turned out right, the rest of his life. We were all touched and amused, I remember, by his enthusiasm.

Now that I know Ralph better, I know that there was nothing strange about his inviting us all to spend the rest of the week with him. Since that day, eight years ago, I've known him to invite a week-end guest, whom he liked, to extend his visit from week to week until it lasted more than two years. But at the time I thought, and I guess all the others thought, that he was crazy. We stayed, though.

We stayed, and we had a lovely time. We fished and sunbathed and swam, and in between times I found out why a man so obviously dry behind the ears should want to bury himself in the woods for the rest of his life. Ever since he was twelve years old, he had been spending his summers at Coburn's, and his winters wishing it were summer so he could go back to Coburn's. Middle Dam was the place in all the world where he was happiest, and he'd always told himself that some day he'd live there permanently. It took a long time and a lot of doing, but finally he'd managed. You see, Ralph, unlike me, has a single-track mind.

My mind, however, did fall into a single track before that week was over. I became obsessed with the idea that if I didn't see more—a lot more—of this Ralph Rich, I'd quietly go into a decline and die. It's a common phenomenon, I believe, both in fact and in fiction. It doesn't need any explanation, if indeed it can be explained. It's seldom fatal, I understand, so probably I'd have recovered if I'd had to. I didn't have to. Almost immediately upon my return to Massachusetts, while I was trying to think up a reasonably plausible excuse for happening back to the Rangeley region at the time of year when people just don't go there, I began getting letters, telegrams, and finally telephone calls, almost daily from Ralph. Then he began spending his time and money on the long and painful trek from Maine to Boston. It was, in short, a Courtship, and ended in the usual manner, with our deciding that this was a lot of expensive nonsense, so why didn't we get married?

I know that everybody who was ever in love has speculated along the following lines, but please bear with me while I do it once again. If, on that trip out of Parmachenee, one of us had stopped on the Carry Road two minutes to tie a shoe string, or if Ralph had split wood just a little bit faster, we would never have laid eyes upon him. He'd have been in the house, and we'd have walked right by. But the timing was perfect, and that's how I happen to live in the woods.

How I happened to be a writer was just as sloppy and haphazard. I wrote a little number about Maine guides, at my sister's suggestion, for *Scribner's* Life in the United States Contest. I finished it in May, and the contest didn't close until September, so I thought I'd try it out on a couple of dogs first. I'd get it back in plenty of time to qualify.

Now this is not mock modesty. I was absolutely stupified when the *Saturday Evening Post* bought it. Ralph was, too. But we rallied sufficiently to write another entry for the *Scribner's* contest, since our first had been scratched, as it were, and it won a prize. This double success so went to our heads that we decided that from then on we would be writers.

We weren't, of course, because being a writer involves a lot more than just thinking it would be nice to be one. We sold our first attempt at fiction—which was probably bad for us as it gave us false confidence—and then we settled down to discover that writing is not all beer and skittles. But I think that now, at last, we are nearly writers. We don't wait for inspiration any more, having found that inspiration is mostly the application of the seat of the pants to the seat of a chair. We stall around, trying to put off writing, which I understand is the occupational disease of writers. We earn most of our living by the written word. And we are utterly impatient with people who say, "I've often thought I could write myself."

It's taken me a great many words, I see, to answer the first questions people always ask us when they come out of the woods and find us here, unaccountably installed in a little clearing that is always full of the smell of pine and the sound of the river. That's a question that always crops up early in the conversation—"Doesn't the river get on your nerves?"—because until you get used to it, the dull roar, like heavy surf, seems to shake the air. It is all-pervading and inescapable, and you find yourself raising your voice higher and higher above it. But after a while, unless the tone changes with the rise and fall of the water, you don't even hear it. You learn to pitch your voice, not louder to carry over it, but lower and deeper, so that it's not shattered by the vibration. And finally all the places in the world that are away from the sound of furious white water come to seem empty and dead.

I don't pretend to know all of the answers. I don't know what to answer when people say, "But isn't the way you live Escapism?" I don't even know, really, what escapism is. We haven't tried to escape from anything. We have only exchanged one set of problems for another:—the problem of keeping out from under car wheels for the problem of not getting lost in the woods, for example; or the problem of being bored to death by one's neighbor for the problem of being bored to death by oneself. I don't know what to answer when someone says, "I should think you'd go insane!" It's too cheap and easy and obvious to retort, "And I should think you would."

But some of the answers, the answers to the easy, matter-of-fact questions, like "Why don't you write a book about it?", I do know. The answer to that is, "Well, I guess maybe I will."

And so I am writing a book about it.

II

⟨flourish⟩

"But How Do You Make a Living?"

I ALWAYS LIKE TO KNOW WHAT PEOPLE DO FOR A LIVING. This is probably just plain nosiness, but I like to call it a scientific interest. I like to argue that research is simply snooping on a high plane and that the village gossip is a student of applied behaviorism just as much as was Pavlov, shut up in his laboratory with his unfortunate dogs. So when I run across one who seems to be existing as a lily of the field, neither toiling nor spinning, I like to find out how it's done.

Since we would seem to be in that class ourselves, I consider "But how can you make a living up there in the woods?" a perfectly legitimate question. By no stretch of the imagination could our two acres be rated as a farm. There is no place of business within a day's hard journey of us. We don't like to kill things, so our trapping activities are confined to a trap-line for mice and rats run by Gerrish and Rufus in the kitchen and corn patch. How we keep body and soul together is a mystery to the uninitiated. At times it's a mystery to us as well.

We make a living in a variety of ways. For one thing,

there's the taxi and transport service from Middle Dam to Sunday Cove and way-stations. The rates are a little bit flexible, depending on a number of things. Very often, in winter, woodsmen who are leaving the lumber camps call on us to take them and their turkeys—woods for knapsacks—up to Middle Dam. If all goes well, the charge is a dollar. After Thanksgiving the road gets more and more treacherous as the snow gets deeper and deeper, and it becomes easier and easier to slide off into the ditch. The passenger then is obliged to help get the car back onto the road. If this is a matter of a few shoves, the rate goes down to seventy-five cents. If it requires a lot of snow shoveling and strenuous heaving, the fare decreases accordingly. Sometimes it vanishes utterly. You can't charge a man for spending half the morning with his shoulder to the tail board of a 1929 Essex truck, getting his clothes plastered with flying snow. When that happens, Ralph just decides to make a social occasion of it and spends the rest of the morning visiting with Larry Parsons. So far the situation has never seemed to demand that he pay the passenger for riding.

I always feel a little apologetic about our being a four-car family. After all, with only five miles of road available, it seems a little ostentatious, in view of our faded denim pants and patched work shirts, to be discussing which car to take to get the mail. It was worse, though, when the Packard was running.

The Packard was a 1917 Twin Six touring car, built on the general lines of a pre-Revolutionary four poster with canopy, and I always felt like Queen Mary—a nice feeling—when I sat enthroned in it. I regret the passing of the Packard. I don't like these modern cars that you have to crawl into, bumping your head in the process. I don't like to crouch in a cockpit, no matter how luxuriously upholstered, and peer through inadequate slits of glass at the waist-lines of the pedestrians. I like to stalk into a car, sit regally aloft, and view the country o'er.

I won't regret the passing of the Marmon, known locally as Rich's Big Green "Mormon," at all. It is a 1924 sports touring model, at least half a block long. Because of its tremendous power, Ralph uses it for hauling, and I have to ride in back and watch through the rear window that we don't lose our load. I hate the thing. There is no place to brace my feet and the frame of the car is so long that a twig in a rut turns it into a catapault that tosses me helplessly into the air. The Carry Road is nothing but bumps, so it's like riding in' a corn-popper. And besides, I have a sneaking notion that Ralph is just a little bit fonder of the "Mormon" than he is of me.

I'd better make it clear at once that we didn't *buy* all of our four present cars. We came by them through a series of deals—all except the Essex which was given to us by a friend who had become too attached to it to be able to bear the thought of selling it down the river for the twenty dollars the dealer would allow him on a trade-in. He wanted to know that it would have a good home with kind people. Men get so emotional about machinery. And the Marmon was a left-over from the days when Ralph lived on The Outside.

The Model T used to belong to Larry Parsons. Larry is very sensible about cars. When they take to swooning in crises he says, "To hell with it," waits until the ice is safe, tows them out into the middle of the lake, and leaves them to go down into a hundred feet of water during the spring break-up. That's what he was doing to this Model T one winter day when Ralph showed up. Gerrish is unhappy driving anything but a Model T—and I might add that anything but a Model T is apt to be unhappy after Gerrish has been driving it. So Ralph ground the valves on the Parsons' snowboat, did something or other about the Parsons' lighting plant, fixed the plug in the Parsons' bath-tub, which had had to be held up with the bather's toe while the water ran out, in return for the Model T. That is what is known as a deal.

The Model A, vintage of 1930, used to belong to Jim Barnett, the local lumber baron. He had it in here one summer when he was getting out hurricane pine for the government. Under the aegis of several non-mechanical-minded straw bosses, clerks, and government scalers, it developed all the ailments that motors are heir to. During its periods of hospitalization, Ralph did Jim's errands for him, and when Jim moved his camp out, he left the Model A in payment. Ralph spent a happy fifty-nine-hour week investigating its innards, with frequent summons for me to come out and view with horror what some damn-fool butcher had perpetrated on the wiring, the pistons or the timing—I was always properly horrified, as a good wife should be, but I never knew quite at what—and now the thing runs.

People always ask how we got all these cars in here, there being no road from The Outside; and we always tell them that we took them apart, packed them in on our backs over the trail, and set them up again. Gratifyingly often we are believed. Of course we really brought them in over the ice, or rafted them in on scows.

The hey-day of the transport business, with this assorted

fleet of animated junk, is summer. That is when the canoe trips go through here. Some guide book of the lakes, which every camper in the world seems to have fallen afoul of, says that one gets from the Lower Richardson to Umbagog by way of the Rapid River. Anyone who can read a contour map can see that that is impossible. It has been accomplished only twice in history, once by mistake—Captain Coburn, when young, got caught in the current and was lucky—and once by design—some guides from up along the border wanted to make a record, but before they got through they wished they'd never started. Cluley's Rips, a mile below us, is the most vicious piece of water I have ever seen. It's frightening just to stand on the bank and look at it. The water pours into a narrow gut, overhung by rocks and dripping spruces, with such force that it has no time to level out. The middle of the river humps up, green and white and snarling, almost to eye-level of the bank-stander. Cluley, whoever he may have been, was drowned there. That's how you get things named after you in this country.

We profit by the guide book's error. Nobody wants to carry a canoe five miles. It would take all day. We can do it in half an hour, if we're lucky. Sometimes we're not lucky.

The most unlucky day we ever had started out all right. Right after breakfast the telephone rang, and it was Cliff, the old guide and trapper who lives down on Umbagog. Sometimes his last name is Wiggin and sometimes it's Wallace, depending on how he's feeling at the time. He was born with one name, but brought up by folks bearing the other. I'm not sure he remembers now himself which was which. He told us that there were two young men at his place who wanted themselves and one canoe taken across the carry, and that they'd be at Sunday Cove at ten o'clock. That was fine. That would give us time to go up to Middle Dam and bring down forty-eight cases of canned goods that we were laying in against the winter.

Forty-eight cases of canned goods fill our trailer to the brim and weigh enough to be a strain on the trailer hitch. It was unfortunate that the hitch chose to give way as we were going around a down-hill curve. We kept to the road, but the trailer went flying off into the woods, dodging a dozen trees with uncanny intelligence and coming up whango! against a house-size boulder. Cases flew in all directions, exploding as they landed. Cans of milk, figs in syrup, salmon, string beans, sliced peaches, clam chowder and what have you littered an acre of ground. We got out and looked at the wreck and at each other.

Ralph said a few things, and then he said, "Help me get the trailer back on the road, and I'll go home and fix the hitch while you pick up this mess."

It should be easy to pick up a few hundred cans and put them in piles. It wasn't. It would have been easier to pick up a covey of partridges. They were under leaves, behind rocks, down holes. While I was grubbing in the underbrush a can walloped me on the top of the head. Probably it had been lodged in a bush, but it seemed to have leaped from the ground with malicious intent. I had been hot and mad and disgusted and now I was hurt as well. And I still couldn't find three cans. I haven't found them yet. I went home.

It was half past eleven and Ralph was still working on the trailer hitch, he having had his troubles, too. Our clients were still, presumably, sitting at Sunday Cove, and almost certainly thinking hard thoughts about us. Just as we were debating what to do next, they walked into the yard, having got tired of waiting.

The least we could do was to invite them to lunch, with apologies and promises that everything would shortly be under control, and that as soon as we had eaten we would go after the canoe. I walked back to the scene of the wreck, collected some corned beef, spinach, and pineapple slices, and threw together a meal, while Ralph finished the hitch and the two youths went swimming. Then we all had a drink of rum, which we all needed, and things seemed more rosy.

They looked so much more rosy, in fact, that I decided to leave the lunch dishes and ride down to the Cove, too. We boarded the Packard, then extant, hitched on the trailer, and set out. The ride was without incident, *mirabile dictu*. But in turning around at the Cove Ralph stalled the motor, and then we were sunk again. The Packard's weakness lay in weak coils, and it wouldn't start when the motor was hot. We waited for a while for it to cool off, during which time Cookie, Kyak's mother and our dog of the moment, managed to find a porcupine and get her mouth full of quills which we had no tools to remove. The Packard still wouldn't start, so we walked the three and a half long, hot miles home after the current Ford, a Model T touring, since deceased.

I declined an invitation to ride back again and stayed home to do the dishes, de-quill the dog, and lick my own wounds. Pretty soon the whole works was back again—Ford, Packard, trailer and canoe. Apparently the Packard had cooled off enough to start the minute our backs were turned. The trip to Middle Dam was successfully accomplished, with the customers only about a day behind schedule. I will say they were wonderfully good-natured about it. They still wanted to pay Ralph for throwing their trip completely out of gear; but there are a few things left for which we don't take money.

The worst and final repercussion was delayed two days. Then the money for that ill-starred trip arrived by mail, with no return address. There wasn't a thing we could do but keep it. We felt like a couple of curs.

Ralph has hauled all sorts of things across the carry. He has hauled anything that will float, from a rubber fold-boat to a steel, gasoline-powered work boat. He has hauled woodsmen suffering from third degree burns, all manner of cuts and fractures, pneumonia, and delirium tremens, known hereabouts as "the horrors." He has hauled a litter of pigs, bound for the garbage disposal department of a lumber camp. He has hauled news-reel men and their cameras, covering the National Championship White Water Races, and fire wardens covering a forest fire. But the ones I like best and he hates the most are the girls' camps.

He hates the girls' camps because he claims that, in spite of the fact that the girls are always under the auspices of a guide and two or three counselors, you might as well try to organize a handful of quicksilver. I like them, because I like to see the old boy get his come-uppence. He gets them all packed in nicely around their canoes and duffle, and someone decides she has to have a picture of the out-fit, but that Tessie's skinned knee and Vera's camp letter won't show, so will everybody please rearrange themselves? Or Muggsy can't find her sweater, so everything has to be unpacked. Or someone has a notion, and the notion spreads, and in a flash the whole works is streaming off into the bushes. It drives him nuts, being, so he says, me raised to the nth degree.

The most recent invasion got even Gerrish down. Ralph went to Middle to get them—fifteen of them from some camp over in Vermont—and stopped here to re-fill his radiator. They swarmed into the yard like a pack of beagles, with an old and completely resigned guide making perfunctory motions of bringing them to heel. While his charges were posing for snap-shots with Kyak, who makes swell local color to show the home folks, he came in to ask permission to build a lunch fire on our land. I asked him how he liked his job. He sighed wearily. "Wal, it ain't no *position*," he said with feeling.

He could have saved his breath about the fire. Gerrish was tarring the seams of a boat and had the tar pot heating over a little fire between two rocks. According to his rather hysterical story, the first thing he knew he was smearing the boat with tomato soup, and then he realized he had somehow become embroiled in a mass culinary operation. He grabbed the tar pot, fought his way clear, and knocked off for dinner. He believes in co-operating with the inevitable.

I was charmed with that lunch, aimed to fill the hollow brought on by ten miles of paddling since breakfast and to generate enough energy to get the whole shebang to the nearest camp-site, ten miles away, before supper. The menu:—Tomato Purée; Cheese Dreams; Lemonade.

Once Ralph got a job with the Geodetic Survey, which was in here for the summer making a contour map of the country. To make a contour map, it seems, you first establish, by some esoteric hocus-pocus with trigonometry, the exact altitude of one point, in this case a stone in Coburn's front yard. (Alt. 1462.27 feet above sea level.) Then, working with surveying instruments, you run in circles from that point, sticking sticks with the new altitudes on them at convenient places along the circumference of the circle. If the reading when you get back to Coburn's stone is 1462.27, you may assume that all points on the circle are correct. You then take any point on the circle and follow the same procedure from there. At the end of the summer the entire country is covered with imaginary circles and actual sticks. Then you start running straight lines across country, re-checking altitude with a barometer at any sticks you may come across—surveyors dignify these sticks by calling them Temporary Bench Marks—and attempting to come out at flags which have been tied according to what system I never did find out, to various inaccessible trees. This is the last step before putting the map on paper, and this is where Ralph came into the picture.

One of the rodmen was taken ill, the appropriation for the survey was almost gone, and the head surveyor was loath to lose time and money waiting for his man to recover. So he appealed to Ralph to help him out, assuring him that all he had to do was stroll through the woods with a string tied to his arm, stop when shouted to, and blaze the nearest tree. He didn't say that they would be working in the B Pond territory.

There is nothing the matter with B Pond. It lies to the south of us, over a beech-covered ridge, and it is lovely and placid and wild. But Ralph loathes B Pond, because the trail over is rough and steep. He'd rather be dead than take a trip over the B Pond trail.

Nevertheless, everyday that he worked for the Survey he

went to B Pond, and he didn't go by trail. That isn't the way the Survey does things. They pick out a point at random, consult their notes and learn that somewhere a mile off to the S.S.W. is a white cloth tied to a yellow birch, take out their compasses, tighten their belts, and start looking for it. The rodman—Ralph—goes ahead, trailing a hundred-yard piece of string. When the end of the string comes abreast of the surveyor, he puts up a shout and the rodman stops and makes his blaze. As soon as the surveyor overtakes him, he sets out again, in theory, at least, letting nothing turn him aside from a perfectly straight line. This would be a cinch on the plains of the West, but this is rough country, and we had a hurricane in 1938.

The results of the hurricane here have to be seen to be believed. Acres of trees are piled up like jackstraws in windrows forty feet high and half a mile long. A rodman doesn't go around these. He goes over and through them. Ralph insists that one whole day he never had his feet on the ground except when he came down for lunch. The despised B Pond trail began to look like a boulevard, especially as he knew it was only a hundred yards off to the west, running parallel to their course. It might as well have been a hundred miles off. It might better have been, because then he could have forgotten it. He tore his clothes to ribbons, and then did the same to his skin. He put a vicious blaze on a little sapling and a porcupine fell out of it, missing him by inches. That's the same as being missed by a twenty-pound ball stuck full of red hot needles. He got three and a half dollars a day and whatever satisfaction went with the chief surveyor's affidavit that (a) Ralph was the best rodman he'd ever had, and that (b) this is the most hellish country he's seen in a career covering every state in the Union.

But I know better than ever again to try to persuade Ralph to take a nice little walk over to B Pond with me.

I have my difficulties, too. I don't much like to cook. I like the results of a morning's hard labor to last more than ten minutes. But once in a while I have to take boarders. This usually happens when I am in the worst possible position to do so. Last spring is a good example.

All three families in Middle Dam had enough food to last, with care, over the break-up and until a load of supplies could be brought in from The Outside. We were feeling pretty good about it, because sometimes we aren't so lucky. Nobody, we fondly thought, could get in to eat up our carefully counted potatoes and beans. We were sitting pretty. I was even entertaining the extravagant idea of making a one-egg chocolate cake instead of a no-egg gingerbread, when the telephone rang. It was Alice Miller, and she was in a dither.

She said, "Louise, how much food have you got? I got a crew of five walked in here along the shore from the Arm to stay over the break-up and do some work on the dam. I ain't got a thing to feed them."

The Millers had helped us out in more pinches than I can remember, and it wasn't often that I had a chance to do much for them. This was a God-given opportunity to lend a hand. I'd peel the larder down to the last bone, and be glad of the chance. If I saved out a dozen eggs and a couple of cans of corned beef, and beans and salt pork and split peas and flour and corn meal, we could eat for the few days until the lake was clear, even if it wasn't a very balanced diet. We had plenty of canned milk and potatoes. I told her what I could let her have.

"Swell! I'll send someone down with a pack-sack!"

She hung up and in due time her emissary arrived. I gave him everything I could spare, and he staggered off up the Carry Road under the load.

Barely was he out of sight when the telephone rang again. A man's voice said pleasantly, "Mis' Rich? This is Ban Barnett. I'm down at Sunday Cove, with a crew of three. We walked in over the old Magalloway trail to fix the Carry Road before the drive comes in, and we'll be right up. We'll stay at your place for two-three days, like always."

"Did you bring any food?" I asked with regrettable lack of hospitality.

"Food? Holy God, Mis' Rich, we had all we could do to get ourselves through that Jees'ly swamp!"

"Ban," I said desperately, "I can't board you. I've hardly got enough food in the house to feed the family. You'll have to—"

He'd have to what? The Millers couldn't feed four more. The Parsons weren't any better off than I was. They couldn't go home, nine miles through the swamp and over a mountain, with nothing under their belts.

"You can feed us," Ban assured me with touching faith. "You got potatoes and salt, ain't you?"

I fed them for three days, and ever since I have had implicit belief in the miracle of the loaves and fishes. We had pea soup, which is very filling. We had baked beans. I sent Gerrish fishing. You can never catch fish when you need them, but he did. We had trout and salmon. We had corn meal mush and molasses. The butter ran out, but we had johnny-cake and the last of the jam I had made the fall before. We had dandelion greens and fiddle-heads, those strange, furry fern fronds that taste something like asparagus and something like swamp water. You boil them and serve them with butter, if you have any butter. My two cans of corned beef made two meals. There are ways of stretching meat enough for three to feed seven, other than Divine multiplication. One can I cut up in cream sauce—a lot of cream sauce—and served on toast. The other I cut up with cold potato—a lot of potato—and browned into hash. The Parsons let me have three cans of tomatoes. One made tomato soup, one went into scalloped tomatoes with bread crumbs—lots of bread crumbs—and the last I strained for Rufus to drink, in lieu of orange juice. You can make one egg take the place of two in scrambled eggs by using too much milk and thickening it with flour. It's not very good, but it's something to eat.

Oh, I fed them. It wasn't according to any known dietetics, but we all survived. And when the ice went out and the first boat came in with supplies, I had left a cup of sugar, five potatoes, three cans of milk, a quart of flour, and one egg.

While I was peeling potatoes paper-thin, diluting canned milk with too much water—we did have plenty of water—and measuring out lard by the quarter teaspoon, Ralph and Gerrish were working with the crew on the road. That's another annual source of income, the reimbursement for which just about covers the taxes. Working out your taxes on the road is routine procedure hereabouts. You spend a week filling in wash-outs, rebuilding caved-in culverts, and leveling out the worst ruts, and the tax sale is forestalled for another twelve months. Oh, you can get along with very little cash money in this country if you know the ropes and are sufficiently adaptable.

I was being very adaptable the day Ted Benson called me up from Pond-in-the-River Dam. Ted is the boss of the dam repair crew that travels about the country from headquarters in Lewiston. They always stay at Miller's when they are in this neck of the woods, and when they are working on Pondy Dam, Alice Miller sends down the makings of dinner, and they prepare it over an open camp-fire. Ted is a Dane, and his name is really Theodore (pronounced Tay-o-dorrr) Bendtsen. He has been in this country ever since, almost half a century ago as an apprentice to the Danish Merchant Marine, he deserted ship at Portland; but when he gets excited he still lapses into Danish on the hard words. He was very much excited on this occasion.

I finally made out that he wanted me to come up to the dam and cook dinner for him and his crew of nine. His long-string-of-Danish cook had been out over the week-end and had too bad a hang-over to be of any use to anyone. It wouldn't be any work at all. Mis' Miller had everything all ready. All I had to do was heat it up. He'd do it himself, only dam repairing had reached a crisis where not a man could be spared. Would I come?

I would be glad to. I like Ted, and I'd like to do him a favor. Ralph had gone to Upton to vote in the state elections, so there was nothing to keep me at home. I locked up the dogs—we had five then; that was when we thought a dog team would be a good idea—put Rufus into a pack-sack—he was too young to walk—loaded him onto my back and went up to the dam.

A fire was already burning under the grate that Ted had

salvaged from an abandoned steamboat and placed on two rocks, and a number of kettles were standing around on the ground. A long-chinned individual named Rush was splitting wood, and Ted was standing by to tell me that the dinner hour was eleven o'clock by the battered Big Ben he had placed conspicuously on a stump. Then he went off down the dam fill, motioning Rush to follow.

Rush put another chunk of wood—only we natives call them "junks"—on his chopping block and reduced it to splinters while Ted moved out of hearing. Then he left his ax in the block and closed in confidentially.

"You want to watch that crazy Dane," he warned me. "I've cooked for him. You know what he does? He gets hungry and comes up and shoves the clock along ten-fifteen minutes. You have to keep an eye on him."

It was half past ten then.

I tied Rufus to a bush and gave him a pannikinful of water and a spoon to play with. Then I looked into the food situation. The big kettle held a boiled dinner—corned beef and cabbage, potatoes, carrots, and turnips. It was all cooked, but it would take at least twenty minutes to heat through again, which left ten minutes in which to make the coffee—at least a gallon in a big, smoke-smudged pot. The grate would hold only one thing at a time. Well, it could be done, with a good hot fire. I set the kettle on and stuffed some dry spruce under it. The flame sprang up with a heartening crackle and I started to unpack the plates and eating tools.

Suddenly I realized that Ted was hovering. He took the cover off the kettle, peered in, put it back, snitched a cookie out of a bag, and wandered back down the dam fill. I looked at the clock. It said ten minutes of eleven. I set it back fifteen minutes and started arranging plates of bread, butter, cookies, apple pie, and cheese in a row on a plank. Alice Miller has a reputation all up the lakes for the abundance and excellence of her fare.

The fire had died down a little, so I put some wood on, saw that the boiled dinner had commenced to steam gently, and took the coffee pot down to the river to fill it with water. When I got back, Ted was again retiring down the dam fill, the clock said five minutes of eleven, Rufus had untied himself and was eating cheese, and there were ants on the pie. I took the cheese away, tied Rufus up, set the clock back fifteen minutes, brushed the ants off, and covered the pies with a clean dish towel. Then I sat down on the stump beside the clock and waited for the boiled dinner to boil. It was quarter of eleven by my time, which by then had nothing to do with any other time on earth.

Pretty soon the big kettle began to rumble quietly, sending out clouds of steam and a delicious odor, and Ted started up from the dam, walking briskly and dangling something in his hand. I took one look and set the clock back five more minutes. It was a two pound salmon, and my prophetic soul informed me, rightly, that he wanted it cooked for his dinner. Boiled, he said, with melted butter on it. I took off the boiled dinner, set the coffee pot on, and went down to the river with an extra pan to get some water for the fish. When I got back the clock again said five minutes of eleven. I set it back to quarter of, edged the coffee pot over to make room for the salmon, and put some butter in a pannikin on the edge of the fire to melt.

Rufus was eating leaves, which might or might not be edible, and although by then I didn't much care which they were, I fished them out of his mouth, getting my finger bitten in the process, and set out the salt, pepper, and vinegar. A loud hissing behind my back indicated that the coffee had boiled over and put out the fire. I took the coffee off, burning my hand, and built up the fire with some birch bark. Ted's fish was boiling, and Ted was coming up from the dam again, so I stuck a fork into it, decided it was near enough done as made no difference, and with no attempt at concealment, shoved the clock along to eleven.

"I guess we're ready," I told Ted, and met his eye. "Right on the dot, too!" I added blandly.

I still take boarders when I have to, but I don't cook out any more. It's too hard on the nerves. I'd rather do something like knitting, which can be confined to the home. I'm a good knitter, and I'm proud of it. I see no point in being modest about things you know you do well. It doesn't indicate humility so much as hypocrisy or lack of perception. So then, I am a very good knitter. I even won first prize at the Andover Fair once for a pair of gloves. Fifty cents, it was, and a blue ribbon. I spent the money, but the ribbon I wouldn't part with for pearls. I can knit while I read, thus staving off boredom and creating an illusion of great efficiency. I can make up my own directions, or I can follow printed directions, which apparently is the harder thing to do, although I don't see why it should be.

I think the difficulty with people who can't follow printed directions for knitting or anything else is that they try to understand them. They read the whole thing through and it doesn't make sense to them, so they start with a defeatist attitude. They try to relate the first few steps to the whole, and there is no obvious relation, so they get discouraged and say, "Oh, I can't learn things out of books. But if you'll just show me—"

You don't have to understand directions. All you have to do is follow them; and you can follow them only one step at a time. What you need is not intelligence, but a blind faith. I never read directions through. I never read beyond the operation I am engaged in, having a simple trust that the person who wrote them knew what he was doing. That trust is usually justified. Oh, there's no trick to following directions, and if I don't teach Sally and Rufus one other thing, I'm going to teach them that. I think it's important.

When I get my own family's sweaters and mittens and socks done for the winter, I knit for whoever will pay me—neighbors, lumberjacks, anyone. Also I sew on buttons and patch clothes for woodsmen, whenever there are lumbering operations in here. I don't like to sew, and I don't sew very well, but I do better than most lumberjacks. Ralph, coming across an article about Father Hubbard, the Glacier Priest, took to calling me Mother Hubbard, the winter I started acting as housemother to the woodsmen. It applied, but not as he meant it to. I'm not a snappy model; I really don't wear Mother Hubbards, but the effect is about the same.

Had Ralph been born a little earlier, he would have been a Yankee horse-trader. As it is, he doesn't do so badly with his car trading, in a country where trading is a religion. Albert Allen, a friend from Upton who has lived all his life in this vicinity, covered the general attitude one day. "Nope," he said, "I'd be ashamed to give it to anybody. 'Tain't good enough. But maybe I can find someone who'll make a trade." No matter what you start with, here, if you stick with it long enough, you'll get what you want. All you need is something to start with. Will Morton, who lives on Rifle Point, off Middle Dam, and who is the oldest working guide in the state, being eighty-two— and one of the best—started out with an electric razor, which one of his sports gave him for Christmas. He ended with a boat, which was what he had in mind all the time. I've forgotten, unfortunately, the intermediate steps.

Ralph's most remarkable operation was the trading of the old Model T touring car. There was a lumber camp over on Sunday Pond three miles north of us then, and one gray November day the clerk of the camp called up and announced that he'd heard Ralph had a lot of cars and would maybe sell one. He wanted it to run up and down Umbagog, now that the ice was safe and the snow hadn't come yet, so he could go out and see his girl.

We'd just acquired the Essex, so Ralph was open to bids on the Model T. The clerk—Mac, his name was—said he'd be over next day to take a look. Ralph spent the intervening time pacing up and down and muttering to himself, trying to decide what price he ought to ask. He concluded finally that he'd ask twenty-five dollars, but would be glad to get fifteen.

The trial run was a huge success. They went everywhere —down to Sunday Cove, across Umbagog to Sturtevant Cove, and up through the woods to the Brown Farm, where they called on Joe Mooney and had a game of ping-pong with the company doctor. Mac was impressed twenty-five dollars' worth, all right, only he didn't have twenty-five dollars to spare. Just as Ralph was about to come big-heartedly down to twenty, Mac advanced a proposition.

"Look, I'll tell you what I'll do. I'll give you fifteen dollars and return the car when the camp moves out."

Every woman occasionally wonders what manner of man she has married. No matter how long she has been living with her husband, once in a while he presents a new face. It's the bunk about women being enigmas and men being just transparent little boys at heart. Or else I'm gullible. I had Ralph down as good old, honest, out-spoken Rich, the guy with the heart of gold; the guy who, offered his price in that frank and open manner, would say, "Oh, hell, fifteen dollars is plenty. She's yours. Drive her away!"

And did he? Oh, my goodness, gracious, no! He hemmed and hawed, while I bit my tongue in an effort not to interfere. Finally he gave in, with the perfectly maddening appearance of granting a favor. "That'll be all right," he said graciously. "When you get through with her, be sure to leave her on this side of the Cove, so I can get her without any trouble." Just like that. And then I swear he went out and measured gas into the tank with a teaspoon, so that Mac could get to the nearest source of supply, but not much further.

That night Mac went to Errol to see his girl. The next day it snowed eighteen inches. The rest of the winter the Ford sat under a drift at Sunday Cove—on this side of the Cove, as requested—and never turned a wheel. In the spring Ralph drove it home. I should think he'd lie awake nights, but he doesn't. He has the horse-trader conscience, I guess.

I haven't. I'm a rotten trader. But I did do one deal that gives me perennial satisfaction. I think I came out all right, but even if I didn't, even if I got gypped out of my eye-teeth as Ralph says I did, I'm very happy about the whole thing.

There are three boats and a canoe that go with the place, and of course everybody uses them. But they really were Ralph's boats. I wanted a boat of my own, to use and possibly abuse as I chose. I wanted a boat I could put into a pool downriver and not be asked, "When are you going to bring that boat back to the Pond? I want to use it." So when the Bernier boat—Bernier was a famous builder of the type of boat called the Rangeley boat—began to go to pieces from neglect, Ralph gave it to me. The idea was that I would fix it up myself and it would be mine.

Well, I just didn't get around to it, somehow, and it continued to lie on the shore of the Pond, with the paint flaking off, the wood drying out, and the caulking falling from the seams. And that's where Gerrish enters the picture.

He said to me casually, "Ralph tells me that Bernier boat belongs to you."

I thought I felt a deal coming on, and I'd observed Ralph long enough to have learned some rudiments of the technique. So I just said, "Yeah."

"You ain't going to have no boat if you don't tend to it."

I said, "Yeah," again, and we sat in companionable silence.

Finally he said, "Have a cigarette." Pause while we lighted up. "What'll you take for it?"

"I don't know. What'll you give for it?"

"It ain't worth much. Needs a lot done on it."

"To tell you the truth," I said frankly, "I don't want to get rid of it. I want to cut the stern off square, when I get the price of an outboard motor, and make a kicker-boat out of it. What'll you take for fixing it up for me?" That was in the classic tradition. I'd registered reluctance to part with my property and made a counter offer.

"Half the boat," he said promptly. "I'll do the work and you furnish the materials and we'll own it together. When you get around to buying a kicker—wal, there's places I'd go if I had a kicker-boat."

"Where, for instance?" I asked. I didn't want my half of the boat hauled down to Mount Desert Island along with his.

"Upper Dam. Or the West Arm. I wouldn't take it off the lakes."

So it was a deal. He scraped the boat, caulked the seams, replaced a broken gunwale and put in a new stem and keel. That took a month. Then he gave it two coats of oil and two coats of paint, and it's the best boat on the place. He did a swell job. I don't see why Ralph thinks it was a skin deal. I didn't pay anything for the boat in the first place.

I didn't pay anything for it in the last place, either, and that might be what gripes him. He seems to have a feeling that I should have paid for the paint and oil and steel wool and marine caulking and nails and copper sheathing. But he has a whole shop full of that kind of stuff. I should think he'd be glad—but he doesn't seem to be. It would bother me a lot more if I didn't remember Mac and the Model T.

My sister and I used to play a game called "Husband's Occupation?" It was a simple-minded game that we made up off application blanks of various sorts. One of us would ask suddenly, "Husband's Occupation?" and the other had to think up a possible but not very probable answer. "Flea trainer," for example. Or "Percheron Faulter." Or "Sealer of Weights and Measures." I guess we were easily entertained.

I guess we still are, because I am amused, spasmodically, at being married to a Maine guide. Oh, yes, Ralph's a guide, too, although he doesn't work at it much.

Of course a guide has to be a good woodsman and canoeman and camp cook and emergency doctor, and the State of Maine ascertains that he is, before issuing him a license to guide. But he could never earn a living if he didn't also make the grade with the sports—same as dudes of the West—as "quite a character." He has to be laconic. He has to be picturesque. Maine guides have a legend of quaintness to uphold, and, boy! do they uphold it. They're so quaint that they creak. They ought to be. They work hard enough at it.

Here's the Maine guide. He wears what amounts to a uniform. It consists of a wool shirt, preferably plaid, nicely faded to soft, warm tones; dark pants, either plus-fours, for some unknown reason, or riding breeches; wool socks and the soleless, Indian-type moccasin, or high laced boots. He carries a bandana in his hip pocket and may or may not wear another knotted around his neck. But he must wear a battered felt hat, with a collection of salmon flies stuck in the band, and he must wear it with an air; and he must wear a hunting knife day and night; and he must look tough and efficient. If he has high cheek bones and tans easily, that is his good luck. He can then admit to part-Indian ancestry, accurately or not. Indian blood is an item highly esteemed by sports. Naturally he could do his work as well in mail-order slacks, or in a tuxedo, for that matter; but the sports wouldn't think so. Sports are funny.

"That fellow there," the sport is supposed to say, showing his vacation movies in his Westchester rumpus room, "was my quarter-breed guide. He's quite a character. Never had any education beyond the seventh grade, but I don't know anyone I'd rather spend a week alone with. That's the real test. He's a genuine natural philosopher. For instance, we were talking about the War, and he said —and I never thought of it this way before—." What the guide said he probably lifted from Shirer's book, but translated into Down East, it wouldn't be recognizable.

A few livid scars are a great asset to a guide. It doesn't matter how he got them. Maybe as a barefoot boy he stepped on a rake. The holes make swell bear-trap scars, acquired one night up in the Allagash, when the thermometer was at thirty below and the nearest settlement was fifty miles away. Maybe he cut his hand peeling potatoes. It sounds much better to say a beaver bit him. Maybe he fell downstairs and gashed his forehead. When asked—and he'll be asked all right—he can tell all about his big fight with the lynx. They all make good stories to tell around the evening camp-fire.

Oh, those evening camp-fires! That's when the good guide gets in his dirty work. That's when he sows the seed for a re-engagement next year.

This is the set-up:—Supper—fresh-caught trout with bacon curls, potatoes baked in the coals and slathered with butter, a kind of biscuit cooked in a frying pan and resembling Yorkshire pudding, canned peas and fruit—is over. The sports, pleasantly stuffed and mildly weary from having "helped" paddle for ten or twelve miles, stretch out around the fire. Down on the shingle that natural philosopher, that real character, Bobcat Bill, washes the dishes. The water glows like blood-stained ebony in the leaping light, and the firs stand up behind, black and motionless. Back in the bush a fox barks and a deer crashes away from the scent of wood-smoke. All around lies the wilderness, dark and unknown and sinister. Inside the little pool of light is all that is left of the safe and familiar—the canoes drawn up on the shore, the piled packsacks and blanket rolls, the forms and faces of friends. A loon sends its lost-soul lament over the darkling water, and a shiver runs around the fire. Then Bobcat Bill strolls up from the lake, throws an armful of dry-ki onto the blaze, and begins tossing blankets toward the group. In the flash of a buck's tail the old magic begins to work. The tight little fire-hearted circle of fellowship is formed. We're all brothers here, united by our common cause against the power of the black beyond. We're all valiant, noble renegades from civilization's chafing bonds. We're dangerous and free!

The loon throws its blood-curdling cry against the mountains once more, and laughs its crazy laughter.

"Never hear one of them critters a-hollerin'," Bobcat Bill drifts easily into his act, "but what it 'minds me of one time I was lost up on them big caribou barrens across the lake. That's how I come by this here scar on my shoulder. Reason I was up in there, a feller had met foul play—"

I'm making guides sound like a bunch of frauds, and I don't mean to. They work hard and they're in a difficult position. Like all merchandisers, they're obliged to give the customer what he wants, and it's their tough luck that the customer wants adventure. Adventure, free of actual risk, is hard to produce; and the state frowns on the actual killing off of sports, even by accident. So the guide has to make the customer believe himself Daniel Boone's contemporary equivalent, without actually letting him stick his neck out too far. A little discomfort, yes. That'll make fine telling back in Westchester. Too much discomfort, no. Actual danger, a thousand times no, not even if he insists with tears and pleading that he really wants to rough it, to get off the beaten track into tough country, to pit his own brains and brawn against death by violence or starvation. It's too easy to meet trouble in this country without deliberately looking for it.

So what's the answer? The answer is atmosphere:—tall tales around the camp-fire, a perpetually grim and watchful bearing, a knife and revolver worn always at the ready. The answer is illusion:—jam into bear's blood, bobcat into Canada lynx, vaccination scar into dagger wound.

Ralph's occasional guiding consists chiefly in taking out fishing parties by the day in this immediate vicinity. That's what he's best fitted for, knowing as he does every fish in the river by its first name, and where it'll most likely be hanging out at two-thirty on any given Wednesday. He always comes home exhausted by suppressed mirth. Sports are funny-ha-ha as well as funny-peculiar.

His prize catch was an outfit of politicians from a medium-sized Massachusetts city. At home they were elaborately teetotal; the W.C.T.U. is a force in that city. But they brought fourteen quarts of Scotch and a case of beer—snake-bite precautions—for their three-day stay in the woods. They managed to get rid of it, and I don't think they dumped it in the river. That would argue a little training somewhere along the line, I should think. They'd never been fly-fishing before, but they'd seen pictures of fly-fishermen. So they had the works:—waders, creels, canvas jackets, tapered lines, collapsible landing nets, everything. Everything, that is, except the ability to cast a fly. Ralph spent the day climbing trees to retrieve flies caught in branches and diving into the river to un-snag them from the bottom. Between times he hauled his sports out of the water—they were great fallers-in—and dodged erratic back-casts. He had a very active day. Along about dusk a great outcry went up. Someone had caught a fish. An enormous salmon, so he said. Ralph netted it. It was a small chub. The chub is a poor relation of the carp family, and we natives look down our noses at them. Even the cats won't eat them. The politician wasn't so choosey. He took it home. Probably he has it mounted over his desk now.

Ralph finally got three of his party put to bed. The fourth—he of the chub—refused to go. He'd tasted blood and he wasn't going to waste time sleeping. Ralph left him sitting on the bank of the river with a quart of Scotch conveniently at hand. It was pitch dark, which not only put him in the legal position of being a breaker of the half-hour-after-sunset law, but also in the impractical position of not being able to see his line. The first consideration didn't bother him. The second he got around by using a powerful flashlight trained on his fly. He caught no fish, but he had fun.

The other thing that we do for a living is write. This is the most important, because we spend the most time on it, and because the larger part of our income is derived from it. Probably if we spent the same amount of time and energy working in a factory or selling brushes from door to door, we'd have more money and fewer headaches. But there are other things we wouldn't have.

In theory, at least, one of the advantages of writing is

that you can work anywhere and any time. You aren't tied down. Actually this is true only within limits. I have found that unless I make myself some office hours and stick to them—8.30 to 11 A.M. and 1 to 3 P.M.—I don't do any writing. I pick some wild flowers and arrange them, wash the dog, and make a cake, and then it's too late to start this morning. So I read another chapter of the book I started last night and get dinner. After dinner I think I might as well finish the book and go swimming. Morning is really the time your mind is clearest, I remember being told. There's no sense in trying to start writing in the afternoon. So I'll write to-morrow. I really will.

But I wouldn't if I didn't have my office hours. If I can't think of anything to write about, I just sit in front of the typewriter and brood.

I couldn't write anywhere, either. I couldn't write on a cruise to the West Indies, or in a mining town in Nevada, or in the bayou country, or any other place where the surroundings were new and unexplored. Putting down words on paper is a very dull substitute for seeing new things and people. On my ninety-ninth cruise I could probably write, or after I'd lived two years in Nevada. The real meaning of "You can write anywhere" is that you can choose a place where you're going to like to be and do your writing there after you've exhausted its other possibilities. Your original choice is free.

Another reason I like to be a writer, aside from the fact that I can live in the backwoods instead of off Times Square, is that I like to see my name in print. This is pure exhibitionism, and we'll say no more about it. I don't like exhibitionists, either. And while I'm baring my girlish heart, I might as well admit that I enjoy having people look respectful when I say, "Oh, I write." I get a kick out of it, even if I do feel like a fraud.

Feeling like a fraud is one of the bad things about being a writer. You have to be a little disparaging about your work sometimes. Because of its nature, it is so closely tied up with your own personality that taking it seriously verges perilously close to the pompous. So there's a lot of talk by writers about just doing pot-boilers until one is financially secure enough to embark on a really serious work. Frankly, this is hooey. Writing pot-boilers implies writing down, and condescension is immediately apparent to, and rightly resented by, the editor. I believe that any writer who sells enough to eat off the proceeds is writing the very best he can all the time. When he stops, he stops eating.

I've read a lot of first-rate writing, and I have some critical sense; so I know where I stand. I'll never be first-rate. I'll improve with practice, I trust, but I haven't got what it takes to reach the top. However, I hope I'll never make the excuse that "it's only a pot-boiler, after all." Everything I write, no matter how lousy it turns out to be, is the very best I am capable of at the time. My writing may be third-rate, but at least it's honest. You can't be even a third-rate writer without taking your work seriously.

But if you take it seriously, chances are that others will, too, and I enjoy having a fool-proof excuse for not doing the things I don't want to do. If I said, "Oh, I can't. I have to do my mending," the answer would be, "You can do it this evening." If I say, "Oh, I can't. I'm working on my book," there's no argument about it at all. It's wonderful. I hardly ever do things I don't want to do any more. Except write.

Writing is hard work, and don't let anybody tell you otherwise. It's hard on the eyes, the back, the fanny, the disposition and the nail-polish. It's hard on the nerves. Your income is so uncertain. You never know, when you're sweating blood over a story, whether the editor is going to hold his nose, or cheer and send you a check for—

And that's another thing. People don't mind asking a writer how much he gets paid for a story. There must be some explanation for such a breach of good taste in otherwise well-bred persons. I have been coping with the situation by stalling. I say, "Well, that depends. It would be impossible to say. Some magazines pay higher rates than others, and some writers are better than others—" And blah, blah, blah.

But I'm not going to stall any more. The next time anyone asks me how much I got for a story, I'm going to tell them. I might even tell them the truth. And then I'm going to say, "And what does *your* husband earn in a year?" That ought to settle that.

Upon reflection, I conclude that probably the best short answer to "How do you earn a living?" would be "From hand to mouth."

III

"But You Don't Live Here All the Year 'Round?"

WHAT PEOPLE REALLY MEAN WHEN THEY ASK US IF WE live here the year 'round, is "But good Lord! Certainly you don't stay in here during the winter? You must be crazy!" Well, all right, we're crazy. I would have thought so myself, before I tried it.

I used to hate winter, too. When I was a child it was because winter meant school, and although I got along reasonably well there, school was something to be considered with nausea. Along about February I used to think of the stretch of time until June and freedom with such a hopeless depression as I have never known since. It just didn't seem possible that I could live that long. The only time in my whole scholastic career that I ever liked school was one spell when I was in the eighth grade; and the reason for my change of heart then had nothing to do with my studies. I fell in love with the boy who sat in front of me, and since he lived over on the other side of town, the only time I got to see him was during school hours. It made a difference in my attitude, but it didn't last very long. In spite of all the sentences I diagrammed for him, and the arithmetic answers I slipped under my desk into his eager palm, come Valentine's Day, he spent all his pocket money on a big lace and ribbon heart for a blonde who sat over in the dumb section, and who didn't know a verb from a common denominator. It soured me on the male for a time, but it taught me a lesson that has been valuable ever since: to wit, men may admire and use brains in a woman, but they don't love them. I reverted to my hatred of winter.

After I grew up, I still hated it, and I think that now I know the reason why. In civilization we try to combat winter. We try to modify it so that we can continue to live the same sort of life that we live in summer. We plow the sidewalks so we can wear low shoes, and the roads so we can use cars. We heat every enclosed space and then, inadequately clad, dash quickly from one little pocket of hot air through a bitter no-man's land of cold to another. We fool around with sun lamps, trying to convince our skins that it is really August, and we eat travel-worn spinach in an attempt to sell the same idea to our stomachs. Naturally, it doesn't work very well. You can neither remodel nor ignore a thing as big as winter.

In the woods we don't try to. We just let winter be winter, and any adjustments that have to be made, we make in ourselves and our way of living. We have to. The skin between outdoors and indoors here is so much thinner than it is even in a small town, that it's sometimes hard to tell where one stops and the other begins. We can't dress, for example, for a day in the house. Such a thing doesn't exist. We have to go outdoors continually—to get in wood, to go to the john, to run down to the other house and put wood on the kitchen fire, to get water, to hack a piece of steak off the frozen deer hanging in the woodshed, or for any one of a dozen other reasons. Outdoors is just another, bigger, colder room. When we get up in the morning we dress with the idea that we'll be using this other room all day. When we step into it we make the concession of putting on mittens—if we're really going to be there long enough.

Everyone in here dresses more or less alike, until it comes to foot gear. We all, male and female, wear plaid wool shirts—two of them sometimes—and wool pants, ski or riding. We wear wool caps and home-made mittens, with leather mittens, called choppers, over them. The choppers don't keep the hands warm, but they keep the mittens dry and prevent their wearing out. We all wear wool socks. And there the great woods schism begins. Everyone has his own pet ideas of the proper footwear for below zero weather. No one will listen to any one else's opinion on the subject. Everyone knows he is right, and no one will dabble with experiments. Feet freeze too easily and frozen feet are too painful and serious to be courted deliberately.

Ralph belongs to the great gum-boot school of thought. Gum-boots have high leather tops sewed on rubber feet. They are loose and roomy, and their addicts wear two or three pairs of heavy wool socks inside them. I guess they're all right, if you like them. Larry Parsons swears by laced, all-rubber knee boots and two pairs of socks. He claims that the leather tops of gum-boots get soaked when there is wet snow, and then where are you? The answer to that is that healthy feet perspire a little, and there is no chance for evaporation through rubber. So by night your socks are going to be wet anyhow, and what difference does it make how you get them wet? The Finnish lumberjacks who brought their equipment from the old country—and there are quite a number of them around here—have a good foot gear, consisting of heavy felt boots, knee high and about an inch thick—too thick to wet through, and much too thick to chill through. They look as though they'd be wonderful, but you can't get them in this country. Some of the native lumberjacks try to achieve the same effect by buying old-fashioned black buckled galoshes, about four sizes too big, and wearing four or five pairs of socks in them. They keep the feet warm, but it's like wearing a bucket on each foot. A few people wear high leather boots, but almost everyone else agrees that they are cold damn things. Nobody would be caught dead in a pair of ski boots. They're too stiff and heavy. Let the city folks have them. They don't know any better.

Myself, I wear one pair of wool socks and the lightest, cheapest pair of sneakers I can buy, and nobody can convince me that this isn't the answer. Everyone else is working on the wrong principle, that of getting more and more layers between their feet and the cold. That's wrong. What they gain in insulation they sacrifice in foot flexibility. Their feet are just two petrified lumps wrapped in wool. According to my system, articulation isn't interfered with, and the blood circulates freely, bringing heat from the body to the feet as a hot water heating system brings heat to the radiators. I haven't been able to win any disciples to my belief, but that's all right. Neither have I ever had my feet frost-bitten.

I seem to have devoted a lot of space to what we wear on our feet in winter, but it's quite in proportion to the amount of time spent talking and thinking about it. It's a very vital matter.

Outside, life takes on pace with the approach of winter. It is the gay season, the season of parties and theatres and all the other things that will help people forget that outdoors something that they can't cope with is going on. Here life slows down, just as the world around us slows down. The leaves fall from the hardwood trees. Spruce and fir and pine stop growing and stand, dormant and black and thick, on mountain-side and lake-shore, their slim tips pointing monotonously to the gray sky. Of course they don't move, but they seem to draw silently in around us. We realize suddenly what we have forgotten: that after all, there are only three families of us—only a dozen puny human souls strung out along the lake and river—against all the forces of nature. To the people Outside, "the forces of nature" is a convenient phrase out of a textbook. To us they are a reality. We know we haven't a Chinaman's chance of controlling them. We only hope we can out-maneuver them.

I always feel like a renegade when the first little powder snow comes. It never lasts long, and it isn't serious, but the proper attitude is the long face, the foreboding shake of the head, and the grim comment that it won't be long now. I would like to act as Kyak does, and go tearing around in circles, scooping up mouthfuls of snow as a fast train scoops up water, and leaping crazily and prodigiously over little snow-covered trees. I don't, partly because any tree I could leap over wouldn't be worth bothering with and I'd probably fall flat on my fanny anyhow, but mostly because I'd simply be too unpopular if anyone suspected my anti-social liking of winter. So I try to remember that in February, when the snow is four feet or more deep on the level and I'm flopping inexpertly around on snowshoes, I'll be cursing the day the stuff was invented and offering my hope of Heaven for a good long look at a patch of bare ground. I turn my attention to the first piece of out-maneuvering that we have to attend to.

That is the circumventing of the freeze-up, our official beginning of winter. That's the fall in-between period, when the lake is just frozen and the ice is too thick to put a boat through and too thin to support a man or a horse or a car. We never know when the freeze-up is going to start or how long it's going to last. The only thing we do know is that while it's going on, we are completely bottled up. The nearest A & P is some forty miles away, but it might as well be in Egypt. Whatever we are going to need over a period of two or three weeks, we have to bring in before the Arm starts to freeze over. Tea, coffee, sugar, flour—I go over the list in my sleep. Oatmeal, canned meat and fish, fruit, and vegetables. And canned milk! Good Lord, if I'd forgotten that again! One year we forgot it and the Parsons forgot it, and the Millers didn't buy any because they keep a cow and didn't have to. So the cow chose that time, of all times, to go dry. We all learned, the hard way, to like black coffee and tea. I still like it, but I don't like to remember how oatmeal tastes without milk on it.

The real problem, though, is fresh meat and eggs and butter. If we bring them in too early and the weather warms up, we have the most horrible phonemena known to the thrifty Yankee heart and soul—good food, slowly spoiling. If we cut the margin too fine, we wake up some morning and find a half an inch of ice—a futile and infuriating amount—on the lakes. So we watch the barometer and thermometer and stars and the thickness of Kyak's pelt and listen to the weather broadcasts on the radio and rush out at all hours of the day and night to hold a wet finger to the wind. And sometimes we guess right and sometimes we don't. So far we've managed to survive the consequences of errors in our computations, but it's a pretty harassing period to go through, all the same.

Luckily for our sanity, the deer-hunting season furnishes a distraction around freeze-up time. Of course, everyone in here goes hunting. It isn't sport with us, though. We want and need the deer meat. (Only snobs and city people say venison, I early learned.) Hunting is a business with us. There are plenty of deer. In the summer, when it's against the law to shoot them, they stand around the yard under foot in romantic, negligent poses, fairly screaming to have their pictures taken. They come into the flower garden at night, and with great discrimination eat the blossoms off all the more difficult flowers to raise, turning up their delicate noses at such common fodder as zinnias and nasturtiums. Again in the dead of winter when their natural foods are buried deep under the snow, they drift into the clearing to eat hay or excelsior or cardboard boxes out of the dump, or anything else they can find. We couldn't shoot them then even if the law allowed; they are too gaunt and pathetic—"too poor," as they say up here. Anyhow they wouldn't be fit to eat. They've already been driven to browsing on cedar, with the result that they taste like furniture polish. During the hunting season, when they are fat and sleek and it's legal to kill them, every deer in the country remembers a man he has to see about a horse back in the thick growth on the highest ridges. It's uncanny. Ralph estimates that by the time he has caught up with one and shot it and dragged it out, estimating his time at the current local wage of thirty-five cents an hour and taking into account expenditure of shoe leather, ammunition, and wear and tear on clothes, but with no charge for loss of temper, the meat comes to about ten dollars a pound. He doesn't like deer meat, anyhow, so probably his figures are padded. He says he'd rather eat an old goat and be done with it. So he goes out only when I drive him out, almost at the point of his own gun.

Larry Parsons was in the same frame of mind one year. We were up there one afternoon when he came in from hunting. He'd been out all day, and he was a rig. His shirt was torn, his face was scratched, and frozen mud caked his boots and pants. He told us in no uncertain terms that that was definitely that. He didn't give a damn if he never shot another deer. For all of him, every unspeakable deer in the State of Maine could go climb a tree—an interesting possibility, zoologically speaking, only Larry wasn't speaking zoologically. He was speaking from the heart. He had been over at Black Cat, got into a swamp, crawled through blowdown for two miles or more, and when he went to eat his lunch, found it gone from his back pocket. So he was through. He'd eat potatoes and salt if he had to. He'd eat nothing, if it came to that. But never, never, so help him Hannah, would he step foot out of the house again, after a deer.

At this point Al, who had been listening with the look of sympathy we all learn to assume to cover up the fact that we are inwardly estimating just how soon it will be safe to broach the subject of deer hunting again, squeaked and pointed out the back window. In the middle of the clothes yard stood an eight-point buck. Larry shattered every existing record in oath-breaking. The kitchen floor smoked as he crossed it. He missed the first shot, and the buck obligingly turned broad-side. He couldn't miss the second time. It must have been a feeble-minded buck. From the eugenic viewpoint, it was undoubtedly better for the race that he didn't live to propagate his kind.

The real excitement of the deer-hunting season isn't hunting deer, though. It's hunting deer-hunters. It's always the same, every year. Any night that Ralph comes in at sunset and says, "It's going to turn cold tonight. We'd better get in some extra fire-place wood," I know what's going to happen. We go out into the lovely still dusk for the wood, but I can't really appreciate the black silhouettes the pines on the western ridge make against the orange and apple-green sky, nor the wreaths of steam that begin to rise from the river as the temperature of the air drops below that of the water. I'm too busy wondering how soon the telephone will start ringing.

It usually starts just at full dusk. It may be the Millers calling, or Cliff Wiggin, or the Brown Farm, but it all amounts to the same thing. "Say, you ain't seen anything of a couple of hunters, have you? Yeah, they're stayin' here. Went out this morning and they'd ought to have been back an hour ago. Well, sort of keep your ears open for signals, will you, and call me up if you hear anything—"

We'll hear something, all right. Just after we've decided that, thank God, they're lost in some other neck of the woods and aren't our responsibility, and have changed into slippers for a quiet evening in the home, Kyak will look interestedly out of the window and indulge in a short "woof." We'll go out onto the porch to listen. Sure enough, faint and far away will come the sound of three grouped shots, the universal woods signal of distress. It's a signal that can't be ignored. I don't know what would happen to a person who turned a deaf ear to three shots, but I more than half believe that the nearest tree would fall and crush him to a pulp. It should, anyhow.

Ralph groans, gets his gun, fires the two answering shots that mean, "O.K. I hear you. Now for the love of Mike, stay where you are and keep on signalling," and starts pulling on his gum-boots again. I go to the telephone to report that the missing have been spoken. Ralph collects his compass, a lantern, his gun with lots of cartridges for signalling, and sets forth into the night.

If lost hunters would only stay put, they'd be fairly easy to find. But they rarely do. If they're inexperienced enough to lose themselves in the first place, they're inexperienced enough to get panicky. The thing to do, once you know you are lost, is to find a good, safe place to build a little fire, build it, fire the three shots, light a cigarette, and sit down and wait. If the shots aren't answered wait a while till you are sure it's late enough for searchers to be out looking for you and shoot again. If you've plenty of shells with you, continue to do so every five minutes; if not, space your volleys further apart or until you hear someone shooting for you. But *before* you have used up all your cartridges, resign yourself to a night in the open and make the best of it. They'll be looking for you in the morning—you don't have to worry about that. They'll come shooting, and you'll answer with the cartridges you've carefully saved, and before ten o'clock you'll be back in camp eating bacon and eggs and drinking hot coffee.

This is such a sane and easy program to follow, but no lost hunter that we ever encountered ever followed it.

They all do the same thing. They start travelling as fast as they can, usually in the wrong direction and always in circles. I've been lost, and I know the feeling. It is hard to be sensible—not to be driven by a nameless terror and urgency—but you have to be sensible. You can't go ramming around in the woods in the pitch dark. The least serious thing that will happen to you is that you'll become completely exhausted and demoralized. Much worse things can happen. You can fall in a hole and break a leg. You can trip and shoot yourself. One hunter over on B Pond ridge went running through the woods at top speed, smacked into a tree, and knocked himself cold. It's better, even if harder, just to sit down and wait.

The procedure for finding lost hunters is always the same. First comes a period of swearing at anyone dumb enough not to get himself out of the woods before dark. (This phase runs concurrently with the assembling of paraphernalia.) Because we live so near the river, the next thing that Ralph does when he has to go out hunter-hunting, is walk up the road to where it's quiet so he can hear the shots as plainly as possible and determine their direction by compass. Then he fires two answering shots and starts off in that direction and keeps on walking until he hears some more shots. He re-checks his direction, finds that the lost one has wandered four points to the northeast, say, corrects his course, fires two more shots, hoping that they will toll the quarry in his direction, and keeps on walking. This may continue for an hour or it may continue most of the night. The first time it happened it was fairly exciting, but after years of it it has become a nuisance.

In the meanwhile I have kept the tea kettle boiling so

that when Ralph gets home, complete with hunter, they can have something hot to drink before going to bed. My inclination, after a half a dozen experiences, is to go hastily to bed as soon as I see their lantern up the road, and let them get their own lunch. Six times is enough to hear the same old story, and it always is the same old story.

After the hunting season is over and the lakes have frozen, we can settle down to winter, which consists not of the problem, primarily, of how to keep ourselves amused, but of the much more interesting problem of keeping ourselves warm and fed.

The first thing that has to be dealt with is the wood situation. You don't have to ask anyone what he's doing for busy-work from November until January. He's getting in his year's supply of firewood. What else would he be doing? The wood has to be cut after the leaves have fallen, but before the snow gets too deep and makes it hard to get around in the woods. It has to be sawed into four-foot lengths, split, and piled for hauling when the snow gets deep enough. The hauling is usually done with horses and sleds, although we use a car and have to build a road for the purpose. It's amazing how good a road can be built out of brush and snow over the roughest terrain. Brush is thrown into the holes and wet snow piled on top. Then it is trodden down and smoothed off. You wouldn't think it would hold up a rabbit, let alone a car or a team of horses and a heavy sled loaded with a couple of cords of hardwood. But as soon as the weather settles down to a steady cold, the whole thing freezes as solid as a rock. It seems to have the permanence of the Appian Way. I'm always surprised when I run across an old hauling road in summer to find it nothing but a series of skids, brush piles, boulders and deep holes. It seems impossible that we ever rode on it smoothly where now it's difficult even to walk.

We put up eight or ten cords of wood, all of it since the hurricane being blowdown along the Carry Road. That is not an editorial we. Gerrish and Ralph do most of the work, but the proudest moments of my life are those occasions upon which Gerrish sidles up to me at lunch time and mumbles, for fear of hurting Ralph's feelings, "You got time to come out this afternoon and give me a hand? I got an old son of a bitch of an old yellow birch to saw up." You see, I'm a much better hand on a two-man cross-cut saw than Ralph is. Gerrish says I'm better than a lot of professional woodsmen he's worked with. This sounds like frightful bragging, but I don't care. It's really something to brag about.

Excellence on a two-man cross-cut has nothing to do with size and strength. It's wholly a matter of method. A two-man cross-cut is a saw blade four and a half or five feet long with a removable handle at each end. The sawyers take their stances at either end and pull the saw back and forth between them. That sounds easy, and it is easy if you can just remember to saw lightly, lightly, oh, so lightly. Ralph's trouble is that he hates to saw wood and he wants to get it over with as soon as possible; so he bears down on the saw, instinctively, I suppose, since intellectually he knows better. A lot of people who know better do the same thing. It doesn't make the saw cut any faster, and it makes it run an awful lot harder. It makes all the difference between pulling a four-pound weight back and forth or a forty pound. A very common admonition from one sawyer to another in this country is, "Pick up your feet, will you?" That is probably meaningless to the uninitiate, but a good sawyer resents it very much. It means that his partner is saying that he doesn't mind riding him back and forth with every stroke of the saw, but he does consider it unnecessary to have to drag his feet along the ground, too. It's the obscure local way of telling a man he's bearing down on his end of the saw and it's an implication that he doesn't know his trade.

I don't know how other sawyers manage to retain the fairy touch, but this is how I do it. First I make sure that I'm going to be comfortable, even if this involves shoveling holes in the snow for my feet and lopping off sundry twigs that might switch me in the face. Then I take my end of the saw and pay very close attention to what we're doing for the first inch or so. It's important to start the kerf straight. If it slants or curves appreciably the friction becomes terrible when you get half way through the log. By the time the cut is well started I've got into the swing of the thing and don't have to think about it any more. Particularly do I not think about the fact that we are sawing a log in two.

These are the things I do think about. First, I think with satisfaction how good this particular exercise is for the waistline. I can feel the muscles roll and any accumulated ounces of superfluous padding melt away. Then I look around the woods and think how lovely they are in winter, with the lavender shadows of the bare trees lying like lace on the snow, and the evergreens standing up black and stiff all around. Everything is as still and sharp as an etching in the thin winter sunlight.

About then Gerrish says "Whoa." We have long since agreed that when either of us says "Whoa," we'll finish the stroke we're on and do one more. This gives both our minds a chance to come back from the vacuum they've been wandering in. This whoa of Gerrish's indicates that we're more than half way through the log and it's time to drive a wedge in the kerf to prevent the saw from being pinched. I sit back on my heels while he drives the wedge, and consider taking my top shirt off. Putting up your own wood is certainly the way to get the most heat out of it. It warms you twice—once while you're sawing it and again while you're burning it. I take my shirt off and pick up my end of the saw again.

Now I think of the deer who will be coming in at night and how glad and surprised they'll be to find a new tree down. They can browse all night long in the moonlight on the buds which yesterday were forty feet above their reach. We'll see their tracks in the morning. I look at the sawdust that is coming out in little spurts from our kerf with every stroke of the saw. If it happens to be a white birch with a red heart, the sawdust is lovely on the snow—pale gold and soft warm rose. White birch is the least satisfactory of the hardwoods for firewood, but it makes the prettiest sawdust. Firewood's excellence in order is this: maple, yellow birch, beech, and white birch. White birch is the most expensive to buy, though. People from the city think it's pretty and romantic, and that puts the price up. I'm just thinking about that when the saw drops and we're through the log. Gerrish hasn't had to tell me to pick my feet up, either.

After the wood has been cut, rough split, and hauled into our yard, it has to be resawed into stove length and split into two sizes, a large size for the heater and a small size for the kitchen stove. The sawing is done by power.

We have a circular saw rig, run by a Model T motor that Ralph fished out of the lake and reconditioned. It's certainly a lot more satisfactory than the old-fashioned hand buck saw, but I refuse to have anything at all to do with it. It terrifies me. Just the sight of the saw spinning viciously around, its teeth a bright blur in the sunlight, and the sound of the queer, inhuman rising shriek it gives as it rips through a piece of wood, make the cold shudders run up and down my spine. I'm really and truly afraid of it. It's unreasonable, I know; but some fears lie beyond reason.

I like to help split the wood, though. It's frozen to the core by now, and splits easily. It's fun to stand a chunk—pronounced "junk" here—up on the chopping block, give it a clip with the axe, and watch it explode. Occasionally a knotty piece will give trouble, but the mere fact of reluctance to split puts the whole thing on a personal basis. So! You won't, huh? Well, we'll see about that! All right. I don't have to use an axe. I can use a maul, if you're going to be that way. There! Dammit!

It's invigorating to win a fight, even if it's only against a stick of wood.

We're still fussing around with one or another phase of the wood question when Christmas comes along.

Christmas in the woods is much better than Christmas on the Outside. We do exactly what we want to do about it, not what we have to do because the neighbors will think it's funny if we don't; or because of the kids, who will judge our efforts not by their own standards but by the standards set up by the parents of the other kids. We don't have any synthetic pre-Christmas build-up—no shop window displays, no carol singers in department stores, no competition in the matter of lighting effects over front doors. At the intersections where the deer-runs cross the Carry Road, no Santa Clauses ring bells in the interest of charity. We didn't even have a Santa Claus until last year. We thought it would be nice if Rufus grew up knowing who gave him presents and bestowing his gratitude in the proper places. So we had never even mentioned the name of You-know-who. However, a visitor at Millers let him in on the secret, explaining to him that Santa Claus is the man who brings things for little boys. Rufus knew very well that Larry Parsons brings in everything we get from the Outside. Q.E.D., Larry is Santa Claus. He still persists in this belief, which makes him perfectly happy and we hope it does Larry, too.

We don't even have a Christmas tree. It seems a little silly, with hundreds of square miles of fir and spruce, from knee-high babies to giants of eighty feet on all sides of us, to cut one down and bring it into the house. It seems almost like vandalism to shake the ice and snow from its branches and hang them with pop-corn strings and cheap tinsel. We have our Christmas tree outdoors, for the benefit of the birds, hanging suet and crusts on the branches of one of the trees in the yard.

But we do have Christmas, just the same, and since we are so far from stores and last minute shopping, we have to start planning for it a long time ahead. With no chance to shop for gadgets, we have to make quite a lot of our presents, and the rest we get from what is known here simply as the Mail Order. I give mittens, hand made by me with the initials of the recipient knit into the design across the back. These don't cost much over and above my time, and no one in this country ever had too many pairs of mittens. For people who live Outside I try to think up things that they couldn't buy in stores. After all, it would be simple-minded to send out and buy something, have it mailed in here, wrap it up, and send it out to someone who, doubtless, lives almost next door to the store where it was bought.

I make little mittens about an inch long and sew them onto a bright fourteen-inch length of cord, as children's mittens are sewed onto a cord. These are bookmarks, in case you haven't guessed. To city people who, I know, have fire-places, I send net bags full of the biggest and best pine cones I can find, to be used as kindling. I make balsam pillows. I know these can be bought at any roadside stand north of the Maine border. But mine don't have pictures of Indians stamped in ink on cheap pink cotton cloth, along with the excruciating sentiment, "For You I Pine and Balsam." I collect old-fashioned patchwork quilt patterns from any source I can find them, and use them to make my pillow covers. In the old quilts, each unit is usually from twelve to fifteen inches square, and that makes a very good size for a balsam pillow. I make them, naturally, by hand, and they look very simple and expensive. They don't cost very much either. And I do love the names of the old patterns—Star of Bethlehem, Wedding Ring, Flower Garden, Log Cabin. They have a nice homely sound. You can think of a lot of things to make out of nothing, if you have to.

But making presents isn't half of Christmas in the woods. I'll never forget the year the lake didn't even begin to freeze until well after the tenth of December. We'd ordered our Mail Order, and presumably the Andover Post Office was harboring our stuff until someone could go out to get it. Finally, the day before Christmas, it was decided that an expedition should go on foot, get the stuff, and then, if at all possible considering the thin ice, drive it all in in Larry's old Model T which was down at the Arm.

We had living with us then a friend named Rush Rogers. He and Ralph and Edward Miller and Arch Hutchins, who was working for Larry, joined forces and set off down the ice on foot dragging a couple of sleds behind them to haul the stuff in on if the ice proved unsafe for the car. They got to the Arm all right, and from there into Andover was easy in Miller's Outside car.

Sure enough, all our stuff—we'd sold a story a short while before and were having a fat Christmas that year—was at the Post Office. In fact, since the Post Office was small and space at a premium during the rush season, our packages were all piled in the front window like a display, and the population of Andover was standing outside guessing at their contents. The Middle Dam delegation continued on to Rumford, stocked up with groceries and Christmas Cheer, picked up the mail and packages on the way back, and arrived back at the Arm in the afternoon. The mail and supplies filled the Ford to bulging. Arch wedged himself into the driver's seat, Edward stood on the running board to watch the high-piled packages, and Rush and Ralph tied the two sleds behind in single file and sat on them. I wish I could have seen them. The sleds were hardly big enough to accommodate their rears, and they had to hunch their knees up under their chins and hang on with both hands for dear life. Arch was driving the old Ford as fast as it would go, snow and ice chips from the chains were flying into their faces, so they couldn't keep their eyes open, and the sleds at the ends of their lines were slewing with terrific swoops. As a final touch they held their bare hunting knives in their teeth so they could cut the sleds loose if the car went through the ice ahead of them. Edward told me later that they were the funniest-looking rig he ever saw.

The ice was really too thin to be safe. It bent and bowed under the weight of the car, and rolled up ahead of them in long flexible swells. But Arch followed the rules for driving a car on thin ice—keep the doors open, go like hell, and be ready to jump—and they got home all right, only a little late for supper.

Then started one of the most hectic evenings I have ever spent. First, everything had to be unpacked; and when the Mail Order packs, it packs, what I mean. Corrugated board, excelsior, paper padding—they certainly give it the works. We decided that Ralph would do the unpacking in the back bedroom, with no lamp. He could see enough by the light through the open door. We didn't want any fire on Christmas Eve, and all that packing material around loose was definitely a fire hazard. Rush would assemble all of Rufus' toys that came knocked down—and that year most of them did—but first he had to put the new batteries, which were in the mess somewhere, into the radio so I could hear the Christmas carols.

I would re-wrap packages prettily. I started out with our present to Renny Miller, a five-cell flashlight, which we thought might come in handy for him. A flashlight is an awkward thing to wrap neatly, but I did a fairly good job and went on to the next thing. Rush was back of the chimney doing something to the radio wires, and in a minute he said, "Hey, Louise, where's that flashlight of Renny's? Lemme have it a second, will you?" I unwrapped, let him have it a second, and wrapped it up again.

I'd barely got the bow tied satisfactorily when a yelp came from the back room, "Good-night, there goes a box of blocks! Hey, Louise, lemme have that flashlight of Renny's a second, will you?" I unwrapped it, let Ralph have it a second, and wrapped it up again. The back bedroom, I noted in passing, looked as if a brisk breeze had swept through it. I wrapped up the snow gliders we'd got for the two younger Miller children and looked around for Rush He had disappeared, so this looked like the opportune time to tie up the mittens I'd made him, and the checked wool shirt that was Ralph's present to him. I got out a suitable piece of Christmas paper and some silver cord.

Then came a rapping on the window, and in the glow of the lamplight I saw Rush's face, framed in icicles and spruce branches. He didn't look like Father Christmas, though. He looked like a man in distress. "Hey, Louise, I can't see a thing out here by this aerial. Bring out that flashlight of Renny's a minute, will you?" I unwrapped it again—carefully, this time, as the paper was getting a little shabby at the creases—and took it out. In passing through the back room I observed that the brisk breeze had risen to gale velocity. I could still see the top of the bureau and of Ralph, but the bed had been drifted under. I held the flashlight while Rush did whatever he had to do. We went back into the house and turned on the radio. A very satisfactory rendition of "Holy Night" rewarded us. I re-wrapped Renny's present, decided it looked pretty moth-eaten, undid it, got fresh paper and ribbon, and did it up again.

"Holy Night" changed to "Oh, Little Town of Bethlehem," and I listened with pleasure, wrapping up presents, while Rush started to put together Rufus' bounce horse. As the music came to an end, I woke up to the fact that Ralph had been shouting for some time from the back room. "Hey, Louise! Bring that flashlight of Renny's—"

Before we went to bed that night I had wrapped that darned flashlight nine times. I had become a much better flashlight wrapper by midnight than I had been at seven o'clock.

At midnight we had some sherry and crackers and cheese. Because this was Christmas, Ralph had a raw egg in his sherry—which I think is barbarous—and Rush brought me a magnificent treat—Camembert cheese, which Ralph considers equally barbarous. We were exhausted and silly and we had a lot of fun. It was the best Christmas Eve I ever had, in spite of the flashlight.

After Christmas, what we call "the long drag" sets in. One day is very like another. The sun rises late over a snow-covered world. It's worth while to get up, even with the thermometer twenty below zero, to see a winter sunrise. The eastern sky flames with red, and the whole world turns rose. The steam, rising from the churning open water of the river, has been freezing all night long on every tiniest twig and spill from the water level to the tops of the tallest trees. Walking down to the kitchen over the squeaking snow is like walking through a fabulous wood where all the trees are wrought silver encrusted with diamonds. It's a marvellous sight, all the more breath-taking because it lasts so short a time. As soon as the sun is up and the wind begins to stir, it is gone and the trees stand again in their winter grays and dark greens.

Getting breakfast in winter is something. The kitchen stove won't hold a fire over night, so in the morning everything in the place is frozen—the wood, the water in the pails, the bread, the butter—everything. Everything you touch is colder than ice—the metal pans, the copper on the drain board, the iron of the stove-cover lifter. You learn very quickly not to take your mittens off until the place has had a chance to thaw out. I can get a whole breakfast wearing my mittens. I think it would be very good training for those occupations, such as surgery, for example, which require unusual manual dexterity.

Dusk draws in early in the winter. We come in for the night about four o'clock, light the lamps, and settle down. I know all about the inconveniences of kerosene lamps. You can't tell me a thing about filling them every morning, about trimming the wicks, about keeping the chimneys bright. But they give such a lovely, soft, golden light that it's worth the bother. I love lamplight.

During the short space between sunrise and sunset, there are a lot of things that have to be tended to. There are the daily chores, chief of which is filling the woodboxes, bringing in the water, and shovelling snow. Snow shovelling sounds like a trivial occupation, but it isn't. It's hard work and it's maddening work. The paths and steps have to be shovelled out, but all the time you're doing it, you know in the back of your mind that (a) it'll probably snow again during the night, and (b) if you could only wait until spring, you wouldn't have to do it at all. I get tired just thinking about shovelling snow. I hate futile activity.

But keeping the paths clear hasn't half the headaches

of keeping the road to Middle open for a car. We can't even choose our time for doing that. We start out in the car as soon as it begins snowing as if it meant business. You can always tell. A really serious snow starts in with fine flakes, which hiss against the windowpane and sting the face. The wind starts moaning up the river, and first the further ridges, then the nearer, then the trees across the river, disappear in a ghostly pall. Probably blizzards start as often at ten o'clock in the morning as at seven o'clock at night, but my impression seems to be that it is always dark when we start out to break out the road. Undoubtedly this is a hangover from my first trip.

It was cold that evening, I remember—too cold, we thought, to snow. We never knew when the sun set; gray afternoon merged slowly into black and starless night. We brought the wood and water in, had supper, fed the dogs, pulled down the shades against the biting cold, and drew up around the lamp with our books. The fire roared softly in the stove; a dog whined in his sleep; outside a tree cracked now and then in the falling temperature. It was a good evening to be inside.

Suddenly Ralph said, "Listen to that wind!" We pulled aside the curtains and peered out into the night. At the bottom of each pane of glass was a little line of white, curving up at the ends. Even as we looked, the lines thickened and something like a handful of smoke momentarily clouded the glass. Ralph dropped his corner of the curtain. "Snow," he said, and reached for his gum-boots. "I'll go get the car started. You'd better put some wood on the kitchen fire. I'll meet you up at the road."

By the time I had put on my sneakers and mended the fire, Ralph was ready to go. He had a cant dog, a couple of shovels, some rope, some empty burlap sacks, and a lantern in the back of the old Model T. I climbed in beside him and we started off. It really didn't seem to me that this was necessary. Only about an inch of snow had fallen so far, and it was crisp and mealy. Why didn't we wait awhile?

I found out. As soon as we got out of the shelter of the buildings, the road vanished. Everything vanished. The headlights showed us only a thick white wall that swayed in the wind, and pretty soon we couldn't even see that. I got out onto the running board and scraped the windshield clean, and we went a few more rods. Then I repeated the performance, and we went on again. It was just like living and trying to work in a heavy, smothering black bag. I hadn't the faintest idea where we were. None of the trees along the side of the road looked familiar. Even our voices sounded odd and muffled. We must be, I thought, about halfway by now. I got out to see if I could find the ruts, and sensed rather than saw something even blacker than the surrounding blackness off to the left. It was the wangan. We'd come only a third of a mile.

Halfway up Wangan Hill we fell off the road. The front left wheel went down with a sickening slump, the rear wheels raced, and there we were. We didn't say anything. We didn't have to. We just lighted the lantern and got out to look. The bottom of the car was resting on the frozen snow shoulder of the road, and neither of the rear wheels had traction. We had to dig the pan and axles free and get her back into the ruts somehow. We did. Don't ask how. I don't know. All I remember is lying for what seemed like hours on my stomach with snow drifting over me, scraping away at that frozen shoulder. Then

I remember shoving for dear life while Ralph gave her the gas. I remember also Ralph's giving me a little lecture on the asininity of anyone my age not being able to drive a car. If I could drive and he might shove, then we might get some place. This annoyed me, as I do feel like a fool to be the only woman east of the Rockies who can't drive a car, and I gave an awful heave. Out she came and I leaped aboard.

The snow had made three inches while we were fooling around, and any last trace of ruts had vanished. Indeed, it had become hard to tell where earth ended and air began. There was only one thing to do. I took the lantern and got out and walked, leading the way. I hadn't thought of it when I decided upon sneakers as the ideal winter foot gear, but this was a place where they were of unparalleled value. No one else could have felt the ruts with the soles of their feet. I walked along one rut, making a track that Ralph could keep a wheel in. That was all he needed to keep him on the road. We made Middle all right—everyone there was in bed—turned around and started home again. The return trip was comparatively easy. Our own tracks were still faintly visible.

We went down to the kitchen, made some coffee, drank it, ate a doughnut apiece, stoked the fire and started out again. It was after eleven o'clock, and snowing harder than ever. We fell off the road three times, and on the return trip the car dragged in the middle all the way. We drank some more coffee, ate some more doughnuts, and set out again. This time we were piling up so much snow with the front of the car that we both got out and stumbled and slid a hundred feet up the middle of the road to break down the crown, came back and rode the distance we had walked, and repeated the performance, until we saw Miller's back pasture gate in front of us. Then we shovelled out a place to turn around in and came home. It was after three o'clock by then, and neither of us could remember a time in our lives when we hadn't breathed snow, and had snow down our necks, up our sleeves, in our faces, and most especially dragging at our feet. And it was still snowing, and we had to keep on making these ghastly expeditions into uncharted space. We set out again.

I can't remember whether this trip, or the next, or the next, was our last. They all blur into one long eon of wallowing and pushing and shovelling, of roaring motors and spinning rear wheels and boiling radiators, of blowing snow and moaning wind, of brief periods in the warmth and light of the kitchen, of scalding coffee, of changing soaked mittens and socks for mittens and socks not quite so wet, and of wishing first that I could go home and go to bed, and, along toward the last, that I could just go to bed under the nearest bush. Somewhere along there, though, we found ourselves standing beside the Ford, tacitly acknowledging that we were licked. We'd shovelled and we'd pushed. We'd practically willed her along the last quarter mile, when she'd been out of the ruts more often than she'd been in. The snow was just too mealy to provide traction, and now it was just too deep to plow through. The last inch had been our undoing, and now we might as well drag ourselves home and go to bed. Ralph drained the radiator. The Ford would keep until spring just where she sat.

I looked around. I could see a little now. The woods were getting, not lighter, but a little less solidly black. I could see a gray smear running away in two directions from where we stood. That would be the road. I could see strange humps and fantastic figures that were trees standing around us in the thinning snow. Yes, thinning. The flakes were falling much slower now. They were big and feathery, and lacked the vicious drive they'd had all night. The storm was definitely letting up. We took one more look at the car, and Ralph shook his head. It was just too late to make any difference. We were on foot now until spring. We might as well accept it.

"Where are we, anyhow?" I asked.

"Top of Birch Hill."

It could have been worse. It was less than a mile home. We could have had to walk all the way from the Parsons' front door. We blew out the lantern and started home through the first beginnings of a beautiful clear dawn.

On foot for the rest of the winter! That's where we always end. Sometimes we're on foot in December, and again we manage to keep the wheels rolling until February, but sooner or later we have to get down the snowshoes from their pegs on the porch and start walking the mail.

When we first came to live here, mail was definitely catch as catch can. The Post Office at Coburn's is a summer office, open only from May 15th until October 1st, and before and after those dates, Middle Dam ceased to exist as far as the Government was concerned. If anyone happened to be going Outside, he took the community letters and brought in whatever postal matter the Andover Post Office had been storing for us. Sometimes we got mail every week. In the dead of winter or when conditions were bad we were lucky if we got it twice a month. Now, however, we have a Star Route to Middle Dam, and we get mail every Tuesday and Friday. It's wonderful for everyone, except possibly Larry, who is the mail carrier. There are times, I imagine, when he'd just as soon stay home as go trekking off down the lake with what he sometimes refers to as "the Christly mail." It's all right while the boat is still running, or after the lake is frozen and he can use his snowboat—an ingenious device that looks like a Black Maria, with skis in place of the front wheels and caterpillar treads behind to furnish the driving power. But in between times he has to carry the sacks around the shore on foot, and that's something else again. The first year he was mail carrier Ralph had two great over-size tires come for the Big Green "Mormon," and, of course, they arrived during the freeze-up. Ralph told Larry he was in no hurry for them and to leave them at the Arm until the ice was safe, but Larry is too conscientious for his own good. He carried and rolled them all the way up from the Arm. That's the kind of a guy Larry is.

On Mondays and Thursdays, then, one of us has to walk to Middle to take up the out-going mail, and again on Tuesdays and Fridays, someone has to go up to bring down the in-coming. I myself don't mind the trip, even on snowshoes, those inventions of the devil. It isn't like breaking a trail through fresh snow. We take pains to tramp down a good, wide, level float up the middle of the road, and in between storms this float is packed so hard that we can sometimes go all the way bare-foot. Bare-foot, I probably don't have to explain, is simply woods for "without skis or snowshoes." It's nice to get away from the house for a while and to visit Al Parsons and Alice Miller, and there's always a lot to think about and look at along the road. There are the woods themselves, which I like better in winter than in summer, because I like the type of design that emphasizes line rather than mass. The bare branches of the hardwood trees look exactly like etchings. There are strange vistas of hill and pond which the foliage blocks out in summer, and which therefore have a rare, new appeal, like glimpses into a far and beautiful country. The view through the bare tree tops from the top of Birch Hill might be a Swiss view, I decide, and the deep black slash between the ranges where the Arm stretches south through its narrowing valley might be a Norwegian fjord. Then I wonder why we all like to pretend that we're somebody else, somewhere else. Why is it more fun to think I'm a Norse woman looking over a fjord than to admit I'm me looking over into South Arm? Probably, because part of being me, looking into South Arm, lies in pretending I'm a Norse woman? This is very involved and gets me nowhere. That's the sort of footling conjecture that I indulge in while walking the mail.

Another great source of entertainment on these mail walks is the tracks in the snow. Sometimes they are just tracks—the clear-cut, chiseled hoof marks of deer, a rabbit's big, spreading pad-marks, with a little dent behind them where its maker squatted in the snow, or the precise line of prints left by a trotting fox. Sometimes they tell of tragedy. You follow the delicate embroidery of a wood-mouse's trail for a quarter of a mile, and then it ends like the snipping off of a thread. Two feathery swept places in the snow, where the wings of an owl brushed as he swooped, tell why. Or you may come to a churned-up, blood-stained spot, with the tracks of a rabbit and a wild cat leading into it, but only the wildcat's tracks leading out. You don't have to have a dictionary to translate that story. Once in a while we see a bear track, but not often. The bears ought to be, and usually are, sleeping somewhere in the winter.

Actually, the only track that has the power to startle us very much is the track of man. We fancy that we know about where everyone belonging to Middle Dam is, at any given hour of the day or night. Moreover, if anyone comes down the Carry Road, it's usually to see us. There isn't any other place to go, in winter. So if nobody has stopped at the house, and yet here's this track on the road—well! It couldn't be any of the Millers. They're all working on their wood. It can't be Larry. He doesn't wear L. L. Bean gum-boots, and only Bean boots have this chain tread. It might be Dorian, who works for Larry. He was talking last week of getting some new boots. But he's supposed to be sawing ice. Maybe it's one of the company timber cruisers, come in from the Outside. Or maybe it's the game warden. Or maybe— It doesn't strike us as odd at all that we have so changed our way of living from that in which we were brought up, that bear and deer and wildcat tracks are all in the day's walk, while a stray human boot-print throws us into a dither.

But that's not all of walking the mail. After we get to Middle there are people to see and talk to. There are all the Millers and both the Parsons, and whoever is working for the Parsons at the time. They may be doing almost anything, but whatever they're doing, it's worth while stopping to watch. Al will probably be sewing or cooking. She's one of the busiest people I ever saw. She's never sewing ordinary things. She runs a gift shop in the summer, for the benefit of Coburn's sports, and she'll be making a very trick apron, or a particularly useful laundry bag. If she's cooking, it won't be just cake and pie and cookies. It will be doughnuts that contain orange juice and grated rind instead of milk and spice—a very tasty dish, by the way—or a spice cake, the basis of which is canned tomato soup, or coconut-chocolate candy, made largely of leftover mashed potato. She gets around among the pages of the women's magazines, all right.

If it's right after New Year's, all the men of Middle Dam will probably be cutting ice. Cutting ice is a man-sized chore. Over two thousand cakes have to be got in for the hotel, so-called, and on top of that there's Larry's own personal ice and Miller's ice. Then they branch out. They go up into the Narrows and fill the ice houses of a couple of summer camps up there, and they fill Mrs. Graves' ice house at the Arm. It's a lot of work, and more involved than would seem at first glance.

First of all, they have to arrange to have the ice the right thickness, a matter that can't be left to Nature alone. This is one of those cases of circumvention. The ice, during the first part of January, is about a foot thick, and that isn't quite thick enough. Before spring it may be three feet thick, but freezing under the insulating blanket of snow that covers the lake after the first of the year is very slow. So in order to speed it up, the snow must be scraped off the cutting area. A couple of below-zero nights after the ice is clear will do the trick. Then the ice field has to be scored for the cutting lines like a pan of fudge, with a tool that looks like an old-fashioned spike harrow with the spikes set sixteen inches apart. Then the cutting begins.

The cutting used to be done with a hand ice-saw, until Larry decided that that was unprogressive. He got hold of a machinist on the Outside who dreamed up an ice-cutting machine for him. This consists of an old Model A motor on steel runners, with a chain-driven circular saw out in front and a handle like a baby carriage handle out behind. The operator walks behind, pushing the rig and raising and lowering the saw as desired. The scored grooves in the ice act as guides for the runners. This ought to have been much easier and faster than hand sawing; and it would have been, if, instead of sawing ahead in a straight line, the thing hadn't inexplicably insisted on sawing backward in a circle. Ice sawing was suspended until the creator could be brought in to take the bugs out of his darling. He came in one week end, toiled long and earnestly, and left Sunday night with assurances that everything was going to be all right, now.

Monday morning ice cutting was resumed. Larry drove his reconditioned labor saver the length of the ice field, parked it for a moment while he organized the hauling and storing brigades, and turned back just in time to see what happened. Ralph was at Middle at the time, and saw it, too. He says it was one of the most impressive sights he ever witnessed.

Larry had unwittingly left the ice cutter on the edge of a triangular floe of free ice, formed by two accidental and invisible cracks and the open water alongside of which he had been sawing. It was a big floe of a thousand square feet or more of ice—too big to be noticeable to a man just walking across it. But it wasn't too big to be affected by the weight of the machine bearing down on its edge. As they looked the point of the triangle rose majestically, and the opposite side dipped. The ice cutter clung for a moment and then started slipping into the lake. It was the slow-motion quality of the thing that made it so impressive. The whole works just hung for a long moment. Then the cutter disappeared into twenty feet of icy water, and the floe settled slowly back. The lake stretched without blemish two miles to the further shore.

They got it out later all right, and sent it out to be overhauled. It's still there, and they're still cutting ice with a hand ice-saw at Middle Dam.

They had some trouble putting the ice in at the Arm one year, too. When a cake of ice has been cut free, naturally it floats and can be hauled up out of the water, loaded on a sled, and taken up to the ice house. The first cake they cut from the ice field at the Arm didn't float, though. It disappeared, leaving a hole. So did the next. Larry stuck his head down the hole to see what went on. He found that he and his men and horses were standing on a sixteen-inch piecrust of solid blue ice, over some three feet of air, with another layer of ice below. The lake had dropped three feet after the top layer had frozen and the lower level had frozen subsequently. Ordinarily the ice would follow the water down, but the ice was so thick it just arched to the shore instead. Larry was relieved to know that the laws of natural science hadn't suddenly been revolutionized. All the same the situation was annoying. One man had to crawl down into the air space and lift up the pieces as they were sawed so they could be hoisted to the top. It was a nasty, cold, cramping job. Nature can think up simply abominable little tricks to pull off unexpectedly.

Some winters we have lumber camps in here. Nobody has to have the general nature of a lumber camp described to him. Literature and the movies have done that quite adequately. They haven't shown, however, what it means to be neighbors to a lumber camp; to have as the boon companions of one's four-year-old son a bunch of the hardest and toughest teamsters, sawyers, border-jumpers and general roustabouts that ever came down a tote road; to find that one is suddenly confronted with a choice of stopping talking or learning an entirely new language—a language consisting of such terms as "bucking up on the landing," "sluiced his team" and "shaking out the road hay." Being what I am, I chose to learn the new language.

I also had to learn to differentiate between a day man, a stump cutter, and a member of a yarding crew. A day man gets paid by the day and does whatever the boss tells him to. He may cut firewood, swamp out roads, pile up brush and tops, anything. A stump cutter is an individualist. He works alone, felling his own trees, limbing them out, sawing them up into four-foot lengths, piling the pieces neatly for the convenience of the scaler, and getting paid by the cord. He's usually pretty good. That's why he works alone. He can make more money that way than he could at day rate or by pooling his ability with that of someone else. Sometimes, however, he's hard to get along with and no one else will work with him. A yarding crew consists of three men and a twitch horse. One of the men cuts down the trees and limbs them, one drives the twitch horse, dragging—or "twitching"—the entire trunk of the tree to a cleared space called a yard, where the third man saws it up with a buck saw and piles it. A good yarding crew can cut and pile an awful lot of wood in a day.

Besides these classifications of woodsmen, who comprise the main population of the camp and who sleep in a long low bunk-house, there are several specialists. There's the boss and the straw boss, who have their own little shack, not because they feel exclusive, but because the men like to sit around their bunk-house in the evening and bellyache about the weather, the food, the administration of the camp, or the way the trees grow, or any one of a thousand other things. The presence of authority would put a definite damper on this favorite of all indoor sports. And while talk is cheap, like other cheap things—air and water, for example—it is invaluable. A man who has cursed the boss all evening to his confreres is almost always a man who goes to bed feeling at peace with the world, and who wakes up ready to put out a good day's work. So the boss lives in his own little hut, dropping over occasionally to join in the poker game that runs continually from supper to bed-time and all day Sunday.

In another little hut, known as the Office, live the clerk and scaler. The scaler, as his name implies, scales the wood for the men. That is, he estimates with the aid of a long marked rule called a scale rule the quantity each man cuts, keeps a record of the scale for the landowners, and reports each man's cut to the clerk, who pays the man accordingly. The clerk keeps the camp books, pays the men, orders supplies, tends the wangan—the little store where tobacco, candy, clothes, saw-blades and axes are sold—and runs the punch board, which is always a part of the camp picture. The clerk and scaler are men of at least some education, and I think they enjoy living alone, because they like to sit up nights and read, and in the bunk-house lights have to be out at nine o'clock.

Behind a partition in the kitchen, which is also the dining-room, and which is by law a separate building, live the cook and his cookees, or helpers. They don't mingle much with the rest of the camp. They're too busy, for one thing. For another they have their discipline to maintain.

If arguments start they're apt to start in the dining-room. That's one reason why no talking is allowed in the dining-room, aside from simple requests to pass the butter, please. And I mean "please." I've eaten a lot of meals in lumber camps, and I've been amazed at the prevalence of "please" and "thank you." I wish my own family were always so punctilious. The other reason for no talking is that the cook doesn't want the men dawdling over their meals. A large percentage of our woodsmen are Canadian Frenchmen, and they can't talk without gesticulating. This means they would have to put down their tools and stop eating, which would slow up the meal considerably. The cook contends that they can do their talking somewhere else. All he wants them to do is eat and get out, so his cookees can get on with their dishes.

Somewhere high on the social scale comes the blacksmith. He sometimes lives with the boss, sometimes with the clerk, and sometimes with the men, depending on his type. He makes the sleds that are used to haul the wood, keeps the horses shod, repairs tools, and is usually an amateur veterinary besides. He and the feeder—woods for stableman—are responsible for the health of the horses, but if anything beyond their ability arises, they take the responsibility of calling a real vet. The feeder waters and feeds the horses, cleans the stable, and keeps an eye on the pigs. Every lumber camp has five or six pigs. They are brought in in the fall, cute little tricks with curly tails, fed all winter on the tons of excellent garbage that are the inevitable by-product of catering to a hundred men or more, and sent out in the spring to be slaughtered. By that time they are simply enormous.

Every lumber camp also has cats. In the fall the cook

brings in a cat to keep the kitchen free of mice and the stable free of rats that come in in the bales of hay. It is always a female cat. If I didn't know our Tom, I'd be inclined to believe the flat statement of an old friend, Beatty Balestier—yes, Kipling's brother-in-law, but he'd kill you if you mentioned it. Beatty told me once when I was trying to locate a tom kitten, "There's no such thing. All cats are female cats, and all kittens are the result of immaculate conception." My observation of lumber camp cats inclines me to believe he had a tenable argument there. But be that as it may, by spring every lumber camp within a radius of ten miles of us has at least a dozen cats—the original and three litters. All the kittens, regardless of their mother's complexion, are black and white. No wonder Tom is such a smuggy.

When a lumber camp first moves in, all the men look alike to me. They're all big and tough-looking and most of them need a shave, which they won't get all winter. They all dress more or less alike, in layers of shabby sweaters and shirts, ragged pants, and wool caps. They all walk along the road with the same swagger, carrying their axes and saws over their shoulders, swearing at their twitch horses, and dropping their eyes upon meeting me. After a while I begin to get them sorted out and those that I meet regularly I start speaking to. The first time I do this the same thing always happens. The man starts obviously, raises his eyes to look at me, looks all around to see if by any chance I mean a couple of other guys, and looks back at me. Then his face lights up in the warmest and friendliest of smiles, and he answers. If he can't speak English, he answers in French or Russian or Finnish. It doesn't make any difference. We both know what we mean:—"Hello, stranger. I'll never get to know you very well. We haven't much in common, but we're both here on this snowy road, with the woods all around us. Stranger, I wish you well." They do wish me well, too. Lumberjacks have a reputation, I know, for being brawlers and roisterers and general trouble-makers, and I guess when they are on the Outside, with their systems full of rot-gut, they often deserve this reputation. But I have never met a lumberjack in the woods who didn't treat me with complete respect and friendliness—and I've met a lot of lumberjacks. What they do Outside, I neither know nor care.

Sometimes, though, we get indications that some individual's conduct before he crossed our ken might not bear the most rigid inspection. This was true, we gathered, of one of Rufus' bosom pals, a big part-Indian named Tony. Tony looked like a ruffian, and was sweet. He rode Rufus on his horse, stopped in the yard to play with him, took him on walks and brought him presents, like partridge feathers or a length of chain carved out of a single piece of wood. I used to worry about these friendships of Rufus' —for Tony was only one of many. After all Rufus was only four and some queer customers do get loose in the woods. I suppose it was the stock maternal stewing. Ralph told me not to worry, and after a while I came to believe him. I'm glad I did. The risk was negligible, I know now, and what Rufus gained in knowledge and poise was considerable.

Then one day the feeder came down to the house at noon simply bursting with excitement. "We got a G-Man, Mis' Rich," he announced, as one would announce the outbreak of a rare and fatal disease. And sure enough, an F.B.I. agent had walked into camp from Upton—a long, hard walk, but you know the F.B.I.—looking for some man. The man had been there, but had left the week before. (I don't know, to keep the record straight, what he was wanted for, or whether they ever caught him.) So the G-Man had some lunch and walked out again. He wasn't in camp more than an hour. But the fact that he came at all was enough.

When the cutting is a mile or more from camp, some of the men carry their lunches with them rather than walk clear in and back again. Tony was one of these. But the man that worked with him preferred to walk back for a hot lunch. He came back to the job that afternoon and told Tony that there was a G-Man in camp. Tony went on with his work but kept deep in the spruce thickets along the back of the cut. When knocking-off time came, he turned his horses loose, with a slap on their rumps to get them started, and let them go into camp, alone—a thing they always did, anyhow. He, himself, didn't go home to supper. He stayed up on the mountain-side, hungry and all alone in the cold and dark until the middle of the night. Then he sneaked into camp and snatched a few hours' sleep. The next morning, bright and early, he was at my kitchen door to say good-bye to Rufus. I didn't recognize him, at first. He'd shaved off the luxuriant beard he'd been nursing along all winter. He didn't know where he was going, he told me cheerfully. He was just going.

These seemed, and still seem to me, to be over-elaborate precautions for complete innocence to take. I still wonder sometimes what Tony had on his conscience.

This visit of the G-Man and Tony's oddly coincidental flight were a source of discussion all the rest of the winter. Nothing is so prized in the woods as a good juicy morsel to hash over. Here is a community of men, practically cut off from the world. Most of them can't read. They have one thing in common—work. They have to talk about something and they'll talk about anything. They'll talk about the number of birds that flew out of a thicket, or the deer they saw eating road-hay—the hay spread on icy places in the hauling roads to prevent loaded sleds from overrunning the horses—or the super-intelligence of their own twitch horse. They'll talk about the snow, which is damned for hindering the cutting, or lack of snow, which is damned for hindering hauling. They'll talk about the food—it was always better at the last camp they were in—or the shelter. That was always better, too. The roof was either higher, permitting better ventilation and air circulation, or lower, conserving heat; or else the floors were warmer, or the lice less numerous. But most of all, they like to talk personalities. In short they like to gossip. They'll take the fact that a man changed his underwear in the middle of the week instead of waiting until Sunday, the conventional underwear-changing day, and make almost an international incident out of it. It's fascinating to observe.

Occasionally there's something worth talking about. Once in a great while someone goes crazy and tries to kill himself or someone else. That's good for a month's talk. Once Rufus got lost, and I, in desperation, called up and asked the clerk if anyone there had seen him. Every man available set out to look. He was finally discovered about five hundred yards from the tar paper shack where the horses are taken to eat their noon-day meals; or as the man. who found him said, "About two and a half good twitches." A good twitch is the distance a horse can drag a full-length pulp log without resting. Distances are frequently measured in twitches or fractions thereof by woodsmen. It's a habit I've got into myself.

This search for Rufus furnished talk for a week. Once a big Swede known as Bow (pronounced as in bow-wow, which is what his brother is called, incidentally) decided to relieve the monotony by putting a set-line through the hole in the ice where the horses were watered at lunch time, and catching himself some fish. The fact that if the game warden had caught him, he'd have probably spent the rest of the winter in jail only added spice to the venture. For days he tended his line night and morning and never caught a thing. Then one evening his luck changed. There was something—a considerable something—down in the water at the end of his line. His shouts brought the whole camp onto the ice in time to witness the landing of the fish. It was fish all right—a can of salmon with the label still adhering, in case proof were needed. They're still talking about that, in the woods.

Sunday is the day of leisure in a lumber camp. That's the day the men do their washing, file their saws and sharpen their axes, get their hair cut, and attend to any other odd personal jobs. It's horse-shoeing day, too, except in emergencies. Sometimes the blacksmith lets Rufus "help" by holding the horse's foot for him. This is a great treat for Rufus, but considerably less of a treat for the blacksmith, I would think. What the horses' views are, I have no way of knowing. Sunday afternoon is recreation time. Then the big stud poker game really gets going, and the Russians and Poles start their interminable gloomy hands of *spadowiecz,* a game completely incomprehensible to non-Slav. Then if the ice is good, the athletically in- clined join Ralph and Rufus and me in skating on the

Pond in the cove where we keep our boat in summer-time. We can't skate for sour apples, but neither can anybody else, so we all have a lot of fun and make a lot of noise falling around on the ice. Then those who can carve, work on their ornamental bottle stoppers and birds in cages, mysteriously cut out of a single block of wood. Then those that are big enough and tough enough to get away with it knit on socks and sweaters.

I never can quite make up my mind whether I like to have the lumber camps move in or not. I really like it best when we're here alone. I've heard enough of the popular Freudian lingo that people in general sling around so carelessly to know that I am no victim of agoraphobia. I like to know that I have miles of unpopulated space around me. The lumber camps don't bother me, but I know they are there. Worse, I know they are cutting down the trees. I feel a great regard for trees; they represent age and beauty and the miracles of life and growth. I don't like to see them destroyed, especially as the cellulose made from them can just as well be made from corn stalks. On the whole, I'd just as soon that the lumber camps went somewhere else.

On the other hand, there are nice things about them. It's nice to have not-too-close neighbors once in a while. But the thing I enjoy most about them is a perfectly silly and inconsequential thing. Our winter bedroom is right next to the road, and I like to hear the men and the horses going to work before we get up. Once in a while a man will whistle or sing, but mostly they go quietly, with only the jingle of a chain, the blowing of the horses, and the squeak of the frozen snow to mark their going. The whole thing doesn't last fifteen minutes, and it really isn't anything to get starry-eyed about. I just like it; that's all.

Winter, to look forward to, is a long, dark, dreary time. To live, it's a time of swirling blizzards and heavenly high blue and white days; of bitter cold and sudden thaws; of hard work outdoors and long, lamp-lit evenings; of frost patterns on the windows and the patterns of deer tracks in the snow. It's the time you expected to drag intolerably, and once in a while you stop and wonder when the drag is going to begin. Next week, you warn yourself, after we've finished doing this job on hand, we'd better be prepared for a siege of boredom. But somehow next week never comes. There's always something to keep it at bay.

Then one day there's a patch of bare ground on a sunny slope, the dog starts going wild with the smell of spring, and someone says that the break-up ought to come early this year. The break-up! But Good Heavens, the lakes only froze up a couple of weeks ago. Well, a little more than that, maybe. Let's see— Why, it's time to tap the maple trees and overhaul the cars and clean house! The next thing you know, the smelts are running and the loons have come back into the growing patch of open water in the Pond-in-the-River. There's an ant hill in the flower garden and a dandelion blossom up by the road. Gerrish has begun talking about a good mess of dandelion greens, cooked with salt pork. It's time to clean up the vegetable garden and paint the boats, and the consensus is that the ice will be out by next Tuesday.

Next Tuesday!

Where has the winter gone?

IV

"Isn't Housekeeping Difficult?"

No. Housekeeping in the woods is—for me—not at all difficult. I'd like to let that statement stand unqualified, testimony to my enormous efficiency and energy. Too many people know the truth about me, though, to make that advisable. The truth is that under the most favorable circumstances—circumstances including linoleum floors, vacuum cleaners, washing machines, and automatic water heating systems—I would still be a rotten housekeeper. My friends would indulgently call me a little bit careless, and my enemies would label me down-right slovenly. My enemies would be the nearer right.

Here I can be a rotten housekeeper, and it doesn't make much difference. After all, this is the woods. People don't expect quite so much in the line of shining silver, polished glass, and spotless woodwork. I can, with a clear conscience —or fairly clear, anyhow—ignore a lot of persnickety details. I can be sensible about these things. I can refuse to allow myself to become the slave of a dustpan and brush. I have learned, because I've had to, to spend money wisely. Now I am learning to spend my time wisely; and I don't think it's very wise to spend two hours waxing the living-room floor on a lovely day when I could be out fishing. If I say this often enough and fast enough, I can convince myself that almost no effort beyond attending to the bare necessities of food, clothing, and shelter is really required of me.

We do have to eat. That I will concede. So I spend a large proportion of my housekeeping time in getting ready to cook, cooking, and recovering from cooking. It makes me tired just to think about it.

This is supposed to be the Independent Life, but as far as getting supplies goes, we're dependent on quite a number of things, ranging from Larry Parsons to the weather. Except during the short summer months, Larry is the one who goes to Rumford and hauls our supplies in by car and boat, and whether or not he goes depends on the weather, the state of the lake, and how much else he has to do. Once Larry goes, whether I have the ingredients to cook what I want to cook, or must, instead, cook what I have the ingredients for, depends on how bright or dull we were while making out the supply list. We try to put in supplies for a week at a time in the summer, and for a month or more, at a time, in the winter. In making out a list of that length, it's very easy to leave off two or three items that are absolutely essential. There is no way of rectifying these errors. Once a thing is forgotten, it's forgotten until next time. Then you find to your surprise that a lot of things you thought were essential aren't essential at all. It's very enlightening.

Try to make a list of all the groceries you're going to be needing for the next four weeks. Go ahead. It won't cost you anything. You aren't in my boots. If you leave off eggs, you won't have to go without, as we do. Remember that fresh fruit, meat, and vegetables won't keep forever, and plan accordingly, listing canned goods for the last part of the month. Remember also all the boxes and bottles in the kitchen that aren't empty, but will be next week. Those are the things I always forget—the vanilla and salt and nutmeg. I used to forget the staples, too, going on the assumption, I guess, that one always has sugar, flour, and tea. It didn't take me very long to learn this little fact of life— one doesn't. Now my lists start with the staples—eggs, butter, milk, oatmeal, cornmeal, molasses, coffee, split peas, beans, salt pork—you go on from there. Next I do the perishables—oranges, bananas, lettuce, whatever vegetables are in stock and good. I leave that to Sam Swett, the manager of the A & P, who, fortunately, is most trustworthy. Rumford is no Babylon, rich in exotic viands. I have to take what I can get. (Once in my ignorance I ordered artichokes, and got back a little note saying, "I heard of these, but I never see one.") Meat next—beef, pork or lamb to start the month with, and then a ham, always, which is only semi-perishable. Then the canned goods—meat, fish, fruit, and vegetables. Then the odds and ends, like cheese and spices and macaroni and rice and cocoa. It sounds easy enough, but I always forget something, like a lemon. So instead of having Eggs Benedict, as I had planned to have as a special treat, I end by having plain ham and eggs which are no treat at all.

I've just been over the foregoing list, and there is a very serious omission, which I'll bet a button no one spots. Of necessity, everyone in the woods makes his own bread. I've left off yeast, which means that we eat corn bread or baking-powder biscuit until Larry goes out again. Almost everyone thinks he likes hot breads, and they are all right once in a while. But they get terribly, terribly tiresome, both to make and to eat, after a week.

The usual supply difficulties are intensified twice a year by the fall freeze-up and the spring break-up, those periods when, as I've explained before, you can't get out of here because the ice isn't safe to cross but is too thick to put a boat through. Cold weather, though, isn't an unmixed curse. When it really gets cold, with a cold you can depend on not to waver, then you can stop vilifying the temperature and begin to use it. You can make ice-cream, for example, following any good recipe and putting it outdoors in a pan to freeze. This involves running out every half hour or so, to stir the custard and scrape what has frozen away from the sides, but it's worth the bother to me. I've loved ice-cream from my childhood, when a cone was an event. I still love it enough not to be too bitter about the fact that here in the woods we almost never can have it in summer, when the weather is hot, but must wait until the time of year when scalding soup and hot buttered rum would be the reasonable man's choice.

The important use of cold, though, is to keep food. Early in December we buy a case of butter—thirty-two pounds— and freeze it. This will last us until spring and the final pound is exactly as sweet and fresh as the first was. We buy meat in quantities and freeze that, too, It's wonderful to know that in the Arctic regions of the summer house living-room, fifty pounds of pork loin dangle from the ceiling, out of reach of dogs and cats, awaiting our pleasure. Frozen meat is all right to eat if care is taken to thaw it slowly. Otherwise it will be tough. And, of course, it can't be thawed and frozen again and thawed and eaten. You're apt to die horribly if you're not careful about that,

I understand—although so far my knowledge of that is hear-say.

Like everyone else in this country, we freeze up a deer whole, if we're lucky enough to get one, and if we get it late enough in the season. We let it hang long enough to be tender—about two weeks—in an above-freezing place, and then we hang it out in the woodshed. There are two advantages to using the woodshed for a cold storage room. One is that it is cold. The other is that we're no butchers, and we need a lot of room and a lot of tools to get a steak off a frozen deer. I found a chart in Fanny Farmer for the guidance of housewives in buying beef, and while a deer doesn't seem to be constructed exactly like a cow, still we can get the general hang of the thing from the chart. So we always take Fanny to the woodshed with us when we're going to butcher. Then we lower the corpse from where we've hoisted it to the peak of the roof, and lay it across the chopping block. By using an axe, the buck saw and once in a while the two-man cross-cut, we manage to worry off what will pass as a roast or a steak or a collection of chops.

If we get the deer early in the season before it's cold enough to freeze it, the problem of keeping it is complicated considerably. The liver and heart are eaten first, by me. Ralph won't eat what he inelegantly calls "guts." Then we save out two or three of the choice cuts to be eaten fresh, and I have to can the rest. The steaks I fry for about a minute, first on one side and then the other, in a good hot spider, so they'll brown. Then I roll each slice in a tight little roll, pack the rolls into jars, semi-seal, and boil the jars in a washboiler full of water for two hours and a half. After the jars are removed from the boiler, I complete the sealing, stand them upside down to cool, scrutinizing them at intervals for tell-tale air bubbles which mean leaks and consequent spoilage, and finally put them away. Later these can be unrolled and broiled or fried as ordinary steaks; but unless they are lightly fried before canning, they'll be nothing more than plain boiled meat.

The tougher cuts, such as the forequarters, I hack up and boil in large kettles. Next day I cut the lean meat from the bones, pack it tightly into pint jars—pints are better for our size family—fill the jars with gravy, partially seal, and go on from there with the same routine as above. This meat can be used in the winter for meat pies, pot roasts, hash, or just plain meat and gravy.

That takes care of the bulk of the deer, but there are still the neck, horns and hoofs to be accounted for, and we're the Thrifty Riches. A live deer, grazing by the riverside, is a beautifully proportioned thing; but the minute that it's dead something happens to its neck. It doubles in length apparently. There's a lot of meat on it, but the meat's no good. It's tough and stringy and can be used for only one thing—mince meat. It makes the best mince meat in the world.

This leaves only the horns and hoofs. No, we don't make our own gelatin. Ralph uses sections of horn for decorating hunting knife handles, and makes gun racks and coat hooks out of the hoofs and thin lower legs. They are bent at the ankle, dried and cured, and driven into holes bored in the walls. We have a dozen or more of them over the house, and they look very nice indeed and are very handy.

And that's that, as far as a deer is concerned.

I always think I'm going to can some partridges, too, but

I never have yet. We don't get very many, and they're so small that it takes several to even make a decent meal. So we never have any left over to can. I've never tried salting fish, either, although it can be done, I guess. We eat them fresh, in season—fried, if they're pan trout, or baked if they are big salmon. Those, and smelts in the spring of the year, are the only kind of fish we get here, except chubs and suckers, which aren't fit to eat. We've never tried eating porcupine, either. We've never had to. We don't kill them, though, even when we find them chewing our houses down. They are edible, and they're the only animal that an unarmed man can kill for food. They're so slow and stupid that they can be clubbed to death if necessary. No woodsman will kill them wantonly. Someday he may be in a spot where a porcupine will save him from starvation. Some states—Montana, for example—have game laws to protect the porcupine, for this very reason.

In Maine, as in all other parts of the world, there's a lot of talk goes around about the excellence of the native country cooking. In Maine, as in all other parts of the world with which I am familiar—not so many, I'll grant you, but enough—this is largely eye-wash. There are a few fine country cooks around here, but most of the food is very undistinguished in character. Most local cooks have two ideas about what to do with food. They either fry it—and I think the steady diet of fried food in Maine accounts largely for the high incidence of chronic indigestion and stomach ulcers—or else they make a chowder out of it. We have a by-word in our family. When confronted with the disposal of almost anything from a dead fish to a pair of worn-out pants, someone is bound to say, "It'd make a nice chowder!" That really isn't stretching the point much, either.

I'm indebted to the local cooks for another expression. That is "smitches and dabs." We have a meal of smitches and dabs about once a week, usually on wash day. This consists of a smitch of this and a dab of that. In other words, that's the meal that cleans up the ice box. It's a family institution by now, and a very useful one. Sometimes these left-overs are just warmed up separately and sometimes they are combined into one dish. You dump some odds and ends of meat, any stray vegetables, a can of beef broth—to make gravy—into a baking dish, top the whole with biscuit dough, bake, and you have a shepherd's pie. Or you put left-over salmon, peas, ham, and a can of mushroom soup into a dish, cover with buttered crumbs, and again bake. I suppose this is some kind of a casserole, but it doesn't really make much difference what it is. It comes under smitches and dabs in our family.

We have Desperation Dishes, too. These are things we eat when we run out of food, for one reason or other. A stand-by, of course, is baked beans, which we have every Saturday night anyhow. In a minute I'm going into the proper baking of beans in detail. It's a subject that deserves attention. Baked beans can be terrible, or they can be swell. In our family Gerrish is the judge. He's a baked bean expert from away-back. If he says after the first forkful, "Your hand slipped a mite this week, didn't it, Louise?", I feel like crawling under the table. But if he says, "You hit it about right this time," my chest swells to the button-bursting point.

Even good baked beans can become tedious. I remember one year when the lake didn't finish freezing and we couldn't get in any supplies, we had them twice a day for ten days. One of these days was Thanksgiving, too. In honor of that day I invented another Desperation Dish. Besides beans, we had in the house a very small can of Vienna sausages and a half a bottle of ketchup. I put a layer of cold baked beans in a baking dish, sprinkled lavishly with ketchup, and arranged half the sausages on it. Then I repeated, ending with a layer of beans, and heated the whole until it bubbled gently. It was really pretty good. We have it now every once in a while, even when we aren't desperate. Desperation Dishes often turn out much better than you'd expect.

Now about the baking of the beans. Baked beans have to be baked. That sounds like a gratuitous restatement of the obvious, but it isn't. Some misguided souls boil beans all day and call the lily-livered result baked beans. I refrain from comment.

We use either New York State or Michigan white beans, because we like them best, although yellow-eyes are very popular, too. I take two generous cups of dry beans, soak over night and put them on to boil early in the morning. When the skins curl off when you blow on them, they've boiled long enough. Then I put in the bottom of the bean pot, or iron kettle with a tight-fitting cover, a six-by-eight-inch square of salt pork, with the rind slashed every quarter of an inch, a quarter of a cup of sugar, half a cup of molasses, a large onion chopped fairly fine, and a heaping teaspoonful of dry mustard. This amount of sugar and molasses may be increased or cut, depending on whether you like your beans sweeter or not so sweet. This is a matter every man has to decide for himself. The beans are dumped in on top of this conglomerate, and enough hot water is added to cover, but only cover. The baking pot should be large enough so there's at least an inch of free-board above the water. Otherwise they'll boil over and smell to high heaven. Cover tightly and put into a medium oven—about 350° is right. They should be in the oven by half past nine in the morning at the latest, and they should stay there until supper time, which in our family is at six.

So far there is no trick in making good baked beans. The trick, if it can be dignified by such a term, lies in the baking, and like a great many trade tricks, it consists only of patience and conscientious care. You have to tend the beans faithfully, adding water whenever the level gets down below the top of the beans, and you have to keep the oven temperature even. If you're lazy, you can put in a lot of water and not have to watch them so closely. But to get the best results, you should add only enough water each time to barely cover the beans. This means that you'll give up all social engagements for the day, as you can't leave the baby for more than half an hour at a time. I think the results are worth it—but then, I haven't anywhere special to go, anyhow. My beans are brown and mealy, and they swim in a thick brown juice. They're good. I always serve them with corn bread, ketchup and pickles.

Another Desperation Dish is Mock Tripe. It is an old home recipe of that almost legendary Norwegian guide, Travis Hoke, and is very useful in disposing of otherwise unusable odds and ends. If you have a fresh salmon you can put its skin in a light brine until you are ready to use it, or the skin of a baked fish, carefully removed, will serve as well. Save the daily leavings of the oatmeal pot and spread them out about a half inch thick to dry. When you have amassed a sufficient quantity and it is covered with a heavy brown crust, season well and wrap in the fish skin. Dredge this with flour and put it in your roasting pan with a small amount of water or milk, cover, and bake at least an hour in a medium oven. The result is truly amazing.

Every cook is supposed to have some short cuts or labor savers that experience has taught her. I ought to have a million, for Lord knows I have learned to cook in a hard school. But I have only a measly little list of discoveries. The first is that an egg beater can be used for a lot of other things than the beating of eggs. I'd almost rather throw my stove away than my egg beater. I use it to take the lumps out of gravy or chocolate cornstarch pudding or cream sauce. When the cereal sinks in a leaden mass to the bottom of the pan, because I didn't have the water boiling briskly, or didn't stir it enough, I beat it up with the egg beater, and it comes out smooth and creamy. I beat mashed potato with it, and squash. I beat anything and everything with an egg beater, and I always put it immediately into a deep pan of cold water to soak. Otherwise all the time it saves will be spent in washing the thing. It's devilish to get clean if it is allowed to dry.

My second little device is a pane of window glass which I put over my open cook book. I'm a messy cook, splashing flour and milk and batter and egg yolk all over the table. If they splash on the book, the pages will stick together and you can't use that recipe again, as I have found to my sorrow. If they splash on the glass, that's all right. Glass washes.

My third and last contribution to the culinary world is a way to crumb fish or croquettes or cutlets or what-have-you easily and quickly. I put my crumbs or flour in a paper bag, drop in the object to be crumbed, close the bag and shake violently. This doesn't sound like much of an invention but it saves an awful lot of mess. When you're through you have nothing to clean up. You just shove the paper bag into the stove and burn up the scanty leavings.

Now I'm probably going to discover that all these things are common practice among cooks everywhere, and that I'm just tagging tardily along behind my brighter sisters.

There are two factors which complicate the cooking situation for me. One is that I never know how many people I am going to have to feed. I always have to allow for at least one more than the family, in case anyone drops in. In the woods the first question you ask anybody, no matter what time of day he arrives, is, "Have you eaten?" This is absolutely obligatory, and the reason is easy to see. A man can't drop into a dog cart for a hamburger or a cup of coffee, if he's hungry. He expects the population to feed him, and in return he expects to feed whoever drops in at his place. It's an understood thing, just as it is understood that in winter, no matter whose house you go into, if they are not at home you immediately look at the fires and add wood if necessary. You do this even if you are a stranger to the householder. It may be serious to let a fire go out. So we feed game wardens and fire wardens and timber cruisers and lost hunters and stray woodsmen and anyone else who happens along, and they tend our fires as required. Once we even fed the census taker, a gentleman whom, by the way, we were very much surprised to see come staggering out of the snowy woods. We'd figured that we would be among the submerged and forgotten one percent, when it came to census taking.

The other difficulty I have to surmount is the kitchen itself. In the country, and even more in the woods, a kitchen is much more than a place to cook. It's the place where people sit, for warmth or sociability, or to do odd jobs. We have the usual kitchen furnishings—straight-backed chairs, table, work bench, sink, ice box, stove and woodbox. We also have a comfortable rocking chair and a pile of books and magazines. Half the time, when I'm cooking, I'm also hurdling over someone's legs, or a dog or cat, or a pile of guns and coats. Or I may have to walk around a landing net that has been left by the stove, or an inner tube that Ralph is patching in the middle of the floor. In all seasons except summer, I have to dodge a line-ful of wool socks, hung up to dry, and skirt two pails of water left by the end of the stove to keep warm for car-starting purposes. Often my pots and pans have to find what space they can around a soldering iron thrust into the firebox and my pot roast is shoved back in the oven to ac-commodate a pair of newly oiled boots that must be dried.

I used to try to keep the kitchen sacred to legitimate kitchen activities, but I finally gave it up. No matter how often I chased Gerrish and his tackle-mending or Ralph and his car-repairing or Rufus and his fleet of trucks into the living-room, they always insidiously filtered back. Ac-tually there's an advantage to having them right there. If they're in the room they can't very well pretend not to hear me when I start hollering to have my water pails filled or some wood brought in from the woodshed. And I might as well break down at last and admit that I like having them underfoot. The few times that they stayed in the living-room when I sent them there, I felt like a social pariah out in the kitchen all alone with my efficiency.

To augment our larder, we have a vegetable garden, and believe me, please, that's quite a feat when you start, as we did, with a little plot of land which has excellent sun and drainage, but which also has a growth of brush and ever-greens all over it, and under that nothing but thin, acid woods soil studded thickly with rocks and boulders and solidly interlaced with a mat of roots. Our garden is splendid now, but it's taken us eight years to get it that way.

The first year was spent in cutting the brush and trees and removing the roots and the worst of the rocks. This was honest-to-God hard labor, particularly as we didn't have the right equipment for it. Ralph and Gerrish and I have spent a whole day getting out a boulder that weighed more than the three of us put together. The first step, always, was to trench around the thing so we could get at it, and Ralph and Gerrish did this. Then they collected an assortment of chains, levers, and cant dogs, and summoned me. My part consisted solely of lending my weight on the end of a twenty-foot beam that served as a pry, or dodging around the edges of the operation with an armful of blocks of assorted sizes. "Over here! Over here!" Ralph and Ger-rish would shout in chorus, their faces red and strained with lifting. "For God's sake, stick a block under her be-fore—" I'd thrust a block in to hold what they'd gained and they'd relax, panting and perspiring, to get their breaths and plan the next step. The general modus oper-andi was to lift the boulder up with levers to ground level, building a scaffolding of blocks under her as she came—I'm catching this "she" habit, too—and then roll her across an extremely precarious bridge of planks to solid earth. Then we worried her onto a stone-drag and dragged her away behind our then current work car, the old twelve-cylinder Packard. Frequently, with only six inches to go before we could roll her out, the entire scaffolding would collapse and drop the boulder back to the bottom of the pit—a perfectly maddening thing to have happen. I do believe in the malevolence of the inanimate, and of all inanimate objects, stones are the most malevolent. In the first place the stones in our section lack symmetry, so if you apply pressure where you think it will do the most good, they are just as apt to roll to the left onto your foot, as to the right where you plan to have them roll. In the second place, they are ponderous, and once they start rolling, you can't stop them. All you can do is jump clear and start swearing. In the third place—and this to my mind is the worst of all— after they have flopped the wrong way and have ruined an entire morning's work, they just lie there. There's something about the bland face of a stone, lying in the middle of a pile of wrecked scaffolding at the bottom of a hole, that makes you want to throw yourself face down on the ground and kick and scream.

We got enough rocks and roots out of the ground that first year so that we could plant a few things in the cleared spaces. But we didn't get them all out, by any means, and haven't even yet, in spite of a yearly session with them. We put in peas and string beans and carrots and beets and corn. Ralph and I were no gardeners but Gerrish had had a garden in one place or another ever since he wore diapers, so in most things we bowed to his superior wisdom. But when it came to corn, he and Ralph disagreed. Ralph contended that the growing season as far north and as high as we are is too short to allow corn to reach maturity, and that it should be started in the house and transplanted into the garden as soon as the weather was warm enough. Gerrish announced categorically that one did not transplant corn. It wouldn't grow, and even if it did, there was no point to it. The season was plenty long enough.

They argued two or three days about this, and then they decided that they'd divide the corn patch, and each would take half to cultivate as he saw fit. Ralph made himself some nice little starting flats, filled them with dirt, and started his corn in the house. Gerrish put his corn away in a drawer and forgot about it until the ground warmed up.

Ralph's corn came up very nicely and he tended it as if it were black orchids. On the same day that Gerrish put his seed into the ground, Ralph transplanted his thriving little shoots. They looked very green and tender and brave out there in the cold world, and he covered them carefully every night, to guard them against a spring frost. They didn't grow very much at first. I suppose they were getting themselves acclimated. After about a week, Gerrish's corn started to come up, and that's where the double-dealing entered the picture.

Gerrish came home from fishing one evening with a whole string of chub. Nobody eats them, so I couldn't imagine why he had saved them, or why he was hiding them so carefully under the back steps. He didn't mind telling me, after swearing me to secrecy. He'd remembered that the Indians used to plant their corn over dead fish, for fertilizer, and he was going to tunnel into his corn hills and put dead chub where they'd do the most good. He'd show Ralph how to raise corn.

Well, a promise is a promise, I know, and I usually try to keep mine. But this was supposed to be a controlled experiment, and I've been brought up to respect the scientific attitude. I couldn't let that go. I told Ralph—swearing him to secrecy, of course—and that night he went chub fishing, with some success. Thereafter the two of them spent a lot of time sneaking fish corpses into the garden and burying them under their respective corn hills. I used to help them both, which was probably traitorous of me, but it afforded me a lot of fun.

We had corn off both sides of the patch on the very same day, and there was nothing to distinguish the one from the other. Now we plant our corn by the Gerrish system. It's a lot easier.

Oh, the troubles we had that first year! No sooner had our vegetables broken ground than the deer started coming in at night and eating the plants. We decided at once that we had to fence the garden, but it was going to take a little time to get the fencing material in from the Outside. In the meantime something had to be done. For a while we worked days cutting and setting fence posts, and sat up nights with a shot gun. But you can't keep that up forever. Then the game warden told us to spread some blood meal around. This is a packing house product that is used primarily for fertilizer. The smell of blood is supposed to frighten the deer away. It didn't, though. On the contrary, I think it attracted them. Then someone told us that if we made a little tent in the garden and kept a lighted lantern in it all night, the deer would keep their distance. The tent material had to be thin, so the light would glow through, and the color had to be changed often, so the deer wouldn't acquire the contempt bred by familiarity. We tried that—we'd have tried anything—and rather surprisingly it worked. At least, it worked for a week. Then one morning we went into the garden and found the tracks of a dozen deer, all converging on our little tent. Apparently they'd held a meeting and decided on a mass investigation. They hadn't touched any of the vegetables, though. I guess they were too intrigued with the light to bother about anything else.

That very afternoon the wire for the fence came, and next morning we put it onto the posts we'd set so fast that it smoked. And that was that.

That wasn't the woodchucks, though, that crawled through the mesh of the wire. We had to set traps for them. *That* wasn't the heavy rain, either, that gullied out the slope of the garden and washed out half the crop. We had to terrace the whole slope, the next year, to prevent a recurrence. But neither fence nor traps nor terracing was any answer to our basic problem, the problem of the soil. It's taken us all these years to lick its thinness and acidity and infertility. We've spaded in tons of manure which we've hauled from Miller's and various lumber camp stables, to add humus and give body to the soil. We've bought hundreds of pounds of lime and raked it in, to counteract the acidity which is always a characteristic of forest mold. We've scattered hundreds of pounds of commercial balanced fertilizers, too. What we've accomplished, really, is to make arable earth out of the rubble heaps of sand and clay and gravel that the great glaciers dumped here ages and ages ago. It may not be a becoming attitude, but all the same, we do point with pride to our vegetable garden. I consider that my skill with a spading fork is just as much a part of my housekeeping ability as is my urban sister's nose for a bargain in canned goods. They both result in putting better, cheaper vegetables on the family table.

The clothing problem causes me very little concern. One of the reasons I like to live here is that I don't have to bother to try to be a snappy number. I couldn't, anyway, no matter where I lived; but in civilization I'd at least have to make the effort, in fairness to Ralph and Rufus. I couldn't humiliate them by putting them in the position of having to answer, when someone asked, "Who's that funny-looking woman?"—"Oh, that's my wife" or "my mother," as the case might be. And, boy! would I be miserable! I can't stand having things tight around my waist or neck or wrists, and you can't be stylish unless you have your clothes anchored in a few places, at least. My idea of an ideal costume is slacks worn low on the hip bones, and a cotton shirt with the sleeves rolled up and the neck band unbuttoned. I can wear that here. I look thoroughly sloppy, but here it doesn't matter. Ralph and Rufus love me—I hope—for my good nature. There wouldn't be even that about me to love if I had to try to be chic.

This is what my entire wardrobe consists of at the moment.

1 pair of blue denim pants
1 pair of canvas pants (my garden, fishing, and berrying pants)
1 pair wool whipcord jodhpurs (Ralph hates them)
1 pair wool ski pants
3 cotton shirts (the 59¢ variety)
3 wool shirts
4 pairs of cotton ankle socks (17¢ a pair)
3 pairs of wool ski socks (I made them myself—39¢ each, but worth a lot more)
2 sweaters

1 wool jacket
1 denim jacket
1 bathing suit and cap
3 changes of underwear and nightclothes
1 very old bathrobe
1 wool bonnet and mittens to match
3 pairs of 79¢ sneakers
1 pair of leather moccasins
1 large kerchief, to use as hat, scarf, berry pail, dog leash, depending on the circumstances.

I did have a belt, but I never wore it, so I gave it to Gerrish. And I have a .22 revolver, but I don't suppose that comes under wardrobe, really, even here. I've also got a tweed suit and a pair of silk stockings and some shoes in case I have to go Outside in a hurry; but it's been a long time since I've even looked at them. They've probably perished of dry rot by now. The last time I had to go out in a hurry was when Kyak became suddenly and terrifyingly ill and needed to be taken at once to the veterinary. It was at night and raining pitchforks, and I had no time or inclination to dress up. I wore my fishing pants and Gerrish's raincoat, which was just as well. The only people besides Ralph that I saw were Larry Parsons and the vet. I didn't really see Larry. He was running the boat, but it was so dark and foggy that he had to make the trip down the lake by compass, and all I could distinguish of him was a dark shadow up in the bow and a faint blur of features when he inhaled on his cigarette or turned the flashlight onto the compass. And later in the car it was almost as dark. The vet was too much interested in Kyak's symptoms to bother about what I had on. I'm sure the next time an emergency arises, the conditions will be duplicated. So I don't have to worry about my Going Out Clothes.

Ralph's wardrobe is about like mine, except he has gum-boots for winter and work shoes for summer and a canvas parka and a mackinaw. He prefers canvas pants the whole year through and refuses to have riding or ski pants. Rufus wears overalls and cotton shirts, or sun suits, for summer, and ski pants and sweaters in the winter. Once when he was very little I did buy him a little wash suit, with shorts and frilled shirt. He looked perfectly adorable in it the one time he had it on. But he and his father and Gerrish all pronounced it sissy, and I could never get him to wear it again. Sally is the best-dressed member of the family. She goes Out to school, so she has to have the usual quota of dresses, presentable shoes, and street coats. At her age, too, these things would matter, I suppose, even if she never went Outside.

There are a few general aspects of the clothes situation that interest me very much. One of them is the growth of ski pants as a national institution. When I was a child, ski pants were absolutely unknown in this country. I realize that they were introduced along with the vogue for winter sports, and that is not surprising. What surprises me is their acceptance by non-skiers of all ages. It has apparently reached the point where everyone owns a pair of ski pants, just as everyone owns a skirt or a pair of trousers. This really is a tribute to the practicability of the garment. People in general don't own baseball caps or football pants. The most non-athletic types own ski pants.

Another thing that interests me is the false notion held by almost all city people that you can get wonderful bargains in the country. Ralph, for example, owns a very handsome red-and-black-checked shirt, made of wool material so thin it tailors marvellously. He calls it his sporting shirt, and wears it only on special occasions. Occasions special enough for the sporting shirt usually involve people from the city, and before long someone will get up the courage to ask, "*Where* did you get that shirt and how much did you pay for it? I want one like it."

The answer is, "My sister-in-law gave it to me for my birthday and she got it at Jordan Marsh's in Boston and I've no idea what she paid for it."

The let-down is always tremendous. "Oh, I hoped you were going to say that you got it at some cross-roads country store for two dollars. You always hear about the wonderful things that people pick up back in the sticks for practically nothing—"

Yes, you do. But there aren't any wonderful things in country stores, for any amount of money. The stock in a country store consists of cheap clothes, cheap food, cheap everything. Usually they cost more than the same article in the city. Cheap things are all that country people can ordinarily afford. If you want marvellous things, you have to go to the luxury trade stores in cities, and pay accordingly. You can't get something for nothing, even in the country. I buy homespun yarn from various farmers' wives around on the Outside, and I pay very little for it. It's all wool, from sheep reared on the place. That sounds like one of those marvellous bargains; but it isn't. It's worth exactly what I pay for it. It's harsh, and it's unevenly spun, and there are only two colors—gray and a tan mixture. For my purpose—work socks and mittens—it's quite all right. But when I want to make a sweater, or a nice pair of socks for

Ralph, I send away to the Mail Order for some decent yarn.

The truth of the matter is that in spite of the literary convention of bursting barns, overflowing larders, and cellars crammed with luscious preserves and delicious smoked hams, in spite of the accepted version of the countryman as being clad in the warmest and best of wools, the thickest and softest of leathers, and the deepest and darkest of furs, country people are clothed much more shoddily and poorly than city people, class for class. In short, the country standard of living is very much lower than the city standard. This is actually not as hard on country people as it would seem to be. You don't mind cheap clothes if everyone else is wearing clothes just as cheap. There are other things that contribute to health besides a balanced diet. There are fresh air and sunlight and lack of nervous tension. I think, probably, whether you're better off in the country or in the city depends, in the final analysis, on where you'd rather be. You're best off where you're the happiest.

As I have said before, we do all our purchasing from the Mail Order—more formally, from Sears, Roebuck and Montgomery Ward. Having been brought up in a medium-sized town within easy reach of Boston, I never had a chance to become familiar with the great American institution of the Mail Order until I came to live in the woods. Now, I couldn't get along without it. It's wonderful as a source of supply, and their catalogs are a fascinating source of entertainment. We sit by the hour looking at the illustrations and reading the descriptions of the thousands of items in the enormous twice-yearly catalogs, and we buy anything from motor parts to ankle socks from

Sears' or Ward's. If, for my sins, I ever have to live at the corner of 42nd and Broadway, I shall still trade with the Mail Order. I'm completely wedded to the idea.

Everybody in this country is thoroughly familiar with the Mail Order. I show up at Middle in a new pair of slacks, and Alice Miller says, "Oh, those are those Ward's slacks. A dollar ninety-eight. I was thinking about getting me some, only in brown." Or somebody comes in from Upton sporting a new hunting shirt, and I can put the price tag and percentage of wool on it with the accuracy of a purchasing agent. Fifty percent wool, and two seventy-five in the big catalog; but he paid only two forty-nine for it. They had them on sale in the latest flyer. There are no secrets between Mail Order devotees.

I never realized how revealing a filled-in order blank can be until one day I happened on the sample order blank in the back of the Sears catalog. This is a facsimile of an order, made out in full, for the guidance of the customer in making out his own order. Very likely the name and address at the top of the blank are fictitious, but the order itself looks genuine. I read it through carefully, and I felt at once that I knew the woman who made it out as well as I know myself.

The goods were to be sent to John T. Jones, R.F.D. No. 1, Tipton, Iowa, but Johnny Jones didn't make out the order. Mrs. Jones did that. She hadn't been married very long, I think, and she didn't have very much money to spend. But she had ideas. She wanted her house to be nice. She lived in the country in Iowa, but she didn't want to let herself go. She wanted to look smart like the town girls. I know just how she conned the catalog night after night, between finishing the supper dishes and going to bed, to be sure she was getting the best possible value for her money. She made a lot of selections and jotted them down —the names of the articles and the prices—on an old envelope, before she made her final choices. I know, because I have done the same thing. She had only thirty dollars to spend. I know that, because the order came to $29.42. That's just about as close as you can come to a specified sum.

I know that this order was important to her, because it is written so carefully and neatly in ink. The penmanship is obviously not her note-to-the-milkman hand. It's her very best penmanship, stiff and careful, with the t's crossed accurately. That's the way I write when I make out an order to Sears' or Ward's. That's the only time I do write that way.

This is what she bought. Four yards of rose-printed chintz, a dusty rose chenille bedspread, and a pair of dusty rose curtains. You see? She was fixing up a bedroom, with spread, curtains, and dressing table to match. Probably it was for the spare room; she'd at last saved enough to redecorate it as a real guest room. None of the articles is the best grade—that I remembered from my own perusals of the catalog. But they're the best she could afford. She wanted her house to be nice.

Then she bought three pairs of flag-red ankle socks— that's how I know she must be young, and therefore newly married—and a green suit, Cat. No. 55H7186, which cost $15.50. I remembered Cat. No. 55H7186. It's a nice suit, very young and dashing. She hesitated a long time before she spent that much money on a suit, I know, but in the end she remembered how proud of her Johnny always acted when he took her to the movies Saturday night before they were married. In the end she sacrificed I don't know what—a two-quart double boiler, perhaps, or an extra pair of sheets—to keep him acting that way.

The last item was a Craftsman hammer, for ninety-eight cents. That was for Johnny. She had a little over a dollar left, and he'd been fussing about that old hammer with the loose head out in the shed— Oh, I know Mrs. John T. Jones of Tipton, Iowa. Perhaps she is just someone dreamed up in the advertising department of Sears' Chicago office! But she's me, too, and a million other women like me, scattered from here to the Rio Grande, who do their shopping through the magic of the Mail Order.

All my life I've had a very clear idea of the kind of living-room I'd like to have. It's the living-room so often described in English novels or novels of country life among the gentlefolk in Virginia or the Berkshires. Everybody knows the room well, with its wide windows, its books and flowers and faded chintz, its open fire and comfortable shabby chairs and sleeping dogs. It sounds attractive and comfortable. It's comfortable, all right, but not necessarily as attractive as it's made out to be. I know. That's the kind of a living-room we have in the summer house.

The trouble with faded chintz, let me tell you, is that instead of looking soft and old and precious, it looks like chintz that should have been replaced two years ago. The trouble with the dogs is that instead of lying in front of the fire and lending atmosphere, they lie in the middle of the floor where you fall over them. Or else they lie in the shabby chairs and look so hurt when you try to oust them that you can't bear it, and you'd almost sit on the floor yourself rather than cause them pain. The trouble with the open fire is that it throws embers onto the rug—a screen holds in the embers, but holds in the heat, too—so that eventually you decide to take up the rug altogether and have a bare floor—unless you've already taken it up because it's too hard to keep clean, what with the men-folks of your family, and the dogs and cats, tracking in mud, sawdust and snow. There's nothing the matter with the flowers and the books and there's nothing the matter with the shabby chairs, if you can accept them as shabby chairs and don't try to make something interesting out of them. BUT —and this is never taken into consideration in the novels— if you're the kind of weak-minded person who will put up with faded chintz and dogs in shabby chairs in the first place, you're too weak-minded to put your foot down there. You allow the corners of this interesting room to become jammed with fishing tackle and guns; the table and mantle are soon buried under a mound of fly-tying material, magazines, odd pieces of rock, and work gloves; the floor is littered with toys and tools; and several pairs of boots for all types of weather are parked at the end of the couch. In short, the place is a mess. The only thing that can be said for it is that there is nothing in it that can be hurt by the roughest usage. It's a room you can let yourself go in, for what that's worth. It's a room where you can put your feet up and relax.

That's the kind of a home Ralph and I have made for ourselves in the backwoods, and that's the kind of marriage we've managed, together, to make, too. There are drawbacks to living off the beaten track, but there is one thing that more than offsets any number of drawbacks: if you can stand this life at all, your marriage has a much greater chance of success than it would have anywhere else. I believe that a great many marriages fail because there is no true dependence between the partners thereof. Somehow, when a well-dressed, well-fed, sleek and contented male says to me—and there have been such occasions in my palmy youth, believe it or not—"I need you!", I just can't quite believe it, much as I'd like to. It's nice to hear, but it's silly. When, however, Ralph comes into the house with the sleeve of his shirt torn and blood dripping from a gash on his arm, and shouts at the top of his lungs, "Damn it, where are you? I need you!", he's obviously telling the truth. He may be interrupting me in the middle of something that I don't want to leave, but that doesn't make any difference. He does need me, and he needs me right then. There isn't any doctor he can go to to tie him up. There isn't any restaurant where he can get his meals, or any laundry to wash his shirts. I'm necessary to him; and by the same token, he's necessary to me. It's a terribly trite thing to say, I know, but most of us have to be needed to be happy.

Is it, then, necessary to live the hard way, just so you can feel you are needed? For me, yes, it is. I know myself too well to be able to delude myself that my wit or my beauty or my wisdom or my intelligence could ever become indispensable to anyone. I have to have things demonstrated in material terms that I can understand. And I have found this to be true: that the material makes a very good and solid foundation for a dependence that cannot be defined, an inter-dependence of mind and spirit which we might never have known had we not first had to depend on each other for the tangible, demonstrable things.

We've managed to make a good marriage. This I say with all humility. It's a marriage in which there is nothing that can be hurt by the roughest usage. It's a marriage that you can let yourself go in, a marriage in which you can put up your feet and relax.

V

~~~

"Aren't the Children a Problem?"

THE TRUE YANKEE ANSWER TO THE QUESTION, "AREN'T THE children a problem?" is, of course, another question: "Aren't children always a problem, no matter where you live?" If they aren't, I've wasted a lot of time in my civilized past listening to the bridge table chat of the young mothers of my acquaintanceship. Unless my memory plays me false, parenthood anywhere from the heart of Texas to the middle of Manhattan is one long coping with maladjusted personalities, crooked teeth, allergies to goose feathers, and lamentable traits inherited from the other side of the family. In short, certainly children are a problem, only in the woods the details of the problem aren't quite the same as they are on the Outside.

The problem starts with getting them born. Of course, with Sally, I skipped this. She's my step-child, and sprang into my life, full-panoplied, as it were, at the age of twelve. I skipped not only the actual giving birth, but also the house-breaking and habit-forming. This advantage is offset to an extent by the fact that I'm responsible for her not only to her father and my own conscience, as I am with

Rufus, but also to her mother as well—no mean responsibility. It would be bad enough to have something happen to your own child. It would be almost impossible to have to go to another woman and say, "So sorry, but I let your daughter get drowned." That's the chief reason that the first thing I did about Sally when I took her over was to insist that she learn to swim. All in all, though, I would say that I came by Sally in the easy way.

Rufus I got the hard way, on the 18th of December at 2.55 A.M., with the thermometer down to 10° above zero. That's a night I won't forget in a hurry. Neither will Ralph, I imagine. Ralph has always been the type that, if he heard it rumored that the wife of one of his friends was going to have a baby eight months from date, took to crossing the street and raising his hat politely from the opposite sidewalk, when he met her. He was taking no chances of having to ride in a taxi with her to the hospital. The mere thought caused him to break out in a cold sweat. Well, the night Rufus was born he didn't have any time to worry about what might happen in a taxi. He was much too busy coping, single handed, with what was happening right then and there. In spite of the temperature, though, he was doing his quota of sweating. I can see him now, with a wool cap pulled down over his ears, his mackinaw collar turned up to meet it, and his mittens on, reading by lantern light a little book called, "If Baby Comes Ahead of the Doctor." Perspiration was running down his face. You see, he knew the doctor couldn't possibly get there for ten hours or more.

Nothing is more tiresome than the details of some other woman's pregnancy, but just bear with me for a minute. I've been wanting to say this for a long time. I don't believe most women need be miserable at all. There are two simple preventive measures to take. First, they can stop regarding themselves as being for the period, interesting and unique and fragile, and treating themselves like rare porcelain. It's very bad for them. No wonder they feel rotten. A coal heaver would feel rotten too, if he kept telling himself that he ought to on general principles. And second, they can just not listen to their married friends' and maiden aunts' tales of the terrible things that may happen to them. Some of the things that otherwise sensible women tell prospective mothers are enough to frighten the wits out of anyone. They won't let you remember that these ghoulish tales are the exceptions and that most babies are born with some discomfort, it's true, but not much else. Personally, I'd almost rather have a baby any day than go to the dentist. My friends tell me that this is just because I was lucky. I think I made my own luck. I felt swell, so why should I alter my normal behavior and curtail my normal activities? And—this I will admit was just plain luck —I was so situated that there were no married friends and maiden aunts to scare the pants off me. Result: I had a very pleasant pregnancy, thank you.

End of Lecture on Prenatal Care, by Mrs. Rich. Thanks for listening.

I was supposed to go out to Rumford to have Rufus; but then he wasn't supposed to be born until the first of the year. The idea was that I would stay in over Christmas, and then in a leisurely way, betake myself to the hospital to wait the necessary week or ten days. Consequently we hadn't moved out of the summer house which is without heat upstairs. Ralph was going to move the things in my absence. In the meantime I pursued my program of

"Business as Usual," and the usual business of a lovely day such as the 17th of December turned out to be, was sliding on the Pond. I never saw such a beautiful winter day. It was warm and sunny, and the ground was covered with a light fluff of snow, which was blue in the shadows, and gold in the sun, and faint rose and purple on the distant hills. On the Pond it had blown into tightly packed patches which were white, as snow is supposed to be, against the sky-reflecting deep blue of the glare ice. We'd started to go to Middle Dam, but when we saw the Pond, we went there instead. The sliding was perfect. We could run on the snow islands and slide across the intervening spaces of ice to more snow. Cookie went with us—she was alive at the time, Kyak's mother—and she had a lovely time, too, racing and barking and falling down and scrambling to her feet. We all fell down dozens of times before we completed the mile circuit of the Lamonts' island, which may have had something to do with Rufus' premature arrival. I don't know. I felt quite all right.

All I know is that I woke up in the middle of the night, out of a sound sleep, with a stomach-ache. Only it wasn't a stomach-ache. It was an emergency, and there were no lights on the Ford, and I didn't have a bag packed. I woke Ralph up, and he went down to telephone the Millers and, of course, woke them up, while I wandered around with an old pair of slippers in one hand and a cake of soap in the other. I couldn't seem to think where I'd put my suitcase or what I should put into it. Pretty soon it became obvious that it didn't matter. I got back into bed just as Ralph came up with the information that the Millers' Ford had no lights either, and since it was pitch black outdoors we wouldn't be going anywhere. This didn't upset me as much as it would have fifteen minutes before. I'd already come to the same conclusion but for an entirely different reason.

I don't want to give the impression that I was calm and unruffled through this whole proceeding. I wasn't. But I took one look at Ralph's face and saw that he was ten times as alarmed as I was. I'd never seen him really alarmed before, and it was the best thing in the world that could have happened to me. I suddenly felt very brave and confident. I remembered that lots of babies are born without benefit of the medical profession, and that the best thing in a crisis is to keep busy. I was busy enough myself. All I had to do was to give Ralph something to occupy his mind.

"You'd better heat up a lot of water," I said. I didn't know quite what for, but I remembered that in books people always heat water under similar circumstances.

He went away and I could hear him rattling away down in the kitchen. By and by he came back and said that he wanted a nice wool blanket to warm over the stove before he put it in the laundry basket. "Got to have some place to park the kid," he explained, and I stopped worrying about him. He was functioning again, that was plain. I told him where to find the blanket, in between pains, and he went away again. When he came back, five minutes later, he was a father.

Usually a father has no immediate responsibilities toward his new off-spring aside from running up to the hospital once a day for a viewing—and of course paying the hospital bill. Ralph's responsibilities, on the contrary, were immediate and pressing. There was the little matter of the umbilical cord to be cut and tied, first of all.

"And don't you wash new babies?" I asked.

"Nope. You grease them." I don't know to this day how he came by this piece of knowledge, but he was right. Perhaps he read it in the *Reader's Digest*. That's where much of our information originates. He folded his new son in a bath towel and went away with him, while I lay in bed and worried. What did he know about greasing babies and tying cords? The new baby was crying, too, a little but furious bellow. I could hear him from away upstairs. What was his father doing to him? Or wait a minute—you were supposed only to worry, weren't you, if they didn't cry. So probably it was all right. It was criminal, I decided, for a grown woman to arrive at motherhood knowing as little about the whole thing as I did. By and by Ralph came back.

"Did you get him greased all right?" I asked anxiously.

He looked offended. "Certainly I did. I should hope, after all the pistons I've oiled in my lifetime—" Pistons, mind you!

"What did you use?" I asked, horrified, "Motor oil?"

"Olive oil, naturally."

"Where did you get it? We haven't any olive oil."

"I've got a can. I use it to make fly-dope out of."

Well, why not, after all? If early experience molds a child's life, I could see from where I lay that I was going to be the mother of another mechanic and fly-fisherman.

"He's all right and he's all there," Ralph went on. "Fingernails, toenails, hair, everything. I went over him carefully. And, my God! is he homely!" He threw out his chest. "I never did like pretty men, anyway," he added complacently. "He's got a grip like a wrestler, and Cookie likes him, so I guess he'll get along all right. And say. What am I supposed to do with all that hot water?"

Oh, yes. The hot water. Well— "Why don't you make some coffee?" Suddenly I was starved. "Make me a sandwich, too—a ham sandwich with a lot of mustard."

Alice Miller came down in the morning, as soon as it was light. Lying in bed, I could hear her laughing down in the kitchen. She laughed all the way upstairs. "What do you suppose Ralph used to tie his cord with?" she demanded before she was halfway into the room. "A piece of rope! That poor little kid! The knot's bigger than he is. I guess I'll call the doctor in Rumford when I get home and tell him there's no need of his coming way in here. No sense in spending twenty dollars for nothing—"

And so Rufus missed his chance of having a doctor look him over. I guess it didn't do any harm. He's never seen a doctor from that day to this, except in a purely social capacity.

I frequently read in magazines articles which begin:—
DO YOU REALIZE—

That blank percent of the homes in America have no running water?

That blank percent have no bathrooms?

That blank percent of our children are born with no doctor in attendance?

These appalling figures show that the huge army of the underprivileged—

I cluck my tongue, suitably appalled for a moment until true realization hits me between the eyes. "My God," I think, and then I am truly appalled. "That's *us* they're talking about! Why—*we're* the underprivileged! Why—Why—"

But are we? I'm not stupid enough to recommend that all, or even any, children be born with only their fathers in attendance. But because it happened to Rufus doesn't make him underprivileged. In fact, I would say he was especially privileged—not in that he was held up by the heels and oiled with piston-oiling technique, but because from that moment on, his father has had a very special feeling for him. All normal fathers love their children, we will assume. They all feel a responsibility toward them. But—and I think I am not being merely sentimental when I say this—that early, primitive responsibility that devolved upon Ralph toward Rufus left its mark. Fatherhood is necessarily a less intimate relationship—physically at least—than motherhood; but Ralph can't think of himself only as the guy who buys Rufus' food and clothes and administers spankings. Fundamentally he is always the guy who tied his cord and greased him, when there was no one else to do it. That is something I wouldn't want Rufus deprived of, for all the hospital treatment in the world.

Nor can I bring myself to believe that our children are hopelessly handicapped because they take baths in washtubs in front of the kitchen range, read by the light of kerosene lamps, and sleep in unheated bedrooms. We'll give them a bathroom and steam heat and electric lights when we get the house rebuilt; but perhaps we'll be making a mistake. Soft living isn't important to them now, because it never has been. They're never going to be miserable because of physical inconveniences. Perhaps the best thing we can give them in a world where the possession of material things becomes more and more precarious, in a world of marching armies and destruction-dealing skies, is a tough-fibered indifference to heat and cold and comfort and discomfort.

What can we give our children then, that won't be out-

moded, that won't, under some eventuality that we can't
foresee, prove to be a handicap to them? I don't know the
answer to that one. Once I would have said "Ideas and
Ideals." But I grew up in the years after the first World
War, when perpetual peace was supposed to be the easily
attainable ideal. I was trained in that ideal, and I believed
in it with all the sincerity of which I was capable. Perhaps
it is still attainable—but if it is, it will be by some different
means than those I was taught to trust in. I don't want my
child ever to feel as lost in the world as I do right now;
nor do I want to inculcate in him the doctrine of force and
aggression at no matter what sacrifice of the rights of
others.

We can give him a happy childhood to remember, a way
of life that he will be willing to die to protect, if the need
arises. That sounds like a grim and Spartan gift to a little
boy, but it's not as dangerous a gift as the belief in
pacifism and universal well-wishing to which my generation was exposed. I don't want to raise my son to be a
soldier—but if he has to be one, I want him to be a good
and capable one. I want him to know what he's fighting
for—and Freedom and Democracy won't mean a thing to
him, unless they are all tied up with memories of things
that he has loved ever since he can remember—things like
the sound of the river, and the way Kyak lies and dreams
in front of the open fire on a crisp autumn evening, and
the picnics we've held at Smooth Ledge. The name of his
country won't be worth fighting for, unless he can remember from experience that his country is the place, not of
equal opportunity, not of universal suffrage, not of any
of those lofty conceptions so far above a little boy's ability
to comprehend, but the place where he walked with his

father down a woods road one evening and saw a doe and twin fawns; or the place where he came in from playing in the snow and found the kitchen warm and fragrant and his mother making pop-corn balls.

That's all that I can give him; that's all that I dare to try to give him—something that he will love enough to want to preserve it for himself and others against whatever danger may threaten from whatever quarter, and the toughness and courage with which to fight for it. To bring him up untouched by war, insofar as is possible in a world where no one is completely unaffected by war today, is about the only contribution that I know how to make for the future.

Even here I am working in the dark. He won't remember the things I expect him to remember. I don't remember from my own childhood the important things that happened; but I can recall a hole in the ground among the roots of a maple tree that grew in front of our house. It was a small hole, about as big as a pint measure, but there was something about it. It was moist and smelled of earth and water when I lay on my stomach and thrust my four-year-old face into it. It was everything that was mysterious and marvellous to me then, and somehow it still is. I couldn't have explained to anyone then what that little hole in the ground meant to me, and I still can't. But the memory of it makes me wonder what Rufus is carrying around in his head that he can't share, and never will be able to share, but which will affect him. Sometimes I get a clue. Sometimes I see him lay his hand on a rock with a special gesture, or I find a piece of broken china that he has carefully hidden away, or I hear him talking to himself about a rabbit. But since I, myself, loath nothing quite so much as having someone prying into my thoughts and feelings, there is nothing I can do but wonder.

I wonder, too, if all the houses he ever reads about in books will be this house, just as all the houses I read about are in the end the house in which I grew up. It was a low, white, old-fashioned house, and some of the houses in books are huge mansions. But no matter how carefully the author explains the arrangement of the rooms, no matter if he goes to the trouble of drawing a floor plan, when his characters go from the drawing-room down long corridors into the dining hall, in my mind's eye they pass from our little living-room through a door to the left directly into the low square room where we ate. I only hope that Rufus won't spend his life picturing lords and ladies taking baths in the middle of the kitchen.

Of course the biggest problem we encounter in bringing up our children in the woods is their formal education. They do have to go to school. Even if there weren't laws requiring their attendance, even if we were quite capable —which we aren't—of giving them a solid foundation in the three R's, we would still have to send them. One of the most important parts of education is learning to get along with other people, and we just can't supply a society of their peers for them to rub up against. Rufus has seen so few children of his own age that he has no idea how to act with them. He lets them walk all over him, he's so happy to be with them. So we'll shortly have to ship him out to his grandmother's where he will learn among other things, I hope, to stand up for his rights. It's going to be rather a painful experience, so the sooner he gets it over with the better.

I certainly hope the school authorities don't start out by giving him an Intelligence Test before he's learned the ropes. If they do, his I.Q. will be about 50. (I don't believe in I.Q's. anyhow. My own is up in the near-genius group, and nobody knows better than I the abysmal depths of dumbness I can plumb. I just happen to have a very good memory for the sort of things they ask on Intelligence Tests.) But poor Rufus! All the questions dealing with such common things as running water, electric lights, hens, and railroad trains will leave him completely in the dark, and they don't ask how to tell a fox track from a dog track —a difficult thing that he can do easily—or how to use a birch hook, or how to employ a cant dog to its utmost efficiency. I suppose that is what the textbooks dismiss blandly as Feeble-mindedness by Deprivation.

Sally's education has been somewhat peculiar. The first twelve years of her life she lived in Southern Illinois and attended school regularly. Then she came with us for a while. Just as she was getting used to our peculiar mode of life, her mother sent for her to come to Liechtenstein— a small country between Switzerland and Austria, in case you didn't know—and she spent two years there and in the West Indies. She didn't go to school at all, but she was being educated, nonetheless. She learned, among other things, not to giggle when a Count kissed her hand, no matter how much it tickled, how to get through the customs with the least trouble, how to wear clothes, and how to order a meal in German. Then came the War, and Sally came back to us. She goes to school in Upton now, boarding with the Allens, who are among Ralph's oldest friends. She certainly ought to be adaptable. She's had a varied enough experience. I think that she is. When she was fifteen, her birthday party was held in the bar of a hotel in Haiti, closed to the public for the occasion. When she was sixteen, her birthday party was held in Allens' kitchen —open to the public for the occasion, I judge. Apparently everyone in town attended. As far as I can tell, she enjoyed both parties equally.

The school in Upton is a two-room school, and I'd forgotten that such a thing existed. If I'd remembered it, I would have delivered a speech beginning, "Well, in this day and age, with all the fine schools available, no child of mine—"; I would have been wrong. Sally learns as much, if not more, in what is known as the Upstairs Room, where Grades 7 to 10 inclusive sit under one teacher, as she could possibly learn in the biggest and best-equipped school in the country. Her Mr. Flanders is a very good teacher. The excellence of a teacher has nothing at all to do with his background, or the amount of salary he is paid, or anything else except his own personality and inherent bent. A good teacher is born, I am convinced, and his presence would make a good school out of a woodshed.

But Sally gets more than book learning out of going to school in Upton. She gets, for the first time in her life, the sense of being a member in a community. This is a thing more easily acquired in a small town than in a large one, and it's very important to feel, I believe, that you are a member of a whole. There's time enough, later, to be an individual. Later, when she gets out into the world, she will be "different" because she went to a rural school. It will make a good story. It will set her apart. We all want something to set us apart from the rest, to make us interesting. It doesn't have to be very much. I, myself, derive a great deal of satisfaction from the fact that I'm the only person I ever encountered who grew up in a family where they had family prayers every morning after breakfast. My sister and I are probably the only people in the world who grew up in a household where the immutable winter Sunday morning breakfast was oyster stew. Ralph says now that he wishes that on the night of Rufus' birth he'd thought to move me out into his work shop. It couldn't have been any colder than the bedroom was, and Rufus might then have had the distinction of being the last American child to be born in a log cabin. Not that it would have made any difference—unless he wants to run for the Presidency of the United States some time, which God forbid—but it would have been something to talk about. That's what I mean.

So Sally, some night in the future when she's sitting in the Stork Club all done up in gold lamé—also God forbid—can smile reminiscently and say, "You know, I got my education in a rural school in the backwoods of Maine." I think the effect will be very piquant.

Right now, though, she's having too much fun to worry about being different. She belongs to the 4H Club, and goes to church and teaches a Sunday School class of infants, and has a boy-friend. In fact, she has a different one every time we see her, practically, which makes it nice. If she stuck to one I'd probably think I had to worry about its being serious. In short, she's living the usual life of a small town American girl, only she's getting a lot more out of it than most small town girls do. She's been around enough to value it at its true worth.

Probably I ought to be able to draw some valuable deductions and conclusions from my special set of circumstances in regard to the problem of child-raising. I'm sorry to say that I can't. The only conclusion that I've come to is pretty general and pretty trite. All any parent can do is to stagger along as best he is able, and trust to luck.

VI

~~~~

"What Do You Do With All Your Spare Time?"

THIS IS WHAT I CAN'T DECIDE:—WHETHER I DON'T HAVE ANY spare time at all, or whether most of my time is spare time. Spare time, as I used to understand it, was the time left over from doing the necessary, unpleasant things, like correcting Sophomore English themes or washing out silk stockings in the bathroom. It was the time I frittered away on useless, entertaining pursuits, like the movies or contract bridge. Now almost everything I do—except cooking —is fun, and it is also useful. There is no line of demarcation between work and play. It makes it hard to explain what I do with my spare time.

Take the matter of smelting, for example. I happen to be among those who consider going smelting a form of sport. Gerrish agrees with me, but Ralph thinks it's hard work. Therefore, since someone has to stay home and mind the fires, he's the one to do it, while Gerrish and I sally forth into the night.

Smelts are not, unfortunately, the most co-operative of

fish. In this country they're about the size of average sardines—the Norwegian kind—and normally they live deep in the lakes, where you never see them. In the spring, however, after the ice is out of the brooks but before the lakes break up, they run up into the brook mouths to spawn. We stand on the bank with dip nets, dip them out into pails, take them home, and eat them. The hitch—and never let anyone tell you that Nature hands over anything without a string attached—is that they don't start running until after dark, and they're extremely coy about the whole thing. You can never tell what night or what time of night they'll pick to run, so you have to be there every night.

We do our smelting at the Head of the Pond, where the upper river empties into it. That's almost two miles from the house, and of course the road is deep in soggy snow at that time of year, so we have to walk. Right after supper Gerrish and I start out, leaving the dishes for Ralph to do, because if we are going to get there before dark, so that we can collect fuel for a fire to keep warm by, we've got no time to waste. It wouldn't be so bad if we had only ourselves to consider, but we have to take lanterns and buckets and nets—fine-meshed dip nets attached to long handles. The walking is terrible, the kind of walking where you can go along fine for a few steps on an old snowshoe float, and then you sink in suddenly to your knees. It's much harder and more nerve-racking than just plain wallowing to your waist at every step, but if you leave the road and start wading in the soft snow at the side, you find there is a foot of running ice water underlying it, and that your boots aren't quite a foot high. It's a most disconcerting discovery to make.

After a while, though, we get there, coming out of the

gloom of the path through the pines onto the shore of the Pond. The snow has shrunk back from the water, here where the sun can reach, and the ice has receded beneath the insistent attack of the current from the river. We stand on bare gray rocks and look out over an open stretch of fretted gray water to the dirty white line of the ice pack. All the delicate and subtle coloring that is a part of the winter landscape—the faded gold of dead grass heads, the fine red lines of the stems of low bushes, the orange of a fungus on a stump, the lavender of distance—has been drained away by the dusk that lies on the surface of the Pond and the darkness that lurks in the enfolding hills. There is nothing at all to be seen but gray—a hundred different tones of gray, from not-quite-white to almost-black. It's dreary and desolate and lonely, and I love it.

In the middle of the river is a little, low, rocky, scrub-covered island, and that is the best place to establish our base, because from it we can cover both channels. We take our impedimenta across, leaping precariously from rock to rock, and then start collecting a pile of firewood. The fire started, we sit down close to it, shivering a little in the penetrating wind that blows across the ice, and talk for an hour or so, while we wait for full dark. The flames leap up, staining the black water crimson. The river gurgles over a reef of gravel with a soft, incessant chattering sound. Off in the open water toward the ice pack a loon, the first of the year, raises its dismal, wailing hoot. A fox barks back in the woods. Finally we light our lanterns and go down to peer into the water.

If luck is against us we see just the clear water, deceptively shallow in the lantern light, running swiftly over the clean stones. We blow out the lanterns and go back to the fire to wait a while, not really expecting that things will be different in half an hour, but because, since we're there, we might as well make sure that tonight is not the night. Our initial opinion that there's no sense in hanging around usually proves to have been correct, so we leave our paraphernalia under a bush and go home. That's one nice thing about living in the woods. You can leave anything anywhere, for any length of time, and be sure of finding it when you come back to it.

But if luck is with us we see the smelts running up against the current, millions and millions of them, like a long black snake, and the fun begins. We scoop frantically, and the fish that were black in the water turn to living silver as we lift them out, struggling in the nets. Water streams from them like silver fire in the unsteady light of the lanterns, and we call back and forth to each other, "Come over here! There's millions of them—" or "How're you doing over there?" We get excited and careless, and misjudge the depth of the water, so that our boots are soon full. But it doesn't make any difference. The pails are filling, too, and the smelts are running thicker than ever. Gerrish freezes suddenly, like a dog going into a point. "Gosh, I think I heard a salmon jump! Let's come over here early tomorrow night and bring our rods." I agree. Suddenly I don't see how I can wait until even tomorrow to feel a three-pound salmon fighting on the other end of a line.

The pails are full. We put out the fire, leave the nets and one of the lanterns, and start home. It is inky black in the woods, and sooner or later, usually sooner, whichever is carrying the remaining lantern falls down and breaks the chimney. Then we flounder around an interminable time, running into trees, falling down and spilling the smelts, gathering them up by the light of matches—until the matches give out—and listening to the loons laugh with a laughter that suddenly has an extremely personal note to it. Eventually, we see the lights of home, and stagger in, exhausted.

Why is this so much fun? I don't know. It just is, if you happen to like it. Even if you don't, it's worth while to go smelting. After the winter's diet, the first fresh fish of the year taste wonderful. Gerrish and Ralph clean them for me, cutting the heads off and slitting the bellies, and I dip them in a thin batter and fry them in deep fat until they're brown and crisp. They look like French-fried potatoes, and served with lemon juice or tartar sauce, taste like manna. We have them every day during the brief fortnight they are running.

The very last time that we go, Gerrish and I always bring home twenty or thirty live ones in a pail of water. These we dump into the wangan spring hole as we go by, to save as bait when we go trolling at B Pond. They'll live there indefinitely, I guess. I've never had a chance to find out. Most of them escape down the brook before very long.

Along about smelting time is usually sugaring-off time, too, and this I don't particularly relish. I like the new maple syrup all right, and I don't have to do any of the work. Ralph and Gerrish tap the trees, going back into the woods across the road on snowshoes, and carrying the pails and spiles by the armload. It takes them about all one morning to get the tapping done. Then one or the other of them goes out morning and evening with two buckets on a shoulder yoke, and brings in the sap. In good years we make enough syrup to last us through the whole twelve months. It's good syrup, too—heavy in weight and delicate in flavor.

Good sap weather is clear weather in which the temperature during the day rises to above fifty and drops well below freezing at night. The sap is supposed to be drawn by the warmth and sun up into the branches daily, and driven by the cold back into the roots at dark. I say *supposed,* because this is the old country-man's explanation of it, and I've gone through life discovering that, no matter how reasonable these homely bits of scientific data sound, often they are completely wrong, and the real explanation is something involved and improbable. That may not be the case here. I don't know anything about it. I'm just protecting myself.

Our equipment is mostly homemade. Some of the spiles are just wooden spouts that Gerrish and Ralph have whittled out by hand. They are driven into the holes bored into the south side of the tree trunks, and the sap drips through them into the pails which are hung beneath. These are simply No. 10 tin cans in which we have bought fruit or vegetables, with covers roughly fitted to them to keep out rain and snow. The rain and snow doesn't do any harm, but it makes that much more water to evaporate before we have syrup. Our evaporating pans are a series of large shallow cookie pans, which we put on the kitchen stove top. They're the reason why I don't like the sugaring-off season. Every time I want to put a stick of wood in the stove, or toast a slice of bread, or heat a flat iron, or fry an egg, I have to move one of those damn syrup pans. If I hang up a pair of mittens over the stove to dry, the chances are that sooner or later they'll fall into a syrup pan.

Briefly, the whole thing is a nuisance, and before we're through, I wish to Heaven I'd never heard of maple syrup.

It's nice to eat, though, on griddle cakes, for supper. Sometimes we boil it down a little more, beyond the aproning consistency which is the standard weight for syrup—syrup is said to apron when it runs off the side of a spoon in a solid sheet, or apron, instead of in rivulets—and pour it hot onto dishes of snow. It congeals as it cools to a thick gumminess, and is wonderful to chew on. It's fun to give it to Kyak for he loves its sweetness so, but at the same time gets his jaws all stuck up, to our great amusement. This over-cooked syrup makes a marvellous sauce for vanilla ice-cream, too. A common country dessert that we sometimes have is fresh raised doughnuts and hot, new syrup. Each member of the family has a cereal dish of syrup, and dips the doughnut into it as he eats. This is not very elegant, but it's very good. Lots of people have hot baking-powder biscuit with butter and new syrup for breakfast, during the syrup season, instead of the more conventional griddle cakes and syrup. Probably this is good, too. I wouldn't know. I have trouble enough getting breakfast on the table without going into hot baking-powder biscuits.

I know one man who drinks a full cup of new syrup every night before he goes to bed, for its medicinal properties. He says it accomplishes the same thing as sulphur and molasses, but a lot more pleasantly. That may be so. I know that all over the countryside here, woodsmen and farmers and trappers drink maple sap out of the pails at the trees. They seem to have a craving for it, which isn't accounted for by its taste. It hasn't much more taste than spring water; it has only what I can best describe as a green feeling in the mouth. I believe, therefore, that it is a natural spring tonic which supplies minerals or vitamins or some other elements that have been lacking in ordinary country winter diet. I can't see, otherwise, why men who usually drink no more than four or five glasses of water a day suddenly take to drinking two or three quarts of maple sap.

To complicate matters in the spring, our semi-annual moving day rolls around. My mother always says that two movings are as good as a fire, when it comes to eliminating unnecessary possessions, and she's about right. All the things that have been collecting in the winter house against a sudden unforeseen need—the leaky gum-boots, the nests of cardboard boxes, the crop ends of boards, the links of chain, and the broken toys—I suddenly see in their true colors, and take them down to the dump. Of course Ralph and Gerrish and Rufus trail me like a pack of hounds and salvage most of the trash, uttering outraged cries of horror at my vandalism, but I manage to accomplish a little thinning out. To take care of the remaining worthless treasures—and of what use is a felt hat with four holes in the crown and no brim to speak of, or a piece of rubber belting six inches square?—I have instituted in the kitchen what is known as the culch corner. This is a sort of exterritorial ground for junk. Anything that's been put in the culch corner—a wide corner shelf with a box on it—I can't touch, much as my fingers may itch to pitch it out. There's everything there—old bolts, old wrought-iron cut nails, bits of unrelated metal, old wool, wiping rags, coffee cans, broken hack saw blades, a divorced work glove or two, parts of a dog team harness, lengths of fish line, a coil or two of synthetic gut leaders (known woodswise as "sympathetic gut"), and some odd wooden wedges. It's a mess, but it's better to have this one big mess in the corner of the kitchen than a patina of messiness spread all over the house. I didn't, by the way, name the culch corner. Culch is the New England word for that clutter of partly worn out or obsolete objects that always gathers, like moss, on a non-rolling household. I don't know who first used the term culch corner, but it stuck. Now we all call it that.

It's nice to be down in the summer house again. There's more space to move around in, and the river is nearer and louder. We wake up in the night and hear it, and for a night or two mistake it for the sound of wind and rain. But real rain is different. It starts slowly, with individual drops striking the roof only three feet over our heads, in an almost ceremonial roulade. Then it comes faster and faster, with the full symphonic orchestration of rising wind in the trees and the river's roar. The walls of the summer house are not ceiled like those of the winter house, and the storm seems much nearer to us when we're living down there. Paradoxically, this makes us feel that much warmer, and safer, and more protected.

There's always one thing I forget on moving day. We manage to shift all the favorite chairs, and the lamps, and the radio, and the typewriters, and footstools, and personal belongings, and ash trays. But come bed-time, Ralph always says, "Where's my sleeping hat?" He thinks his head gets cold at night without it, although he goes around bareheaded all day. It's always in the same place—hanging on the head of the bed in the winter house bedroom. Sometime I'm going to establish a record and remember it—unless he establishes the same record first.

As spring moves into summer, the berries start getting

ripe. All through the woods, wherever there is enough of a clearing to let the sun in, acres and acres of raspberries and blueberries come into fruit. I never can quite believe that this dour and grudging country has suddenly suffered such a complete reversal of form. This princely generosity seems just too good to be true. I feel we must go berrying right now, right this minute, before all the berries vanish again.

Ralph loathes picking berries. I used to try to sell him on the idea that since for once we were getting something for free, it was his *duty*— But my wifely pep-talks never raised his enthusiasm above a Laodicean luke-warmness, which started cooling the first time he tripped and stretched his six-feet-two in a bramble patch, and from then on declined rapidly to absolute zero. So I gave up. He just isn't the type. Fortunately, Gerrish is the type.

Gerrish always refers to me as She, just as he always refers to Ralph as The Boss. He'll say to Ralph, "She claims She wants to go ras'berryin' t'morrer mornin', so if you ain't got nothin' special in mind—"

Ralph never has. He's only too thankful that I don't try to enlist him.

To get to the best raspberry patch, we have to take a boat and row about a mile across the Pond to where the dead stub of an old "punkin" pine stands on a ridge, dwarfing with its towering height the by no means insignificant growth along the shore. From the boat, the shore line is an unbroken wall of forest, but we know that if we land near a maple a little to the left of the stub, and scrambled up a steep, spruce-covered slope to the foot of the pumpkin pine, we'll come out into an old, overgrown birch cutting. Here the raspberries grow on tall rank canes among the rocks and fallen trees and rotten birch tops and around clumps of young spruce and fir. It is a quiet place, sheltered from the wind, and when we arrive there early in the morning, it is wet with dew and laced with long shadows from the surrounding forest. It is cool and full of the stir of birds and the scoldings of red squirrels and little striped chipmunks. That's why we always go there early. Later, when the sun is high, the place is like a furnace, breathless and so hot that even the birds and squirrels retire to the shade of the woods. It is silent then, and dead, except for the hum of insects; but the heat and stillness account for the size and quality of the berries. If you stand still and listen, you can almost hear them grow, swelling and stretching as the rich red juice fills them.

The minute we get into the clearing, I find that I am alone. Gerrish has vanished. I hear a dry stick snap somewhere, but the bushes are so high I can't see him. It would be useless to call. He wouldn't answer. Like me, when he goes berrying, he wants to berry, not stand around doing what he calls "jawrin'." When his pail is full, he'll whistle and I'll go down and meet him at the boat. My pail will lack a half an inch of being full. Gerrish takes a proper pride in being the best and fastest picker he ever saw, and there's nothing I can do about it, try as I will.

The raspberries hang on the underside of the canes, glowing like jewels against the green of the leaves. They are dead ripe, and will drop off at the lightest touch. Raspberries are the most care-demanding of all berries to pick. They mash easily, so they must be handled lightly. Even setting the pail down too often and too hard will result in a shapeless mush in the bottom. That's why Gerrish and

I suspend our pails from our belts; thus we'll have both hands free to pick and avoid constant jarring of the berries. The canes have to be lifted delicately. It's infuriating to raise one and have all the fruit tumble off to be lost among the rocks and debris on the ground.

I don't know where Gerrish goes after he shakes me. I keep away from the south side of the cutting. That is, by tacit consent, his stamping ground. I don't even know what's over there. I have my own beat to patrol, working slowly up a vague remnant of hauling road near the middle of the clearing to the top of the ridge, and coming back down along the edge of the woods on the north side. At the top of the loop the earth is thin and shallow and the bushes aren't very big or productive, but I always go there just the same. There is an outcropping of ledge there, gray and weathered and warm with sun under the hand. I love stone. I won't try to explain why, because I don't know. But everybody loves the feel and quality and essence of some material. It may be leather, or wood, or fine porcelain. It may be satin or bronze or tweed. Whatever it is, there is almost a spiritual kinship between that substance and that person. That's the way I feel about stone, and that's why I always go up to the top of the raspberry patch.

We're not the only ones that pick berries. The birds eat them, of course, and the foxes. Bears love them. One day I followed in the path of a bear down my north side of the cut. I could see by the bent bushes where he'd been ambling happily along, stripping the canes as he went, minding his own business and thinking his own thoughts, even as I was doing. Suddenly I came to a place that looked as though a tornado had hit it. The undergrowth was all flat-

tened out, the ground was torn up, and a couple of sap-
lings were broken off. Right smack in the middle of the
devastation, dangling from a low branch, was what was
left of a big hornets' nest, gutted and destroyed by one
furious sweep of a huge paw. The poor old cuss had evidently been attacked by a squadron of dive bombers before he knew what it was all about. I could see where he
had started for the Pond. He certainly hadn't stood on the
order of his going either. Every jump must have been ten
feet long. I'd like to have seen him, clearing rocks and
bushes and fallen trees like a bird on the wing. There, but
for the Grace of God, might have gone Louise Rich. Well,
better him than me. I have only two legs, and it would
have broken my heart to have had to jettison a pail half
full of raspberries.

On the way back across the Pond, I always think about
the delicious jam and preserves I'm going to make out of
our twelve or fifteen quarts of berries. This is purely
mental exercise, but it makes me feel smug and thrifty, and
I might as well enjoy the feeling while I can. In our family
everybody, even the dog, will eat raspberries until their
eyes pop, so there aren't ever enough left after twenty-four
hours to do anything fancy with. I do, though, usually manage to squeeze out a couple of pies, making a special effort to have the crust flaky and sprinkling flour over the
berries lightly before baking to prevent the juices all
stewing out. Too much flour is bad. It takes all the juice
up. With the remnants of crust I make turn-overs for be-
tween-meal snacks. If the weather is sultry and the berries
start to mold, I stew them up with sugar for supper-sauce,
to be eaten with cake or cookies. Then if there are still
some left, I make jam, to be put away against the winter.

There is really only one dessert to be made out of raspberries, when there aren't enough to go around. This is a sort of cooked up-side-down shortcake. In the bottom of a cake pan I melt a little butter, add about a half a cup of sugar, and a cup or two of raspberries—whatever I have left after saving out a cupful. Then I mix up a good short biscuit dough, using two cups of flour, four teaspoons of baking powder, a generous third of a cup of shortening and a half a cup of milk. This I roll out about a half an inch thick, cover with the raspberries I've held out and some more sugar, roll up into a jelly roll, and slice into inch slices, which I put cut-side-down in the pan. I bake in a hot oven and serve hot with milk or cream and the hot cooked berries from the bottom of the pan. It's nothing, really, to write home about, but it accomplishes its purpose, which is to keep the family from hollering too loudly and long about the inferior desserts that are being handed out to them recently.

Blueberries are more common and therefore much less highly esteemed than raspberries. We don't have to go on any boat trips to get plenty of blueberries. They grow all along the Carry Road, and in a half an hour I can pick enough for a couple of pies, some blueberry muffins, and a little spiced blueberry jam. The only trick about pies is to add a little salt and lemon juice to the berries to give them zip. Blueberries are apt to be flat. The only trick about blueberry muffins is to roll the berries in flour so they won't sink in a sodden mass to the bottom of the batter. Blueberry jam is easy to make. Add sugar to the blueberries, pound for pound, and boil until the mixture starts to thicken. Then add cinnamon, nutmeg, and allspice—a pinch of each to the pound—and pour into glasses.

It jellies readily—I think there must be a lot of natural pectin in blueberries—and is good with hot or cold roasts and fowl.

There are plenty of other things to do, too, to fill in spare time. Before the ice goes out all the boats and the canoe have to be overhauled and painted. Usually one or more of the boats has sprung a leak somewhere and we have to find out just where and repair it. Usually, too, someone during the preceding season—probably I—has left a boat improperly secured on a windward shore, and it has chafed badly on the rocks. This rough spot has to be sandpapered smooth and oiled before the painting can begin. Any broken thwarts and gunwales have to be mended, and missing irons replaced and oarlocks repaired. Anchor ropes have to be examined for frayed places, and Ralph's trick anchor control gadgets have to be gone over to see that they are in working order. These rigs, which he invented and made himself, are very clever The rope feeds over a pulley wheel in a bracket bolted on the bow and back through a special casting attached to the rower's seat, which allows the rope to be locked any where by a cam lever. If you're handling a boat alone in a current, jockeying for the right fly-casting position, it's a great advantage to be able to drop your anchor without leaving the seat or missing a stroke. It's also a great advantage, when you have somehow become involved with a six-pound salmon who is either going to break your rod or run your line all out unless you do something and do it fast, to be able to up-anchor without putting your rod down.

I like to paint boats. Ours are all painted the same, like our houses, which are a soft Nile green with buff doors and window sashes. Our boats are green outside and buff inside. The basic principle—to put on several thin coats instead of one thick coat—applies to boats as well as to any other paint job, and you have to be careful not to let drops form along the edges of the strakes. But after a while you can paint automatically and let your mind wander where it will. It's sunny and sheltered down on the boat float, and it's a nice place to be in the early spring. The birches along the shore of the Pond are beginning to show the faint and tender green that is so different from the black-green of the conifers, and the maples are blossoming red. The water, in the patches where the ice has gone out, is a deep indigo blue, and the ice pack in the distance is a line of snowy white. The wind smells of spring.

Ralph spends the before-break-up period, which is also the period when the road is hub deep in mud and therefore impassable for anything but foot traffic, in overhauling the cars. This I won't attempt to go into. I don't know anything about it, except that it involves lying in mud and dirt under the cars, and coming into the house with simply filthy hands, and moving my potatoes to the back of the stove, where they stop boiling, so that some motor part or can of oil can have the place of honor. It also involves dozens of trial runs around the loop of the driveway, and a great deal of breathless listening to what sounds, to my untutored ear, like a perfect performance, and then a flood of language and another taking down of the motor to locate the seat of a murmur that may some day develop into a bad chest cough. It's a very trying period for everyone except Rufus, who crawls under the cars right along with his father, and sticks his nose into gudgeon grease, and gets his clothes plastered with mud and oil, and has a wonderful time.

About two years ago Gerrish and I took up fly tying. There were several reasons for this. We thought it would be nice to have a hobby for our evenings, for one thing. For another, flies are expensive to buy if you fish as much as we do. We're always losing flies, or having them ruined by a big fish, and it's always the fifty-cent types that meet with grief. It runs into money in the course of a season. Besides that, it was getting embarrassing for us to have to look respectful when city sports said, "Oh, of course I tie all my own flies!" as though that were a feat beyond such inept souls as we. So we took up fly tying.

I, myself, didn't intend to become a slave to the habit. I thought I'd just dabble in it, but it didn't work out that way. We were too proud to ask anyone how to go about tying flies, so we got ourselves a book of instructions and a batch of feathers and set out to teach ourselves. Gerrish gave me fair warning before we started that he couldn't learn things from books. He had to be shown; but if he could just see someone actually *do* a thing once, then he could do it all right the next time. I can follow printed directions fairly well, so the idea was that I would follow the book and Gerrish would follow me, and in that way we'd both learn. We both did, but what started out as a hobby became almost an obsession, especially with Gerrish. He's a rabid fly tyer now, and I might add, a very good one. He makes a much better fly than I do, for all that his hands are bigger and look clumsier than mine. The heads of his flies are small and smooth, while mine sometimes get beyond me and turn out large and rough. That's where the amateur betrays himself.

We thought at first that we'd be satisfied if we could make a few streamers and some of the simpler stock patterns of wet flies. We weren't going into anything complicated. We weren't even going to consider tying dry flies. We knew our own limitations. Neither of us was going to invest a lot of money in equipment. Ralph had a small vise he'd lend us, and I had nail scissors and some odds and ends of embroidery silk and yarn for bodies. There was plenty of black thread around the house, and some silver and gold string left over from Christmas wrappings, and Ralph had some beeswax in his sailmaker's outfit. He also had shellac, and we could probably find plenty of feathers and fur around the woods. All we'd have to buy was two or three dozen hooks and maybe a few feathers not indigenous to this soil, such as jungle cocks for eyes. We wouldn't have to spend more than fifty cents, all told. That's what we thought, at first.

That state of mind lasted about a month. During that month we saw everything in the light of possible fly-tying material. We brought home dead birds, and the tails of deceased flying squirrels we found, and quills out of other people's feather dusters. We clipped stiff fur from Kyak to make buck tails, and went hunting with my .22 revolver for red squirrels. (We never managed to get one.) We hounded chance acquaintances from Upton to bring us in hen feathers and hackle feathers from roosters the next time they came. And we tied up enough Plymouth Rock streamers to last us a lifetime. We had plenty of Plymouth Rock feathers, you see. Then we faced the truth. The bug had got us. We'd have to buy some more equipment—not very much, of course; just a few necessary things. After all, this was partly an economy measure. We'd just spend a dollar or two.

Last spring our feather bill was over fifteen dollars. We'd already spent five or six dollars on special scissors, a pair of hackle pliers, a bottle of head varnish, a special wax preparation, and a box of assorted hooks. Heaven knows what our bill would have been if some friends hadn't presented us with a fly-tying vise. That's what fly tying can do to you. It can make you lose all sense of proportion. We even lost our pride. When a professional fly tyer, Frank Walker, of Oxford, Maine, came to stay at Millers' that summer and offered to show us a few tricks of the trade, we forgot all about our lofty ideas of independence, and spent all one Sunday afternoon with him. He's an old man, and he's tied thousands of flies, over the course of years. He's found short cuts and practical methods that the books never dreamed of, and that it would have taken us twenty years to dope out for ourselves. And even if I never intended to tie a fly in my life, I would have enjoyed watching him work. It was really something to see him tie a Black Gnat on a No. 14 hook, with his big hands, a little stiff from rheumatism, moving slowly and delicately and surely around the almost invisible little object in the vise. Great skill and competence in any line is always impressive.

It's hard to tell exactly where the great fascination of tying flies lies. Of course, there is the satisfaction in creative work. It's fun to take a pile of raw materials and make something out of them. The more demanding the work, the greater is the satisfaction. It's fun to finish shellacking the head of a fly, hold it up, and be able to think,

"There! I'll bet nobody could tell that from a bought fly!" You feel so pleased with yourself.

But that's only the beginning. People are easy to fool. The real test comes when you try the fly out on a fish. If you can catch a fish on a fly you tied yourself, then you can commence to regard yourself as a fly tyer. Still, there are always a few fool fish about that will rise to anything, so it's better to get several strikes on the fly before you indulge in too much own-back patting. But that isn't the end, either. Pretty soon you start regarding the copying of the proven, standard patterns as mere tyro's work. Anybody can copy a fly, you think. Most people know the Yellow May is good at this time of year in these waters. So there's nothing remarkable about catching a good fish on a Yellow May, no matter who tied it. Now if YOU could think up a new pattern that would catch fish, that would really be something.

So you start watching the fish. Tonight they're rising to some silvery gray little bugs that are flying up the river. If you could tie a fly that looked something like that, with perhaps a touch of yellow in the body— You reel in and go home. By working fast, you can get it done in time to try it out before dark. Perhaps it won't catch fish. All right; maybe if you used a little tinsel in the tail— There's no end to it, as you can see. And there's no feeling quite like the lift you get when eventually you hit on the right combination, and a walloping big trout comes surging up out of the shadows and grabs your very own fly, the fly you conceived and executed all by yourself.

One of the things that always surprises people who visit us, anticipating, prepared for, or resigned to—according to their various natures—a period of total quiet, is the number of excursions and alarums which preclude any chance of monotony. Something is always cropping up, and you never know when you get up in the morning what will have happened before you go to bed at night. It may be nothing more momentous than a visit from the game or the fire warden, but they always have something of interest to offer.

Our fire warden lives with his wife and dog on Pine Island at the upper end of the Narrows between the two Richardson Lakes, and he and Ralph are kindred souls. They both collect junk. Fortunately, where Ralph collects car motors, Amby Hines collects motor boat parts, so they don't chisel in on each other's rackets. I haven't been up at Pine Island lately, but I gather that Amby is running into the same trouble that Ralph is—not enough space to store his loot and a wife that objects to having to clamber over a pile of cold metal when she gets out of bed in the morning. She won't let him make a junk pile out of her boudoir. (I won't let Ralph, either, but he does, just the same.) Amby is really in a worse position than Ralph. The Island isn't very big, and he's used up about all the available space. He's loath to start a boat motor dump on the mainland. "They'll rob 'em off me," he explains matter-of-factly.

The last time he was down, he was having trouble with his dog, a young terrier, who had not yet encountered a porcupine. Amby thought, quite rightly, that the sooner the pup got that over with and learned better, the happier they'd all be; but there weren't any porcupines on the Island. However, while patrolling his beat down the Lower Richardson, he stopped in at Spirit Island, where a group of boys were camping, and found that they'd caught a porcupine and had it in a box. It is against the law to confine a wild animal without official permission, although ordinarily Amby wouldn't have bothered about a porcupine, because he knows that whenever it got ready a porcupine could gnaw its way in half an hour out of any box ever made. This time, however, he needed it himself, so he confiscated it and took it home in a water pail.

When he got to the Island he turned it loose and called his dog. Porcupines are slow and clumsy, but nevertheless it managed to scramble up a tall pine before the dog caught up with it, which is probably just as well for the dog. This was about four o'clock in the afternoon, and the dog sat at the foot of the tree and howled until half past three the next morning, ignoring all commands to come into the house and forget it, and completely shattering any ideas of sleep that the Hineses might have been entertaining. At half past three the dog called it a day and retired under the porch to rest. As soon as the coast was clear, the porcupine came down, swam to the mainland, and vanished. Amby was discouraged when he stopped at our house. He had to start his porcupine hunt all over again, and this time he wasn't going to be lucky enough to find one all crated for him.

A fire warden has to work hard. He has an area to patrol, and he has to see that no one builds a fire within that area, except at State-designated camp grounds. You just can't go into the woods and camp anywhere, for obvious reasons of safety. Then if there is a lumbering operation going on, he has to manage to show up in the slashes, unheralded and ghost-like, often enough to deter the men from smoking in the woods. This involves a lot of walking in the course of a week, and lots of patrolling around the lakes in a kicker boat. If a forest fire starts in his territory, he has to organize the fighters, and if it's in someone else's territory, he has to go over there and help. He has to co-operate with the game warden in seeing that the game laws are observed, although naturally this is a reciprocal arrangement, and he can call on the game warden for help whenever he needs it. If someone gets lost, they both have to join the search, along with whatever talent they can scrape up around the countryside. But the really rush period in a fire warden's life comes when the State does what is colloquially known as "slap a band on the woods."

The band is slapped on whenever there is a protracted drought, and the woods are consequently tinder-dry. Actually the Governor proclaims that the woods are closed to hunters, fishermen, campers, and any other unauthorized persons; in other words, it *bans* use of the forest areas, and forbids building of fires or smoking by anyone whatsoever. The fire warden is like a cat on a hot griddle when a "band" is on. He has to be everywhere at once, telling people to leave the woods immediately, and riding herd on legitimate occupants like us, who belong there, and on himself. Neither he nor we want a forest fire—he, because it's his business not to have one, and we because we naturally don't want to burn up. But you'd be surprised how easy it is, if you are an habitual smoker, suddenly to find yourself in the middle of a dangerous area with a half-smoked cigarette in your hand and no recollection at all of having lighted it. We just stop carrying smoking materials when a "band" is on, and so does the warden. If you haven't got them, you can't smoke them. The result is that every now and then he appears at our door with the announcement, "My tongue's hanging out for a smoke. Mind if I bum a cigarette and come inside and smoke it?" It's all right to smoke in the house during a "band."

Our game warden, in spite of the fact that he is a respectable married man with four children—including a pair of twins—looks like the scenario writer's dream of the perfect Northwestern Mountie. He wears his uniform with style—he's got the right build for a uniform, with wide shoulders and slim hips—and he walks with a sort of cat-footed swagger. His face is lean and handsome and dark, and he has a tough and reckless air about him. I guess he is tough, if he wants to be. Fortunately, we keep on excellent terms with him, simply by observing the game laws. I don't want to sound holy and smug about this, but we do make a point of not breaking them, because we believe in them. In fact we believe some of them are not rigid enough. They are necessary laws and if we weren't convinced that this is so, we'd probably be the worst poachers in the county.

We always ask the game warden how business is, and often he has an unusual arrest to tell us about. He tells a story well. A recent adventure happened over on the other side of his territory. He was up on a mountain patrolling a closed brook when he came on a boy fishing with his pockets crammed with short trout, about twenty of them. Naturally, he took the offender into custody and led him down the mountain to where his car was parked by the road. But he saw no reason why he should carry the four or five pounds of illegal fish over the rough trail. Let the guilty party do it. The guilty party had other ideas, however, and managed to put them into effect. By the time they had reached the road, he had surreptitiously got rid of the evidence, dropping the little fish quietly at intervals along the trail. So there was our Mr. Leon Wilson with a prisoner, but with no evidence and no case. He was pretty mad about the whole thing.

But not for long. Presently the boy's father came out of the woods, having apparently been just behind them all the way down, all ignorant of his son's arrest. He didn't notice the bad company his son was keeping. (By most people around here, a game warden is generally considered about the worst company to be found in.) "Hey, Bud," he hailed. "You must have a hole in your pocket. I been picking up your fish along the trail for the last couple of miles!" He had the missing illegal fish in his creel.

Ho-hum! Possession is all that needs to be proved against you, according to the law. It didn't make any difference to Leon whom he pinched. Both of them knew better.

We used to set our guests to work helping pull porcupine quills out of the dogs. This was when we had five dogs, and ideas about a dog team. They didn't work out. In the first place, it cost more to feed five huskies than to feed the whole Rich tribe. In the second place, we were always in hot water with those darn dogs. Either they'd get loose and chase game, or else they'd scare people going along the road—the dogs were perfectly harmless, but some people are timid—or they'd tear the wash off the line and chew it up. And one or the other of them was always coming in full of porcupine quills. They always chose the most inconvenient times for these forays into the sporting life, and you can't postpone a de-quilling operation. The longer you wait, the deeper the quills work in, until you can't get them out at all. This won't necessarily prove fatal, as often they fester and eventually come out by themselves, after a week or so. But if you love your dog—and we loved each and every one of that wolf pack of ours—you can't stand seeing him suffer. So we've delayed dinner three hours on occasion, to pull quills. We've even arisen at one o'clock in the morning and worked until daylight, with me sitting on a dog's head in my nightgown, while Ralph wielded the plyers.

We don't have that trouble any more. Thor we had to shoot, because he tried to swallow a porcupine. Cookie, the dearest and smartest dog that ever lived, was struck by lightning. Metak and Mukluk we finally had to give away. It doesn't take long to write those four lines, but every word of them represents heartbreak. We loved the big bums, even if they did keep us in a continuous turmoil. Now we only have Kyak, the art dog, left. Kyak's stupidity doesn't extend to sticking his own neck out. He ran afoul of a porcupine just once, when he was very young. A great many dogs never learn to leave them alone, but will go through the agonizing experience of quills weekly until the day of their death. Not so Kyak. He'll look, but he's never touched one since that long ago disaster.

I have referred to the dogs and a dog team and I suppose I'd better clear up the matter once and for all. We thought at one time it would be a good idea to have a dog team. In this country the cars go out of use after the deep snows come, there being no possible way of keeping the road open, and that means that every pound of mail and food and material must either be carried on someone's back, or dragged on a hand sled, the two long, hilly miles from Middle Dam to here. And that's no fun. It's really mysterious how a reasonable load of groceries can multiply its weight so enormously in the time it takes to walk it two miles.

The second winter that we lived here, in the middle of February—a very well chosen time, since we were just about fed to the teeth with lugging things on our backs— Stumpy Crocker and Norman Vaughn came in to see us, and they came from below South Arm by dog team. Norman had been a dog driver on Admiral Byrd's first Antarctic Expedition, and he was full of enthusiasm for this particular mode of travel. His team consisted of nine dogs. I had always been led to suppose that huskies were vicious brutes, but these nine weren't. They were sweet. Of course, they periodically fought terribly among themselves, but as far as humans were concerned, they were a bunch of softies. Ralph and I fell in love with every last one of them. Our infatuation blinded us to the fact that for three days' stay, Norman brought in over a hundred pounds of food just for the dogs, and we fell easy victims to the notion that a dog team was just what we needed and wanted most of anything in the world. This notion was clinched after Norman had ridden us up to Middle a couple of times. It was marvellous just to sit and be whisked up Wangan Hill. Besides, we didn't really need nine dogs, Norman assured us. Five would be plenty.

So when, the next spring, Stumpy offered us a husky pup, offspring of one of Norman's team, we accepted with alacrity. That was Cookie. From the same source the Millers acquired another husky, Karlok—he was an albino, and one of the most beautiful dogs I have ever seen—so what could be more natural than a match between them when they grew up? The final result was a litter of four pups, of which Kyak was one. And there was our dog team in embryo. Nothing could have been simpler.

The pups grew. Norman had told us that when they were about half grown was the time to start training them; so when they were five or six months old, we put them in harness. He had said nothing, though, about the desirability of having an experienced dog with them to show them the ropes. So we just hitched them up and told them to mush. Cookie looked at us in amazement. This was a new game, and one she wasn't sure she liked. Kyak lay down on his back and went limp, his legs like boiled macaroni. Nothing we could do would get him onto his feet. Every time we stood him up he just collapsed. Metak and Richard just stood and shivered. Only Mukluk got the idea, and he very soon became bored with pulling not only the light sled we had, but all his relations as well. He finally sat down and looked disgusted, and I didn't blame him.

We might have given up the idea then if Stumpy hadn't made a fevered telephone call from Fitchburg, where he lives. Would we give one of his dogs a home? (He was a victim of the dog team obsession at the time, too.) We wanted to know, naturally, what was the matter with the dog. People don't give valuable dogs away without any reason. It seemed that nothing was the matter with the dog except boyish high spirits. He was a wonderful dog—gentle, obedient, well-trained to harness. The only trouble was that he was a little too powerful. He'd run away with Stumpy's young son Weyman, and had frightened some saddle horses on a back road. Unfortunately the saddle horses were complete with riders, and, even more unfortunate, one of the riders was Stumpy's boss, who didn't appreciate the situation at all. Hell was about to pop unless something was done about Thor. Now we had no saddle horses up our way, so— We'd really stopped listening at the "well-trained to harness" clause. Here was the answer. Thor could be a sort of tutor to the other dogs. We said, "Yes." It seemed evident that Providence wanted us to have a dog team. No sooner did a problem arise than the solution appeared right behind it.

Thor arrived and we immediately renamed him the Hound of the Baskervilles. He was almost as big as a Shetland pony, and had a head like a basket ball. He didn't have teeth. He had fangs. He looked horrible, and he was the biggest bowl of mush I ever saw. He thought he was a lap dog, and tried to sit in my lap whenever I sat down. I just haven't got enough lap for that, so he finally compromised by sitting beside me by the hour with that huge head on my knees, gazing adoringly into my face. My legs would grow numb under the weight, and consciousness of all my shortcomings would rise to the surface under that worshipful regard. Nobody could be that wonderful, me least of all. It was very embarrassing for me. I could have stood it, though, if Thor had been a good teacher. He wasn't. He was perfectly willing to work, and the others were willing to let him. Our dog team, obviously, was going to consist of Thor and Mukluk. Kyak, instead of being shamed by this example of usefulness, just grew limper and limper. It got so that whenever he saw one of us with a harness in hand, he fainted. The dog team, as such, was getting no place fast.

On top of this, it was costing more to feed the dogs than to feed us, and we were continually deluged with complaints by a lot of damn fools about keeping dangerous animals—definitely untrue. My Monday laundry was periodically ripped from the line and torn up, and the only way to insure keeping a whole pair of shoes in the house was to hang them by the laces from the ceiling beams, where the dogs couldn't reach them. In short, we had nothing but trouble and expense in connection with those darn dogs. We were told by experts that we'd never have a dog team unless we stopped making pets of the dogs. It was all wrong to feed them twice a day and let them have the run of the house. Dogs won't work unless they are half starved and kept tied up outside, away from human association. Working dogs aren't pets; they are slaves and should be treated as such. Well! That doesn't go for us. Neither Ralph nor I could ever treat any dog like that—certainly not our own dear dogs that we loved. So we gave up the dog team idea. But we still had the dogs.

Then one by one, things began to happen to them, and, viewed cosmically, it was probably just as well, much as it hurt at the time. After every disaster I said my little say—"Here we had six dogs, and five of them were swell. We're going to end by being left with the only lemon in the bunch, just you wait and see." And so we were. Oh, well, Kyak isn't much of a dog; but he suits us. He's nice with Rufus, and we love him dearly. And that's all we want.

Lots of things crop up to entertain us and our guests. There was the time for instance that we enlivened my sister Alice's visit with a fox hunt. Don't be thinking of red coats and Irish hunters, because it wasn't like that at all. We wore our night clothes and raincoats and rode in a Model T, our sole weapon was a landing net, and while Alice and I strove to establish the right note by shouting "View halloo" and "Yoicks" at intervals, Ralph rather ruined the effect with his insistence upon bellowing in moments of stress, "There goes the little son of a bitch!"

You see, he'd gone up to Middle Dam late to mail an important letter, and he'd got talking. By the time he arrived back home, Alice and I had gone to bed. He came busting into the house with the news that at the foot of Birch Hill he'd seen, gamboling in the glow of his headlights, a whole litter of fox pups, apparently strayed from their den while their mother was away, and quite evidently having a time for themselves. In fact, he'd had to stop the car to keep from running over them, and when he got out to look, they'd just sat down in the road and looked right back.

"They're so tame," he concluded, "that I could have picked them right up, only I remembered in time that they bite like the devil."

This inspired Alice. "Look, why couldn't we take a landing net and a big box to put them in—" She didn't have to finish. We got the idea. Before we quite realized what we were about, we were headed up the road, complete with net, box, and flashlight. Ralph was driving, Alice was standing on one running board with the light, and I was on the other with the net. The plot was that as soon as a fox was sighted—or is "viewed" the right term? —the viewer would shout, the car would stop, and we'd all three pile off for the kill—or capture, in this case.

We saw the foxes all right. They were the cutest little articles that ever ran the woods—round and fluffy, with little pointed masked faces, up-standing ears, and wide grins. But they weren't to be caught. The moment we tried to clap the net over one, he just eased off into the darkness where the beam from our flashlight, which wasn't very good anyhow, couldn't pick him up. We spent hours riding up and down the road, shouting and laughing and jumping on and off the car, until we were exhausted. I've always doubted the English theory that the fox enjoys the hunt as much as the hunters, but I do believe these foxes did. They knew perfectly well that they were in no jeopardy whatsoever, which isn't true of a fox with a pack of hounds after him. They kept coming back into the road for more. When we finally decided that if we didn't go home we'd all get pneumonia, they were still dodging back and forth in front of the car, daring us to try to catch them. But we knew when we were licked. We went home, built up a fire, and spent the rest of the night drinking coffee and Barbados rum. (Courtesy of Alice.)

Ralph and Gerrish are forever needing a third person to lend a hand in furtherance of one of their projects, and I'm invariably elected. A plank has to be held while they saw it, or the combined weight of the two of them is just too little to push a crippled car out of the driveway, and will I please come and lean on it, too? Or they want me to hold a rock drill for them. I don't know whether they don't trust each other, or whether they figure that if someone has to get hit on the head with a sledge hammer, I can best be spared. Whatever it is, I have sat for more hours than I care to count, with a sledge whistling down past my nose as I concentrated on holding the top of the drill steady, while giving it a quarter turn between blows. I have got so I can tell by instinct just when to shout "Mud!"—when the water that has been poured into the hole has just exactly been taken up by the rock dust, and the whole works can be lifted out on the drill, leaving the hole dry and clean. Or they want me to be handy with a cant dog in case a motor they are shifting from one cradle to another starts to tip; or to block up a rock as they raise it; or take down the figures while they scale a pile of pine logs; or read a spirit level while they do the leveling. If it isn't one thing, it's another.

And, after all, I'm supposed to be a writer, so I do have to spend a little time writing. Some of the work of writing can, of course, be done concurrently with other things. You can figure out, while washing the dishes, just how to get around the difficulty of having Her discourage His suit without having Her appear to the reader just silly, and also without forcing Her to reverse Her attitude, along toward the end of the story, so completely as to seem actually feeble-minded. You see, there are certain ill-defined but nonetheless definite rules that have to be followed in the writing of magazine stories. There are some things you simply can't do, and some subjects you simply can't touch upon. Within the frame-work of these rules, you have to try to produce the illusion of some originality. It's not as hard as it sounds, but it does require a little figuring, just as it requires a little figuring to get a grand piano up a stair case with two turns in it. I might add that these rules apply to poor, medium, and good stories. If you have a simply swell story in mind, you can forget the rules. A swell story takes care of itself.

VII

~⌒~

"Don't You Ever Get Bored?"

WE ARE OFTEN ASKED IF WE NEVER GET TERRIBLY BORED here and I'm a little diffident about telling the truth. There is something so smug about people who say, with horror and umbrage at the very suggestion, "Oh, no! I'm never bored!" It sounds a little like, "Who, me? With my rich mine of inner resources? ME? With all my rare memories and rich philosophy?" I hate people like that. They're infuriating, and I think they are liars as well. Everyone is bored sometimes. It's a very painful illness, and completely undeserving of moral censure.

But be that as it may, the answer still is no. We're almost never bored. In winter we work too hard. In the summer we still work hard, and there are always distractions to fill in the chinks between jobs—things like guests, and fishing, and swimming. Nobody could be bored in autumn, when the air is like wine, and the hills are hazy tapestries with the red and gold thread of the frost-touched maple and birch embroidering a breath-taking design on the permanent dark fabric of the evergreens. The lakes then are unbelievably blue. All the things you've meant to do all summer but didn't get around to suddenly start crying to get done, and the days aren't long enough to crowd them all in before the first snow.

The only time left to be bored in is spring, when winter is over but it's still too early to plant the garden or move to the big house, and there's nothing very much to do but wait. Spring, as far as I'm concerned, is a vastly over-rated season, and I'd be bored to death with it, for all its burgeoning buds and returning birds and coy extremes of temperature, were it not for the spring log drive. The log drive was not designed solely for my entertainment; that's what is so remarkable and providential about its falling, as it does, in the slump of the year.

The idea of the drive is simple. All up the lakes, from Umbagog to the Little Kennebago, that tiny lost pond in the mountains fifty miles to the north, the winter's cut of four-foot pulp-wood lies boomed on the thick ice, waiting for the spring break-up. Before the first step of the metamorphosis from so many sticks of wood to so many Sunday Supplements, or high explosives, or evening gowns can begin, it must be got to the mills in Berlin, N. H., on the Androscoggin. The obvious method is to float the wood down. So even before the ice is out, the driving crews start filtering into the woods, to the company wangans along the chain of lakes. There is a lot to be done before the wood can start south.

I should explain "wangan." It is an Indian word, and can mean almost anything, like the Latin *res*. It can mean a camp or building. Pond-in-the-River wangan—or Pondy wangan, as the drivers call it—is a long, low shack a third of a mile above us, where the Rapid River crew lives during the drive. There is a sign in the bunk-house that reads,

"Wangan open an hour after supper." That refers to the store where the cook sells candy, tobacco, snuff, and clothing. (It really is a big box in the kitchen, and the reason it isn't open all the time is that the cook doesn't want to be bothered in the middle of his baking to hand out and charge against wages a nickel's worth of makings.) The cook may say, "I lost my wangan when the work boat swamped," and that means that his dishes are at the bottom of the lake. Or he may complain, "The wangan's runnin' low," meaning this time that he's short of food. Or a man may take his wangan and fly—leave the job with his little bundle of personal belongings. You can tell only by the context what the word means, and it's a very convenient word to know. I use it myself a lot, in non-driving connections.

The first year I was here, I couldn't wait for the drive to begin. I knew all about log drives, having subsisted at one time on a literary diet consisting exclusively of Stewart Edward White and Holman Day. I knew all about the thrill and perils of white-water driving—the big jam, the narrow escapes, the cat-footed agility of the drivers on the huge, plunging logs. I knew just what a river driver would look like. He should be big and bold and dark, with plaid shirt, well-cut riding breeches, caulked boots, and a mouthful of picturesque curses and ribald songs.

There is a stir that goes through the woods just before the drive moves in that is difficult to explain. Actually it consists only of suddenly increased activity on the telephone. The telephone man, Fred Bennett, who has long, blowing white hair, the delicate and transparent fragility of great age, and the toughness and staying-powers of a cross between a Shetland pony and a camel, comes slogging in through the woods and swamps and wet snow between here and the Brown Farm, and adds a half-dozen phones to our line. There is one at Middle Dam wangan, one at Pondy wangan, above us, and one at Hedgehog wangan, below, at the mouth of the river. The rest are hung in tar-paper cubicles on trees, in places where crises demanding immediate aid may arise.

Almost as soon as the phones are in, they begin to ring, strange numbers that have nothing to do with our simple, year-round, one, two, three, and four. They ring all the time, and I, neglecting my housework and throwing overboard all ethical scruples that first year, listened in. (That's all right to do, here. Often when I ask someone where they got a piece of news, they say quite frankly and shamelessly, "Oh, rubbering on the telephone.") Just by standing in the kitchen with the receiver to my ear, I could see the drive get under way all up the length of the lakes.

At first all the calls were to Joe Mooney at the Brown Farm, who acts as a sort of liaison officer. First of all came the reports as to the condition of the ice in the various lakes. "She's pretty rotten here on Umbagog this morning. If a west wind comes up she'll be clear by night. The river's all open and we've got the steamer *Diamond* in."— "She's blackin' up fast toward the Narrows. Give her two or three days of hot sun and she'll be out of the Richardsons." (Why are things like ice that won't melt, or inclement weather, or balky motors always "she" to the men who deal with them?) "They brought a horse 'n' sled down the big lake this morning. She won't go out for a week-ten days."

Then—"She's out of Pondy River, and we're puttin' in the *Alligator* tomorrow."—"The *Rowell's* in at Upper

Dam."—"The *Frost's* just goin' off the ways at Cupsuptic."

Then it speeds up. "This is Henry Mullen at Pondy. The cook claims he wants a barrel of flour, couple of crates of eggs, an' a half dozen hams. We got about thirty to feed tonight."—"Middle Dam talkin'. I got to have some inch an' a quarter line and a bunch of pick poles."—"I need ten more men. Thurston's boom's broke loose in the Arm, 'n' it's scattered all over Hell."—"I gotta have some pitch. This bateau at Middle leaks like a sieve."—"Where's that cookee? The cook's raving."—"I gotta close Pondy dam. I can't string no sluice boom with all this water runnin'." And finally, "When's that first boom comin' down? We're ready any time."

The ice is out; the winch boats are in; the crews have come; the ground work is done. The drive is ready to start.

That first year, when the news came over the telephone that they were going to launch the *Alligator,* we thought we'd go up and watch. We had seen her sitting patiently on her ways on the shore of the Pond all winter long, a big, twin-screw, square-ended craft, with a flat deck and a tall wheel-house perched on top. She was ugly and clumsy, but we felt a sympathy for her. We had watched the red leaves of autumn sift down on her deck and lie in fading, flattening windrows. We had seen the snow drift higher and higher about her, the wind-sculptured curves lending her a false and fleeting beauty. We had seen it shrink in the March sun, leaving her exposed and ugly again. We wanted to see her come to life.

Alligator is both the name of this winch boat in the Pond and the name of her type of amphibian boat. Alligators are built like barges, flat and rectangular, but they have a huge steel cable running from a winch in the bow.

The anchor is dropped, the winch unwinds as the *Alligator* runs backward to the boom, and hooks on; then the winch winds up the *Alligator* to the anchor, trailing behind her the boomful of pulp-wood which it is her business to move from the Head of the Pond to Pondy dam, at the foot. When the cable is wound up the anchor is run ahead again and the process repeated. At the foot of the Pond the boom is opened and the wood turned loose and sluiced into Rapid River, to be corralled three miles below in a catch boom, which the *Diamond* will winch to Errol Dam on the Androscoggin. Meanwhile the *Alligator* has gone back to the Head of the Pond for the boom that the *Rowell* has winched down the Richardsons from Upper Dam to Middle Dam and which has been sluiced down the upper section of Rapid River into the Pond. It sounds complicated, but it's just the old bucket brigade principle.

In Canada, where they hail from, an alligator doesn't stick necessarily to one lake, but goes right down the chain. Between lakes they pull themselves across bare ground by fastening their cable ahead to a stump and winding the boat up to it with its own winch. Many of the old pines along the Carry Road have deep girdling scars from the cable on their trunks, left from when they brought the *Alligator* in here.

As we were walking up the road to my first *Alligator* launching, we heard sounds of activity on the Pond-in-the-River Dam, so we swung off down the side trail that leads to it. I'll admit I was in a dither. The men in my life to date had been distinguished more for their intelligence, good citizenship, and consideration for their mothers than for dashing and romantic attributes. The most athletic played good tennis. The most daring crossed streets between traffic lights and talked back to cops. I'd never known any men in the business of danger.

We came out of the woods onto the dam. A tall, sad, thin man with a long upper lip was drooping on the rail, staring morosely across to where the sluice-booms were being strung—two long, floating log walkways from the dam up into the Pond, to guide the pulp-wood down to the open gate of the dam after the *Alligator* let it go. Presumably the stringers were river drivers, those daring heroes of song and legend. They looked like—

They looked like any gang of men going about a routine job, except they were a little shabbier, a little more nondescript, a little less arresting than any bunch of road menders I ever saw. There wasn't a plaid shirt in the crew. Some of them had on faded cotton shirts, but most of them were covered from the waist up with what my grandmother used to call "nice, sensible, woolen underwear," of the long-sleeved, knitted variety. Nothing is less glamorous, especially when south of them is worn a pair of ordinary, store-bought suit pants, which have seen better days, and which have been cut off, with a hack saw, apparently, just below the knee. (I later learned to say "stagged" below the knee. One stags one's pants, one's shirt sleeves, anything that needs to be abbreviated quickly, even one's hair.) The head-gear, too, was strange without managing to be piquant. First, tied like a baby's bonnet under the chin and tucked into the shirt at the back of the neck, was a bandanna handkerchief or, failing that, just an old piece of cloth, such as a shirt tail or a square of flour sacking. On top of that was the hat proper, which might be a cheap felt, a visored cap, or a battered derby.

They didn't even do the job with a dash. They just walked apathetically up and down the logs, boring holes, driving pegs and fastening ropes.

Of course I should have remembered that people who do things well almost always do them without flourish. That's the trouble with expert performances; they look too easy to be exciting, unless you can do them a little yourself. I can't skate much, so to me Sonja Henie's stuff looks pretty simple to have so much fuss made about it. But I can shoot and swim and cast a fly fairly well, so a champion in those fields has me standing on my chair. I'd never tried to walk a floating spruce log, so I would have been a little more impressed had there been some arm-waving and catching of balance. I've tried it since, and I know enough now to be plenty impressed, especially since I now know that very few river-hogs can swim.

(Blow No. 2 to my romantic notions:—river-drivers live in books; in life the term is river-hog. And I might as well deliver Blow No. 3 right now:—in a pulp drive there are no log jams; the wood is too short.)

To get back to the log-walking—I can imagine nothing worse than being out on the sluice boom in the middle of the night, as is sometimes necessary, with the black water snarling three inches from my feet. The current goes by with express train speed when the gates are open, and the wood hurtles past in the dark. The boom, although two or three logs wide lashed together, is wet and slippery and anything but steady. Even if a man could swim, he would have little chance. No one would see him go, except by great luck. No one would hear him call, if he had time to call before being knocked senseless. The first time he would be missed would be when the men came back off the boom. And the water is like ice. It would be a cold and lonely way to die.

I also found later that the peculiarities of costume are not merely a misguided attempt at quaintness. Riding breeches bind the knees, and long pants catch on brush and trip the wearer and get wet around the bottoms. The simple solution is long pants stagged. Black flies and gnats can make life Hell in springtime in the woods, and the best protection against them is to keep covered. Hence the woolen underwear and the bandannas. The hats are added, not as a sop to convention, but to keep the neck covering up and the glare out of the eyes.

The sad man spat dourly into the water and looked at us, so Ralph said, "Nice day."

The man said, "Yeah," as though he were cursing it.

So Ralph said, "I'm Rich. I live down below here."

"Yeah, I know," the man said. "I'm Mullen." He didn't have to add that he was the Pondy boss. We knew that from our illicit listening on the telephone. I'd pictured him as being what they call here a "bull of the woods"— a big swaggering bravo who could lick his weight in wild-cats. He didn't look to me as though he could lick Rufus, who was six months old at the time.

Ralph rallied first. "Drop in sometime if you're cold or wet and have a drink. I've got some pretty good liquor."

Mullen shook his head and winced. "Not me. Thanking you all the same." He squinted at his crew out on the booms. "I'm off the stuff," he stated violently, and spat again. "I was down to Berlin last week an' I bought me a quart. Then me an' another joker split another quart. Then a feller give me a pint. It was all good stuff too," he explained defensively. "Cost ninety cents a bottle. Then

I went into a lunch room an' got me a can of beer." His face twisted. "You know that God-damned Jees'ly beer pizened me," he concluded simply. "So I'm just through with all that stuff."

We left him alone with his hangover and continued up to the *Alligator*.

There was a great deal of commotion there. Steam was up, and the winch cable was hitched to a dead-man across the cove. The *Alligator* was creaking and groaning and rumbling and not budging an inch. A head appeared through the afterhatch. The sulphurous blue haze of profanity thinned a little when the owner saw me, out of respect to my sex. It simmered down to a few heart-felt "Comical Christs," "God-damned blue-bottomed old tubs," "Desprit Jesuses," and "Christless onery bitches," which in the woods is practically parlor conversation. What he needed, it seemed, was some grease for the ways.

"You ain't got no grease?" he asked Ralph hopefully. "If I had a little grease—"

This didn't seem to be my department, but it wouldn't hurt to ask. "I've got some old doughnut fat, if that would do you any good—"

"How much you got?"

"A kettleful. Ten pounds, about."

He climbed down onto the ground. "Lady, you saved my life. I'll have the cook return it to you, soon's he gets his in."

So the *Alligator*, that first year we were here, slid down cinnamon-scented ways into the Pond, and a few days later the cookee delivered at our door an equal quantity of lard and an invitation from the cook to come to lunch.

"Either first or second lunch. Ten o'clock or two. Don't

matter." On the drive there are four meals a day, breakfast at six, first and second lunch, supper at five, and then, if the men have to sluice after dark, another lunch before they go to bed, which may be anywhere from ten P.M. until two the next morning.

We decided we'd go to second lunch, because Rufus would be asleep and we could leave him. Before we started up to the wangan, Ralph said, "Now look. There's a guy up there named Casey that has My Ideal of a hat. It's a swell hat and I want to make a deal with him if I can for it. So I'll point him out to you, and if you could sort of be nice to him—you know, soften him up—"

I knew, and I knew too without asking, what the Ideal Hat of Casey would look like. It would be a battered felt, of no recognizable style, with the crown squashed out of shape and the brim drooping dejectedly. Ralph had been working on one of his old city hats for years, trying to achieve that special abandoned and disreputable look; but it takes a long time to get it. "All right," I said resignedly. "What is he, an Irishman?"

Every married woman knows the look he gave me—the very special look husbands save for their wives when they say something more than usually stupid; the look combining in equal proportions disgust, resignation and nausea, with a dash of dismay at the prospect of living to be a grandfather with such a half-wit.

"With a name like Casey?" he asked. "What do you suppose he is, a Frenchman?"

The meals on the drive are buffet affairs, unlike the sitting-down meals in a logging camp. All the food is laid out on a long trestle table in the kitchen, with the knives and forks and tin plates and pannikins stacked at the end.

You get your tools first, and then go down the table, filling up your plate with whatever looks good to you. The trouble is everything looks good. There are always two kinds of meat—a hot beef pot-roast, for example, and cold sliced ham—and potatoes and three other vegetables. Then there are always baked beans, and fresh bread, and pickles, and applesauce, and, to top off with, three kinds of pie, cake, cookies, and doughnuts. When you can't get any more onto your plate, you look for a place to sit down and eat it. The cook wanted us, as company, to sit at the table, but I saw a hat that could belong to no one but Casey. So I said I'd rather do as the river-hogs did, if he didn't mind, and went outdoors and sat down beside the man with the hat, under a pine tree.

He looked a little terrified, but he couldn't get away, as there was a man on the other side of him.

"Lovely day," I said cordially, and he grunted. "Good cook you've got," I went on, and he showed the whites of his eyes like a nervous horse. "Been working in the woods long?" I asked with neighborly interest, and he definitely shied.

The man on the other side took pity on us both. "He don't understand no English, lady," he explained kindly. "He's a Frenchman."

I gaped at him. This was absolutely too marvellous to be true. After that look Ralph had given me— "With a name like Casey?" I asked.

"Oh, they just call him Casey. He's got some frog name nobody can pronounce. So when he went to work for the company, they put him down as Casey. Sounds as near like his real name as they could get."

I beamed on Casey, not minding that he didn't beam

back. He was unshaven, and ragged and dirty, but he looked wonderful to me. He'd given me a weapon I could use in domestic crises for years to come. I loved him like a brother.

Apparently he misunderstood my intentions, because he got up in a panic and fled. Incidentally, Ralph never did make the hat deal, because next day Casey asked to be transferred to the Middle Dam wangan. I don't know whether it was I who scared him, or whether it was the predatory way Ralph kept looking at his hat.

The remaining driver said to me comfortingly, "Don't mind him, lady. He's bashful. All us fellers is bashful. Lots of folks think we're tough, but we ain't. Any time you want to come up here or to the dam, you come right ahead. Nobody'll hurt you. An' any time you want some chores done down to your place, like splittin' wood, say, you just call me. Just call the cook on the phone and say you want to get hold of Venus."

Would I not! Not every woman has a chance to confound her husband by saying, "Oh, don't bother, if you're busy. I'll get Venus to do it."

We thanked the cook kindly for his hospitality, and said we had to get home, because the baby would be waking up.

"You got a baby?" His eyes lighted. "Bring him up here. There's nothing I like so much as a baby. Any time you want to go any place, you leave the baby here with me an' the cookee."

He meant it too, and I took him up on it a dozen times. I'd come back from an afternoon off, to find Rufus propped up on the cook's bunk, chewing a piece of dried apple, with a circle of men around him, trying to make him laugh. They were wonderful with him—much better than I was. Most of them were homeless and familyless, and a baby was a treat. As a matter of fact the first picture ever taken of Rufus was taken in front of the wangan in the arms of Jonesy, the drive cook.

That cook, Jonesy, and his cookee, Frank, were the first of a long line of woods cooks that I now know, and I hold them in especial esteem. Jonesy and I used to hold long conclaves on the culinary art, and he taught me how to make a tough pot-roast tender by smothering it with raw onions and adding a cup of canned tomatoes, salt, pepper, and a little water. Then you cover it tightly and leave in a slow oven for hours. The acid in the tomatoes, so Jonesy claimed, eats the tough fibre in the meat. Anyhow, it works. Another valuable thing he taught me was how to cut fresh bread into thin slices—a neat trick if you can do it, as everyone who has hacked jagged chunks off a warm loaf can testify. The knife must be reasonably sharp, of course, but the trick is to have it hot. Lay it on top of the stove for a minute, every four or five slices. This also works.

In return I bootlegged vanilla extract for him. Extracts aren't allowed in woods camps, and "you know yourself, Mis' Rich—you're a cook—you know a cake tastes like sawdust without no extract."

I thought this was a senseless regulation, and said so.

Jonesy sighed. "They have to have it that way. Fellers'll drink it up as fast as they can tote it in, an' there's nothing meaner'n a vanilla drunk, 'less it's a canned heat drunk."

"But imitation vanilla has no alcohol. That I just gave—"

"Sure. But lots of the woodsmen can't read. It smells like vanilla and tastes like vanilla, so they drink it and get drunk anyhow."

I was glad to hear this, as it confirmed an opinion of mine that getting drunk is fifty percent wishful thinking.

As a cookee, Frank wasn't too good, but he was entertaining in an unintentional way. He spent most of the time when he should have been peeling potatoes and washing dishes—a cookee's lot in life—strumming on a guitar and singing cowboy songs. His ambition was to get onto the Radio, on a hill-billy program. I've heard worse than he, though that isn't saying much. So he'd drone "When the Work's All Done This Fall" happily through his nose while Jonesy and Ralph and I peeled his potatoes.

We were all thus engaged one day when he discovered that by calling the Brown Farm and asking Joe to switch him onto a Magalloway line he could talk to the Camerons. The Camerons have some very pretty daughters, one of whom Frank had met at a dance. He put his guitar away under the bunk and began to bustle around.

"You got a flat-iron, Mrs. Rich?" he asked. "Can I borrow it? I got to press my pants."

I said, "Yes," and Ralph said, "Aren't you a little ambitious, young feller? It's fourteen miles from here to Camerons', and most of it's uphill. You can't walk that distance and back after supper."

Frank was surprised. "Oh, I wasn't planning on it. I'm just going to call her up. An' I ain't going to talk to no girl on the telephone with my pants looking like I'd slept in 'em."

That remains to this day the yard-stick by which I measure all chivalry.

Frank's, I'm sure, was the only singing I ever heard in a driving camp, in spite of the fictional convention that rivermen and loggers top off a hard, twelve or more hour day by sitting around a camp-fire singing French-Canadian chansons and talking about Paul Bunyan. Our river-hogs come in from work, eat their suppers, and go to bed. On the days that there is no boom to sluice or other work to be done, they wash their clothes and mend them, and play stud poker, and sleep. A few that have licenses go fishing and some pitch horse-shoes in the wangan yard, and a very few, since so many are illiterate, read old magazines that we give the cook. But none sing.

The only stories that are told are woods gossip. Nobody ever heard of Paul Bunyan. The nearest thing to him is Sock Saunders, who is more of a poltergeist than a hero. If a man drops a picaroon into the river he says, "Well, take it, Sock Saunders!" If he slips on a log, but catches himself in time, he says, "Foxed you that time, Sock Saunders." If he cuts his foot, he explains, "Sock Saunders got me." There are no stories about Sock Saunders. He's just the guy who hangs around and makes life complicated.

But nobody sings as they walk the boom in at Middle Dam, an event that should call for a chanty, with the boss lining out the verse and the walkers roaring the chorus. At Middle the *Rowell* can't get in close enough to the dam for the current to take the boom in, so on either side of the inlet above the dam is a headworks—a big log raft with a capstan on it. Hawsers are hitched to the boom, and four or more men man the capstan and walk the boom in. It comes reluctantly, inch by inch, as they walk doggedly round and round. It's hard, monotonous, drugging work. But nobody sings.

Around the camp the cook is the boss, no matter who the boss of the rest of the job is. What he says, goes. One year we had a cook named Scotty Maxwell, a veteran of the Boer War, who was at the relief of Ladysmith. How he landed in the Maine woods I don't know, but he is a good cook and he brought British Army discipline right along with him. He's a holy terror in the kitchen. He always has a meat cleaver handy, but he never has to do more than glance at it. He liked sit-down meals, where he could get people lined up in orderly rows instead of having them sprawled every which way, all over the yard. But nobody could sit down if his face and hands and fingernails couldn't pass Scotty's inspection. Whoever fell below his impossibly high standards went back and washed, ten times, if necessary. I went into the kitchen one day at first lunch and found five terrified Frenchmen sitting in a row on the floor with their plates between their knees. They'd worn their hats to the table, and were being taught gentlemanly conduct the hard way.

The third functionary around the drive is the bull-cook. This title puzzled me, as I never saw the bull-cook, a wizened little man answering to Bones, cooking. Jonesy cleared the matter up. "He's called the bull-cook, but he's really the barroom man."

"*Barroom?* But if you can't even have vanilla—"

"Oh, not that kind of a barroom. It's where the men sleep."

"Bunk-house?"

"Well, city folks might call it that." City folks also call a place to eat a mess-hall. In the woods it's the kitchen.

The barroom man is a combined chore-boy and chambermaid, and his job is no sinecure. He has to keep the barroom clean, keep a fire going in cold weather and a smudge going on nights when the bugs are bad. He also has to keep an outside fire going under an oil drum of water, so the men can bathe and launder. The cook won't have people using his hot water. Then he has to saw wood for his own and sometimes the cook's fires and row the lunches out to the *Alligator* crew when meal-time overtakes them in the middle of a haul.

This last was Bones' cross, because he couldn't row a boat. We used to make book on how long it would take him to get near enough to the *Alligator* to catch a line thrown him by the crew. But his sea-faring career ended one day when the wind came up while he was waiting on the *Alligator* for the crew to finish eating, so he could bring back the dishes. He was afraid to come ashore in the rowboat and spent the rest of the day on the Pond. The barroom fires went out and the boss was raging as was the cook. The *Alligator* crew missed two meals as he sat there and were not pleased. After that Frank rowed the meals out, and Bones helped with the potato peeling.

As May wore on toward June, we became used to waking up in the morning to the hollow *thunk* of the wood as it bumped down the rapids in front of the house. It is a pleasant sound, like distant, slow-beaten drums. We learned to watch the dam from our porch, and to grab our fly-rods and run when a boom came in. In the short interval between the arrival of a boom and the opening of the gates to sluice it, there is often a quarter hour's glorious fishing. The big trout and salmon follow the wood down out of the Pond, feeding on the grubs and insects that drop from the rotting bark. They come up from the green shade below with that powerful and accurate surge that so delights the heart to behold. Standing on the sluice-booms, one sometimes forgets to fish, so lost in awe and admiration does one become for their vicious grace.

After a little the water at our feet begins to stir almost imperceptibly, tugging gently at the wood that is held back by the "trip"—a single long log swung like a gate across the channel. That means the boss has had the gate raised a few inches to warn any fishermen who may be on the river below that they'd better high-tail it for the bank.

We had a boss once named Phil Haley who would not observe this convention. Fishermen got in his hair. They were always underfoot, walking out on the sluice-boom, snagging his men with their backcasts, and asking foolish questions. They disrupted work, because everyone always stopped everything in the hopes of seeing a hundred dollars' worth of Abercrombie & Fitch fall into the river and maybe drown. So when it came time to hoist, Phil hoisted. Let the jokers scramble. Phil it was who once gave Ralph ten dollars to hold for him as safeguard against losing it in a stud game. He said he might need it when he got Outside. He observed that "a ten dollar bill is an awful handy rig to have 'round," which seems to me to cover that both simply and adequately.

Most bosses, though, will warn the fishermen, so when we begin to see the boom stir and the drivers start climbing down onto the sluice-booms with their pick-poles, ready to pole the wood along toward the gate, we reel in our lines and climb up onto the dam to watch them hoist (pronounced heist) the gates.

Pond-in-the-River Dam is an old-fashioned wooden dam with a long, unpainted shed over the center section sheltering the gate-works. The gates are raised by man power, teams of several men each manning the big wheels at the ends of the heavy timber gates. They start turning the wheels over slowly, and the gates creak as they move against the enormous pressure against them. Then, as the tempo increases, the gates come up slowly, dark and dripping, groaning and protesting, and the water begins to flow under them, impatient to be free. The first white spate deepens and greens, and the low whispering rustle changes to a roar. The whole dam vibrates as the gates clear the water, and the boss shouts, "Let go your trip!" The men who have been on the gates come out on the dam, their chests heaving, their faces glistening with sweat, and watch the first wood go through. "She's runnin' good," they will say; and "Ain't that handsome pulp, though? Comes from up back of Metalluc. I was cuttin' on the stump up there last winter."

It's lovely on the dam on a bright spring morning, with the wind blowing down across the boom and filling the air with the sharp smell of resin, so strong and fresh that you can taste it. The planks tremble under your feet, and the roar of the river and the thumping of the wood fills the ears. The river is deep blue and crisping white, and the cut ends of the pulp are like raw gold in the sun. All the senses come alive, even that strange rare sense that tells you, half a dozen times between birth and death—if you are lucky—that right now, right in this spot, you have fallen into the pattern of the universe.

We would like to spit on the last log of the last boom of the drive as it goes through the dam, but we're not sure that this brings luck to any but those who have worked on the drive. So we give the good spitting spots to the river-hogs, who put a lot of store by the ceremony. They spit copiously and accurately, and I hope the charm works. I thought I'd discovered a new folk-way when I saw a driver last year throw an almost new pair of work gloves into the sluice after the last log.

"Is that good luck, too?" I asked.

"Nope. I ain't needin' 'em any more, that's all. I'm through."

"Aren't you going on the rear?"

"Nope. I got a date over at the college in West Stewartstown."

That is the euphemism for the county jail, and so I started to cluck the sympathetic tongue.

But my man threw out his chest. "They can't get along without me over there, when it comes time to plant the gardens," he said with modest pride. "I bossed the plantin' there now five years runnin'. Just happened I got picked up in Berlin every year there for a spell in the middle of May, for drunk an' disorderly. Last year I missed. We didn't get off the Diamond till late, an', Hairy Jesus, what a mess they made of them gardens! So when I got pinched last Christmas they turned me loose—deferred my sentence, the judge called it—till planting time. They weren't takin' no chances this year. Tomorrow mornin' there'll be a boat at Cedar Stump for me, an' I gotta be there."

After the last log has gone through the dam, there are still two or three days of "rearin'" before the drive moves out. Rearing is going down the river and cleaning up all the wood that has been left in the rear, caught on rocks or washed up on the banks. It is pitched back into the river again and finally gathered in the catch boom below. It's the hardest part of the drive. By that time it is hot, and the bugs are bad, the water is still like ice, and the men are wet from morning to night. But it marks the point at which you can begin to think definitely about getting drunk in Berlin, so the crew works with great speed and good humor. Before we know it the flash boards are off the dam, the river is clean as a whistle again, the roar of the rapids is back to normal, instead of rising thunderously one hour and startling us by sinking to a whisper in the next. (Here silence is an uncanny noise.) The men start trekking to Sunday Cove, where the work boat will pick them up and take them out. They call to us as they go by, "My regards to the little feller!" and "See you next year."

The cook does not walk to the Cove. He has his position to think of. He comes in, strange and formal without his white clothes and apron and in a store hat, and asks Ralph to drive him down. "I'll pay you," he says.

That's a pathetic thing about woodsmen. If they ask you a favor, they make it clear at once that they can and will pay for it. It's a telling comment on the treatment they receive on the Outside, where they are considered bums, and are always asked to pay as they enter, as it were. "I'll pay you," they say, protesting their self-respect. They are always so pleased and puzzled when we won't take money, pointing to all the favors they have done us. "Oh, that! That wa'n't nothin'."

So Ralph says to the cook, "Naw, you can't pay me. I'm going down that way anyhow."

The cook climbs into the car, and at the last minute leans out and says to me, "I left a few odds an' ends for you up at the wangan. No sense of throwing good food to the squirrels." I'm used to woods computations now, but the first year I was flabbergasted at the loot. There were a half a dozen pies, a flour barrel almost full of cookies and doughnuts, and ten huge loaves of bread—the cook's idea of a few odds and ends.

The first two or three days after the drive goes out we always feel a little lonely and lost. The wangan looks so forlorn as we go past, with no smoke coming out of the chimneys, no sound of Bones' axe ringing crisply from out back by the wood-pile, no men sitting on the long bench in front, or rinsing their clothes in the brook where it flows under the Carry Road. The windows are shuttered once more, and the benches have been taken inside. By the brook a forgotten pair of socks droops from an alder bush where they were hung up to dry. The trampled grass in the yard is beginning to spring upright again. Down by the Pond, the *Alligator* is high and dry again on her ways.

The drive is over. It wasn't what I had expected it to be. The men weren't romantic, or daring, or glamorous. But they were something much better. They were good neighbors. We're going to miss them.

But not for a week or so. Not until Fred Bennett comes in again and takes the phones out. While they stay we'll be too busy to miss anyone. The fishermen have begun to swarm into the woods. "Sports" the natives call them here; it is a term like the cowboy's "dudes" or the stage farmer's "city slickers." Fishing up and down the river, deep, so they think, in the wilds of Maine, they are amazed and baffled to find telephones hanging on trees.

I know just what they say. They say, "Well, for crying out loud! Look at the telephone! Gee, let's ring it and see if anyone answers."

So they ring it. Naturally they ring one, which is our number, and by the time Fred Bennett gets in we are half insane with trying to explain in a million well-chosen words the whys and wherefores of the situation.

But now, I think we have at last evolved a system. We've got now so we can tell a "sport's" ring from a native's. It has a feeble, wavering quality, quite unlike that of the firm hand accustomed to cranking a battery phone. So when that kind of a ring comes over the line, we take down the receiver, say briskly, "Grand Central Station, Information Booth," and hang up. It almost always stops them.

To be fair to the writers of the romantic school of logging fiction, what they invariably dealt with is the long-log drive, which is quite different from the pulp drive of today. They used to drive long logs—and by that I mean whole trees, sometimes as long as sixty feet—here. But those days were a decade or more ago. We would never see their like again, the old river-hogs mourned. And we never would have, if it hadn't been for the hurricane that hit New England in 1938.

The hurricane blew down millions of feet of pine. Pine isn't used for pulp, so there was no chance of its being cleaned up on the next pulp operation. Nobody would gamble on taking it out as the market would be glutted with pine after the hurricane. The prospects were that it would just lie where it had fallen in crazy jack-pots. Inside of a year the worms would be in it, unless a forest fire got there first; and what the worms and fire missed would burn in the slower, surer fire of decay. It's a truly sad thing to see a big tree lying on the ground, even if you know that the bringing low of so much beauty and majesty will serve some useful end. It's heart-breaking when nothing but waste will result.

And then the Government had a good idea—"for the

Gov'ment," as they say up here. They set up a Timber Salvage Administration for the saving of the pine. The lumbering was let out to local contractors who would get the blowdown out of the woods and into Government storage booms in specified ponds and lakes, whence its release onto the market could be controlled. Worms will not attack wood that is in the water, and water won't injure it for years. The Government paid a fixed price, depending on grade, and Government scalers and graders oversaw the work, and presumably prevented the woodsmen, who were paid on a piece-work basis, from cutting any standing pine. It's a lot easier to cut a standing tree than one that is not only down, but also tangled up in a half a dozen others. It's a lot safer, too. You can never tell what a blowdown will do when you get a saw almost through it. It may drop as you plan it's going to. On the other hand the stresses may be such that it will jump with the force of a forty-mule-kick and knock you galley-west. You never can tell, and maybe you won't get a chance to make a second guess.

The nearest Government storage booms were below us in Umbagog, and Jim Barnett contracted to get out the pine lying on the slopes along Rapid River and into the booms before winter set in. He moved his men and wangan into the Pond-in-the-River driving camp in early summer, and by the first of October he was ready to drive the logs, which he had temporarily boomed up in the Pond, down the river to the Government booms. I, personally, was looking forward to this drive with a great deal of interest, because I had long since given up hope of ever seeing a long-log drive. I wasn't glad the trees had blown down, you understand, but since they had, I was glad to be on the spot to see them driven.

And then the Government had another idea. We should have been warned when we read in a two-week-old Boston Sunday paper a feature article on the Romance of Hurricane Timber—that was what they were calling our blowdown Outside—and the Revival of the Old Long-Log Days. We should have been warned, but we were only entertained. We had no inkling of what was in store for us until Jim came in from Outside one day and began telling about meeting the Timber Salvage agent, who, it seemed, had discovered a publicity angle to the pine drive. This long-log drive on Rapid River would probably be the very last of the old time drives ever to be held, and he thought it should be perpetuated for posterity. He was going to bring in a bunch of newspaper reporters and newsreel cameramen to make a living record of this rapidly dying bit of the American scene—his verbiage, not Jim's or mine—and Jim's share in the project was to give them something to take pictures of and write about. It would be interesting to people, he said, and it would be good publicity—for whom he carefully didn't specify. The tax payers were footing the bill for the salvage, after all.

All this seemed fair enough to Jim, and he was perfectly willing to co-operate. The only trouble was that the agent seemed to take for granted deeds of derring-do, heart-stopping crises, and a plethora of almost legendary figures whose prowess had been told in song and story all up and down the rivers of Maine. In the fall of the year there isn't enough water in the lakes to put much of a head on the river, so it was going to be impossible to open the festivities with the expected forty-foot wall of water racing down the channel, the long logs turning end over end along its face like match sticks. And as for legendary figures, Jim was fresh out of them. The men he had had working for him all summer were just natives who knew how to use an axe and a two-man cross-cut, and he'd planned to use the same men on the drive. They were strong and willing, and they could get the pine down the river all right, if allowed to go about it in their own way. But they weren't old-time river-hogs. Most of those boys were either dead or retired to parts unknown. The only legendary figure Jim knew anything about was reposing at the moment at the county jail. However, he was willing to make a stab at putting on a show for the Fourth Estate.

The first requirement seemed to be more water, so Jim had a couple of courses of flash-boards added to those already on Pondy Dam, and stopped driving altogether for two days to give the Pond a chance to fill up. The second requirement seemed to be a prima donna for the occasion. The man over in the jail—whose name I have forgotten but whom I'll call Black John—seemed to be the logical choice. He was presumably available through the simple expedient of paying off his fine; and he had plenty of legends clustered around his name. He was said to have crossed the Androscoggin on floating logs, once when young and drunk, just to give one example. So Roy Bragg, who was bossing the drive and had a drag at the jail, went over to get him.

He came back with Black John all right, but announced that they'd have to return him in good condition as soon as the emergency was over. Black John had been arrested during the preceding month and it was now the last of

September and the court records were closed and couldn't be opened again. They were terribly sorry, over at the jail, and they wanted to oblige; but they didn't make the laws. However, if Roy wanted to *borrow* Black for a couple of days, they'd be glad to lend him, if Roy would be sure to return him in good order. Roy was sure. Why wouldn't he be? There would be no liquor and he had plenty of strong-arm boys to keep their eyes on Black.

Early the next day the work boat brought in the camera-men and reporters. None of the woodsmen had ever been exposed to the gentlemen of the press before, and they were fascinated. So was I. They were exactly what I hoped they'd be, from reading and movie-going. They got every-body in a dither by running around poking their noses into everything and asking questions. The woodsmen were all ready to go out and start driving the logs, and I think they were a little baffled when it developed that first they were to take off their coats and sit around the camp and barroom occupying themselves with their usual Sunday diversions—stud poker, clothes mending, saw filing, read-ing, and sleeping—while they had their pictures taken.

Then the newsmen got a look at Black John, the star of the show. He wasn't much to look at, I'll admit—just a wizened up little old man with a grizzly stubble of beard, a bleary eye, and a slept-in suit of clothes. So the press went to work on him. They combed the camp for a suitable out-fit for him, snatching riding pants—known in the woods as puff-panties—off someone, making someone else kick in with his hat, and assembling every plaid shirt in the outfit until they found one that would not only fit reasonably well, but that would also photograph well. By the time they were through, Black John did look a little legendary, and he'd begun to act legendary, too. I don't think he'd ever in his life had such a fuss made over him. But he rated it. We all realized that, as soon as the gates were hoisted and the river began to roar.

There is a lot of difference between a river full of pulp-wood and a river full of long-logs. Pulp is just thousands of chunks—pronounced "junks" in our country—of wood. There is nothing particularly impressive about it, and it can be a nuisance, collecting in our swimming pool, clogging up the little basin between two rocks where I rinse my Monday washing, and spoiling the fishing. But long-logs—well, they come surging down the current like express trains, shedding green water from their backs, and leaping over boulders. There's something vicious about their bulk and speed—something alive and dangerous. Of pulp you say, "There's a lot of wood." Of a long-log you find yourself thinking, "There was a tree."

Black John climbed down through the dam and clung to the pier, waiting, his feet in their caulked boots a few inches above the racing water. Pretty soon he saw what he wanted plunging down upon him—a big high-riding pine butt. He leaped, and when he landed, light as a cat, his feet were going in a little dance step. The log spun and twisted and water boiled up to his knees, but he kept right side up. He didn't even seem to be paying much attention to what he was doing, and, to give him credit, he wasn't paying attention to the cameras, either. He was just standing there motionless except for his dancing feet. But when his log crashed onto a reef and half its length reared out of water, Black John was in the air a split second before the crash, and as the two wings of water flung out by the settling log collapsed, he was ten feet away on another log, still poker faced, still keeping his feet moving. He was good, all right.

After the cameramen had taken what they considered enough feet of that, they announced to Jim that now they wanted a log jam. So the boss went downriver to find one. With the amount of water running, that should be easy, but just to play it safe, Jim told him to take a crew, and if they couldn't find one ready-made, to make one. In the meantime he suggested that maybe the newsmen would like to see Black John go through the sluice of the dam on a log. Black John balked, however. He'd go for ten dollars, but he wouldn't go for nothing. In the first place this was supposed to be a vacation from jail, and he wasn't going to exert himself too much. He could work back at the clink. In the second place, if he fell into the river, as he was likely to do, it would cost him money. He'd have to reimburse the owners of his borrowed finery, and he'd have to buy himself a bottle of pneumonia preventative. However, he did finally compromise to the extent of agreeing to go down the sluice in a bateau if Jim would get him a crew. By the time the crew was found and had been taken out of their overalls and put into something more suitable, and the sluice had been successfully negotiated, the boss was back with the news that he hadn't been able to find a jam, but he'd managed to start a honey on the rips just above Long Pool. So we all adjourned the half mile down the river.

It was a pretty good jam. The logs were coming around the bend and hurling themselves onto the key log that the men had managed to lodge across the current, hitting with a hollow booming and jumping clear out of water when they struck. The newsreel men set up their cameras and the reporters got out their pencils, and the entire personnel of the camp swarmed out onto the jam to break it up. Half of the men had never seen a log jam before (pulpwood doesn't jam), but by this time they were all infected with the desire to get into the movies, so it wasn't very surprising that almost immediately some real action began. Somebody heaved too hard, and somebody else who was watching the cameras instead of what he was doing fell down into the crack between two logs. It was no joke. He went down to his armpits in the icy water, and all that prevented him from going further was the fact that he flung his arms around the logs. And the logs kept piling up from above, and nothing was giving an inch below. It's not very pleasant to stand on a river bank and watch a man being crushed within twenty feet of you, especially when there's not a thing you can do about it except yell. We all yelled, except the cameramen. They just kept on turning their cranks. That was their job, and I decided then that it wasn't a job I'd care for. It requires too much nerve.

And then Black John ran out onto the jam. He looked frail and ineffectual beside some of the woodsmen already there, but he was a river-hog from 'way back. He knew what to do. It was a very telling demonstration of the superiority of brains and experience over brawn. One heave with a cant dog, and the jaws of the nutcracker opened six inches. Six inches was enough. Out came the nut, so to speak, and high-tailed it for shore, leaving his cant dog behind him. Another heave or two, and the whole jam started downriver.

This I will say for Black John. He didn't let the situation die like that, with a bunch of logs floating off into the unknown. He threw back his head and howled, "Never mind the man! Grab his cant dog! That cost the company money!" That was the old river-hogs' battle cry. It put the finishing touch on the episode. Black John had a true feeling for style.

That about ended the famous long-log drive—except, of course, for the actual driving of the logs down to Umbagog. Its like will never be seen again. As a matter of fact, I doubt if its like was ever seen before in the annals of lumbering; it was unique. But everybody was satisfied. The newshawks—to quote *Time*—got their stories; the cameramen got their pictures; the salvage agent got his publicity; the woodsmen got their faces in the "moom-pitchers"; and the rest of us got a field day. I'm not sure what Jim Barnett got, except a lot of trouble and expense. If it's any comfort to him, we Riches think he managed the whole affair with graciousness and tact.

P.S. Black John was returned safely and in good condition.

VIII

⁕

"Aren't You Ever Frightened?"

THERE'S NOTHING TO BE AFRAID OF IN THE WOODS—EXCEPT
yourself. Nothing is going to hurt you—except yourself.
This, like all sweeping statements, is subject to a few
amendments; but the basic idea still holds. There is nothing at all to be afraid of in the woods—excepting always
yourself.

When I investigate what lies back of the statement, "I'd
be simply terrified most of the time, living the way you
do," I usually find bears. For some reason the non-woods-
wise expect to be eaten by a bear the minute they get out
of calling distance of a main highway. If it isn't a bear
that's going to attack them, it's a wildcat, and if it isn't a
wildcat, it's probably a rabbit. There may be a little more
danger from a bear than from a rabbit; after all, a bear
is larger. Animals in the woods aren't out looking for
trouble. They don't have to look for it. Their lives are
nothing but one trouble after another. The sentimental
view is that wild animals live an idyll, doing what they
want, browsing on herbs and flowers, wandering happily
along woodland glades, and sleeping where night overtakes

them. Actually the poor devils must live in a constant state of terror. So many things can, and do, happen to them. They can starve or freeze in winter. They are fly-ridden in the summer. Men and larger animals constantly harass them. Their young may be taken from them by any number of means, all violent. They know trouble too well to be interested in making any more. I pity all animals, but especially wild animals, from the bottom of my heart; and it's very hard to be afraid of anything that arouses pity.

I don't want to pose as an expert in animal life. In other words, I want to hedge a little. I don't know anything about lions or rogue elephants or hippopotamuses. People who know about them claim they're something to steer clear of, and I'll take their word for it. I've never happened to get in between a she-bear and her cubs, but I understand that that's not a good thing to do. I'm just talking about the Maine woods and the animals you ordinarily encounter there.

The way to see wild animals to the best advantage is to see without being seen. As a matter of fact, that's about the only possible way to see them. They don't stand around, if they see you first. I always wonder as I walk down the road, how many pairs of eyes have me under surveillance, how many hearts beat with suffocating rapidity until it is certain that I am going straight along the Carry on my own harmless business. I can feel that constant mute and questioning regard from hillside and thicket and roadside tangle of grasses and weeds; deer and bear and coon, and fox, mink and partridge and little white-footed, bat-eared mouse—they all stand and watch.

My favorite animals to watch are the deer and foxes. They are both so quick and pretty and well co-ordinated, and they're both such a lovely red color in the summer. We don't see foxes very often. They do their sleeping by day and their prowling by night. Once I saw one, though, eating blueberries off a bush. Usually we see them trotting their precise and dainty trot along the road. This one looked so informal, with his feet braced and his head out-thrust, pulling the clusters of ripe berries off the bushes, and ducking as the branch snapped back.

We see deer all the time, but we never get tired of them—or almost never. The exception was a deer we named Joe. He started coming into the yard when he was just a young spike-horn, and we took such pains not to frighten him that he soon became very tame. He'd stand around and watch us work. Deer are very curious, and it almost got to the point where before Ralph could drive a nail into a board, he had to shove Joe's nose out of the way. That was all right; what finally fed us up with Joe was his destructive attitude toward our flower gardens.

We'd worked hard on those gardens. One was an old ant hill, which we'd chosen as the site for a bed because it had good exposure and didn't need clearing. All it needed was to have the ants exterminated. Before we got through with that little chore, we wished we'd never been born. Two or three of the beds just had to have the underbrush and roots and rocks cleared away—and, of course, the soil changed over from acid woods mold to good garden earth. But the last of them we made on the vestigial remains of an ancient bridge pier. No one has ever been able to account for that pier. It is just above the house on the river bank and apparently once there was a very sizable bridge there. The pier is made of huge boulders, much too large to have been moved by anything less than an ox team, so the bridge was more than a temporary structure. There must have been a road through there once, but there is no record of there ever having been such a road. Where would it have come from and where would it have gone to? Nobody knows. There is no trace of it now. Someone once advanced the theory that Arnold might have built it on his way to Quebec, but I think his route is pretty well established as having been well to the east and north of here. Whatever the reason for the bridge, it was built a long, long time ago. We had to cut trees with six-inch butts when we cleared off the pier for our flower garden.

But that was only the beginning. When we got the trees cut and the roots and sod cleared away, there was nothing left but bare rock. We had to haul dirt in, from any place we could scrape it up, to fill the pockets in the rocks, and we had to haul in about an even amount of stable dressing to make the earth arable. We'd been all through this with the vegetable garden, but this was worse, because there was no hauling the trailer with the Packard to the scene of the operation and pitching the load off. It all had to be transshipped from the road by wheelbarrow, down narrow planks laid on a steep bank. It was a lot of work, and when we got it done and planted we didn't appreciate having Joe go in there to stamp down all our seedlings and later eat all the blossoms off any plants that survived his first treatment.

It may well be asked why we bother with a flower garden, considering all the sweat involved, especially when we have a whole forest full of wild flowers for the picking. The answer may sound a little silly, especially to those people to whom we have so carefully explained that no, we don't miss seeing other people. We don't miss them at all.

It may sound a little pixyish and whimsical to say that what we do sometimes get lonesome for are civilized flowers, and stretches of lawn and ordered gardens. Our tangles of zinnias and larkspur and violas, slopping over into rather shaggy grass paths, may be a pretty far cry from shell walks and clipped hedges and roses around a sun dial; but we love them and I can have tame flowers to put on my dinner table and around the living-room part of the year.

I hope the foregoing explains why we got bored with Joe. Unfortunately, he didn't get bored with us. He'd go back onto the ridges every fall, and we'd hope for the best. But every spring he'd show up again, bigger and lustier than ever. It didn't make us much happier to learn that a full grown buck makes a dangerous pet. After he has reached maturity, he may, without a moment's warning, turn definitely nasty, lashing out with horns and hoofs for no reason at all. The Durkees in Upton had a tame buck that, after living off their bounty for several years, suddenly chased someone into the lake—it was fall, too, and the water was cold—and wouldn't let him out until someone put a bullet through his head. We didn't want that to happen to us. The situation was solved when we developed that dog team idea. The smell and sound of a pack of huskies was enough to scare Joe into the next county. So some good did come out of that impractical dog-dream after all.

Probably the cutest, sweetest animals in the woods are new born fawns. They aren't red like their mothers, but spotted tan and white, so that when they stand still—as they do, instinctively, in the presence of danger—they look like just another patch of sun-dappled shadow. There is nothing quite so defenseless as a new little fawn, so Nature takes over its protection until it can at least outrun the more deadly of its enemies. Not only does a fawn become practically invisible when it stands still, but it has no scent whatever to betray its presence. A dog that can smell a deer a half a mile away will pass a fawn almost within touching distance, and never turn its head. Oddly enough, the fathers of most of the wilderness young are hell bent on their destruction, so Nature attends to that, too. During the spring and early summer, when the does are dropping their fawns, the bucks are in the velvet. They have shed their antlers during the previous winter, and on their heads are the beginnings of the new horns—two swollen, velvet-covered knobs, which are not only soft, but are also extremely sensitive. The mildest-mannered doe, inspired by mother love, has no trouble at all during the velvet season in bull-dozing the toughest buck that ever breathed. Nobody ever told us that this is the reason for the apparently extravagant antler-dropping, but to us it seems obvious, and I mention it because so many people have remarked to us that they didn't see any point in a buck's growing a fine set of horns only to lose them before the next spring.

Some people who should know better—like some guides and woodsmen—believe that a doe will desert her fawn if she detects the man scent on it, and they warn you not to touch a spotted fawn. I'm happy to be in a position to state authoritatively that this isn't so. This is how I happen to know.

One day in the early summer, Ralph was coming down from Middle Dam in our old Model T, and, as usual, he wasn't sparing the horses. He broke over the crest of

Wangan Hill and around the bend in the road, and there in front of him right in the middle of the road was a doe and a fawn that couldn't have been more than a few hours old. Its spots were bright and it wavered on its slender, impossibly delicate little legs. Ralph slammed on everything and skidded to a halt just as the doe, who stuck until the radiator was almost touching her, jumped clear. She had courage, poor thing. The fawn couldn't jump. It was too little and weak and confused. It went down in the road. Ralph swarmed over the door, heart-broken. He's often hardboiled in his attitude toward his own kind, but when it comes to animals, he's just a bowl of custard. Then he saw that he'd stopped well short of the fawn. It hadn't been touched. It had simply obeyed a command from something that had been born within it—a command to play possum. It lay flat on its belly with its hind legs under its body in a crouch and its front legs stretched straight out, its head between them. The grass between the ruts arched over it, and it lay perfectly supine, even when Ralph bent over it. Only its eyes moved, rolling back to follow his movements. Even when he ran his hand along its spine, to make sure it was all right, the only sign of life it gave was an uncontrollable shrugging of the loose skin on its back. It didn't know what this was all about; after all, it had had only since about dawn to get used to this world; it had nothing to go by except that inner voice; but it was doing its poor little best to follow instructions.

It was obvious that it would go on lying there until snow flew, unless something was done, and Ralph had to get home to dinner. So he picked it up in his arms and started to carry it to the side of the road. Then it came to life. Legs flew in all directions. It was like trying to cuddle an indignant centipede, Ralph informed me later. He put it down off the road in a hollow by a large rock, and leaped into the Ford.

The first thing I knew about the affair was when I heard the car come into the yard, and Ralph's voice shouting for me to come quick and ask no questions. Fortunately, I have long been accustomed to following orders first and finding out afterwards, so I set the pudding I was making back off the fire and ran. On the way back to Wangan Hill, Ralph explained what had happened, so I was all prepared when we left the car at the foot of the hill and walked the last hundred yards to where he had left the fawn. The hollow by the rock was empty.

Then we looked up. There, not twenty feet from us, were the doe and fawn, standing in a little patch of sunlight. It was one of the prettiest sights I ever saw. The little fellow was standing perfectly still while its mother lapped it over from head to tail, to get the obnoxious human smell off it. They both stared at us gravely for a long moment, and then the doe wheeled and trotted away—not frightened, not even nervous—with her child galloping obediently at her heels. If I'd been a mother then—which I wasn't—I'd have known that this was all that would have happened. There have been times since when Rufus didn't smell exactly like a lily, but I've never considered abandoning him for that reason.

The animals we see most, next to deer, are porcupines. I can't seem to find it in my heart to love a porcupine. They're perfectly harmless—they *don't* throw quills, by the way—but they're stupid and ugly, and besides, they do a lot of damage. They fill the dogs full of quills, which is the dogs' fault, I'm willing to grant—and they try to gnaw our houses down around our ears, and they climb trees and sometimes girdle the tops, thereby killing them. The quills stick up all over their backs in an untidy mess, and they have blunt rodent faces with dull, slow eyes. They don't make any noise, except a rattling sound, which I've read is made by clacking their quills, but which I think, myself, they make with their teeth. I can't vouch for this. I don't have much traffic with them. I did catch one once and put it under a water pail in the middle of the garage, so that when Ralph went to back the car in, he'd have to get out and move the pail. I knew what his frame of mind would be toward the blankety blank so-and-so that would leave a pail there, and I thought it would be fun to have him kick it viciously aside, only to unveil a furious porcupine. It didn't work. The porcupine escaped by a sapping operation, and Ralph didn't get home until after dark and never saw the pail. We did have an albino porcupine that lived for a while out back of Gerrish's house, and that, being rather rare, was interesting enough. But porcupines as a tribe are very, very dull. We had a weasel living in the chimney base once, too, but we never could get very matey with him, either. He was too quick for us. We'd see him, brown in summer and white in winter, flowing like quicksilver in and out of the rocks and bristling his whiskers at us. He always gave me the shivers. He was so deadly purposeful, and he had such a vicious eye. I was glad when he moved away.

We've never seen a wildcat, though there are plenty of them around. We see their tracks often enough, and sometimes hear them yowling on the ridges. They aren't dangerous, unless cornered, but they like to make you think they are. One of their tricks is to follow you along the road, just about dusk. They don't stay out in the open, where you can turn around and heave a rock at them. They keep in the bushes at the side. When you stop, they stop. When you hurry, they hurry. After a while it gets on your nerves.

Once in the late fall I was sitting in the living-room of an evening with Ralph and our friend Rush Rogers, knitting. It was a very peaceful scene. For once the room was reasonably tidy, and for once the dogs—we had two then, Kyak and Mukluk—were sensible of their responsibilities, and were lying in picturesque postures in front of the fire, instead of trying to crowd us out of our best chairs. The firelight glanced off the backs of the books on their shelves in a satisfactorily colorful manner, and a little light snow brushed the window panes gently from time to time. The radio was coming in well, and the room was full of music. I should have been purring like a cat, with contentment, but I was uncomfortable, for some reason. I couldn't settle down.

Rush said, "Good Lord, Louise, what ails you? I never saw you twitchy before."

I said, "I don't know. I just feel someone looking at me."

Ralph hooted. "I suppose so. Who, for instance?"

I said stubbornly, "I don't know. I only know someone's looking at me. I can feel it."

I didn't get any sympathy. I just got told that neither of them could stand notional females, and if I was planning to develop a temperament, I'd better go somewhere else and develop it. They both knew a lot of sure-fire cures for temperament.

But I still felt someone looking at me.

Finally I couldn't stand it any longer. I got up, lighted a lantern, and went out on the porch. The dogs raised their heads somnolently, and Ralph and Rush exchanged looks of bored amusement. It was snowing lightly outside and the porch floor on the open end was sugared thinly over—all except for a little spot where a furry rump had been planked, and two smaller ones that were clearly paw marks, directly outside the window at which I was sitting. A scramble in the snow told of a hasty departure when I had opened the door. The evidence was easy to read. A wildcat had been sitting within three feet of me all evening, watching me knit. I learned later that this is not at all uncommon. They love to look in at lighted windows. I can't imagine why. I can't imagine, either, what ailed the dogs that they didn't put up a howl—except that they have a real talent for always doing the wrong thing, even when the wrong thing is nothing.

We see bears only once in a while, although there are plenty of them around here. They are shy animals, not easily caught unaware. We usually come on them in various berry patches, when their attention is concentrated on picking berries and they are off guard. These encounters are carried off with a minimum of excitement. We say, "Oh," and start south, and the bear says, "Oh," and starts north. Not that anybody is afraid of anybody, you understand. We just don't like to intrude on each other's privacy.

We don't believe in confining wild animals. Nothing makes me madder than to see a lion in a cage or some luckless racoon chained up at a gas station. I'm not a reformer by nature, but that's one thing I will crusade about. I think it's all right to kill animals if you have to, or even if you want to, but it's not all right to imprison

them. I always feel like declaring a holiday, and Ralph
does declare one, when we hear about a service station's
confined bear running amok and maiming a few attend-
ants and customers. It serves them darn well right. So,
feeling as we do, we never try to make pets of the wild
life around us. Just once did we make an exception, and
that was none of our seeking. It was more or less wished
on us by circumstances.

This is the way it happened. I had asked Coburn's driver
to bring me in three lemons, so when Ralph came home
with the mail and handed me a little paper bag, I thought
I knew what was in it. I tipped it up and dumped the contents out on the kitchen work bench. Then I did a typical
female, clutching my pant legs and shrieking, "Eeeee!
Take that thing away from here." My lemons had suffered
a sea-change into a two- or three-day-old skunk.

When I recovered my composure enough to look the
thing over, I had to admit it was cute. It was about three
inches long, with an equally long tail and about half inch
legs, and it was striped black and white like any other
skunk. Ralph had seen it in the road when he went up to
get the mail, and when he came back over an hour later,
it was still there. By then it had fallen into a deep rut
and was unable to get out. He stopped the car to help it,
and found that it was almost too weak to stand. We
discovered later that, the day before, a mother skunk,
accompanied by her new and numerous offspring, had had
a skirmish there with one of Coburn's guest's dogs. (The
dog lost, incidentally.) In the fracas, this little fellow,
whom we named Rollo, got lost.

You can't go off and leave a young thing to die of
starvation, naturally, so Ralph picked it up and brought

it home. He put it in the lemon bag so he could hold it without hurting it while he drove with one hand. He thought he could probably figure out some way to feed it after he got it home.

Cookie, Kyak's mother and the best dog we ever had, was our dog of the moment. Not to put too strong a point on it, she was the best dog anybody ever had, bar none. Kyak and the other pups were a couple of weeks old, and we were still keeping them in a pen in the corner of the kitchen, where they'd be warm and where Cookie could reach them easily. While we were debating the skunk commissary question, she came in to dispense the evening meal to her family. That seemed to be the answer. We found an unoccupied nipple, told Cookie everything was under control, and added Rollo to the roster. She looked a little startled, but, being the dog she was, took our word for it that the situation was entirely *comme il faut*. That's the kind of a good dog she was.

Cookie was willing, and Rollo had the right idea, but a husky is built on a somewhat grander scale than a skunk, so it wouldn't work. Then we thought of a medicine dropper, and that did work. Poor little Rollo went at it, clutching the dropper frenziedly with both front paws, and never stopped drinking the warmed canned milk and water until his little stomach was as round and hard—and about as large—as a golf ball. By this time Cookie's four pups were gorged and asleep, so we dumped Rollo in with them. Cookie looked at us, smelled of him, and looked at us again, trying to understand what was expected of her. Cookie definitely was a lady, and she always tried to live up to her station in life. She understood that we meant that she was to take care of this odd-looking addition to her family. So she rolled him over with her nose and, despite his struggles, lapped Rollo thoroughly from stem to stern, just as she washed her own children. After that Rollo belonged. Nobody was going to accuse Cookie of favoritism; and from that day on, Rollo was just another husky puppy, as far as she was concerned.

I think he, himself, thought he was a dog. Certainly the other pups treated him like one of themselves. The whole lot of them played together as puppies do, roughhousing and mock-fighting, chewing each other's tails and ears, and attempting mayhem in any form. At first we used to try to rescue Rollo. The pups were almost ten times as big as he was, and I was afraid he'd get killed. But he didn't thank me at all for my solicitude. When I put him down again at a safe distance from the fray, he'd stamp his hind legs in a towering rage—the skunk method of expressing extreme irritation, and the last step before the gas attack—and rush back to fling himself into the battle. I still don't understand why he didn't get completely ruined. I've often seen one dog grab him by the scruff of the neck while another grabbed his tail, pulling him in opposite directions with all their might, growling and shaking him as puppies will do with a piece of rope. It made my stomach ache to watch, but he apparently loved it for when they released him, he'd always rush in for more. It's my opinion that that twenty-four hours of being lost in the wilderness so early in life left a bad scar on his subconscious, so that he valued any attention as preferable to no attention. He'd never let himself be left alone for a moment, if he could help it, and when the pups slept, he was never content to sleep on the edge of the heap. He'd always burrow down into the center, completely out of sight.

He used to follow me around like a shadow as I did my housework. He'd be at full gallop never more than six inches behind my heels, and if I reversed my field, he'd side-step and fall right in again. It was lucky he was so fast on his feet. Half the time I'd never know he was there and, if I'd ever stepped on him, there wouldn't have been even a grease spot left. He was so tiny he could easily curl up in one of my shoes and have plenty of room left. It made him simply furious to have me go upstairs. The risers of the steps were much too high for him to negotiate, and I'd come back down again to find him stamping back and forth in a dudgeon below the first step. That stamping never failed to amuse me. He'd not only be mad—he'd be just damn good and mad! And yet, though he obviously wanted to make a noise like thunder and stamp the house down, the best he could make was a little pattering sound on the floor. If you're ever gone out of a room in a fury and slammed the door behind you with what was supposed to be a shattering crash, only to find it was equipped with a pneumatic check and so eased soundlessly into place, you can appreciate how he probably felt. Still despite his rages, he never in all the time he was with us made the slightest smell in the house. We thought some of having him operated on, but the vet in Rumford said frankly he had never done such an operation, so we let it go. We are glad now that we didn't find someone who could do it. He was cleaner around the house than any cat we ever had and he never, even in his infancy, made a single error.

Only once that we know of did he ever make a smell and we couldn't blame him for that; in fact, Ralph applauded him. We had at that time a cat named Jane, and she and Rollo had always hated each other, for no good reason that we could ever see, for they always left each other strictly alone. One evening I had made a chocolate malted milk for Rollo—that was his favorite food—and set it out. Rollo was just starting in on it when Jane appeared around the corner. Rollo stamped violently but Jane continued to approach and sniffed at the saucer. She wasn't going to touch the contents, I'm sure; she was just curious. But he had warned her and she had paid no attention. Faster than the eye could follow, he turned end for end, arched his tail over his back, and—whisht! smack into Jane's face at a range of less than a foot. She rolled right over backward, scrambled to her feet, and went off like a bullet. She never came back. Presently she took up her abode at the nearest lumber camp.

We had been afraid that after the pups and the skunk reached the age where they could eat solid food, Rollo would starve unless we fed him separately. He could never hold his own, we thought, against that gang of ruffians. We might as well have spared ourselves the worry. He was quite capable of looking out for himself. When the crush around the communal pan of puppy biscuit and milk became too great, he would wade right into the middle of the dish, forcing the pups to eat along the edges while he stuffed himself practically into a coma.

Rollo became a terribly spoiled brat before the summer had advanced very far. We gave him too much attention, and so did the dogs, and so did the sports who kept coming in in increasing numbers as the news of our pet skunk spread. I never thought to have my social career sponsored by a skunk, but that is what it amounted to. I met more new people during that summer than I ever have before or since in the same length of time. Perfect strangers, they'd come drifting into the yard from God knows where, say "Good morning" and then come to the point:—"We heard you've got a pet skunk." The upshot was always the same:—would it be all right for them to have their pictures taken holding Rollo? The folks back home— Rollo became as camera conscious as a child movie star, and as objectionable. He'd look bored and sulky—but he'd never miss the chance to have his picture taken. His complete composure served as an excellent foil, I might add, to the nervous apprehension on the faces of his picture-companions. Nobody ever seemed to quite take our word for it that he was perfectly safe.

Skunks are a horribly maligned animal. Everyone shuns them. Everyone accuses them, and without ascertaining the facts, of various crimes, such as hen-killing and egg sucking. They do no such things. Actually they do no damage at all; on the contrary, they are the natural enemies of vermin of all sorts and among man's best friends in the country. They are naturally gentle and easily tamed. A skunk will never attack until he is sure his person is in danger, or unless he is suddenly startled. I wish more people would bother to be nice to skunks. We were, and it paid. Rollo, in spite of being spoiled, made a perfect house pet while he was with us.

We never made any effort to confine him so it couldn't last forever. He was always free to come and go as he pleased. We even untacked a corner of the screen in the kitchen door so he could get in and out at will. As he grew older, he began to revert to nature, and the skunk nature is nocturnal. He slept more days, and roamed about nights. When we went out to the woodshed in the early, dewy morning to get kindling to start the breakfast fire, we would more and more often meet him, just coming home from a night's ramble. Then for a while he wouldn't come home for two or three days at a time, and finally he didn't come home at all. We'd meet him sometimes a mile or more down the Carry Road, and he'd run up to us and we'd pick him up. He never forgot us, and we never forgot him. We just grew apart, as those whose interests diverge always grow apart. Finally we stopped seeing him altogether. I don't know what eventually did happen to him—whether he wandered away, or whether he met with an accident. Very few wild animals die of old age. One thing we were glad of then—that if he did meet with death in any of the common swift wilderness forms, at least he was able to go down fighting. We hadn't rendered him defenseless.

Actually I've only been frightened once by animals since I came here to live. That was up at Miller's, and was a completely silly performance. It happened a long time ago, when Cookie was only a puppy. She had an enemy—Miller's older cow—who never overlooked an opportunity to chase her. I don't know how the feud started, and I don't know whether the cow would have hurt Cookie if she had caught her. It may have been just her bovine idea of a game. However, that may be, she certainly looked like business as she thundered after that terrified little ball of fur, with her head down, her nostrils flaring, and her tail out stiff behind. I don't blame Cookie for putting her tail between her legs and scuttling.

It was in June, and Alice Miller had a houseful. There were her sister Amy and two small girls, a half dozen men who were working repairing the dam, a woman named Polly Gould who was doing the cooking for them, and her little girl, besides Alice's own family. We went up there one evening to visit with the assembled multitude, and in the course of events, Alice, Amy, Polly and I took the collection of five small children and my small dog up into the back pasture to see if the blueberries were ripe. The two cows and Betty, the horse, were grazing off toward the edge of the woods, but we didn't pay any attention to them. Betty is as cross-grained a piece of horse-flesh as ever drew breath, but usually she minds her own affairs.

Cookie saw her old enemy in the distance, too, and I suppose she thought that now her inning had come. She'd been the chasee all too often. Now she was with me, the all-powerful; it was her turn to be the chaser. I don't suppose it ever entered her addled little head that the creature lived and breathed that would have the temerity even to think of attacking me or Ralph. We were God, as far as she was concerned. If you're walking with God, there's nothing you don't dare. You even dare to run yapping after a dragon and nip at its heels.

Unfortunately, neither the cows nor that limb of Satan, Betty, were True Believers. As one, they threw back their heads in affronted amazement, snorted, and took off after Cookie, who knew only one thing to do. She turned in her tracks and sought sanctuary under the shadow of my wing.

The first I knew about the whole business was when Amy shrieked, seized her youngest by the arm, and started running for the gate. The rest of us looked up. I don't know how two cows and a horse could create the illusion of being a whole herd of Texas longhorns gone loco, but they did. We each grabbed a child, and the whole bunch of us streamed off across the field, women shouting for help, children screaming with terror, and poor little ki-yi-ing Cookie bringing up the rear. None of us up to that time had been famous for her track work, but that evening, in spite of the rough ground, the boulders, and the bushes, we shattered all records for a two-hundred-yard dash. I swear that as we fell over the rail fence, hot breath was fanning the backs of our necks and horns were grazing our posteriors.

That's the only time I've been frightened in a country where bear and wildcats are common, and cows and horses extremely rare; and because I was so scared, and the whole thing so ridiculous, my immediate reaction, once we were safe, was unbounded rage. I was mad at Miller's livestock, at Cookie for bringing them down on us like a wolf on the fold, and at myself for running. But I was maddest of all at Ralph and Renny Miller and the crew of workmen off the dam. When we had got our breaths, and the spots had stopped dancing around in front of our eyes, did we see them running anxiously to our aid? We did not! We saw them all lying helpless on Miller's back stoop, weak with laughter.

Classed with animals as an A Number One Menace, by females from the city, are what they always refer to as "drunken lumberjacks." I am not a psychiatrist, but as a writer whose stock in trade is human nature, I am interested in all its various manifestations. One of the least explicable to me is the phenomenon of the woman who would not allow such a crude and lusty word as "rape" to pass her well-bred lips, but whose every inflection indicates that that is what she is hoping to be told about when she asks obliquely and with bated breath if I am not afraid of drunken lumberjacks. Well, I'm not. In the first place, very few of the lumberjacks I see are drunken. They may have been when they left civilization, but by the time they get in here, they're only sick and sorry, and in no state to menace anything larger than a day-old chick. In the second place, drunk or sober, they're twice as scared of me as I am of them. I hope that settles that question once and for all. I'm just a little bored with women who claim to be afraid of men, or who feel either inferior or superior to men, or who consider men as being anything other than so many more people.

There are, of course, a few things in the woods that anyone with sense is afraid of. So are there in the city, or on a farm, or at the seashore, or anywhere else, except possibly in the grave. A reasonable amount of danger is part of the price of living.

The hurricane of September 21st, 1938, was something to be afraid of—only none of us except Ralph had ever been in a hurricane before, so we didn't know enough to be afraid until it was all over. Then there was so much else to do that there didn't seem to be any time for fear. I'm not going to go into any great detail about the hurricane. Everybody who lives in New England has his own version of that cataclysm; and everybody in the world knows somebody in New England, and has therefore heard all about it, probably *ad nauseam*. Let me just say that after three days of pouring rain, along about dusk of the fourth day the wind started to blow very, very hard. Ralph was at Middle with Fred Tibbott, who was visiting us, and Edith Tibbott and I were at home with Rufus. After we'd waited supper half an hour, they called up from Miller's to say they couldn't get the car started, so they'd have to walk home, and for us not to worry. Up to then we hadn't considered worrying. We'd heard quite a lot of noise outside, but the woods are always noisy when the wind blows.

I decided that this was as good a time as any for me to go to the john, so I threw open the kitchen door, and almost walked into the top of a tree that was lying where the porch had been. The porch was at the bottom of the cellar hole, twelve feet below. That was the big birch at the corner of the house, I made mental note, and Ralph was going to be good and mad when he saw it down. In the meanwhile I still had my errand to perform, and there was still the front door. I turned the knob, the door crashed back against the wall, and I stepped out into the top of a pine that lay across that porch. This was no night, I concluded, to go ramming around in the dark. I shut the door and tried to call up Miller's, to tell Ralph and Fred not to start home. The line was dead. With rare perspicacity I diagnosed it as trees down across the wire. There was nothing to do, so Edith and I ate our supper, brought Rufus downstairs to sleep—a tree had fallen across the roof right over his crib, waking him up and starting a leak that dripped onto his pillow—and sat down to read. This sounds like courage and composure, but it was only ignorance.

After a while Fred and Ralph came in, soaking wet and full of tales about dodging falling trees all the way from Middle Dam. There must be, they said, at least two dozen blowdowns across the road. Ralph was, as I had foreseen, sick about the trees in the yard blowing down, but since there was nothing to be done about it, the two of them ate their supper, we all had a game of Mah-jongg, and went to bed.

In the morning we woke to a ruined world. We couldn't even get across the yard; trees lay criss-crossed in a giant tangle from the back steps to the road. The sky line all around us was unrecognizable. Where had towered tops that I regarded as personal friends and eternal landmarks, now gaped ugly holes. It was heart-breaking. A house you can rebuild; a bridge you can restring; a washed-out road you can fill in. But there is nothing you can do about a tree but mourn, and we had lost twenty-eight of our largest trees right in our front yard. Somehow it made it worse that the sun shone brightly, and that the still, washed air was as soft and warm as down. The day was like a bland and lovely child under whose beauty lay the horror of idiocy.

Fred and Ralph worked all day with axes and a two-man cross-cut, cutting a way through the mess to the road, the woodshed, and other frequently used points. Late in the afternoon, one of the dam crew staying at Miller's managed to get through from above with the news that instead of two dozen trees across the road, there were over two hundred. We needn't let it worry us, he concluded comfortingly. There was no reason for us to go up to Middle anyhow. The Lake Road to the Arm from Andover was plugged, too, and the mail wouldn't be coming through until God knew when. By that time they'd have the Carry Road open, for they had to be able to use it to get back and forth to Pondy Dam which they were repairing.

I thought then, and I still think, that it was a terrible waste that no one was murdered on the night of the hurricane. The writers of the whodunits work dreadfully hard thinking up and presenting plausibly the very strict frameworks of their stories. Here we had it all handed to us on a silver platter. We were a very limited group; we were cut off from the police and from all outside help; there was no way of escape for the murderer; the night and storm served not only as suitable atmosphere for crime, but created the confusion necessary for the successful perpetration of that crime. And nobody even got hit by a flying branch.

We don't have hurricanes more than once in a century in New England, so they rate rather as an exciting novelty than a true source of apprehension. We've had our allotment of hurricane. What we have to worry about now are the consequences of it.

The consequences are not all bad, we discover, in spite of our initial myopia to silver linings. The birds, deer, and small animals have increased greatly in numbers around here since the Blow; the condition of the woods has made it difficult for hunters to get around, and the great windrows of blowdown afford marvellous cover. I'm all for anything that will conserve wild life, even if it incidentally jeopardizes my own roof-tree. And actually my own roof-tree will profit, too. Old opportunist Rich immediately saw the possibilities.

After the hurricane, as I have explained before, the Government organized a pine-salvaging project. However the pines that had blown down across the Carry Road couldn't be salvaged by them because they had been butchered into every imaginable odd length when the road was cleared out. The idea then was to open a thoroughfare, so every tree lying across the road was cut twice—where the gutters would be, if we had gutters—and the piece in the middle was rolled off to one side. The result was several hundred good pine logs of no commercial value because they were in crazy, hit-or-miss, non-saleable lengths. We had long been planning extensive remodelling of the summer house, building a new shed for the rolling stock, and what not. We didn't object to unorthodox lengths for the jobs we had in mind. So Ralph made a deal with the landowners whereby he acquired them to the benefit of all concerned. All the next summer he and Gerrish worked like dogs getting these logs into a boom they strung in our boat cove in the Pond, where they would be safe from worms, fire, and rot.

That's easy to write, but it wasn't easy for two men to do. What they lacked in numbers, they had to make up in ingenuity. They finally worked out a rig that was the marvel of all beholders to take the place of the rest of a four-man crew. They took the front axle of the deceased Packard, complete with wheels and tires, and equipped it with a drawbar that could be fastened to the rear of the Big Green "Mormon." The butt ends of the logs rode on this, while the top ends dragged. But two men can't lift a three-foot green butt eighteen inches off the ground and roll a pair of wheels under it. So they built a portable ramp which they carried along in the car, studded with spikes to prevent slipping, and rolled the ends of the logs up onto this, using a combination of cant dog leverage and roll hitches. Once the log end lay on top of the ramp, projecting sufficiently ahead, the axle was rolled under, the log was dropped on it and secured with ordinary logging chains, and off they went, as merry as could be. At the Pond they had built a log rollway, and it was comparatively easy to unchain the log, haul the axle out from under it with a quick jerk of the car, roll it over to the top of the rollway with cant dogs, and let her go. I used to go up and watch them unload and roll in for the simple and elemental pleasure of seeing the big splash. I felt a little sheepish about this at first, and advanced the excuse that I really went because Rufus liked to watch the water fly. Very soon, however, I noticed that many of the crew that worked on the pine drive managed to be around kibitzing when unloading time came, and that, while they were interested in the mechanics of the operation, they always cheered when the great fan of water rose twenty feet into the air. After that I didn't apologize for my simple tastes. After all, where would Niagara's popularity be if people didn't like to see water splash?

This landing the logs in the Pond, however, wasn't even the beginning, since we aren't planning to build a deluxe log cabin. We're planning to rebuild a house, with pine paneling throughout the common rooms. So the logs in the Pond have to be transmuted into boards and timbers, and since that is impractical to do by hand with a broad-axe, we have to build a small sawmill. You see how one thing leads to another, when you can't just call up a dealer. At present the foundation of the mill is partially built, and sooner or later it will be running, powered by the old Packard Twin Six motor. I can already foresee the end. The logs in the Pond will be hauled out and sawed up, and the paneling will be made and put up, and the house will be finished. Then we'll have a sawmill with nothing to saw. This will be a challenge to Ralph, and he'll start thinking up other things to build, so he can use the mill. Then after every available inch of our property is covered with buildings of one sort or another, we'll probably end with an eighty-foot schooner, or something.

The most immediate result of the hurricane is really a legitimate worry—or rather, an increasing of one of our few standard dangers—the danger of forest fire. That's a thing that is never out of our minds, and a thing we have a right to fear, because we have so little control over the starting of a fire. We, ourselves, are almost fanatically careful about matches, and cigarette butts, and lunch fires. Everyone who lives in the woods is. I've known men to get to worrying over whether every ember of a fire they'd made at noon was out, and to back-track eight miles, after dark, just to make sure. But these were woodsmen. People from the Outside aren't conditioned to the fire hazard as we are. They don't mean to be careless, probably. They just don't know any better. If you're used to throwing a cigarette butt down wherever you happen to finish it, it doesn't register whether it lands on an asphalt pavement or in a brush pile. (Just thinking about the latter makes my palms sweat.) And fires aren't always started by humans. There are plenty of instances where they have been started by lightning, or even by a bit of broken bottle, acting as a burning glass. This chance element is what brings our heads up and sends us running for the field glasses to scan the horizon at the suspicion of a whiff of wood smoke.

It was bad enough before the hurricane, but now it is a hundred times worse. Now the woods are full of dried, dead tops that will burn like tinder. If a fire should start over back of a mountain somewhere, it might take a half a day or more for the fire fighters to get in to it through the blowdown, instead of two hours as formerly. With a brisk breeze behind it, and bone-dry brush to feed on, a fire can travel ten or twelve miles an hour, or even faster. You see, it doesn't burn evenly. It may jump a half a mile over the heads of the fighters, leaving them in an extremely unenviable position. That's why, when a pillar of smoke

arises somewhere off in the bush, the telephone begins to
ring, and we get out a compass and a map to determine,
by comparing the sightings of Joe Mooney and Upper
Dam, say, just exactly where it is. If no ponds or barrens
lie between it and us, and the wind is in our direction, we
get ready to start to collect the things we're going to
evacuate.

We don't have to discuss what we'll take with us when
we leave. That was all decided long ago. We don't have
to discuss where we'll go. If the fire is below us we'll go
to Middle, where there are boats to get us out onto the
lake. If the fire should be above us or cut us off from the
lake, we'll go to the Pond-in-the-River and take to our own
rowboats and canoe. If it's a big fire it will get pretty hot
and smoky out on the Pond, but we can always submerge
ourselves. We won't be very comfortable, but the odds will
be in favor of our surviving. For just such an emergency
Ralph always aims to have at least one car in good running
condition, regardless. The first load out of here will consist of all of us, Kyak, Tom (if we can catch him), the
typewriters (which are our living), an envelope containing
birth certificates, will, deeds, and other documents, and
Ralph's cedar box of Scotch flies (which he sets great store
by and which are practically irreplaceable). If there is time
to come back for more loads, we can get clothes, guns, and
fishing tackle. It's very illuminating to have to make a list,
which you will very possibly have occasion to use, of the
things you'd save in an extremity. It reduces one's material possessions to their proper place.

Since the hurricane, we have had two or three fires
within danger-distance of Forest Lodge. One was over by
Magalloway, and the fire-fighters got it under control be-

fore it burned over very much woodland. These fire-fighters may be volunteers, but they are as likely as not conscripts. The wardens have a right to draft any able-bodied male they may run across and oblige him to fight a forest fire for thirty cents an hour and meals—if the meals can be got to him at his post of duty. Often they can't. Fire wardens are only human, and it's my opinion that nothing delights them more than to force some stray sport, all done up in the expensive outfit that goes with a fifty-thousand-dollar income, to dirty his hands and burn his clothes for a measly thirty cents an hour. I'm a meany, too; I, too, think it's funny.

The other fires were across the river from us between C Pond and Upton. They were started through the care-lessness of the river drivers on the Dead Cambridge. We could see the smoke, travelling fast and low on the wind, about four miles away, and at night the skyline pulsed with light. When you can see that variation of glow caused by a whole tree suddenly exploding into flame, then you know the fire is too close for comfort. If the wind had shifted and come drawing up the river valley, as up a gigantic flue, nothing could have saved Forest Lodge. We sat up late nights, during that time.

Then the wind died down and a slow and drizzling rain started, the sort of rain that people living as we do actually pray for, forgetting the fashionable scepticism with which education has veneered us. It was a steady, quiet, increasing rain, with the promise of a long wet night in it and, come morning, the surety of sodden woods through which no fire could travel. We tipped the porch rockers against the wall to keep the seats dry, and brought the deck chairs up out of the garden. We closed the windows on the southeast side of the house, and placed a pan on the floor under the annoying gable that always leaks a little after a long drought has shrunk the shingles. We dashed out after forgotten clothes on the line, and brought in logs and kindling for the fire-place. It would be safe to have a fire this evening; the roof would be well soaked and inhospitable to sparks. And everything we did, we did with a sense of reprieve, with the realization that doing these homely things was a privilege of which we might have been deprived. We knew then that it is true that the only way to know how much you love a thing is to see it in peril of being lost.

Another legitimate worry in the woods is sickness and unavoidable accidents. Fortunately, woods life is very healthful. We are never sick, literally. Aside from the period directly following Rufus' birth—and I count that as a natural phenomenon, not an illness—I haven't spent a day in bed since I've lived here. Ralph has spent only two, with a bad cold. He doesn't count that against himself, as he didn't cook up his own cold, but caught it from some Outsider who came in here teeming with germs. If ever medical science wants data on the nature of the common cold, we're the persons who can supply it. We do all the things that are supposed to cause colds—things like walking half a day through wet snow with our clothes sopping wet, or not changing our shoes after coming in after a day in the rain, or sitting on cold stones, or lying full length on damp grass—and the only time we have colds is when someone brings them in from the Outside to us. We don't have things like mumps or measles, because people with ailments like that aren't fit to travel in here. What it amounts to is that we are living in a sort of reverse quarantine, with the germs locked out instead of in. It's wonderful—although I can't help feeling that the minute we get Outside among the coccuses and viruses that are rampant there, we'll be bowled over like nine-pins. Any immunity we may have built up in previous years has probably long since atrophied.

Almost every accident that can happen to you in the woods is avoidable, and soon you learn to avoid them. You have to, with a doctor usually no nearer than twenty miles—and twenty pretty tough miles, at that. You learn to hold wood that you are splitting by the edge and not by the top, so you won't take off a thumb. I don't have to remember here to look both ways before crossing the road —but I do have to remember always to keep an axe on the off side of the log when I'm limbing out, to carry it over my shoulder with the blade away from my head, and never, never, to take a full swing with it unless I've made sure first that I've got plenty of room behind and above me. These things I no longer have to remind myself to do; I do them quite automatically; and if this seems like odd habitual behavior for one who was brought up more or less as a lady, I can only say that there's no comfort in being a lady with a few inches of cold blue steel inbedded in your skull.

If you get cut by an axe in the woods, all you can do about it is to try to stop the bleeding, disinfect the wound —with salt, probably, as that is most easily available—and tie it up to get well by itself. If you can't stop the bleeding, you can send for the doctor, if it will make you feel any better in your mind. Almost certainly, however, the bleeding will have stopped by itself, or the patient will have bled to death, before the doctor can get in, unless the accident occurs in the summertime and there happens to be a doctor staying at Coburn's. The three weapons to use against axe cuts then are: (a) sense enough not to get cut, (b) a good working knowledge of how to apply a tourniquet, if the worst occurs, and (c) a philosophical attitude.

Burns are fairly common in the woods, and they're almost always the result of carelessness, too. You can easily get burned pouring kerosene into a stove to boost up a slow fire, or by tripping over the cat while carrying a kettle of scalding raspberry jam, or by unscrewing the cap of a boiling car or tractor radiator, or in any one of a dozen other damn fool ways. The only time I ever heard of anyone getting burned in complete innocence was last winter when a lumberjack was walking by the stove in the barroom, minding his own business, and for no reason at all the stove tipped over at that moment and dumped its blazing contents onto his feet. That was just tough luck, but it didn't make it any the less painful. As usual in an emergency of that sort, we were summoned, and we applied our sole remedy for burns—compresses of strong, cold, freshly made tea. This may sound like witch doctoring, but of course it's really the standard tannic acid treatment. He got well. Our burn patients always get well if they stick with the tea treatment faithfully.

Tea, therefore, besides being a beverage in our house, is a permanent item in our medicine cabinet. So is iodine, for small cuts and bruises. So is a five-pound package of Epsom salts, which we wouldn't dream of administering to our worst enemy internally. We use it solely in hot saturate solution for soaking infections. Because our lives are far from sedentary, and our diet is correct, we never need what are euphemistically known as "little pink pills," but we do keep on hand a bottle of Castoria, in case Rufus needs it, and one other laxative, for the use of visitors. We also have a bottle of fruit salts for alkalizing the system after we have been exposed to someone else's cold. I keep aspirin on hand, and take perhaps three tablets a year. Ralph takes none. Gerrish sometimes suffers from neuritis, and he takes the rest. Add a jar of some soothing salve, some gauze bandage, some adhesive tape and absorbent cotton, and baking soda for insect stings, and you have our complete medical equipment. Ralph also keeps a couple of pound cans of anaesthetic ether on hand in case the doctor if called for broken bones should forget to bring any. Our equipment isn't elaborate, but it's quite adequate.

You can break bones in the woods, by not paying attention to what you are doing or where you are going. You can drown, by the same method, or freeze to death, or smash yourself up in the rapids, or lose yourself in the woods. It always boils down to the same thing, though— you weren't using decent judgment. So I still insist that, aside from forest fire, there's nothing to be afraid of in the woods, except yourself. If you've got sense, you can keep out of trouble. If you haven't got sense, you'll get into trouble, here or anywhere else.

I lost myself just once, and I'm glad I did. It was an experience worth having, since it turned out all right. It was, of course, my own fault, from the very beginning. The reason I made up my mind to go to B Pond three days after the hurricane was because the day before one of Coburn's old guides started out for there, got lost, never even saw B Pond, and after hours and hours of wandering, finally came out on the Dead Cambridge, some four miles beyond his goal. From there he eventually got out to Upton. I decided to show the world that I was a better guide than he was; and that, I submit, is the world's least worthy excuse for taking a chance. I would even have gone without a compass, if Ralph hadn't made me take one. Me get lost just stepping over the ridge to B Pond? Don't be silly. I don't need a compass. But I took it to save argument, pinning it into my shirt pocket with a safety pin, because Ralph said he'd scalp me if I lost it.

Well, I got to B Pond all right. It took a lot of doing. The trees were down across the trail in windrows, some of them twenty feet high. I could see how Coburn's guide got lost. He did what I did—went around the piles instead of over them. I did what he didn't do—always worked back to the trail again before trying to go forward. Therefore I never piled up any considerable drift away from the correct line, as he did. His error eventually added up to several miles. Mine was never over a hundred yards, a fact for which I take no credit. I was only profiting by his mistakes. I got to B Pond. There was a watchman, Fred Davis, staying in the lumber camp over there, so I have his affidavit to prove it.

It was on the way back that I got lost. Fred Davis fed me doughnuts and coffee and advice before I left for home. I think he was a little doubtful of my sanity, because he talked to me as if I were a child. "You've got a compass? All right. If you have to use it, remember it's *right*. A compass is always right. Remember that. You've got matches? All right. If you find yourself hurrying, sit down and smoke a cigarette. Smoke it slowly, right down to the end. Don't get scared, no matter what happens." I listened politely. He meant well, even if I didn't need his advice.

I'd already been over the ridge once, hadn't I? Well, then—

It was that cocky attitude that lost me. I didn't think it was necessary to follow the trail quite as closely as I had coming over. That was primer stuff. I knew roughly where the trail was. I could get back to it any time I wanted to.

Only I couldn't, I found. Suddenly nothing was familiar. I was in the middle of a black-growth swamp that I hadn't even known existed. I had no idea whether I was east or west of the trail. I thought I was on the west side, but I could have crossed the trail unwittingly while crawling through or over one of the tangles of blowdown. There was just one thing to do—get out the compass and go by it. If I went slightly east of north, I'd come out somewhere on the river, and from there I could find my way home.

My first look at the compass shocked me. I was going directly southeast, according to it, and that was obviously crazy. The compass was wrong. I must have broken it coming over. Or else there were mineral deposits around here that no one knew about. Whatever the reason, the compass was obviously wrong. I *knew* I was going in the right direction. Then I remembered what Fred Davis had said. "The compass is always right." Ralph had told me the same thing many times. "*Always* believe the compass." All right, then, I'd give it a try, in spite of my better judgment. I lined up a topless maple about a hundred feet away, pinned the compass back into my pocket, and started across the tangle of spruce and fir blowdown.

That was the most hellish trip I ever took. I was almost never on the ground. Sometimes I was twenty feet in the air, with nothing to step on, with twigs scraping my face, and with the knowledge in my mind that if I slipped here, I could easily break my back and die slowly and horribly, with not a chance in the world of being found. But worse than that was something that wasn't mind or heart or anything else that I've ever felt before, pulling me irresistibly around to the southeast. To go against it, to follow the compass, was almost physical agony. It was something that can't be conveyed to anyone who hasn't experienced it. I would climb laboriously over a tangled jack-pot, and stop and get my breath. All around me, hemming me in, were more towering piles of blown down trees. I would start over a pile of them, and then remember that I was supposed to be following the compass. I would unpin my pocket, take the damn thing out, and look at it. If it was right, my proper route lay almost at right angles to the way I was going. But it *couldn't* be that way! However— I'd pick a landmark by it, put the compass back in my pocket, pin it in and start climbing; and all the time that thing inside me was twisting and turning and pulling me over to the right. Fighting it was harder than fighting the blowdown. I've talked with other people who have been lost, and they all agree with me that the feeling is something that can't be conveyed. It's like being under a spell.

Then at long last I heard the river. It wasn't where it should be at all. It was where the compass said it would be, which was something quite different. I came over one last gigantic windrow, and could see it shining through the branches. I heard an axe. There, only a few rods above me on the other side was home. I could see Ralph chopping away at a tree in the yard, and Edith Tibbott sitting with Rufus on the porch. They looked like people in a mirage, small and clear and unconcerned. I felt as if, should they glance in my direction, they wouldn't see me at all. If I shouted, they wouldn't hear me. They couldn't really be there. I took a long drink of river water, washed my face, wiped it on my shirt tail, and started up the shore toward the dam.

I'm glad I got lost; it was an experience. I hope I never, never get lost again, and I don't think I ever shall. You see, there's nothing in the woods that can hurt you, except yourself. I know better now than to hurt myself that way again.

IX

"Don't You Get Awfully Out of Touch?"

SOME TURNS OF SPEECH ARE USED SO FREQUENTLY THAT THE meaning has worn off them, just as a hero's head wears off an old, much-used coin. They still pass as legal tender between one mind and another, but they are really only blank and worthless tokens for what once were ideas. We use them just as we use a thin dime; we accept them for what they represent, not for what they are; but if we stop to weigh and examine them on the scales of sense and in the light of reason, we see by how much time and rough usage have reduced them.

I know perfectly well what people mean when they say, "I should think you'd get frightfully out of touch!", but it's a silly expression all the same. Out of touch, indeed! I don't see how anybody, actually, can be "out of touch." The demented are in touch with some world of their own. The castaway is in touch with his physical surroundings, his material needs, his thoughts and his memories. The sleeper has his dreams; and the dead—who can say surely what or where the dead touch?

So I ask sourly, "Out of touch with what?"

The answer is always the same, and always delivered a little vaguely, it seems to me, in my annoyed and hypercritical mood. "Oh, the new books, and plays, and music. You know. Culture and world affairs. Your own sort of people."

There's no answer to that, except, "Oh, nuts!", and ordinarily I don't go around saying "Oh, nuts" to anybody outside the family.

The reasons I feel like saying "Oh, nuts" are manifold. Just as a starter, I have often read more new and old books during the preceding year than my interlocutor, and I might add, read them with considerably more attention and appreciation. I don't have to do my reading, you see, for any other reason than my own enjoyment. We happen to have a great many new books, because we are lucky enough to have a rather tenuous connection, through my librarian sister, with a book shop in Boston, and one of the owners—feeling sorry, no doubt, for "Miss Dickinson's poor sister, stuck way off up there in the woods"—sends us, at intervals, boxes of advance copies which are given her by the publishers. These are occasionally bound galley proofs and sometimes regular copies as they will appear on the book stands, except that they have paper covers. Now this, I know, is childish, but I get an awful kick out of reading books in galley proof, in spite of the fact that they are tough on the eyes. It makes me feel tremendously in the know and *au courant* of literary matters. If I happen to find in the book, as we often do, a little slip of paper announcing the first day of sale to the public, and if that date happens to be, as it sometimes is, some time week after next, then my cup of bliss is full. Not only am I reading a new book, but I'm reading it before my friends in the city, so enviably "in touch," can possibly get it. All right; I admitted it was childish, didn't I?

Then, too, I actually do have time to read those books that I always planned to read, but never got around to, or that I have read once hastily—in the days when I lived in civilization and had to read the books "everybody" was reading, or else suffer looks down the nose because of my ignorance—and always planned to go back to for more intelligent perusal. I have read all of Proust, for example, under this scheme (I didn't think very much of it, either), and "The Education of Henry Adams" (which I think very highly of indeed), and I've reread "The Case of Sergeant Grischa," which I remembered rightly over the years as containing some passages of extremely beautiful and moving prose—notably the description of the march to face the firing squad. I memorize a lot of poetry, too, so I'll have something to be saying to myself on long walks. A poem to repeat, either aloud or silently, will help you over a hill or on a long mile as surely as a neighbor who stops his team and gives you a lift.

I never can get over the power of some combinations of words to stir the heart. They are, after all, just words, and taken separately they don't quicken the pulse at all. But there's something about certain alliances—. Take for example "Fills the shadows and windy places with the lisp of leaves and ripple of rain." Take almost all of "The Garden of Proserpine," which doesn't even make sense, but is so musical and beautiful that it doesn't have to mean anything. It is full of such lines as "Blind buds that snows have shaken" and "Red strays of ruined springs." Bertrand Russell can make my scalp crawl any old day with such examples of his own particular brand of cold and chiseled prose as the last paragraph of "A Free Man's Worship," which begins "Brief and powerless is man's life; on him and all his race the slow, sure doom falls pitiless and dark," and ends "—to sustain alone, a weary but unyielding Atlas, the world that his own ideals have fashioned despite the trampling march of unconscious power."

What wouldn't I give to be able to write like that!

I'm very sorry to say—and I mean this; I am truly sorry, because I know I miss a lot—that I don't appreciate good music. I don't understand it and it doesn't speak to me at all. I wish it did, but about the most complicated compositions I can enjoy are Sibelius' "Finlandia" and something called "Kammenoi-Ostrow" by Rubinstein, and these I can hear on the radio often enough to satisfy me. If I did comprehend and love classical music, I could still hear it on the radio, for I could listen to the Philharmonic, and it would cost me neither money nor effort. I could sit in my pet rocker with my ski-panted legs folded under me and smoke a cigarette and have a fine binge for myself; but that just isn't my kind of binge.

The same applies to plays. I never was a theater fan. When I lived in cities, I missed a great deal of possible pleasure because of this blind spot of mine; but since I have lived here, it has proved to be a blessing. I'd be miserable if I read of the opening of something new and enormously good, and knew that there was no possible way I could get to see it. As it is, my appetite for the dramatic has to be satisfied with the situations that arise in my own life, or the lives of my friends, or in the general world condition. These bits of theater are less artistic and well-shaped than the scenes that appear on the stage, but since

I don't know enough about good theater to be critical, they keep me happy.

If the foregoing is a confession of self-centeredness, lack of imagination, of taste, and of background, I can't help it. It's the truth.

I don't see how people living in cities, instead of off in the woods as we are, can really know so very much more about world affairs than we do. If living in civilization meant that they were in the confidence of Winston Churchill or had daily tête-a-têtes with even a second under-secretary of an under-secretary of the Secretary of the Navy—maybe yes. But as a matter of fact, they know only what they read or hear, and that's exactly what we know. The only difference is that in the city you can get ten conflicting reports a day on any given situation, while we have to wait until *Time* comes in the Friday mail to find out what the whole thing really boils down to. We get our news a little late, but I wouldn't be surprised if in the long run we have a clearer and more sensible idea of what is going on than those who read every special edition and listen to the special spot-news broadcasts on the radio all day long. Frankly, I don't see how they can possibly know where they're at from one moment to the next, and I should think they'd all go raving mad.

We have a radio, too, of course, so if we wanted to, we could hear news broadcasts every half hour or so. But we don't want to. We have too much else to do; and, since ours is, perforce, a battery set, we have to consider before turning the radio on whether what we are about to hear is worth running the battery down that much. It's amazing how much you decide can be eliminated under those circumstances. If it would help humanity or the course of the War by so much as one iota, I would gladly sit all day long and listen to eye-witness accounts of air raids and hour by hour reports on the progress made or not made along the numerous fronts. But it wouldn't help anything, and it would keep me in a constant state of turmoil and indigestion. So we have our fifteen minute dose of everything's-going-to-hell each evening, and the rest of the day we try to forget about it. There's not very much tranquillity left in the world today. It may be that in striving to preserve a little of it we are making the best contributions within our powers. Or it may be that this is pure rationalizing, and we are guilty of the most abysmal selfishness.

In our house, when you turn the radio on, it's because someone wants to listen to something specific. As the batteries get low, we listen to fewer and fewer things, saving the power, until the batteries we have ordered arrive, for what we want most to hear. Elmer Davis, Ezra Stone in "The Aldrich Family," and "Information Please" are the very last things to go. No matter where they stand nationally, they're at the top of the Rich Poll. If we have a little more leeway, we listen to Jack Benny's program, partly because we think it's extremely funny, and partly because we're always in hopes of being able to put our finger on the reason why it's so funny. Then there's a program called "I Love a Mystery," which probably hasn't anything to recommend it at all from an artistic point of view—except the sound-effects—but which we adore. It's full of creeps and horrors and hair-breadth escapes, and the actors are splendid. If there's a prize fight of importance, we listen to that. Ralph and I could once take or leave prize fights, but they are Gerrish's meat, and he's finally managed to get us into the same frame of mind. The idea is that we try to keep our radio in its place. It is our servant, and we try not to let ourselves become its slaves.

I'm not decrying the radio at all. I think it's marvellous —so marvellous that I won't let anyone try to explain to me how it works. We explain too much, in this day and age. Even if I could understand all about wave lengths, which is doubtful, I'd much rather not. I like to feel myself in the presence of a miracle when I turn a switch and the voice of a man in California comes all the way across a continent of snow-covered farms and frozen rivers and mountain ranges and empty plains to fill our living-room with song. Perhaps the miracle would be even greater to me, if I knew just how it's done, but that's a chance I don't dare to take.

In the summer we have a daily paper from Boston, and all the rest of the family read it religiously. I have to admit, though, that aside from reading the headlines and the Household Page, I use it mainly for a game that I play with myself. Like all the rest of my solitary games, it is simple-minded; but, like the rest of them, it entertains me. It consists of scanning the pages carefully and deciding which of the events reported I am gladest I didn't have to attend. Usually there's a wide choice of material, and I'm hard put to it to choose between the Girl Scout Jamboree at Old Orchard Beach (five thousand Scouts between the ages of twelve and sixteen were there, and mustn't that have been a headache for someone!) or the Forty-and-Eight Costume Parade in East Fairview Centre (where three women fainted, and if I know my costume parades, feuds for a generation to come were started over the charges and counter-charges that the judges had been suborned). If this game served no other purpose, it would serve to make me—if such were necessary—satisfied with my lot well off the beaten track.

Another thing that I am happily aware of being "out of touch" with is the world of fashion. I was never very clothes conscious, so my best efforts at chic were never very satisfactory, when I was in circulation. If I looked smart, I felt most uncomfortable and self-conscious; and if I felt at my ease, my appearance was such that my friends would feel called upon to explain to their friends, "You mustn't expect her to look too snappy; but she's awfully good-hearted. When you get to know her, you'll like her."

It's wonderful to sit up here in the woods and look at the pictures in the advertisements of the hats I don't have to wear. (It's my belief that a hat should help your face, not do its best to increase a Simple Simon effect.) My sole attempt at glamor so far has been the purchase and use of a ten cent bottle of red nail enamel, and this was somewhat less than successful in its purpose. I put it on twice, and both times was rewarded by shudders and averted eyes on the parts of Ralph and Gerrish, and wails from Rufus because "Mummy hurt self!" I finally abandoned it and Rufus appropriated it. He painted Kyak's toenails red and slopped some on his fur. The game warden came in, gave the dog one look and said, "I thought you told me your dog wasn't a deer killer." It took some demonstrating to prove to him that Kyak wasn't reeking with the blood of innocent victims, and when that was over I pitched what was left of the enamel into the river.

There has been just one time in my life that I regretted bitterly not being beautiful and glamorous and marvellously apparelled; and that happened, as of course it would happen, just before the spring break-up. At that moment my wardrobe was at its very lowest ebb as the transition from winter to summer clothes had not yet taken place. It consisted of a pair of worn flannel slacks, a pair of really impossible ski pants, and some faded wool shirts. Moreover, I was about twenty pounds overweight, my hair was as straight as a string, and I couldn't get Outside to have a permanent—not that a permanent would have helped much, but I think it would have given me moral courage in a situation that I think any woman would have found difficult.

This is the way it happened, and I'll have to go back a little to fill in the background. Ralph has a great many qualities which I love and admire, but tact is not among them. He is just about as intuitive and sensitive to nuances of feeling as an iron hitching post. This works as much for me as against me. If he sometimes seems insensitive to my feelings, I by the same token don't have to worry about his being wounded by a chance word or look of mine. The result is a sort of rough-and-ready understanding of each other that I wouldn't exchange for all the romantic twaddle in the world. But it was not always thus. When we were first married, Ralph used to tell me occasionally what a good cook and sempstress and conversationalist and what-not Sally's mother was. I did have sense enough not to burst into tears, in the bride tradition, and accuse him of not loving me. But all the same, I felt inferior.

Then Sally came to live with us, and she sang her mother's praises, too. There was no reason in the world why she shouldn't and every reason why she should. She naturally loves her mother dearly, and moreover, it is greatly to her mother's credit that Sally never showed the slightest resentment of me as her father's second wife. Intellectually I could see that; but emotionally I developed a simply horrible case of jealousy. I'll never underestimate the power of jealousy to drive its victim to any length. It's a dreadful thing to be jealous. It distorts your whole mental outlook. I, who know, say so. Ralph, the insensitive cluck, of course never sensed that I felt that way, for which I now give thanks.

Then Sally went to Europe to join her mother, and I managed to forget about the whole thing, most of the time. I had Ralph, and then Rufus, too, and a life of my own that was proving more and more absorbing. In short I began to get sense. And then—

Then one fine early April day, Alice Miller called me up on the telephone and said with an air that chilled my blood even before I heard the message, "Well, I've got some news for you that you're not going to like! At least, *I* wouldn't like it, if I were in your boots."

My heart sank. "Now what?" I asked.

"Well, we just had a call from Baltimore on our Outside phone. It was really for you, but of course we took the message as they can't get you on that phone." She was deliberately keeping me in suspense. Before break-up is a slow time in the woods. Then she threw her bomb. "It was from Ralph's first wife. She and Sally are coming in to visit you."

I had thought Sally and her mother were in Haiti. I don't remember what I said to Alice. I do remember, to my shame, walking around the kitchen telling Ralph, "I won't have it. You've got to do something. I simply won't have it!" It really wasn't so much that I *wouldn't* have it, as that I *couldn't* have it. I just couldn't cope with the situation. Here I was, plain, everyday Louise, with a shiny, wind-burned nose and chapped hands, expected on practically no notice to compete with a beautiful cosmopolitan, fresh from the salons of Europe. I didn't have any clothes. I didn't have any conversation. I hadn't been anywhere or done anything interesting. She'd been everywhere. She'd have lots of interesting experiences to talk about. She'd have trunks full of gorgeous clothes. She'd be witty and fascinating.

"I won't have it," I repeated. "You've got to do something."

I know Ralph was stunned by this sudden metamorphosis of house cat into tigress. He just looked at me as though he didn't know me. "But what can I—"

The upshot of it was that poor old Ralph walked up to Middle and called practically every hotel in Baltimore until he found the one at which Sally and her mother had been registered. They'd left half an hour before for Boston. And that, as it turned out, was one of the best breaks I ever had.

Even I in my half-maddened condition—and I can see now that I was being impossible, although I think that almost every woman can understand how I felt—couldn't refuse hospitality to a guest who had come all the way from the West Indies. It was really a compliment to me, I suppose, that Terp felt she could come. Whatever Sally had told her mother about me must have been at least reassuring. Now, after it is all over, I can feel pleased about that.

At the time, though, I simply felt defeated and hopeless when Ralph made his report. "What'll I do now?" he asked.

"Nothing," I said. "There's nothing you can do. Don't worry about it. I'll be nice." I gritted my mental teeth. "If it kills me," I added silently.

It didn't come anywhere near killing me, because as soon as I met Terp, I liked her. I'd better make that absolutely clear at once. Naturally, everybody within a radius of about fifty miles knew about the whole situation before forty-eight hours had gone by. The local grape vine smoked, and the taxi driver who brought Terp and Sally up to the Arm from Rumford must have stopped at every village and farm on his way back, as near as I can figure it, to make his report. I could actually feel a wall of suspense and anticipation tightening up all around us.

Everybody knew who had gone in to Rich's, and they were just sitting waiting to see who would come out. Some probably thought it would be Terp, with a black eye and most of her hair pulled out. Some thought it would be me, with my chin elevated righteously above the folds of a cloak of outraged virtue. But none thought it would be possible for us to live two minutes under the same roof. That it was possible is owing chiefly to Terp's tact and absolute honesty of purpose. She was the perfect house guest, and she had no ideas whatsoever of breaking up my home. She wanted to leave Sally with us again, and she wanted, before she did it, to ascertain what manner of woman she was handing her child over to for a longer or shorter period. This is a motive that anyone can respect.

I'm afraid, however, that locally I got most of the credit for preserving the status quo. I know exactly what everyone was saying and thinking all around us. I know all about the interminable analyses of the situation, and the speculation that was rife, and the inevitable final conclusion—"Well, all I can say is that Louise is better natured than I'd ever be. *I* wouldn't put up with it!" I began to feel like a character in a Russian novel. There was the snow and the deep woods and the surrounding waste spaces, and in the middle of it we sat, a man and his two wives and assorted children. Terp even has red hair, and in Russian novels someone is always a beautiful redhead. All that was needed to complete the picture was a troika and a wolf pack.

It's always nice to have made a new friend, but this visit gave me more than that. It gave me freedom. It made me realize that the things we fear are almost always things which needn't be feared at all. They are creatures of our imagination. There was never anybody like the Terp of whom I was so jealous, but I would still believe in her and make myself miserable on her account, but for the fortunate chance that Ralph got that hotel in Baltimore on the telephone half an hour too late.

Not long ago, a friend who was about to marry a widower said to me, "Tell me honestly, weren't you ever insanely jealous of Ralph's first wife?"

The idea was amusing. I started to say, "No, of course not."

Then I remembered, dimly at first and then with increasing vividness. Yes, I had been exactly that—insanely jealous. I hope I never forget it. As long as I can remember that particular needless hell, there isn't much chance of allowing myself to repeat the experience for any fancied provocation.

We're supposed also to be objects of commiseration because we are out of touch with what are referred to as "your sort of people." There are two major weaknesses in this premise. The first is that I haven't been able to find out in thirty-odd years of living exactly what sort of a person I am. I think that this is a fairly common difficulty. It's hard to evaluate oneself, and self-evaluation is usually tiresomely self-conscious and absolutely inaccurate. When I hear someone say, in all honesty, "Now I'm the sort of person who'd give the shirt off my back," I decide immediately never to ask him for the loan of a common pin. If the analysis runs, "I never forget an injury," I know that I can count on immediate and generous forgiveness and forgetfulness for any injuries I may have inflicted. The only clue I have to my own character is a family saying which runs something like this—"That old loafer! Sure, he's a bosom pal of Louise's. The bigger the bum, the surer he is to be one of Louise's friends."

As a matter of fact, I don't know exactly what is meant by "your sort of people." There are plenty of people around here that we would be highly complimented to be classed with. Perhaps they didn't come from Boston, and perhaps they aren't college graduates. So what? They have the qualities—generosity and honesty and humor—that we would be happy to feel we shared.

The other weakness is that we aren't out of touch with anybody that we want to stay in touch with. After all, the U. S. Mail still operates. Because we have more leisure to write letters than we had in civilization, we are actually closer to a great many people than we ever were before. I know all about the great efficiency of the telephone and telegraph, but I still think it's too bad that the old-fashioned habit of long letters has fallen into desuetude. Brevity and speed are all right in business matters, but friendships can't be put on a business basis, even in the matter of communication. I like to know what my friends are thinking and feeling. If too long a time elapses without my checking up on these things, I find that where once was a friend there is now a pleasant stranger. When I lived in the city, I had lunch and went to the theater with these strangers at fairly frequent intervals. Since I took to the woods, I haven't seen them at all, but some of them have become my friends again. We've had to fall back on letter writing, you see.

There is this to be said for writing a letter instead of having lunch downtown: when you are writing a letter, you are thinking only of the person who is going to receive it. Nothing else is bidding for a share of your attention—neither the funny hat on the woman at the next table, nor the quality of the service, nor the nagging worry as to whether that odd sensation around the calf of your leg a moment ago was or was not a run starting in your new stockings. In short, there is no static. In addition to this, I find it very difficult to discuss intimate matters with anyone. It is embarrassing for me. I start talking about the weather as soon as the conversation shows a tendency to get personal. On paper though there's nothing I wouldn't hash over. Any of my correspondents will probably be glad to corroborate this.

Since I have to depend on letters for many of my contacts, especially in the winter, when, perforce, we have very few visitors, I have developed a few loose rules for being a good correspondent. I don't have to point out, I'm sure, that letters received should be answered within a reasonable time—say a month; but there is such a thing as answering too promptly and writing too long a letter. It makes answering a burden to your correspondent, who will feel obliged to do at least as well as you have done, and will soon be heartily sick of the whole thing. I always try, at least, to answer any questions that have been asked me in a letter I am replying to. Nothing makes me madder, myself, than to have people ignore my questions. I wouldn't have bothered to write them if I didn't want to know the answers. I try also, in order to avoid my frequent difficulty of sitting down to write a letter in which I had thought I had plenty to say and suddenly finding that I've forgotten all the gems I was going to pass along, to make notes from time to time on the back of the envelope of the latest letter received from my correspondent. These make odd reading—"Spare ribs, O. K."; "C. V. arrested for stealing bear out of trap"; "Al's report on Jake" —but I know what they mean. This is a little trouble, but not so much trouble as trying to make the brick of a letter without the straw of subject matter. And finally, I don't expect to get any answer to a letter. Then I'm never disappointed or annoyed when nothing comes of it, and I'm delightfully surprised when something does. This same attitude can be adopted with profit toward almost any aspect of life, I have found.

Not only do the mails run, but the boat still runs, and when in winter it has been hauled out, Larry's snowboat runs. So we can and actually do see some of our Outside friends in the flesh, from time to time. Naturally, we feel drawn to anybody who cares enough about seeing us to make the long, hard trip in here, and most of all to our very favorite flock of loons from Massachusetts whom we refer to as "The Crocks." This isn't a reference to their physical condition, but to the fact that a couple of them are named Crocker. Actually they're a rugged crew. They come in here, singly or collectively, at any time of the year, and by every conceivable method, snowboat, snowshoe, dog team (Stumpy once owned a dog team, but like us decided it wasn't worth the trouble), boat, canoe (Stumpy has some aluminum canoes with outboard motors, that are the marvel of all beholders), and, if necessary, on foot through the woods. They haven't arrived by airplane yet, but that will come as Ralph Smart was a pilot in the last war. It doesn't make any difference how or when they come, we're always enchanted to see Stump and Big and Bill and Ralph. It makes it nice that one of them is named Ralph, too, since that is also Gerrish's first name. When the Crocks are here, all I have to do is request, "Ralph, get me a pail of water, will you?" and I get three. I accomplish this by carefully not looking directly at any one of the three Ralphs.

The Crocks presumably come in here for a rest, but they have the strangest notions of resting that I ever heard of. They must endorse the theory that a change is a rest. The minute they get here, they start splitting wood, or going on jaunts to B Pond, or helping with whatever is the current project around the place. Stumpy and I always plan to go to Sunday Pond across country by compass, just to show it can be done, but so far the world has still to be shown, by us, at least. Meanwhile, my Ralph and the others sneer audibly. Bill is the most normal in his choice of amusements. If it's summer, he goes fishing, which is all right. It's even all right to fish as he does, about ten hours a day. Gerrish adores Bill because he's always crazy to fish, and goes too. Big spent all one Sunday morning, when Ralph was cleaning up the hurricane pine along the Carry, understudying the driver of a tractor that Jim Barnett had very kindly let Ralph have the use of that day. I can see how anybody who has never driven a tractor might want to try it once, but Big started at nine o'clock in the morning and, with Ralph, was two hours late for lunch, while Bill and I waited. That's quite a stretch for a man who ordinarily spends his day behind a desk. And it wasn't as if this was his one chance of a lifetime to horse a tractor around. Big's company in Fitchburg, Mass., owns a dozen tractors, and he could go out and run one any old time he chose. But I suppose that would be work.

Besides themselves, which would be amply sufficient, The Crocks always bring us all the new stories that are going the rounds Outside—and they hear them all and tell them well—and a collection of swell food, always including exotic viands, such as caviar, shad roe, artichokes or palm hearts. I know these things aren't really necessary to the sustaining of life, but it certainly does something for you in the middle of winter, when you have been living on pot roast and carrots, to drink a Cuba Libre and then sit down to a really sophisticated meal—the sort of meal that you have always before eaten off snowy linen, under soft lights, and to the accompaniment of muted music. It doesn't, surprisingly perhaps, taste any the worse for being eaten by kerosene lamp light, off a linoleum table top, to the sound of sleet against the window. If anything, it tastes better for this seasoning of incongruity.

The general impression which seems to be shared by most of our city friends is that we live in the middle of a desert and never see anybody. This obviously isn't true, as I think I have made apparent. We see lots of people, ranging in rectitude from the game warden to border jumpers and notorious poachers. (One thing I have noticed that all poachers have in common is a manner that can best be described as piety put through a collander, a sort of purée of noble thoughts and too-good-to-be-true motives.) Our friends and acquaintances range in geographical origin from Alice Miller, who was born in Andover, Maine, to a lumber camp cook named Roland Thibault, who was born in Saskatchewan and arrived here via Alaska and the West Coast.

In addition to the people we see, we also have friends whom I, at least, have never seen. Joe Mooney at the Brown Farm is one of these. I've talked with Joe countless times on the telephone; we have some very spirited encounters, yet I've never laid eyes on him. Joe is quick on the trigger. He can and does come back instantly with a pertinent comment upon any situation; but unfortunately for purposes of illustration it is usually unprintable. Joe is a swell guy. Johnny West was another. I never spoke to him in my life; I wouldn't have known who he was if I'd met him face to face on the Carry Road; I don't imagine he knew any more about me than my name and where I lived, if he knew that. But I always felt comfortable in my mind when I heard Johnny West go over.

Johnny West was a flyer who ran an air service out of Berlin, N. H., up through the lake country, and anywhere else for that matter. It wasn't a very big business and it didn't run on any regular schedules, but if you had to go somewhere in a hurry, either into or out of the woods, you could call up the Brown Farm, who would call Berlin, and get Johnny to come and get you. His plane had pontoons in the summer and skiis in the winter—he could always find a lake to set his crate down on in our country where landing fields don't exist—and it was always painted red. We'd hear an airplane motor and go out and look. There high up through the tree tops we'd see a flash of scarlet.

"There goes Johnny West," we'd say to each other. "Wonder where he's going."

We might well wonder. He did the oddest business, I should imagine, of any pilot in New England. He flew lumberjacks into camps, when they'd missed the tote team on account of too much conviviality. He came into camps in the winter and flew out cases of the horrors or compound fracture. Once he went into Upper Dam, in the middle of the spring break-up when Upper Dam was inaccessible, to get an old man who was very, very ill. This was to be the old man's first time in the air, after almost eighty years of living. He died before Johnny West got there, but he still got his ride. The body had to be taken out somehow.

Johnny West flew fishermen, and he also flew fish. When the State put about eight thousand stock trout into B Pond, he flew them in in milk cans lashed to the pontoons. That was the only practical way they could be brought in alive. The alternative was to pack the cans in on the backs of guides, which would have been too expensive, and trout die if too many are confined in too little water, unless the water is aerated. Even the sloshing around in the cans that the water would get on the B Pond trail, probably wouldn't be enough to keep the air supply replenished. But they could be flown in in five minutes from South Arm, where they arrived in special tanks with aerating blower attachments. It worked out very well.

I'm not awfully sure, though, that I approve of the

whole thing, on general principles. If you fly fish into B Pond, the next step is flying fishermen in to catch them, and that puts B Pond in the class with any little mud hole on the State Highway. I think a few places ought to be left in a hard-to-get-to condition. There should be some reward for willingness to make an effort. I wouldn't climb a mountain for anything I could think of, off-hand. I loathe mountain climbing. But still I don't think motor roads should be built to the tops of the best peaks. I'd be awfully annoyed if, after a ten-hour scramble up the side of a mountain, I arrived breathless and exhausted at my goal just in time to see a fat dowager in printed chiffon drive up in a limousine to park between me and the view. I'm going to be awfully annoyed if some day I stagger out of the woods onto the shore of B Pond, after negotiating that rough trail, just in time to see a plane full of playboys and girls make a landing.

Johnny West was a beautiful flyer. When he set his plane down on a lake, it was like seeing a red maple leaf flutter to the water. He was company for us, and he made us feel secure. We knew that if something perfectly dreadful happened—something beyond our ability to handle, like double pneumonia or a broken back—we could always get Johnny West to fly a doctor in, or fly us out. He saved a woman's life up in Parmachenee by flying a doctor in in the middle of a bitter winter night, about a year before his death.

Johnny West is dead. He died when his plane struck a high tension wire in the course of a forced landing, just as the early winter night was drawing in. I hope it was the way he would have chosen to die, but I don't know. I didn't know Johnny West. He was nothing to me but a flash of red across a lonely sky, and a thin, steady throbbing over the noise of the river. He was nothing to me but a name—and our margin of safety.

Aunt Hat is even further removed from my orbit than Johnny West was; she must have died years before I ever dreamed of coming into Maine. She didn't even live here. Her place of business was in Bangor, when that was still a lumber town. But Aunt Hat nonetheless is a very real person to me. You see, instead of going to the theater, we who have taken to the woods while away some of our long winter evenings sitting around each other's kitchens, drinking coffee, eating doughnuts, and talking. Talk is the backbone of our social life. It was during one of these evenings in the Millers' kitchen, when the wind was swooping down across the back pasture and the loose snow was driving across the lake like an army of gigantic ghosts, that Renny Miller brought Aunt Hat to life for us. We've loved her ever since.

Renny has his own way of telling a story. He starts slowly with no emphasis, filling in all the details as he goes along. That night he was telling us about his boyhood on a farm near Bangor, and how his first job was in a livery stable in town. "That's how I met Aunt Hat," he threw in casually. "Aunt Hat? Why, in them days Aunt Hat was the toniest Madam in the State of Maine. She ran a house up on the Orono car line. There wasn't a more respected businessman in Penobscot County than Aunt Hat, for all she wore skirts. She ran her place right, too. You didn't find no drunken lumberjacks in her house, like you did down the other side of Bangor. She kept the place clean and quiet, and it was furnished elegant—all gold furniture with red plush upholstery. And her girls were ladies, every one of 'em.

"Just to show you how smart she was— One Hallowe'en night a bunch of boys moved one of them little waiting stations the trolley car company had strung all along the line for the customers to take shelter in during bad weather. They lugged it down from a couple of miles up the track and set it up on the edge of Aunt Hat's front lawn. Now a lot of women in Aunt Hat's business would have been sore, figuring they was being guyed. But not Aunt Hat. She was real pleased. She seen right off what a good idea it was, and she made the company leave it there. They had to build themselves a new one, up where that one was robbed from. She was a smart woman."

"Were you one of her customers?" Ralph asked.

Renny grinned. "Aunt Hat and me was just like that." He crossed two fingers. "We set an awful lot of store by each other. Like I told you, I was working for a feller that ran a livery stable in Bangor. I was a pretty good hand with horses, and after he'd sort of tried me out with the old hacks he had in there for two-three weeks, he figured he could trust me, and he put me in charge of his show rig."

Renny sighed and his blue eyes grew dreamy. "Now there was something you don't see no more," he said nostalgically. "That rig was the prettiest sight I ever laid eyes on. Four coal black horses, he had—not a white hair nor a blemish on any one of 'em. Just like peas in a pod, they were. Them horses was curried twice a day till they shone, and the boss kept 'em so full of oats they danced, instead of walking. Them horses was so proud of themselves, by God, they made a man proud to be seen with 'em. He had a set of white harness with silver buckles made special, and it was as much as my job was worth to let a speck of dust get on that rigging. Every time it was used, I had to clean it and do it up in fresh tissue paper. White plumes it had, too, kind of sprouting off them four black foreheads, and he had a big white carry-all, with black cushions and silver trimmings. On either side of the driver's seat was a big silver lamp, and the whip set in a silver whip-socket. The driver had a uniform, sort of, that he had to wear, in keeping with the rest of it—tight, white britches, and a black cut-away coat and white gloves, and a silk hat with a bunch of white ribbons on the side of it. You'd thought I'd have felt like a fool in that outfit, me being about seventeen at the time, and fresh off the farm. But after I got to know them horses, I wouldn't have any more disgraced them by making them appear in a public place with me in my work clothes than I'd have let them go hungry. The boss hired this rig out for swell picnics and such, and I guess the biggest times of my life then was to go spanking down the main street of Bangor on that high seat, with the silver shining and the plumes tossing and them four big horses arching their necks and stepping high, wide, and handsome. Swell cars is all right—but there was a turn-out!"

That was before my time, but I could see it, too, prancing across the kitchen floor.

"Then," Renny continued, "then come September and Fair time and the Boss busted his arm. He called me into the office one day and said, 'Renny, I don't see no way out of it but that you got to drive Aunt Hat and her girls over to the Fair. I always do it myself, but no one-armed man can hold that team of hell-raisers, and there's no one else I'd trust them with. So it looks like you're elected.'

"Well, for all I was young and green, I knowed all about Aunt Hat. Every year she took her girls over to the Fair in this rig. She'd lease space and set up a swell striped tent she had, and she did a rushing business, besides giving the girls an outing.

"'I won't do it,' I says to him. 'I won't drive them hussies clear out there in broad daylight and on a public road. I won't be made no laughing-stock.' He pled with me, but I wouldn't listen, so finally he says he'd appeal to Father. My father was a God-fearing man, so I thought that'd settle that.

"But Father took me to one side and says to me, 'Renny, your mother and I ain't going to like this any better than you do. It's going to cause a lot of talk. But it would hurt us a sight worse if we thought we had a son that backed out of a job he'd undertook. Jim's hurt and he's depending on you to take his place. He's been good to you, and don't you go back on him.'

"Aunt Hat wanted to get out to the Fair Grounds the day before the Fair opened, so's to get settled and ready for business. I was out to her place at daylight, planning on getting an early start, before there was too many people on the streets. But she thought different.

"'What?' she says. 'Go sneaking through town like that at this ungodly hour and throw away all that free advertising? Like Hell, young man! You come back here at ten o'clock; and you can put in the time till then on that silver-work. It may shine bright enough for the Methodist Sunday School picnic, but it ain't bright enough for Aunt Hat!'

"We got going about half past ten. There was four seats besides the driver's, and Aunt Hat piled three girls in each seat. They was all dressed alike in black satin, and they had white feather boas around their necks and big black hats with white willow plumes. Sounds kind of plain, but believe me, it wasn't. Must have been the way they wore them outfits, but they looked a sight flashier than any red dress I ever see. Aunt Hat was dressed the same, only she had a big gold chain around her neck and a watch pinned on her bosom. I was wondering where she was going to sit, she not being spare, exactly, when she hollered to me, 'Where's your manners? Get that rump of yours off that seat and give a lady a hand. I'm sitting up in front with you.'

"I'd counted on skirting around the center of town, but I see there was no use even thinking about that. So I hunched my head down into my collar and tried to look inconspicuous, while I let the horses out a little, so's to get it over with quick. Next I knew, Aunt Hat had her elbow in my ribs; and for a woman as well larded as she was, she had a right sharp elbow.

"'You hold in them horses, or I'll skin you. Hold up your chin and throw out your chest. There ain't a man on this street that wouldn't swap places with you right now, and don't you think different. You'll drive this rig and be proud of it, or, by God, I'll pitch you off this seat and drive it myself.'"

Renny smiled reminiscently. "She'd 'a' done it, too," he assured us. "So I see there was no use. I threw back my shoulders and set up straight and cocked my silk hat a mite to one side, and Aunt Hat threw out her chest until the seams of her dress strained. I had the checks and the martingales both on; the horses bent their necks pretty nigh into bows, and they trotted as though the street was paved with eggs. When we went by the Bangor House, I see our reflection in them big front windows, and we was something to look at. Them twelve girls looked just as proud and well curried as the horses. They looked the passers-by over, not brash, you understand, like you might expect, nor giggling like some of the girls I'd drove on picnics, but sort of dignified like. I tell you folks that before I got out of town, I'm damned if I wasn't proud to be driving them."

We could all understand that, I think. Renny made us feel just as he must have felt on that long ago September day.

"After we left town Aunt Hat turned to me. 'You done fine, Renny,' she says, and after a minute we was chatting together like old friends. She was a real nice woman, once you got to know her. When we got out to the Fair Grounds, the gates was closed as the Fair wasn't officially open yet. I made to hand the reins to Aunt Hat, so's I could get down and open them, but she put her hand in its black kid glove on my arm.

" 'You set still, Renny. I'll tend to this.' And she stood right up and shouted, so's you could hear her all over the grounds, 'Open up these gates, you sons of bitches! Here comes Aunt Hat and all her whores!' "

Renny laughed aloud at the memory. "I like to died," he said. "I tell you, I never hear that there hymn, 'Unfold, Ye Portals Everlasting,' but what it brings to mind them gates. Unfold—that's just what they did do, and we drove through with a flourish. The Grounds was full of folks getting their exhibits ready, and Aunt Hat says, 'Drive around the race track, and drive like you did back in Bangor.' She shoved my hat over one ear, and off we started. The crowd all come running to the rail to see us, and somebody started to cheer. Round we went, and the cheer growing louder all the time, till when we come around again and drove off, it was bedlam let loose. Aunt Hat never batted an eyelash. When we pulled up in front of her tent she ordered the girls down, kind of crisp like, but pleased, too. Then she says to me, 'Thank you, Renny. You come back and get us Saturday night,' as genteel as you could ask.

"She was a great Aunt Hat. After that I took her and the girls out on plenty of airings and picnics. She'd always ask for me when she ordered the rig. The Boss didn't have a look-in, no more."

Ralph said, just to keep the record straight, "Then you weren't a customer of Aunt Hat's, at all?"

Renny looked at him. "Customer, hell. Anybody could be a customer. I was a friend!"

No, poor Riches, we don't have plays and music and contact with sophisticated minds, and a round of social engagements. All we have are sun and wind and rain, and space in which to move and breathe. All we have are the forests, and the calm expanses of the lakes, and time to call our own. All we have are the hunting and fishing and the swimming, and each other.

We don't see pictures in famous galleries. But the other day, after a sleet storm that had coated the world with a sheath of ice, I saw a pine grosbeak in a little poplar tree. The setting sun slanted through a gap in the black wall of the forest, and held bird and tree in a celestial spot-light.

Every twig turned to diamond encrusted-gold, and the red of the bird's breast glowed like a huge ruby as he fluffed his feathers in the wind. I could hardly believe it. I could only stand still and stare.

And then I repeated to myself again something that I once learned in the hope that it would safeguard me from ever becoming hardened to beauty and wonder. I found it long ago, when I had to study Emerson.

"If the stars should appear one night in a thousand years, how men would believe and adore; and preserve for many generations the remembrance of the City of God which has been shown!"

X

"Do You Get Out Very Often?"

THE FIRST WINTER THAT I LIVED HERE, CLIFF WIGGIN-Wallace used to call me up. He still does, for that matter, whenever he gets bored with his own society and that of his several cats. I'd only seen him once, but we'd have a good gossip every now and then, and about once a month he'd ask me what day of the week it was. I'd tell him, shaking my head and clucking my tongue to myself. You see, Cliff hadn't been Outside for three years, and I thought I recognized the first sign of his going woods queer. Woods queerness is a real and serious and fairly common thing here, brought on by solitude and a growing awareness of the emptiness all around. It starts in little ways, and gets worse and worse, until finally it may end in raving insanity. Every now and then, someone along the lakes is taken out to an asylum. I thought Cliff ought to go out on a spree. Three years is too long a time to stay in the woods.

Or so I thought then. I didn't know that it would be over four years before I myself saw the Outside; and if I had known it, I wouldn't have believed that the time could pass so quickly and lightly, that season could roll so smoothly into season, and year into year.

I didn't spend the whole four years sitting in my own back yard, of course, unless you interpret back yard loosely as stretching from here to the border. I covered the territory hereabouts fairly thoroughly.

For example, Gerrish and I make at least one annual trip to B Pond. It's supposed to be a fishing trip, but we've never yet caught any fish. There are some enormous old trout in there, and once in a while someone brings one out. They're pretty cagey—that's why they've lived to be enormous—but we always hope. This hope is one of the reasons why we continue to go. The other is that we like B Pond.

B Pond deserves a better name. It should be called Benediction Pond, or Sanctuary Lake. It might even be called the Pool of Proserpine:

> "Here, where the world is quiet,
> Here, where all trouble seems
> Dead winds' and spent waves' riot
> In doubtful dreams of dreams . . ."

There is that feeling of remoteness and calm and timelessness about it that makes the scramble of ordinary life seem like a half-forgotten and completely pointless dream. It just lies there in a fold in the hills, open to the sky and wind and weather. Ducks and loons breed in its coves, the gulls fly over it in great white arcs, and the great fish go their secret ways in its dim depths. Once in a while human beings, like Gerrish and me, invade its privacy, but we don't make any impression on B Pond. I always have the feeling that the whole valley in which it lies—the hillsides and the deer on the hills, the trees that grow down to the water and the birds that build in them, the pond itself with all its myriad life—simply waits for us to go. I always want to turn back, after we have entered the woods on our homeward trek, to see what enchanting things take place the minute our backs are turned. It's that kind of pond. There must be many like it in Maine, that the map-makers could so callously label it B Pond, simply because it lies in what was once B Township, and pass along to other matters. There must be, but I can't believe it.

I hope that when I'm sixty and Gerrish is eighty, we'll still be going to B Pond every spring. We'll still politely invite Ralph to go too, of course; and he, of course, will still refuse to have any part of the expedition. That's one of the things I can't fathom about the spouse of my bosom—why he won't go to B Pond. He says it's because of the walk over the steep, rough trail, and because you never catch any fish there, and because he doesn't like trolling anyhow, being a fly-fishing addict, and because he just doesn't like B Pond. The last is probably the real reason. Somewhere he has acquired a deep-seated aversion to the place, so there's no point in arguing with him about it, or trying to understand it. He just doesn't like B Pond.

Let me tell you about the best trip we ever made to B Pond. Some days are enchanted, as everybody knows. Every detail of the day, even the most trivial, falls into exquisite juxtaposition with the next. Commonplace things take on significance and beauty. Perhaps it's a matter of timing. Perhaps for once one walks in sympathetic vibration with the earth, disturbing nothing as one treads. However that may be, this was one of those days.

We got up before dawn and ate breakfast by lamp-light. The stove didn't sulk or smoke, and neither the oatmeal nor the bacon burned. The coffee was good—hot, strong, and clear. When I put up our lunch, the bread sliced without crumbling, and the ham curled pink and thin from under the knife. The butter was just right to spread, firm but not hard. I found a box at once that was just the correct size for our sandwiches and bananas, and I didn't forget sugar and canned milk for the coffee we would make at noon over a camp-fire. Gerrish came in from the garden with a canful of the liveliest, juiciest worms a fish could hope to see. The shiners that we had been keeping in a minnow trap down in the river had neither escaped nor died, and we found a tobacco box that was ideal for carrying them. None of our tackle had been mislaid or broken, and Ralph didn't wake up and come down and sneer at us for going to B Pond.

We went up the road and across Pond-in-the-River Dam just as the sunlight struck the tops of the trees on the ridge. The valley was still in shadow, with steam rising white from the churning water and turning to a lovely pearly pink as it reached the sun-shot air above. I knew how fish feel as they swim about in the depths and look up to see the light of day above them. We went into the woods and climbed the ridge, with the sound of the river fading behind and below us. I never can tell exactly when I stop hearing the river. It fades and fades, but still is there. Then suddenly it is there no longer, and the silence is much louder than the roar ever was.

For once I could keep up with Gerrish with no effort. Usually he has to dawdle, which is terrible for him; or I trot, which is terrible for me; or we strike a working compromise whereby each goes his own pace and we have a reunion at our destination. This morning we moved along together swiftly and silently, watching our footing on what passes for a trail, admiring the woods in the early gray light, and not talking. That's one of the good things about Gerrish. I can talk to him or not, and silence is as comfortable for both of us as speech. When we got to the top of the ridge we met the sun. The woods were suddenly pierced with long, green-gold lances of light, and instantly a thousand birds began to sing. They sang us right down to the shore of B Pond. I'm not a bird lover by trade, but that morning I felt like St. Francis. I felt like an angel coming down a heavenly stair, with the air alive and alight around me with music and the rustle of wings.

The boat slid smoothly out of the lean-to where we keep it and into the water, without the usual knuckle-barking struggle. We sat down on the shore to assemble our tackle, and a shelldrake came flying in from the east, not seeing us at all. The sun was behind it, and as it spread its wings and tail to brake for a three point landing almost in our laps, the delicate rib of every feather was silhouetted black and single, and the down along the ribs was gold and translucent. We could see how wonderfully and intricately it was made. Spray flew up like a fountain of jewels as it plowed the water. It was a bird of fire, coming to rest among diamonds and emeralds.

We got into the boat and pulled slowly away from the shore, paying our lines out behind. The rods vibrated as the spoons began to turn beneath the glass-smooth surface. No breath disturbed the water. Each pine and spruce and budding maple on the shore stood upright on its perfect, unbroken reflection. We went around the pond once— about two miles—and then it was my turn to row. The boat seemed to have no weight at all. The slow and steady pull and recovery were like an opiate, and time stopped.

Two loons appeared from somewhere and swam out to look us over.

Loons are my very favorite birds in all the world. This pair circled around us, curious and unafraid, turning their big hammer-heads pertly and halloo-ing back and forth about us. They showed off, diving and staying under water for incredible periods, and bobbing back to the surface in unexpected places. They stood on their tails and stretched their huge wings, and rolled from side to side, smoothing and preening their broad white bosoms. Then they looked at us again. We were really just as funny as they had thought in the first place. They exchanged glances and their weird laughter echoed from the hills. My eye caught Gerrish's, and in a flash there were four of us laughing crazily instead of two.

Nothing could go wrong that day. A breeze came up, but it only crisped the surface of the water, without making rowing a chore. Big, fleece-topped clouds rolled up from the horizon, breaking the smooth blue of the sky into lovely patterns and sending their shadows chasing over the far hillsides; but they never came near the sun. We went by a little point, and I said, "Isn't that a pretty place!" It was. It was covered with grass and a low growth of scarlet-stemmed bushes. A gray ledge cropped out along the water's edge, and a little clump of white birches, budding misty green, leaned over its own image. Just as Gerrish turned his head to look, a red doe stepped out of the black spruce copse behind and stood with her head high, looking at us. That would never happen again in a hundred years, and I'm glad I have a witness that it happened then.

Finally Gerrish said, " 'Bout time we were leaving, ain't

it?" He rowed a few strokes. "Noticed anything missing?"

"The gulls!" I exclaimed. "They haven't come yet."

We turned toward the rock that serves as a landing. And then we heard a faint and faraway crying. Through a high gap in the mountains the gulls came winging from the east, a dozen of them, screaming with excitement. They flew around the pond three times, white against the dark hills. They swooped to the water and soared to dizzy heights, riding the currents of air up and up without moving a wing, their plaintive mewing filling the air. Then they settled down on the rocks which have been their breeding grounds for centuries.

I'm glad that we didn't catch any fish. I'm not sentimental about fish. I'd just as soon kill them as not. But that day we had enough to bring home with us without adding any corpses.

Trips to B Pond aren't always so idyllic. Fairness demands that I should report on the most horrible one we ever took.

We didn't get started until after lunch. It had been threatening rain all morning, so we should have known enough to stay at home. But the ice had been out two or three days, and we had a theory that now was the time when the fish would be rising. After lunch the clouds looked thinner, so we hastily scratched together our tackle and set out.

I don't know how we did it—we'd each been to B Pond a hundred times—but we got lost. There were some new woods-roads criss-crossing the ridge from the winter before's cut, but we knew the country. We shouldn't have become confused. However, we were. We wandered all over the ridge for an hour, trying to find something that led somewhere. We always brought up in a pulp-yard. Finally we went back to the dam and started all over again, and this time we made it.

We came out at the lean-to, hot and disgusted and tired, and Gerrish held out his hand for the key. Of course—oh, so utterly and completely of course! I didn't have the key. It was too good a padlock to break, although by then only its strength, and no ethical consideration, deterred us from breaking it. We were mad. We'd come to B Pond to fish, and we were going to fish, if we had to build a raft and paddle it with our hands.

It didn't quite come to that. We found an abandoned and water-logged old boat drawn up in the bushes, along with a pair of home-made oars. It leaked quite a lot, but by bailing with our bait can—we dumped the worms out into the boat, where they squirmed around our feet—we thought we could keep afloat.

"We ain't got much time," Gerrish said. "You start rowing while I set the tackle up."

There was a nasty, biting little wind blowing, and the water was gray and choppy. The boat handled very badly, and pretty soon a fine, chilling rain set in. I didn't chill much. I was working too hard keeping up steerage-way. Every time I seemed to be getting somewhere, the water started coming in over the tops of my boots and I had to bail, while the wind drifted us back the way we had come. I could feel a blister developing.

Gerrish in the meantime had his gear laid out on the stern seat and was assembling it. He had a gang-hook full of worms on the end, and along the leader a couple of drop hooks, Archer spinners, spoons, and various gadgets. It was a very imposing and lethal array.

"There!" he said finally, with a craftsman's satisfaction, and threw it grandly over the side.

He hadn't tied it to the line. Paralyzed, we watched it sink irrevocably out of sight. Then we looked dumbly at each other.

Gerrish found words first. He had a very sound suggestion to make. "What say we tie some stones around our necks and jump overboard, Louise?"

And that's the other side of the B Pond story.

There are lots of places to go, all in the woods, it's true, but all different. There's Prospect, a logged-off, burned-over point, eight miles up the lakes, near Upper Dam. You go by boat, past unfamiliar coves and promontories. At one place is a walled cellar hole, now under water, which is all that remains to show where Richardson, for whom the lake is named, tried to establish his ill-fated colony. The fields that the score of families who went with him cleared so laboriously have all gone back to the forest. Nobody knows anything about Richardson—what vision inspired his undertaking, or what lay at the root of its failure. All that remains of him is a piece of excellent dry-masonry and a name curving down a map. A man could have worse memorials. "He was strong and patient and honest," the painstakingly laid stones bear silent witness. "He had courage and imagination," say the letters of his name, so strange and incongruous on the map between Mooselookmeguntic and Umbagog.

From the entrance to the Narrows you can look back across the hills and see Mount Washington, a whole state away, and so faint and lofty as to seem more like an idea than a mountain. From nowhere else on the lakes can you see it. And nowhere else are there blueberries like the blueberries of Prospect, which are what you go there for in the first place. They grow as large as your thumb nail, and have a peculiar dull black lustre under the bright surface bloom, as though soot from the old fire still stains and sweetens them. There are acres and acres of them, and no matter how long and fast you pick, working in the ceaseless wind that blows across the barren from the lake, loud with the lovely sound of water lapping on stones, you can no more than scratch the surface of the plenitude. We come home, wind-burned and juice-stained, with forty or fifty quarts; but no one could tell we had ever been there.

At night, after being at Prospect, I lie in bed and see great clusters of berries slide by endlessly against my closed lids. They haunt me. There are so many of them yet unpicked, so many that never will be picked. The birds and bears and foxes will eat a few, but most of them will drop off at the first frost, to return to the sparse soil of Prospect whatever of value they borrowed from it. Nature is strictly moral. There is no attempt to cheat the earth by means of steel vault or bronze coffin. I hope that when I die I too may be permitted to pay at once my oldest outstanding debt, to restore promptly the minerals and salts that have been lent to me for the little while that I have use for blood and bone and flesh.

Then there is Sunday Pond, small and remote, with a cliff on the north shore. You can see right across the Carry from that cliff, from Richardson to Umbagog. There is the Sandbank across the lake, where the best swimming is; and Smooth Ledge, with the river raging around a great out-cropping of rock. The loveliest pool on the river is at the Foot of the Island, and at Long Pool the deer come to drink and a disreputable old bank-beaver lives. There is the Pocket of the Pond, running up through a hellish black cedar swamp to a tiny icy spring. And there is rumored to be a nameless little pond somewhere up on the hog-back between the Carry Road and Sunday Brook. No one knows exactly where it is. No one knows, really, if it exists at all. But some day soon I'm going to find out. If I get lost, perhaps they'll name the pond after me—if there is a pond. That's the surest way to achieve immortality in this country. Who would have heard of Cluley if he hadn't been drowned in the rips?

I spent four years ramming around the woods, and I could have gone on for the rest of my life in the same way, if it hadn't been for Alice Miller.

She called me up one day in April to tell me that she was going out over the break-up to visit her sister in Lewiston. I said, for something to say, "Well, see a couple of movies for me. I haven't seen one for myself for over four years." I was just talking. I can take movies, but I can just as well leave them alone.

"You'd ought to go out, Louise," she said. "First thing you know, you'll be going woods queer."

I laughed, but she didn't.

"I'm not fooling," she said. "You can laugh, but how do you know you ain't queer already? For all you know, come to get you in crowds and traffic, you'll act like one of these farm dogs in a town, running into doorways and shivering and howling. You'd ought to go out."

I continued to think that was pretty funny for about five minutes after she'd hung up, and then I wasn't quite so sure it was so very funny. After all, she'd spoken with conviction. She'd really snatched at an opportunity to make the suggestion. Maybe she'd noticed something about me— Or maybe Renny had. Renny'd been around the woods most of his life. He knew the symptoms. Maybe he'd said to her, "If you get a chance, drop a hint to Ralph about Louise. It's time she went Outside. Or if it comes right, say something to her—" How did I know? The clerk at Barnett's Number One camp the winter before had thought he was all right long after even I could see that he wasn't. So had that big Russian up in the Narrows, and it had taken four men to tie him and get him aboard Larry's boat. So had the lumberjack who had tried to hang himself in the horse hovel down by the *Alligator,* and the woman up on Mooselookmeguntic. And so did I.

It's ghastly to wonder seriously about your own sanity. First you start remembering things. I remembered breaking my pet needle the week before, and all the talking I had done about it.

"Haven't you got another one?" Ralph asked.

"Certainly. I've got dozens. But this one was different. It was balanced just right."

"Well, for God's sake! Whoever heard of a balanced needle? You're nuts."

Of course, he often says "You're nuts" to me. But hadn't he looked at me queerly this time? *Was* it odd to think that a needle could have correct balance? I didn't think so—but how could I tell?

I thought of my Columbiana Pump pencil. It was painted cream-color with gold lettering on it, and it was round. I don't like hexagonal pencils. They hurt my fingers. Most round ones, especially free, advertising pencils, have specks of grit in the graphite. Not my Columbiana Pump pencil, though. The lead was soft and smooth. It was the best pencil I had ever taken in hand, so I said it was mine. I hid it in my mending basket, and nobody was supposed even to think about it. And then one day it was gone.

I flew into a froth. You know:—"Considering the very few things I'm fussy about around here, I should certainly think that when I ask to have a measly little pencil left alone, it could be left alone. I'll find out who took my Columbiana Pump pencil, and when I do—" You can imagine.

It didn't seem to me to be an unreasonable attitude, but how could I be sure? Do sane people go into rages about pencils? Do they make horrible threats? I didn't know, and whom could I depend on to tell me honestly? I remembered the clerk from Number One saying pitifully, "I think I'm going crazy. Do you think I am?" I remembered my answer. "Of course not. Crazy people don't wonder if they're crazy. You're all right." I remembered wondering what I'd do if he suddenly went into a violent phase.

There was only one answer. I had to go Outside. If I weren't on the way to woods queerness already, I soon would be if I began to question and scrutinize my every act and thought. I'd begin to see hidden meanings in what people said to me and in the way they looked at me, or in the things they didn't say or look. Merna and Albert Allen, with whom Sally was boarding while going to school in Upton, had invited me repeatedly to come out with Rufus and stay over night. I'd have to see if I couldn't manage somehow to get out there.

The ease with which my going was arranged, once I let it be known that I wanted to go, did nothing to re-establish my peace of mind. Actually, of course, people were just being nice. In spite of all that is said, and more especially written, about the crabbed New Englander, New Englanders, like all ordinary people, are nice. Their manner of proffering a favor is sometimes on the crusty side, but that is much more often diffidence than surliness. I shouldn't have been surprised and suspicious at all at the co-operation I received after Ralph asked one of Barnett's tractor drivers to ask Merna the next time he was out in Upton if it would be convenient to have me some time during the next week. Ordinarily I wouldn't have been. But I couldn't help remembering how hard we'd all worked, the winter before, to get that clerk out on a legitimate pretext before a strait-jacket was necessary.

The tractor driver, Edgar Worster, said that he knew it would be all right. He lives next door to the Allens and he'd seen Merna two days before. She'd told him to bring me out on the tractor the next time he came, and as it happened, he was going the next day. The camps were breaking up, and he had to take out the beds, stoves, some lumber, and the pigs, and there was no reason in the world why he couldn't add Rufus and me to the load. If I'd just be ready to start around noon—

Ordinarily to get to Upton from here is a problem. You can walk seven terrible miles, or you can go down Umbagog in a boat—if you can get a boat and the ice is out—or you can go to the Arm and then drive thirty-odd miles around over East B Hill. To be able to ride out on the tractor was a break. You can't do it just any old time. There is no road at all. It's possible only when there is enough snow to pack into a reasonably smooth surface. There are limits to what even a tractor will do. So I accepted the invitation with alacrity.

Then the question of what to wear reared its ugly head. Rufus was all right. He had a fairly new snow suit. But as for me—

"Don't give me any of that 'I haven't got a thing that's fit to be seen' business," Ralph begged. "That's what women always say."

Maybe it is, but for once it was absolutely and literally true. I *didn't* have a thing that was fit to be seen, even in far from dressy Upton. I almost didn't have a thing, period. I hadn't bought anything but woods clothes for five years. Woods clothes would have been all right, but even Upton has prejudices in favor of reasonable neatness and cleanliness. My old ski pants had holes in the knees and seat, and my newer ones were filthy and I didn't have time to wash them. I thought briefly of the days gone by when I had worried over such esoteric details as the exact shade of my stockings. Now I had one pair of silk stockings, five years old, and when I put them on, they went to pieces, rotten from lying in the drawer. Mice had eaten the shoe-strings out of my one pair of Outside shoes.

Well, that was all right. I didn't have any overshoes, anyhow, so I could wear what was left of the silk stockings, for something to fasten my garters to and hold my unaccustomed girdle down, some wool knee socks, for decency and warmth, and my gum-boots. So far, so good. Then I had a twelve-year-old Harris tweed top-coat. God bless a good tweed! It's passable as long as two threads hold together. I didn't have a hat, of course, or gloves, but nobody wears them in Upton anyhow, except to church. I had no notion of going to church. And I had a suit. It was seven years old, completely out of style, and slightly on the snug side. But if I moved the buttons of the jacket over so it would close, took up the hem, and eked out the waist-band of the skirt with a piece of twine, and then was careful not to ever unbutton the jacket, it would do. It would have to do.

It did do, although when I was ready to go, I understood fully for the first time the term "a haywire rig." Since haywire is a fairly common commodity in the woods, it is used universally for emergency repairs. Therefore anything that is held together with haywire is a haywire rig. Broadening the scope of the term, so is any makeshift expedient whatsoever. If you run out of cornstarch and have to thicken a chocolate pudding with flour, that's a haywire rig. As I walked through the snow down to where the tractors were waiting, I was the haywirest rig north of Boston.

Two tractors were going instead of one, and the driver of the second tractor I had never seen before. Now, I'm shy. I know that's old stuff. I know I'm awfully tired, too, of having just plain snooty people excused to me by their friends on the grounds of a fundamental shyness. But I stick to my story. I am shy. So I said to Ralph, "You'd better introduce that man to me, if we're going to ride out together." If Ralph knows a person, he is apt to assume that by a sort of social osmosis I know him too.

He said now, "Why, that's Paul Fuller. You know him."

I didn't. I knew he had a wife named Linda, who was one of Jim Barnett's daughters, and that he had four children, one of whom was Rufus' age almost to the day. I knew these things as I know who isn't speaking to whom in Upton, and why, without ever having seen any of the characters in the drama. But I didn't know Paul Fuller.

It didn't make any difference. "Hi, Louise," he said before Ralph could go into his introduction. "Four years since you been out, isn't it; and Rufus hasn't ever been out at all. Well, he's going to get an eyeful. You can ride on the big sled, next to the pig crates. Keep an eye on them, will you? Don't want to lose the pigs off. Let's see, the last time you was out must have been when you and Ralph—"

I don't know where I ever got the impression that the

grapevine only works one way—that I sit up in the woods, invisible and inaudible, collecting my data. It came as a distinct shock that, while I knew that the youngest Fuller child is allergic to tomatoes, the Fuller family undoubtedly knew all about the loose filling in my second left upper molar.

We crossed the river on a corduroy bridge that bowed and quivered under the weight of the tractors. I sat on a pile of lumber, beds, and horse-blankets, twelve feet above the ground. There was no road and the sled had no springs. Very shortly I felt as if my spine were coming through the top of my head. I looked forward to where Edgar was hunched in the saddle of the tractor, fighting his machine. It would crawl slowly and powerfully up an outcropping of ledge, balance, and come down *zoonk!* on the other side. Every time that happened—and it happened about every sixty seconds—I saw six inches of daylight between Edgar and the seat. I shuddered for him and took a look at the pig crates, which were inching toward the rear of the load. The pigs weren't happy, either. The only one who was happy, as far as I could see, was Rufus. Tractors are his passion and tractor drivers his gods. He was in seventh heaven.

We crossed a high, beech-covered ridge and came down to B Pond, and from then on it was new territory to me. We left the shore of the pond at the outlet and struck out through a long narrow swamp, between dark, crouching ridges. I had never been there, and yet it was familiar. After a while I realized that it was exactly like that terrible and desolate country of "Childe Roland to the Dark Tower Came," which has always been for me one of the most diabolically inspired pieces of horror writing in English.

It was a level, somber place, with stunted cedars growing out of the swamp, and the snow wasting away from about black bog holes. As for the grass, Browning covered that:

". . . it grew as scant as hair
   In leprosy; thin dry blades pricked the mud
   Which underneath looked kneaded up with blood."

There was even the sudden little river, which crossed our path as unexpected and as vicious as an adder. Then came a place where a forest fire had passed. Nothing grew there any more. Black, limbless stubs pointed to the gray sky. It was neither swamp nor forest—"mere earth, desperate and done with." The tractors, lumbering along like prehistoric monsters, were not incongruous. They were like the incarnation of mindless brutality in this mindless, brutal place. The whole thing got me down, which probably proves that too much education doesn't pay. Rufus and Edgar and Paul hadn't read Browning, and were all innocent of literary connotations. They seemed perfectly happy and unimpressed.

It was odd to be Outside. It was odd to see modern cars, looking like a bunch of water-bugs scooting up and down the road, after our collection of angular antiques. It was odd to go into a house that had electric lights, and to have Merna say, "Sally, run up to the store and get two pounds of sugar." I had forgotten that people lived near enough stores to be able to run up to them at a moment's notice. I ran, too, for the novelty of it, and we took Rufus along. He'd never been in a store before, and he couldn't believe his eyes. I bought him his first candy bar, and he didn't quite know what to do with it. It didn't take him long to find out, though. Probably buying it was an example of misguided motherly indulgence.

There were several people in the store, and they all said, "Hi, Louise. How does it seem to be out?" Sally told me their names, which were familiar to me, and now I sorted them out to go with the right faces. They didn't seem like strangers and they didn't treat me like a stranger. I had a fine time. Albert Allen gave me a bag of carrots to take home, and Jim Barnett tried to give Rufus a pair of white rats, but there I drew the line. White rats give me the creeps. Rufus forgot his disappointment in the excitement of viewing the Allens' hens. Horses, cows and pigs he had seen before, but never a hen. He was fascinated. We kept losing him and finding him leaning transfixed against the hen-yard fence. He watched the cows being milked, too, with amazement. Milk heretofore had been something that came out of a can. He saw a new little calf and a lot of things that turned out to be dogs. I suppose it is news to one whose entire dog experience has been Kyak that a Cocker spaniel is a dog, and, surprisingly, so are such divergent types as setters and toy bulls. It must be baffling. But he loved best of all the other children. It was a discovery that he and Junior Miller weren't carrying the whole burden of perpetuating the race.

The things I loved best, next to watching Rufus react, were eating someone else's cooking and meeting so many friendly people. It wasn't until we were half-way home the next morning that I remembered to be relieved that in a traffic jam in front of the store—three cars and an ox-team all at once—I felt no compulsion to scuttle into the doorway and shiver and howl.

Our one legitimate reason for going to Upton is to attend Town Meeting, which all over New England comes on the first Monday in March. Town Meeting is supposed to be a political phenomenon, the purest form of self-government, or something. That sounds a little overwhelming. It sounds as though the citizens ought to put on their best clothes and pace solemnly to the Town Hall on Town Meeting Day, in full consciousness that they are about to share in the freeman's most priceless privilege and most sacred responsibility, that of determining their own destiny. It sounds, in short, a little stuffy and dull.

It's nothing of the sort, in Upton. Town Meeting Day there combines all the better features of Old Home Week, a session of the Lower House, a barbecue, and an encounter between the Montagues and the Capulets.

When we arrived a half an hour before the meeting was called to order, everyone in the township who could stand on his feet was present at the big, bare town hall, perched on top of Upton Hill. The village half-wit and the town drunkard stood on the steps, shaking hands with all comers, a self-constituted welcoming committee. A wave of noise, as solid as water, met us at the door. School was out for the day, and the children chased around the room. Around the red-hot, air-tight stove at one end the women sat, exchanging gossip, recipes, and symptoms. At the other end, around the speaker's table, stood the white-collar class, the minister, the school-teacher, the hotel proprietor, and the storekeeper—postmaster-telephone-operator. They were white-collar in name only, as, like the rest of us, they wore flannel shirts, sheep-skins, and corduroys. Half-way between, a group of farmers exchanged views on politics, crops, and the price of grain, while over in a corner the ribald lumberjack element swapped dirty stories and lent color to the scene with their bright mackinaws and high boots. The game warden, tough and trim in his blue uniform, came in and sat down beside our leading poacher. The one had had the other thrown into jail the preceding fall, over a little matter of an untagged deer, but that didn't seem to shadow their social relations. The town's oldest citizen, Silas Peasley, from whom Rufus gets his middle name and in whom every one of us took an affectionate pride, held court down one side of the room. We all went up and spoke to him, and we all got together later and sadly agreed that he had failed considerable. Last year, on his eighty-second birthday, he had been able to leap into the air and click his heels three times. It would be a wonder if he could manage twice this year.

When the meeting was called to order, things simmered down. The children went out-doors, the men tip-toed to seats, and the women lowered their voices. In theory, they have a hand in the town government, but unless a really bitter issue is at stake they sacrifice the franchise for speculation as to whether the town's latest marriage was a shotgun affair or not. The first business on the Warrant was the electing of a moderator, and someone nominated Cedric Judkin, who runs the store, the post-office, and the telephone exchange. (They are all under one roof, along with his living quarters, so this doesn't require the ubiquitousness that would seem to be implied.) This nomination was routine. Cedric has been moderator since the memory of man runeth not to the contrary. This year he dealt precedent a mortal blow.

"Nope, I can't do it," he announced from the stove that he was stoking. "I'd like to, but my mother-in-law is sick, and my wife has to stay with her, so there's no one to tend store and sort the mail. I got to be back and forth 'twixt here and there all day. You'll be obliged to get someone else."

"But, gosh-a'mighty, no one else knows this here parliamentary procedure!"

"Well, I'll be in and out. If you get sluiced, I'll help out," Cedric promised.

There was a flurry of nominations, all declined. Nobody wanted to stick his neck out. Finally the hotel proprietor allowed himself to be persuaded, because if somebody didn't, the meeting would never get going. He made it clear that nothing that happened was to be held against him, and climbed onto the platform with the well-mixed metaphor, "Don't know how this is going to pan out, but I guess we'll get through somehow."

We got through the electing of the town officers very nicely, since this is largely a matter of re-electing the present incumbents, the most suitable candidate for each office having been determined days ago. Only death can dislodge one. In that event, the office is apt to rotate for a few years until its predestined occupant is discovered, when it again becomes stabilized. The exception is the three selectmen, who, having the most to do, are most liable to censure. But we have a neat system to take care of that. To fill the three positions we have four suitable men. Each year the one in greatest disfavor at the moment is deposed, and the current spare elected to his place. By the following March his crime has been eclipsed by the blacker, newer indiscretions of one of the trio in office, and back he comes. It's a sort of political Musical Chairs. It works out very well.

This year Article 10 of the Warrant was the Fighting Article. We always have a Fighting Article. Once it was whether the constable should receive a salary of three dollars a year, or whether, instead, the town should buy him a star instead of making him furnish his own. One year it

had to do with the licensing of a beer parlor. And once—
oh, lovely year of which fables are still told and Rabelaisian
quips repeated—it was whether or not the town should
appropriate money to hire the services of a bull for the
convenience of the cow-owning citizens. This year the
Article read: To see what sum of money the town will
grant and raise to purchase or repair snow-removal equipment. Snow removal—"breaking out the roads"—is an impressive item on a Maine town's budget. It costs more than
the education of the young.

"Mr. Moderator."

"Mr. Hart."

"Look, I been running that damn plow for seven years,
ever since we bought her, and she was second-hand then.
She ain't going to go through another winter. She's all
tied together with haywire, and every time I take her out,
something new falls off. I'm sick and tired of the whole
rig."

"I don't see where Bill's got any kick coming," a voice
from the rear proclaimed. "He gets paid by the hour,
whether he's plowing or tinkering. Far as that goes, he was
hired with the idea he'd keep her in good shape, and if he
ain't done it, that's skin off his own nose."

"God A'mighty, there's limits to what a man can do
with a bunch of junk. If you or any of the rest of your
shiftless tribe can do any better—"

"Shiftless! At least my woman makes her own bread, instead of traipsin' up to the store for it, like some I know."

"Address the chair!" the moderator shouted.

"We need a new plow!"

"We don't! We can send her back to the factory and
have them undo the damage Bill's done her."

"*I* done her!" There was more to this speech, but no

one heard it, because a perfectly deafening uproar started outside one of the long windows. A lanky farmer looked out and turned to report.

"Hey, Bill, that spotted heifer of yourn's stuck in a drift outside, bellerin' her fool head off and doing her damnedest to break a leg. You'd better see to her."

"How in hell did she get out?" and Bill streaked for the door. The meeting waited until he got back. The battle with his live-stock in thigh-deep wet snow had improved his temper.

"Look, folks," he said reasonably, "why don't we buy a new snow-plow? We'd be money-in-pocket in the end. Patching up this one's just pouring cash down a skunk hole."

"Couldn't we appropriate some money and let the selectmen study into it and decide—" a mild little man suggested.

"No," one of the selectmen said with finality. "That's what was done fifteen years ago when we put in that cement bridge down by Durkee's. I happened to be selectman at the time and we built the best bridge we could for the money. A good sound bridge, too, 'tis. But there's talk about it to this day. So it's up to you folks to decide what to do, and us selectmen will see it's done."

Bill Hart said hastily, "I move we appropriate three thousand dollars and buy a new plow." His sister-in-law's husband seconded the motion and one of the Hart uncles-by-marriage called for a vote before the opposition could collect itself.

The votes were written on slips of paper brought from home—no sense in wasting the tax-payers' money on printed ballots—and a straggling procession started for the ballot-box, over which the moderator and clerk stood to insure an honest vote. The town half-wit cast his ballot with the rest, and as soon as his back was turned the clerk fished it out and pocketed it, a flagrantly illegal act condoned by everyone present on the premise that there warn't no need to hurt his feelings. It was a close matter, but the new plow won.

A weather-beaten man with a rather fine and intelligent face, who had been figuring feverishly on the back of an old envelope, rose to his feet. "Mr. Moderator, we hadn't ought to do this. It's going to raise taxes sixty percent. I got the figures right here. We'd ought to do a little more considering before we act."

There was a stunned silence, and then a roar. The moderator pounded frantically, and then cut loose with a bellow. "There ain't no use losing our tempers now," he pointed out, demonstrating the derivation of his title. "We voted the money, and it's too late to change our minds."

"Why is it, if we want to?" demanded some untamed spirit.

"I don't know. But seems like it's against the rules."

"Where's Cedric at? Get Cedric."

Cedric had gone over to his store, but when the summons went out, he came splashing across in the March mud and slush with his coat-tails flying. His bearing was rather that of a mother whose better judgment had been telling her all along that she shouldn't have left the children alone with the buzz-saw.

"I don't recall anything about that in the rules," he said when the problem had been put to him. "But I don't see why we can't rig it up. How many want to back water?"

The walls bulged.

"All right. If someone will put it in the form of a motion, just so's it'll be legal—"

The haste with which the matter was put through was indecent. Then the conservative sum of two hundred dollars was voted to repair the old plow, and the Fighting Article was history.

The women had withdrawn some time before, and now one spoke to the moderator from the doorway. "Lee, if you've come to a good resting-place, dinner's on upstairs."

Town Meeting dinner is an event in the year. The food is all donated, and the proceeds—the charge is thirty-five cents—go to the Ladies' Aid. Everyone puts her best culinary foot forward. There were ham and chicken, scalloped potatoes, salad, and hot rolls; the pies were cut in quarters, in the generous country style, and the layer cakes were laced with jam and topped with yellow whipped cream. The coffee was hot and clear. It was insulting to the committee not to have second helpings, and thirds and fourths were subtle compliments. At first everyone concentrated on the food, but after a while the talk broke out.

"—ain't layin' now. Guess I'll hire me a dozen Rhode Island Reds to see me through till spring."

"Extravagant! My land, you'd ought to take one look in her garbage pail!"

"—lost his shirt on that cut in the Diamond. Had to haul five miles—"

"Sure I hired out to them. When them crazy Democrats come around and shove money at me, what'm I supposed to do? Sit on my hands? But when it comes to voting for any such tom-fool notion—"

Maybe the effects of the meal were soporific. At any rate, the afternoon session was as calm as a Quaker Meeting. There was a little discussion about the appropriation for the Poor Account, which is our version of Relief. This was during the depression, so perhaps the argument deserves a note, as being unique. The customary amount granted is five hundred dollars, but since it is never wholly expended, the Poor Account was getting top-heavy, having reached a total of about a thousand dollars, which is MONEY in Upton. Someone therefore suggested that it would be a good idea to skip the Poor Account this year, and let it feed off its hump, so to speak.

The first selectman was doubtful. "I dunno. 'Course, we never do spend it all, but still, it's good to have a backlog, case of emergency. We could cut down, say, to two hundred—"

This was the year when Relief money was running out all over the country, and when food riots were common in the big cities, but that's what we did, all the same. And that doesn't prove, either, that New England didn't feel the depression. What it proves is that rural New England, with its starved farms and hand-to-mouth living, is chronically so near depression that a big slump doesn't matter much. It simply means pulling in the belt another notch, wearing the same clothes one or two or three more years, and going without butter. We don't get guns for our butter, either. We get something even more necessary to the safe-guarding of Democracy. We get self-respect and the right to spit in anyone's eye and tell them to go climb a tree.

And that about covers Town Meeting. Ralph goes every year, since he considers it his duty as a citizen. His sense of responsibility doesn't carry him to the point of taking office, though. It was suggested to him one year that he'd be a good Health Officer. He didn't see why, until his one very special qualification was pointed out to him. He lives a long way from the village. "No one wants the job," they said earnestly. "You're in trouble all the time. Folks get mad if you light into them about the way their out-houses smell, or where they dump their tin cans. Next thing, you may find the air let out of your tires, or a hole in your boat. Now living way off up there, you could come in every so often and raise hell, and then go back to the woods till it sort of blew over—"

P.S. He didn't take the job.

As a matter of fact, there's really no point in our going Outside since for three months of the year the Outside comes in here, in the form of guests at what we call the Hotel, but which is, as I have said, Captain Coburn's Lakewood Camps at Middle Dam. That's two miles away from us, and that's a good distance for it to be. We can see the Outsiders whenever we want to, but they don't cramp our style. If I want to wear shorts, which is an error no one over eighteen should commit in public, I can do so. I can also run my household as badly as I please, and our house guests can sun-bathe in the altogether without let or hindrance. It's ideal.

The Outsiders who frequent Coburn's are known, of course, as sports—even the fat lady who comes here against her will, because if she doesn't spend two weeks in summer here with her husband, he won't spend two weeks in Florida in the winter with her. She's quite a gal. She's down, but she isn't out. She'd much rather be home in the suburbs, but since she can't be, she does her best to bring the suburbs along with her to the woods. She wears spike heels and flowing lavender chiffon draperies, and gives bridge parties every afternoon, at which she serves the nearest a fishing camp chef can come to a dainty fruit salad. She herself supplies the cut-up marshmallow and maraschino cherries to top off this dish. She gives cute prizes. I find her very tiresome at close range, but at a distance I rather admire her spirit. And to be honest, she's just as much interested in maintaining this distance as I am. She finds me impossible, too.

One thing about living in the backwoods—You Meet Such Interesting People! Or else you meet so few, and have so much more time to talk with them, that they seem interesting. Maybe everybody is interesting, if you get a chance to hash things over with them while they're in their old clothes and have their mental hair down. I met a woman on the dam the other day. She was sitting in the sun, knitting, while her husband fished. If I had met her at a tea, she would have been wearing a rather dowdy beige lace, a harassed expression, and an unbecoming hat, and we would never have got beyond "How do you do?" because I would have been feeling inadequate and lacking in chic, too. As it was, we covered everything, finally getting around to methods of coping with insomnia.

I'm not an expert, being the kind that seldom remembers hitting the bed; but I advanced my formula. Lying awake in the dark, I plan a trip. It's usually to the West Indies. I start at the very beginning and go shopping. I buy everything, from toothpaste to the exclusive little model that's going to knock them dead at the captain's dinner. Then I buy the very smartest luggage and pack. In theory I also conjure up all the people I meet on the boat, and what we do and say to each other. Actually I have yet to stay awake long enough to get myself aboard.

Her method promises even more entertainment. She starts from the present and moves backward in time, remembering every dress she ever owned and the most important thing that happened to her while she was wearing each one. She says a lot of things come back to her that she had completely forgotten.

I can believe it. I gave the idea a trial spin while I was washing dishes. I remembered dresses I wouldn't be found dead in now. That black evening gown of 1930, for instance, with a hemline above my knees in front and down to the floor in back, forming a sort of show-case for my legs, which were modishly clad in very light stockings. (Why some of my friends didn't tell me?!) I broke my ankle while wearing that dress, which probably served me right.

Then there was a dress—about the only one I can still contemplate without writhing—made of men's heavy silk shirting, striped ivory-color. (Ralph says how can a solid color be striped, but that comes under What Every Woman Knows and means alternate dull and shiny stripes.) It was softly tailored and becoming and lucky, as some dresses are lucky. I first brought my golf score down into the eighties while I was wearing it.

When I get more time, I'm going to play this dress game some more. I still don't know the name of the woman who told me about it, but I owe her a vote of thanks. I collect one-handed means of entertainment. They come in handy in the woods.

There are a few things that sports do that make me mad, such as wearing smoked glasses the first time I meet them. I hate to talk to strangers in dark glasses. I can see the quirk of the mouth, but without the corroborative evidence of the eyes, I can't tell whether it's a friendly quirk or a cynical one. I feel like snarling, "Take those damn things off, so I can tell what's going on behind them."

It doesn't make me mad, though, to have them patronize and laugh at us quaint natives. They don't know it, but we're laughing and patronizing right straight back. They think our clothes are just too picturesque and amusing; and we think beach pajamas a hundred miles from a beach, and waders worn for boat fishing, and shorts and halters in black-fly season are amusing. (You can skip the "just too picturesque." We don't talk like that, and besides, I don't think we're supposed to know what picturesque means.) Their delight in our naivete can't exceed our delight in their gullibility. They ask us what makes the lake look streaked. All right, that's a silly question. Any fool should know it's the wind. So all right, it calls for a silly answer, and we have one all ready, because that's a stock question. "Oh, that's where the sled tracks cross the ice in winter," we say, and they usually believe us.

Pete and Ira Brown and I had a lot of fun with a whole porchful of sports one evening. Pete and Ira are two old guides, friends of mine. They were sitting outside the hotel with a dozen fishermen when Ralph and I arrived for the mail.

Pete said, "Hi, Louise. Been to B Pond lately?"

I said, "Yup. Gerrish and I went over Saturday."

"Catch any fish?"

"Nope. I don't think there are any fish over there."

Ira stated flatly, "You don't fish the right place. There are plenty of fish there."

"Well, I fished everywhere, so I must have been in the right place part of the time."

Ira squinted at me through a cloud of cigarette smoke. His eye had a warning gleam. "Bet you didn't fish under the island."

The silence on the porch was electric. Every eye was turned out over the lake, but every ear was cocked in our direction. I had to play this right.

"Why, no," I said uncertainly. "I forgot all about under the island."

Ira looked relieved. "That's where the fish are, this time of year. In them caverns. Last time I was over, I camped overnight on the island. Couldn't hardly get a wink of sleep from the racket they was making, feeding off the roots of the grass. You try there next time."

I couldn't take it any longer. I couldn't stand the bland expressions on the Brown brothers' faces, and the puzzled credulity on the sports'. I said hastily, "Thanks. I will," and went inside.

I love some of the sports. I used to love old Dr. Aldrich, who came up yearly to fish and play poker. He liked to fish, but he also liked his comfort. There's nothing very cozy about sitting on a hard cold rock, surrounded by a cloud of black flies and mosquitoes, so Dr. Aldrich didn't do it. Every evening he'd go down to Harbeck, a good pool just below Middle Dam, weighed down with impedimenta. First he inflated an air cushion, a process which left him purple of face and bulging of eye, arranged it on a rock, and arranged himself on it. Then he tucked a steamer rug carefully around his legs and placed a Flit gun beside him, its handle, like that of Lady Macbeth's dagger, to his hand. Then he was ready to fish. He'd work out fifteen or twenty feet of line and make a dozen casts. Suddenly he'd reel in furiously, lay down his rod, and snatch up the Flit gun. A fog of insecticide all but obscured him, and the black-fly corpses fell like rain. Then down with the gun and up with the rod, until dark. I used to walk clear up to Harbeck of an evening to watch Dr. Aldrich fish. It was worth the effort.

Something else that is worth the effort once—and it is an effort—are the National Championship White Water Races that are held here on the Fourth of July. I'm not awfully sure they are worth tagging along after more than once. After all, one guy getting dumped into the river is much like another guy getting dumped into the river, and this is one sport that is as hard on the spectators as on the entrants. Harder, maybe. All that can happen to a contestant is getting wet, getting bruised on rocks, and getting drowned. All these things can happen to the spectators, and in addition they can get bug-bites, heel blisters, scratched, sun-struck, exhausted, and lost. So I do my race-watching from my own front porch, knitting and dispensing food and drink to those of our friends who drop in in passing. But I am in the minority. People come from all over the country to spend three days chasing up and down the river.

The reason that these races are held on the Rapid River is that the flow of water can be regulated here. A flood or a drought doesn't matter. Renny Miller can just raise or lower a gate in the dam. And the river, while actually not navigable, is so nearly so that there is always the sporting hope that by some combination of luck and skill someone might get through in a canoe. Most of the races are not canoe races, though. They are run in fold-boats, which are exactly what the name suggests—light little collapsible boats built like kyaks. The frames are made of short pieces of wood with metal sockets on the ends and can be fitted together into the skeleton of a boat. Over this is drawn a rubberized canvas cover, which comes up over the bow and stern, leaving a cock-pit for the operator, who sits flat on the bottom, on a couple of slats, and wields a double-bladed paddle. A rubber apron buttons tight about his waist. With this apron it is almost impossible to swamp the boat. It draws so little water that it can slide over submerged ledges, and the construction is so flexible that it bounces off rocks instead of cracking up on them. So it is comparatively easy to run the river in a fold-boat. But only comparatively, you understand. I don't want to try.

What fascinates me is not the races themselves, although they are exciting, what with spills, hair-breadth escapes, and near-drownings. The real interest lies for me in what I will 'call the White Water Crowd. Travis Hoke, a friend of ours, is always talking about the various crowds—the Wedding Crowd, for example, college classmates who make a life work of attending each other's weddings, and whose conversation is filled with references of how stinko dear old Pinko got at Blinko's bachelor dinner. Or the Doggy Crowd, with their dead-serious discussions of that little bitch of the Squires', Faux Pas, by Social Climber out of Emily Post.

Me, I adore the White Water Crowd. All day long they slide down the river in their little boats, looking grim and desperate, and stagger back to Coburn's, battered and exhausted, to start all over again. They talk about haystacks when they mean swells, and about amazingly clever bowwork, and about Skowhegan Guide's Models, and they talk about nothing else. Tense and distraught, they come into the yard and ask to borrow some inner-tube patches and rubber cement, so they can mend their boats in time for the next race. They're so deadly earnest about the whole thing. I feel like saying, "Take it easy. It's supposed to be sport." But I know that would be considered a wrong attitude. I know the reason I'm no good at games is that I can never forget that they are games. It never seems very important whether I win or not, as long as I'm having fun playing. I spinelessly don't mind if someone else can hit a tennis ball harder and more often than I can. So I don't dare to suggest that maybe river running isn't exactly as important as they think it is.

They don't even slip into something loose and relax in the evening. Oh, my, no! When it gets too dark to risk life and limb any longer on the river, they trail back to Coburn's, take off their foot-ball helmets, life preservers, and sodden shorts and sneakers—regulation river-running costume—paint their wounds with iodine, and assemble in the lobby of the main lodge to look at each other's river-running movies. The movies are very good, actually. I like to look at them, too. But most of all I like to sit in the dark with all these hearty souls sprawled around me on the floor and hear them talk. I am sorry to say that I can never believe that floor-sprawling is anything but a pose; I have tried it, and it is *not* comfortable; but it looks well in the flickering fire-light, and is in good magazine-story tradition.

"That's Pussy on the Housatonic," someone will say of a fast-moving streak on the film. "Remember? That's the first time Pussy was ever in a fold-boat."

"Sure. But Pussy was always a good canoeman."

"Where is old Pussy now?"

"Pussy? Oh, Pussy's out on the Great Snake in Idaho, trying to make a record. Heart-broken not to be here, of course, but when this thing came up—"

"Ooooh, look! Ace, there's you. Look, Ace! I told you you were putting too much beef in your back-water. See what I mean now? See how your bow weaves and— Oh! Hey, can't we have that run over again? I want to show Ace—"

It all adds up to lunacy. And the lovely lunatic pay-off is that they do all this for a little bronze medal with a picture of a man in a fold-boat on the front and the date, place and occasion engraved on the back; and I, who never wet a foot or scraped a knee, I, with my wrong attitude, get one, too. I get one because Ralph was helpful about carrying them and their boats repeatedly from the finish back to the start in his cars. So when the Presentation of Medals came along, and they had one left over, they gave it to him, ceremoniously, to show their appreciation, which was very nice of them. And he came home to where I was sitting and reading and pitched it into my lap, saying, "Here, Mama. Here's something to add to that charm bracelet you've been claiming you're going to collect." Rubies wouldn't have pleased me more. I like a dash of irony in my dish.

So after all, why should we bother to go Outside? There would be only one reason, to see our friends; and our friends come here instead. We have swell friends, as I suppose everyone has, and we'd much rather see them here, undiluted by people we don't like, than Outside. So if they are willing to put up with my off-hand meals for the sake of lounging around in their oldest clothes and being free to do and say what they please; if they are willing to swap their own good beds for our not-so-good ones plus a lot of excellent scenery and fishing; if they want to take the long, involved trip in with nothing much at the end except us and the assurance that they are very much more than welcome, why, that's the way we want it, too. And that's the way we have it.

Once in a while the river gets to sounding like the wake of a steamer, and then I think maybe I'd like to go somewhere on a boat. I've only been on boats a little—one trip to Europe, long ago—and I love boats. But where in the world could I go to-day? Where is there peace and quiet and contentment? Where—except here.

XI

"Is It Worth-while?"

NOBODY EVER ASKS ME, "IS THIS LIFE YOU ARE LIVING worth-while?" That's a question that I ask myself, occasionally.

I ask it when I get up on a twenty-below-zero morning to find the kitchen stove in one of its sullen moods. Smoke oozes from every crack, but the top won't heat enough to melt the ice in the tea kettle. A cup of hot coffee is a long way in the future. I bang the oven door and the stove pipe falls down, raining buckets of soot over everything, including the butter that I have put on the stove shelf to warm to a spreadable consistency. Smoke pours out of the down chimney in clouds, and I have to open the door and all the windows, or suffocate. My eyes smart and run water, and my hands and feet slowly and painfully turn to ice, and the answer is, "No! Nothing is worth this!"

I ask it when, at the end of a long, hot summer, everyone in Middle Dam has used up his entire ice supply, and I want a glass of ice water. I can't have it. Moreover, the meat is going to spoil unless I do something about it at once, and the butter is unattractively liquid, and the lettuce has wilted, and the tomato aspic that I made this morning isn't going to set. I think of tall, frosted glasses, and salads that are crisp and noisy under the fork, and lemon sherbet, and decide I'd swap the whole north woods for one properly refrigerated meal.

I ask it when Rufus, all snowy and rosy, comes in from a day with his lumberjack pals and croons lovingly, "Mummy nice old son of a bitch." I ask it when I've got the lunch dishes done and the kitchen tidy and am all set for an hour's leisurely reading before going swimming, and a whole hungry gang drops in. Anywhere else, we could drive to the nearest hot-dog stand, but here I have to start from scratch and throw together another complete meal. I ask it when I look at the hands of Coburn's women guests and then at my own, with their short nails, calloused palms, and the burns from the oven door across the backs. The answer is always "No. It's not worth it."

You can't very well stop operations to ponder the problem of worth-whileness when you have a big salmon on the end of a light line. When the reel starts screaming and the rod bends into a vibrating bow and you suddenly remember that you meant to change that frayed leader and didn't; you have enough to think about. The fish starts away from the boat, and you burn your thumb braking the line. Then the water explodes fifty feet away, and you see him, a furious arc in the air, shaking his head viciously in an effort to dislodge the fly. He's a whale! He's easily the biggest fish that— He starts for the boat, and you reel in frantically. The sun is in your eyes, and the landing net is just out of reach—not that you'll ever bring him to the net; your arms are numb already—and then, abruptly, there he is, right up under the gunwale, just as tired as you are. You find that you can reach the net after all, and you ease it over the side, taking care not to hit the leader —and he's yours! He doesn't weigh the seven pounds you thought he did when you saw him break water, but the pocket scales say four and a half, and four and a half isn't so bad. You wet your hands carefully before taking him off the hook, and slide him over the side. You don't think to ask yourself then if that was worth-while. It's enough that it was fun.

"Is it worth-while?" is not a question that I think to ask myself when I am out in the middle of B Pond, watching the gulls inscribe their white scrolls against the sky. I don't ask it when I see a deer drinking at Long Pool, or hear a loon laugh, or when I compare Rufus with other children of his age and discover that he is two inches taller and five pounds heavier than most of them, and that he doesn't enter rooms with a piercing shriek of "It's Superman!" I don't ask it when I get a check for a story, or find that my $1.98 mail order bathing suit looks much nicer than the $15.00 model I saw on a woman up at the hotel— or does it only seem that way because I'm browner and thinner and can swim better than that woman? I don't ask it when friends have such a good time with us that they hate to leave as much as we hate to see them go; or when we all sit on the porch in the evening with our feet on the rail, and watch the tide of the dusk rise from the valleys up the hills and across the sky. The stars come out one by one, and the moon swings up above Pondy Dam, changing the river to a road of restless gold. It isn't a moment to be asking yourself questions. It's a moment to enjoy.

It amounts to this. "Is it worth-while to live like this?"

is a question that I never ask myself under fair conditions. I ask it only when exasperation or discomfort or exhaustion pre-determine *No* as an answer. That's about ten times a year. On the other three hundred and fifty-five days of the year, I don't question anything. Happy people aren't given to soul searching, I find. Revolt and reform, whether private or general, are always bred in misery and discontent. So now, sitting here quietly with nothing to annoy me and nothing to exhilarate me—except that I am at long last on the final chapter of this book I undertook so light-heartedly to write—I will once and for all try to find the answer.

Why did we come to live here in the first place? We thought it was because we liked the woods, because we wanted to find a simple, leisurely way of life. Now, looking back, I think that we were unconsciously seeking to find a lost sense of our own identity. Looking back through the telescope of the last six years, I can see myself as I was and realize how living here has changed me. I hope it has changed me for the better. Certainly I am happier than I was then. Certainly I am more at home in this world that we have created than ever I was in that vast and confusing maelstrom that we call civilization.

Here I dare to be myself. I don't see why it should ever again be important to me what I wear, or whether I have read the latest book or seen the latest play, or know the newest catch word. I don't see why I should ever care again what people think of me. It seems silly now, but those things were once important. I don't see why it should ever matter to me again who does or does not invite me to her house, who does or does not speak to me, who does or does not have more money than I have. Those things used to matter, though, because I had no identity of my own. I had nothing to go by but the standards someone else had set up. To define freedom, for which men and women and children are dying all over the world, in terms of indifference to clothes and social contacts and popular attitudes seems so trivial and irresponsible a thing to do that I am ashamed of it, as of a gross impertinence; but that is what living here adds up to, for me. I am free.

It adds up to more than that. All ordinary people like us, everywhere, are trying to find the same things. It makes no difference whether they are New Englanders or Texans or Malayans or Finns. They all want to be left alone to conduct their own private search for a personal peace, a reasonable security, a little love, a chance to attain happiness through achievement. It isn't much to want; but I never came anywhere near to getting most of those things until we took to the woods.

I have peace here. It may suffer surface disruptions when I forget to put my bread to rise, or Ralph discovers that Rufus has drained the radiator of the Big Green "Mormon" and poured the water into the gas tank; but the depths of that peace can't be shaken. We have a reasonable security. Sometimes we may have to figure a little closely to pay the taxes and outfit the kids and put the groceries in for the winter; but the things that matter— our feeling of entity, our sense of belonging—are never in danger here. Neither is the contentment that comes through accomplishment. What we have achieved isn't important to the world. No lives will be saved or unborn generations rise up to call us blessed for our six years' work here. All we've done is to take a little slice of wild land and force it to produce; to take some old ramshackle buildings and make them livable; to take land and buildings and two diametrically opposite personalities and make them into a home.

A great many people ask me if Ralph and I don't get on each other's nerves horribly during the long periods when we see only each other. That's a legitimate question. Everyone knows the corroding effect too great familiarity has on even the strongest attachment. It should have an even more devastating effect on me, as I am, I know, not quite normal in my loathing for having anyone crowd in on me, either literally or figuratively. I can't stand being jostled physically, and I can't stand having my actions questioned or commented upon. I could, quite literally, kill anyone who says to me, "A penny for your thoughts." I'm a New Englander, so I can't talk about love. The only way I can explain why I never feel like killing Ralph is open to unflattering misinterpretation; but I'll try to explain, all the same.

Emily Dickinson once said of a little niece who had been shut up in a closet as punishment, and was discovered there hours later, perfectly composed and happy, "But no one could ever punish a Dickinson by shutting her up alone!" That applied to Emily herself, and it applies to this obscure Dickinson. It applies to my ability to be contented here, away from the world, and to the truth underlying Ralph's and my relationship: that being with Ralph is just exactly as good as being alone.

Now that that's written, it looks terrible; and I meant it to be the nicest thing I could say!

And what about Ralph himself? Does he feel as I feel about our life here? I can't answer for him. No one can truly answer for another person's thoughts and feelings. I can only go by what external evidence I have.

Last summer a visitor, Barbara Wing, asked Ralph a purely hypothetical question, during one of those long rambling discussions that kindred souls get into: "If you had a million dollars left you to-morrow, what would be the first thing you'd do?"

Ralph thought for a long time, and I thought right along with him, wondering whether it would be an island in the South Seas—this was before Pearl Harbor—or a ranch in the Argentine. Finally he said slowly, "Well—that's a hard question to answer. I can't make up my mind whether a bathroom or a new roof for the woodshed comes first." He was serious, so we all laughed; but I don't worry any more about whether he really likes it here as much as I do.

I'd spend my million dollars on Forest Lodge, too, except for a fund I'd invest in letting the kids see the world. I'd send them everywhere and let them taste everything, so that at last they'd come to know what we have here to value. Discontent is only the fear of missing something. Content is the knowledge that you aren't missing a thing worth-while.

I know that many people—perhaps most people—couldn't feel that, living here, they held within their grasp all the best of life. So for them it wouldn't be the best. For us, it is.

And that's the final answer.

THE END

THE RANGELEY DISTRICT

Map courtesy of Susan Renwick Driver

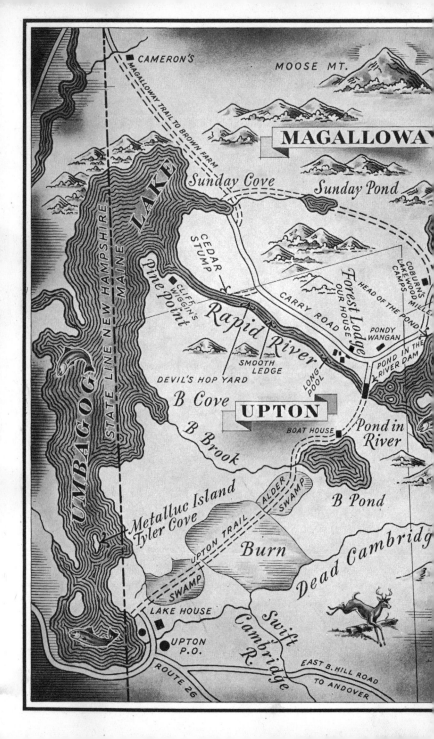

My Neck of the Woods

Contents

1

The North Country

SPEAKING RELATIVELY, I live in the far north—in the top, left-hand corner of Maine, just below the Canadian border—and there seems to be something about that country that fascinates people, even people who have never been there and never intend to go. Perhaps it's an inheritance passed down through the centuries from the time when for those who ventured away from the known coasts, the familiar landmarks, there was only one fixed point to steer by, the Pole Star, only one sure thing to guide them, the trembling needle pointing North. Or perhaps the North represents an idea, a state of mind, cold, detached, lonely and austere, sanctuary from the heat and confusion and indulgence of the modern world. Or perhaps again—and this is by far the most probable explanation—I'm making much ado about nothing, and the thing that interests chance acquaintances and sets them to asking questions about the North when they find out where I live is nothing more nor less than pure astonishment that anyone could be so misguided, and a natural curiosity about such a life. So I try to tell them what the North is like.

In the first place, it is very, very beautiful. It's a country of lakes and forested mountains and tumbling rivers. It's beautiful all the time. In the spring the new leaves of the birches and the blossoms of the maples look like wisps of green and red smoke blowing across the staid dark background of the fir and spruce, and the forest floor is carpeted with flowers—huge purple violets and tiny white ones, and the fragile wood sorrel, and the pink twin-sisters. The leafless rhodora blazes in the swamps. Then the thrushes sing high on the ridges in the arrowy light from the setting sun, and the red deer come down the slopes, stepping daintily, into the dusk of the valleys to drink. In the little villages and cross-roads around the lofty plateau of the lakes, the ancient lilacs break in a frenzy of bloom like lavender surf over the low houses against which they lean. Even when it rains—and it rains quite a lot in Maine in the spring—it's beautiful. The curtains of the clouds hide the mountains, and all the world is gray and dim and full of the sound of water, and of the high, sweet voices of the peepers in the bogs.

Summer is lovely, too, rich and full-blown. Cool, crisp nights follow blue sun-drenched days. Thunderstorms rattle around the mountains, rolling up one valley and down the next. The wild blueberries and raspberries ripen in hot clearings back in the woods, and the bear and foxes eat their fill. Everything smells wonderful—the pine, aromatic under the sun, the breeze blowing across a rock-ribbed pasture of cut hay, the very earth itself.

You have to see autumn in the North to believe it. The lakes are incredibly blue and the hillsides shout with color—orange and scarlet, yellow, and a crimson that is almost purple. In the night, the wild geese honk overhead beneath a full, burnished moon, fleeing south over the silvered ridges from the smell of winter. The Borealis crackles up from the northern horizon, sending unearthly streamers of light a thousand miles long to waver and fade at the zenith. At sunrise the ground is white with hoar-frost, against which the tracks of the rabbits and deer and bob-cats are black and precise, and the water in the ruts of the woodsroad is skimmed lightly with ice. The air is like wine, thin and dry and chilled; and like wine, it exhilarates body and mind, so that the performance of great tasks and the dreaming of great dreams are as easy as turning over your hand.

And winter—what can I say about winter, when the wind, clean and knife-edged, pours down from the northwest, and the country is held in the grip of an iron cold? The snow falls and falls, steadily and soundlessly; or it drives down the bitter wind, scourging the land. The houses in the villages huddle together like sheep under its lash. The ice on the lakes silently thickens—one foot, eighteen inches, three feet—until it is as solid as living ledge under the heaviest load. In the dead silence of a windless night, it surrenders to the strain of its own increasing pressure, and as the rift runs across a lake—two, four, ten miles—a great half-human howl echoes through the mountains and up to the stars. It's a blood-chilling sound to hear, wild and lost and despairing.

It doesn't snow all the time. Between storms the sky is deep sapphire, and all the shadows on the glittering white earth are violet. Nothing is familiar. The drifted snow lends grace and softness even to the stark architecture of a woodshed. In the villages and cross-roads, the windows of the besieged houses peer over eight-foot walls of snow at cars passing on the cleared roads, and every chimney wears constantly a plume of blue wood-smoke. Men shoveling paths and mittened women hanging out their stiffly frozen sheets call back and forth, and their voices are clear and bell-like in the crystal air. But winter is more than a time of ice and snow and cold. It's a time when more than the land is drained of life and emotion. It's a time for sitting and thinking, for being quiet, as the trees and rivers and lakes are quiet.

That's what the North is like, I try to tell people, although of course there's a lot more to it than that. Almost nobody could be satisfied to live forever without human contacts, immersed in and sustained solely by natural beauty. That wouldn't be living at all. Such an existence would end in either stagnation, or in madness brought on by the terrible loneliness. There are some, like Elmer Rhodes, who do go mad, although not necessarily from loneliness. But people go insane in cities, too, and who hasn't been lonely at some time during his life, no matter where he lives? Elmer Rhodes was an exception. Cliff Wiggin, my next-door neighbor on the west, five miles down and across the river, sometimes goes for months on end without seeing a soul, and he's far from crazy. He's far from stagnant, too. He's full of ambition and busy as a beaver all the time. But maybe he's an exception, too, and anyhow, nobody wants to hear about Cliff. Everybody wants to know—and they smile insinuatingly and knowingly when they ask—if it isn't true that we backwoodsmen eat fresh venison every month in the year.

It so happens that I never ate a piece of illegal deer meat in my life, partly because I consider it just slightly more palatable than old goat meat, partly because I really disapprove of poaching, and also partly, I must admit, because I'm afraid of the game warden, Leon Wilson. He's a nice guy as long as he's sure you're on his team, but he can get awfully tough awfully fast when he suspects that you aren't. I don't want him getting tough with me, the way he did with Morgan Twitchell— But I've lost my audience, which is demanding how cold it gets in winter.

It gets pretty cold, sometimes, down to forty or more below zero. But most of the time it doesn't get much colder than ten below in the day-time, which is a good snappy temperature in which to work outdoors. Once, though, Alys Parsons and Frances Greenwood and I, with our assorted husbands and hired help, walked the four miles across the lake in twenty below weather, and we were too hot when we got to South Arm, where the road to the Outside begins. Of course there was no wind, and in this altitude the air is dry and doesn't seem so cold, and we were walking pretty fast. Frances had on her new Easter hat, all covered with flowers— but no one is interested in Frances' hat.

No one is interested in Rienza Trimback's aprons, either, or in the Crew twins, or in what happened to Fred Kilgore. They're just people, and people are a dime a dozen Out-in-the-States—which is what we sometimes call the large part of the Union outside the backwater in which we live. People are no treat. Everybody knows hundreds of them, and they're all the same, aren't they? So skip the people, and tell us about the North. Nobody lives there anyhow. That's what makes it so fascinating.

Well, it's always interesting to hear another point of view outlined, as my sister says when she thoroughly disagrees with someone, but doesn't feel up to a fight. I suppose from one viewpoint, five and a half persons per square mile, which is about what we average, does add up to nobody. As for me, I consider that an ideal population, thick enough to be comforting, yet not so thick as to be cramping. Some of the five and a half have lived here all their lives, some were born here, moved elsewhere for a while, and then came back, and some came from Away originally to settle here; but they all have a quality in common. I'm not sure whether it's a cause or an effect. To put it in the simple and unflattering words of a friend, Mabel Sias, "Do you people get the way you are from living here, or were you all peculiar to start with? Why you all even look alike."

We really don't, of course, but I can see what she means. There is a prevalence of the long Yankee face, with its lean jaw, uncompromising mouth, and observant eyes, but the universal resemblance is more than that. It lies in the expression on the faces, which do not give themselves over easily to the polite smile or the grimace of facile grief. It lies in the handling of the body—in the deceptively leisurely stride and the economy of gesture, in the almost animal-like ability to relax and to spring from relaxation into action. It lies, too, in the speech, which is laconic, and the manner of speaking, which is deliberate and usually unimpassioned, and I'm afraid, frequently unintelligible to the Outsider. But these are only the visible clues to some fundamental common denominator.

What that denominator is, I find it hard to say; and anyhow, I'm tired of talking about my friends and acquaintances in terms of population averages and generic types, because they're a large part of the reason why I like the North. The landscape is very beautiful, as I have said, but it's the figures in the landscape that make it interesting. To me they are different from people anywhere else I have been, and they make more sense in the things they do and say. Whether this is because there are so few of us here that we know practically everything there is to be known about each other, and so understand almost everything, or whether Mabel Sias is right and it takes an eccentric to understand an eccentric, I'm neither prepared nor willing to state. All I'm going to do is just for once forget about the scenery and the weather and tell about the people.

2

The People Next Door

ONE OF THE very few things that a probably misspent life has taught me is that no matter how tough the going may become at times, you do manage to get along somehow, by the Grace of God and a long-handled spoon. Even so, I don't see how I could possibly get along without my next-door neighbors, Alys and Larry Parsons. The very thought of having to try makes my blood run cold. It isn't only because of the material aid and comfort they give me, either. I suppose that if all came to all (the local variation of "if worse came to worst") I'd be able to get someone to carry my mail and groceries and freight up and down the lake, give me a hand at loading a barrel of kerosene into and out of the back of the Ford, tell me what ails my washing machine motor when it won't start, and advise me what to use to get raspberry stains out of a white shirt. But the people who can do all those things aren't always, or even very often, people that feel the same way you do about the country you call home, with whom you can arrive at conclusions through a peculiar, truncated language which consists as much of what is not said as of what is said, who agree with you about what is funny and what is sad, or who can and will play along with you in your simple-minded little games and diversions. The Parsonses are the exceptions. I'd probably be able to maintain life in this feeble frame without them, but I'd be awfully lonesome and I wouldn't have much fun.

The label "next-door neighbor" here doesn't mean the same thing that it does in civilized communities. Al and I don't do any gossiping over back fences as we hang out our washings. We both have pretty good lungs, but not good enough to make shouting over a distance of two uninhabited miles of wilderness feasible. The Parsonses live at Middle Dam proper, where from May through September they operate a sporting camp, and I live down below Lower Dam at Forest Lodge on the Rapid River. We're connected by the Carry Road, which is more of a carry than a road, consisting as it does of rocks and ruts and dilapidated corduroy culverts, and wandering irresponsibly through Black Valley and over Birch Hill and past the Devil's Hopyard to provide a passage between two large lakes—Lower Richardson and Umbagog—the Rapid River being unnavigable for canoes. We're also connected by a catch-as-catch-can telephone line, privately owned by a lumber company, powered by dry batteries, and running about fifteen miles from Middle Dam down along the road, through a swamp and over a mountain to the Brown Farm in Magalloway Plantation. The Carry Road offers no access to the Outside; for that you have to take a boat from Middle Dam across Lower Richardson to the South Arm, where another road takes off for Civilization.

In summer when the hotel, so-called, is open and the mail comes In every day except Sunday, I see the Parsonses at least six times a week, but I don't know them very well. After the first of October, when we go on to our winter schedule of mail on Tuesdays and Fridays only, I see them twice a week, but I know them much better. In winter I talk with Al over the telephone, too, at least once a day. Since Ralph died and the children are Outside at school, I live alone in winter. I have raved and sworn so loudly and at such length on the subject of the criminal folly of anyone's living alone in the woods and making himself a burden and a responsibility to the neighbors that the least I can do, I feel, is to save my own neighbors worry by checking in every twenty-four hours with the information that I'm still alive and kicking. In summer I never call Al up unless I have something important to say to her. She's too busy running her business to welcome idle chat from me or anyone else.

The hotel at Middle Dam is constructed on the general plan of many sporting camps throughout the country. There is a large central building, painted white, wide-porched, and rambling over the greater part of half an acre, which houses the lobby or office, the dining room, the kitchen, and back-hall, or helps' dining room, and on the second floor the sleeping quarters of the women employees. The male employees sleep in the guides' house, up back, and up back, too, are the barns, shop, engine house for the lighting and pump systems, the storehouse, icehouse, woodsheds, and laundry. North and south along the lake shore, spread out like wings from the main building, are the nineteen individual cabins for the guests, each with its own bath and living room, with fireplace or Franklin stove, and from one to three bedrooms. It is really quite a large and elaborate establishment, completely independent when it comes to the common public utilities like light and water, and it requires a great deal of work and thought and ingenuity to keep it running smoothly.

The thought and planning go on all the time, but the concentration of hard labor, as far as the Parsonses personally are concerned, comes in the spring when the place has to be opened for business after a long winter. Then there is only a skeleton staff on the premises, the rotten condition of the ice precludes getting more help In, and there is so much to be done. In Larry's department the boats must be repaired and painted and launched, the plumbing must be overhauled and connected, chimneys and leaky roofs must be patched, and a million minor repairs must be made. He usually has, in addition to his year-round man, Swene Meisener, two or three extra men to help him, and the Lord knows he needs them. Under Al's aegis come the more domestic aspects of opening the place: the cleaning of the cabins, the setting up of the dining room, in which the tables and chairs have all been piled on top of each other to make room for the winter storage of rowboats, the organizing of the kitchen and store-room, and the policing of the flower beds. She usually has one woman to help her, and that woman's time is pretty well taken up in preparing meals for Larry's crew.

So, very often on a nice spring day I go up to help Al, more for her company's sake than anything else. The sight of a dandelion in bloom on a sunny south bank or of snow fleas hopping merrily about on a melting drift, or the wild and disturbing cry of the loons flying up-river in the night to find the first stretches of open water in Pond-in-the-River have sufficiently infected me with spring fever so that I don't want to stay home where I belong. Besides, there is no really good reason why I should stay home. I can do my own house-cleaning any time before the middle of June, when the children come In from school, and the silver lining of the dark cloud of living alone is that you aren't tied down to three meals a day and a ten o'clock bedtime. If you want to leave your breakfast dishes in the sink, shut the drafts of the stove tight, close the door behind you, and walk two miles to help a neighbor wash windows, you are at liberty to do so, returning when you feel like it, be it late that night or not until the next day or the day after.

It was while Al and I were feverishly cleaning Petticoat Alley, the wing of the hotel in which the waitresses and cabin girls sleep, making up beds and hanging fresh curtains, that she said to me a little distraughtly, "I'd certainly like to know how it happened that I woke up one morning and found myself in the hotel business way Back of Beyond. I'm very sure I never planned—" She pounded her thumb with a tack hammer and broke off to shake it and swear.

I laughed, pounded my own thumb, and said, "Damnation!" When order had been restored, I told her, "I know just how it happened. The same way I happened to wake up and find myself a writer living way Back of That. We married the men."

And that, of course, is exactly what did happen. Al, like me, is a native only by circumstance, choice, and—at long last—tenure of office. She was born and lived all her life Out-in-the-States, and probably had every intention of continuing to do so, until her college roommate suggested one summer that they both get jobs way off at this quaint and unlikely place in the woods, just for the fun of it and for something different to do to kill the vacation. So they did, the roommate as a waitress and Al as a cabin girl. I remember seeing her that first summer—my career as a native is a few years longer than hers—walking around with an armload of clean towels or sun bathing on the float. Her name was Alys Grua then, which I thought was one of the strangest and prettiest names I'd ever seen written or heard spoken, and which would probably have been the only thing I knew or remembered about her, if it hadn't been for Larry. At that time Captain and Mrs. Coburn owned and ran the hotel, and Larry had been their boatman in summer and caretaker in winter for several years. He started paying attention to Al, and she was interested enough so that she came back to work the next summer, and the winter after that they were married. She came In to live this odd and sometimes difficult life for the same reason that I did: because the men we married wouldn't be happy anywhere else, and we preferred to be miserable with them than comfortable without them. Or at least that's what we both probably thought at the time. It was so long ago and so much has happened since that it's hard for us to say just exactly how we did feel as brides.

The Parsonses built a very nice little house for their year-round home up above the tennis court, where the Carry Road begins, on the C Township side of the Magalloway line, and they have lived there ever since. I like their house. It stands among the trees, with a lawn and flower bed in front, and flower boxes outside the kitchen. You can look out of their front windows over the roofs of the cabins along the shore and see the whole length and breadth of the lake from the Narrows almost into South Arm, and the great northwest flank of Old Blue, with cloud shadows chasing over it and snow on its summit in the fall when it's raining down below.

It's a view that is never twice the same, but always lovely, no matter what the weather or the season of the year.

For a few years Larry continued to work for Captain Coburn and Al stayed home and ran a gift shop in her living room for the benefit of the guests in summer, and in winter kept house for her husband, like anyone else. Then one fine April day, when the air was soft from the south, shrinking the snow and turning the ice blacker and blacker, word was received from Mrs. Coburn that the Captain had died suddenly on his way home from Florida. There were already reservations for people who were panting expectantly on the Outside, waiting to come In for the spring fishing as soon as the ice was out, and the hotel had to open. The Coburns were childless, so the mantle of proprietorship fell on Al and Larry, and they have continued to wear it to this day, when Mrs. Coburn too is dead.

That's how Al happened to wake up one day and find herself in the hotel business, and I thank God whenever it occurs to me to do so that it's she and not I. But that's all right. I have more than a suspicion that she considers my means of livelihood with the same feeling of inadequacy and horror with which I regard hers. What we have in common is a way of life and a frame of reference in which to conduct our respective enterprises, and a healthy and, I hope, mutual respect for each other's special temperaments and abilities.

I long ago gave up describing my friends to people, because I'm apparently no judge of what they look like. All of my friends are either beautiful or handsome, depending on their sex. They really are, although I'm told that it's just because I'm glad to see them that they look so wonderful. I'm sure Al is a beautiful woman, though, even discounting my natural bias. She is tall and slim and carries herself well, and she wears her clothes with style. I don't pretend to be stylish, so my admiration when she appears looking like something out of *Vogue* is untinged by envy. It does burn me up slightly, however, when she infringes on my sartorial territory of dungarees and plaid shirts, and continues to look chic. I forgive her, though, for the sake of her voice, which is low and flexible, a rare thing among women in this country; and for the sake of her eyes, which are among the loveliest I have ever seen, large and gray-blue and eloquent, with dark lashes; and for the sake of her smile, which contains an almost angelic sweetness, in contrast with her sometimes salty conversation.

She has a way of saying, when I'm stewing and fussing about something, "You certainly have a terrible time, don't you, Louise? And enjoy every minute of it," in an amiable but astringent tone that makes me suspect that I'm raising an awful hoo-rah about nothing. She's very good for me. But over and above all that, she possesses the two qualities which I think I admire and envy above all others, whenever I encounter them. One is great physical courage, which it has become fashionable among those who lack it to rate second to moral courage. I don't. Moral courage is fine, and Al has plenty of that, too; but physical courage is not the common commodity that the books would have us believe, and I am always impressed and moved by any demonstration of it. The other quality is the simple, old-fashioned, and increasingly rare virtue of not being afraid of hard, dirty work. I simply *love* a good worker.

Of course, I think Larry is handsome, in a charming, masculine way. He is dark, and he laughs a lot, giving the impression of great good nature. As is not always the case, this impression is founded in fact, as far as Larry is concerned. He is about the best-natured and most obliging person I have ever known. He's much too accommodating for his own good. People—me included—impose on him terribly. Or at least, they impose on him up to a point. When this point is reached, long after anyone else would have flown into a thousand exasperated bits, Larry is all through for good. After that there's no sense in asking him for favors, because he won't do them, and I admire him for it. I've known him longer than I have anyone else in this country except John Lavorgna, and the longer I know him, the better I like him and the more I respect him. When I was new to this country and didn't realize that according to rural morality it is improper for a woman to entertain affection for any male other than members of her very immediate family, I once made the grave error of stating publicly that I was very fond of Larry. Fortunately the only two people whose opinion mattered to me, Al and Ralph, had been around and understood what I meant; and it didn't seem worth while to explain to the others that our very tenderest passages consisted of Larry's showing me how to fix the faulty generator of my Reo with a bit of zinc out of a common flashlight battery, or of my lending him my three-and-a-half ton chain hoist to haul out the rear end of his Chris-craft.

Larry and I see eye to eye about this country. I remember once in November he was driving me over to Upton to see my children, in school there. We started over East B Hill just as it began to spit a little snow. The leaden clouds, heavy and dull, pressed down almost onto the tops of the trees, and the woods on either side of the narrow dirt road were drab

and as still as painted pictures, in the hush preluding the
storm, the evergreens black and rigid with frost, the hardwoods bare-branched and lifeless. A little dirty snow lay in
ragged patches along the way, and the dank chill of the air
penetrated even into the station wagon. It was a bleak and
desolate scene, and I shivered involuntarily as I looked out
at it.

"It sure looks Godforsaken," Larry remarked. "I don't
know why we don't give it back to the Indians."

"I don't either," I agreed. "They didn't know any better,
and we do. Or at least we ought to. I never saw such a
dreary hunk of geography in my life. And right this minute
some people we know are swimming in Florida."

Larry shifted gears as we started to climb toward where
the road disappeared into the low-hanging, snow-swollen
clouds. "Want to join them?"

"Good God, no!" I exclaimed, appalled at the thought.

"Me neither. This country's not so much to look at, maybe,
but it suits me."

Several years later he and Al did go to Florida for a
month's vacation. When they returned, looking very brown
and healthy, I asked whether they'd had a good time; and it
seemed that they had, a very good time indeed.

"But how was it really?" I insisted, entertaining ideas of
their having been seduced into desertion by the hot sands
of the South while I'd been up to my ears in snow, and practically freezing to death.

Larry shrugged. "Nothing there but climate, and we've
got plenty of that at home. Better here, too. More variety to
it." And that settled Florida's hash.

To run a business that is in operation only a little more

than four months of the year sounds like a sinecure. It sounds like the lazy man's dream. Sure, you do a little work during those four months, if keeping a few books and giving a few orders to the help and chatting with the guests occasionally can be called work. And think of the other eight months! Nothing to do except loaf and spend the easy profits. It sounds too good to be true; and I have news for anyone who's thinking of trying it: it is too good to be true. I don't know all about it, naturally, but I have been deeply enough involved from time to time with various phases of the business to know that it's no bed of roses.

The first thing to be done in the spring is to get the Ice Out announcements ready to mail. The announcements that the Parsonses send are little folders with the literature describing the camp on the inside, and "The Ice Is Out at Lakewood Camps" on part of the outside. The rest of the outside is reserved for the address. For a week or two after we hear the first crow cawing off somewhere in the woods—the first infallible sign, if not exactly of spring, at least of the prospect of spring some time—Al keeps her typewriter alerted with a stack of announcements and the address book beside it, so that in spare moments while she is waiting for the potatoes to boil or for Larry and Swene to come in from the woodshed, she can address a few more announcements. There are hundreds of the things and it's a terrible chore. In the meantime, on one of his trips for the mail, Larry has bought six or eight sheets of cent-and-a-half stamps, and the plot is that anyone who has time on his hands can sit down and fold the addressed announcements, sealing them shut by folding and pasting a stamp over the free edges. I do that quite a lot while I'm killing time at the Parsonses', because it takes no special intelligence, and you can carry on a conversation at the same time. Al and I have decided a lot of weighty problems while getting the Ice Out announcements ready to mail, such as what to do about the pink sweater with black sequins on it that someone gave her, and whether or not I should let my hair grow. We also decided, after wading through several addresses like 375 W. 57th St., New York 21, N. Y., that we couldn't stand living in a place that was identified merely by a series of numbers and abbreviations. We'd feel as lacking in individuality as cards in a steel index. Give us addresses like Wounded Knee, or Pretty Prairie, Kansas. Or even, for that matter, Middle Dam, Maine.

When the announcements are all sealed and stamped, they are put into an empty canned-milk case and shoved under Al's bed to be forgotten until the ice actually does go out and Larry mails them. I would like to add that it is a good idea to carry a roll of Lifesavers in your pocket at this stage of the game, because the Government glue on cent-and-a-half stamps tastes horrible.

The iris bed *always* needs weeding, but in the spring it is even worse than usual, so while it is still too early to start to open cabins, but warm and sunny enough to make working outdoors a joy, Al and I give it a good cleaning out. It lies in a strategic position, commanding a view of almost every building on the place, as well as the lake and dock. No one can go anywhere or do anything without our seeing him from the iris bed, so we combine the pleasures of accomplishing something and satisfying our curiosity. We can chat with Larry as he goes by with a Stillson wrench to where he is connecting the water pipes to the cabins, shout up to Whit Roberts, mending the hotel roof, to ask if he can see any open water over by the Sandbanks from his vantage point, and annoy Swene, painting boats on the lawn. The weeding of the iris bed is more of a social function than a chore.

It was while we were thus employed one April afternoon that we instituted our Fifty Year Bird Plan. Up to that time we could both identify robins, crows, sea gulls, blue jays, and shelldrakes. I was kneeling on a sportsman's discarded magazine, and discovered that the cover-picture, although it said American merganser under it, was actually nothing but a stupid-looking old shelldrake.

"Ooh, look, Al," I said. "Now when people ask us what kind of ducks those are, we can show off."

"We really ought to know the names of the commoner birds here," she said. "After all, we're natives and supposed to know our own country. People are always asking—"

"My system," I told her truthfully, "is to say it's a yellow-bellied sapsucker if it's small. If it's large, I say it's an osprey. Nobody ever knows the difference."

"Yes, but still— I've bought a bird book," she confessed.

Just then Nugget, the cat, came strolling by with a dead bird in his mouth, so apropos that we considered him an instrument of Fate. We hi-jacked the bird, found the bird book, and identified it as a myrtle warbler. Then we decided that although obviously all small birds were going to be myrtle warblers that summer, we'd learn a new bird a year for the next fifty years, and die ornithologists. The next year I found a dead pine grosbeak, and last year a bird became trapped in the office and we caught it and discovered that it was a redpoll. I don't know what chance is going to provide us with This Year's Bird, but something will doubtless turn up.

After the iris bed, it's time to open a few cabins, enough

to take care of the really eager beavers who come In the minute the lake is free, before the regular cabin girls are ready to take over. I won't go into detail about that; it's just plain house-cleaning, washing windows, brushing down walls, and scrubbing floors. It's at this time that I begin to regard Al with awe. All the blankets and linen and draperies have been washed the fall before and stored in a couple of rooms in the hotel proper, and I go up to where she is sorting them into piles and say, "I've finished Metalluc and I'm ready for the curtains and bedding now."

She sits back on her heels. "Metalluc. Yes. Those blue curtains there belong in Metalluc and the gray foot-blankets. And let's see—the cushions there are slip-covered. Right over on that chair." Since there are nineteen cabins and the draperies are not interchangeable, as the windows differ in size and number, it is important to get the right ones. Al never makes a mistake. The inside of her head must look like the files of the FBI.

Once in a while I think that I've caught her in error, and I say smugly, "These slip-covers that you gave me don't belong in Turnstile. All the chairs there are plain wooden rockers." Then I prepare to gloat in a lady-like manner.

"Are you sure? Oh! That bride and groom we had in Allston in September! He didn't think anything was good enough for her, so he swiped furniture out of unoccupied cabins from all over, when we weren't looking. You'll find the Turnstile chair in there, and when you come to Comfort, there'll be a reading lamp missing. That's in Allston, too. I *wish* people would leave things alone." So I trudge meekly back to Allston, and sure enough, I find it crammed with stuff that obviously doesn't belong there. *I* wish I knew how Al does it.

By the time the ice actually does go out, the place is ready to roll, and I figuratively kiss Al good-bye for the duration. While I'll be seeing her every day throughout the summer, things won't be the same. Our encounters will be brief and business-like transactions dealing with my mail and milk and groceries, or else they'll carry about them the flavor of assignations. It's a very rare occasion when I can catch her alone and free to talk. She's a very busy woman.

Her day starts with a six-thirty breakfast with the help, out in the back-hall, and at six-forty she is tidying the office, vacuuming the rugs, running the dust mop around, straightening magazines, and fixing the flowers. The main dining room opens at seven, and when the guests start streaming in, she's at the desk, putting up the mail, getting her daily shopping list ready, answering questions, and finding a box and a piece of string for the lady who wants to send home to her sister in Philadelphia some attractive moss that she's found. Then she has a little conference with the stage driver (who has left his stage across the lake at South Arm), telling him to stop in at Stevens' after he's left the mail, on his way to Rumford, to see if they have any green corn to sell, to be sure and call at Buster's for the tire Mrs. Rich sent out to be vulcanized, to try to match this sample of blue thread for one of the guests, and above all things not to forget that he's to collect some people who are arriving on the three-thirty train. Then if he has time after he's finished his regular shopping list and stopped at Hood's for the special milk for the Gaston baby, will he go around to the Rumford Public Library and see if he can find a quotation for Judge Endicott.

The Judge thinks it comes from Demosthenes and starts out "Like the diet prescribed by doctors." Anyhow, he says it has something to do with the unsoundness of public relief. The stage driver looks defeated but says he'll try.

By this time it is almost eight-thirty, the time the boat has to leave in order to make mail connections, and the Smiths, who are leaving this morning, are still in the dining room. Al goes in and asks tactfully if their baggage is strapped, so that the cabin boy can take it down to the boat. This has the desired effect of hurrying them up, and she walks out onto the dock with them and sees them off, expressing appropriate sentiments and waving good-bye until the boat is halfway to the Ledge. It's all right then to stop and go back to the office for the list of people who want to lunch out to-day. The back-hall girl, who waits on the helps' table and does the helps' dishes, also puts up the lunches, so Al goes into a huddle with her, imparting the information that while most of the lunches will be standard, there are a few deviations. Dr. Spaulding is allergic to butter. Mr. Peters is a Catholic and to-day is Friday, so give him either egg or tuna salad instead of the ham, and Mrs. Keane wants milk instead of coffee in her thermos. Then she hunts for the chef, who is discovered in the big refrigerator counting lamb chops, and starts taking down the things he's going to need from the storehouse during the day. It's a long list, so she impresses his helper to carry the heavy things, and goes back to consult with Rosella, the pastry cook, about desserts. They decide that everyone likes apple pie, and now about that pudding that didn't go so well last night. It's really good, only of course everybody ordered the strawberry short-cake, so how about running it again under a different name?

That settled, Rosella says, "There's still some coffee in the pot. Here, have a cup along with one of these chocolate doughnuts. I just made them and they came out extra good." So Al pours herself some coffee and bites into a doughnut, just as a cabin boy, shielding his eyes with cupped hands, peers in through the screen.

"Mrs. Parsons in there? Someone wants her on the telephone."

Al runs, leaving her coffee but taking her doughnut with her. It's Joe Mooney at the Brown Farm, saying that the Union Water Power Company wants someone to tow their scow to Upper Dam, and then go over to Mill Brook and pick up a load of lumber. The boatman is at South Arm with the big boat, so that means that Larry will have to go with the half-cabin. No one has seen Larry for at least half an hour, so Al starts looking for him and finds him up in the engine room tinkering on the light plant, which showed symptoms of low blood-pressure or something the evening before. She goes back and arranges to have a lunch put up for him, because there's no telling when he will be back, and decides that maybe now is the time to sneak off home and make her bed and perhaps wash out a few stockings. But the laundress catches her before she can escape, to complain that there's no hot water. By the time they discover it was just a question of not having let it run long enough, one of the cabin girls comes in with the report that the kids in Trail's End have broken a window, and what is she supposed to do about it? Al finds Swene and a piece of glass and some putty, and now it's after eleven and time to type the luncheon menus. Then a canoe trip from a boys' camp lands, demanding post cards, soft drinks and candy bars. She rediscovers the great

.ruth that it takes a twelve-year-old about the same length
of time to decide between a Sky-bar and an Oh Henry as it
does his father to weigh the merits of a Pontiac against a
Studebaker, and before they're on their way again, the lunch
hour is half over. Larry won't be back for hours, so she goes
into the dining room and eats alone.

Now might be the time to make her own bed, she thinks,
and starts maneuvering into a position behind the fireplace
chimney from which she can make an unobtrusive exit via
the cold drink room and the back door. But the kids from
Trail's End troup out of the dining room, announcing that
they are going to play ping-pong, and may they have the
balls? While she is getting them out from under the counter,
the telephone rings. Andover announces that a party of two
by the name of Baffinland or something like that is on the
way In. No, they're not expected; that's why they stopped
to have the call put through; but they want the boat to meet
them right away. So Al finds the boatman (long since
back from South Arm) who is improving each shining hour
by cultivating the vegetable garden, sends him on his way,
and goes to tell the north-side cabin girl that she'll be
having occupants in Birch Lodge, so will she please check
it. As she goes quietly past the iris bed, looking neither to
the right nor left in the ostrich-hope that if she doesn't
see anybody, nobody will see her, the woman in Sunshine
hails her, waving a half-knit sock.

"You said you'd help me when I came to turning the heel."

So Al forgets about making her bed for the time being
and about washing stockings for the day. While she is explaining patiently, "No, you slip one, knit two together,
knit one, and turn," the Coreys come up a little apologetically.

"We know we should have told you before, but we've de cided to picnic out to-night instead of going into the dining room. So just this once could you make an exception and have a lunch put up for us?"

Al refrains from commenting that the Coreys are the fifth exception this week and says she guesses it can be arranged Then she goes out into the kitchen and puts up the lunch herself, since the back-hall girl, thinking that her work is al done until suppertime, has gone blueberrying with the wait resses. Just as she ties the string around the box, she glances out the window and sees the boat out by the Ledge. That means that the Baffinlands-or-whatever-their-name-is are aboard, and she hasn't done a thing about her face and hair since before breakfast. She dashes out of the kitchen and along the path to her own house as fast as she can—and she can run faster than anyone I ever saw—slams into the house, washes her face, puts on fresh lip-stick, runs a comb through her hair, and races down in time to greet the Baffinlands ade quately, although a little breathlessly. She shows them to their cabin, answers their seventy-nine questions, and returns to the office, because it's time to type the dinner menus. The chef comes in to say that he's terribly sorry, but he forgot this morning that he was going to need a new bottle of Worcester shire sauce, and will she please get him one from the store room. After that, the Baffinlands come in to register and buy fishing licenses, and in the course of that transaction she discovers that their name is really Boardman; so she goes about for five minutes muttering it under her breath, because she believes it's good business to call people by their correct names. Then the people who went over to B Pond yesterday call up from Lower Dam to say that they are back that far, and will she send the command car down after them. She finds Swene, dispatches him down the Carry, and looks down the lake to see the big boat returning from the Arm. Presumably the guests who were to arrive by the afternoon train are aboard, so she goes down to meet the boat, greet them, and get them settled. The B Pond people drive into the yard, jubilant over the fish they have caught. She admires them extravagantly, although she's seen seven thousand fish in her hotel career, and never did think they were particularly fascinating phenomena in the first place. But she shows the fishermen where the fish-box is, and explains that they can send word to the chef by their waitress as to when and how they want the fish cooked.

Just as she has got around to sorting the mail, I come in from down the road, and she says, "Hi. Your tire is out by the iris bed, and here's your mail. What have you been doing all day?"

"Oh, I've been working like a dog," I tell her complacently. "I've finished a chapter of my book, and done some washing, and made bread. Then I finally got my tomato plants tied up, and picked a couple of quarts of raspberries, and of course went swimming with the kids two or three times. I've done a lot. And what have you accomplished for your country?"

"Nothing," she tells me bitterly. "I've just frittered the whole day away. I haven't even made my bed."

That's what goes on with Al all summer long, when things are running smoothly; but sometimes a little sand gets into the gear-box. The laundress has a bilious spell, for instance, and Al has to do the laundry. Or the white-dishwasher goes to her cousin's funeral, and Al does the dishes. Things like that.

The Parsonses used to have an elderly gentleman named Dean working for them, tending the garden, milking the cows, and driving the old car that carries fishermen to the more remote pools along the river. I liked Dean a lot. He was a little teched, as we say, and given to charming illusions. He told me once in the fall that he'd seen sixteen snow-white foxes running a foot race along the shore of the lake in the early morning—purtiest sight he ever see against the deep blue of the water and the scarlet of the maples. Of course it was all in his head, but I thought how lucky he was to have a head like that. One Christmas he made some enormous wreaths and long swags of trailing pine and black alder berries and hung them all over the barn, because he thought that the horses and cattle, whose kind had been present at the birth of the Christ child, should share in the season's celebration. I thought that was a lovely idea; but possibly I wouldn't have been so enchanted with Dean if he'd been working for me, since one of his illusions was that there was no need of his writing anything down, because he had a good memory. Actually he had a memory like a sieve.

He would come into my house and say, "Louise, you seen anything of a couple of sports?"

"Sure, I've seen eight or ten go by to-day. What do yours look like?"

"They got on red-and-black checked shirts." Since nine out of ten sports wear red-and-black checked shirts, this wasn't very helpful. "I'm supposed to pick them up and take them back to the hotel."

"When and where?" I'd ask.

"Seems to me 'twas four o'clock at Lower Dam. Yes, that's what 'twas. Maybe I better write it down." And he'd get out his note-book and stub of a pencil and lean on my ice-box and write down, "Lower Dam, four P.M.," and go away. In about an hour Al would call me up to ask if I'd seen anything of Dean.

"Sure, he was in here a while ago. He said he had to pick up some people at Lower Dam at four o'clock."

"Oh, Lord! They wanted to be picked up at the Hopyard at two. They're going to be furious and I don't blame them."

"I'll run up to the dam and tell him," I'd offer, and she'd thank me.

When I'd delivered the message, Dean would look disgusted. "Pity folks can't make up their minds and keep them made up," he'd snort. "Look, I got it written down right here, Lower Dam, four P.M. Sports are all hen-heads is what I think." During his regime, Dean certainly gave variety and interest to Al's day.

As to what Larry does all summer, I have only a vague idea. Every time I ask where he is, he's either driven to Portland to pick up the Lyonses off the night train, or he's taking a party to Pine Island, or he's helping the electrician fix the mangle in the laundry, or he's asleep because he was up all night taking the man who had a heart attack to the hospital. The few times I do lay eyes on him toward the end of the summer, all he'll talk about anyhow is the World Series and what I think of the Red Sox' chances. He goes temporarily insane every fall, along with most of the guests, male and female. Al and I share a complete indifference to the ability of one group of overgrown schoolboys to hit a ball harder and oftener than another group can, and after having listened to that sort of nonsense far too long and patiently, we have developed a defense. When someone starts, "I've just been

listening to the ball game. It's the last of the eighth, Yankees
at bat, two on and one down," we move in with our counter-
offensive.

"I've just been listening to the radio, Louise," Al will say.
"Pepper Young's Family at bat, with Portia Facing Life on
third."

"The boy to watch is Young Doctor Kildare," I'll tell her,
"although John's Other Wife is batting over three hundred.
Do you suppose The Goldbergs will really trade The Woman
in White?" While this doesn't precisely endear us to the fans,
it does sometimes discourage them a little from talking about
baseball, to us at least, and is one of the silly games we play
to make life tolerable.

Finally the hotel closes for the season and everything that
was taken out for use in the spring has to be washed and
ironed and put back into storage. The pipes have to be disconnected and drained, and everything freezable has to be
taken out of the storehouse and put into guides' house cellar.
The windows of all the cabins have to be checked and
unlocked, because the buildings heave with frost in the winter
and unless the window sashes are free to move a little, all
the glass will be cracked by spring. It's just as much work to
close a camp as to open it, but there is a different attitude
toward the whole thing. We have fun in the fall. We all feel
free and irresponsible. The summer is over, none of the guests
has drowned, the pressure is off. I can go up to see Al any
time I want to, knowing that even if she is washing blankets,
I won't be bothering her. I can help her, and then we can
bum a cup of coffee from the cook and take it outdoors to
drink in the sun. Everyone is in fine careless fettle in the fall.

The only time I ever saw Al really mad, though, was in

the fall. I went up the Carry one afternoon and found her sitting on her steps with her hands clasped over her knees, staring out over the lake with a grim expression on her face. "What ails you?" I asked diffidently.

After a minute she said tightly, "You know those damn horses."

I knew the damn horses well, and I knew that she didn't feel much more kindly toward them than I did. They're really nice animals, but they're what is known in this country as gawmy. That means well-intentioned, but clumsy and accident-prone. What I had against them was that the week before Larry had told me that if I wanted some carrots, I was free to take what I cared to dig in his garden. So I found a spading fork and went to work. I big-heartedly decided to dig them all, take the few I wanted, and sack up the rest for the Parsonses. My plan was to go down the rows digging, leaving them lying on the ground, and then to go back and pick them up. When I reached the end of the first row, which was about fifty feet long, and turned around to go back up the next, I found Prince breathing down the back of my neck with the top of the last carrot I'd dug dangling attractively from the corner of his mouth, and Chub right behind him. I'd forgotten that Larry lets them out of pasture in the fall. They'd followed me right down the line, eating carrots as fast as I uncovered them. I was mad, so I banged them over the noses with the fork handle and they galloped away, laughing at me. But the minute I started digging again, they came back and I couldn't get rid of them, so I had to give up.

What Al had against them was this: For some strange reason, she can't learn to braid her hair. She is about the most capable person I know, not only when real labor or brainwork is involved, but in handicraft as well. So it strikes me as being amusing and rather appealing that braiding, which even I can do, baffles her. She decided one day to try doing her hair coronet style, and being unable to braid herself, she appealed to Larry. He said he didn't know how to braid either. But a few days later she surprised him up in the barn braiding the horses' manes and tails, simply to make them look pretty. Larry is really a little soft about those horses; but she thought, and so do I, that if he could braid them, he could braid her. So the horses were slightly in disgrace already on the day that Al lost her temper.

She had spent the whole morning laundering the white sash curtains from the cabin bedrooms, about forty pair, and instead of hanging them on the lines, she'd spread them on the grass to bleach. The next thing she knew, someone had let the horses out and they had not only walked all over the curtains, muddying and tearing them, but had finished the job by lying down and rolling all over them. They were a mess. When I found her, she was trying to make up her mind whether to shoot the horses or shoot herself. In the end, of course, she did neither; but now no one lets the horses out of the pasture without first asking Al if she's planning to bleach curtains.

Now we're in the eight months of the year when hypothetically the owner of a summer resort can relax and cultivate his ethos. There is a great difference between hypothesis and practice in this country, however. It takes until November to get snugged down for winter, with the houses banked, the gardens cleaned, the boats stored, and all tools and equipment under cover. Then there are still eighty-five cords of wood

—more, if it's been a cold summer that has depleted the supply —to cut, haul, saw, split, and stack, and tons of ice to be put up. Those jobs, along with incidental chores and emergencies that are bound to crop up, fill the winter very nicely. Larry sacrifices two days of every week to the carrying of the mail. In summer this is simply a matter of going to Andover by boat and car, and in deep winter, although it isn't quite that easy, it still can be done safely enough, provided that you're sufficiently rugged to stand the trip across the lake in a twenty-below gale. Larry is. He can and frequently does take the kind of physical pounding that would kill a moose.

But nobody is immune from the dangers of the thin ice of the fall, and so twice a week until the ice is safe, he has to walk the mail around the shore. This just about doubles the four-mile trek to the Arm, and it's a horrible trip. The rocks are covered with glare ice, and the going is rough. You look at a point two hundred feet and two minutes away, test the ice, know it won't hold, and struggle three-quarters of a mile around a deep cove. I've walked around the shore to get Out, and my tongue was dragging by the time I reached the Arm. I wasn't carrying a seventy-pound pack-sack, either, and I didn't have to turn around and come back the same way the same day.

Larry's courage, stamina, and sweet temper were demonstrated yet once again on the day that Wade Thurston was killed. It was late in the day and already dark when he got In with the mail, and he looked tired, as well he might. He had just taken off his boots and put on dry socks and slippers when the telephone rang. It was Joe Mooney to tell Al that Wade had been killed by a runaway sled. "And will some of you folks get word to Lee Thurston? He's logging up on

Elephant Back, and they want him to come right Out. I hate to ask you this time of night, but he hasn't got a phone yet, and you're nearest."

Larry was stretched out reading the paper, with the look of a man all settled in for the evening about him, when Al gave him the message. "Jesus, that's too bad," he said. "Poor Wade." He reached for his boots and started putting them on again. "I can't wait for supper. Could you make me a sandwich and some coffee, Al?"

"Oh, Larry," she protested, "you can't go. You've already walked the shore twice to-day, besides the trip to Andover. Can't you send Swene or Louis? It must be an eight-mile walk onto Elephant Back, after you get off the lake. It's too much—"

Larry stood up, tucked in his shirt, and tightened his belt. "Nope, I can't ask the boys to do a chore like this. I don't pay them that kind of money, and I'm not expecting it of them. On top of the trip, which is going to be long and hard enough, it's not going to be any easy chore to break the news to Lee. This is one of those things a joker has to do himself." He drank a cup of coffee. "Where's my good flashlight? It's going to be blacker'n the inside of God's pocket up on that mountain. Well— Expect me when you see me, and don't worry. I might have to go Out to Andover with Lee. He's going to take this hard."

We watched the little spark of the flashlight move slowly along the dark shore of the lake, growing smaller and smaller against the black and starless immensity of the night, disappearing now and then around a point of land, and then reappearing and always going steadily forward. Finally, when we could see it no longer, I said to Al, "Want to know something? You're married to one hell of a swell guy."

She kept her eyes fixed on the point in the darkness where we'd last seen the light. "Do you think that's any news to me?" she asked. She did her ironing that night, knowing that it would be senseless to go to bed to lie tossing and worrying about Larry. Of course, he got back all right the next day; but that's the sort of thing that makes living in the woods hard, much more than the inconvenience and physical effort involved.

Sometimes I used to wonder, before I knew her well, what the percentage for Al was in this life. She was used to civilization, where the flick of a finger floods a room with light and a call to the laundry takes care of the problem of clean sheets. Here we spend hours a week trimming and filling lamps, and washing their chimneys, and at least a day and a half a week getting the dirty clothes washed and out and in again and ironed and put away. In winter it's more than that, because you can't dry them outdoors half the time, so you spend the rest of the week playing The Winter Game of hanging a few at a time over the stove and hoping to get them all dry before the next wash-day. Al is younger than I, and I thought that with her looks and intelligence and background, she ought to be Outside, seeing life. I couldn't make up my mind whether she really was contented here, or whether it was simply a case of her being old-fashioned enough to believe in whither thou goest.

Then about three years ago, when she was recuperating from an operation in Boston, Mabel Sias and I went to see her. We tried to persuade her to go to New York with us before returning to the woods. I'd just come down from Middle

Dam, and I was able to assure her that Larry was getting along all right; and Mabel had just come up from New York, full of all the wonderful things we could do and see there. We three would have a marvelous time, we told her, and there was no reason in the world why she couldn't go, as soon as the doctor would let her.

She said yes, she knew she'd enjoy it, and yes, she knew Larry would be all right, but—

"But what?" Mabel demanded. "Come on now, Butch, give me one good reason why you can't come."

Al raised her lashes and looked at us squarely with her beautiful eyes, speaking with an almost child-like simplicity and wistfulness. "I know you're going to think I'm silly—but I just want to go home!"

Of course that was the one really good reason for which there was no answer, so we stopped pestering her and gave up the whole notion. But since that day I haven't wasted any more of my time worrying about Al. I haven't felt it necessary.

3

Planned Economy for One

WHENEVER PEOPLE TALK to me about Maine and the backwoods, they seem to expect a hermit, and it so happens that we have one, or a reasonable facsimile thereof. I was a little bit confused about our hermit when first I knew him. This was long before I ever met him, in the days when our acquaintance was confined to telephone conversations. It's true that he's my next-door neighbor on the west, but since he lives five miles down on the other side of the river, with no road and no bridge between us, he might as well have been living on the Azores as far as I was concerned, except for the telephone. This is a single strand of uninsulated wire wandering over the river and through the woods, which makes it more or less possible for us to talk to each other: more when the weather is good and the batteries fairly new, and less when the line is bogged down with snow or fallen fir-tops or the batteries are old and weak.

The first time he called me up he introduced himself as Cliff Wiggin and wanted to know whether it was Monday or Tuesday, since he'd lost track of the days. I told him that it was Tuesday the seventeenth. He asked if I were sure, because if it was Tuesday at all, it must be Tuesday the tenth.

45

By this time I didn't know myself what the day or date was, although we did agree that the month was October, so I said I'd find out and call him back. By looking at the cover of the last week's *Time*, I determined that it was indeed the seventeenth, and cranked the four long peals that would summon him back to his phone. A voice said, "Wallace speaking," so I asked the voice please to tell Mr. Wiggin that it was Tuesday the seventeenth, and the voice laughed and said that it would. And that took care of that.

During the next two or three months I talked occasionally with Mr. Wallace and occasionally with Mr. Wiggin about the weather, the hunting, and the proper proportions of soda and cream of tartar to use when you ran out of baking powder and wanted to make biscuits. From these exchanges I built up for myself a cozy little picture of those two old cronies holed up in their snug little cabin at the foot of the falls, sharing their tasks and pleasures. Mr. Wiggin apparently was the one who did most of the outdoor work—at least, he mentioned things like banking the house for winter and digging the root crops—and for some reason I thought of him as tall and broad-shouldered, with a full beard. Mr. Wallace did the cooking and inside work—he told me how to make molasses pie and how to bleach flour sacks with lye—and he was round and apple-cheeked. Since everybody in this country plays cribbage, I could just see them on stormy winter evenings, when the wind whooped off the lake and the snow drifted high on their window sills, bent over the cribbage board in the golden light of a kerosene lamp, pegging away like mad, slapping their knees and laughing companionably when either made a killing. It was a very pretty picture indeed. The only trouble with it was that it was completely false. There weren't both Mr. Wiggin and Mr. Wallace. There was just Old Cliff, who lived alone and sometimes called himself by one name and sometimes by the other. He did all the work, both indoors and out, and spent his evenings catching up on his mending, reading, and playing with the cat.

When I found this out from the game warden, Leon Wilson, I called him up to upbraid him. "You've made me look like an awful fool," I said. "Why did you let me go on and on—?"

He laughed. "Wal, I'll tell you, Miz Rich. First-off, I didn't tumble myself. Then I thought I'd see how long it took you to catch on. It got to be kind of a game. You know how 'tis, livin' back here. Don't take a hell of a lot to keep a feller amused."

I know exactly how it was. I myself was becoming pretty adept at the simpler, one-handed forms of entertainment, and if I could have found anybody gullible enough to believe that I was two other people, I'd have played the role to the hilt. So I told him that all was forgiven, and how did he come by two surnames in the first place? That turned out to be a matter very easily explained.

Cliff was born a Wallace, but he was brought up from his orphan babyhood by a family named Wiggin, over around Magalloway Plantation, near the foot of the Peaks of the Diamond. A Wallace he remained, legally, since he was never adopted, but for easy identification with his foster family, he was more often called Cliff Wiggin while he was growing up. He answered to either name, and gave whichever came first to his tongue when asked. Like most of the boys who were born into this country seventy-odd years ago and like many who are born here now, he took to the woods about as soon as he could walk, which is not surprising, since the woods started within a stone's throw of the kitchen door and ended somewhere up around the Arctic Circle. He learned to hunt and to trap and to fish, and had shot his first deer, long before he was in his teens; and not long after, he was guiding parties from the city during the season, and working in the lumber camps during the winter. At sixteen he was a grown man, doing a man's work and carrying a man's responsibility, a thing not unusual in that time and place.

When he was about twenty, he decided to see the world. He'd come in contact with people from the Outside, and he'd heard their talk and observed their ways. These observations led him to the conclusion that he was as smart as they were. Some of the hen-heads he guided owned five-hundred-dollar rifles and leather jackets as soft and pliable as a piece of old cotton waste, and they couldn't run a compass line through an open pasture. A really up-and-coming joker should be able to do all right Out-in-the-States. Besides, he was curious to find out what lay beyond mountain and lake. So he went up to Massachusetts. Here people always speak of down Maine and up Massachusetts-way, and that used to bother me, as by my reckoning anything on the top of the map is up and anything toward the bottom of the map is down. But Cliff explained that to me once out of his large fund of miscellaneous information. It seems that in the old sailing days, the prevailing wind being south-westerly, you sailed down the wind from Boston to Portland and up the wind when you wanted to go back. Cliff didn't sail up to Massachusetts, though. He walked most of the distance, working his way as he went along.

A sport once told me that he had it all figured out that if Cliff had done all the things he claimed to have done in his lifetime, he'd be one hundred and forty-eight years old the coming spring. What he failed to take into consideration was the essential versatility of any frontiersman. Cliff had no trouble in working his way to Massachusetts. He could cook, pitch hay, handle horses, milk, repair almost anything devised by man, and turn his hand to any one of the scores of other skills included in the liberal education of a pioneer life. He hadn't decided exactly where he was heading, except that it was somewhere far away and exciting. He thought that he'd keep an open mind, take one step at a time, and hold himself ready to recognize and grasp opportunities. This plan, he felt, would lead him to wealth and adventure.

Probably it would have, too, if he hadn't fallen in love shortly after reaching Massachusetts. No Casanova, he found a good steady job in a factory, established himself as a sober, solid citizen and good provider, and armed with these sterling qualifications, wooed and won the girl of his dreams. This should have been the end of the story, and for about twenty-five years it seemed as though it might be. He worked hard and saved his money. He received promotions and raises with encouraging regularity. He bought a house with hardwood floors in every room and a half-acre lot around it. It began to look as though this were just another Horatio Alger story of rags to riches.

Then something happened. Perhaps he woke one night and heard the faint, sweet, discordant cry of the wild geese going over, beating their way northward through the rare, pure altitudes with the moonlight on their backs. Perhaps, walking down the crowded street, he caught a pungent whiff of the alien scent of cut pine, from a building under construction. Perhaps it was nothing more than a dandelion blooming bravely on a starved plot of city grass. Whatever it was, it brought Cliff up short. He asked himself, as we all must do at one time or another, "What in tarnation am I doing here?" This wasn't where he belonged. This wasn't any place he'd ever intended to be, or any life he'd ever intended to live. He realized with surprise and an overwhelming sense of dismay that half his days had been spent, and that middle age found him possessed of nothing that he really wanted. It never occurred to him that he had passed the point of no return.

He wrote a letter to his wife, handing over to her the mortgage-free house and the very respectable bank account, told the boss that he was quitting as of that moment, went down to the station, bought a ticket, got on the train, and came home. It didn't take so very much longer to do than it does to tell about it, and while this course may seem to have been a little ruthless, you can't make an angel cake without smashing a lot of eggs and maybe even throwing away some of the yolks. How his wife took this cavalier treatment, I have no way of knowing for certain. Since Cliff never heard a word from her from that day to this—and he wouldn't have been hard to trace, returning as he did to the green pastures of his youth—I accept his opinion that she didn't really mind having him go.

"I was just a bad habit she'd got into," he explained. "She was used to having me around, just like you get used to a window that jams. Must have been a relief to her, after a while, not havin' me trackin' up her clean floors. I ain't none of these here indispensable men; never was, nor ever aim to be."

When at last he stood again in the shadow of the Peaks, he had no money and only the clothes that he stood in, but this didn't worry him. He figured that he was almost exactly as well off as he had been on that day a quarter of a century before, when he had set out to see the world. True, he had lost twenty-five years and the physical qualities of youth; but he had gained something of greater value, something a surprising number of people never acquire. He knew now exactly what he wanted from life. He wanted peace and freedom, and he intended to have them. He knew what he was about. He realized that peace and freedom are almost incompatible: that if you want freeom, you'll almost surely have to fight for it, but if you'd rather have peace, you can probably have it by selling yourself into some form of bondage. Well, he was prepared to do a little fighting when necessary—he'd already fought and won the Battle of Massachusetts; and he was prepared to accept a few temporary bonds while he was establishing the conditions under which he would, by his own definition, feel free and at peace. The thing that worried him most was time. He'd frittered away half his life, and he didn't intend to waste the other half.

He could have gone back to what he had been, an itinerant woodsman and guide, but there was no future in that, and not much of a present. The thing for him to do, he decided, was to acquire a fishing and hunting camp and set himself up in the sports business. Thus he'd have a home of his own and a source of the small income he needed for his very few wants. He'd be his own boss, and he'd be what he called "shed of folks." He'd had enough bosses, and folks crowding in on him, during the past twenty-five years to last him the rest of his life.

He cruised about the country, familiar from old time, and finally located a set—as we say in Maine—of run-down camps, so far gone that he was able to lease them very cheaply. There was a four-room cabin with a pitch-roofed loft, outhouses, an icehouse, and a woodshed. The roofs leaked like sieves, the floor of the porch was rotted away, some of the windows were broken, porcupines had been at the thresholds, and there was no plumbing of any description. But the sills and timbers were sound, there was a good place for a garden, once it was cleared of encroaching brush and grubbed free of roots, and plenty of hardwood for fuel stood within easy hauling distance. The site was as perfect as possible in a world of imperfections. The buildings were on a tongue of land running out between Lake Umbagog and the river, with water on three sides of it. At the back, the deep sheltered reach of the river offered perfect anchorage for boats, and the view from the porch across the open lake to the mountains of New Hampshire was superb. Every breeze that blew crossed the point, and on the hottest day it was cool there. The territory offered excellent hunting, and the fishing was good and varied—trolling on the lake or fly-fishing in the five miles of river pools behind. Perhaps best of all, no road or trail led within miles of the place. It was exactly what Cliff wanted.

So he went to work for somebody else in the woods long enough to earn money for a year's rental and a modest grubstake, and moved in. There was plenty of work on the buildings that he could do alone to keep him busy for a long time; but he soon realized that he was going to need more money than he had estimated. The cost of lumber and building materials had risen fantastically on account of the war—the first World War, that was. The place was in no condition as yet for paying guests. Cliff could have gone back to work in the woods, or more profitable still, in a war plant; but he thought it was too dangerous, even for a short time. "You climb a little way out on a limb, and first thing off the pickle boat, you find yourself in a bear trap," he said, with a fine free mixing of metaphors. "I done that once, and look at the mess I got into. I warn't takin' no more chances. Not me. I'd finally got back to home base, and I made up my mind I was goin' to hang snug, if I had to live off potatoes and salt."

Just about then, when the potatoes and salt appeared to be developing into more than a manner of speaking, National Prohibition became a fact. Now the rural districts of Maine have always been, and probably always will be, peopled by a fairly large body of inspired and two-fisted drinkers. I suppose this is true, possibly, of most places where the work is back-breaking and monotonous, and the opportunities for recreation few and far between. Maine, moreover, had been a temperance state ever since it was a state at all, and the citizens from the backwoods, who stayed at home and minded their own affairs, had always nursed a dark suspicion that State Prohibition was a burden that had been foisted on them when their backs were turned by smart-aleck legislators down in 'Gusta. The injustice of this charge is beside the point. The point is that drinking was more than an escape or a pleasure; it came pretty near to being a duty of the right-minded.

Now it became apparent that the day was about to dawn when passable drinking liquor was going to be even harder-come-by than ever. The close proximity of the Canadian Border made it inevitable that a surprising number of upright citizens should decide that smuggling wasn't really a crime, especially if you didn't get caught. On the nights of the dark of the moon, the narrow little secret trails across ridges and along hidden valleys knew well the silent footsteps of shadowy men who shouldered heavy pack-sacks which they handled like crates of eggs. The trouble with that liquor was that it was expensive—definitely not the poor man's potion. The poor man could resort to the lumberjack special, canned heat, or he could hunt up a farmer with a full silo, and persuade him to tap it and drain off the juice at the bottom. Neither of these drinks was very expensive initially, but the consequences of drinking them might be before long, providing you could choke them down at all. They were never palatable, and they were often lethal.

It occurred to Cliff that what this neck of the woods needed was a safe, not too costly, drinkable liquor, and that by the long arm of Providence, he was the man to provide it. Years before he had guided the vice-president of a famous old distillery, and one night over the campfire the man had talked shop to him. He'd told how rum was made, growing almost poetic about it, as men who are absorbed in their work will do. He'd been eloquent enough so that Cliff, who is like a magpie when it comes to collecting and storing away miscellaneous and glittering, although possibly useless, bits of information, remembered the formula and process. It was the famous one, the one which contributed so largely to New England commerce and wealth in the old, bad, swashbuckling molasses-slave-and-rum trading days. Cliff decided that it might as well contribute to his wealth, too.

He knew the perfect place to conduct his new enterprise, over in the deep woods by Sunday Brook. There he had everything he needed, a steady flow of icy water, plenty of fuel, and complete privacy. He could get over there by boat and trail in three-quarters of an hour, and nobody the wiser. So he bought some barrels of black molasses, set up a hay-wire, or homemade, still, and went into production. Larry Parsons once told me that Cliff made wonderful rum, smooth, dark, and powerful, and that he didn't charge half enough for it. "He could have cleaned up a fortune," Larry told me, "but you know how Cliff is. You can't tell him anything, once he's got his mind made up. He figured on making a fair profit, and that's all he'd take. Not that anybody tried very hard to talk him into doubling his prices. If he wanted to play Santa Claus, nobody was going to stop him." Larry laughed reminiscently. "You know what the old joker did? He even gave a rebate if you brought back the empty jug."

I truly believe that this fair-trade policy was dictated by honesty, and that just goes to show that honesty is really the best policy after all. Not only did the good word quickly get around, so that the drinking world started beating a track to Cliff's door, but all of his customers were so grateful and well satisfied that they took the greatest pains to do nothing that would involve him in the toils of the law. In a surprisingly short time he was making money hand over fist, and he could have made a lot more, if he'd been reasonable.

His unreasonableness lay in his refusal to increase the volume of production. As he viewed it, things were all right just as they stood. He wasn't in the moonshine business. His real business was getting his sporting camp into running order, and the still was a small, though necessary, side line, unimportant except that it enabled him to buy kegs of nails, matched siding, and other necessities. He didn't want to spend too much time running off his rum. He had too much work to do at home, important work like painting and setting glass and clearing up his garden plot. He didn't mind taking his boat over to Sunday Cove two-three times a week. It was a pretty ride and sometimes he caught a fish or found a useful piece of flotsam or jetsam, such as a cantdog, lost on the drive, or a good sound piece of eight-by-eight off one of the dams. He could mull things over during the boat ride. The drone of the outboard and the sight of the familiar shore sliding by were conducive to clear thinking, and the solution to such problems as how to place a new sill under the kitchen single-handed without wrecking the place swam easily to the top of his mind. He didn't object to the walk up Sunday Brook to the still, as long as he didn't have to take it too often. There were blueberries and raspberries to be picked in season as he went along, and in the fall he could take his gun and knock off a partridge or two for a stew, or get a shot at a deer. Later he took a few traps along and put in some mink and beaver sets, as much for fun as for the cash the pelts would bring. It was all pleasant enough, but he wasn't going to be diverted from his primary object of getting his camp into shape by tying himself down to another still. It was pointed out to him that by enlarging his business he could make enough money to hire half a dozen carpenters to help him, if he wanted to, but he dismissed this idea as the purest folly.

"What would I want with a mess of carpenters diddling 'round doin' everything wrong the minute my back was turned? If you want a dog hung right, hang him yourself, I always say. Top of that, they'd be expectin' their meals on time. I might just as well be back punchin' a time-clock in the factory as tied down to a cook-stove. Me, I eat when I get hungry. And s'posin' I'd get hung up some place—wound a a deer, say, and have to track it all day—and didn't get home when they expected me. They'd be a-worryin' and a-frettin' and a-gettin' out a posse after me. One thing I can't abide, it's knowin' someone's home stewin' about me. Takes all the pleasure out of life. Then take evenin's. They'd want to be jawrin' and yarnin', and sometimes a man don't want his ears all hacked up with a lot of foolish talk. Might just as well be married again as shacked up with a gang of carpenters. Nope, I aim to keep on the way I am, and what folks don't like, they can lump."

That was that.

But the money kept coming in and the time arrived when Cliff decided that he had all he needed. His camps were now in good repair, with tight roofs and firm foundations. He'd bought a new boat to replace the old wreck he'd been using, and he had material on hand for a new float and boathouse. He'd bought simple but adequate furnishings for the camp, and there was no object in wasting any more time fooling around. Spring was just around the corner, and he wanted to open up for business as soon as the ice went out. He had yet to get the last of his wood under cover and do his spring cleaning. After that there'd be his garden to plant and his sports to look after. He'd be a very busy man.

So one morning he arose very early, while it was still pitch dark. He took a look at the thermometer and the sky and decided that if he started at once, he'd be back before the sun had risen high enough to soften the crust. It had thawed the day before, but after sunset the mercury had plunged down nearly to zero. So this morning conditions were ideal for hauling a heavy sled, and the Lord only knew when they'd be so again. He put on his creepers, got the sled out of the lean-to, put a box of necessary tools aboard it, and set out for Sunday Brook. The going was good. His creepers bit crisply into the crust, and the sled followed easily, its runners squeaking and whispering on the snow, a low accompaniment to his tuneless whistling. His breath streamed like a white scarf over his shoulder, freezing on his parka hood, but his blood coursed warm and vigorous through his veins, and he felt wonderful. This was a great day, he thought as he strode along, watching the familiar pine- and spruce-tops along the shore emerge from night against the graying eastern sky. This was the last time he'd be taking this trip for a long while to come, perhaps forever, unless he felt like dropping over this way sometimes in the fall, deer hunting. Well, he was glad to be shed of the business, although in all fairness it had served him a good turn. He couldn't rightly say otherwise.

He was at work before the sun was up, dismantling the still, pausing now and then to blow on his fingers or thrust his hands into the warmth of his armpits. Handling the icy metal and tools was a cold business. He'd heard and read about Government agents smashing stills, and he thought maybe it would be more fitting if he did the same, just to show he was through. It would be kind of dramatic and give him a lot of satisfaction for a few minutes, but it wasn't a very sensible thing to do—not when so much of the stuff was perfectly good and would come in awful handy around the camp. He loaded the sled with salvaged parts, dug up a few gallons of rum he'd cached under a snowdrift and added them to the pile, lashed his load secure, and started out for home.

The sun was up, gilding the tops of the trees on the other side of the cove, and he'd have to hurry if he didn't want to end up floundering hip-deep in wet snow. The downhill run through the woods to the shore was easy, but when he started along the level of the lake, the sled began to hang back. He stuffed his mittens under the ropes where they dragged on his shoulders, to ease the bite, and plodded on. To-morrow, he thought, maybe, if the weather held good and he felt like it, he'd try to get over the mountain to Magalloway and start the word going that he wasn't making no more rum. After he'd sold this piddling little eight-ten gallons, he was through. No need of inconveniencing folks to come clean into his place for nothing. No need of inconveniencing himself, either, having them interrupting his work.

It wasn't quite as simple as all that, though. To his surprise and indignation—because what he did was his own business, he considered—his clients put up what he termed an awful holler. "They come cryin' 'round, beggin' and pleadin' with me. 'Ain't no use your arguin',' I told them. 'Might as well save your breath. I don't cal'late to make no more liquor. Don't drink myself, and don't hold with drinkin'. Wine is a mocker,' I said. Didn't mean to put it on so thick, but they was all dingin' at me, and I lost my temper. Don't see no harm in the other feller's takin' a drink, if he's so minded, so long as he don't try to make me go agin my principles. But there warn't no need to get nasty like some of them jokers did, sayin' I was a good one to preach after runnin' a still all that time. Like I told them, that warn't law-breakin'. That was necessity. Now that 'twarn't necessary no longer, I didn't aim to go breakin' the law. 'You can have what liquor I got here,' I told them, 'at the reg'lar price, but when it's gone, there ain't no more.' Couldn't seem to get it through their thick heads. They kept tellin' me I was crazy, passin' up an easy livin' like that. What did I want with an easy livin' and money in the bank? Had money in the bank once, I told them. Plenty of it, too, and what good did it do me? 'Nope,' I told them, 'you might as well make up your minds to it and quit pesterin' me. I got things to do and no time to waste.' "

Finally he managed to convince them that he meant what he said. It was a tough fight, but I guess it was worth it. More than thirty years have elapsed since, and during that time no one has tried to argue Cliff into or out of anything, once he has announced his attitude and intentions.

I saw Cliff for the first time about twelve years ago. Of course we'd been carrying on over the telephone for five years or so before that. We'd swapped recipes, local gossip, home remedies, and advice. We'd joined in cursing dog-days and the Wright brothers, whose irresponsible antics were going to end in ruining the lakes and any chance of privacy a man might have left to him. The occasion for this was when nobody had been able to get Cliff on the telephone for five days. It was in the middle of winter, and he was living alone, of course. In this country when anyone lives alone and off the beaten track, the neighbors—the term is loose; a neighbor is the nearest person, be he one or twenty miles away—try to keep a casual check on him. It's easy to break a leg or contract double pneumonia in the woods, and if you're alone, either can be disastrous. I'd tried to call Cliff a couple of times myself with no success, and so, apparently, had Joe Mooney at the Brown Farm. Joe called me one evening and wanted to know when I'd last talked with Cliff. It had been several days before.

"Maybe his line's out of order," I suggested.

"Maybe," Joe said, "but I don't think so. It was all right last Sunday, and we haven't had any snow or high winds since. Nobody else's line is down. We'll give him one more try. Help me ring, will you, Louise?" Helping anyone ring probably needs some explanation, since I'm sure it's a custom peculiar to lines like ours. When the batteries are weak or the lines are wet, you can crank your arm off, but the result at the other end may be nothing louder than a faint tinkle. However, if two people ring together on different phones, it boosts the decibels—or whatever else you call it—and a quite respectable clangor issues from the third. This night, however, Joe and I rang in concert for ten minutes, and nothing happened.

"Well, I dunno," Joe said at last from his post fifteen miles away over the mountain. "Seems like that ought to have waked the dead. Guess we'll send a plane In in the morning, just to be sure he's all right. A plane ought to be able to land on the ice, hadn't it?"

I said I thought so, if you could judge Umbagog by the Richardsons. The snow was deep, but it was packed hard and smooth, and if the pilot got In early, before it softened up enough to cake on his skis, he shouldn't have any trouble. So the next morning at about six o'clock, when it was barely light, I hear the drone of a motor high in the air over Umbagog-way.

At noon Cliff called me up. I was glad to hear his voice sounding hale and hearty, but he didn't seem any too pleased to hear mine. "They claim you and Joe been worryin' about me," he accused.

"Yes, we have," I said. "Where've you been? I've tried and tried to get you."

"I been right here where I belong."

"Have you been sick?"

"Nope, never better in my life. I been busy."

"Well, then why couldn't we get you? Was your line down?"

"Nope. Oh, I heard it a-clatterin' away all right, off and on all week, but I didn't feel like answerin' it. Didn't feel like talkin' to nobody, so I let the damn thing ring. Then that flyin' fool comes bargin' In, right when I'm gettin' my feet braced to overhaul my saw rig. I sure gave him his go-on-home-a-cryin'. Seems like a man can't have no peace a-tall 'round here no more."

And that's how we happened to be condemning the Wright brothers; because Cliff prophesied darkly that it wasn't going to end with a joker's having his breakfast hour all shot to hell. Next thing they'd be running regular taxi services In to the lakes, to ruin the fishing and scare the bejesus out of the game, and how would I like that? I said meekly that I wouldn't like it at all. He informed me that furthermore he wouldn't stand for havin' folks a-worryin' and a-frettin' about him, because it made him as oneasy as a cat. He hung up with finality.

Eventually Ralph and I acquired a boat down on Umbagog, and so widened our field of action to include Cliff's bailiwick. We were slatting down the lake one day when he appeared on his dock and waved us in. He wanted to know whether I wanted some rhubarb to stew up. He had all kinds of it, he said, and I was welcome to as much as I cared to pull. He looked, I am happy to report, exactly as I had finally made up my mind that he should—tall, lanky, ageless, and durable. After I'd picked my rhubarb and admired his garden and tame rabbits, we inspected the new peeled-log bunkhouse he was building so that he could accommodate a few more sports.

"I ain't makin' it too big," he said. "Just big enough. I don't aim to have no more sports than I can cook for myself without bustin' a gut. Minute you start hirin' people to work for you, you stop bein' boss. I aim to be boss."

We sat on the porch for a while, drinking tea and taking turns looking through his spyglass at passing boats on the lake. It was a real spyglass, the single-barreled kind that you can stretch out to a length of two feet, and Cliff kept it on the porch, he said, so that he could identify approaching craft and decide at his leisure whether he wanted to bother with the occupants, or whether he'd rather go hide in the bush until they were gone. Life was too short to waste any of it on fools, and while he was hiding in the woods, he could be improving his time in any number of ways. Then he rose to his feet and said he'd better be getting at his chores. I'd heard about Cliff's methods, so I knew we'd better be going.

The three of us walked down to the dock together along the narrow little grass-grown path in the pleasant shade of the few big birches he'd left standing for beauty's sake, and all the time I was wondering whether I dared to offer to bring down some horse-radish roots for him to heel in, the next time we went by. I was afraid he might think I was being forward. He'd gone to quite a lot of trouble to eliminate social contacts from his life, and I cherish privacy too much myself to risk infringing upon another's right to it. My broodings and soul searchings were interrupted by the approach of a kicker-boat around the point from the lake.

In the stern was Ben Bennett, an old guide whom we all knew, with two sports in the center and bow seats. We knew they were sports because they had on beautiful Pendleton shirts, high waders, and life belts. Ben throttled his motor down and drew alongside. He wanted to know, he said, if he could borrow a couple of shear pins. He didn't have a spare, and he aimed to go up the river to fish. He didn't cal'late to hit any rocks, but in that river you never could tell, and if he sheared a pin, he sure as hell didn't aim to row all the way back to Chandler's. Cliff said he didn't blame him a mite, and started searching under the seat of his own kicker-boat, drawn up on the float, for the ditty-box in which he kept his spare parts. In the meantime the sports began making conversation.

"It seems impossible to believe that there are places like this," one said enthusiastically. "It does a man good to get away once in a while, to live close to Nature, to forget his worries. Why, I'm a new man since I've been up here." He leaned forward, carried away, and Ben prudently shifted his weight to trim the boat. "Do you realize," the sport went on impressively, "do you *realize* that it's been eight days since we've heard the whistle of a train?" He leaned back expectantly, and we were saved the necessity of replying as Cliff found the shear pins, thrust them into Ben's hand, and shoved the boat off with scant ceremony. We watched them recede up the river.

Then Cliff blew out his breath. "Wal, now, ain't he the little wonder of the ages?" he demanded. "Ain't he the copper-riveted modern marvel? Eight whole days he ain't heard a train a-whistlin'." He turned to me. "When'd you hear your last train, Miz Rich?"

I did a little rapid thinking back. "Let's see. About four and a half years ago, as nearly as I can remember; and if it's another four and a half years to come, that'll still be too soon."

"Barrin' one time I was down to Berlin ten years ago, I ain't heard one myself for well nigh onto sixteen years. Used to hear them all night long when I was livin' up in Massachusetts. If there's a more Godforsaken sound, I don't know about it."

"I don't either," I agreed wholeheartedly. "People who visit us get the shivers when they hear a loon, they say it's so eerie—"

"Or a lynx yowlin' back on the ridge in the night," he took up the tale. "Or geese honkin' over. Why, them's all real home-like sounds, comfortable and natural as broke-in boots." He stopped and changed the subject abruptly. "Come see me again. Drop in any time. Door ain't never locked, in case I ain't around."

"Thank you," I said, genuinely pleased. "We will. I'll bring you down some horse-radish roots, if you want them." He said he did, and after that we did call on him occasionally, but not often enough to wear out our welcome. He only came to see us once, and that was only because he was guiding a sport who wanted to meet an author. Cliff was self-admittedly not much of a hand for visitin' 'round. On this occasion he did the honors punctiliously, but as soon as he decently could, he oozed out the door and spent the rest of the call inspecting the V-belt arrangement on the saw rig, with the idea of rebuilding his own. In that way he could figure that the visit hadn't been a total waste of time.

The last time I saw Cliff was down at Errol Dam, the western gate to the lake region from the Outside. He was unloading four rather puzzled- and disgruntled-looking men from his boat onto the landing, tossing their duffle out after them with a fine no-nonsense-now air. After they had climbed into their cars and gone away, he lowered his boat down the current alongside ours, so we could pass the time of day.

"I thought that party was going to stay until the end of the week," I remarked, "and here it is only Wednesday. What happened? Did they get called home?"

He spat into the water and started winding his motor cord. "Nope."

"Didn't they like your place?"

"Yep, liked it fine. But I'll tell you how it was, Miz Rich. I got sick an' tired of hearin' them gab, so this mornin' I told them to pack up their gear, I didn't want them 'round under foot any more. An' they did."

"Why, Cliff!" I exclaimed, horrified. "You're in business! You can't do a thing like that."

"Wal, mebbe not, but I done it. I ain't beholden to them nor to nobody. 'Tain't worth the twenty dollars a day to me to put up with their clatter. Got up this mornin' with a notion I'd like to go trollin' in the Deep Hole, an' I'd like to go alone. An' by the great horn spoon, that's what I'm a-goin' to do."

He yanked on the cord of the outboard, and it roared into life. He lifted his hand in casual salute and started off up the river, an old, shabby, lonely figure, looking very small in his little boat on the wide waters between the somnolent summer shores—but for all that, the figure of a free man.

4

Paid Notice

IN THIS COUNTRY, so sparsely settled and so little traveled, you often hear for years about people without ever having seen them. You know their names and their characters and how they're getting on in the world, and finally you feel as though you were acquainted with them, and you develop a true interest in them. We have so little to amuse us here—no plays, no movies, no concerts—that we have to extract what drama we can out of the life around us. Our chief diversion is talking, and what is there more interesting to talk about than people? I suppose this comes under the heading of gossip, and I must admit that much of the talk is unkind and destructive. But this is not, I believe, so much because the majority of people wish ill to others as because exaggerated tales of double-dealing and misfortune and villainy are in themselves more exciting than accurate reports of the doings of the God-fearing and hard-working. However that may be, all I knew for a long time about Jones Corners and the Crews I got second-hand from Catherine Jacobs, who once lived over around there. Catherine worked for me for four years during the war, and in the course of four years under the same roof we managed to cover quite a bit of territory, orally, neither one of us being exactly a strong silent type.

I don't know why, of all the people in Jones Corners that Catherine talked about, I became especially interested in the career of the Crews, since here, certainly, was a family about whom nothing scandalous or derogatory could be said. They were decent and self-respecting, and they worked like dogs to make a living off their poor little farm. Perhaps the reason that I sympathized with Betty Crew was that I too had once been a schoolteacher from Away, and that I too knew what it was to be poor and to work hard. I knew what it meant to come from a life made easy by modern plumbing and electric lights to a life complicated by kerosene lamp chimneys to be washed every day and a balky pump, with hot water something to be hoarded, since every drop had to be heated on the top of a wood-burning kitchen range. So although I had never laid eyes on the woman in my life, I was always glad to hear news of Betty Crew of Jones Corners.

The place hasn't changed much in the thirty years since Betty Freeman went there, fresh out of Normal School, to teach in the little three-room school. It was then the tiny civic center of a scattered farming community, and it still is. The main road through the village has been hard-surfaced since then, and what used to be the blacksmith's shop now has a gas pump out in front and a free air hose hung up beside the wide door. Perhaps some of the half dozen houses clustered around the cross-roads wear a newer coat of paint, and surely the lilac bushes and rambler roses have grown taller and rambled further; but these are the only visible signs of change. The stone Union soldier still presents arms tirelessly upon his pedestal in the grassy enclosure where the roads cross; the harsh-toned bell of the white church still sends out its summons through the Sunday morning air; and the citizens of the town still assemble in the combined General Store and Post Office at four in the afternoon, when the mail stage is due. Very few of them expect mail, but the arrival of the stage is a good excuse to drop work and go down to the store to pick up the news and trade in their butter and eggs for sugar and tea.

The chief difference between the Jones Corners of fifty or seventy-five years ago and the Jones Corners of to-day is that then it had a future and now you might almost say that it hasn't even a past. The bright dreams of the settlers never materialized. It never grew beyond its early stages. The world simply went another way and left it, as it has so many northern New England towns, little more than a survival. The same buildings stand; the same customs and attitudes are adhered to; descendants of the same families farm the same grudging fields that their forebears wrested from the forest. If anything, the place has retrogressed. Some of the family names current fifty years ago exist now only on the dim slate markers in the village cemetery. The descendants of many buried there have gone away, defeated by the stubborn Maine soil and the ruthless Maine climate. The second growth has taken back their fields, the heaving frost has overthrown their boundary walls, and time and neglect have leveled their buildings. It's not much of a loss. They weren't very good farms anyway, just marginal land from which only those more stubborn and ruthless than soil and climate could possibly make a living—people like the Bennetts and the Bartletts, the Hodges and the Abbotts, the Hazens and the Crews.

It was a Crew whom Betty married after her second year

of teaching: Bert, the last of the family and sole heir to the stony, up-ended, impoverished Crew acres and the shabby old Crew homestead, stuck away on a dirt road three miles from the center. Everybody in town said that Bert was making a terrible mistake. The schoolteacher didn't know anything about hard work, and all she'd do would be fritter away Bert's money on foolishness, and, in the end, probably leave him. He'd do better to stick to his own kind, they said; there were plenty of girls around town who'd be more than willing. And I guess that was true, because Bert was likeable and dependable and attractive, in an unspectacular, slow-spoken way. As for Betty's friends, they thought she was just plain crazy to bury herself for the rest of her life way back in the sticks. She'd be miserable, they said; and it wasn't as if there were any hope of influencing Bert to move somewhere else. That was true, too. The farm was his home and the home of his forefathers, and he took a wordless pride in hanging onto it. He had roots going down into the thin soil of the Crew land far deeper probably than he himself realized. It would be easier to move the granite ledge back of the barn to another location than it would be to move Bert Crew off the Crew farm.

Betty didn't care what anybody said. She loved Bert and he loved her, and that was all that mattered. She was going into this thing with her eyes open. She'd lived in the community for two years, she'd seen what being a farmer's wife meant, and she was prepared to be one. Given time, she was sure that she could correct all the wrong impressions about her.

And she did. Off the beaten track though the Crew place was, before the summer was over every woman in town had found or made occasion to call on Betty Crew. How casual callers could know about the absence of dust from the tops of the picture frames or the state of their hostess' bureau drawers I wouldn't be in a position to say; but know they did, and the reports brought back were favorable. Betty was said to be a good housekeeper. She put out a nice white wash, too, and I, who know, tell you that that is quite a feat when you have no washing machine and have to heat the water on the stove in an old copper boiler. In the time between Bert's mother's death and his marriage to Betty, the rule that a patch is no disgrace but a hole is a scandal had been in abeyance. After all, Bert was trying to run the farm and do his own cooking, housework, and laundry, so he deserved a little lenience. But now it came back into operation again, full force. The first time after the wedding that Bert showed up at the store, every woman in the place maneuvered herself into a position behind him from which she could study the patch on the shoulder of his faded blue shirt. It was a work of art, with the edges turned neatly under and the stitches tiny and even. When he told Sam Abbott to stop saving him a loaf of bread every other day and bought yeast instead, heads were nodded in approval. Only slatterns allowed boughten bread on their tables—sleazy stuff with no body to it that won't stand by a man any time at all. Self-respecting housewives make their own honest bread. Then in the fall Betty turned her old winter coat and dyed it, instead of buying a new one; and from then on she was less and less criticized, until in a surprisingly short time she was accepted.

"How do you mean, a short time?" I asked Catherine, when she told me that. I'd had some experience myself in storming the local citadels.

"Oh, seven or eight years. No time at all, really."

I said, "You mean her troubles were over? Nobody talked about her any more? She lived happily ever after?"

Catherine snorted. "Of course not. Nobody lives happily ever after. Where there's life, there's always something to worry over and something to criticize. You know how people are. And besides, by that time she had the twins, Freeman and Carolyn, and whenever there was nothing else to talk about, the old hens would start ripping into Betty for the way she spoiled Carolyn."

"Well, did she spoil Carolyn, really?" I asked.

"I don't know, Louise. It would be hard to say. Maybe she did and maybe she didn't. If she did, I don't know that I blame her much. Carolyn was the cutest kid you ever laid eyes on, the kind it would be awful hard not to spoil. She was fair like her mother, though of course Betty's faded a lot now. But Carolyn's hair was the only really gold hair I ever saw in my life, and it curled all over her head like a halo. She had the sweetest little face. She had a sweet nature, too, so sunny and obliging and sort of *giving*. Freeman took after his father, and you'd never know those children were twins. He was dark and serious and thoughtful, and I think he was the *best* child—you know how some children are just *born* good?"

I said no, I didn't know. In my experience, every child was capable of devilishness, my own not excepted.

"Well, you ought to have known Freeman Crew. If ever a child was a little angel—"

I said, probably inspired by jealousy, that he sounded like a smug piece to me, too good to be true, or else a little lacking.

"No, really, he wasn't like that. He was bright—both kids were bright as buttons—and full of fun, but he was just *good*.

I don't mean that Carolyn was *bad*. It was just that she was a born tumble-heels, the way some people are. If one of them fell into a brook or out of a tree, it was always Carolyn. If a glass of milk got tipped over at table, it had to be Carolyn's. Look, I took care of them once for two-three days, when Betty's mother died and she had to go down-country to the funeral, and I'll tell you how it was—"

This is how it was. For all she had been prepared for, and accepted readily and without mental reservations, the life she'd married into, Betty did find the existence on the farm bleak and austere. Perhaps she herself didn't realize it. She took pride in her increasing competence and derived a great deal of satisfaction from her own and Bert's accomplishments, and found reward in Bert's love and admiration. Still it was a pretty Spartan life, stripped of the small extras over and above the necessities, the silly little things that make living fun. She didn't go much of anywhere, partly because at the end of the day she was too tired to make the effort required to change her clothes and drive over the rough road to the village to attend Church Suppers and meetings of the Grange, getting back late to a shortened night's sleep; and partly because, whether she would admit it or not, she found it depressing always to be one of the less-well-dressed women there, always to hear about some other housewife's having acquired a new linoleum or a water-heater, while she was making-do with what she had. She wasn't envious and she didn't complain; but there it was, all the same.

Then, after all this time of putting up with second-bests, the twins were born, and at last she and Bert had something a little bit finer than anyone else in town had. There is something special about twins, and these were such beautiful babies. It was no wonder that she and Bert took delight in them. Delight—that's the word: great pleasure, joyful satisfaction. Those were the things that had been lacking from the farm, and as the twins grew a little older and could follow their mother and father around on eager, uncertain feet, those were the things that came to the Crews in ever-increasing measure.

Now feeding the poultry became a pleasure instead of a routine chore, because the twins were there—Carolyn toddling shrieking into the flock, trying to catch a pullet to cuddle, while Freeman squatted on his heels as still as a little stone, holding out a handful of grain until he had lured one under his hand. The big old trout that had been caught and put into the well by Bert's father, to keep the water pure, was remembered again after many years and given a name, Mr. Higgins; and it became a game to try to see him as he hung, self-sufficient and supercilious, in the icy depths at the bottom of the fern-fringed stone-lined shaft. Freeman often saw him, for he learned quickly that the greatest care must be taken not to startle Mr. Higgins. He would inch his dark little head over the coping by imperceptible degrees, and there the great fish would be. But when he called Carolyn, she would run up laughing and thrust her shining head over the opening—and there would be nothing to see at all except the two faces, the one so dark and grave, the other so fair and gay, reflected far below against the blue reflected sky, in a frame of dripping stonework and greenery. Everything on the farm took on new meaning and significance with the coming of the twins, and even Bert, who had lived there all his life and loved the place to his very bones, found new things to marvel at and rejoice in almost daily. For the first time since he could remember, he discovered himself standing and staring at an apple tree in bloom, seeing it not in terms of possible bushels of saleable fruit, but as the children saw it, a miracle of transitory loveliness, its own excuse for fragrant being.

Then the twins were old enough to go to school, and the horizons of the farm broadened. Because they were so quick and eager and intelligent, from the very first they were included in all the little school programs. The teacher knew that when The Day came, Freeman and Carolyn would be line-perfect and immaculate in the beautiful clothes that Betty made them out of the hand-me-downs which her city sister, unseen now for years and virtually lost to her, sent to the farm. That was when the criticism started. "The way she dresses that child! You'd think she was Somebody!" and "Takes the clothes right off her own back," and "I only hope she don't live to regret it." But Bert and Betty, sitting in the audience in their shabby decent wear, looking and listening with all their eyes and ears to the charming—and it almost seemed sometimes charmed—pair on the platform, were unconscious of comment. Freeman would stand there as serious and responsible as a little judge; but Carolyn's eyes would seek out her parents, and then her whole face would break into a smile that carried her entire heart with it. Betty's gaze would meet Bert's shyly, seeking confirmation of the incredible fact that these were indeed their very own. ("Look at the way they smirk at those young-ones, like they were little tin gods!" and "There is such a thing as making a fool of yourself over your children.")

Perhaps Betty was wrong. Perhaps she should have punished Carolyn more often—"Spare the rod, I always say"—for the childish disasters into which her impetuous spirit so often impelled her. But she believed that she knew her daughter, and that she was one to be driven with a light rein.

The twins were graduated with honors from the Jones Corners Grammar School, and went, along with the rest of their classmates, to the High School in the nearest large town. They were both immediately popular, and that's not so easy for a "bussy," a transported pupil whose schoolday starts with the ringing of the eight forty-five bell and ends promptly with the one-thirty dismissal gong, when the buses are champing to be gone, leaving no time for extracurricular activities or the cultivation of new friends.

"I know," said Catherine to me. "I was a bussy once myself and it's a tough life. You just never get to know any of the other pupils, except the kids from your own town, and you knew them anyhow. But Carolyn and Freeman do all right. He plays on all the teams and Tim Bartlett has taken to beauing her around. He lives at the Corners, a couple of miles back from the Crews. The kids have known each other all their lives, but you know how it is. He never paid her much mind until he saw how the other new boys flocked around her. They're really awfully cute together. They're simply crazy over each other, kid-fashion."

"What does her mother think about it?" I asked.

"Oh, I guess she doesn't take it very seriously. She has ideas about the twins. She's planning to send them to college somehow."

But it wasn't to work out that way.

Immediately after graduation, when he was barely seventeen, Freeman came home one day and announced that he had decided to enlist. He needed his parents' permission, he said; but if they wouldn't give it, he'd just run away and lie about his age. His reason was typical of him: "I've decided I ought to."

His mother wrung her hands, literally. That's a phrase I've read often, and in print it sounds very false and melodramatic. But have you ever seen anyone do it? It's the most pitiful gesture in the world, especially when it is used by a woman like Betty Crew, who has depended on her hands to meet all the crises of her adult life, and who is confronted with a situation where all the strength and patience and skill and tenderness of her ten fingers and roughened palms can be of no avail. Here is my defense against the world, the gesture seems to say, rendered invalid. "But, Freeman," she said, "why? Can't you wait for the draft? You won't like that kind of life. It may sound very exciting and adventurous, but it won't be. You'll hate being crowded into barracks. You've always had your own room and done as you chose—"

"I know it," said Freeman. "That's the reason. I know what I'm losing if we don't win. A lot of guys don't, not really. Mother, I have to go."

Of course, he went; and of course, Bert and Betty were proud of him. His education, they told each other, could wait until he came back. He was young and there was plenty of time. In the meantime Carolyn would enter college in the fall as had been planned, in spite of the fact that she herself was all for going to South Portland or Brunswick and getting a job in the shipyards. "It won't be any fun in college without Free," she said. "Mother, you've no idea the murder we get away with, with our twin act. And anyhow, have you heard what they pay down there? Even to dopes like me? Why, I could come back simply awash with mink and pearls, and lift the mortgage from the old homestead." Carolyn read omnivorously.

Her father looked at her. "There has never been and never will be a mortgage on this place. I don't like to hear you talk that way, even joking. If you're so set on working, there'll be plenty to do around here this summer, with Free gone. In the fall, you'll go to college, like we always said."

She missed her brother dreadfully that summer. She never once saw Mr. Higgins, although Tim Bartlett reported that he was still alive and well. Tim was what Bert termed "around under foot," and he had the patient nature necessary for a viewing of the ancient trout. Betty was frankly glad of Tim now. He kept Carolyn entertained and helped fill the gap made in her life by her brother's departure. He took her to dances and the movies or just plain riding in his old Chevvy. Both of them had to work during the day, Carolyn helping her mother with the house or the hens, or hoeing the corn or the beans—tasks which would naturally have fallen to Freeman, but which were not too hard for a country girl; and Tim had his own farm to run, another little half-starved ancestral piece hardly worth the bother, except that this year was a good potato year and the Government was paying all-out prices for potatoes to be made into medical alcohol. Tim's father had suffered a stroke in the early spring, so Tim was left with the care of the farm and his father, his mother being long dead. The only time Betty ever heard him complain of his lot, which was not too happy a one for a twenty-year-old, was the day the draft board turned him down. "Agricultural Deferment," he said bitterly. "So I hoe those damn potatoes while Free takes a pop at the bastards. Excuse me, Mrs. Crew."

"That's all right, Tim," Betty said serenely. "I don't like

rough language, but this time I guess you're justified. You're a nice boy."

On the twenty-seventh of August of that year, at ten o'clock in the evening, she had occasion to change her opinion. She was sitting in the kitchen with the Lewiston *Sun* spread out before her on the red-checked tablecloth, looking over the headlines. She and Carolyn had been canning raspberries all day, and she was tired. Carolyn had gone out with Tim; but Bert had stepped on a hay-rake, and half the evening had been spent in soaking and dressing his foot. So this was the first time in over sixteen hours that she had had time to call her soul her own, and she was enjoying it. Bert was asleep, and Carolyn wouldn't be in for an hour or so; but she was all right, because she was with Tim. Betty thought that maybe in a minute she'd get herself a nice cold glass of buttermilk out of the springhouse, to drink slowly as she read the local items, and then before Carolyn came in, she'd take a bath and go to bed. The prospect seemed good to her.

She heard the screen door creak and turned quickly. You never knew when tramps might be around. But it was only Carolyn, with her soft, white, impracticable coat over her arm, and her young face more drawn and pale than Betty had ever seen it. She looked ill and almost old.

"Mother," she said, "I have to speak to you. Tim and I have decided to get married, right away."

This is too much, Betty thought. I'm too tired. But when she spoke, her voice was even. "Let's not talk about it now, dear. You know as well as I do that what you're saying is out of the question. After you're through college, if you still feel the same way about Tim, perhaps— Let's both have a drink of buttermilk and a piece of cake and go to bed." She smiled, but Carolyn, always so responsive, didn't answer her smile.

"A piece of cake," she said despairingly. "Mother, you don't understand. I—I've *got* to marry Tim. I'm going to have a baby."

Betty closed her eyes. In a minute she knew that she wasn't going to die, much as she willed to, so she drew a deep breath and opened them again. Carolyn was still leaning against the door, the planes of her face flat and marble white in the lamplight, her eyes dry and bright. She said thinly, "Mother! Don't look at me like that."

"And how do you expect me to look at you?" Betty didn't recognize her own voice. "I—I just can't understand. This will kill your father, Carolyn. He's set such store by you and Free, and we've done our best for you children, and now you thank us by acting like any common little—"

Carolyn's chin came up. "Don't you say that. It wasn't like that at all. It was— Oh, what's the use? Mother, I am truly sorry about hurting you and Daddy. But I'm not sorry about anything else, and"—her voice rose dangerously—"and don't you try to make me sorry. Don't you blame Tim for this, either. He already feels awful enough about it."

"Then why isn't he in here with you where he belongs, instead of making you face the music alone?"

"He wanted to come in, but I wouldn't let him. I knew how it would be, and— Oh, Mother, do we have to talk like this to each other?" At last the difficult tears streamed down her face, but she still held herself erect. The little Carolyn who had so often flung herself weeping into her mother's arms, sick and sorry to have made her mother sad, was gone forever now; and in her own heartsickness and sorrow, Betty looked at the new Carolyn and saw only defiance and the shameful death of all her dreams.

"It must have been a terrible time for Betty," I said to Catherine at this point. "What did they do? Send Carolyn away to have her baby or—?"

"I'll give the kid credit," Catherine told me. "Probably she could have gone away, but she didn't. She married Tim and stayed right there in town and faced all the talk that always follows a seven months' baby. Gee, you know, Louise, it must have been plain hell for her. She was used to having a good time for herself, running around with the other kids and sort of being queen bee, and all of a sudden here she was, disgraced and saddled with the care of a baby and an old helpless man, besides the housework and all. And while she wasn't really on the outs with her own family—Betty wouldn't let it be said that she turned her back on her own daughter—still and all, Betty didn't exactly wear her shoes out running over to Carolyn's house."

"But couldn't Carolyn and Tim have moved to another town, or at least couldn't Tim have got a job in the shipyards for a year or two, until it all blew over? Seems to me she was leading with her chin, staying there."

"No." Catherine was definite about it. "In the first place, you forget he was frozen—what an expression!—on the farm by the Government on account of his darned old potatoes. And in the second place, he's like Bert, hipped on the subject of the family homestead. No, she had to stay there if she was to be with Tim. And she was. She's crazy about him."

"Is he crazy about her?"

"He thinks the sun rises and sets in her, which is all right, too; only it didn't make things any easier for her when it came to getting the wash out and cleaning up Tim's father—she had to change and wash his bedding sometimes two or three times a day, and that's no joke—and being snubbed by the Ladies' Aid. Tim did all he could to help her, but after all, he had his own work cut out for him. I saw her down to the store for a minute last time I was over to the Corners, and, my Lord, what a change! She used to be sort of bubbly and full of life, but now you'd never know her. She isn't twenty yet, but she seemed so sort of settled. Her hands looked old. She had the baby with her, and I will say she keeps him nice. While I was there, some of the bunch she used to train with came in, and they stood around drinking pop and joking and arguing about whether to go to a dance up-country that night, or to the movies in Farmington. Honestly, Louise, I could have cried for Carolyn. Not much more than a year before, she'd been the ring-leader, and they'd all been listening to her, and in the end, doing what she wanted to do. Now she might just as well not have been there at all. She just stood off to one side and listened. I don't blame the other kids. They all spoke to her friendly enough when they came in. But then they forgot her, as why shouldn't they? She didn't have anything in common with them any more, but still it was—" Catherine fumbled for the word and produced rather uncertainly "—sad. The ones I'm really sorry for, though, are Bert and Betty. It's been terrible for them both, even if they do take it in different ways."

Bert, that quiet and patient man, took it the way an ox takes a blow with a sledge hammer, wielded by one whom he has trusted, between the eyes. He was numbed and staggered and bewildered, but he went on because nowhere in his philosophy was included the clause that a man was permitted to give

up while yet there remained one deep spring of vitality un-
drained. He never went to the store any more. Infrequent
late-passers on the road reported seeing his lantern, a steady
golden point against the lofty black of the hills, as he sat in
the open shed, cutting seed potatoes in the chill of an early
spring midnight. He attacked the stony High Pasture, which
had always been considered impossible for anything but grazing, prying out the rocks which for decades had increased in
number as they worked to the surface under the action of
heaving frost and eroding weather, worrying them with a
crowbar until they were free. Then he would throw the bar
down, and before the sweet high clang of iron on stone had
died, he was assaulting the insensible masses of granite with
his bare hands, performing prodigious feats of brute strength
as he bullied them onto the stone-drag. Even then he could
not rest, but, wiping the sweat from his haggard face, spoke
hoarsely to Belle, the old nag, urging her to where the wall,
which was to serve the double purpose of disposing of the
stones and fencing the field, grew daily. He seemed a man
driven by the Furies as he rolled the stones off the drag and
fitted them into their appointed places.

Yet Betty, watching from the kitchen window, sometimes
saw him stand, a gaunt silhouette against the skyline, motionless for long periods, a small filling-rock held forgotten in his
hand as he gazed away across the valley toward the hidden
house that Carolyn now called home.

And once Nate Pease, hunting a strayed cow up in the
Crew woodlot, came out from under the canopy of tender
green and glowing red birch and maple buds, across the faded
carpet of last year's down leaves, onto the tough, short, blu-
ette-sprinkled turf of the High Pasture, and found Bert there,

engaged in Herculean struggle with a boulder twice his weight. As any man would, he lent a hand, throwing his bulk where it would do the most good, until the stubborn rock rested firmly on the drag. Then he squatted for a breather on his heels, balancing easily, forearms on thighs, hands hanging limp between his knees, and spoke for the first time as he surveyed the pitted acreage. "Quite a job you done here. What you plannin' to put her into?"

He told about it later, down at the store. "Bert just looked at me like he didn't rightly understand what I meant, or didn't know the answer. 'Course, that's foolish. No man goes to all that trouble to clean up a field, lessen he's got some idee in mind what he's goin' to do with it. Finally I said, 'If 'twas mine, I'd put her into rye the first year, and plow her under, come fall. Then next year, I'd put her into a cash-crop.' He looked at me and looked at the pasture, and then he nodded his head. 'That's what I'll do,' he said. ''Twas as if he hadn't thought to ask himself till right that minute what he was cleanin' up that pasture for. But that don't make sense."

Of course it didn't make sense to Nate. Like all farmers, and especially New England farmers, he had more work ahead of him constantly than he could see his way clear to doing. The undertaking of a gruelling unnecessary task, purely as a therapy for despair, was beyond his understanding.

Betty fought. With head high and lips tight, she attended every meeting of the Ladies' Aid and the Sewing Circle, showing only by the heightened flush on her cheekbones that she noticed the sudden cessation of conversation and the not-quite-quick-enough seizing of a safe topic like the weather that attended her entrance. She knew exactly what "they" had been talking about. They had been talking about Carolyn, and while for decency's sake a show of regret that such a thing should have happened to so nice a girl might have been maintained, and sympathy for Betty might have been punctiliously protested, she knew that underneath these conventional attitudes lay a deep and malicious satisfaction that what had so long been prophesied had come true. They were glad that all the work and planning and purpose of Betty's life had come to naught. She hated them as she sat there, smiling and chatting Spartanly; and sometimes as she went home, head still high and weary shoulders still square, she hated Carolyn.

She shouldn't have to go through this, to have to pretend that everything was fine, that she and Bert were pleased that Carolyn was married to a good boy like Tim Bartlett, that the whole thing had been done with their knowledge and approval, and that, because Carolyn fell on the cellar stairs, the baby had really arrived two months early. Who ever heard of a seven months' baby with hair and fingernails complete? An expression of Freeman's came to her mind: "Who do they think they're fooling?" Who indeed did she think she was fooling? Nobody; nobody at all; but she had to keep on trying, even though sometimes as she lay sleepless in the small hours she recognized with that peculiar light-headed clarity that comes to an exhausted mind and body that it would be better if she simply admitted to the facts. Then perhaps— then almost certainly—the chase ended, the moral victory theirs, the hounds of Virtue would bay on another trail. The talk would stop and people would begin to forget.

Then something happened that made all the fuss and worry about Carolyn's predicament seem trivial. Betty was listlessly washing her breakfast dishes when the radio program to which she was half-listening was interrupted. The announcer, excitement shaking the careful control of his usual professional tones, announced the attacking of the beaches of Normandy by Allied task forces. Betty froze, dishmop suspended, eyes wide, breath held. That meant Freeman. Nobody had to tell her. She knew. After a minute she put the mop down, took off her apron—she couldn't have said why—hung it carefully on the hook by the sink, and walked out the door and up the hill to where Bert was harrowing the High Pasture.

He saw her coming, and waited for her at the end of the furrow. After she had given him the news, he stood looking for a long moment out over the countryside spread below this high field. It was a beautiful day; oh, what a beautiful June day it was, warm for Maine, and still and golden. The hills around the valley were softened in a slight haze, and their gentle, flowing contours melted into each other with an almost poetic rhythm, leading the eye easily up and up to the faint far mountains of the West. The bark of a dog drifted clearly up from the valley, and the sound of a hammer pounding briskly. The empty milk-blue sky bent softly over all. Bert sighed deeply and put his hand on Betty's shoulder in an unaccustomed gesture of tenderness. "Try not to fret," he said. "I know it's hard, but—" He broke off, at a loss, and gazed around again at the lovely, smiling world. "An awful lot of good boys are dying to-day for this," he said heavily. "I dunno. Maybe they could do worse." It was a strange sort of comfort; but somehow Betty was comforted.

It was odd how many people had excuses that day to drop in at the Crew farm. Nobody had very much to say. One or two blurted awkwardly that they sure hoped Free was makin' it all right. That was all; but somehow through the casual laconic talk of crops and weather and recipes and canning it was borne in upon Betty that the tide had turned, that this sympathy that was being offered wordlessly had the unmistakable ring of authenticity.

When Freeman came home that fall—for he did come home, with a decoration for valor which he tried to conceal and a slight limp which he could not—he found to his intense dismay that he was a hero. He was the first boy from town to come back, and Jones Corners went all-out to welcome him. Catherine told me about it.

"I guess folks were a little ashamed of themselves for the way they had acted about Carolyn and thought that this was a good chance to sort of make it up to Bert and Betty. I heard a lot of talk about how nice it was that Freeman had turned out so well to kind of balance up for the disappointment his sister had been. They were inclined to be willing to let bygones be bygones. Everybody in town that had a car that would run trimmed it all up with bunting and signs about 'Welcome to Our Hero' and drove over to Livermore to meet the train. The Corners is off the railroad. The band went in one car—it's only five pieces but it doesn't sound too bad outdoors—and all the school kids went in the school bus. They had flags and paper hats and a song to sing that the teacher wrote to the tune of 'Hail the Conquering Hero Comes.' The rest of the cars were packed with everybody in town and his dog, all done up in their best clothes. Freeman, poor kid—I never saw anyone so flusterated. He had to stand there with his ears turning purple and take it, the works—song, speech by the first selectman, cheers, being kissed, by all the girls—heck, I kissed him myself; no wonder he was embarrassed. On top of that, the train crew wasn't going to miss anything, so they held the train till it was over, half an hour at least, with the passengers hanging out the windows. Finally they piled him into the first car with the selectman and his parents and drove back—"

"Wait a minute," I said. "Where was Carolyn all this time?"

"Oh, she was around. Came in a car with Tim and some of his cousins. There wasn't room for her in the car with Freeman." She slanted her handsome eyes at me. "I said folks forgave, but I guess they didn't forget. Or maybe there really wasn't room. I don't know. Anyhow, back at the Corners they gave a banquet in the church basement for Freeman, with more speeches and presentation of gifts, and Lord knows what-all; and everything was peaches and cream. Freeman's getting a medical discharge and he's going on with his education. Of course it won't be the same really as he'd planned. Carolyn won't be with him. Those kids were so close, and they had such a wonderful time together, and of course now that's all over." She examined a fingernail moodily and then burst out, "That's what I hate about war. It spoils everything. None of this would have happened if Freeman hadn't had to go. I know it wouldn't have. It's not only the combat zones that take a pounding. Look at the Crew family. The one thing they did have that amounted to anything was the way they felt about each other. Now it's gone and they haven't anything to put in its place."

Probably she was right, I thought. What was there that could take the place of the kind of natural and spontaneous affection and enjoyment that bound the Crews together? I couldn't find the answer to that one. As it turned out, I didn't have to, because Bert and Betty found it for me. I suppose they spent many evenings seated together in the lamplight by the red-clothed kitchen table, writing and crossing out and rewriting, as they sought the exact and proper wording for the little item that appeared in the Paid Notice column of the *County Journal*, a weekly paper to which Catherine subscribed. She read it aloud to me one evening after supper.

"Mr. and Mrs. Herbert Crew of Jones Corners wish to thank all those who helped to make the welcome home of their son Freeman a success, and they wish to announce that they are also very proud of his twin sister, Carolyn Crew Bartlett of Jones Corners."

I shouldn't have worried. I should have remembered that the Crews, like all the rugged stock from which they sprang, were like the land they lived on. Close under the thin, flower-frothing top-soil that covers the New England hills lies bedrock, which will be neither moved nor altered by any storm that rages over the countryside. All was well with the Crews. They'd got down to the bedrock of character.

5

The Clerks at Spike and Pondy

DURING THE FIRST ten years of my life in this wild and lovely country which I call home, our winter activities were carried on against the background of the lumbering industry. There was never a time when there wasn't a logging camp within walking distance of us, and we were accustomed to the sound of axes ringing through the woods and of trees crashing, back on the ridge. Every morning we were awakened at daylight by the crews going past our bedroom windows to the cuttings, to the jangle and creak of harness, to the voices of men speaking in French or Finnish or the flat Yankee of the locality, to a snatch of song or a fragment of whistled tune. It was a pleasant way to wake up, and I have missed it since this region has been logged off and the camps have moved elsewhere.

The season when I knew Russell Reed and Elmer Rhodes started out as all lumbering seasons start, with the construction crews coming In early in the fall to build the new camps, one a quarter of a mile above us and the other two miles below us, on road and river. A lumber camp consists of at least six buildings. The largest is the bar-room, which is woods parlance for bunkhouse. Then there is the cookhouse, or kitchen, where meals are prepared and served, with a partitioned-off corner where the cook and his helpers sleep, and an unheated ell, called the dingle, for the cold storage of meat. There are the hovel, or stable, and the blacksmith's shop. The office is just what you would expect, a smaller separate shack where the bookwork is done, only in the woods the office also houses the wangan (the store where candy and tobacco and tools and clothes are sold), and the inevitable punchboard; and the clerk usually sleeps as well as works there. The smallest building, except for certain unmentionable little outhouses, is the bosses' shack, where the straw and walking bosses sleep. As you can see, a lumber camp is quite a self-sufficient colony.

When these two camps were done, they had to be called something, for purposes of identification. The one above us, because it overlooked Pond-in-the-River, was called naturally enough simply Pondy. Woodsmen can't be bothered with the intricacies of a name like Pond-in-the-River. The camp below us was called Spike, a fact that baffled Ralph and me for a while, until Syd Abbott, who drove a bulldozer for the contractor, set us right. It turned out that the little spade-bearded French-Canadian carpenter who bossed the construction was named Lebreque. Syd explained reasonably, "You can't very well call a camp Camp Lebreque, can you? So we just named it Spike." And Spike it has remained to this day, when the camp is torn down and the site grown up to raspberry canes and little fir trees as tall as your head. When you live in the middle of one of the blank spaces on the map, any point of reference is valuable, and it's much easier to say, "I saw a bear track down near Spike" than to go into detail like, "about two miles down the Carry, beyond the foot of that long hill, where the river runs along the road."

In the late fall, when the lakes were still open and the ground still free of snow, although the leaves were all down and every sunrise showed a world white with hoar-frost, the personnel of the camps began to filter In. There were the cooks and their helpers, the cookees, and the bosses and the blacksmiths. There were the teamsters, driving the pairs of great horses, and the feeders, who tended the horses and kept the hovels clean. There were the bar-room men—men too old to go into the woods, or else partly incapacitated by some accident when for a moment they had been careless with an ax or with contemptuous familiarity had taken a six-cord load down a slick pitch without snub-line or bridle-chains, but men who could still split wood for the many camp stoves, and keep the bar-room swept and warm. There were the stampers, young men who walked all day alone through the bleak and frozen woods with their little branding hammers in their mittened hands, going from one pile of corded pulp to another, scattered over a fifteen-square-mile area, swinging the stamping iron interminably, imprinting on the ends of each one of the million pieces of four-foot pulpwood the symbol representing the name of the contractor in charge of this particular operation. There were the scalers, lonely men too, with their Bangor scales, who measured the piled wood and accredited to each man the amount he had cut. There were the daymen, paid by the day at a fixed rate for doing whatever the boss told them to do—swamp out, spread road-hay, or work on the landings. There were the yarding crews, working in groups of three as teams, and the stump-cutters, who were so competent that they could make more money working alone on piece rates, or else so at odds with the world that they would rather work alone with only deer and foxes for company than be annoyed with the modern conveniences of co-operation, conversation, and having to put up with their fellow men. And there were the clerks, the white collar class of the lumber camps, who kept the books, ran the wangan, supervised the punchboard, distributed mail, wrote letters for the illiterate, and issued pay in the form of time slips, which in this country are tender as legal as silver dollars anywhere you go.

The first time Ralph and I ever saw Elmer Rhodes, the clerk at Pondy, he was standing in the road in front of the office shack with a little sheaf of letters in his hand, evidently having been warned of our approach by the ungodly clattering of our ancient Model T as it careened over the rutted, stony road. He was in his shirt sleeves, shivering a little in the edged wind that came off the pond to stir his thin gray hair. He looked old and frail and small, alone there against the somber backdrop of woods and mountain and slate-gray open water, as we drew up beside him.

"You're the Riches, aren't you?" he asked. "I'm Rhodes. Wonder if you'd mail these letters for me? Thought I'd get up to Middle myself this afternoon, but the work's piled up on me. You know how 'tis in the fall. The men don't settle down till after the first big snow. Keep shifting from camp to camp, trying to find—I don't know what. One lumber camp's about the same as another, and none of them's perfect. I'd ought to know. Been clerking in them the biggest part of my life. Went into the woods before I was twenty and been in them ever since. You'd think I ought to know my job backwards; used to think so myself. But things ain't like they was in the old days. Comes of the Gov'ment dipping in where it don't belong. All this Social Security." He shook his head. "Complicates the books, and on top of that, half these jokers never heard of the thing. When I make out their time slips, taking out the Gov'ment money, they figure I'm giving them a short scale and put up an argument. Takes up my time trying to explain to the chowderheads. And I ain't as young as I was, nor as patient, for all you'd cal'late I'd be, having reared seventeen children of my own, not to mention a flock of grandchildren—"

I found my voice, which had been startled out of me, temporarily. "Seventeen children!" I exclaimed. "Not *really*, Mr. Rhodes! Or do you mean they seem like seventeen?"

"Nope, there's seventeen of them—or was at last count." He looked both proud and embarrassed. "Keeps my wife busy, now I can tell you, specially since a couple of the married daughters have come home with their young-ones while the husbands are in the Service. Course, they're not all home now, not more'n ten or a dozen—" His voice trailed off. "They go through a lot of shoe leather." He dismissed the subject. "Keeps me hopping, all right. On top of everything else, they've hired a green clerk down below. Never been north of Boston in his life, a city kid fresh out of High School, and I'm obliged to show him the ropes. Reed his name is. Brash little joker. Oh, well." He sighed and handed me the letters. "No sense keeping you here and catching my own never-get-over while I tell you my troubles. If you'd just mail these, and if there's anything for us, bring it down?"

We assured him that we certainly would do that; and after that day, until the snow became so deep that we had to put up the Ford and carry the twice-weekly mail and groceries

down the two miles of road on our backs, we often did Elmer's errands for him.

I became familiar with the voice of the brash little joker
from Boston quite a while before we ever met him, and probably I'd better explain the local custom that made that almost
inevitable. I realize that I risk censure in so doing; but here
goes, anyhow.

First, it is necessary to make you understand what happens
to this country after Labor Day. All summer long it is as
though we were giving a large house party, with the entire
lake region our house, and much of the civilized world our
guests. For three months there is a worldliness and bustle
about the countryside. The cars parked at South Arm, the
jumping-off point into the wilderness, are Cadillacs and
cream-colored Chrysler convertibles with red leather cushions, bearing number plates from New York and Florida and
Ontario. The people who knock at your door to ask for a
drink of water, or beside whom you fish the river in the fresh-
ness of the morning, wear beautiful sports clothes and talk to
you beautifully of books and politics and travel, using words
which we never use here: words like "predicating" and
"casuistry" and "hegira." The mail comes In every single
day except Sunday, and when Alys Parsons up-ends the
bulging canvas sack onto the counter in the hotel office, pre-
liminary to sorting the day's take, copies of *Kiplinger's Letter*
and of the *Herald Tribune* spill out, along with boxes of
candy from Bailey's and little packages from Abercrombie's
and especially ordered loaves of Pepperidge Farm bread. The
lakes are lively with little boats, and it's never safe to go
swimming nude in the river. Everything is very gala.

Then comes Labor Day, and it is as if the party had ended

abruptly and all the guests had gone home, leaving the members of the family alone in the vast empty house. Now the mail comes In only twice a week, and the mail sack is a sad, limp affair, with three envelopes and a small package cowering in one corner. The letters are a note to Al from her mother and two bills, and the package is the torn moccasin I sent Out to be stitched. The blue surface of the lake is empty except for Larry's big white boat, slatting to and from the Arm with loads of provisions for the winter. The countryside seems to echo, and for a little while, until we can readjust ourselves to loneliness, we have to reach out for human contacts, to reassure ourselves that we have not been completely deserted. It's the same feeling that prompts the members of the family to draw their chairs up close to the dying fire, after the party is over, for a last chat before going to bed.

That's why we "rubber on the phone," as it is called. It's exactly what it sounds like. When the telephone rings some other number than your own, you carefully remove the receiver from the hook, clamp a muffling hand over the mouthpiece, and listen to whatever conversation may be going over the makeshift line. This I know would be reprehensible in a civilized community, being nothing more nor less than eavesdropping; but it is accepted here, and no one feels guilty about it. You can admit quite shamelessly that you came by any given piece of information "rubbering on the phone." It was by rubbering that I came to know Russell Reed's voice.

It was a fresh young voice—fresh in both senses—lively and gay, a voice incapable of taking anything seriously. Sometimes an excellent mimicry of the Fall-of-Doom manner of Gabriel Heatter would delight my ear. "Oh, there'll be

ad hearts in the Home Office this week, yes, tears will flow
n the Woods Department. For to-day, as it must to all men,
omes to Russell Reed the time when he can't balance his
ime sheet. Born eighteen years ago in Boston, Reed—"

Elmer was patently less delighted than I. "Cut it out.
'm busy. Bring your books up this afternoon and I'll help
ou."

"Oh, it's not that serious. Feller came in Wednesday night
efore supper and signed on, and Thursday after breakfast
e decided he didn't like it here. Can you imagine that, Elmer,
fter all we'd done—? Anyhow, he went Out without paying
or the two meals he'd eaten and what am I supposed to do
bout it?"

"Little late to worry about that," Elmer told him with dry
atisfaction. "You should have made him pay, and if he didn't
ave any money, you should have made him stay till he'd
vorked it out."

"*Made* him, you say!" Russell's voice rose in horror. "He
vas twice as big as me. Three times as big. *Made* him! Ha!
Well, what do I do now? Just forget him?"

It was Elmer's turn to be horrified. "You can't— He had
wo meals and someone's got to pay."

"Wouldn't it be simpler—?" Russell began wistfully, and
dded hastily on Elmer's outraged, indrawn breath: "All
ight, all right, I'll pay myself; but I still think—"

The first time I ever saw Russell Reed he was on horse-
ack. I was up in the top of the woodshed, getting down
he snowshoes that we hang on wires there during the sumner, to keep them dry and safe from mice, when I heard a
listant drifting cry of "Hi-yo, Silver!" My first reaction
vas that I'd gone woods queer at last. When you start hear-

ing voices, it's supposed to be bad. But before I had time to worry much, one of the big, shaggy twitch horses from Spike wheeled into the driveway. I knew the rider must be the new clerk. Woodsmen seldom ride the horses, and never wear blue serge suits and unbuckled galoshes. So I pitched the snowshoes down onto the sawdust pile and swung myself down after them.

"Hello," I said. "You must be Reed. What can I do for you?"

"Well, frankly, it wasn't my idea to turn in here. This is the first time I've ever been on horseback, and nobody told me horses have minds of their own. You got any helpful suggestions?"

I laughed. "It's considered easier to do with a saddle, but if you want to learn the hard way, bareback—"

"Nobody's got a saddle. Say, you haven't got a pair of skates I can borrow? I want to go skating before the snow covers the ice. Do you know anything about skiing? I've ordered some skis. I'm going to do a lot of skiing this winter. Maybe I'd better get some snowshoes, too." He looked at the pairs on the sawdust. "Never saw a pair like that. What's the advantage?"

I explained that they were bear-paws, and although I myself didn't like them much, as they always seemed to me to be nose-heavy, they were considered good off the trails, as they had no tails to tangle in the brush.

"I guess I'd better get that kind then. I want to explore this whole country while I'm here. Oh, and look. Have you got any books I could borrow? Time sort of drags in the evening."

I assured him that we had all kinds of books and asked

him if he wanted to come in right then and pick some out.

"Gee, I'd like to, but if I ever get off this beast now, I'll never get on again. Besides, I thought I'd go up to Pondy and heckle Elmer. What a guy! Nothing but work, work, work. What's the percentage in that? What does he want to sit in the office all the time for, adding up columns?"

I thought of poor Elmer, bowed eternally over his books, his pale face forever puckered with worry. "Maybe Elmer wants to hold his job," I said meanly. "Maybe you'd better not make too many plans, because it's just possible that the company didn't hire you to ride horseback and ski and skate and explore."

He laughed. "Don't worry. I get my work done. I got system, see. Trouble with Elmer is he takes things too serious. It drives him nuts to see anyone have a good time."

"Oh, I don't think that's quite fair. He just feels responsible for you and doesn't want you to get fired."

"Don't kid yourself. He's just fussy. I'm trying to teach him to have a flexible mind, like mine."

"You'll have flexible employment if you're not careful," I told him. "Not that it's any of my business."

"Nope," he agreed cheerfully, and clucked to the horse, who seemed to have fallen asleep on its feet. "Can't find the starter on this thing. Give him a bat on the rear, will you, Mrs. Rich?" I delivered the bat, and he went off, hi-yoing at a great rate. He was a cute kid, I thought, even if he was a little too cocky; but he wouldn't last very long on this job.

I was wrong. The deer season ended and the lakes sealed over and the snow piled deeper and deeper in the woods. The sun rose later and later, and, barely skimming the ridges to the south, set earlier and earlier. Christmas passed, and the cold strengthened, striking deeper and deeper toward the heart of heat which means life in the North, whether it is the core of warmth that a man carries about in his own body, or the carefully tended fires of his dwellings. Russell Reed should have, by my reckoning, long since run home, defeated, to the city streets that he knew, to the steam-heated apartment, the easy entertainment of movies and Saturday night dates, to the comfortable, gregarious job as soda jerk in the neighborhood drugstore for which his undeniable good looks and sassy manner so well fitted him. But still he rollicked about the country. His rather weedy frame filled out and he took on an appearance of great physical well-being, probably because of the gigantic lumber camp meals and the many hours he spent in the open. He acquired a suitable wardrobe of heavy pants and buffalo-checked shirts, along with remarkable proficiency on skis and snowshoes, and became in short a good woodsman, although slightly in the Hollywood tradition. So I gave up worrying about him, if ever I did worry, partly because he didn't need my concern, but mostly because along about this time we came to realize the truly desperate circumstances that engulfed Elmer.

I guess we'd been pretty blind. We'd see Elmer a couple of times a week as we went past the Pondy office, bending over his desk, working on his books; but as Russell was now carrying his mail, since we were all on foot, we very seldom had occasion to more than wave at him through the window, or at most drop in to buy cigarettes or candy from the wangan. He seemed about the same as usual—possibly a little thinner and grayer, with a nervous habit of licking his lips and cracking his knuckles—so we didn't think much about him, except that he ought to get out in the fresh air more.

Then one still, bitter night I found myself sitting bolt upright in bed. I could hear Ralph breathing deeply and quietly, and the snap of a timber as it contracted in the cold. The white light of the moon lay in a slim wedge on the counterpane, and the cold flowed in an almost visible current through the window which stood open onto the road, ten feet away. There was nothing that could have awakened me, I thought, as I listened and checked off the familiar, natural sounds. Then I heard the slow, spaced squeaking of footsteps on the frozen snow of the Carry. Something was outside, walking back and forth; a bear, perhaps—and the window was only three feet from the ground. I slid out of bed and tiptoed across the floor, intent on closing the window quietly. I'd seen what a bear can do, once it gets inside a camp, and I wanted to be no part of any such shambles.

But it wasn't a bear outside. It was Elmer, thin and black as the shadow of a dead tamarack in the unearthly cold light of the moon. There was something about him that frightened me, although I can't say now what it was. I was only half awake, and I guess I thought that he was a ghost, silly as that sounds. He must have heard me, because he turned his head in my direction. His face was blue in the moonlight, and his eyes seemed sightless. My mouth was dry, and I was cold to my bones. Then I knew how ridiculous I was being, and I spoke to him. "Hello, Elmer. What's the trouble?"

Behind me Ralph asked, his voice blurred with sleep, "Wassa ma'er?" but Elmer only looked at me out of his hollow eyes.

"Elmer," I said sharply, "I'm freezing to death. Go around to the door and I'll let you in. It's warm in the living room."

"I'll let him in." Ralph was awake now. "Poke up the fire and start some coffee. Maybe he's sick."

The living room *was* warm, and I had everything I needed on hand. There were even some sugar cookies in a tin. I lighted all the lights, and the golden glow of kerosene lamps was soft and warm after the icy moonlight into which I had been staring. Elmer stood inside the door, shivering, with his cap in his hands, his shoulders hunched, his chin down, until Ralph said, "Take off your jacket and sit down. In a minute we'll have some coffee. We haven't seen you to talk to for a coon's age. What's new?"

He raised his head. "I—I think I'm going crazy. I-I can't think. I can't sleep or eat or— Do you think I'm going crazy?" His eyes blazed directly at me, and I thought: I have Ralph, and in an emergency a good stout piece of stove wood to stash his head in.

So I said, "For Heaven's sake! I never heard of anything so foolish. Of course you're not going crazy— Here, sit down and drink this coffee. Sugar? Cream? Have a cookie— Don't you know that when people think they are going crazy, it's a sure sign that they aren't? Everybody says so. But if you're really worried about yourself, why don't you go Out for a week end? Not that you need to, but you haven't seen your family for ages, and the change would do you good."

"Do you really think so?" he asked eagerly. Then his shoulders sagged. "I can't. I can't take the time off. I'm be-hind in my work now, and if I ever lose my job, I don't know what would become of the folks. I have to keep my job, if it kills me."

"You won't be much good to your folks dead," Ralph

stated a little brutally. "Do what Louise says. Take a vacation. Russell can do your work for a few days."

He jumped to his feet, spilling coffee. "I—I don't want him to do my work! It's bad enough to have him rubbing it in all the time that he can do his own easier than I can. I—I won't have him monkeying with my books! You hear me?"

"Oh, take it easy," Ralph said. "He's not a bad kid—just a little young and fresh, that's all. He'd be glad—"

"I won't have it! I'd rather—almost anything—than go meeching around him, asking favors. He makes fun of me all the time—"

"Why, no, he doesn't either," I remonstrated. "Or at least, no more than he does everyone. It's just his idea of a joke, to ride people. Just ignore him."

But Elmer was beyond speech. He stood there trembling. Then he snatched up his cap. "Well, I've got to get back to work," he said dully. "Thanks for the coffee. I feel a little better now. Good-night."

Ralph and I sat up until daybreak, discussing the situation, but the only conclusion that we could come to was that one of us had better speak to Russell, and suggest that he stop pestering Elmer for a while. As Ralph had said, he was a good kid—just a little too young to have much imagination.

As it happened, it wasn't necessary, because Russell brought the matter up himself the next afternoon, when he stopped in to change some books. We heard him talking to the dog as he took his skis off outside, and then stamping the snow off his boots on the porch. He banged once on the door and entered, as is the custom of the country. For once his handsome face was serious, and his greeting restrained. He came at once to the matter that was bothering him.

"You folks seen Elmer lately? What ails him? I think he's going crazy."

"What makes you think that?" I asked cautiously.

"Well, I was just up there, and he was raving and tearing and carrying on. What started it—when I went in he was adding up a column of figures for the third time, and he'd got a different answer every time. All I said was, 'Why don't you do like I do?'—and he never even gave me a chance to finish. He threw his pencil on the floor and started yelling about how everybody was in a plot to make his work harder. He didn't make much sense, but it sounded as though he thought I was responsible for starting Social Security, just to foul him up. Just then the scaler came in, so I got out. Gee, what an excitable guy! Has he always been like that?"

"I don't think so." I told him. "But you see, he has a lot of family responsibility, and he worries. Then of course he's been keeping books one way for over forty years, and he can't get used to a new way. You must remember he's an old man, and it's hard for him to change, and I suppose it hurts his pride to have a new clerk like you do the work so easily, and—"

"Gee, why didn't someone tell me? I'd be glad to help him, only when I first came here, he acted as if he'd invented the books, always telling me what was wrong with mine. I didn't think he'd relish any suggestions from me. Why, I could bring my adding machine up a couple of days a week, and—"

"You could bring what up?" I asked.

"My adding machine. I rented one for the winter, when I found out what I had to do. Why, I'd *never* get done without it. Of course, it won't do all the work for you, but it sure saves a lot of time and mistakes."

I looked at him bitterly. "And I've been giving you credit for being so smart!"

"Well, isn't it smart to do your work the easiest way? But like I was saying— I could lend him— Only now he's so sore at me, probably he wouldn't use it anyhow. He's in a terrible state. If I'd known— You don't suppose my kidding him really bothers him, do you?"

I decided to tell the truth. "Yes, I do; but I think it would help his morale just to know you've been using an adding machine, whether he wants to use it himself or not. He's lost confidence in himself, I guess, and if he could get it back—"

The next day along about sunset Russell knocked on the window. "Can't take time to get my skis off and come in, or I'll be late for supper. Just wanted to tell you Elmer has the adder, and I've showed him how to run it. He's all pepped up about it, and everything's under control."

For a few days it did seem that way. Elmer stopped walking the Carry in the night, and when we waved to him through his window, he seemed almost cheerful. But unfortunately things aren't that easy of solution in real life, no matter how neatly they may work out on paper. The next thing that happened was that Elmer began distrusting the adding machine. It didn't seem sensible to him, so he said, that a gadget could do brainwork; so he checked every total himself, and it wasn't long before he was worse off than ever.

"I try and try to tell him," Russell said to us, "that that machine doesn't make mistakes, but he won't listen. Honest, I'm worried about him. I feel to blame—"

"I don't think you should," I said. And I really didn't.

"After all, most people can take a little riding without going off their base. It isn't your fault. It's just that everything's too much for him."

Russell looked grateful for this reassurance. "I'd certainly hate to think— You know, I must have been an awful little stinker when I came in here. Gee, it seems a long time ago!"

It did to me, too. "You've grown up some," I told him. "What made you come here in the first place?" I'd been wanting to know for a long time.

"I guess I read too many books. I wanted to go some place where there was room and mountains and snow and adventure, and the only jobs I could get in the city were dumb. So I answered an ad in the paper— Well, I got what I wanted all right, and now I'll never be satisfied with anything else, I guess." He brooded. "Well, I've got to get going. I told Elmer I'd stop in this afternoon."

It was only a few days after that that the telephone rang early in the morning. It was the scaler at Pondy. "Elmer down there?"

"No. Why would he be down here at this time of day?"

"Couldn't say. Only he isn't around here, and his bed hasn't been slept in. They haven't seen anything of him at Middle, either. I'll call Spike. Might be he went down there." I stayed on the line while he put his call through and heard Russell say that he hadn't seen Elmer since day before yesterday. "I'll come right up," he added. "Maybe I'll meet him on the road." Shortly after I saw him going by the house fast on his skis, and after what I considered a decent interval, I called Pondy back.

The scaler answered. "Nope, we ain't found him yet, but most of his stuff is gone, including his snowshoes, and Russell says there's fresh snowshoe tracks turning off the road onto the B Pond trail. Any of you been over that way in the past day or two? No? Then it looks like he just packed his switchel and flew. He could make Upton all right, and from there he could catch the stage to Bethel and get home." A muffled colloquy followed, and the scaler came back on again. "Russell's worried for fear he's jumped into the river or something foolish. He's going to follow the tracks and make sure he's okay." He hung up.

Russell was back by mid-afternoon, with his mackinaw swinging open and his cap shoved back on his head, in spite of the freezing weather. "Whew, that's hot work," he said. "I made time. Went clear over to the highway that leads into Upton. I lost his tracks there. There'd been a lot of traffic over the road. Anyhow, I figured that if he got that far, he was all right. It's only a mile into town, and all good road. What I was afraid of was that he'd made up his mind to do away with himself, and I kept expecting to find— But I didn't." He leaned on his ski poles, dug into the snow. "I'm sort of relieved. He needed a vacation, although it was kind of funny, his going off without saying a word. But probably the notion hit him, and he just went. He'll be okay when he gets back." He thrust his poles powerfully, setting himself into motion. "Got to get back to the salt mines. Haven't done a stroke of work to-day, and what with my own books and Elmer's, Mrs. Reed's little boy is going to be busy."

But the days went by and Elmer didn't come back, nor was any word of him received. A couple of letters came In from his wife, the last one mailed long after Elmer should have arrived home; so finally the boss decided reluctantly, because he was loath to interfere with the private life of anyone as harmless as Elmer, that something ought to be done. "I hate to set the state cops on his trail," he said. "He ain't done nothing wrong. Russell says his books and money balance. Only if anything's happened to him, his folks ought to know. Before I call the cops, cal'late I'll go over to Upton and see what they know about him there."

Nobody in Upton had seen hide nor hair of him, and in a town of that size someone would have, if he'd been there at all. It was as if he had been snatched into thin air at the point where his snowshoe tracks ended on the beaten surface of the road. He'd never gone into the village; that was certain. Where, then, had he gone? There was no other town within walking distance, and a canvass of the farms along the highway revealed nothing. It seemed obvious that he had been given a lift by a passing car, and in that case it was a problem for the police. Woodsmen had, before then, been picked up and robbed and murdered for their few belongings, and their bodies dumped off in the woods or thrust under the ice of lake or river. So for a short while there was a feverish search for Elmer, with the usual futile excursions and false alarums; but it all came to exactly nothing. After a while the excitement died down, there was a new clerk at Pondy, and we didn't even talk about Elmer very often, except, when conversation lagged, to speculate idly on what did actually happen to him.

Late in March the camps closed and the crews went Out. Russell Reed, one of the last to leave, came in one morning to tell us good-bye. "We'll miss you," I told him sincerely. "I suppose you're going home to Boston?"

"Sooner or later. I thought I'd sort of look the rest of this country over a little, as long as I'm up this way. I thought I'd go over into New Hampshire and Vermont, and maybe do a little real skiing. Some of the winter sports places are still open. I'll let you know how I'm getting on; and if you happen to hear anything about Elmer, will you let me know? I've kind of got him on my mind still."

I didn't realize until much later just how much on Russell's mind Elmer really was; so much, in fact, that the proposed skiing trip was merely a blind for what actually amounted to a personal, one-man search for him. I met Russell quite by accident one day, after the ice had gone out, on Congress Street in Rumford, where I'd gone to shop for the first time in eight months. After we'd greeted each other and he'd informed me that he'd never before seen me in a skirt and I looked funny, we decided that he had time for a quick cup of coffee before he had to catch the afternoon train down-country. We have two trains a day, and the first one leaves too early in the morning for most people.

"Where've you been and how've you been and all about it?" I said after we were seated. "Don't ask me about things up on the lakes, because everything is the same as usual, and everybody's fine, and—I know you're going to ask—nothing has ever been heard from Elmer."

He stirred his coffee thoughtfully, his head bent. Then he looked at me. "Mrs. Rich, how good are you at keeping your mouth shut?"

"I'm not sure." I told him truthfully. "Pretty good, I guess, if it's important that I should."

"Well, this is important." He looked around in a conspiratorial manner and lowered his voice. "I found Elmer. Shhh!" he admonished hastily as I started to exclaim. He really was an awful kid still, I thought; all this elaborate hush-hush business. "You see," he went on, "I knew he couldn't have much money with him, so I figured that if he was still alive, he'd have to get a job somewhere. He'd have to go far enough away so he wouldn't run much risk of meeting someone who knew him, but he couldn't go too far, because he didn't have the price. I figured that he'd try for a lumber-camp clerking job, since that was all he knew how to do, and he'd probably pick some small job, run by an independent operator, because that way he'd run less chance of being recognized by the regular woodsmen who float around from company camp to company camp. Then I inquired around where there might be a set-up like that. New Hampshire was too near, so I decided to take a look around northern Vermont and York State. Part of the time I made out like I was looking for work myself, and part of the time I pretended I was just a skiing nut. I didn't take anyone's word for anything, because I figured maybe he'd be using another name, and whatever it was wouldn't mean anything to me. I had to see for myself. And sure enough, I found him over in Vermont in a little camp back in the hills."

He looked to me for approval, so I said, meaning every word of it, "I think you're wonderful, Russell! Tell me, how does he look, and how *is* he, *really?*"

"He looks swell. He's grown a beard and put on some weight, and he says he likes his job. He's only got twenty-five men, and he can handle that easy enough. I'm not going to tell you the name he's going by, or where he is. Not that I don't trust you," he added politely, "only the fewer people that know a secret, the better, I think. Don't you?"

I said that I certainly did. "But why does it have to be

a secret? If he's all right now, I think his family ought to know—"

"*No!* If you could have seen the look on his face when I walked in—like a wild animal in a cage! I thought he was going to jump through the window. *No.* Don't you see? He feels free now, for the first time since he was twenty, and if he has to go back to the cage—"

"Now really, Russell," I said tartly. "Aren't you being a little melodramatic? And remember, it's a cage—if you must call it that—that he made himself. What about his poor wife, worrying about him, and for all you know, starving to death? At least she ought to be told that he's alive and well, even if you don't want to go into details. I don't think it's fair—"

"She's got millions of grown-up kids to take care of her. She won't starve. And if they know he's alive, they'll find him. They'll mean well, but— If I'd thought you were going to be like this, I'd never have told you. Give the poor devil a break, Mrs. Rich. I *tell* you that if they catch up with him and make him go back now, he'll go stark, staring mad!" He shook his head impatiently and started again. "Look, give him time. Maybe after a while he'll go back of his own accord; and even if he doesn't, isn't it better to have his family worry a little—they'll get over it; they're probably through the worst of it already—than to have him shut up in Augusta the rest of his life? Then they really would have something to worry about."

"Well," I said slowly, "I don't know." I looked at him. All the things that I had thought made him such an attractive kid were completely wiped out of his face—the impudence, the insouciance, the gay recklessness. He looked a little stern and very serious. And suddenly I wondered why I was in such a dither. Why, it wasn't my problem at all. That fresh brat Russell Reed had made it his, had taken over the full responsibility, and it had made a man of him, a man whose judgment should and could be trusted. There was no excuse at all for me to interfere.

"Okay," I said. "Now if you intend to catch that train—"

All this was quite a while ago, and there isn't very much to add, except that the next Christmas Eve, Elmer walked into his own home unannounced, more hale and hearty and happy than he had been in years. It made quite a stir at the time, and the final official verdict was temporary amnesia. He bought a little store with the money he'd saved during his mysterious absence and has done very well with it. And last Christmas I got a card from Russell Reed. He'd spent the war with the ski-troopers, where the going had been rugged but interesting, I gathered. At the writing, he was in Alaska, which he assured me was much better than Maine. Maine was all right, of course, for kids such as he'd been, and for old ladies. He didn't say "like you," but I suspect that's what he meant. Yes, Maine was all right; but Alaska, now, was real country.

6

And She Be Fair

WHEN THE TELEPHONE rang on that gray November morning, I was just finishing up the last of the breakfast dishes. I tossed the wiper over the line near the stove with one hand, took down the receiver with the other, and said, "Hello, Joe" into the ugly, battery-powered, and completely indispensable wall set. There are five families strung out along the fifteen miles of single, uninsulated wire that loops and sags through the woods from the Parsonses' at Middle Dam to the Brown Farm in Magalloway Plantation, and after you've lived with the rather makeshift contraption for a while, you get so you can identify each individual on the line by his ring. Sure enough, Joe Mooney's beautiful, deep voice —which was all I knew of him, since I had never seen him— drifted easily over the miles of swamp and mountain that separated us to mingle in my kitchen with the singing of the tea-kettle, the crackling of the fire in the range, and the whine of the dog wanting-in at the door.

"Louise," he said, "have you people seen anything of a young couple over your way? They went into the woods ten days ago, and they were supposed to be back at the end of the week. They haven't showed up, and their folks are getting worried."

That was easy to answer. We hadn't seen a strange face or heard a strange voice for over a month. "But they might be up at Middle," I added. "What are they doing anyhow, hunting?"

"I've already called the Parsonses and Millers and they're not around there. Yeah, they're hunting. They're on their honeymoon. Struck off up-country right after the ceremony. The fellow's on leave from the Army, and he's going to be AWOL in another ten minutes, more or less, if he isn't already. Their car's still where they left it, parked in True Durkee's field in Upton, so— Look, Louise, is Ralph doing anything special this morning? Maybe he'd drive down to Sunday Cove and take a look around? You see, they set off in a boat up Umbagog—"

"Sure," I promised. Joe's asking was the emptiest formality. When anybody gets lost in this country, everybody drops everything to look for them. We all realize more fully than any town-dweller possibly can that man is pretty insignificant when pitted against the forces of Nature, and that knowledge binds us into a mutually protective fraternity. We know that in spite of our best efforts and precautions, the time may well come when any one of us will be lying on the back of a desolate ridge with a broken ankle and night drawing in, and then the only thing that will stand between us and pure panic will be the certainty that if we just sit tight, someone will come and get us out. So I said, "Sure. I'll let you know when we get back, Joe."

Looking for people lost in a hundred square miles of woods isn't quite the hopeless task that it sounds. Actually there are only a few places where they are likely to be. This young man and his bride should be easier than most to find, equipped as they were with a boat, which they would have to draw up somewhere along the lake, and all of the paraphernalia for a week's camping, which they certainly weren't going to carry about on their backs all day. They'd have to leave it at one of the few possible camp sites, which they would undoubtedly use as a base. So Ralph and I didn't bother much about beating the bush and hallooing on the three-mile trip to Sunday Cove. We made one side excursion to Smooth Ledge, because that is a lovely place to camp, but there was nothing there except the green water pouring smoothly over the ledges, a cold fireplace with the ashes still soggy from the rain of ten days before, and a partridge sitting in a stunted cedar.

As we coasted down the last long rough hill to the cove, we heard the sound of an outboard, throttled low, and I felt a lift of the spirit. Everything was all right. These people, whoever they were, were safe. They'd just lost track of the time, an easy thing to do in the woods, especially if you're on your honeymoon. Each day flows smoothly into the next, with nothing to distinguish one from the other except a change in the weather or some outstanding event, like the shooting of a deer or the blooming of the first dandelion. But when we came out of the woods and drew up beside the caved-in remains of an old lumber camp, we saw Cliff Wiggin-Wallace hunched in the stern of his battered old boat, slowly circling the glassy waters of the cove. We gave him a hail, and he came in to where we were standing on the steeply shelving ledge that serves as a landing.

"Mornin'," he said, cutting his motor. "What you folks

doin' down here so early?" We told him and he nodded. "Me, too. Joe give me a ring a while ago. I've been over every inch of shoreline 'twixt here and my place, and I ain't seen hide nor hair of a livin' soul. I figure now on goin' over and follow in' the New Hampshire side down. Might be they're over there." He squinted at the sky from under the brim of his disreputable old hat. "She's brewin' up some weather. Don't like the looks of it. Come to-morrow, we'll have snow." He changed the subject abruptly. "You ain't got a piece of two-inch angle-iron up to your place, Ralph? I'm fixin' up my saw rig—"

They were off. Where in towns people meet and chat on corners, or in the drugstore or post office, we carry on our casual social contacts on lonely shores or boat landings, or along trails leading to nowhere of importance, or occasionally in the middle of lakes, shouting from boat to boat. When Cliff and Ralph began to show signs of staying there the rest of the morning arguing about V-belts, I whistled to the dog, off on some private errand, to create a diversion. Cliff knew Kyak was a boat-riding fool, and that if once he got aboard it would take more than the three of us to get him back ashore; so he started winding the cord of his outboard.

"I'll be gettin' along," he said. "You might let Joe know where I'm at; save me the trouble of callin' him." He yanked on the cord, the motor roared into life, and he lifted a limp hand in farewell and headed out of the cove toward New Hampshire.

To tell the truth, I didn't think much more about the lost young couple that day, after I'd called Joe up and given him my report. I was busy with the housework and all the tasks outdoors and in that have to be done in November, in preparation for the long winter ahead. If I had any attitude about the whole affair, it was that everything possible was being done to find them, backed by a sort of subconscious confidence that they'd turn up safe and sound eventually. I'd lived through dozens of excursions and alarums centering about lost hunters during my ten years of life in the backwoods. Sooner or later they always showed up none the worse for wear, and my sweat, blood, and tears were so much wasted energy. But along about sunset there was a knock on the kitchen door, and I opened it to find Fred Judkin, from Upton, standing on the step with an older man, a stranger, at his shoulder.

I hadn't seen Fred since before he went into the Army, so I greeted him with great enthusiasm, telling him how nice he looked in uniform—which probably disgusted him—and asking him if they'd got their deer. I assumed he was home on leave and was improving his time by hunting. But when he stepped into the mellow light of the kitchen, I saw that he wasn't carrying a gun and that his face was tired and serious. He introduced his companion as Mr. Kennicott, and they both sank down wearily into chairs by the stove, with the air of men who had a long hard day behind them. "Ralph will be right in," I said, "and then we'll have supper. You'll sleep here, of course? You can't start back to Upton at this time of day. It'll be pitch-black in half an hour."

"That's what I was wondering, Louise—if we could stay the night here. When we started out, we planned on getting home to-night, but it's taken us longer than we thought, and anyhow—" He nodded significantly at Mr. Kennicott, who was sitting with his head bowed and his eyes closed in one of the straight, uncomfortable kitchen chairs. His face was gray with fatigue and his lips looked pinched. So far he had made no comment beyond a courteous greeting, but now he remarked a little apologetically, "I'm not as young as I was. It's taken it out of me, the walking and the worrying, but I had to come—"

"It's Mr. Kennicott's boy that's lost," Fred broke in quietly. "He's in my outfit. I know this country, so the Army gave me emergency leave—"

The door opened, and Ralph and Kyak came in on a wave of cold air. I explained our guests to him, and he said, "Wow! You mean you've followed the shore of Umbagog all the way up to here? It must be twenty miles."

"Not quite," Fred told him. "A couple of other parties started out to search the shore nearer Upton, so we took the old Magalloway Trail as far as the town line, and cut down to the lake from there. Even so, it was tough enough. I was counting on Cliff to set us across the river, but he wasn't home. We had to walk up the other side as far as the dam, before we could get across. You been over there lately? Nothing but blowdown and swamp holes."

"It's been that way ever since the hurricane," Ralph told him. "You must be half starved. When do we eat, Louise?"

I hastily put two more plates and a handful of silver onto the table. "Right now. Ralph, see who wants coffee and who wants tea, and I'll call Cliff and Joe up to hear if there's any news." But Joe didn't answer the two long rings that were his signal, and I remembered then that he closed the switchboard at six and went home, at that time of the year. So I rang four times for Cliff. After a minute he said, "Hello."

"Any news of those people who are lost?" I asked, and he said that there wasn't.

"Went down the New Hampshire side as far as Moll's Rock, and all in through Leonard's Pond, and I didn't see a trace of no one. So I come along home. I figure no news is good news." I said yes, that's what I figured, too, and hung up.

After supper, rested and relaxed by the hot meal, we moved into the living room and drew chairs up around the open fire. The wind had started to whine down-river, whuffling around the corners of the house like a coursing hound. I went from window to window, pulling the faded red draperies together with a muted clash of rings on rods, to shut out the night. At the last one I stood for a moment in the shadow beyond the circle of firelight and looked at the room. Outside in the lonely darkness the wind beat insistently against the glass, and the wild roar of the river swelled and faded on the gusts. Inside it was quiet, except for the rustle of the fire on the hearth and the quiet breathing of the sleeping dog. The three men sat silent, sunk low in their chairs, their long legs stretched out to the blaze and their eyes fixed on the leaping flames. A window rattled behind the drawn curtains and I shivered, although the room was warm.

As though he knew what I was thinking, Mr. Kennicott said in his quiet voice, "I hope they're warm enough to-night."

Ralph spoke quickly. "It isn't really cold out—not much below freezing. It'll be easy to keep comfortable to-night, if they know anything at all about the woods." He made it a question.

"Oh, yes. Yes. All their lives they've been crazy about the woods, both of them. Why, even when they were kids—" his eyes lighted and his tired face came alive—"even when they were kids, they knew the woods better than some guides.

They'd light out as soon as they'd had their breakfasts, and sometimes we wouldn't see them again until sun-down. We've got some pretty rough country down our way—not like this, of course, but wild enough—but we never worried about them. My boy got his first deer when he was twelve." He laughed. "That was a proud day for him. I can see him now, trying to act as if it were nothing, and him not much taller than his gun. Couldn't touch him with a ten-foot pole all that fall. Kind of put Mary's nose out of joint—Mary's his wife now—but she got an eight-point buck two years later. She was thirteen then, a skinny little thing with her hair all every-which-way, running around in work pants and a plaid shirt. You couldn't hardly tell her from another boy. It wasn't till she was sixteen or so that she turned pretty all of a sudden.

"It's a funny thing how some girls do that. She came into the house one morning—she and Jack were planning on going fishing that day—and I looked at her and thought to myself, 'Well, son, it won't be long now. You're going to get used to a little competition pretty soon.' When they get as good-looking as Mary is, they usually lose interest in hunting and fishing and scrambling up mountains and knocking around in boats. It's only natural that they outgrow their tom-boy days. Jack had never shown Mary any special consideration, and I didn't imagine it would occur to him to start now. The first time they ever went fishing—he was seven and she was six—'twas down to the mill-pond. They cut two poles and rigged them up with twine and some old hooks they found 'round the house and dug themselves a canful of worms. Mary baited her own hook, you'd better believe. They caught a mess of little perch, and you'd better believe too that Mary

cleaned her own. Don't know but what she cleaned his, too.
He was just enough older, and a boy—you know how it is.
The way a little girl like that would look at it, he was doing
her a favor letting her hang around with him, and she felt
she'd ought to pay her way by doing more'n her share of the
dirty work. Not that he was mean or hateful to her, ever.
He wasn't. It was just that he treated her like a kid brother;
and her folks and Ma and me, we were glad it was that way.
Made it nice all around, living next door to each other, the
way we do." He smiled into the fire. After a minute he
went on.

"That's why in a way I was sorry that day she turned
pretty. Oh, I don't suppose it was as fast as all that, but it
seemed so to me. I'd seen her just the day before, and she'd
looked the same as always—little thing with eyes too big for
her face and her hair cut short and curly. She kept it short to
save bother, but it curled of its own accord. Then the next
morning—" he paused, looking a little puzzled— "next morning it was still short and curly. Come to think of it, she even
had on the same clothes—blue jeans rolled half-way up to her
knees and an old shirt Jack had outgrown, with the sleeves
pushed up above her elbows. But out of a clear sky it struck
me that there was one awful pretty girl. Maybe it was the
way she laughed, with her head thrown back; or maybe it
was how she handled herself, quick and business-like, but at
the same time as graceful as a swallow. Whatever it was, I
thought to myself that the boys would be flocking around
her pretty soon, taking her to the movies and buying her
sodas. Naturally she'd like it, and who could blame her; but
then where would Jack be? He'd think it was silly to offer
to carry one little bit of a half-pound book home from school

for her, when he knew she could walk all day with a thirty-pound pack on her back.

"Mary's awful deceptive to look at. She's little; looks as though you could break her in two with your bare hands. But she's tough as nails. She can do anything my boy can do, and some things she can do better'n he can. Swim, for instance. Jack's a good swimmer, but Mary—she's a champion. She's as much at home in the water as on dry land. That's one reason I'm not worried as much as I might be about them now. Allowing their boat swamped—though I don't know any reason why it should have, with them brought up around boats and knowing how to handle them—but allowing it did, they'd get ashore as easy as rolling off a log. No, I'm not worried about that."

He fell silent while Ralph hauled himself to his feet and put another birch log on the fire. The sparks flew up the chimney as the loose bark caught, and the room was suddenly flooded with leaping red light. Somewhere a shutter banged dully, and at the window over the river the curtain swayed slightly in the draft around the sash. But the air in the room remained so still that the smoke from our cigarettes rose unwavering toward the raftered ceiling. It was as though we four were in a sheltered pool of quiet, safe from the rushing torrent of the wind passing over us. Then the fire settled down to a slow, steady burning, and Mr. Kennicott went on, almost as though he were talking to himself.

"What I figure has happened, one of them got hurt. It's easy to do in the woods. You slip on a mossy rock and break your leg, or you catch your foot in a crevice and sprain your ankle. I don't figure they had a shooting accident. They both know too much about guns for that. No, one of them is hurt, and the other can't leave to get help. They don't know this country at all. They don't know where people live, or how to get to them. If it were down home now— But it isn't, and all they can do is the sensible thing: wait to be found. They know that as soon as they're over due, we'll be out searching. Just as sure as I'm sitting here, they're holed in somewhere, snug as you please. They've got good warm sleeping bags and plenty of food, and they know how to set up a comfortable camp. I always say, and it's true, that you don't have to worry about two people in the woods. Two people can get out of almost anything. It's when a man's alone that you have to worry."

We all nodded, because what he said was reasonable and had in the past proven true, except in a very few, exceptional cases; and we all thought, although no one said it, that they both must be alive, since in the event of a fatality, the survivor would have made his way to help immediately. I wanted to hear the rest of the story of Jack and Mary, so I asked, "And did Mary's growing up pretty work out the way you thought it would?"

Mr. Kennicott brought his mind back from wherever it had gone. "Well, no. Not exactly." He chuckled. He had a nice chuckle, low and amused. He was a nice man. "Oh, the other boys began noticing Mary all right, but they didn't seem to make much headway with her. Once in a while she'd go to the movies with one of them, if Jack was off somewhere playing basketball or something. But it didn't mean anything. As for Jack, he never looked at another girl in his life, although if you come right down to it, I don't suppose he really thought of Mary as a girl. Most kids, when they get into High School, go through a girl-crazy stage, but Jack never did. He's a nice-looking boy, if I do say it as shouldn't, big and handsome with a wide grin—takes after his mother in looks—and he's got a nice way with him, too. Mannerly. Ma saw to that. He played on all the school teams and he was pretty good in his studies, too. I don't want to brag, but he's a boy any parent could be proud of, and I am proud of him." He laughed apologetically.

"I've been telling you about Mary, and how popular with the boys she got to be in High School. Well, the same thing goes for Jack. Being good-looking and captain of the football team, the girls chased after him something terrible. One spell there, Ma threatened to have the telephone taken out, the way it rang all the time with some girl calling up to say she'd lost her assignment book and would Jack please tell her what geometry problems they were supposed to do. He never caught on, either. It wasn't that he's dumb. He isn't. He was just so busy with one thing or another—sports, and studies, and an old car he rebuilt, and hunting and fishing—he was just so busy he didn't have time to think about girls. He was always polite enough to them, but his mind was on other things. Mostly they were things Mary was mixed up in, and I don't wonder he never thought of her as a girl. That jallopy, for instance. When he couldn't raise the price of a new set of spark plugs, she'd chip in and then they'd change them together. She knows as much about a Ford motor as most garage mechanics. Many's the time I've seen her, grease from head to foot, taking up the brakes or fiddling with the timing. When he wasn't using it, she'd use it; and when he graduated from High School and went into the Army, he gave it to her. That was a year and a half ago, when he was eighteen.

"First leave he had, Mary skipped school—she was a year

behind him—and spent the whole morning getting that jallopy tuned up. She and Ma went down to the station in it to meet the train, since I was at work and Ma don't drive. Ma told me about it later. Time had got away from Mary, so she hadn't had a chance to so much as wash her face, and she had on a pair of overalls, covered with oil. It didn't make any difference to her, nor to Jack. He jumped off the train, hugged his mother, and said to Mary, 'How's she running? Have you changed the oil yet?' Mary said, 'Yup. Gee, Jack, I'm glad you're home! There's something wrong with the wiring. We're getting a short.' As far as Ma could see, they started right in where they'd left off, and I guess that's the way it seemed to them, too. Except for Jack's being in uniform and not being in school, things were exactly the way they had been for the past ten or twelve years. Jack would go down-town and hang around the stores visiting with his old friends mornings, but he was back by the time Mary got out of school. Once in a while he'd bring her home in the jallopy, but only if he happened to be in that neighborhood. Then he'd go over and wait while she ate her lunch, or sometimes she'd come into our kitchen after she'd changed out of her school clothes into pants and make herself a sandwich to eat while they decided what to do that afternoon. It was like old times. Mary's mother said as much to Ma. 'Carrie,' she said, 'seems good to have Jack home, like old times, when we used to wonder which child belonged to who.' We always joked about that, because it always did seem as though both of them belonged to both families. You see, neither one of them had any brothers or sisters, and I suppose that made them closer than lots of next-door neighbors.

"Well, things went along about as usual until last June. The kids wrote to each other. Mary used to pass the letters she got from Jack around. No reason why she shouldn't. He'd ask questions about the families and the folks he knew. Once he wrote a whole letter about painting the boat and having the outboard overhauled. He and she'd built the boat together and they were pretty proud of it. It's the boat they're using now— not very big, so's they could carry it around to different lakes on a trailer they patched up, but a nice tight little boat, for all that. It wasn't what anyone could call a romantic correspondence, by any stretch of the imagination. Then June came, and Mary was all set to graduate. The Friday before graduation was the Senior Ball, and that's a big affair in our town, about the biggest of the year. For one thing, it's the only dance except the Elks' Easter Ball that everybody really dresses up for. The men and boys wear their good dark suits and the girls wear long dresses."

I knew how it was because it is the same in all rural communities. None of the men own evening clothes—such an extravagance would never occur to them; what's the sense of spending good money on an outfit you can wear only once or twice a year? But the girls and women do usually have one long dress, which they often make themselves and which they wear when occasion arises for several years, changing its appearance from time to time by altering the neckline or hem, or by dyeing it and adding a corsage of artificial flowers. Since it is the custom of the country to attend the ordinary run-of-the-mill dances in whatever you happen to have on when the notion to go hits you—polo shirts and corduroys, cotton dresses, pleated skirts and sweaters, anything—the unusual spectacle of a solid front of decent dark suits, with matching trousers and jackets, and of trailing skirts and bare arms creates a very gala and formal effect. People not only look different, but they act differently, so that the whole atmosphere surrounding the event is very special.

"Jack not being at home," Mr. Kennicott went on, "Mary went to the dance with Steve Proctor. Naturally she didn't want to miss it, it being one of the big events of her whole High School career, as you might say. I don't know why she picked Steve, specially, out of the herd, except maybe because all the girls were after him and it was sort of a feather in her cap, that he asked her. You know how young girls are about things like that, even Mary, who is more sensible than most. Steve's all right—well-raised and all. Only thing wrong with him is maybe he's always had a little too much money and he's a little too handsome. That's a combination that can spoil any boy, and I guess Steve's done pretty well not to be any more spoiled than he is. He did things up brown for Mary— sent her flowers to wear and called for her in the new convertible his folks had managed to get somehow in spite of the war for his graduation present. We saw the whole performance out our living room window, with him handing her into the car like she was spun glass, and walking around to the driver's seat after tucking her skirt in and closing the door for her. Ma had to laugh, it was so different from when she went places with Jack. Then she has to swarm in the best she can under her own power, usually over the door which got jammed somehow and won't open, and more than half the time with the jallopy already under way. She can do it, too, neat as a cat; although I must say she took to Steve's methods like a duck takes to water. That's the woman of it for you."

He looked at me sideways, but I refused to rise to the bait.

"Along about ten o'clock, when Ma and I were just about

ready to turn off the radio and call it a day, someone ran up the steps and across the porch. Ma said, 'Land of Mercy, here's Jack!' and sure enough it was. He'd got leave unexpected and hitch-hiked home to surprise us. Ma bustled around getting him something to eat, and he said he guessed he'd call up Mary, since the lights were still on next door, and ask her over for a bite. So we told him where she was, and he said, 'Oh, sure. Did she get the boat painted, do you know?' We sat around talking and drinking Cokes for an hour or so, and then we started thinking about bed again. Just as we were all in the front hall, a car door slammed out front and someone came running up the walk. We stepped out and saw that it was Mary. 'Oh, Jack,' she said, 'someone at the dance said they saw you get out of a truck down on Main Street, and Steve wouldn't bring me home to see, so I swiped his car and I guess he's going to be mad, but I don't care; he can't push me around—' all in one breath and mixed up. Jack started to laugh, and then he got a good look at her and stopped.

"He'd never seen her in a long dress before. Maybe he'd never really seen her at all before. She sure was worth looking at. The dress was white with a great full skirt that made her waist look about six inches around, where it was tied with a silver ribbon. It was sort of old-fashioned around the top, like it was falling off her shoulders, only it was supposed to be that way. She was so tanned that her neck and shoulders looked dark against all that white and it gave her a look—glamorous, maybe you'd call it, or exotic. She was mad and excited, so her eyes snapped and her color was high, almost as bright as the flowers in her hair. She looked—well, beautiful. That's the only word for her. Jack just stood there, and then Steve Proctor came busting up the path. He was mad, too, and when you come right down to it, I don't know but what he had a right to be, with Mary running out on him and swiping his car to boot. He said, in that high-handed tone of his that always gets people's backs up, although I don't guess he means any harm, 'What's going on here? I don't appreciate having any girl of mine—'

"Mary looked at him and said, just as high and mighty as him, 'I'll have you understand I'm no girl of yours, Steve Proctor!' Then she turned her back on him and started up the steps toward Jack. I guess that's what did it, the way she came up those steps. With the women running around in short skirts and pants the way they do nowadays, you don't often get to see one of them go up steps the way my mother used to, bending and picking up her skirt just a little in front with both hands so she won't trip on it. I didn't know how much I'd missed it until I saw Mary do it, and then it occurred to me that it was one of the prettiest gestures a woman can make —graceful and womanly and—well, just plain pretty. I guess it struck Jack the same way. Next thing I knew, she was in his arms and he was hugging her as though he'd never let her go. He took time out to say over her head to Steve, 'Sorry, Bud, but Mary's my girl,' and then he kissed her.

"I'll say for Steve, he took it well, or maybe he knew when he was licked. He looked a little surprised, but then he laughed, not mad but real pleasant, and said, 'Okie-doke, my mistake.' Then he went and climbed into his car and drove away. About then Ma and I came to that we weren't needed, so we went back into the house.

"The kids wanted to get married right away, but we—her folks and Ma and me—persuaded them to wait till this fall. We were all so pleased, we wanted a bang-up wedding, and anyhow, they seemed so young. They're still pretty young, nineteen and twenty, but the way times are now, with Jack liable to be shipped overseas any day— So the wedding was a week ago last Friday, and it was real nice. Mary wore her Senior Ball dress—the one that caused all the trouble, if you want to put it that way—and her mother's veil, and with Jack in uniform they made a handsome couple. They'd always wanted to come up this way hunting, having heard a lot about the country, but of course it wasn't very feasible before they were married. So they planned this trip for their honeymoon. We joked about it a lot—seemed as if they were a lot more interested in getting their gear together for this trip than they were in the details of the wedding. If Mary's mother would have let her, I'll bet she'd have been perfectly satisfied to be married in her hunting clothes, so's not to delay starting up-country by having to change. They had the boat all loaded on the trailer the night before, and their duffle packed, and as soon as the reception was over, they struck north. That was the last we saw of them, waving and laughing in the old jallopy, with the trailer bobbling along behind."

Fred Judkin took up the tale. "They pulled into Durkee's along the early part of the afternoon. True helped them get their boat into the water, and showed them where they could leave the car, out of the way. The last he saw of them, they were headed down the Cambridge, following the channel stakes the way he told them. Of course, he couldn't see them much beyond Lakeside. The river takes a big bend there before it empties into Umbagog. But they were going along fine, as long as he could see them. They had plenty of daylight left so they should have made any camp site on the lake they saw fit, that night." He yawned. "It's past my bedtime. We want to get an early start to-morrow and cover some of the places we missed to-day." He got to his feet slowly and the rest of us followed suit. I said I'd have breakfast ready by six-thirty, so they could be on their way, and showed them where to sleep.

"Thank you for telling us about your son and his wife," I said to Mr. Kennicott. "They sound swell. I'm sure they're all right. Sleep well, and try not to worry."

His voice came back strong and confident. "Oh, I shall. I'm sure they're all right, too."

That was one of the noisy nights we sometimes get in the woods. Sometimes the wind can blow a gale, and all we hear is a distant roaring in the tree-tops and an occasional faint, faraway report as a fir-top snaps. At other times, as on that night, when the wind is in the right quarter, it kicks up a terrific clatter. It rattled shutters and riffled the shingles, sounding like a great beast clawing to get through the roof, sloping so close over our heads. The trees near the house tossed and groaned, and branches crashed to the ground. Sometime after midnight the wind went down and a still cold set in, making the timbers of the house creak and snap as they contracted. Used as I am to the woods and all its moods, I didn't sleep very well. I kept thinking of that boy and girl somewhere out in the vast night. They weren't just a couple of lost hunters to me any more, just a couple of nameless, faceless strangers who were no responsibility of mine. I knew them now, and so I worried about them. Supposing it were Rufus or Dinah? I abandoned that line quickly. It wouldn't bear thinking on, so I thought of Mr. Kennicott instead. If I were worried, what must he be going through, now that he was alone, without the barrier of human speech and companionship to stand between him and the cold, logical doubts that pounce in the night? I was glad when the window showed gray, and I could get up and build the fire and start breakfast.

I was still alone when Mr. Kennicott came into the kitchen. Last night he'd looked old and tired and troubled, but this morning his face was as gray and composed as stone. I showed him where he could wash and gave him a clean towel, and he thanked me. Then he said calmly, "I've made up my mind that my boy is dead."

"Oh, no!" I protested. "No!" I couldn't bear to think that the laughing, ardent boy and girl whom I had met the night before were not living and laughing still somewhere near to us.

"Yes. I guess I've known it all along, but I wouldn't let myself believe it. During the night I saw there was no use in trying to run away from it any longer. I appreciate your sympathy, Mrs. Rich, but I'm certain. I've had all night to think, and now I'm—reconciled." The last word was almost inaudible, weighted as it was with sorrow; and now I didn't see how I could bear the knowledge of this man's bitter cup, which he must accept and drink alone, among strangers. We heard Ralph and Fred thumping down the stairs, and Mr. Kennicott added quickly, "No need of upsetting them. I ought not to have told you—only you seemed so interested last night in the children." I guess it was his using the word "children" for the first time in all our talk that illogically convinced me that his intuition was not playing him false. Then his tone became almost brisk as the others entered the room. "Starting to spit a little snow. We've got no time to waste." I looked out the window and saw the first fine flakes which presage a serious storm slanting down against the black wall of the forest across the river.

I shall never forget that breakfast. You don't ever forget an overwhelming demonstration of the incredible extent of human fortitude. No one would have suspected, unless like me he knew, down what bleak prospect those mild eyes were gazing as Mr. Kennicott drank his orange juice. His obedient fingers handled knife and fork without a tremor as he ate his bacon and eggs. He made an observation or two about the weather and the war; he answered comments naturally, giving his full and tranquil attention to the speaker; once he even laughed. I do not know, I cannot imagine, upon what secret reservoir of strength he was drawing, nor can I comprehend the extent of a natural dignity and consideration that forbade, even under those Spartan circumstances, making others uncomfortable by a parade of grief. He seemed just an ordinary man, heroic in neither appearance nor manner; but I learned then that Courage sometimes chooses just such a simple face to wear.

Over the last cups of coffee, he and Fred discussed their program for the day. They had planned to go back the way they had come, covering that part of the shore of Umbagog that they had missed by taking the short-cut the day before. But the snow was making on the ground so fast by that time that the sensible course was obvious: to abandon the idea of scrambling over the fifteen miles or so of icy rocks which comprise the shoreline, and to take the more direct and sheltered B Pond Trail to Upton. Then they would surely get back before traveling became impossible. Fred and Ralph went back upstairs to put their boots on, and I started slapping together a few sandwiches for them to take with them. Mr.

Kennicott finished his coffee, and then he asked me rather diffidently how much he owed me for the lodging and meals.

I was surprised, and a little hurt, so I spoke more abruptly than I intended to. "Why, nothing. Do you think we'd take money for helping people in trouble? We've had our troubles, too, when we've had to accept help, and the least we can do is help others—" I broke off, ashamed of myself. I was afraid I sounded a little smug, and anyhow, the occasion didn't call for a stump speech from me.

He said simply, "Thank you," and then Ralph and Fred came back. In a few minutes the three of them started out of the yard, heads bent against the blowing snow, because Ralph thought he knew where there was a piece of angle-iron for Cliff in a deserted shack over by B Pond, and this was a good time to go and see. I had just turned away from the window when the telephone emitted Joe's distinctive ring.

"Hello, Louise," he said. "Trouble, trouble, trouble. Now we've lost Fred Judkin and that boy's father, Kennicott. You haven't seen anything of them?"

I said that I had indeed, and that they were already on their way home.

"Well, thank God for that, anyhow," he commented piously. "Things are bad enough already. Louise, they just found the boat that young couple set out in, all stove up on the shore opposite Big Island. Guess there's no doubt but what they're at the bottom of Umbagog. Judging from where the boat was found, they couldn't have any more than got started when they swamped or capsized. It's too bad, a young couple like that."

"But maybe they got ashore, Joe. Maybe they're trying to find their way—"

"I'm afraid not. Where they found the boat wasn't more'n half an hour's walk through the woods to Durkee's, and if they swam ashore to the New Hampshire side, they'd have landed right in front of Mrs. Potter's. She's gone South, but her farmer's still there. I guess they're drowned all right."

"But, Joe, Mr. Kennicott said they both were wonderful swimmers, and it was a seaworthy little boat."

He sighed. "Louise, you'd ought to know by now that no one can swim ten strokes in these lakes in November, specially in the kind of clothes you have to wear at this time of year to keep from freezing to death. Like as not they had high boots on, along with heavy coats and pants." I did know it, of course. The water is paralyzingly cold, just above the freezing point. "And about the boat—boats that are all right in other lakes, aren't all right in Umbagog. You know that, too, or you'd ought to. That's a mean lake." I was still silent, because everything he said was perfectly true, and too many people had already been drowned in Umbagog for ignoring those facts. Joe went on, "What they figure happened, they were going along all right until after they got past Davis Landing. It's sheltered in there, and they didn't realize how rough it was until they come out into the main lake, there by Potter's. Then it was too late. They've got a party going out this morning to drag for the bodies, but I don't think there's much hope of finding them till spring. The lake will be froze over in a couple of days, soon as we get a still night. It's too bad. Why, they couldn't have been married more'n two-three hours."

"But, Joe, why didn't they find the boat before, if it was so near Upton?"

"It was too near. No one thought anything could have happened to them so quick, so they all started searching farther afield."

I hung up, feeling that most futile of all emotions, rebellious anger at the lack of discrimination shown by Death. With all the people in the world who wanted to die, who were better off dead, or who deserved to die, why did it have to be these? It was so stupid. It was so wasteful. There was nothing either original or constructive about these reflections, and I knew it, but that didn't prevent me from indulging in them. I was working myself up into a fine frenzy when a knock on the door brought me up short. I opened it to find Mr. Kennicott, his cap and shoulders powdered white, standing there in the falling snow.

"I had to come back," he said. "I got to thinking about you feeling so bad. Don't. The way I look at it, you go when your time comes, and their time had come. If it had to happen, it couldn't have happened better. Really it couldn't, Mrs. Rich. They were head-over-heels in love, and they were together, the way they wanted to be, looking forward to life. If they'd lived, maybe they'd never have been so happy again. Likely things wouldn't have been anywhere near as wonderful as they planned. Life never is. Things go wrong. At least they'll never have to go through what Ma and me and her folks have been through in these last three days." He hesitated, trying to think of something more to say, but there wasn't anything more; so he turned half-away. "Just don't feel so bad, Mrs. Rich."

I promised that I'd try not to. It never occurred to me to tell him about Joe's call. He knew the truth already, and he'd made his own terms with it. We said good-bye again, and he hurried off after the others. After he was out of sight, I closed the door slowly, thinking about what he had said. There was a lot of truth in it, I thought; but mostly I thought about Mr. Kennicott's taking the trouble, burdened as he was, to come way back to say a few words of comfort to a woman he'd never seen before and would never see again. The dead boy had been cheated out of something a lot more valuable than the few short hours of happiness which had been Life's final gift to him. The real tragedy was that now he'd never have the chance to grow, to develop through living and suffering, into the kind and gentle man his father was.

7

Rienza Trimback

HERE IN THE backcountry, a far larger percentage of women are married than in urban areas. This is, I believe, because neither men nor women get along very well here alone. In the first place, there are very few lines of endeavor in which a woman can support herself. Almost the only job she can get, unless she is trained to teach school, is keeping house for a widower with children, and then she usually ends by marrying him. In order to eat, a girl either has to marry or move away to some town or city where opportunities for women are more varied and numerous. In the few cases where a woman inherits enough property to live on, she still needs a man around the place. It's a rare woman who can shingle the barn roof or plow the back pasture herself; and the hiring of occasional help isn't too satisfactory. It always turns out that on the three days when she really needs someone to put up the hay for her, every man in the community is busy in his own hay fields; and on the fourth, it rains.

This is not a one-sided proposition. A man needs a woman to look after him, too. There are no convenient restaurants where he can get his meals, no laundries with mending service to take care of his clothes, no women-by-the-day to clean up his house, no Visiting Nurse to tend him when he is sick. A man alone is a pretty sad object in the country, with buttons dangling, pants held up with safety pins, the lean and hungry look that comes of a diet of fried foods, and a neglected house where the beds are never made and no flowers grow in the dooryard or on the kitchen window sills.

This doesn't mean that country marriages are simply marriages of convenience. In the country more than anywhere else marriage includes true companionship, based not only on mutual dependence in material matters, but in matters of the mind and spirit as well. Here where in winter the countryside is so bleak and white that even the roofs look lonely, where for days, sometimes, a farm is cut off from the world by drifted roads, the society of another human being whose aims and interests and affections are one's own is a constant and necessary bulwark against the forces of loneliness and despair. Marriage here is the natural state, an axiom of satisfactory living, and it is a rare person who is not married by the time he or she reaches the upper twenties. Exceptions do occur, and Rienza Trimback is one of them. Her story, with no important differences, is the story of almost every unmarried woman hereabouts.

We have, as my more worldly friends often point out to me, some peculiar names in Maine. I like them myself, the names like Laurel and Ivy and Maple and Fern, bestowed through a love of the green growing things. I like the biblical names—Bathsheba, Serepta, Joshua, and Nahum. Some of the names are old-fashioned and prim, like Prudence and Araminta and Charity, and some of them are just made up and fanciful, designed, I suppose, to bring beauty and poetry to a Spartan existence—Lunetta, Velzora, Jolene. I know one young man who was named for a can of peaches. His mother, wracking her brains for a name for the new baby, happened to see the can on the kitchen shelf, so his name is Delmonte. Then there are the names that were originally brought home from the far places of the earth by sea-faring ancestors and handed down from generation to generation, so that to-day I know a Persia, a Casindania, a Ceylon, and, of course, Rienza Trimback.

Rienza Trimback was a very attractive girl forty-odd years ago, when she was eighteen. I've seen pictures of her and I've heard people talk about her. The pictures show a girl with dark eyes, wide with innocent question, over a mouth, large and sweet, that seems disciplined with difficulty into gravity. Her dark hair is swept up into a pompadour that leaves bare the broad serene forehead and little, close-set ears. Her chin is round and young, and she's a pretty thing, with the unfinished, soft prettiness of youth.

"The good times I used to have with Rienza!" one great-grandmother who was a girl with her told me, shaking her head and smiling. "Didn't take anything to set us off in them days. Giggle, giggle, giggle from morning till night. It got so our mothers wouldn't let us set together in church, we behaved so unseemly. Not that we meant any harm or disrespect to the minister, but you know how young girls are. We found a tee-hee's nest in every ha-ha bush. That girl could dance the shoes off the devil himself. That was when I was engaged to Oren, and she was runnin' 'round with Barrett Ames. There wasn't a dance within thirty miles that we didn't take in. We had an awful good time. She might have married Barry, too—although I dunno; she had a drove of them after her, and could have taken her pick of half a dozen—only that winter, when she was goin' on nineteen—"

The winter when Rienza was almost nineteen, her mother caught cold on the way home from a funeral and was dead of pneumonia within the week. Pneumonia took a terrific toll in those days, when a doctor was seldom called until the patient was desperately ill, and sometimes, overworked, exhausted, delayed by bad roads, couldn't get there until the day after that, when it would have been too late even had he had modern drugs to rely upon; and one funeral, with the long committal service in a barren and sleet-swept graveyard, was all too frequently closely followed by at least one other. Rienza's mother was a victim of the times; and so, no less, was Rienza. She was the youngest of nine children and the only unmarried girl in the family, so it was taken for granted that she would be the one to stay at home and keep house for her father. She didn't rebel against the edict of her brothers and sisters and the neighbors. Probably there wasn't any edict, when it comes to that. She simply fell into the accepted pattern of the day. If a man had an unmarried daughter, naturally she looked after him, if his wife died. It was her duty.

Rienza's father, old Ephraim Trimback, had been ailing vaguely ever since he'd fallen out of a haymow a year or two before, and after the blow of the death of his wife, he began to fail visibly. The consensus was that he wasn't long for this world. Three or four years would see Rienza free to live her own life, everybody said, and what a comfort it would be to her in after years to know that she had done her duty well. It was wonderful, they all said, how a flibbertigibbet like she'd always been could settle down in the traces. She was turning out to be as good a housekeeper as her mother had been before her, and that was saying a lot. She kept a big flock of hens herself, for the egg money, and her married brothers came over regularly to help her father with the heavy chores. It was a very good arrangement all around. Of course, during the period of mourning for her mother she couldn't attend any public gathering except church, and some of the young men who had been attentive to her drifted away to other girls, who were free to go dancing and sleigh-riding. But Clyde Matthews and Barrett Ames and Wilbur Pottle remained faithful, even if it did mean spending long evenings talking to old Eph. Confined to the farmhouse by his respect for convention and what was becoming semi-invalidism, he developed a thirst for sociability and a tendency to monopolize Rienza's callers.

When the conventional year was over, Rienza prepared to resume her own social life. She'd agreed to go to the Valentine Day dance in Bethel with Clyde, and she was looking forward to it eagerly. It seemed a long time since she'd danced. She altered her last year's flowered challis, which she'd had little occasion to wear, and washed her hair and brushed it until it shone. She looked very pretty when Clyde called for her, with her eyes sparkling and her cheeks flushed with excitement. She put on her coat and turned to say good-night to her father.

"Now don't you wait up for me, Pa," she admonished him. "You go to bed when you get ready. I won't be very late."

"Have a good time," he said. He gave a slight grimace of pain. "I—I guess I'll go to bed now. I don't seem to feel very spry. No, no, don't you bother none about me. I'll be all right. Just you go along and have a good time."

That time she went, but of course she didn't have a good time. She couldn't help worrying about her father, alone and sick, and long before the dance was over, she told Clyde that she was terribly sorry, but she thought that she ought to go home. He was very nice and understanding about it, even after they discovered when they got back to the Trimback place that old Eph was sleeping the sleep commonly accredited to the just, after having, from the evidence, disposed of a glass or two of milk and almost half a mince pie. But the same thing happened again and again, until it became apparent to everyone except Rienza that her father simply didn't want her to go anywhere. Whether this was just because he was lonely without her, or because of a deeper-seated fear that she would marry and upset his well-established way of life, there is no way of knowing. Whatever the case, no sooner would she start getting ready to go out than he would develop a symptom.

"Gol-ram it, Rienza," he'd moan, "my back's killin' me. Don't seems if I can stand it. Maybe a hot soap stone—" And she'd drop everything to build up the kitchen fire and heat the stone and get him into bed.

Or he'd say, "By Jim Hill, Rienza, I knew when I et them beans you'd sneaked some mustard in. You know I can't stomach mustard, an' now I got the cramps. Gol-ram it, can't you do nothin' for me? Stir up some ginger tea or sompthin'?" Eph Trimback was a very religious man. He'd been a deacon of the church in his better days, and no more violent oath than Gol-ram or Jim Hill was ever heard to cross his lips. He could put a lot of feeling into those innocuous expressions, though. They never left you in any doubt as to his attitude toward anything that displeased him.

"To hear the old goat Gol-ramming and Jim-hilling around," Barrett Ames said bitterly one night down at the store, "you'd think he was dying and it was Rienza who was killing him." Barry was the only one left of Rienza's train of beaux. The others had become discouraged. He had been counting on taking her to the Strawberry Festival at the Grange that night, and his disappointment when she couldn't go because her father seemed to be suffering from the combined effects of food poisoning and galloping consumption had left him in a violent and outspoken mood. "There's nothing more the matter with him than there is with me, and probably not as much. He'll outlive the whole of us. It makes me mad, the way he puts it over on Rienza. What she'd ought to do is just walk out on him once or twice when he starts throwing a fit, and let him fend for himself. By the time she came home, he'd have got over what ailed him. But she won't. He's got her buffaloed."

Finally even he couldn't stand it any longer. He begged her to marry him and put an end to an impossible situation. "Your father could come and live with us," he said. "Or he could go live with one of your brothers or sisters. You've done your share. Let them do theirs."

"But, Barry, this is his home. He wouldn't be happy anywhere else. Besides, I couldn't ask my brothers to take him, even if he'd go. All the burden would fall on their wives, and that wouldn't be right. They're not blood kin. My sisters all have big families and more worry and expense already than—"

"Then board him out somewhere. I'd be willing to help pay—"

"I couldn't do that!" Rienza looked at him with shocked eyes. "My own father. I'm surprised that you'd suggest it. Oh, Barry, it isn't that I don't love you. I do, I do, more than I can say! But it would kill him to move, even to your place. If you could only see your way clear to come and live here, just until— We're young. We've got lots of time ahead of us."

"No." Barry was sure about that. "I feel the same way as he does about my own place, and I can't live anywhere that I'm not the boss. It wouldn't work out. Rienza, can't you *see?* You're only twenty-three, but I'm over thirty. I haven't got all the time in the world. He's had his life. It's only fair that he should step down now and let us have our chance!"

But Rienza couldn't see it. Her duty was her duty.

"All right. I guess that settles it. I won't be hanging around here any more, Rienza. I can stand only just so much, and I've reached the end of my tether. If you change your mind—"

Rienza didn't believe him, really, when he said he wouldn't be back. She kept expecting him for a long time, until at last she heard that he was taking Winona Frayle around to all the dances. Then it was too late to change her mind, even if she would. Barry married Winona five years after Rienza's mother died, and that was the year when people began to say that Rienza was starting to show her age. The round softness of her face changed, and her jawline began to show fine and firm. Her lips thinned a little and looked less ready to laugh, and her eyes took on a steadfastness. She wasn't pretty any longer, but there were those who thought she'd grown into a very handsome woman, handsomer than her young prettiness had promised.

One thing Barry had been wrong about. Old Eph didn't outlive them all. Under Rienza's excellent care, he outlasted his wife by fifteen years, and died at the age of eighty, of a heart attack. He left Rienza the farm and a little money, which everyone including her brothers and sisters agreed was only right, and the satisfaction of knowing that no one could possibly accuse her of dereliction. If she found that knowledge rather cold comfort sometimes, nobody ever suspected it. Rienza had never been one to complain.

She was thirty-four, which was pretty old for marriage in the country in those days, but the friends of her girlhood, all married and mothers by this time, undertook to find Rienza a nice beau and marry her off. All her old admirers were settled down, of course, but as one friend said, "There are plenty more fish in the sea." Their good offices weren't really necessary. Rienza was a good-looking woman with property of her own now. Pretty soon she had two eligible suitors calling on her. One was Lee Miller, a widower of forty with two small children and a farm of his own, and the other was the new minister, William Stoddard, a handsome man of about Rienza's age, and miraculously unmarried. Opinion was divided as to which was the more suitable. Some held that Rienza was farm born and bred, and ought to stick to a life that she knew. Others maintained that she was naturally high-minded and smart as a whip and would make a wonderful minister's wife. Her experience with the ill and elderly would come in handy, and she could make a lot of the pastoral calls and be a real help to her husband.

What she thought herself it was difficult to guess. At the Ladies' Aid chicken pie supper it was observed that she sat with Lee Miller and was perfectly lovely to his children, always a good sign. But when she and Mr. Stoddard were invited over to the Freeman Howards' for Thursday night boiled dinner, it came out in the conversation that she'd helped him with the Scott Evans funeral sermon which had been so well-thought-of by everyone. Of course, someone would have to help him, he being so new and all. He couldn't be expected to know about certain episodes in Scott's life to which it would have been unfortunate to make even accidental reference. But that he had chosen Rienza for this task was considered highly significant. She herself parried all questions and hints blandly. She agreed that the Miller young-ones ought to have a woman to take care of them, and in the next breath agreed that the Reverend was a fine man and should have a wife to help him in his work. Nobody got much change out of Rienza, as Winona Ames told Barrett, adding that in her opinion Rienza took a rather spiteful delight in keeping everyone on tenterhooks. Winona, after ten years of marriage to Barry, wasn't exactly jealous of Rienza, but she couldn't have been called precisely her kindest critic.

Which one she would have married—and almost certainly she would have married one or the other—it is impossible for anyone, probably even Rienza, to say at this late date. The matter was never settled. At the time when it might have been, Rienza's Aunt Martha suffered a stroke. Aunt Martha and Uncle Widd were childless, and it never occurred to anyone, least of all to Rienza herself, that she had done her share for the family. She was single; she was accustomed to taking care of older people; she was the obvious one to step into the breach. So she moved over to the next farm and undertook the nursing of her aunt and the housekeeping for her uncle.

At first she must have believed, or tried to believe, or hoped, at least, that the arrangement was only temporary, that Aunt Martha would get better or someone else would be found to take over the responsibility. She never said so to a living soul, but she took with her only a few of her clothes, and ran home across the fields and over the brook every day or so for something she hadn't thought she'd need. For a long time she took Thursday afternoons to herself, to go over to her own house and tidy it up and air out the rooms. Occasionally she settled Aunt Martha comfortably for several hours, prepared and served an early supper for easygoing Uncle Widd, and went over home, as she called it, to get ready a meal and entertain her friends under her own roof. Sometimes she included Lee Miller in these gatherings, and sometimes William Stoddard, and sometimes both of them.

These evenings had little in common with the old laughing, rollicking days when she had gone dancing with Barrett Ames. They were all older and settled now, and married couples of those days didn't attend dances and race over country roads beneath the setting moon. There were the children to think of, at home in the care of an obliging relative or neighbor who didn't want to be kept up much later than ten o'clock; and the countryman's day starts too early to make late hours attractive. After supper they usually played whist or fan-tan—for matches, of course, or just for fun. When the game was over, they drank sweet cider or lemonade and ate sugar cookies and hermits, and talked for a few moments. Then someone said, "Well, much as I hate to break up the party—"; and someone else said, "Let me help you with these dishes, Rienza. The two of us, it won't take any time at all." This offer was a courteous gesture, and was always rejected with equal courtesy. "Oh, my, no. There are only a few. It won't take me a minute—or I might leave them till morning."

By ten o'clock the sedate party was over, the guests were going down the steps, and the country stillness was broken with "Had a *lovely* time, Rienza!" and "You come over to our house next week," and, distance-diminished, "Good-night, good-night!" Then Rienza would do up her dishes, and plump up cushions, and put out lights; and if sometimes she dawdled over these tasks, pretending that when they were done she would go up-stairs to her own bed, to a sleep untroubled by the necessity of keeping one ear alert for an invalid's call, no one ever knew. She'd go about the house one last time, twitching a curtain straight, lingering in the last heat of the stove; and then she'd put on her coat, lock the door behind her, and trudge off across the fields to where the light in Aunt Martha's window beckoned, her head held high, her shoulders square, denying herself the useless indulgence of a backward glance at the low white house sleeping in the starlight.

At the end of three years, William Stoddard received a call to a larger church. He talked with Rienza before he accepted it, asking, although he already knew what the answer must be, whether she wouldn't accompany him. She was truly fond of him—not with the headlong passion which she'd felt for Barry Ames, but with a maturer, quieter affection none the less genuine. But she couldn't go with him. God had appointed her to a post which she couldn't desert, she told him; and she couldn't urge him to stay, living in a hope which might never be realized, when he'd been summoned to a field of greater usefulness. It sounds like a stilted little speech for anyone as practical and down-to-earth as Rienza was, but it came from the bottom of her heart, and William Stoddard came away from the interview very much moved. Years later, after he'd married and become a successful city pastor, they still exchanged letters at Christmastime; and sometimes on Sunday afternoons—this was much later—she'd listen to his beautiful voice, trained and polished now, come in over her battery-operated radio, and wonder that she was so little affected by anything except a faint and natural curiosity as to how well she would have fitted into the life he had made for himself.

Not very well, she concluded, giving herself less credit than she deserved.

After the Reverend Stoddard went away, Lee Miller increased his attentions. Rienza liked him and she really loved his two little girls, who were being brought up more or less haphazardly by a series of Lee's female relations, who came and did for him and the children for as long or short periods as their own domestic arrangements would allow. Rienza realized that this was not an ideal, or even a very good, situation for two little girls approaching adolescence and its problems. Completely ignorant of modern psychiatry, she was nevertheless informed by her common sense that the girls lacked the emotional security and the consistent discipline and routine that were necessary to their welfare. That isn't the way she put it, the day she saw Saba, a precocious twelve-year-old, down at the store in lipstick and near-silk stockings, carrying on, as Rienza put it, with one of the Barlow boys, who was seventeen if he was a day. Rienza, whom few things shocked any more, was shocked that day. She left her basket of groceries to be called for later and marched up the dirt road to the Miller farm, heedless alike of the dust raised by her determined progress and of the hot July sun beating down on her bare head. Lee was hoeing in his bean field, and she summoned him to the wall with a shout and an imperative wave of the arm. She wasted no time on the amenities.

"Lee, if you don't do something pretty quick about those girls of yours, the first thing you know they're going to get into about the worst kind of trouble a girl can get into. I guess you know what I mean without my saying any more about that, but I'm too fond of them and of you to let them go the way they're going without at least having my say-so. I don't know what in tunket your sister Liz is thinking of to let a child like Saba rig herself up the way I just saw her down to the store, but—"

"Whoa-back, Rienza," Lee said in understandable bewilderment. "What's biting you? You seem a little up-sot."

"I am up-set. When I see a nice child that I've known from the cradle rolling her eyes and batting her lashes and swinging her hips at a man old enough to be her father, like a—a—well, a movie star, I figure I've got a right to be up-set. What Liz—"

"Now wait. Let's get this straight. In the first place, Liz had to go home yesterday. Her mother-in-law's sick. My cousin Fawnie'll come over from Sumner as soon's her oldest girl gets back from Boston, and—"

"That's just what I'm talking about. What kind of a way for those poor young-ones to live is that? Never knowing who's going to be bossing them from one day to the next, having to change their ideas and their habits every ten minutes— Yesterday Liz, who's a wonderful woman, I'll grant you, but inclined to be a little bit too strict; and to-morrow Fawnie, who I must say, much as I like her, is downright slack about a lot of things. When I think—"

"Now wait." Lee was a patient and methodical man. "Let's get back to the store. Who's this man old enough to be her father that Saba's flirting with?"

"Maybe I did exaggerate that a little. It was Wade Barlow, and if he isn't old enough to be her father, he's a lot too old for her to be fooling with, even if it's only in fun. I wouldn't trust those Barlow boys as far as I could throw them, but this time I will say that it's not all his fault. Saba may be only twelve, but got up the way she is, with silk stockings and lipstick and a tight dress, she looks older and—"

"Lipstick? I don't know anything about any lipstick and silk stockings. Where'd she get those?"

"How do I know where she got them? That's what I'm trying to tell you. You ought to have a woman in the house that'll look after those girls. They're good girls, but they're getting to the silly age. I know all about it. I was that age once myself." She stopped short, looking comically startled. "If you can believe it," she added dryly. "But that's not the point. The point is that they haven't got anyone to tell them things. No man, no matter how hard he tries—and you do try, Lee; you're a good father—can bring up two girls alone. What you'd ought to do is get married to a nice, good-hearted, sensible woman. There." She folded her arms and scowled at him.

Lee straightened up and shoved his broad-brimmed straw hat onto the back of his head. "I'm glad you brought it out into the open, Rienza. I been trying to work up to it gradual for the past couple of years, but I never seem to be able to find the right time to ask you. You'd be pretty near perfect, and I guess you know I think the world and all of you."

"That wasn't what I was leading up to at all. You know I can't marry anybody, with Aunt Martha the way she is, getting more helpless all the time and no telling how long it'll last. I've given up any idea of ever marrying." The minute she said it, she knew it was true, had been true for quite a while, although never before had she faced it, and right now she was too busy and concerned to spare any time indulging in regret that it should be so. "You're a good man, an awful good man, and if things were different, I'd be pleased to— But there's no use in thinking about that. No use at all." She had a sudden tired feeling that she'd been through this too many times before, and that the sooner it was over, the better.

"You've got to pick out someone else that's suitable and just go ahead and marry her."

"Sounds easy," Lee commented with mild cynicism.

"Well, it is easy. Any woman in her right mind would be glad to marry you, if you'd just get up enough gumption to go after her."

"I'm interested to hear it," said Lee, and added with humorous intent: "And I suppose you've got her all picked out for me."

"Since you mention it, yes, I have." Rienza recognized the humor but decided to ignore it; this was too good an opportunity to waste. "Marge Abbott. She's a widow with no children of her own, and she's good with young-ones or she wouldn't be such a successful schoolteacher. She's just about the right age, and she's nice-looking and capable. Besides, I've seen her casting sheep's eyes at you—"

The next day she started closing up her own house, which had stood ready for immediate occupancy for five years. She took down the curtains and washed them and put them away in bureau drawers. She aired and sunned the blankets and quilts and packed them in trunks, with cedar boughs to keep out moths. She rolled up the rugs, and turned the mattresses over the foots of the beds, and oiled the stoves against rust, and spread newspapers over the parlor carpet, and pulled all the shades down to the window sills, and disconnected the pump. Then she turned the key in the kitchen door, and picked up the bushel basket of odds and ends, such as the egg-beater that was better than Aunt Martha's and the iron gem pans to which she attributed her fame as a maker of pop-overs, and went once more across the fields and over the brook to Uncle Widd's, with the dead house staring at her inflexible back from blind eyes.

It was at about this time that she began to acquire her reputation for being—well, not exactly queer, but for sometimes doing odd and unaccountable things, like walking alone on stormy nights when all sensible folk were safely and warmly housed. She herself couldn't have explained why she did it. She'd stand in the window, listening to the wind pour over the house and away across the pastures, thinking how far it had come and how far it was going. She'd think of the things it had seen, the lakes and mountains to the north, the endless stretches of forest where rabbit and wildcat and deer felt its lash, and suddenly she'd feel that she couldn't tolerate being shut away here, behind glass, a moment longer. She'd snatch her coat and rush out to walk swiftly, head lifted and long back straight, over the empty wind-washed fields and roads. "Her age," her friends said wisely. "Old maids of a certain age get notions." But it wasn't her age that sometimes gave her the trapped feeling that forced her to stride the open countryside with only the friendly wind for company.

At about this time, too, people began to notice that Rienza's speech and manner, which had always been tactful and ladylike, were undergoing a change. She was always pleasant still, but people began to say that you'd better not ask Rienza's opinion unless you were prepared to hear exactly what she thought, expressed in plain terms. It wasn't that she was ever rude. It was more as if she had decided that, while she was clearing her life of unessentials like the care of a house she never used and the attentions of men she could never marry, she might as well make a clean sweep and throw overboard all the affectations and poses to which she had been trained.

And eight months after her interview with him, Lee Miller and Marge Abbott were married. It turned out very well, too. Aunt Martha died about four years later, but of course Uncle Widd still needed someone to do for him, especially now that his arthritis was getting so bad; so Rienza stayed on. The amount of housework involved didn't fill her time, so she increased her flock and started raising fancy poultry and eggs for market. The farm was not at all isolated now that most roads were hard-surfaced and everyone had cars, and she had a good business established by the time Uncle Widd died. He left her his farm and eight thousand dollars in the bank, which is quite a lot of money by local standards.

For the first time in her adult life, Rienza was free of responsibility. She was fifty-five years old, financially independent—what is known here as very well-fixed—and a good-looking woman for her age or any other age, for that matter. There was quite a lot of gray in her hair, but her eyes looked bigger and darker than ever since her face had grown thinner. Her figure and erect carriage were the envy of her friends, who had to a woman paid the price of child-bearing and hard work. Not that Rienza didn't work hard. She did. She enlarged her poultry farm to include much of Uncle Widd's land, moved back to her own house, and took advantage of the times and easier transportation to rent Uncle Widd's house to a man with a family, who worked in the mills in Rumford. He only wanted enough land for a garden, so it was a good deal for her. She began selling her poultry and eggs to wholesalers who called for them twice a week in trucks, and before long she was adding to Uncle Widd's bank account instead of living on it. Oh, yes, she worked hard, but it was the strenuous kind of outdoor work that kept her slim and brown. She appeared at the store one day in dungarees and a work shirt, and the disapproving comment was that from the back you could hardly tell her from one of those young summer women. Usually, though, she didn't wear her work clothes off the farm, and that one lapse was forgiven her when Winona Ames died of influenza and, after a decent interval, Barrett began calling on her, taking up, as one commentator put it, right where he'd left off thirty years before.

There was something right about this second flowering of the old romance, something fitting about the completion of the interrupted cycle, that appealed to the drama-starved hearts of the country people. To a man and woman they were pleased and gratified, and they did everything in their power to nurture the affair. "It's nice after all this time that they should get together at last. Just like a movie. Let's have them over for Sunday dinner," or "Makes you feel things are planned. Here she's stayed single all these years, and he's alone now, with his young-ones all married off. I'm plannin' on makin' a crocheted pop-corn spread for her a weddin' present."

But the Sunday chicken was slaughtered in vain and the pop-corn spread went to the maker's granddaughter when she married, because for some reason the romance failed to mature. Rienza scandalized the neighbors by having her hair cut and buying a station wagon and a pedigreed police dog, and Barry's second son and his wife took over the Ames place and made a home for Barry. Nobody could understand it at all, and it's only by luck that I do. Larry Parsons was buying the considerable amounts of eggs and poultry required in the hotel business from Rienza, and one day when I was riding to Rumford with him on business, we went around by the Trimback place to pick up some crates of eggs.

Rienza was dressing broilers in the woodshed when we drove into the yard, and came out to meet us, tall and lithe in her dungarees, her short gray hair curling close to her beautifully shaped head, and her fine lean face as keen as a hawk's. "Oh, it's only you," she said to Larry. "Though I don't know what difference it would make who it was. I'd look just the same. Times have changed since I was a girl. My mother always wore four aprons, one on top of another, and when the doorbell rang she'd send one of us young-ones to peek before she'd answer the door. If 'twas only one of the neighbors, she'd just take off the top apron, which was made of flour sacking that she wouldn't be caught dead in by anyone, and go to the door in the second apron, which was clean, but maybe faded or patched. If 'twas someone she didn't know quite so well, she'd take that off and go in the one underneath, which was bright and new, but still only percale or calico. But if 'twas a stranger or the minister, she'd peel down to the last one, one of these dress-up aprons, pretty as could be, but only half as big as a handkerchief and no earthly use except for decoration. But I can't very well take these pants off—or at least, I can, but I'm not going to. There's enough talk about me already without my throwing kerosene on the flame."

"Now what've you been doing?" Larry wanted to know.

"Nothing," she stated vigorously. "Not one darned thing, unless you count having a new bathroom put in, with a shower in it. It's the shower that sticks in their craws, I guess. Unwomanly. But I've always read about showers and thought I'd like one. I do, too, and since I earned the money that paid for it, I don't see how anyone's got any call to kick. Then of course I've been talking about hiring that G.I. and his wife that live in Uncle Widd's house to tend the chickens a couple of months this winter, so I can go to Florida. I'm going to do it, too. Might even take him into the business, if he pans out all right. But of course the talk all goes back eight-nine years to when I didn't marry Barrett Ames after all. That's at the bottom of it all."

"Why didn't you marry him, Rienza?" Larry asked. "I've often wondered." It wasn't an impertinent question. There was something so frank and friendly and sensible about the woman that even I, who didn't know her, would have felt free to ask her almost anything, knowing that if she didn't want to tell me, she'd say so with perfect good nature.

"Well, I almost did. At my age you don't fall madly in love all over again, but I'd always been awful fond of Barry. I still am. I was sick and tired of paddling my own canoe all those years, and he looked like a nice strong shoulder to lean on. You must know how 'tis, Mrs. Rich, you being a widow with small children," she said to me. "Don't you sometimes feel like you'd give anything to have someone else decide things for you?"

I said I did indeed.

"There's worse things than having to stand on your own two feet," she warned me. "But like I was saying, I'd pretty near made up my mind to marry Barry, when one day I noticed the way he got up out of a low chair, easy and careful, for all the world like Uncle Widd used to, and my father before him. It came to me then that Barry is twelve years older than I am, and while he was hale and hearty then, 'twouldn't be long before he was an old man. I've spent my entire life seeing old people through their last illnesses—not that I'm complaining—and I decided that I'd had enough of it. I missed my youth, if you want to call it that, and marrying Barry or anyone else wouldn't bring it back. I'd got along single for fifty-six years, and I decided I might as well tough it out to the end."

"Don't you ever get lonesome?" I asked out of my own experience.

"Of course I get lonesome. Who doesn't? But when I start feeling droopy and down-at-the-mouth, I clean the chicken runs or wash the down-stairs paint. There's nothing like a good job of work to cure anyone of the collywobbles. When I get done, I put my feet in the oven and pull my skirt up higher over my knees than would be decent with a man in the house, and count my blessings. I'm self-supporting and self-respecting, and beholden to no one. Any time, day or night, I can do just exactly what I feel like doing. I look over all the married women I know, and pretty soon I stop feeling sorry for myself and start thanking my lucky stars that a sense of duty prevented me from getting married. And you can take that smug look off your face, and stop laughing up your sleeve at me and thinking 'Sour Grapes,' Larry Parsons, because I mean what I say. How many eggs do you want this trip?"

Larry loaded the eggs, and we drove off. "She's a great Rienza," he said. "I think she's a little bit cracked."

I told him that if she were, I hoped I'd go crazy the same way as soon as possible. It seemed a sensible sort of lunacy to me to take the fabric of one's existence, no matter how unpromising material it seemed to be, and build as good a life of it as Rienza Trimback had done. Looking at her, I could agree with her that there are worse things than having to stand on your own two feet.

8

No Position

ONE DAY LAST spring when I was up at Middle Dam negotiating the loan of a quart of No. 30 motor oil for my rather down-at-heels Model A pick-up, I encountered John Lavorgna for the first time this season. It was the kind of day we often get in Maine in May. A gentle rain, hardly more than a drizzle, was falling steadily, and while the Carry was a little soupy in spots, the maples and birches along the way were beginning to put out their first misty red and green leaves, and the huge purple violets were blossoming in the grass between the ruts. In the swampy places the leafless rhodora blazed magenta and the shag-bush shook out a silver cloud. The mellow oboe-like notes of the white-throated sparrows' rainy-day song drifted through the hush of the dripping woods, and everything smelled of greenery and growth and the awakening earth. It was a lovely day in its own subdued fashion, and I was feeling fine as I came into the hotel lobby, shaking the water off my slicker and stamping the mud off my boots. When I saw John, sitting in the corner between two windows overlooking the lake and playing cribbage with a strange man, the day looked even better than ever to me, as it always does to all of us when we un-expectedly run across an old friend.

"John!" I cried delightedly. "When did you come In? How long are you going to stay?"

He laid his cards face down on the table, rose, and came over to shake my hand. "Came In on last night's boat. We was plannin' on stayin' a week, but unless the weather clears up so we can get some fishin'—"

I looked at him. Get some fishing indeed! It was a good day to fish, as well he should know, since he'd taught me most of what I know about fly-fishing. I started to ask him if he'd gone crazy, but something distraught in his expression stopped me. It occurred to me then that his heartiness had been slight-ly feverish, and I made a rapid diagnosis. He was having sports trouble.

So instead of inquiring for his wife, as I naturally would have done next, I improvised rapidly. "Oh, the barometer's started to rise. I'm going fishing myself this afternoon. They'll take anything on a rising barometer, especially at this time of year," and left him to employ that nonsense as best he could to his own advantage. We both knew that the state of the barometer has little, if anything, to do with the state of the fishing, learned opinion to the contrary, and that either the fish are rising or they aren't, depending entirely upon fish psychology, which passeth human understanding. But I did appreciate the seriousness of his position. There is nothing worse in a guide's life than a disgruntled sport, who must be babied along and kidded into thinking he's having a good time. If John could only pry his sport loose from the fireside and get him out into the nice fresh air, where he could whip the river to a lather and start the blood circulating through his veins, maybe he'd feel enough better to decide not to go home on the next train after all. But it had to be managed tactfully and there was nothing more I could do to further the campaign. So I left the warmth of the open fire and went over to where Al Parsons was sorting and labeling merchandise in her haven behind the counter.

She looked up at me and shook her head slowly, her beautiful and expressive eyes lively with suppressed laughter. "Poor John," she murmured. "His sport's getting him down. I've been sitting here all morning listening to him put on his Maine guide act. He's an artist." She raised her voice. "Since you're going fishing this afternoon, Louise, you really ought to stock up on these Carrie Stevens Gray Ghosts. They're killers. Only seventy-five cents, too. I'm sorry I can't go with you, but Larry's Outside on business and I can't leave the office."

"That'll be the Day," I told her, unimpressed. Al is about as much interested in fishing as I am in feather-stitching. "Besides, I'm not going fishing. I just said that. I'm really going to clean my kitchen cupboards and maybe wash a little paint in the living room. As you undoubtedly suspected."

She wrote the price neatly on a box of Montreals. "You and John. The great Maine nature writer and the great Maine guide. Listen to him now."

John's voice, vibrant with sincerity and conviction, rose above the snapping of the fire and the drumming of rain on the roof. "—believe there's a lot in it. I rec'lect one time up on the Allegash—just such a day as this it was, too—we started in fishin' right after lunch on a risin' barometer, an' I never saw the beat of it—"

"Well, this isn't getting any potatoes sprouted," I told

Al. "What I came up for was to see if I could borrow some motor oil."

"Sure. Swene's up in the engine house. Ask him about it."

My oil deal completed, I went back into the office to say good-bye to Al, but she was busy selling some Gray Ghosts to John's sport, so that they could take advantage of the wholly mythical rise of the barometer to go fishing after lunch. She winked at me over the bowed head of her customer and then turned the bland and innocent eye of an old con man on him. There was nothing to be gained by hanging around, so I started the Ford and went home, laughing to myself and thinking that what John had once said to me about a guide's job was certainly true.

"Wal, it ain't no position," he'd said. "It sure ain't no position!"

I've known John for seventeen years, ever since I first came to Maine as a schoolteacher-on-vacation. He was the first Maine guide I'd ever laid eyes on, and I still consider him the best, after having known more guides than you could shake a stick at. The first thing about John to impress me was that he looked like a guide, or at least like my idea at the time of how a guide should look. Since then I've discovered that a guide can look like practically anything from a Judge of the Supreme Court to a housewife. I'm a licensed guide myself, now, so I ought to know. In those days, however, my notions about Maine were derived entirely from reading. John was dark, with the Indian cast to his features which all the books had led me to expect—his profile would look very well on a coin; and he dressed properly, too, in soft, soleless moccasins, faded plaid shirts, and a battered old felt hat with salmon flies stuck carelessly into the crown.

I met him during the month of August, when the fishing isn't very good and the guides, instead of taking out fishermen, which is comparatively easy, have to choose between loafing or conducting what amounts to sight-seeing tours of the country. That's hard work. Fishermen may be monomaniacs, but their peculiar obsession at least keeps them amused and tied down to one spot and one easily answered set of questions, like "Do you think I'd better change to a Royal Coachman?" The August canoe-trippers want to cover territory, experience in four days everything the woods have to offer, and learn every single last bit of available data on anything they see or hear about. I know all about that, too, because during the first phase of my acquaintanceship with John, I was a sight-seeing sport myself, with all the attitudes that I have since come to deplore in others. That's how I met John. He guided four or five of us starry-eyed and palpitating nature lovers up to Little Boy Falls, above Parmachene, near the Canadian border.

We thought he was simply wonderful. One of the more romantic-minded and effusive young women of the party said he was an unspoiled son of the wilderness, living in tune with the earth and the elements. She said she couldn't imagine his ever being tamed and shackled by civilization and convention. She said he was brother of all that was wild and free and natural, one with wind and wave. She really did say all those things, and the funny part of it is that the rest of us, men and women alike, secretly agreed with her, even though we did think it sounded a little bit silly spoken out loud. It was obvious that John did love the woods and lakes. He apparently found the spectacle of an old vixen playing with her cubs on a sunny ledge overlooking Cupsuptic just as appealing and entertaining as the rest of us did, although to him it was a commonplace. His accustomed eyes saw a thousand things that escaped ours—twin, coin-spotted fawns standing motionless in the shade of a tree, blending perfectly with the sun-shot shadow; two tiny song-birds darting and crying in a frenzy about the head of a great hawk, driving it in ignominious retreat from the neighborhood of their nest; an enormous bald eagle perched majestically on the tip of a dead pumpkin pine. To us these things were strange and new, so it isn't surprising that we found them marvelous. It is surprising that he too found them something to marvel at, for all their familiarity. Nobody who didn't truly love the wilderness could have counterfeited the pure delight John took in everything about it, from the fall of light across a far mountain range to the anxious industry of the ants among the crumbs about our feet as we ate lunch on a lake shore. Nobody who didn't love the wilderness to his very bones would have put up with us as the price for the privilege of moving along the high valleys, as most people move through the rooms of their houses. John could have had a nice peaceful life working in a mill, after all.

I don't think we were any worse than most of the August parties, but I'm very sure John didn't return the compliment by thinking we were wonderful. We were, I'm sure, indistinguishable from the scores of other safaris that he's conducted through the same country from year to year. We wore the same unsuitable clothes—shorts in black-fly season and pleated slacks in brush terrain. We had the same dietary peculiarities—the man with ulcers who couldn't eat fried food and the woman who had to have Sanka. We had the gentleman with the sacroiliac which precluded him from helping with the hard work, and the camera fiend who periodically put a spoke in the wheels of progress by making us freeze in our tracks, usually when John had a heavy work canoe on his shoulders, while he took pictures. We got tired and too hot or too cold, and some of us complained. All of us expected the guide to be either ignorant of or indifferent to the concept of an eight-hour working day. Just because he'd served breakfast at six A.M. didn't seem to us to be any logical reason why he shouldn't take us fishing until dark, even if it did mean he was doing dishes and making up bough beds at ten forty-five P.M. And we asked the same old questions, inevitably, that John had answered a thousand times before and knew he was going to answer a couple of thousand times to come. We certainly were no treat to him; but I guess he was wonderful at that, because he never let us suspect the truth. He gave us a good time, and if it was with the ease of long practice that he did so, we were never aware of it.

Let me give you a sample day in John's life. It doesn't make much difference what day or who is taking the current trip, because the days and the sports vary very little. It is John's first responsibility to get his party out and back without allowing anyone to come to greater grief than a few black-fly bites, minor cuts and abrasions, and medium-painful sunburns. But the fundamental safety precautions have become automatic with him, so that his chief conscious concern is to keep his sports happy, contented, and reasonably comfortable.

To this end, he arises between half past four and five in the morning, builds a fire, and starts the coffee. Long ago he discovered that there are people in the world whom it is as much as your life is worth to speak to or even look at until after they have had their coffee, and that this condition is aggravated by their having spent a restless night under unaccustomed sleeping conditions. When John makes coffee, he makes coffee, what I mean. He puts a pound of grounds into a gallon pot, breaks in an egg, throws the shell and some salt in after it, and stirs it up into a nauseating-looking mess. Then he fills the pot with cold water and sets it on to boil. When it has boiled up once, he sets it back to keep hot and settle, pouring a little cold water down the spout to hasten the process. It comes out strong as lye and clear as crystal. It's wonderful. Once when I complimented him on it, he said he didn't believe in no shadow coffee. He liked his drinks to have some authority. "Take Scotch now," he said. "If the Lord intended there should be water in it, He'd have put it in in the first place. I don't drink much, but when I do, I don't do no tamperin' with Divine Will."

I asked him what shadow coffee was. "Why, you know," he said. "It's when a feller sets a pan of water on the fire and hangs a bag of coffee over it. When the shadow of the bag has crossed the water, he calls the coffee done." I did indeed know what he meant.

Then John eats his own breakfast, because after his sports get up, he won't have time. The Maine guide's idea of breakfast is Something: oranges, bacon or ham and eggs, fried potatoes, toast and griddle cakes with maple syrup, doughnuts and a lot of coffee. All the sports who say, "But I *never* have anything except fruit juice and coffee for breakfast!" end by eating everything. Then the dishes have to be washed, and because the hot water supply is limited, they are first rinsed in the lake and scoured with sand. Then they can be scalded, dried, and packed. Next the blankets have to be shaken out and rolled and put into the canoes, and the camp waste has to be burned. At last everything is done, and John takes a last survey of the camp-site, because too often in his career he has had to turn back after two hours of paddling into a head wind to retrieve a camera someone has left hanging on a bush, or a bottle of vitamin pills someone else cached in a tree crotch for safe and handy keeping. On these final reconnoiterings he always collects a sweater or two, a pair of moccasins, and a few bath towels. Then the fire is doused with a pail of water, and all is ready for the shove-off.

The morning is spent in paddling to the lunch ground, probably six miles away, and this isn't as easy on the guide as it sounds. If the fleet consists of more than two canoes, he has to try to keep within easy reach of all of them, in case of accident. Very few sports know much about paddling—oh, they can shove a keeled canoe around Norumbega Park, all right, but the keelless work canoes of the woods are something else again, and the sustained effort required to cover fifteen miles a day of open lake is not quite like dallying around a duck pond—and they have a tendency to lag and scatter. The guide needs eyes in the back of his head to keep them all under supervision. Furthermore, he has, for safety's sake, taken the least proficient member of the party for his own bowman, and there are times when he concludes that he could do better alone, paddling a dishpan with a slotted mixing spoon. He may be just sitting still in a canoe, but he's pretty busy all the same.

The noon meal is the simplest of the day, in the interests of making time. It usually consists of a chowder or stew, topped off with fruit and cookies. John encourages his sports to go swimming while he's preparing lunch. It's something to keep them amused and out from under foot. In spite of good intentions and great zeal, they sometimes hinder more than they help. So John tells them to swim and get cool and rested, and afterwards, if they want to, they can help clean up. It works out very well, and an hour later the expedition is afloat again, with eight or ten miles to cover before pulling out for the night.

The afternoon is like the morning, only harder on the guide, because his sports are now tired and more inclined than ever to loaf and straggle. If this routine of just pushing a canoe around all day sounds a little dull, let me assure you that it isn't. The country is so beautiful, so ever-changing, that boredom is impossible. Then there is always the fascination—to me at least—of entering new country under my own power, country that is inaccessible to the sissies that depend on railroad trains and hard-surfaced roads. New vistas are opened with every promontory that is rounded, and the light changes continually on the mountains. The other traffic on the lake provides matter for speculation. Where in the world did that woman in a Mother Hubbard and a flowered hat come from and where does she think she's going in that leaky old rowboat? Or why are those two men just sitting and drifting in the middle of the lake, miles from shore, talking to each other so earnestly and seriously? Maybe they're plotting murder and chose this place as being eavesdropper-proof. It's fun to think so, anyhow. There's a point with a dead pine on it. It must be the one John was telling about at lunch, where the three men were drowned last year, just off shore. Oh, there's plenty to keep one entertained on a canoe trip.

At about half past five, while the sun is still high, the night's camp site is reached. Dinner won't be until seven or so, so this is the recreation period. That is, for everyone except John. Others can go swimming or fishing, or lie on the grass swapping stories or just smoking and relaxing, or write in their diaries, or change into clean clothes and wash their others, or prowl around with bird books in their hands, snooping on the private lives of hermit thrushes, or collect botanical specimens, or read pocket mysteries, or make daisy chains, for that matter; but not John. He has to prepare dinner. He peels the potatoes and vegetables and sets them on to boil, gets the steaks salted and ready for last-minute broiling, starts the coffee, opens cans of peaches and finds the boxed chocolate cake for dessert, and decides he has time to make hot biscuits. Since he has no oven, this is accomplished in a heavy, covered, iron spider—or frying pan, if you prefer—balanced on two stones near the flame, but not too near, and turned occasionally to insure even baking. It's quite a trick, much harder than, but nowhere near as spectacular as, turning pancakes by flipping them.

I happened on John once while he was mixing his biscuit dough, and I was shocked and disillusioned to find that he was using a prepared commercial mix, simply adding water as the directions said. "Why, John," I said, more in sorrow than in anger, "I'm disappointed. I thought only greenhorns used that stuff."

His composure was unruffled. "Heed what I say," he told me. "It's the greenhorns that make work for themselves, totin' lard an' flour an' bakin' powder 'round all day an' spendin' half the evenin' mixin' them up. You see a feller doin' it the easy way, you'll know you're lookin' at an old hand. There's enough trouble connected with guidin' that can't be helped without lookin' for more." I've remembered this, and I've found it to be true. The experienced old woodsmen have no false pride about being caught with modern conveniences in their duffle. The only reason they don't pack electric blankets is that they can't plug them into a tree.

After dinner is over and the dishes done, John has to cut boughs and make bough beds. This is not a matter of just throwing down a few branches in a heap, but of laying the small feathery twigs in courses, like shingles, with the tips curled up. Then he has to dole out the blankets, because there's always someone whose mother was frightened by a snowdrift or something, so he thinks he's entitled to more blankets than normal people. After this, if John is lucky, nobody happens to think how much fun it would be to go paddling by moonlight or jacking deer with a flashlight. If he's unlucky in these respects, he doesn't get his party to bed until midnight. Then he goes around picking up all the shoes that are lying on the ground in spite of his warning about porcupines' dietary habits and hanging them on bushes. He takes one last look around camp, rakes the fire into a compact heart so that there will be a bed of coals in the morning, and turns in. During the average night he is aroused three times to explain that the crackling and blowing and snorting in the bushes is only a deer, startled by the smell of smoke; that nobody is yelling for help out on the lake, it's just a loon; and that porcupines neither bite nor throw quills. Just as everyone seems finally to have settled down, it's five o'clock and time to start the breakfast coffee.

I've forgotten a great many things about that first trip with John, and many of the details I have confused with the events of subsequent trips; for the first one was so successful that it led to others during the next three years. I've forgotten the names and the faces of most of the other people who went, for example, and why we had to wait for two hours once at Aziscoos Dam, and how it happened that we were sitting in a row one day on the tumbled-down wall of an ancient, lost, and forgotten cemetery, smoking and talking. But some things I'll never forget.

I'll never forget the riddle John asked us that day at Aziscoos, to keep us amused after we'd exhausted the possibilities of the water front, skipped flat stones across the lake until our arms were lame, and played stick-knife for half an hour. Some delays on trips are inevitable, and then it's up to the guide to keep his sports from becoming restive as best he can. John said suddenly, "There was a feller out on a huntin' trip. He left his camp early in the mornin' an' walked three miles due south. He see a bear there, an' shot it an' dressed it out. Then he walked three miles due west, without seein' no game. He was gettin' hungry by this time, so he turned north an' walked three miles till he come to his camp, where he cooked lunch. What color was the bear?"

"What do you mean, what color was the bear?" we demanded. "You can't tell what color was the bear from the facts you've given."

"Yes, you can, too," John stated positively.

"Say it again. Say it slow this time." So he said it again, slow, and we still didn't know what color the bear was.

"It was white," John announced confidently, and we all asked indignantly how he got that way. He must have left something out of the story. "No, I didn't neither leave nothin' out of the story," he said. "Look. He went south, he went west, he went north." He drew an isosceles triangle on the sun-bleached boards of the landing with the point of his sheath knife, and labeled them respectively S, W, and N. "There's only one place in the world you can do that an' come back to where you started, an' that's right at the North Pole. So the bear must have been white, because the only kind of bear lives up there is a polar bear."

I don't know where John picked that up, but it served its purpose. By the time we'd got it through our thick heads, and then memorized it for use against the unwary, the boat that was supposed to pick us up came along, and the situation was saved.

The day we were sitting on the cemetery wall, he remarked that he took an interest in cemeteries because he used to have charge of one, over near Paris. We took this in our stride, since Maine is full of names like Paris and Norway and Calais—only that's pronounced Careless, here—and China. "Paris, France, I mean," John added as an afterthought.

"Paris, *France?* What were you doing in a cemetery there?"

"Oh, it was right after the last war, an' there was this big American military cemetery near Paris. It come under the Army's say-so, an' they happened to put a bunch from my outfit to work in it. I was straw-boss, as you might say. It was real nice work. I enjoyed it. That was how I come to make the acquaintance of President Wilson."

"You mean Woodrow Wilson?"

"Yup. Seems he was over there tendin' out on some kind of a Peace Conference. Wal, one mornin' early I was out in the cemetery, an' I see this feller walkin' around among the graves. It was real pretty out there that mornin'—dew all over the grass an' the flowers bright an' fresh. I thought prob'ly he was lookin' for some special grave—someone that belonged to him, maybe—so I went up an' asked him if I could help him. Course I didn't realize who he was, though he did look a little familiar, or I wouldn't have bothered him. He said no, he doubted I could help him. He needed some help, but it warn't the kind no one else could give him, so he'd come out there alone to sort of mull things over and get them straight in his mind. He said it was a good place to think, quiet, with all the boys lyin' there, bringin' to mind things best not forgot. Then it come to me who he was, an' I started away, but he wouldn't have it. He wanted to know what we were plannin' on doin' in the cemetery; he seemed interested and had some good suggestions to give. He was real nice-spoken, an' we had a good talk. He seemed sort of a sad man, an' I liked him an' felt sorry for him both at the same time, that mornin' in the cemetery near Paris, France."

I'll never forget the first and fundamental rules of fishing that John taught me. We were up at Little Boy, camped there for three days just below the lovely little falls, and he was employing a free half-hour before supper to catch a mess of pan trout in the pool. Most of the party were stretched out on the blanket-rolls, resting, or washing out socks in the river.

"Hey," I said, watching him cast. "Let me try that. It looks easy as pie." I made two mistakes in those few words. The first one I discovered almost at once: it was not easy as pie. The second I didn't recognize until a long time later, because John was too polite to point it out to me, and besides, the guide is supposed to take a beating. That's what he's hired for. I should never have expected him to let me use his rod. Devout fishermen will give away anything they own, sooner than loan their pet rod for even a few minutes. I feel the same way about my own now, and I'd cut my tongue out rather than ask to borrow anyone else's. But I didn't know any better then.

"I'll teach you how to cast," said John, reeling in, "if you'll promise me three things. I don't aim to set loose on the world none of these here uneducated fishermen. There's enough of them foulin' up the works already. If you're hell-bent to fish, you're goin' to fish like a gentleman. The first rule: Don't *never* ask a feller what kind of a fly or lure he's usin'. Sets you down as ignorant right off the bat. Second: Don't *never* lay your line down across another feller's nor fish close enough to him to crowd him. An' third: Don't ever kill no more fish than you're plannin' on usin'. That's bein' a fish-hog. That's about all the important rules, an' if you stick by 'em, you'll come out all right."

I promised, and I've stuck by it, and so far at least I guess I've come out all right.

It seems incredible to me now that I once had to be taught how to pronounce the names of the places which are to-day practically extensions of my own backyard, names which I use as commonly as a New Yorker uses Madison or Broadway. But it's true, and John was the one who corrected me kindly—me and about a thousand others like me—when I said "*Um*bagog." It's Um-*bay*-gog. He taught me that Aziscoos has four syllables, Az-iss-coe-hoss, and that the Dead Cambridge and the Dead Diamond aren't called that because corpses were found on their banks, but only to distinguish them from the Swift Cambridge and the Swift Diamond, rivers with rapids in them where the dead rivers have none. With endless patience he explained, probably for about the seven-hundredth time, that only city slickers say "venison."

Natives call it deer-meat, unless they've been living on it all winter, when they're apt to refer to it as old goat. That was a lesson I've found very valuable since I've set up shop as a native myself.

I remember one day when John had been dragooned into guiding a party on a mountain-climbing trip, although I can't remember what possible contingency had involved me in any such project, since I regard mountain climbing with loathing. All that work for what? A view. I know where there are plenty of views that I can enjoy without having to half-kill myself to get to them. We were resting—probably at my insistence—beside a little pond part way up the darned mountain, when John pointed to what looked to me like a heap of sticks and brush, but which was actually a beaver house. Naturally we were all fascinated, and John was interested, too, but for a different reason.

"Crimus," he said, "there's a lot of beaver in there. I'd ought to put in some beaver sets here this winter—only this year I've swore off trappin' beaver."

We'd heard about swearing off a lot of things, but never beaver trapping, so we wanted to know why.

"Wal, I'll tell you how 'tis. I was down to Boston to the Sportsman's Show last winter, workin' on the State of Maine exhibit. Never put in such a turrible ten days in my life, not even countin' the second time I had pneumonia. It sure was fierce. They'll never get me down there again."

"Why? What was the matter with it?"

"Everything was the matter with it," he stated sweepingly. "Place was crowded with a million people all tryin' to think up a sillier question to ask than the next feller. An' I couldn't stand all them critters in cages. I shoot an' trap animals, but

I don't hold with torturin' them, shuttin' them up for people to gawk at, an' poke at, an' scare half to death. That ain't right. An' when you went outside the buildin', it was as much as your life was worth. Cars goin' every-which-way, sixty miles a minute. I sure was glad when I got back to God's country. Only one good thing happened all the time I was there.

"Like I say I was workin' on the State of Maine exhibit. We had a good exhibit, too, if I do say it as shouldn't. We'd brought down a mess of live beaver, an' we built a place for them. We had a brook fallin' down over some rocks into a little pool-like, an' all around the edge we stuck up some little trees, like they was growin'. Looked real natural. You couldn't see the wire fence on account of the trees, an' we hid the drain the water ran out of with some bushes an' tall grass. Best exhibit in the show—though New Hampshire was pretty good, too. They had a moose an' an albino porcupine. Last thing the night before the show opened, we put the beaver in the pool an' left them to make theirselves to home."

He laughed, his teeth white in his dark face, his eyes narrowed and bright. "They sure made themselves to home all right. When we come in next mornin', the whole place was flooded, with water runnin' out under the doors. Them little devils had gnawed down half the trees an' dammed up the drain. By golly, they must have flew right at it, to get all that work done in one night. Took all hands till noon to get the place cleaned an' dried up enough to open the show. I sure had to laugh, though there were some who didn't think it was very comical. We had to post a guard every night after that, to discourage them."

He threw his cigarette end into the water and stood up in one flowing motion. "Then 'twas that I decided to lay off beaver trappin' this winter. It seemed kind of ungrateful to kill the little cusses after they give me the only laugh I got out of the whole ten days of the show."

The next year we took a trip up into this country, I met and married Ralph, and my days as a sport were over. I became one of the few to pass over and stand on the other side of the great gulf that is fixed between the native and the sport minds, and my relationship with John changed completely. Then it was that I discovered to my surprise that he leads a double life. Heretofore I had seen him only in his professional capacity, as the type of *coureur de bois*, dashing, gay, glamorous. Now I found out about the other aspect of his life.

When John was about twenty or so, he had occasion to spend some time up around Jackman. Two people seem to have made an impression on him during that period. The first was Mary Pickford, who was spending the summer at a camp on Moosehead. When I asked him what she looked like in the flesh, he said that she had pretty hair, adding, "She'd ought to have. She combed it enough. All she done was comb her hair. Every time I went past the place, there she was settin' out by the lake, combin' an' combin' an' combin'." The other person was Mabel, and I wouldn't be surprised at all if Mabel, at sixteen, had just as pretty hair as Mary Pickford. It's still pretty, short and dark and curly, around a high-cheekboned little face with big dark eyes gazing out of it. At sixteen she must have been cute as a button. John thought she was, anyhow, and apparently he wasn't the only one. He had plenty of rivals when he started to tend out on her, as we say here. He did the usual—bought her candy, took her canoeing, and escorted her to dances. I'll bet he was no slouch for looks himself in those days; and pretty soon they had arrived at what I believe is called "an understanding." This is not quite as serious as a formal betrothal, but in this country it's considered fairly binding, just the same.

Then one night she went to a dance with someone else. I don't blame her at all. She was quite within her rights, and there is nothing more infuriating than being taken for granted. But John didn't adopt my broader view. He thought it was terrible. If she was going to be his girl, she was going to *be* his girl, and no two ways about it. He laid it down to her that he wouldn't stand for any of this shilly-shallying around, and the upshot was that they eloped and were married that very day. AND have lived happily ever after.

John and Mabel started out as most young people in this country do, without much money, but with a great willingness to work, an understanding of what hard work is, and a good idea of what they wanted. They wanted a nice home, a good life together, and a large enough savings account to see them safely through their old age. They bought an old house in a state of disrepair, and set about fixing it up. John could do much of the carpentry himself, and Mabel could paint and hang paper, so the project shouldn't cost too much. But it was rather slow work at that, because during the summer Mabel worked as a cabin girl at a near-by camp, and of course John was away guiding much of the time. Out of their earnings they gradually replaced the things they'd set up housekeeping with, by buying a piece at a time, preferring to make-do with what they had until they could afford what they wanted. They installed a bathroom and a modern kitchen, and planted little fruit trees alongside the house. John reclaimed the big garden that had gone back to grass and put in every vegetable that can be grown in this climate and some that people said couldn't; and Mabel spent many of her summer evenings, when she was through at the camp for the day, and more long autumn days, canning and preserving.

I was down in her cellar once, and I never saw such a sight. The walls were lined from floor to ceiling with shelves crammed with jars, each labeled with the contents and the date. There were glowing red beets, scarlet tomatoes, and little golden carrots no bigger than your finger. There were pints of dark dandelion greens, which she'd dug in field and meadow when they were still young and tender in the early spring, and of lighter green Swiss chard, and slender string beans and young peas. There were rows and rows of blue-berries and wild raspberries and cranberries, which you can have for the picking in this country, and smooth peach halves, and pale spiced pears in syrup. There was shelf after shelf of relishes, and picallili, and chutney, and jewel-toned jellies, and all kinds of pickles—mustard, dill, bread-and-butter, gherkin, and plain sweet and sour. Then there was an entire section given over to game—whole little partridges in jellied stock, rabbit meat that looked like chicken, deer steaks which had been browned lightly and rolled before being packed in glass, rich deer-meat stew, and jars of mincemeat, made from the necks and scraps of the deer. Some of the labels said "John's Deer" and some said "Mabel's Deer," with the year, because they both hunted during the season, and

Mabel was a better shot than John, although she wouldn't admit it.

I once saw her make an impossible long shot at a rabbit, shooting quickly from an off-balance position as it ran across an opening in the trees. When it rolled over and over and then lay still, we all stood in stunned and incredulous silence for a moment before bursting into cheers. "Luck," said Mabel. "You ought to see John—" Well, I've seen John shoot, and he's good. But I've seen Mabel make shots like that more than once, and she's better. John says so, too. He brags about it. The day I was in Mabel's cellar, I turned from the rows of sparkling glass and said, "Good Lord, Mabel, I hate to think of all the hours and hours of work that went into this." And I did, too. I don't mind picking berries or beans and pulling carrots or beets, although you can get an awful crick in your back doing either; but if there's anything I hate, it's stewing over a hot stove, sterilizing jars and testing seals, when the day outdoors is blue and gold and everyone else has gone swimming. Things always arrive at the perfect canning stage just when the weather is best outside, for some perverse reason. "Anyway," I comforted both of us, "you won't go hungry this winter."

"No, we don't aim to. When John gets the potatoes and root-crops dug, and the cabbages and squashes in, and the apples picked, we'll be pretty well fixed for everything except coffee and sugar and flour. You never have to go hungry in the country, if you're willing to work." She led the way upstairs. "I'm planning to make a big braided rug for the living room this winter. I've been saving material for a year. And John's going to build me some bookshelves and another kitchen cupboard to keep my new aluminum in. We're finally getting pretty well straightened out. Like everybody, we've had some set-backs—sickness to be paid for and the pipes freezing and bursting winter before last—so it's taken a long time. But it looks now like we're in the clear at last."

And the next thing I knew, the house had burned flat, one evening when they were out for a short time. They didn't save a thing. All that they had worked so hard for over a period of more than a quarter of a century was reduced to a heap of smoking rubble and broken Mason jars in the bottom of an open cellar hole. Even the fruit trees were charred and killed by the heat.

I saw John shortly after that, and he was a little discouraged, but not unduly so. "Folks have been awful good to us," he said. "Those Wilmots that I've guided sent us a pair of wonderful Hudson Bay blankets, and the Grabeys sent a half a dozen sheets and pillow cases. And folks around town— Why, you wouldn't believe it! They turned out their attics and give us everything they could spare. Course, the chairs don't all match—but we can set on them just the same. Some of the pots and pans are a little dented, but they'll hold water. Like I said to Mabel, they're better'n what we started out with, an' what we done once, we can do again. Chief thing I feel bad about—Mabel had just bought herself a new dress. She put an awful store by it. Liked it best of any dress she ever had. She was savin' it to wear somewhere special—an' now of course she never will get to put it on."

"That is too bad," I said. "What are you going to do now, John? Rebuild?"

"Nope. I'm buyin' another house—that one next to the schoolhouse, down home. It's in turrible shape, but when we get done with it— You know, you learn a lot, fixin' up a house.

We made plenty of mistakes on the old one. Things look like they'd work out fine sometimes, but they don't when you come to live with them. There's a lot of mistakes we won't make again. Course, this has set us back some. Guess I won't be retirin' now, when I get to be sixty, like I always said I was goin' to. But I dunno what I'd do with myself anyhow, settin' around all day suckin' my thumb. An' this way, when we get done we'll have a home worth ownin'."

Since then I've been through the town where he lives several times. It's only a little town, and you can see practically all of it as you sit in the lone day coach, which with a baggage car, makes up the train. You have a very good view of John's house, across some fields and a shady road. At first it looked pretty shabby and bare, but it wasn't long before I noticed new shingles on the roof and the start of a new paint job. A year or so later, the chimneys had been repointed and I could see flower beds blazing bright beside the front door and a big vegetable garden laid out in the side lot. The whole place was beginning to look well-cared-for and prosperous, with the windows gleaming and white curtains crisp behind them. The last time I went through, there was a big porch under construction; so I concluded, safely I think, that the important inside remodeling had been completed, and that John and Mabel were well on their way to seeing their goal achieved.

It was at about that time that I developed my theory concerning John. Like most of my theories, it embraces a little fact and a lot of assumption, so it shouldn't be taken too seriously. The fact is that John is part Indian, part Italian, and part Yankee. According to my theory, his Indian blood accounts for his love of and skill in the woods, his Italian blood accounts for his poise and fluency and social grace, and his

Yankee blood accounts for his dependability, industry, and integrity. Since we all have known woods-stupid Indians, surly Italians, and no-good Yankees, this theory obviously won't bear too close inspection; but, though a poor thing, it is mine own, and I like it.

I saw John last only a few days ago. I'd driven up to Middle for the mail, but when I arrived there, the boat wasn't in. In fact, it hadn't even started for South Arm, because it had to go to Upper Dam first to pick up John and a party he was guiding. I looked around for Al Parsons, but she was in conference with the chef, and after that she had to type the dinner menus. I have very strong principles against bothering people when they are trying to do their work. One of the very hardest things about living in any resort country is finding time to attend to your own business. Everyone is in a carefree vacation mood, with no responsibilities, and they don't see any reason why you can't enter into the spirit of play. So I wandered down to the dock, and when the boat came in from Upper Dam, got aboard with the idea of going down to the Arm just for the ride. John was aboard with his sports, and greeted me with a casual nod, not missing a syllable of what he was saying to a gentleman who looked as though he might have a bad sacroiliac as well as a predilection for Sanka. I winked at John and went forward to discuss with Swene Meisener, the boatman, the case of my ailing Reo truck. My principles against bothering men at work extend to John.

I could hear his voice running on behind me as I outlined the Reo's symptoms to Swene, and just as we had decided that there was probably a pinhole in the carbureter float, I heard John say composedly, "It's called Metallic Island because it's full of mineral deposits. It's practically a solid junk of metal. An' I'll tell you another thing: It's a good place to stay 'way from in a thunderstorm. If lightenin's goin' to strike anywhere, that's the first place it heads for." There were impressed murmurs from his audience, and Swene and I exchanged guarded grins. We both knew that the island in question had about as much metal on it as you'd find in a newborn rabbit's ear, and that it was in fact not named Metallic at all, but Metalluc, after an Indian who used to live there.

In a few minutes John came forward to join us, and I muttered under my breath, "You ought to be ashamed of yourself, John Lavorgna. All that eye-wash about Metalluc."

"Sure, I suppose so," he said a little wearily. "But my God, Louise, you get sick of the same old questions and the same old answers. You like a change once in a while. They don't care what you tell them, just so long's you tell them somethin'. There's only one wrong answer a guide can give. Just so long's you don't say, '*I don't know*,' you're doin' all right. But the minute you admit you don't know, you're a gone gosling."

I said I could see what he meant. "Have you got your new porch done yet?" I changed the subject.

"Yup. Looks good, too." He glanced at his watch. "We're makin' pretty good time to-day. I'm hopin' to get home in time to put a coat of paint on it, an' maybe do some work in my garden before dark. The weeds are catchin' up with me somethin' fierce this weather, an' I don't like to have Mabel workin' out there in the hot sun. 'Tain't a woman's place."

"Did you have a good trip this time?" I inquired.

" 'Bout the same as usual." His face lighted up. "We did see one thing worth a long day's voyage. Fawn triplets. I've seen plenty of twins, but this is the first time I ever see triplets. It was a real pretty sight. Wal—I gotta get back to the salt mines." He went aft, and in a minute I heard him saying, "Look at the loon! No, right over there. Whoops, there he goes. Now watch yonder, in line with that cedar stump. That's where he'll come up. You see, loons always come up in the direction they was facin' when they dived. They can't turn around under water. See? There he is."

"Isn't he wonderful?" a feminine voice breathed; and I thought, You can say that again, Lady. Because she only knew the half of it. She had no suspicion that the John who knew loons couldn't turn around under water was only a façade for John, the solid citizen who worked in his garden until dark and got up at dawn to paint his new porch. You had to know both Johns really to appreciate him.

9

The Old She-Coon

In what my children call "the olden days," which may mean a time not more than eight years gone, lumbering was a very different proposition than it is now in this country. Those were the days of the bigger jobbers, the men who undertook on their own responsibility and cognizance to log off for the company a tract of company-owned timberland at a set price per cord for wood landed. They supplied their own equipment, met their own pay-rolls, built and ran their own camps, and used their own methods. A jobber's success depended on the soundness of his judgment, based on experience and the reports of his cruisers, when he put in his bid to the company. If he made no great error in estimating the amount of pulpwood available in a given area, or in the operating cost of his camp, or in the expense of hauling to the landing, the probability was that he would make a lot of money.

A cruiser's report can be taken at face value. If he says, after walking through the woods and observing the size and density of the blackgrowth, that the area in question will yield fifty thousand cords, you can safely assume that it will yield just about fifty thousand cords; because the cruiser is an expert, and his continuance in his job rests upon his infallibility. Any experienced jobber does not make mistakes about operating costs. He has the figures at his fingertips. He does not make mistakes either about the hauling, although it was the hauling that most often licked a jobber, for reasons that I'll explain shortly.

The contract with the company always specified that the wood would be paid for after it was delivered at the landing, which in this country is always a river or lake. The teamsters dumped it on the ice, and there the jobber's responsibility ended. Along toward spring, the company crews came in and strung booms around the winter's cut, to keep it from drifting away when the ice went out; and as soon as the lakes were clear and the wood was water-borne, it was driven to the mills fifty or a hundred miles away in New Hampshire, down the Androscoggin. But it was—and is—the jobber's business to get it from where it stood in the woods to where it was to lie on the ice. Obviously a short down-hill haul is better and cheaper than a long haul over a mountain, and a good jobber knows how many cents per cord per mile he should add on to his price to the company for the landed wood. The catch —as is always the case in any enterprise in this country, be it raising a row of radishes or running a resort hotel—is the weather, one of the few things over which the individual has no control.

Here we average, year in and year out, an aggregate snowfall of one hundred and ten inches, or almost ten feet. Of course this doesn't all lie on the ground at once, but in spite of thaws and settling, in the normal year we never see bare ground between November and April, and there is at any time three or four feet of snow coverage. This is absolutely essential to the success of a lumbering operation. Wood can't be hauled on bare ground, and roads can't be built, except at prohibitive cost, without snow. A hauling road through the woods is a remarkable thing, to me at least. The terrain here is very rough, little more than a gigantic heap of enormous boulders pushed up by the ice cap and left where it lay by the recession of the great glacier, to be covered with a thin layer of leaf mold and soil. Great pits lie between the boulders and big trees thrust up among them. When the ground is bare, it's difficult even to walk through the woods, off the trails, let alone drive a team of horses and a sled through them. The snow changes all that. The boss decides where the roads are to run and sets to work a crew of daymen. First they cut down the trees that stand in the way, and then they fill the pits with brush and anything else they can lay hands on. Then when the snow comes, they shovel it in and trample it down until the road is as level as a floor and frozen as hard as concrete. Of course, when spring comes and the snow melts, the road vanishes into thin air; but it has served its purpose.

The best road I ever saw in the woods was one Roy Bragg had running the mile from Sunday Pond to Sunday Cove. He kept a crew working on it all the time, leveling the sunken spots, watering the ruts in places where the going was hard, and spreading road-hay on the slippery down-pitches, where a heavy load might overrun the horses. Road-hay has to be spread every day, because the deer come out and eat it every night, and shaken up between loads, because it gets trodden down and slick. Roy's road was so good that it inspired his teamsters to run a contest as to who could haul the largest load without sluicing his team. I sat all one afternoon with the scaler in the office, waiting for the teams to come down the valley and pause in the camp yard, so that the load could be scaled, before going along to the landing. The scaler and I were not the only ones who rushed out of the overheated little tar-paper shacks into the pinching dry cold of the clearing when we heard the jangle of harness and the shouts of the teamsters approaching. Doors slammed everywhere, and the entire stay-at-home personnel of the camp—the cook and cookees and bull-cook, the clerk and stamper and feeders—all streamed out to stand shivering while the scale was taken. The winner that afternoon brought down six and a half cords behind a team of four wiry, half-wild little bays, who showed the whites of their eyes and blew out their breaths through red-lined nostrils as they leaned into the collars and pawed for purchase with their sharp-shod hooves. Six and a half cords of green wood is a lot to haul on one load, and everyone cheered the stouthearted little team when the scale was read. It was exciting and somehow moving.

An open winter, such as we sometimes get, made it impossible for a jobber to build roads like that, and the result was likely to be that spring found him with half his cut still piled back in the woods, and the company adamant on the subject of paying for pulp as yet unlanded. This wasn't as serious as it sounds, in practice. The wood wasn't going to spoil in a year, and it wasn't eating its head off. The jobber could go back the next year and haul it out, and in the meantime it served as collateral if he had to borrow money, as he usually did. Things were different in those olden days of twenty years ago. It was easy to raise money, and if the jobber went into the red this year, next year he'd probably clean up twenty thousand dollars. Business was more of a gamble then, and the jobbers acted like gamblers. They tightened their belts and borrowed a stake at the end of a bad season, and at the end of a good one they rode around in Packard Straight Eights and their women wore mink. And it was in those days that Bill Greenwood—only he was Bill Boisvert then, just as Joe Field was Joe de la Pasture—married Frances, a Canadian woman with a dash of Indian blood.

Then times changed, and the jobber had greater obstacles to overcome than the vagaries of the weather. Federal regulations made the borrowing of money from the banks more difficult, and the Federal income tax devoured larger and larger slices of the good years' profits. The flow of cheap labor from across the border was cut off. You could still bring men over, but only under bond, and these bonded men—or Canadian prisoners, as they were, with fair accuracy, called—were often more bother than they were worth. They got into trouble, breaking the game laws or being drunk and disorderly, and had to be rescued from jail; and when it came time to return them to Canada, sometimes they couldn't be found. New wage and hour laws were enacted, although because lumbering comes under the same heading as agricultural and seasonal employment, this didn't affect the logging as much as it did some other industries. But it had some effect, as did the new state health regulations of camps, and the Social Security acts. The days when a jobber was absolute monarch in his own territory were over. He now had to do what one Government or another said, and it was a hard lesson to learn for men who had never taken orders from anyone. In addition to all that, the good places had been logged off, leaving only those areas where the timber was so difficult of access that it would take a very smart man to job it at a profit.

One by one the big jobbers, whose names had been synonymous with power and wealth, who were almost legends in the country, folded. Roy Bragg, who had for sentiment's sake kept on his pay-roll a roistering, bawdy crew of old lumberjacks and river-hogs past their working days, is dead and most of his bravos are on old-age pensions. Silas Huntoon, a deceptively mild and gentle-mannered man whom his woodsmen loved, broke his heart and lost his shirt on the ledges of Grafton Notch, trying to run an impossible operation among the sparse growth and icy cliff-faces of that evil place. He lives alone now in a great old house, not speaking to anyone, adrift in some world of his own. The Thurstons are gone, one crushed by a runaway sled and the other helpless in bed. A few of the others work for the company now, running the camps on wages under company auspices, little more than straw-bosses, no longer solely responsible for the success or failure of the job, no longer very much interested. It was only a matter of time, everyone said, before Bill Greenwood went the way of the rest.

But Bill Greenwood didn't fold. Instead he took a job down in South Arm, and built a big camp on a narrow bench above the lake, with the abrupt shore dropping into the deep and quiet waters almost from the office steps, and the mountain rising steep and forbidding behind the cookhouse. The whole Arm is a forbidding place in winter at best. There the mountains around the lake draw together until they pinch it off into nothing at the Pocket. You can feel them closing in on you as you come down from the open lake above, almost— or so it seems to me—like the jaws of a trap. The late-rising sun of winter never clears the east wall of the mountains until almost noon, and then marches briefly across the slit of sky to drop behind the west ridge and leave the place to a long and cheerless twilight. You can stand in the Arm at three o'clock in the afternoon and see sunlight golden on the ice two miles to the north, where the lake spreads out; but it looks like a picture of another, happier country from where you shiver in a bone-chilling gloom. The knife-edged wind howls down from the northwest, driving before it towering spectres of loose snow, keening and moaning as it comes. It's a hard-bitten, ill-visaged place, and it's the place where Frances Greenwood came to live for two winters.

I met her first in October. The Arm isn't so bad at that time of year. Some of the autumn coloring still clings to the hardwood trees, flaming against the blackgrowth on the mountain sides, and the westering sun shines on the east shore, where Larry's dock is, until quite late in the afternoon. The lake is a deep indigo laced with half-hearted whitecaps, and the sky is an azure vault. Frances could have no premonition of the rigors to come, even if she had been simply sitting, as I was, waiting for the boat to be loaded. She wasn't. She was supervising the loading of half a ton of food and a bunch of drunken woodsmen. Most crews come into the woods drunk, having fortified themselves against the great drought to come, and they often constitute a problem. They were no problem to Frances. She stood there, short and square in wool breeches, high-laced boots, and a lumberman's jacket, looking all Indian with her flat cheekbones and straight black hair, and issued curt orders, sometimes in English and sometimes in French. Larry and Swene had been standing by to lend a hand in case she needed help, but they soon went back to their own business, confident that she could handle the situation.

A bandy-legged little Frenchman with a knocked-down bucksaw frame under his arm came over to me and started telling me how pretty I was; he was well lubricated and obviously seeing things through an extremely rosy haze. Before I could gather my surprised wits, Frances was beside him, quick and light-footed as a cat. She snapped her fingers and pointed to a bench. "Shut up and sit down," she said quietly. He shut up and sat down. "I'm sorry," she apologized. "He's been drinking. They behave themselves when they're sober, but when they're drunk—" She shrugged expressively. "I'm sorry he bothered you."

"He didn't bother me any," I assured her. "After living more than ten years in the woods, it would take more than a drunken woodsman to bother me. I've seen too many of them. They're harmless."

She smiled quickly. Her teeth were very white. "Then you must be Mrs. Parsons or Mrs. Rich."

"Mrs. Rich. And you're Mrs. Greenwood." We exchanged amenities, and she went back to work. She was too busy restraining her crew from falling overboard to indulge in conversation, until the boat slacked speed and edged in close to the shore under the camp. The landing lay in the shadow of the mountain, and the water was black and still as a pool of ink, with a few red maple leaves floating on it. The air was chilly here, but there was something rather cheerful about the way the light of the kerosene lamps glowed in the windows of the buildings and a handful of men streamed down the bank to meet the boat. She got her crew safely ashore without anyone's wetting more than his feet, and turned her attention to a young man with a pencil over his ear and a clipboard on his arm, the badges of office of the clerk. They started checking the load as it was put ashore.

"Where's Bill?" he asked. "Didn't he come back with you?"

She finished a count she was making before she answered.

"A dozen cases of milk— No; he'll be In Friday." She turned to Larry. "You won't forget to pick him up Friday?"

Larry said, "Nope, I won't forget. Friday. I'll get your beef from Armours at the same time. All set? Then we've got to be getting along."

The clerk cast off the mooring lines, and she called to me over the widening strip of water, "Stop in and see me when you go past. Any time. The coffee pot is always on." I said I would, and returned the invitation.

After we were out of earshot, Larry shook his head. "Bill Greenwood has gone to the hospital for a check-up. I hope he makes it back by Friday. She probably knows what she's doing."

"She probably does," I agreed. "She looks competent to me. But what about the job? Who's in charge if Bill's away?"

Larry shrugged. "I guess she is. Seems like an awful lot for her to take on, managing that bunch of halligans. Running a lumber camp's no job for any woman. It's too hard. But it'll only be till Friday."

That's what he thought. Oh, Bill came In Friday, all right, but he was a sick man and by the time he'd recovered enough to take an interest in practical matters, the habit of Frances' authority had been established. It was to her that the cook came when he needed another crate of eggs, although she was as apt as not to say, "All right. But you're using too many eggs. I want you to cut down. There's no need of twenty-egg cake every day. Ten-egg cake is good enough." A ten-egg cake, in a lumber camp where food is prepared in pro-digious quantities and a bushel-batch is a standard frying of doughnuts, is about the equivalent of a normal two-egg cake. Frances ran the cookhouse as most housewives run their own kitchens, watching the butter and the eggs and the left-overs like a hawk, trying to establish a truce between economy and ample, appetizing meals. This sounds like the Bride's First Lesson, but it was against all woods tradition, where the food is always good and plentiful, but the waste is often terrific. Most woods cooks don't bother too much about costs. They operate on the theory that the boss is rich, and probably too busy to notice a spoiled side of mutton here or fifty pounds of lard more or less there. Frances wouldn't tolerate needless waste, and her cook knew it, but still he kept on bringing his problems to her rather than to Bill. He ended by boasting of the low-cost kitchen he ran. "Twenty-seven cents a head a day," he'd say. "And meat every meal. Can't many do better'n that." Since lumberjacks have enormous appetites, he was without doubt right.

But it wasn't only in domestic matters, which might very well come under Frances' management, that her word prevailed. Bill was still nominally the boss, but he was often away, and when a man wanted a job, it was to Frances that he applied as often as not. There is a tale about her method of hiring a man. The story is that she'd hand him her own ax, which always had an edge like a razor, and a piece of hardwood and tell him to split it fine.

"There's the chopping block," she'd say, indicating a flat block of granite near the office door. Unless he could split the wood without putting a nick in the blade, he couldn't handle an ax well enough to work for her.

"But she's fair," the woodsman who told me this tale admitted. "A joker come in the other day and wanted to be hired on. She give him the ax and the junk of firewood, like always, and he flew at it. Split it up fine as matchwood without turnin' the edge a hair, so she told him he was hired. Then he hauled off and braced his feet and brung that there ax down on the stone with all his might. It'll be a long day before that ax cuts any more wood. She was a mite put out, because naturally nobody wants their good ax ruined, so she asked him what the cryin' hell he meant by that foolishness. 'I'll tell you, ma'am,' he says, cool as you please. 'When I get through with an ax, I always leave it in the choppin' block,' and he picked up his frock and started walkin' away, because he figured he was fired before he was rightly hired. She kept him on, though. Said 'twas her own fault, that she'd asked for it."

My informant offered to show me the block of granite used as a testing ground as proof of his story, but I told him that wouldn't be necessary. I'd made up my mind at about the third sentence that it was apocryphal. But like most apocryphal tales, it had its basis in truth. Frances was a hard woman to please, and an eminently just woman in her dealings.

Whenever a new man came into camp, she herself took him up on the mountain and showed him where he was to cut. On an operation, you don't just go out and cut where you want to. You cut where the boss tells you to. The entire area has already been divided into workable units before the job starts, by the boss, who sometimes spots lines to show the divisions and sometimes carries them in his head. During the time when Bill was going to come In Friday, Frances had laid out all the cuts, so I suppose she was the logical one to take charge of that department. It does make a difference to a man where he cuts. In some places the goin' is good, as the lumberjacks say. They mean that the trees are large and bunched, so they can make a good wage at piece rates. Sometimes the goin' is lousy. The blackgrowth is scattered and interspersed with hardwood. A man can work all day hard, and never put up a full cord. In that case he may prefer to work on day, rather than piece, rates. It's not permissible to skip the poor spots and cut only where the goin' is good. When a jobber undertakes to log an area, he must cut it clean. The good jobber tries to divide his territory so that everyone has about the same chance —some good and some poor cutting. This keeps the men satisfied and reduces labor turnover, which is costly in any industry. Frances' turnover was low, so I guess she did a good job in laying out the cuts.

The telephone line which connects Middle Dam with the Outside crosses the Arm below the Greenwood camp and runs along the foot of the mountain on the west shore. One day I wanted to call up someone on the Outside, so I went up to Middle to use the Parsonses' second phone. Mine is just a woods phone, on a private wire that runs about fifteen miles from Middle Dam to the Brown Farm, and I can't talk to the Outside over it. The Parsonses have two phones, one like mine and another, beside it on the wall, that connects with Andover. It's a fascinating arrangement, especially when they both ring at the same time and you have to conduct two conversations at once, like a city editor or a movie mogul. This day I asked Al if I might use her Outside phone, and she said I could try, but it probably wouldn't do any good, as the line seemed to be out of order and was deader than a haddock.

"This is the third time this week that something's been wrong with it. Larry's gone down along the line to see if he can find the trouble. Stick around a while. He ought to be back pretty soon, and maybe he'll have fixed it."

So I stuck around, eating hot cookies and gossiping, and by and by Larry came in and threw his pliers, come-along, and other line-repairing tools on the wood-box. He was in a fine frame of mind, laughing to himself like a loony. "The line's fixed," he said. "I guess it'll stay that way now, barring Acts of God."

"What was the matter with it, and what are you giggling about?" Al wanted to know.

"Nothing special. Frances Greenwood tickles me, that's all." He picked up a handful of cookies and started eating them. "I found out what the trouble was as soon as I got down to Bill's works. The wire's strung low all the way along there, not more'n four feet off the ground, which is all right, because it's easy-reached and usually not in anybody's way. But it's too low to drive a horse under, so instead of propping it up with a pole as they ought to—there's plenty of slack; they could do it easy enough—those lazy jokers just cut it."

"Well, that's a hell of a thing to do," I commented elegantly.

"Yeah, that's what Frances thought. I was giving them my opinions on the subject when she came along. She keeps a pretty snug watch on what's going on. She's in the woods most of the time. Nobody loafs much on that job. The old she-coon's right on their tails all the time."

"The old she-coon" is not a term of disrespect in this country; or at least, I hope it's not. My children and employees often call me that when I go on the warpath. I hope it means what I think it does; the woman in charge.

"What's Bill doing all day long?" Al wanted to know, her tone bristling with sex solidarity. "Sitting home with his feet in the oven?"

"Bill's a sick man," he said. "I don't know what ails him. Maybe he's got ulcers, or diabetes, or high blood-pressure. I don't know. He looks like the Wrath-to-Come, whatever it is. Anyhow," he continued, reaching for another cookie, "along comes Frances and wants to know what the trouble is, so I told her. Did she blow her top! Climbed up one side of them and down the other. Crimus, she sure knows all the words and how to use them!" His tone was awed and respectful. "I wouldn't have dared to say the things she said to them. They'd have beat the tar out of me."

"How did they take it from her?" Al wanted to know.

"Oh, they said yes'm and no'm. Maybe it's partly because most of them wouldn't take a poke at a woman anyhow; but it's more than that, too. They're afraid of her. I don't blame them. I'm damn sure I wouldn't want to tangle with her, when she gets red-headed. She's a rugged hunk of woman, and she isn't afraid of the devil himself. That's the best-run camp I ever saw. There's less trouble there, and more work done, than in any other camp in the district. And I'll pretty near guarantee there won't be any more telephone lines cut."

And there weren't.

I stopped in there one day near the end of February. I'd been Out to see the kids, and Larry had to put in at the camp to leave the mail and some supplies. I was just as well pleased, since I was half-frozen from sitting on an open sled behind the slow-pacing horses in the sub-zero wind. Larry went into the office to deliver the mail, and I ran across the icy yard to knock on the door of the one-room shack that was Bill's and Frances' own. A voice called to me to come in, so I tore open the door, whirled inside, and slammed it behind me against the cold.

You hear a lot about Woman's Touch, and the softening influence it exercises on the most uncompromising surroundings. If this were fiction, I'd be telling you about frilled curtains at the windows of that bare little room, about geraniums blooming on window sills, and bright covers on the bunks. There'd probably be a sweet-grass sewing-basket overflowing with filmy this-and-thats somewhere around, and in all likelihood a transfigured Frances would be swishing gracefully about in a flame-colored velvet hostess gown. I'm sorry, but this is Life. The room was as bare as a barracks, and as neat. The plain gray blankets on the bunks were pulled tight and unwrinkled, the uncurtained windows shone, and you could have eaten off the floor. A few clothes hung on pegs along the wall, and in the corner by the door stood an ax, a crosscut saw, and a pair of snowshoes. There were some magazines and an ash-tray arranged neatly on a plank table, foot-lockers shoved under the bunks, and some homemade straight chairs and three-legged stools against the walls. The only wall decoration was a large poster explaining in French, English, and Russian the first principles of First Aid, and the dainty scrap of needlework in this case was a wooden cheese firkin full of rough gray socks to be mended. A large kerosene lamp with a reflector hung from the ceiling, and a little pot-bellied stove glowed cherry-red in the middle of the floor. They were the quarters of a person too busy to fuss with nonessentials, and probably too tired, at the end of the day, to do more than fall into bed.

Frances, clad in her usual costume of wool pants and a buffalo-checked shirt, was seated on a stool under the lamp, her head bent over the hand of a woodsman who was sitting on another. "This clumsy one," she said to me. "This know-nothing. First he cuts his hand and then he neglects it. No thanks to him it doesn't have to be taken off. And how would you like that, eh?" Her fingers moved gently and surely about the wound, bathing it, probing, applying salve.

The woodsman looked at me sheepishly, grimacing a little as the ointment bit. "It was an accident," he said. "Could have happened to anyone, and not worth fussin' about anyhow. Don't mind what she says. She's got an awful bark, but her bite—"

"What do you know about my bite? Have I bitten you yet? When I do, you'll know it." She started winding bandage expertly. "There, now get out of here. Vamoos. Next time you do a thing like that, you'll get your walking papers."

The woodsman picked up his hat from the floor. "She means it, too," he told me. "She don't fool around." He moved to the door. "But one thing I'll say for the old she-coon, if you're sick or hurt, she sure can be awful good to you."

"Thanks for nothing," Frances said. "What good would a camp full of cripples be to me?" But she smiled a little as the door closed behind the man. "It's good to see you, Mrs. Rich. How did you find the children?"

I said they were wonderful, and inquired for her health and Bill's. I'd seem him at the Arm when I went Out, and he didn't look at all well to me.

"Oh, me, I'm always well, like a horse. But my poor man! He can't get rid of that cough and he's miserable all over." Her eyes clouded. "The doctors don't help him. When it comes spring, I'll fix him up. I'll find the things to mend him, when the snow goes. I'll brew him up a tea that'll put hair on his chest, like my grandmother taught me." She brooded a moment and then said briskly, "Supper'll be soon. You'll stay and eat, you and Mr. Parsons?"

I said that I was sorry, but I didn't think that we could. It was already getting dark, and I'd still have two miles to snow-shoe after I got to Middle Dam, and my fire would probably be out and my house cold.

"Another time, then," she said, and I suddenly liked her a lot. She didn't try to talk me out of doing what I said I had to do, and she didn't go into a routine about "But you aren't going to walk all that way through the woods in the dark *alone!*" It was nice for once to find someone who took it for granted that I knew what I was about. I wasn't half the woman Frances Greenwood was, and I never would be; but it was heartening to have her treat me as an equal.

"She's an awfully nice woman," I said to Larry when we were out on the lake again.

"Yup, she is that. Plays a good hand of poker, too. I've been down a couple of nights to sit in on their games. She's taken two-three dollars off me. I don't like female poker players as a rule. They always want to play deuces and one-eyed Jacks wild, and that's no kind of a game. Not Frances, though. She comes across when she loses, too. Most women expect you to pay when you lose, and forget it when they do." He looked at me sideways, but I didn't rise. He could have been right. Card games bore me so that I never play them, so I wouldn't know.

Instead I said, "But how does she maintain discipline if she fraternizes with the men? If that's the heading playing poker with them comes under."

He laughed. "Don't worry about her discipline. Nobody steps over the line. Couple of weeks ago I stopped in with the mail, and I was getting my feet warm in the cookhouse when hell broke loose in the bar-room." (In the woods, that simply means the bunkhouse. For some reason the term "bunk-house" is considered as sissified as "venison" for deer-meat and "blaze" for spot a trail.) "The cook and I went running out, but Frances was ahead of us. She busted into the bar-room with an ax-handle swinging, laying it on right and left, not bothering to ask any questions and not pulling any punches, either. When she cracked a head, she cracked a head, what I mean. She sure broke up that fight in no-time flat. I never saw a meeker bunch than that gang of hellions was when she got through with them, in about thirty seconds. She didn't waste any breath bawling them out when it was over, either. Just stood there, swinging that ax-handle in her hand and looking at them. Finally she asked, 'Anybody got anything he wants to say?' They just looked at the floor and shuffled their feet. After a minute she said, 'All right, then,' and went out and shut the door. By the time she got over to where the cook and I were standing with our mouths open, she was laughing her head off. She's a great Frances."

She certainly was. During that year and the next, three other jobbers in this vicinity went broke, but Bill Greenwood stayed in the black, and nobody had any doubts as to whom the credit belonged.

The last time I ever saw Frances Greenwood was on a March day down at South Arm. I was going to ride Out with Larry and Al to spend Easter with the children, and we'd walked the four miles down from Middle Dam on the ice, enjoying the scenery and the thin brightness of the spring sun. The thermometer stood a little above zero, but there was no wind and we were dressed in the winter uniform of the country, ski pants and sheepskins, so we were very comfortable—comfortable enough, in fact, so that we didn't stop in at Greenwoods' to get warm, as we usually did. We saw sled tracks leading across the snow from the camp to the Arm, so we concluded that some of the crew must be going Out, too; and when we were about half a mile from Larry's landing, we saw a cluster of black specks that were people milling around the garages. As we drew nearer, Al snatched off her sunglasses, which we all wear as protection against the terrible glare from the snow.

"Hey, Louise," she said. "Am I going woods queer at last, or do you see what I see?"

I looked, and took off my glasses and looked again. "Who in the world—? Al, if anyone's crazy, it isn't us. Where did she come from? She'd better go back there, wherever it is, before she dies of exposure." Because we were looking at a very smartly dressed woman, a sight to see indeed on the shore of the Arm in the winter. She had on a sheered beaver jacket, a dark wool dress, and a silly and enchanting little hat all covered with flowers.

"Hello," she said, and then we saw that it was Frances Greenwood. She'd let her hair grow, and now it wasn't crowwing black any more, but streaked with gray. She looked very distinguished indeed, as though she were Somebody—as in fact she was, if anybody ever was.

"We didn't know you in your Outside clothes," I said. "You look lovely!"

"Thank you." She smoothed her white suede gloves. "I feel foolish. It's been so long since I've worn regular clothes, but we're going down to spend Easter with our son, and I don't want him to be ashamed before his wife's folks." She laughed and looked down at her sheer silk stockings. "I feel as if I was naked, after wearing breeches all winter."

"Aren't you cold?" I asked, but she said she wasn't. She'd come down on the sled, wrapped in blankets.

"The camp's about closed," she said. "The clerk can finish up. We won't be In again."

"But we'll see you next year!" Al exclaimed.

"No, we won't be back at all. We've decided to get out of the logging business. We've done pretty well, and we've saved some money. We're buying a boarding house down-country, and we're going to run that for a change. It'll be a lot easier."

Al and I said that that was fine; that the life she had been leading was much too hard for any woman.

Just then Bill joined us to say that he had the car shoveled out of the garage and ready to go. I'd never happened to have seen him and Frances together before, and I was surprised at the way Frances looked up at him with eyes as soft and liquid as a doe's, and a little wild-rose flush on her high cheekbones.

"That's what the Boss says," she told us. "I wanted to go on for at least another winter. I don't mind life in a camp. But the Boss says, 'Let the company finish the cut.' He says it's time I had it easier, and what the Boss says, goes." And Bill's chest expansion increased by inches as he took her arm to help her over the roughness of the road; to help Frances Greenwood, the old she-coon, who could cross the worst ridge in the country faster than any man alive, over a few measly little ruts and humps of snow!

"We'll miss you!" Al and I called after her truthfully, and then we looked at each other and back to where she was clinging to his arm, picking her way and exclaiming fearfully and smiling up into his face. We didn't have to say what was in both our minds. There was no doubt about it at all. Frances Greenwood was a smart woman.

10

A Policeman's Lot

In this country, we are probably the least policed group of people in the world, with the possible exception of the native tribes back in the hills of places like New Guinea. Our conduct—like theirs, I presume—is governed by expediency and our own good sense, rather than by the outside pressure of the law. It isn't very sensible or expedient to subject your neighbor to murder, theft, or arson, just because he can't yell for the cop on the corner. He could turn right around and do even worse to you, and obviously a state of anarchy would soon ensue, in which nobody would be either safe or happy. We practice the doctrine of do unto others, not because of religious conviction, but because we have found it to be the only rule under which a reasonably good life is possible. We don't necessarily have to love our neighbors, but we do have to treat them decently; and it is an interesting fact that usually the people whom you start out by being decent to on principle, you end by liking in practice. I don't know whether this system would work on a universal scale or not, and since there is very little likelihood of the experiment's being tried, I'm not bothering my head about it. It's enough for me that it works here.

Of course, we are technically subject to the general law of the State of Maine, so once in a while we have to evoke the legal forces. In the case of a violent or sudden death, for example, we have to call the sheriff and the coroner. This sounds a little terrifying, but since the sheriff is Bob Milton, whom we've all known for years, and the coroner is nice old Dr. Greene, who has seen the children through infected blisters and tonsilitis, you can dismiss whatever pictures of police grillings have been forming in your mind. With perfect courtesy and great consideration, they ask whatever questions are pertinent, formulate their opinion, and go back to where they came from. The only other officers of the law we ever see are the game and fire wardens, and in winter, when the woods are so deep under snow that you couldn't start a forest fire if you tried, we don't even have a fire warden.

For a while I was in the bad graces of our game warden, Leon Wilson, because I once stated in the public prints that he was handsome and romantic-looking. I don't think he believed that I was buttering him up so that he would take a broad-minded view of any infractions of the law I might be contemplating. And I wasn't either. In the first place, I knew better. Any time he thought I needed it, he'd just as soon arrest me as look at me; me, or the President of the United States. In the second place, among the few laws of the land that I wouldn't break if I felt like it and thought I could get away with it are the game laws. I believe in them. No, the reason he objected to my remarks was purely professional. He felt that I had undermined his authority. He didn't like having incipient poachers addressing him as Glamour-puss or Gorgeous. I'd feel a lot worse about the whole thing if I thought I had really done him an injury. As it happens, I am perfectly confident that he can handle with neatness and dispatch any situation which might arise from my remarks. All I was trying to do at the time of writing was a piece of accurate reporting.

That's what I'm still trying to do, so I guess I'll have to jeopardize our re-established amicable relations by saying again that I think Leon is handsome. He is tall and lean and dark, with a tough, competent, hard-bitten way about him, and he wears his uniform with a swashbuckling air. He looks like a modern pirate, but actually he is the father of four, including a pair of twins, and a conscientious, capable, indefatigable officer of the law. His official duties, as far as the Parsonses and I are concerned, aren't too wearing. The first time after New Year's that he sees us, he writes down the numbers of our new guides' licenses, which carry with them hunting and fishing privileges, in his little black note-book. This is so that we won't have to carry them with us for the rest of the year, as the law insists. It's an obvious legal provision, but in our cases not a very practical one. Most of us are continually falling into the river by mistake or wading into the lake on purpose to help launch a boat, and any documents in our hip pockets would shortly disintegrate under that treatment. As Leon once pointed out to me, it is not his business to make people's lives miserable over the picayune letter of the law, but to see that the spirit is observed. This was on an occasion when I had hooked and landed a short salmon, and he happened to be present.

Usually a fish is hooked through the membrane surrounding its mouth, a thin, tough, parchment-like tissue without any blood veins in it, and can be taken off the hook with no damage done to it. Occasionally, as in this case, the hook penetrates the flesh and it's impossible to remove it without causing bleeding. I said to Leon, "I suppose I've got to throw this fish back, since it's under legal size; but I might as well tell you right now that if you weren't here, I'd keep it. It's bleeding, and it's going to die anyhow." Even if a fish is bleeding only a little, it does die very soon after you return it to the water, and floats belly-up and malodorous in some back eddy until it rots away.

He inspected the fish. "I guess it is," he said. "That being the case, you might as well kill it and get some good out of it, instead of having it go to waste." So I tapped it smartly at the base of the skull with a sheath-knife handle, and cooked and ate it for lunch. That's what I call being a sensible cop.

Once he has taken our license numbers, Leon can wipe off his official expression, sit down with a cup of coffee, relax and tell us the news. He covers a large territory and has sources of information denied us, isolated as we are. He knows who isn't speaking to whom in Upton and why, and where those people who used to live on the Byron Road moved to. We consider him a friend who happens to wear a uniform, rather than a policeman; and in my case, the fact that I once bought a secondhand kerosene refrigerator from his mother-in-law, through his kind offices, forms a sort of third-cousinly family tie. He annually inquires, for the former owner, as to the health of the refrigerator; and since I can always report happily that it never causes me a moment's worry and is the best buy I ever made, as I honestly don't know how I'd get along without it, an aura of general good feeling is generated. Then I start picking his brains, because in my business gold is where you find it, and he knows and has done a lot of things that I can use. He's aware of my intentions, but he doesn't seem to mind. I once wrote a book for teen-age boys, based partly on stories that Leon had told me. It was kindly received by reviewers and actually won a literary prize, which I found extremely gratifying. My real triumph came, however, when Leon read it and informed me that he hadn't found one technical or factual error in it. I was *really* set up about that.

When Leon was young and didn't know any better, so he says, he was one of the worst poachers in the State of Maine. At that time he lived up near Fort Kent, along the Canadian border, and if anyone thinks it's uncivilized where we live, he ought to go up there. That's really wild country, so wild that even the wardens pay no attention to the Sunday hunting law. Most of the time they don't even know it's Sunday; and if they did, it wouldn't make any difference. The Sunday law isn't necessary up there. It's not a blue law, contrary to common belief, but simply a precautionary measure against race suicide. Sunday is the only day that lots of people are free to hunt—people who work in mills and offices—and but for the Sunday law, the woods would be full of trigger-happy individuals, popping away at anything that stirred without stopping to determine whether it was four-legged, two-legged, or merely a breeze in a bush. This law is a little hard on the regularly employed lovers of the chase, but not as hard as a bullet through the head would be. The woods along the border, though, are too remote to be accessible to Sunday-only hunters, so the law has been allowed to fall more or less into abeyance.

But the classes with more leisure at their disposal can and do take time off to go on a week's hunting trip that far from the beaten track. Sometimes they are not too successful in bagging any quarry, so on the day before they must start for home, they'll go looking for an amenable native who will sell them a deer. This is strictly against the law, and all parties involved are liable to severe punishment if caught. However, since the price of a deer is ten dollars and up, and since ten dollars is a lot of money back here in the sticks, a lively traffic in dead deer does exist, and Leon used to be an especially successful operator. He told me once that it is one of the seven wonders of the modern world that he was never caught. He used to have as many as six or eight deer strung up on a cross-pole just a little way back in the forest from where he lived, and if anyone came asking to buy one, he'd take them out there and let them have their pick. He didn't bother much about their credentials, but simply trusted to instinct to warn him which strangers were all right and which were either disguised officers or stool pigeons. He was just lucky that his instinct was so good.

Finally, in desperation possibly, the V.I.P.'s decided to put him on the other side of the fence by making him a warden. Probably they figured, so Leon says, that there's nothing like setting a thief to catch a thief, so to speak, and this time they were absolutely right. His really extraordinary talents, diverted into the channels of the right, and the instinct that used to inform him when the law was near now just as unerringly communicates the presence of lawlessness to him. Of people who look and act like perfectly upright citizens to me, he will say, "I don't know what they're up to *yet*, but there's something off-color there." Sooner or later he catches them with the evidence upon them. Then some thuggish-looking character whom I wouldn't trust around the first bend in the river comes along, and Leon says, "Him? He's okay." And it turns out that he is. I don't know how

Leon does it, but I suspect that he smells poachers, just as a dog can tell by the sense of smell who is afraid of him.

But all this was a long time ago and is probably just as well forgotten, except that it illustrates the point that once a renegade doesn't necessarily mean always a renegade. Leon continued as a good and able warden up along the Allegash and St. John rivers until the day came, as it must to all of us backwoods parents, when his children reached school age. We are then, all of us, faced with a choice of parting with our offspring for ten months of the year—if we can find a suitable place for them to live, with wise and responsible people, which is not as easy as it may sound—or of moving with them to civilization. The Wilsons chose to move, so Leon asked for a transfer, and now they live over in Newry. I think he still feels a little homesick for the border, judging by the way he talks about life up there. He sounds exactly the way I feel when I'm away from here and get to thinking that the river is still curling over the ledges, and the big mossy rock by my door still acts as pivot for its arcing shadow as the sun goes over from east to west, and the pines across the rapids still toss their cone-heavy heads against the windy sky, and I'm not there to see. It's a desolate feeling, and he has my sympathy. What he misses most, I guess, is his dogs. Up in that country the warden uses a dog team to get around in winter, but of course in this time and place that isn't necessary; and I don't care what anyone says, you simply cannot become as attached to a jeep as you can to a bunch of big, vicious-looking, loving-hearted huskies. I know, because I used to have a dog team myself, and I adored every one of the brutes.

The game warden's duties consist primarily of seeing that the game laws are observed, and I would say, off-hand, that

that is a full-time job for any man. Maine is a comparatively poor state and can't afford battalions of wardens, so each man's territory is pretty large and, up here where there are no roads, difficult to cover. He has to depend on canoes to a large extent, and on his feet even more. To complicate matters, it is extremely desirable that he remain as nearly invisible as is possible for the corporeal; so he wastes a great deal of time hiding in thickets or lying flat in swamps, so that the news of his presence in the neighborhood won't be broadcast. By certain elements he is considered Public Enemy Number One, and if he is sighted, the grapevine gets to work.

I was down at the Foot-of-the-Falls one morning, hauling out a canoe that I'd left there, when I saw written in letters three feet tall on a sand bar, for anyone who might be interested to read, "Warden Up the River." It was impossible for anyone landing a boat at the head of the slack water or walking along the bank to miss it. I went home, and late that afternoon Leon came knocking at the kitchen door to see if he could have supper with us.

"Oh, hello," I said. "I've been expecting you."

"And why would you be expecting me? I'm supposed to be over at Sturtevant Pond. At least, I've tried hard to give that impression."

I told him, and the air was pretty blue for a few minutes. Finally he simmered down enough to make sense. "God damn it," he said, "I'd like to know who saw me. I've been after a certain party all summer, and when I found out that they were planning to fish the Rapid River to-day, I thought for sure my time had come. I spent half the night walking through the woods from over in New Hampshire and the rest of it Indian-paddling in the pitch dark across Umbagog. Then I've been lying in the bushes and rocks all day long without a thing to eat, getting cricks in my back and being chewed up by black flies, all for nothing. The party I'm after acted like a bunch of preachers, bending over backward to stay inside the law, when ordinarily they're the damnedest poachers unhung. I knew it wasn't natural, but I couldn't figure out how they could have been tipped off. When I find out who wrote that, I'll—" His discourse reverted to the unprintable, and I learned about several forms of torture that had never come to my attention before.

On the other hand, one October day I was up at Middle Dam visiting with Al Parsons when Leon blew in. "Well, for the love of peace," I said. "The Law, by gum. Hel-*lo*! I haven't laid eyes on a warden since August. I thought you were dead."

"The warden's laid eyes on you, though," he told me in a rather sinister manner. "Several times."

I passed my activities since August in quick mental review and decided that I dared to ask, "What was I doing?"

"Never mind what you were doing," he said darkly. "You weren't breaking the law, anyhow, or you'd have soon found out I was around." That's all he'd tell me, and I don't know yet, and never will know, what I was doing under his surveillance. A good warden keeps his affairs to himself.

The work is hard enough during the fishing season, but it gets harder after the hunting season opens. Then the warden has to work at night as well as during the daytime. An easy, but illegal, way to shoot a deer is to sneak into an old orchard or field after dark with a jack-light, lie in hiding until the deer come down to feed, then turn on the light—

usually a seven-cell flashlight with a reflector—and shoot the deer as he stands bewitched and bedazzled in the glare. This is completely unsporting, of course, besides being unlawful, and arouses the warden's humane, as well as his professional, instincts. So all through the long fall he spends his nights lying out on the frosty ground, courting pneumonia and rheumatism. He also catches quite a grist of malefactors, which is what makes the game worth the candle.

We had an inveterate and highly talented poacher in our midst a few years ago, whom I will call Morgan Twitchell. Leon knew what he was up to, all right, but he was never able to catch him red-handed, a fact which drove him mad with outraged pride. He spent a great deal of time on Morgan, laying traps for him, following him around, and using all his skill to bring him to book. Finally, acting on information and a sixth sense of his own, he had a warrant sworn out and searched the Twitchell home, finding there enough evidence in the form of untagged deer to put Morgan in jail for the rest of the season. Morgan wasn't at home at the time, and he was as well endowed with sixth senses as Leon. Sniffing danger—that's the only way I can account for it—he circled around his house and vanished into the blue. He could have been a wonderful warden, himself; but he was truly incorrigible. He preferred to break the law, to satisfy some craving for adventure, I suppose, and would rather poach a half-starved rabbit than kill legally the fattest buck that ever ran the woods.

A great hue and cry was raised, and everyone for miles around speculated for days as to the whereabouts of Morgan Twitchell, including Catherine, who was working for me, and me. I was spending the weekend out at Rumford Point, where we had rented a house so that the children could attend school, and we were whiling away a Sunday afternoon sitting in the living-room, talking. I said, "I'd just like to know where Morgan is right now." I knew him and I rather liked him. He was a personable and obliging and merry young man, aside from his lawless proclivities.

"Well," Catherine said thoughtfully, staring out the window, "if you *really* want to know, he's just driving into our driveway."

"You're not even a clever liar," I told her, because it didn't seem to me to be very smart to tell a lie that could be quickly exposed by my simply turning my head and looking out the window myself. So I did look out, and there was Morgan crossing the lawn unhurriedly with his wife and son. They knocked at the door and came in, laughing at our exclamations.

"First," said Morgan, "where's the back door, in case I have to leave in a hurry? And second, may we use your telephone? We've been over calling on some relatives in Milton Plantation, and my wife left her glasses there. We want to ask them if they'll mail them to-morrow." The second part of his speech was so at odds with the first, and with my ideas of what a fugitive from justice should have on his mind, that I burst into helpless laughter. When that was over and the phone call had been completed, we sat down to visit over cups of coffee.

"But where have you been?" I asked. "Every warden in three counties has been looking for you for days."

"Sure, I know it. I've seen them. I'll tell you how to keep from being arrested, if you want. Who knows? It might come in handy for you to know sometime. You just find out where the cops are and start following *them* around. They never think to look behind them. I've been on their tails ever since Friday night."

"That's all very well," I said, unimpressed. "But it can't go on forever. Sooner or later, probably sooner, they're going to catch you, so I can't see what you're gaining by playing games with them."

"Oh, sure they'll catch me. I know that. But what I'm gaining is time. I don't want to be pinched until Tuesday," Morgan explained with sweet reasonableness. I've known about some strange compromises with the law since I came to Maine to live, including the case of a casual acquaintance of mine from the next county, whom the sheriff wouldn't arrest for murder until after the sheriff's daughter's marriage, because the suspect was going to be best man, and his arrest would upset the wedding plans and give the mother of the bride one of her famous sick headaches. But I didn't see at first glance why it should make any difference to Morgan whether he were arrested right that minute or two days later, and I said so.

"Well, you see, I haven't tagged my deer yet." We tacitly omitted any reference to the untagged deer found in his house. They'd been confiscated, anyhow. "As soon as they get me, they'll suspend my license until my case comes up in court. If I'm found guilty, they'll take it away altogether, and I can't hunt any more this year. I want a deer to see us through the winter. I can't hunt to-day, with them so hot on my trail, but if I can have to-morrow to hunt legally, I'll guarantee to get my deer. Then I don't care what they do to me."

Morgan overestimated his skill or luck. He didn't get his

deer Monday, and Tuesday they arrested him anyhow. However, his case was dismissed on a legal technicality— poachers usually know more about the law and its loopholes than lawyers do—and he was set free, presumably to continue his evil practices. A week later I saw Leon, who didn't seem to be as full of wrath and frustration as I had anticipated. I'd expected him to be frothing at the mouth at the latest proof of Morgan's wiliness.

"He's not going to be bothering me any more this season," Leon explained. "Didn't you hear? He broke his leg in two places day before yesterday, down at the birch mill. That'll keep him quiet for a while. You know, Louise, sometimes I think there is a certain amount of justice in life, after all."

He crowed too soon. Two weeks later Morgan was riding along in his car with his rifle beside him, not because he hoped to use it but because he felt undressed without it, when a big bear ambled out into the road. Morgan pulled on the hand brake, reached for his crutches, maneuvered himself into the road, loaded his gun, and put a bullet between the animal's eyes. It was a perfectly legal proceeding; but what made Leon speechless with rage was that Morgan collected the usual twenty-five dollar bounty on bear. This Leon thought was adding insult to injury, and I can see how he felt.

The wardens' duties don't end with enforcing the game laws. Among other things they have to check periodically on empty camps to see that they haven't been broken into, recover stolen property like guns and boats, assist the fire wardens and immigration authorities when necessary, and search for lost persons. It keeps them pretty busy, and I am inclined to agree that the policeman's lot, at times, is indeed not a happy one, even if it is occasionally colorful and exciting. One case Leon had a few years ago especially fired my imagination, and I haven't got over it yet.

At that time Bill and Frances Greenwood were running their logging operation down in South Arm, and late one stormy night the clerk came In with thirteen woodsmen that he'd gone Outside to hire. In accordance with custom, he'd found them by making a survey of the bar-rooms and beer joints of the nearest large town, and of course they were all roaring drunk. It was not only dark, but bitterly cold, with a terrible wind driving the snow straight down the lake. The clerk, who was sober, knew that he would never be able to walk his charges the mile across the ice to camp that night, so he herded them into a cabin on the east shore, built them up a good fire, put the least intoxicated man in charge, and went over to get a good night's sleep in his own bed at camp. He needed it after the day he'd put in with his drunks, and he felt sure they'd be all right until someone came over to get them with a sled in the morning.

In the morning there were only twelve men there. The clerk had not made a mistake in counting. He was cold sober, and he wasn't the kind of man who makes mistakes like that. Nobody could have walked back to civilization on a night like that, even if he'd been sober and fresh; and anyhow the missing man never showed up in Andover, the first village. He couldn't have fallen into the lake, because the ice was thirty inches thick, with no holes in it. The only conclusion possible was that he'd gone outside the cabin, become confused, and just wandered around until he was overcome with cold and exhaustion. So Bill Greenwood started yelling for the warden.

The man was never found. Every drift on the lake was

investigated, in spite of the crotch-deep snow; the woods were scoured for two miles around the cabin, and the high banks of snow on both sides of the road were levelled all the way to Cedar Hill. No trace of him was uncovered. It then became the warden's business to send out word asking anyone who knew of the man's whereabouts—or the man himself, in case by some miracle he had survived to gain the Outside— to communicate with the authorities; and here he arrived at another impasse. No one knew who the man was. Usually the woodsmen all know each other. They run into each other continually on various operations or in the bars and dives of the towns where they spend the off-season. But no one had ever seen this man before. Sure, they remembered his being with them in the truck on the way to the lake; and they gave more or less consistent descriptions of him. But no one could remember just when or where he had joined the party, no one had any idea what his name was or where he came from, and everyone insisted that he couldn't have left the cabin at all, because they had a chair wedged under the door latch to keep the wind from blowing it open.

That's all there is to that story. Of course, the woodsmen believe that he wasn't a mortal man at all, and there are times when I'm not sure that I believe he was, either. This is such a strange, wild country, and sometimes when the wind is moaning up the river and the ghostly fingers of the sleet are tapping on the windows— But that's the purest nonsense, of course, considered in the sane light of day! The facts are queer enough without embroidery. *Who* was he, this thirteenth man whose orbit touched ours so briefly; what manner of man? What did he think about, and what was important to him? Where did he go? The problem seduces my mind into endless speculation.

When I first knew Leon, I used to be shy of him. He was so tough and hard-boiled and business-like. He'd come to the door with a look on his face that immediately convinced me that I was guilty. I certainly felt ill-at-ease and constrained enough. After about two years of telling myself not to be silly, that my strength ought to be as the strength of ten because my heart was pure, I got over blushing and stammering whenever I saw him; but I still couldn't feel exactly matey toward him. He seemed so cold-blooded and ruthless and inhuman. And then the Squareheads moved into the Notch.

Grafton Notch is a forbidding place that greatly intrigues me, although I'm happy to say that my experience with it is limited. It's a high pass in the mountains that you have to go over in order to get from the valley of the Androscoggin to the basin of Umbagog. A brook threads through it, and there are starved fields and abandoned orchards and deserted farms squeezed against the road by the towering cliffs on either side. Once it was inhabited, but the early settlers were driven out by the impossibility of making a living there, which has always seemed sad to me. They worked so hard, clearing the land and building their stone walls and low farmhouses; and then even the seasons betrayed them. They discovered that because of the altitude and the walls of the mountains cutting off the sun for all except a few hours in the middle of the day, not a month of the year goes by without bringing a black, killing frost to the Notch. So they had to move away, leaving their homes and their hopes behind them. Most of the buildings have long since fallen down, but one or two of the more sturdily built still stand, their cedar shingles black and curling, their broken windows gaping idiotically. It was into one of these that the Squareheads moved.

What their name really was I never knew, nor what their nationality. In this country, everyone who isn't a Yankee or a French-Canadian is a Squarehead. The family consisted of a mother and father and a large brood of children ranging from almost man-grown down to a toddler of about three, who was not, so Leon reported to me, too young to cut seed potatoes and help clear the gullied and overgrown fields of the smaller stones and bushes. They had a few hens and ducks, a scrubby little cow, a team of gaunt old horses, and not much else in the line of possessions with which to bless themselves.

"They've got their courage with them, that I will say," Leon told me, "trying to make a go of farming that rock-heap. I'll give them credit, they certainly know what work means. They're at it all day long and half into the night, and considering that they've got almost nothing to do with, they're accomplishing an awful lot. But you know what the Notch is. It takes more than work to make a living there. It would take a crying miracle. I'd almost feel sorry for them, except—"

"Except what?"

"I wish I knew. There's something wrong with them. People with clear consciences don't act the way they do. I sure as hell would like to know what they've got on their minds. It must be something pretty bad, the way they act."

"How do you mean, the way they act?" I demanded, and he shrugged his shoulders.

"I can't tell you. It's nothing you can put your finger on.

It's just the way they look at me, answering my questions like butter wouldn't melt in their mouths. You know yourself that's not natural, not unless they're hiding something. Oh, well, give me time; I'll find out what it is. I haven't started giving them the real working-over yet."

The next time I saw him, a few weeks later, I asked him about the Squareheads, more to make conversation than anything else. We were sitting on the porch at Forest Lodge with our feet on the deacon seat that runs along the rail, smoking and watching the river tumble down-hill. He brought his feet down with a crash and spat over the pole railing.

"Those so-and-sos!" he said savagely. "I came damn near beating up that oldest son of theirs the other day, regulations or no regulations. Nobody can pull a knife on me and make me like it. Nothing makes me madder, except being shot at. I suppose that'll be the next thing. Maybe I ought to go back and pound the tar out of him anyhow, on general principles."

"Pulled a knife on you! Why, Leon, that's—that's—" I sputtered into shocked silence.

"I'll tell you how it was. I was following the brook up the Notch, when I stumbled onto one of the middle young-ones—twelve or so, he is—fishing one of the pools. He was fishing legal, all right; but this year that brook is closed. I latched onto him and started up to the house, holding him by the arm because he'd tried to run away. I wasn't going to do anything about it, except warn the old man. That brook's been open so long I figured maybe they didn't realize they weren't supposed to fish it this year. I've caught a lot of folks in there since spring, and the first time I always let them go with a warning, things being as they are. I aimed to be fair and give the Squareheads the same chance as I would anyone else, much as I don't like them. And besides, to be honest with you, I didn't want to mess around with a piddling little thing like a kid fishing a closed stream. I'm waiting to get them on something really serious. And I will, too."

He brooded for a minute. "Anyhow, when we got up near the barn where the old man and the biggest boy were mending harness, the kid started to scream and jabber something in that outlandish language of theirs. Did I tell you they don't speak English very well? Well, they don't, except the old man. He's not so bad. So the kid starts screaming— sounded like he was warning them about something—and I gave him a little shake to shut him up. I didn't hurt him, honest! But the big boy reaches for his knife.

"I got set for trouble, let me tell you. But the old man snapped something in his own language, and the boy sort of hesitated and then made out like he was just going to cut a piece of strap with the knife. He didn't fool me any, but there wasn't much I could do. The old man put on that smooth face of his and started apologizing for the kid before he'd even found out what he'd done. You know yourself, Louise, that isn't the way people act normally. I explained the situation, and he palavered around a while, waving his hands and almost busting into tears, till I got sick of it and left. But don't worry; I'll go back. They can't always be lucky."

But time went on, and I didn't learn about anything untowards happening to the Squareheads in the Notch, although I read the Police News in the local paper religiously every week, as I always do to see if any of my friends among the lumberjacks have fallen afoul of the law. Leon himself I didn't see for a long time, as much as six weeks or so, and by the time he drifted in one autumn day, I'd almost forgotten the whole affair. Finally, though, I did think to inquire, "How are your pals over in the Notch?"

"Oh, them." To my surprise, he started to laugh with genuine good humor. "I found out what ailed them at last, thank God. It was getting me down, not being able to pin something on anybody as guilty-acting as they were. I began to think I was slipping and ought to turn in my badge."

"For Heaven's sake, what was it?"

"It's a long story, and you're not going to believe it. I didn't myself at first. I never ran into anything quite like it, and— Well, to start with, right after I saw you last I began a sort of war of nerves, like you're always reading about in the papers nowadays. I'd show up at funny times in funny places, sometimes a couple of times a day for a spell. Then I'd leave them alone for a while, and then I'd be living in their back pockets again. I figured that if I got them edgy enough, they'd be sure to make a break. And by God, they did. I walked into their kitchen one morning at about five o'clock, while they were eating breakfast—they begin the day early—and just stood looking at them."

I could well imagine that look, and I cringed in sympathy with the Squareheads. Leon doesn't realize, I guess, how well he can impersonate righteous and terrible retribution.

"They just froze in their tracks," he went on. "One kid had a spoonful of mush halfway to her mouth, and it just stayed there with the milk dropping off into the dish, slow. The biggest boy looked right at me, and if anybody ever hated my guts— He had his hands on the table, and the fingers started to curl as if he had hold of my throat. The old man just got whiter and whiter. It sort of fascinated me, to see anybody get that white. The old lady was the one that broke down. All of a sudden she started crying and carrying on. I couldn't understand what she was saying, of course, but the old man got up and patted her on the shoulder and talked to her, and in a minute she calmed down a little. To tell the truth, I was beginning to wish I was somewhere else. I didn't actually have a thing on them, when you came right down to it, except *knowing* there was something wrong with them; and you can't take that kind of evidence into court, not if you don't want the judge splitting his sides laughing at you. Just as I was wondering what I was supposed to do next, the old boy took matters in his own hands.

"He straightened up and looked at me and started talking. It was the first time I ever saw him without that hound-dog look on his face, or heard him speak without apologizing all over the place about nothing, and it made a lot of difference. He started out on the wrong foot, though. He said he didn't know what I was after, because they didn't have any money; but if I'd just go away and leave them alone, I could have the cow and those old crow-bait horses.

"That made me mad. It always does, when someone offers me a five spot to forget about a short fish or an unstamped beaver pelt. Sweet Simon, what's the point of having wardens if you can buy them off? So I told him I didn't want his jeesley livestock or anything else that belonged to him, and what was more, I had a good mind to run him in for trying to bribe an officer. I laid it on thick, because I was pretty disgusted. I told him I didn't know how it was where he came from, but here you couldn't get away with that stuff, and the sooner he realized it the better for him. I said people who kept their noses clean didn't go around offering bribes, because they knew there was no need of it. Then I asked him if he had anything to say for himself.

"For once he did. It was queer. He stood there with tears running down his face, but for once he didn't act afraid of me. He said— Oh, I can't put it in his words, because he talks funny, sort of broken English with an accent, but educated, like he'd learned it out of a book. But the gist of it was that there wasn't one damn thing I could do to them." Leon laughed. "That's the kind of talk I can understand. I get it all the time, and sometimes it's true, but oftener it isn't. I started to blast him, like I would anybody, but he held up his hand and I shut up." He looked a little surprised. "I don't know why, but I did, and he went on raving. He said they'd been chased from country to country over across, and somewhere along the line one of his sons had been killed and his mother and oldest girl taken away, and at last they'd managed somehow to get to this country. He thought they'd be all right here, and could live in peace without men in big black boots with guns on their hips busting into their house at all hours of the day and night—"

Leon looked at his beautifully polished boots, propped on the fender, and at the heavy revolver in its holster as if they didn't belong to him. He shook his head, and after a minute went on. "He said he didn't give a damn what I did, that nothing I could cook up would be any worse than what they'd already had. I could torture them and kill them and burn their buildings, but he wasn't going to run away again. There wasn't any place left to run to, if this country was rotten too, and he'd rather be dead anyhow than live in a world where there was no room for innocent people who only wanted to be left alone. I thought he was kidding—about me torturing them, I mean—but by God, he wasn't. He believed I might, and he really didn't care."

He sat looking into the open fire for a long minute. "I knew all along there was something awful wrong with that bunch; but hell, Louise, how could I guess? You read about people being persecuted, and you know it's true, but you don't really *believe* it. I've had plenty of guys afraid of me in my time, for the good reason that they damn well knew they were off-side the law; and I enjoyed making them sweat. They had it coming to them. But I never ran across anyone before who was just plain *afraid*. It sort of threw me off. It was something I couldn't understand."

I looked at him, and suddenly I liked him better than I ever had before, because he really was the sort of person who couldn't understand how such a terrible thing could be, how a clear conscience could possibly fail to drive out fear. "How are you getting along with them now?" I asked.

He laughed. "Oh, swell. I drop in there once in a while and stay for a meal. The old lady's a good cook, though she does stir up some awful funny foreign dishes. Good, though, for a change. I'm going to miss them when they're gone."

"Gone?" I said blankly. "But I thought they refused to move again."

"They're not going far. They've begun to realize what the Notch is like, so when I heard about this old farm down below Sumner, going cheap at a tax sale, I told the old man. 'Tisn't much, pretty run-down, but compared to what they've got— The way they all sail into a job of work, they'll have a nice place there in a few years. They're going to move before snowfall. They're out of my district over there, but I guess they'll be all right. The last time I saw them I had to bawl one of the kids out for tickling trout, and he answered me back sassy, just like any kid."

"What did you do then?" I asked, laughing.

"What do you think? I climbed up one side of him and down the other, and threatened to throw him in the can. I wouldn't have, of course. He wasn't doing any real harm. Anyhow, I felt too good about him talking back to me so natural to get really nasty with him." He took his feet down, rose to his considerable height, settled his holster, and tightened his belt. "Well, I've got to shove along. Guess I'll go up to Upper Dam and see what I can uncover in the line of a crime wave there."

And he went off up the Carry, striding along and looking very tough and hard-boiled and ruthless, and even a little bit cold-blooded and inhuman.

11

The Hired Help

RIGHT AT THE start let's have it clearly understood that up here in the backwoods there is no such thing as a servant, in the popular sense. Those persons employed in the households of others are the hired help, and there is a vast difference between being one of the help and being a servant, the difference implicit in the two terms. In the course of seventeen years of living in this country, I have employed probably a dozen different individuals, and in no case can a person be said to have *served* me. Rather they have *helped* me. We have worked together on an equal footing, exchanging the two equally valuable commodities of labor and money, to the end of furthering the common welfare. Somewhere Cervantes remarked, "One of the most considerable advantages the great have over their inferiors is to have servants as good as themselves." My only claim to greatness lies in the fact that the rest of the remark certainly applies to my situation. My hired help has invariably been as good as I am, from any point of view, and in some cases, I'll have to admit, a whole lot better.

That's the way it has to be in this country, because simple geography makes the spending together of most of the waking hours compulsory for people living under the same roof.

In towns and cities on the maid's night out, she can go to the movies or over to see her girl-friend. Here there simply isn't anywhere to go, no form of easy entertainment, and nobody to see. After the supper dishes are dried, there's nothing to do except go into the living room and read or sew or play cribbage or talk. Therefore a very sound principle to follow in hiring help in the backwoods is that anyone who isn't good enough to eat at the same table and sit in the same living room with you just isn't good enough to work for you in the first place. The rule has rather an arbitrary sound, but it works out very well. Of all the people I've ever hired, I've only had to fire one man.

I was sorry about that for two reasons. The first one was that the necessity for firing him showed that my judgment was not infallible, a fact that I hated to admit. The other was that we really liked him. He was good-natured and willing and truly amusing. He had a quick wit and a lively intelligence and true acting ability. We never laughed so hard as during the time Etienne worked for us and enlivened our mealtimes with his exuberant and dramatic re-enactments of various episodes in his career. But unfortunately he was not very reliable. We parted company after a few weeks, and we've never seen him since.

We remember him, though, every time something too much to be borne with equanimity happens. Then someone says viciously, "Astramonia!" hissing the *s* and bearing down, tight-lipped, on the *m*. That was an oath of Etienne's, which we all picked up. He told us that it was Polish and all right for us to use, since it didn't mean anything worse than son-of-a-bitch, which is one of the milder imprecations of this country; and it sounds better, too. I hope he was telling the truth, but I wouldn't bet money on it. Etienne had the kind of sense of humor that might easily have led him into thinking it very funny to hear Gertie Roberts, who was also working for me at the time and who is a pillar of respectability and looks it, ripping out a really nasty word, in all innocence. If that is the case, I only hope nobody who understands Polish happens along in one of our crises. Be that as it may, I am grateful to Etienne for Astramonia. When things get bad enough to call for its use, the next step is either demoralizing tears or helpless laughter, and Astramonia always tips the scales in favor of the tension-relieving laughter.

Of the others who have worked for me, one, Gerrish, of whom I have written before, I lost by death. All the rest left when the job in hand was done, or when September came and the kids had to go Out to school, and I didn't need help any more. We always parted friends, and I do truly mean friends, on a corresponding, visiting-back-and-forth, truly-interested-in-each-others'-affairs basis; that is, all except two men whose names I never did know, who once worked for me for a week in the spring. Brief as our contract was, and in spite of the fact that we never exchanged one word that was intelligible to me, at least, I'll never forget them.

This is the way it happened. It was May, and the ice had just gone out, and the log-drive had started. I'd been living alone all winter, contented as a well-fed woodchuck with the world in general. Then one day Al Parsons called me up to remind me that the Siases, dear friends of mine, were arriving in two days to stay at the hotel for the spring fishing. I went outdoors and suddenly saw the familiar yard through their eyes, or the eyes of any Outsider. It looked awful. Dead leaves lay all over everything, the vegetable garden was a mess, un-

spaded and littered with last year's stalks and vines that I
hadn't got around to cleaning up before snowfall, and worst
of all, the remains of an old log cabin that I'd had torn down
the summer before were piled untidily alongside the woodshed. The logs were pine, sound and dry, and it had been my
opinion that they were too good to waste, that they'd make
wonderful kindling wood, when, as and if they were worked
up into more suitable lengths than twenty feet.

For a moment my heart failed me. The yard I could rake,
the garden I could spade, but the shambles by the woodshed
I could never clean up in less than ten years. The people
whom I had hired for the summer weren't coming In until
the middle of June, which did me no good in my present
straights, and I knew that I couldn't borrow a man from
Larry, because he was in the midst of a busy spell. Then I
thought of the log-drive and the river-hogs. Sometimes on a
drive there are periods of several days when there is no work
for the men, because the booms of logs that are coming down
from the lakes up above have been held up by head winds.
Until they arrive, the river-hogs—or log-drivers, if you prefer
—just kill time, washing out their socks, playing poker, carv-
ing fancy bottle stoppers, and in general becoming more and
more bored with themselves. We were in such a period then.
So I called up the company clerk at the Middle Dam wangan
and asked him if he had a couple of men who'd like to make a
little money on the side cutting wood for me. He said he
didn't know, but he'd inquire; and pretty soon two river-hogs
came knocking at the door. They looked like ninety percent
of the hundreds of their kind whom I have known in the time
I have lived here, dressed in torn shirts, stagged pants, battered hats, gumboots, and four-day stubbles. They looked as

though they'd just as soon murder you for a nickel as not; but I knew from experience that this appearance was deceptive, so I didn't yell bloody murder and slam the door in their faces. I went out into the yard and started to tell them what I wanted done.

That clerk apparently fancied himself as a humorist. Of the fifty men at his disposal, he sent me one who didn't have a word of English to his name, and one who was that rare thing, literally stone deaf. Of course neither of them could read, and the less said about my French the better. And there they stood looking at me, as eager to understand and to please as a pair of spaniels. I could cheerfully have garrotted that clerk. There was nothing for it but to resort to sign language, to get them started on the job, and then to take a quick trip to Middle Dam for a conference with Louie Boutin, who was working for Larry. He'd be willing to give me a brief boot-course in basic woods French. So I pointed to the wood, pointed to the saws and axes, pointed to the space where I wanted the split wood stacked, and made sawing, splitting, and stacking motions. I probably looked as silly as I felt, but their faces broke into sunny smiles, and they nodded vigorously and burst into a spate of French. It seemed to me that the intelligent question for men in their position to be asking should be into what lengths I wanted the wood sawed, so I held my hands about a foot apart, dived deep into my subconscious, and dragged up the phrase, "Comme ça." It worked. They seized a two-man crosscut and a saw horse, and did what is locally termed "flew at it." I flew into the Ford and up to Middle, besieged by misgivings.

I never had two more satisfactory people work for me. They ignored me almost completely and concentrated on the job. The Siases showed up a day early, so I started eating most of my meals and spending most of my time at the hotel, two miles away from my henchmen. It didn't make any difference to them. Judging from the results, I would say that they worked even harder when I wasn't around to keep an eye on them. I came home one afternoon to change my shirt and found that they'd finished the wood, raked up the yard without being told to, and were busy shoring up the top part of the woodshed, which I use for storage, and which needed bracing badly. When they heard me coming they rushed out into the driveway, obviously filled with glee and pride about something or other, although the only word I could catch out of the stream of French that was bubbling out of them was *porc-epic*. It developed that they'd done me the favor of killing four porcupines that were chewing the house down around my ears.

"Bonne!" I exclaimed, my courage, if not my French, fortified by my few sessions with Louie; and to be on the safe side grammatically, I added, "Très bien." This seemed inadequate, so I threw in for free, "Ah, mes braves hommes!" They burst into pleased laughter, which changed to guffaws when I let success go to my head and developed the theme: "Mes braves, aimants hommes." I should have let well enough alone. I meant *aimables*, I guess. They were gentlemen, though. They realized that anybody could make a slight error like that, saying "loving" when she meant "kind."

The next morning they showed up right after their breakfast to see what else I wanted done; or at least, I assumed that's what they wanted. I led them out to the garden and made a sweeping gesture. "Le jardin des legumes," I said grandly, and to be sure they understood, I showed them a boxful of gaudily illustrated packets of seeds I'd bought, cucumbers, lettuce, carrots, stringbeans, and what-all. They nodded, wreathed in smiles, and went off to the shop to get spading forks and rakes. After I'd eaten my own breakfast, I went off up to the hotel to play with my friends, leaving them hard at work. As it happened, I didn't get back until after dark, so I didn't see the garden again until morning. They had not only spaded it, but they'd banked it into raised beds, European style, and planted it for me. I never saw such a neat and attractive garden in my life, with the smallest pebbles raked off, and the empty packets fastened to whittled sticks at the end of each row, gaily indicating the nature of the future crop.

That was all the work I had for them to do, so I called up the clerk again and asked him to tell them to come down and get their pay. He laughed in what I thought was rather a snide manner. "What's the matter?" he asked. "Don't you like them?"

"Certainly I like them. They've been wonderful. They've worked themselves out of a job, that's all." I thought that ought to spoil his joke for him, but I added for good measure, "Gave me a chance to brush up on my French, too." That would fix his red wagon.

We had a little trouble over the pay. In the first place, I couldn't understand what they were trying to tell me, with the aid of the clock and held-up fingers except that it was the number of hours they had worked and the rate per hour. I kept saying "Combien?" which I thought meant "How much?"—and maybe it does; but that didn't get me anywhere. So finally I spread out all the cash I had, about twenty dollars, on the kitchen table, and indicated that they should take what was right. They picked up four and a half dollars apiece.

That was perfectly ridiculous for the amount of work they had done, so I started shaking my head and saying, "No, not enough." A little wistfully, they handed back the fifty cent pieces. I gave up, with a loud cry of "Mon Dieu!" took all the money away from them, and gave them each seven dollars. They were apparently pleased, and I certainly was. I'd never bought a bigger fourteen dollars' worth of labor. Until the drive ended and they took off for parts unknown, they " 'Ça-va?"-ed me enthusiastically every time they saw me along the road, and twice came down and weeded the garden, in which I suppose they took a proprietary interest, just for fun. They were nice men. They proved to me, at least, that a language barrier and the barrier of widely divergent backgrounds and interests need not prevent mutual understanding and esteem, if good will and a common goal exist.

They also demonstrated nicely two of the characteristics shared by everyone who has ever worked for me. One is absolute honesty in material matters. People lean over backwards to be honest. Once Whit Roberts ran out of cigarettes, so I loaned him a pack to see him through until the next day. About two months later, when I came to pay him off for the season, I added up my figures, showed them to him, and asked him if they were correct.

"Pretty near," he said. "Take off fifteen cents for them cigarettes I got off you back 'round the Fourth of July, and we'll call it square." I'd long ago forgotten all about them, and would have been glad to give them to him anyhow; but Whit wouldn't have it. He owed me for them and he was bound he'd pay. I've had women who worked for me trail me clear up to the spring on the ridge back of the house, through brambles and swamp, to ask me if it would be all right for them to borrow a length of my black thread with which to sew on a button. They knew perfectly well that it would be all right, but they weren't going meddling around other people's belongings without asking first. That's a very nice attitude to live with.

The other characteristic is absolute honesty in ethical matters. People around here don't seem to worry lest they do a little more work than they are paid for, or to try to goldbrick on the job, which is just the same as stealing money, since they are collecting pay for the time spent in loafing. Instead of considering things in the light of so much money for so much time put in, they see it as a unit of work to be done, and don't consider themselves through until it is done. I've more than once come upon one of the help doing something I had not told her to do. When I commented upon it, she'd be sure to say, "Well, you asked me to tidy up this cupboard, and when I got the dishes out, the paint looked kind of smudgy, so I thought I might as well make a job of it and wash it now, while it's handy." It's very comforting to know that you don't have to be a Simon Legree; that you don't have to hound and spy upon your help constantly; that they are not just going through motions, but are actually looking for things to do.

I remember only once having to give a direct order and insist upon its being carried out. It was one Sunday noon, when Whit and Gertie Roberts were working for me. Larry called up and wanted to know if Whit would be willing to take a boat down to South Arm that afternoon to make an emergency repair on the dock; and when I asked Whit, he said sure, tell Larry he'd leave right after dinner.

"You go, too, Gert," I said. "You haven't been off the

reservation for weeks, and it's a lovely day for a boat-ride. You can visit with Mrs. Graves while Whit fixes the float."

She looked at me, and at the sink piled with pots and pans, and at the uncleared table. "And who's going to do the dishes and get supper?" she asked, on a climbing inflection.

"I am," I told her.

"Well, I don't know—I hate to— Is that an *order?*"

"That's an order," I said. "Now get out from under my feet. Go on and have a good time."

She went, but I don't think she felt right about it.

Whit and Gertie have worked for me summers for a long time, and the longer I know them, the more I respect them. They are not young, being well into their sixties, with not too easy a life behind them. After all, they are the parents of seven adult children, and the grandparents of I don't know how many more; and by this time they may easily be great-grandparents as well. They've fed and clothed and educated their children, and seen them through long illnesses and expensive accidents, all on the not-exactly-stupendous wages of a country carpenter. What's more, every one of their children has turned out well, at least by my standards. It's true that none of them has become President of the United States, or amassed a million dollars, or won the Nobel Prize. But none of them has been in jail, or on public relief, or deported from the country, either. They are, each and every one of them, law-abiding, self-supporting, and self-respecting; in short, good, solid citizens. To me, beset by the problems and worries of bringing up only two children to be a credit to me—and more important, to themselves—and painfully conscious of how easily the best-intentioned parent can fail, it is a wonerful thing not to find one bad egg in a basket of seven.

Now that their children are all married or working away from home, Whit and Gertie are relaxing and pampering themselves a little. They are finally doing and having things that they have looked forward to all their lives. They own their own home in Andover, and it is a model of convenience and neatness, with a gorgeous big flower garden out to one side. They've put in a bathroom and electricity, and the reason that Gertie started working for me was that she'd made up her mind that she wanted an electric washing machine and refrigerator. She considered them luxuries—she'd got along for fifty years with a big family, without them—so she didn't feel justified in asking Whit to buy them for her. Her view was that he worked hard enough already, without killing himself to keep her in expensive and unnecessary gadgets. She was able-bodied and would earn her own fripperies, thank you. And she did. Her husband was already working for me, and I was looking for a cook, so it seemed only sensible that she should enter my employ; sensible, and pleasant all around.

She gets through a terrific amount of work in a day, even up here, where housework isn't easy. We have no electricity, so when we do the washing, we use a gasoline washing machine. That's all right, but sometimes you waste half the morning fooling with needle-valves and spark plugs, before you can start the motor and get on with your laundry. You have to heat all the water in copper boilers on a wood-burning range. Wash-day is a shambles around here, with the household completely disorganized and a catch-as-catch-can dinner at noon, consisting of yesterday's cold roast, warmed-over potatoes and vegetables, and an assortment of desserts: one stray piece of pie, what was left of the brown-betty, one dish of chocolate pudding, and some cookies. As you can see, it's

refrigerator-cleaning day, as well as wash-day. Then the ironing! We have to use what are fittingly named sad-irons, old-
fashioned irons that must be heated on top of the range. They
make for a long, hard ironing, I'm here to tell you.

I went into the kitchen one day and found Gertie painstakingly ironing what I thought was Rufus' underwear. "For
the love of peace, Gert," I said, "what are you wasting time
and energy on that kid's underwear for, the way he treats it?
He doesn't have to have it ironed."

She went on ironing, looking a little embarrassed as she put
a knife crease into a pair of shorts. "It isn't Rufus'," she admitted. "It's Whitney's. I suppose it's foolish, but even when
the children were little and goodness knows I had my hands
full, I've always ironed his underwear. Not that he'd complain if I didn't; but I know he likes it ironed, and it seems
little enough to do for him." That's the sort of trivial but important thing that makes so many marriages in this country
last for fifty years, growing better all the time.

I think Whit and Gert are wonderful together anyhow, although they probably won't thank me for saying so. I envy
them lots of times, as for example one Sunday late in September, when my children had gone Out to school and the three
of us were here alone. It was a simply heavenly day, bright
and blue, with the sun gilding the first-turning autumn leaves,
and the air sparkling and crisp. After breakfast I decided I
would go up to Middle Dam to see the Siases, who had come
back for the fall fishing. Gertie was just getting the roast for
dinner out of the refrigerator when I announced this plan.

"Are you going to eat up there?" she asked.

"I don't know yet," I told her. "I haven't got that far.
Why?"

"Well, nothing, really. Only if you weren't going to be home, I wouldn't cook this meat until to-morrow."

"But you and Whit have to eat."

"Well, yes. But if you were going to eat at the hotel, we thought we'd put up a lunch and go off somewhere on a picnic. I do love a picnic."

"For Heaven's sake!" I said. "Why didn't you say so before? You go ahead. I will eat at Middle."

I got home before they did, late in the afternoon, and pretty soon I heard them coming up the Carry, laughing together like a couple of kids. They came in with their hair windblown and their noses sunburned, carrying Whit's hat full of late blueberries, a big bunch of goldenrod and wild asters, and a little homemade birch-bark basket full of ferns, which they gave me for the fireplace mantel. And I thought then that if I could look forward with any certainty to having such a good time as they had, twenty-five years hence, I'd be willing to go through all the work and grief and worry they must have gone through together.

Whit is the best workman I have ever seen, bar none. There is something completely fascinating to me in watching anyone who knows his trade, whatever it may be. I think I admire competence in any line more than I do any other attribute. I like people who know what they're doing, and who go about doing it with no fuss or feathers. There is something proud and integrated about them, some quality of modesty and assurance that sets them apart from ordinary dubs in an aristocracy of their own, no matter how humble that trade may be considered generally. Whit is supposed to be a carpenter, but he would be called a cabinet-maker anywhere else. Apparently he can't do a slap-dash piece of work. I once asked him if he'd please nail up a few old boards into a hutch for some rabbits the children owned, and when I examined the finished product, I almost wouldn't let the rabbits set foot in it. It was too beautiful to waste on rabbits, with the corners mitred perfectly and finished with quarter-rounds, and the rough edges of the boards planed down to a satin smoothness. But since I couldn't get into it myself, I finally let them have it.

My kitchen floor had long been a source of pain to me. It had been put down originally as a temporary expedient, and was made of rough planks. Not only did it look terrible, but it was impossible to keep clean, and furthermore had a tendency to warp and curl, presenting hazards to trip the unwary. I finally decided I couldn't put up with it a minute longer, and after a conference with Whit, I went up to Middle Dam to use their Outside line to call the lumberyard. Whit and I had decided that soft wood was good enough for a kitchen, but when I went into a huddle with Lester Farrington, the dealer, over the telephone, I discovered that the price of even second-grade soft wood was appalling. It was the war, Lester said.

"I might just as well pave my floor with gold bricks and be done with it," I said. "That's altogether too much money." He said he agreed with me completely, and, if he were I, he'd wait until after the war, when prices would probably go down. I went home and gave Whit the bad news. He said, "Oh," and sat on a chopping block, whistling under his breath and jiggling his foot up and down. Experience had taught me that these were the outward manifestations of deep thought, so I went away.

Finally he came looking for me, and announced, "You know, Louise, you've got that left-over hardwood flooring

up in the shop attic." I didn't know any such thing. I leave
matters like that to those who understand them. "I've just
measured it up, and there's almost enough for the kitchen. I
know hardwood's dear, but 'twouldn't cost you much to buy
what little more you need. Only thing is, that flooring was
bought a long time ago, when things were better. It's really
too good to put down in a kitchen. Seems a shame to abuse
it."

I said we might as well use it in the kitchen where we needed
it, rather than let it lie idle in the shop forever, so that's what
we did. Whit laid it, scraped it down, and put on a coat of
pre-war tung oil finish that I got from Larry. We ate sandwiches on the porch that day, instead of a nice hot dinner, to
avoid conflict with his project. When it was done, it looked
wonderful—the color of dark honey, with the straight, fine
grain brought up nicely—and I said so.

"Really ought to have another coat," he said. "One coat
won't stand up good, especially in a kitchen, with people
tracking in and spilling water all over. It'd pay you to let me
put on a second coat." This sounded sensible to me, so a
couple of days later we had another cold dinner, and Whit
put on another coat. The floor looked even more wonderful
than before. We hated to walk on it. But Whit took to eyeing
it moodily. At last, out of a clear sky, he said, "What this
floor really ought to have is a rubbing down with fine sand-
paper, and a top coat of finish. Then you'd really have a floor."

"It looks better than any other floor in the house already,"
I said. "Is it really necessary?"

"Well, no. Not what you might call necessary. But that
there's beautiful wood, not like the trash they sell you nowadays, and it seems kind of a pity—"

"If it's not necessary, I guess we won't bother," I announced heartlessly. "I've got too many other things in mind that I want to get done this season." And that seemed to be that.

That evening when Gertie and I sat on the porch after supper, reading the paper and relaxing, Whit failed to join us. I assumed he'd gone fishing, and even when it became dark enough for us to move into the house and light the lamps, I didn't question his not putting in an appearance. He quite often goes to bed before it's dark under the table, as we say here. But at ten o'clock, when I went down into the kitchen to get a drink of water, I heard a strange, steady, shushing sound going on down there. It was Whit, busily sanding down the floor by lamplight. He just couldn't bear to allow a good job to fall short of being beautiful, just for lack of a little more time and care spent on it. He rubbed the floor down and put on the extra coat of finish on his own time, and felt that his personal satisfaction in a job done right was ample pay.

Whit can do anything, even if he is supposed to be only a carpenter. He can paint and tinker gasoline motors into running and handle any kind of a boat and hunt and fish and trap and knit socks and garden, among other things. The only thing he can't do is drive a car. I was trying, one day, to talk him into learning to drive the Ford. I pointed out that it would be much more convenient and perhaps even safer if there were two of us in the household who could drive. He said no. He didn't want to learn. He'd rather walk where he had to go than drive a car. He didn't have any sympathy with automobiles, so he doubted if he'd be able to learn anyhow.

"That's nonsense, Whitney," I said. "You're crazy about motorboats. You run them all the time. If you want to go across the lake, you don't feel that you have to row—or swim. What's the difference? And as for not being able to learn to drive: anybody who can run that damn kicker-boat of yours can run anything."

"I ever tell you about my grandfather?" he asked, in what seemed to be a non sequitur, but I was sure was not. Whit either talks to the point or keeps still.

"The one that took one drink a year, before Christmas dinner?"

"Nope, that was my father. Wouldn't eat his dinner, either, 'less his drink was forthcoming. No, my grandfather that put me in the habit of eating my pie backwards."

"Oh, sure." I knew about that grandfather. When Whit was a child, almost seventy years ago, his grandfather had always made him eat a piece of pie from the thick end of the wedge toward the point, so that there'd be no last-minute decisions that he was too full to finish the crust. Whit does it automatically to this day, and so do my own children, who learned the trick from him. "What about him?"

"Well, he used to work for the Whitneys, owned that big summer place up by Mosquito Brook in the Narrows. Worked there for years. That's how I got my name, Whitney, after them. Anyway, one thing my grandfather wouldn't do was wheel a wheelbarrow. Don't know the whys and wherefores of it, but somewhere or other he'd got a terrible nif against the things, and he wouldn't have no truck with them. Old Man Whitney naturally found out about it in the course of the years, and he'd try to finagle things so my grandfather'd have to give in and use a wheelbarrow, but my grandfather always managed somehow to weasel out of it. Finally the Old Man bought one, a big enormous heavy one, and had the boatman put it together on the boat, coming up from the Arm. When the boat come in, Old Man Whitney told my grandfather to go down to the dock and bring up the freight, like he always done. You ever been up to Whitney's? Then you know what a long, up-hill haul it is from the landing to the house. Well, my grandfather went down, all unsuspecting, and the Old Man and the family and the guests lined up on the porch to see the fun and give my grandfather a horse-laugh. Bimeby they see my grandfather coming up from the dock. He had the wheelbarrow, all right. But he was carrying it on his back. Awkward thing to carry, too, and it must have weighed over a hundred pounds. Old Man Whitney give up, after that."

I laughed. I could just see that stubborn old Yankee struggling up the steep and stony trail, bowed under the load, but unbroken in spirit.

Whit looked dreamily out across the river. "There's an awful lot of my grandfather in me," he remarked softly.

I never again brought up the subject of his learning to drive the Ford.

Of all the people who have worked for me, I guess I entertain as kindly a feeling for Merle Hodge as for any, in spite of the fact that he worked here only one summer. He had been guiding at the hotel, but when the warmer weather spoiled the fishing, the guiding business went into a slump. One night when I was collecting my mail at Middle, I asked Al if she knew of anyone I could hire to help Whit with a fieldstone fireplace and chimney he was building for me. That's a two-man job. She said Merle was leaving, and maybe he'd like the job; and it turned out that he would. So he came down and stayed until October. He was in his late twenties, a veteran, and possessed the same kind of sense of humor I fancy I have. I had a lot of fun with Merle, especially after I discovered that it annoyed him when I prefaced any bit of advice I was going to hand out by saying, "Now, Merle, I'm almost old enough to be your mother, and I want you to pay attention to what I say."

But that isn't why I esteemed Merle so. It started with the Reo. I have an old Model A pick-up which everybody uses for errands and running up and down the road, and what used to be a Reo Speed-wagon, about twenty years ago. Ralph however rebuilt it, stripping it down, removing the back springs so that the rear end would stay down if you happened to be dragging logs behind it, and putting in a second transmission. This gives it forty-seven speeds forward and twenty-nine backwards, more or less, by various combinations of gears, and makes it possible to haul tons of dead weight at any speed from two miles an hour to a hundred. It is an awkward, homely-looking thing, and uncomfortable for anyone except the driver to ride in, but I love the Reo. It simply shouts of power, and I like to feel all those horses at my command. When I start out for anywhere in the Reo, I'm always sure I'm going to get there.

When Merle first came down to Forest Lodge, I took him around and showed him the equipment he'd be using. "The Ford you know about," I said, "but I'll have to explain the Reo to you." I showed him how it worked, and concluded my little homily, "She's *my* baby. I'm very much attached to this old jallopy."

Merle looked at it coldly. "I'll take the Ford," he said.

One Sunday afternoon about a month later, I decided to take the kids swimming down-river. I told everyone where I was going, and Merle asked, "Do you mind if I take one of the cars and go up to Middle to shoot the breeze with the boys?" I said of course not, and which car did he want?

"Makes no difference to me," he said. "Which one are you going to use?"

I said it made no difference to me either. I'd take the one he didn't want. We batted that back and forth for a while, until I could see that we were both being too polite to get us anywhere, so I said I'd take the Ford. It was more comfortable for the kids, riding in back.

"Good," said Merle, looking happy.

"What do you mean, *good?*" I demanded. "I thought you didn't like the Reo."

He had the grace to look slightly abashed. "Well, I'll tell you, Louise. That Reo sort of grows on you." It did me a lot of good to find someone, at last, after all the sneers and scorn that have been heaped on the Reo, that felt the same way about it that I do.

Then Larry called up one day and wanted to know what Merle was doing. I told him, and he asked if I could possibly spare him for a few days. A party wanted a guide, and he was fresh out of guides. If I'd loan him Merle— We're always loaning our help back and forth, and it always makes me feel slightly guilty, as though I were Trafficking in Human Flesh. However, I said sure, if Merle wanted to be loaned. He did, changed from his old blue concrete-mixing shirt into his bright plaid guiding shirt, and went off up to Middle Dam. In the evening after work he came home to make a call on us. He sat down in the living room with a purposeful air, and said, "Louise, teach me about fishing."

That did it. That made Merle my friend for life. Actually

he knows much more about fishing than I do, and all he wanted
to learn was where in these waters, which are unfamiliar to him,
the best places are in the fall. But I don't care what the ex-
tenuating circumstances may be. Someone has asked *me* to
teach him about fishing.

These men—these and others like them—are the people with
whom I live in closest intimacy, an intimacy unavoidable in
this country no matter how large your house may be, between
employer and employed. We have to live in each others'
pockets, as we say. During working hours we may retire
each to his own private world of interest; but when the work
is done and the sun drops down behind Inlet Ridge and the
forest starts inching closer and closer to the house, then we
are driven inside the stockade, inside the four walls and the
roof that keep at bay the wilderness and the weather. It is
then, under the merciless test of familiarity, that our weaknesses are exposed to each other and our strengths revealed.
Whether the house stands or falls depends upon the nature of
those strengths and weaknesses. My house still stands. I have
been fortunate in my hired help.

12

Well You May Ask

IT IS UNFORTUNATELY true that the writer seldom does what
he wants to do; he only does the best he can. Within his heart
and mind are feelings and ideas which he wishes to convey;
which, indeed, he *must* at least attempt to convey, since he
acts under a real compulsion which he cannot deny and remain whole. These ideas may not be important to anyone else,
but they are important enough to the writer so that he is willing to spend a great deal of time and energy—and yes, mental
anguish, exaggerated as that may sound—on their proper expression, in order that they may be shared with others. Usually
he is only partly successful, and that is what makes writing,
much of the time, a painful and frustrating occupation: the
fact that the product of the labor, in cold print, falls so far
short of the living, glowing concept. When I read over what
I have written, I ordinarily feel just as I do when I try to sing,
only worse, because I don't pretend to be a singer and I do
try to think that I'm a writer. I can run through whole arias
in my head, hearing the full, rich, pear-shaped tones as clearly
as anything; and then when I open my mouth all that comes
out is a thin, reedy, pitiful squawk. It's damn discouraging.
The compensation of writing, I ought to add, comes once in a

blue moon, when you recognize with a certainty that nothing can shake that you have somehow managed, for once, to say exactly what you wanted to say, have portrayed a character exactly as he is, have painted a scene in its true colors. Those are the moments which deter a writer from pitching his typewriter into the river and starting to take in washing, as being an easier and surer way of earning a living.

When I set out to write this book, I knew exactly what I wanted to do. It had occurred to me that while I had written before of my life and the country here, I had been too selfishly preoccupied with my own problems and the background against which they have been—more or less—successfully solved to have paid proper attention to one of the chief factors in making that life good, or even possible for me: my friends and neighbors. I wanted—and it sounds quite simple—to tell about them in such a way that others could know and appreciate what kind of people they are and why I admire them so much. I wish, in justice to my friends, that I could have done better; but perhaps God is the only one with the necessary knowledge and equipment to do justice to even ordinary people.

And these people are ordinary people, like the large majority of their compatriots, quietly going about their business from day to day, doing their best to get along. Not one of them is individually significant on the national scene, or even on the miniature scene of local affairs. Not one of them wants to be, or tries to be, "important." But it seems to me that they are nevertheless important, because they are, in a time and country where so many are selling themselves down the river for a materialistic and shoddy way of life, the last exponents of the qualities and standards and virtues upon which this nation was founded. I do not say that here alone still exists the attitude that puts character above personality, principle above expediency, duty above pleasure, and independence above ease. It may easily be true of other places. I think that it must be true of other places where people live as we do here, close to the soil and seasons, close to each other, if not geographically, certainly spiritually, far enough removed from the stress and speed of modern living so that we have time to form our own considered opinions and freedom to act in accordance with them.

I read something in Ruskin once that seems to me to apply to the kind of people this country breeds, the simple, deliberate, durable people: "No changing of place at a hundred miles an hour will make us one whit stronger, happier or wiser. The really precious things are thought and sight, not pace. It does a bullet no good to go fast; and a man, if he be truly a man, no harm to go slow; for his glory is not at all in going, but in being."

It may be that these qualities which I so admire and which were commonly possessed in the early days of this country's history survive here as an anachronism. It may be that they are no longer necessary in the world of to-day, where man's worst enemies are himself and his misuse of his own expanding knowledge, enemies which possibly must be fought with different and more subtle weapons than the simple ones necessary to keep at bay the simpler foes, the wilderness and the weather. But it seems to me equally possible that these qualities possessed by my people, the kind of people whom I like and understand, may be the pinch of yeast in the bit of dough, with which, when the time is ripe, the whole mass will become leaven. When humanity gets tired enough of being hounded from pillar to post, when the powerful have suffi-ciently persecuted the weak and the envious weak have suffi-ciently obstructed the strong, perhaps our way of life will come to seem the true one, the good one; and people every-where will awake in astonishment at having for so long neg-lected its simple wisdom.

THE END